Praise for Edward Rutherfurd

The Forest

"Not all good things come in small packages. If you like books that are big, Edward Rutherfurd is your man. He writes wonderful sagas, tales that cover centuries, always keeping these long stories lively by telling us about the events and conflicts of people's lives. Rutherfurd does the painstaking research; the reader has all the fun."

—Seattle Times

"Many of the most memorable characters are women—Adela the Norman, bold in the face of injustice; her descendant Alice Albion, almost brave enough to defeat the hatred of the civil war; tough old Adelaide, so loyal to ancient grievances that she can't let her sweet niece Fanny take hold of love."

—The Kansas City Star

"The novel covers 10 centuries, tracking a half-dozen or so families and their fates, their fortunes, and intrigues moving the stories along. But the trees have tales to tell, too. As fiction, it works like a charm. . . . English majors will love this, and so will almost anyone else who starts page 1 and follows Puckle, Godwin Pride, Cola the Huntsman and their descendents along Rutherfurd's twisting road."

—New York Daily News

*Please turn the page
for more reviews. . . .*

London

"Remarkable . . . Grand."
>—*The New York Times*

"Rutherfurd is a skilled storyteller with respect for his readers. . . . No tourist will look at London through quite the same eyes after following its history through two millennia."
>—*The Washington Post Book World*

"Hold your breath suspense, buccaneering adventure, and passionate tales of love and war."
>—*The Times* (London)

"Engrossing . . . Real people dance across the pages, as multidimensional as Rutherfurd's invented characters."
>—*Miami Herald*

"A tour de force . . . *London* tracks the history of the English capital from the days of the Celts until the present time. . . . Breathtaking."
>—*The Orlando Sentinel*

Also by Edward Rutherfurd

SARUM
RUSSKA
LONDON

THE FOREST

A Novel

Edward Rutherfurd

BALLANTINE BOOKS · NEW YORK

A Ballantine Book
Published by The Ballantine Publishing Group

www.Ballantinebooks.com

This edition published by arrangement with Crown Publishers, a division of Random House, Inc.

Library of Congress Cataloging-in-Publication Data available upon request

ISBN 0-345-44722-0

Manufactured in the United States of America

First Ballantine Books Canadian Edition: July 2001

10 9 8 7 6 5 4 3 2 1

This book is dedicated to the New Forest Museum.
An inspiration and a joy.

Contents

Preface

THE FOREST is a novel. The families whose fortunes the story follows are fictitious, as are their parts in the historical events described. I have tried, however, at all times to set their stories amongst people and events that either did exist or might have done.

Albion House, Albion Park and the hamlet of Oakley are invented. All other places in the book are real. Most of these New Forest place-names have remained constant for a thousand years: where they have changed, I have used the names by which they are known today. Similarly, though I have tried to avoid anachronisms, it has occasionally been necessary to use a modern term where a historical one would only confuse the reader.

The family of Albion is invented. Cola the huntsman did exist, however, though Walter Tyrrell's cousin Adela did not. The name of Seagull is pure invention; Totton and Furzey are local place-names. The element Puck is often found in southern English place-names, from which I have constructed Puckle. Martell appears both in place-names and in medieval records and suggests a knightly origin. Grockle is a pejorative New Forest term for an ignorant outsider, from which I have derived Grockleton. Finally, the name of Pride, though found in many parts of England, I have chosen to suggest the intense and justifiable pride which the ancient Forest families take in their heritage. The description of Godwin Pride, the archetypal Forest commoner, was suggested by a photograph of the late Mr Frank Kitcher; but the same physical type is to be found in photographs of members of many ancient Forest families

xi

including those of Mansbridge, Smith, Stride and Purkiss. I suspect that the Forest roots of these old families go back to pre-Roman times.

A few historical notes may be appropriate.

KING WILLIAM RUFUS: No one will ever know the exact truth about the killing of Rufus; but we probably do know where it took place. I have followed the arguments set out by the distinguished New Forest historian, Mr Arthur Lloyd, which place the killing down at Througham and not at the site of the Rufus stone. As to the part played by the family of Purkiss, I have followed Mr Lloyd and Mr David Stagg in suggesting that the legend of Purkiss carting the body away derives from a later date. The conversation between Purkiss and King Charles is my own invention; the enterprise of this ancient family is attested today by a notable food emporium in Brockenhurst, without a visit to which no trip to the Forest would be complete.

WITCHCRAFT: The New Forest has long been associated in many people's imagination with the practice of witchcraft. We cannot know what form this might have taken in past centuries. I have no personal experience of witchcraft, nor any desire to have; but there is nowadays such an extensive available literature on the subject of Wicca, as it is usually termed, that I have drawn upon this to create a tale that I hope will seem plausible. I note with interest that many of the ingredients of the witch's cauldron of fable are in fact hallucinogens.

THE BISTERNE DRAGON: I am most grateful to Major General G. H. Mills for explaining to me what this dragon really was.

ALICE LISLE: This famous trial is well recorded. For the purposes of this novel I have allowed myself to interpose the fictitious families of Albion and Martell into the historical families of Lisle and Penruddock at this point of the story, but not in a way that does any violence to history. Research also showed that there are inconsistencies in the usual version of the legend. John Lisle did not in fact sentence Colonel Penruddock; and the legend confuses the two branches of the Penruddocks living in the area. I believe that the slightly amended version given in this novel is very much closer to historical truth. Alice Lisle's daughters existed, as stated, except for Betty whom I have invented.

THE MIRACULOUS OAK TREES: I am grateful to Mr Richard Reeves for drawing the existence of the three miraculous oaks to my attention.

THE SPANISH TREASURE SHIP: There seems to be no official record of this ship, yet local evidence strongly suggests that it did exist. The connection of Hurst and Longford castles is unproven; though I believe it.

BATH: It may interest readers to know that the story of the theft of lace in Bath is based upon a real accusation made against Jane Austen's aunt.

LORD MONTAGU: The scenes involving Lord Henry (the first Lord Montagu of Beaulieu) are invented; but the part he played in saving the New Forest was very real, as indicated in the story.

Acknowledgements

I am deeply indebted to the following, who have so kindly helped me in the preparation of this book. Georgina Babey; Louise Bessant; Sylvia Branford; Peter Brown; Ewan Clayton; Maldwin Drummond; the Deputy Surveyor and staff of the Forestry Commission; Jonathan Gerrelli; Bridget Hall; Barbara Hare; Paul Hibbard; Peggy James; Major General Giles Hallam Mills; Lord Montagu and the staff of Beaulieu Abbey and Buckler's Hard; Edward Morant; the staff of the New Forest Museum and New Forest Ninth Centenary Trust; Gerald Ponting; Lord Radnor; Peter Roberts; Robert Sharland; David Stagg; Caroline Stride; Ian Young.

I should like to record my debt to the published works of A. J. Holland, Dom Frederick Hockey, Jude James, F. E. Kenchington, Arthur Lloyd, Anthony Pasmore, and David Stagg, without which the writing of this book would not have been possible. Also I should like to record my thanks and admiration for the many invaluable articles to be found in *Nova Foresta Magazine*.

No thanks can be enough for Mrs Jenny Wood whose miraculous typing skills made sense of my manuscript. Nor to Kate Elton and, above all, Anna Dalton-Knott for the preparation of the manuscript.

Special thanks once again to Andrew Thompson for his wonderful maps.

As always I should be lost without my agent Gill Coleridge, and my two editors Kate Parkin and Betty Prashker whose patience, kindness, encouragement and creative help made this novel possible.

To my wife Susan, my children Edward and Elizabeth, and my mother, I owe a huge debt for their respective patience, support and hospitality.

Finally and greatest of all, I should like to place on record my extraordinary debt to two scholars: Mr Jude James and Mr Richard Reeves. Their kindness to me, their guidance and their astounding intellectual generosity are not only to be found in every part of this book, but have also made its preparation the most delightful experience of my professional life to date. Any faults that remain in the text are mine alone.

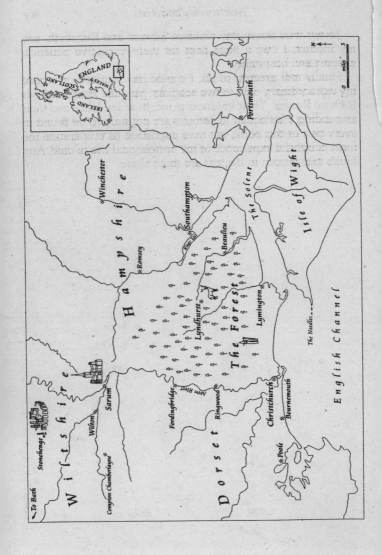

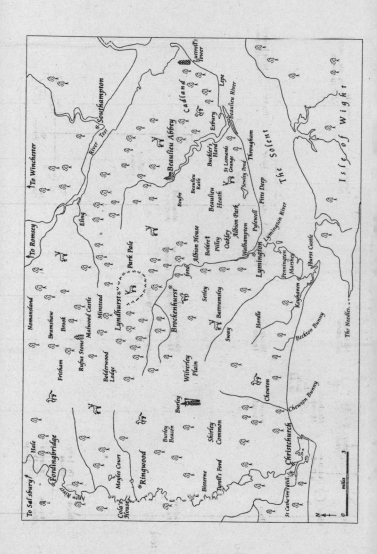

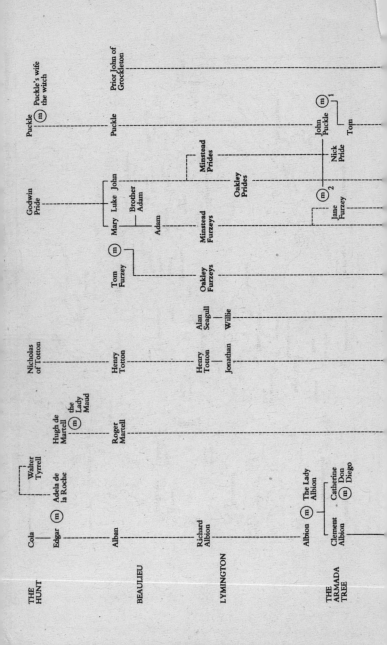

THE HUNT

Cola

Walter Tyrrell
Adela de la Roche

Edgar (m) Adela de la Roche

Alban

Richard Albion

Albion (m) The Lady Albion

Clement Albion
Catherine (m) Don Diego

Nicholas of Totton

Henry Totton

Henry Totton
Jonathan

Alan Seagull
Willie

Hugh de Martell (m) the Lady Maud

Roger Martell

Tom Furzey (m)

Oakley Furzeys

Godwin Pride

Mary ── Luke ── John

Brother Adam

Adam

Minstead Furzeys

Minstead Prides

Oakley Prides

Nick Pride

Jane Furzey (m) 2

Puckle (m) Puckle's wife the witch

Puckle

John Puckle (m) 1

Tom

Prior John of Grockleton

BEAULIEU

LYMINGTON

THE ARMADA TREE

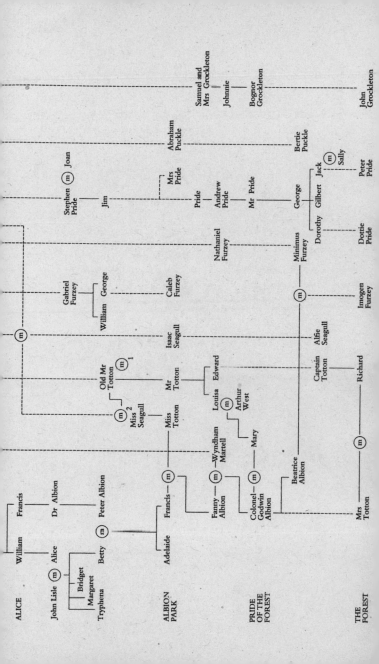

The Rufus Stone

April 2000

High over Sarum the small plane flew. Below, the graceful cathedral with its soaring spire rested on the sweeping green lawns like a huge model. Beyond the cathedral precincts, the medieval city of Salisbury lay peacefully in the sun. Earlier that morning there had been an April shower, but now the sky was clear, a pale washed blue. A perfect day, thought Dottie Pride, to fly a reconnaissance mission. Not for the first time, she was grateful for the fact she worked in television.

Say what you like about her boss – and there were those who said John Grockleton was a brute – he was good about things like chartering planes. "He just wants to get on the right side of you," one of the cameramen had remarked. She couldn't help that. The main thing was that she was in the Cessna now, and it was a beautiful morning.

From Sarum, the beautiful Avon valley continued due south through lush green meadows for over twenty miles until it reached the sheltered waters of Christchurch harbour. On its western side lay the rolling ridges of Dorset; to the east, the huge county of Hampshire with its ancient capital of Winchester and great port of Southampton. Dottie glanced at the map. There were only two small market towns on the Avon between here and the sea. Fordingbridge, eight miles south, and Ringwood, another five beyond that. A few miles below Ringwood, she noted, there was a place called Tyrrell's Ford.

They had not even reached Fordingbridge before the plane

1

banked and turned towards the south-east. They passed a low ridge, crested with oak trees.

And there it was below them; huge, magnificent, mysterious. The New Forest.

It had been Grockleton's idea to do a feature on the Forest. There had been controversy in the area recently: angry public meetings; local people starting fires. Television cameras had already been down there a few months before.

But it was another news item that had sparked off Grockleton's interest. An historical surprise. A piece of ancient pageantry.

"We'll cover this at least," he had decided. "But there may be something larger here: a full feature, in depth. Have a look at it, Dottie. Take a few days. It's a beautiful place."

He really was trying to get on the right side of her, Dottie mused.

Perhaps there was something else in it for her boss, though. It had come out the day before.

"Do you have any connections with the Forest?" he had asked her.

"Not that I know of, John," she replied. "Why, do you?"

"Funnily enough, I do. My family was pretty big down there in the last century. There's a whole wood named after us, I believe." He gave her a smile. "You might like to work that in, perhaps. If it fits, of course."

"Yes, John," she had said wryly. "I'll see what I can do."

They flew over plantations and brown heather heath for ten miles. The terrain was wilder and barer than she had expected; but as they came to Lyndhurst, at the Forest centre, the landscape changed. Groves of oak, green glades, open lawns cropped by stocky little New Forest ponies; pretty thatched cottages with brick or whitewashed walls. This was the New Forest she knew from picture postcards. They followed the line of the old road that led south through the middle of the Forest. The oak woods were thick below them. In a glade, she caught sight of some deer. They passed over a village in a huge clearing, its open green lawns dotted with ponies. Brockenhurst. A small river appeared now, flowing south, through a lush valley with steep sides. Here and there she saw pleasant houses with paddocks and orchards. Prosperous. On a high knoll on the valley's wooded eastern side, she saw a squat little parish church, obviously ancient. Boldre church. She should visit that.

A minute later they were over the harbour town on Lymington and its crowded marina. To the right, on the edge of some marshes, a sign on a large boathouse proclaimed: SEAGULL'S BOATYARD.

The English Channel lay a few miles away to the west. Beneath them was the pleasant stretch of the Solent water with the green slopes of the Isle of Wight beyond. As they flew eastwards now she looked from the map to the coastline.

"There," she said with satisfaction. "That must be it."

The pilot glanced across at her. "What?"

"Througham."

"Never heard of it."

"Nobody has. You will, though."

"Do you want to fly over Beaulieu?"

"Of course." This would be the setting for the opening sequence. Far below them the lovely old abbey precincts lay tranquil in the sun. Behind, screened by trees, was the famous Motor Museum. They circled it once, then headed north again towards Lyndhurst.

They had just passed Lyndhurst and were flying north-west towards Sarum when Dottie asked the pilot to circle again. Peering down, it took her a few moments to locate her target; but there could be no mistaking it.

A single stone, set near the edge of a woodland glade. A couple of cars were parked in the little gravel car park nearby and she could see their occupants standing by the small monument.

"The Rufus stone," she said.

"Ah. I've heard of that," said the pilot.

Few of the hundreds of thousands who went to wander or camp in the New Forest each year failed to pay the curious site a visit. The stone marked the spot where, according to the nine-hundred-year-old tale, King William Rufus, the Norman king – called Rufus on account of his red hair – had been killed by an arrow in mysterious circumstances while hunting deer. After Stonehenge, it was probably the most famous standing stone in southern England.

"Wasn't there a tree there once?" asked the pilot. "The arrow glanced off it and hit the king?"

"That's the story." Dottie saw another car make its way into the gravel car park. "Only it seems," she said, "that he wasn't shot there at all."

The Hunt

1099

The deer started. She trembled for a moment, then listened. A grey-black spring night still lay like a blanket over the sky. Along the edge of the wood, in the damp air, the peaty scent of the heath beyond mingled with the faint mustiness of last year's fallen leaves. It was quiet, as if the whole island of Britain were waiting for something to happen in the silence before the dawn.

Then suddenly, a skylark started singing in the dark. Only he had seen the hint of paleness on the horizon.

The deer turned her head, not satisfied. Something was approaching.

Puckle made his way through the wood. There was no need to move silently. As his feet brushed the leaves or snapped a twig, he might have been mistaken for a badger, wild pig or some other denizen of the Forest.

Away on his left, the screech of a tawny owl careened through the dark tunnels and sweeping arches of the oaks.

Puckle: was it his father, or his grandfather, or someone further back who had been known by the name of Puckle? Puck: it was one of those strange old names that grew, mysteriously, out of the English landscape. Puck Hill: there were several along the southern shores. Perhaps the name came from that. Or perhaps it was a diminutive: little Puck. Nobody knew. But having got one name, the family had never seemed to bother with any more. Old Puckle, young Puckle, the other Puckle:

there was always a certain vagueness about which was which. When he and his family had been kicked out of their hamlet by the servants of the new Norman king, they had wandered across the Forest and finally set up a ramshackle camp by one of the streams that ran down to the River Avon at the Forest's western edge. Recently they had moved several miles south to another stream.

Puckle. The name suited him. Thickset, gnarled like an oak, his powerful shoulders stooped forward as though he was pulling some great weight, he often worked with the charcoal burners. Even to the Forest people his comings and goings were mysterious. Sometimes, when the firelight caught his oaken face in its reddish glow, he looked like a goblin. Yet the children would cluster round him when he came to the hamlets to make gates or wattle fences, which he did better than anyone else. They liked his quiet ways. Women found themselves strangely drawn to some deep inner heat they sensed in the woodsman. At his camp by the water, there were always pigeons hanging, and the skin of a hare or some other small creature neatly stretched on pegs; or perhaps the remains of one of the trout who ventured up the little brown streams. Yet the forest animals hardly troubled to avoid him, almost as if they sensed that he was one of them.

As he moved through the darkness now, a rough leather jerkin covering his torso, his bare legs thrust into stout leather boots, he might have been a figure from the very dawn of time.

The deer remained, head raised. She had wandered a little apart from the rest of the group who were still feeding peacefully in the new spring grasses near the woodland edge.

Though deer have good vision, and a highly developed sense of smell, it is on their hearing – their outer ears being very large in relation to the skull – that they often rely to detect danger, especially if it is downwind. Deer can pick up even the snap of a twig at huge distances. Already, she could tell that Puckle's footsteps were moving away from her.

She was a fallow deer. There were three kinds of deer in the Forest. The great red deer with their russet-brown coats were the ancient princes of the place. Then, in certain corners there were the curious roe deer – delicate little creatures, hardly bigger than a dog. Recently, however, the Norman conquerors had introduced a new and lovely breed: the elegant fallow deer.

She was nearly two years old. Her coat was patchy, prior to changing from its winter mulberry colour to the summer camouflage – a pale, creamy brown with white spots. Like almost all fallow deer, she had a white rump and a black-fringed white tail. But for some reason nature had made her coat a little paler than was usual.

To another deer she would, almost certainly, have been identifiable without this peculiarity: the hindquarter markings of every deer are subtly different from those of every other. Each carries, as it were, a coded marking as individual as a human fingerprint – and far more visible. She was, therefore, already unique. But nature had added, perhaps for man's pleasure, this paleness as well. She was a pretty animal. This year, at the autumn rutting season, she would find a mate. As long as the hunters did not kill her.

Her instincts warned her still to be cautious. She turned her head left and right, listening for other sounds. Then she stared. The dark trees turned into shadows in the distant gloom. A little way off a fallen branch, stripped of its bark, glimmered like a pair of antlers. Behind, a small hazel bush might have been an animal.

Things were not always what they seemed in the Forest. Long seconds passed before, satisfied at last, she slowly lowered her head.

And now the dawn chorus began. Out on the heather, a stone chat joined in with a whistling chatter from its perch on a gorse bush – a faint spike of yellow in the darkness. The light was breaking in the eastern sky. Now a warbler tried to interrupt, its chinking trills filling the air; then a blackbird started fluting from the leafy trees. From somewhere behind the blackbird came the sharp drilling of a woodpecker, in two short bursts on a bark drum; moments later, the gentle cooing of a turtle dove. And then, still in the darkness, followed the cuckoo, an echo floating down the woodland edge. Thus each proclaimed its little kingdom before the time of mating in the spring.

Over the heath, rising higher and higher, the lark sang louder still, above them all. For he had glimpsed the rising sun.

Horses snorted. Men stamped their feet. The hounds panted impatiently. The smell of horse and woodsmoke permeated the yard.

It was time to go hunting.

Adela watched them. A dozen men had already gathered: the huntsmen in green with feathers in their caps; several knights and squires from the area. She had pleaded hard to be allowed to ride with them, but her cousin Walter had only grudgingly agreed when she reminded him: "At least I shall be seen. You are supposed, you know, to be finding me a husband."

It was not easy for a young woman in her position. Only a year had passed since that cold, blank time when her father had died. Her mother, pale, suddenly rather drawn, had entered a convent. "It preserves my dignity," she told Adela as she entrusted the girl to her relatives, thus leaving her with nothing but her good name and a few dozen poor acres in Normandy to recommend her. The relations had done their best for her; and it had not been long before their thoughts had turned to the kingdom of England where, since the Norman Duke William had conquered it, many sons of Norman families had found estates – sons who might be glad of a French-speaking wife from their native land. "Of all your kinsmen," she was told, "your cousin Walter Tyrrell is the best placed to help you. He made a brilliant marriage himself." Walter had married into the mighty family of Clare: their estates in England were huge. "Walter will find you a husband," they said. But he hadn't so far. She was not sure she really trusted Walter.

The yard was typical of the Saxon manors in the region. Large timber, barn-like buildings with thatched roofs surrounded it on three sides. Their walls were made of great darkened planks. In the centre, the great hall was marked by an elaborately carved doorway and an outside staircase to reach the upper floor. The manor was sited only a short distance from the clear and quiet waters of the River Avon, as it flowed down from the chalk ridges by the castle of Sarum, fifteen miles to the north. A few miles upstream lay the village of

Fordingbridge; downstream the little town of Ringwood and, eight miles beyond, the Avon entered the shallow harbour protected by its headland and thence out to the open sea.

"Here they come!" A shout went up as a movement of the door of the hall indicated that the leaders of the party were about to emerge. Walter came first, looking cheerful; then a squire; and behind them, the man they were waiting for: Cola.

Cola the Huntsman, lord of the manor, master of the Forest: he was silver-haired, now; his long, drooping moustache grey. But he was still a splendid figure. Tall, broad-chested, his athletic frame might not be lithe any longer, but he walked with the grace of an old lion. He was every inch a Saxon noble. And if, perhaps, there was something about him that suggested that, deep within, he felt some loss of dignity since the Normans came, Adela guessed that his old eyes could still flash fire.

It was not Cola, however, at whom she found herself staring. It was his sons who followed just behind him. There were two of them, both in their twenties but one, she estimated, three or four years older than the other. Tall and handsome, with their long blond hair, short beards and bright blue eyes, she supposed that each must be a replica of the man their father once had been. They walked lightly, athletically, with such an air of noble breeding that she instinctively felt glad that these Saxons, at least, had kept their manor, unlike the many others who had lost out to her own people. As her eyes continued to rest upon them she even had to check herself with an inward smile. Dear God, she realised what she had been thinking: in their natural state these young men must be . . . absolutely beautiful.

A few moments later, just as the sun was tipping over the oak trees on the horizon, the whole party, some twenty of them, moved off.

The valley of the River Avon, which they were about to leave, was a delightful region. Across the broad coastal plain, which lies below the bare chalk ridges of Sarum, past geological ages had left a swathe of gravel beds. Since then the descending river had carved a broad, shallow path southwards, its banks becoming low gravel ridges clothed with trees, into which, over countless centuries, it had gently deposited a rich alluvium. Between Fordingbridge and Ringwood the valley was about two miles wide; and if the placid river which now made its way through the lush fields was only a trickle compared with its former state, it would sometimes, after the spring rains, overflow its banks and cover all the surrounding meadows with a sheet of sparkling water as if to remind the world that it was still the ancient owner of the place.

Adela had never ridden out with a hunt like this and she felt excited. She was also curious. Their destination, she knew, lay just over the eastern ridge of the Avon valley; and part of the reason why she had begged to go that day was the chance to explore this wild region about which she had often heard. It was not long before they came to the foot of the ridge, passing a little stream and a huge old oak tree standing alone. They walked their horses up a winding track with oak and holly trees and scrub on either side. She noticed, as they got higher, that there were patches of exposed gravel on the track.

Yet it still caught her unawares and made her give a little gasp of surprise as, coming out over the top of the ridge, the wood abruptly ended and then, suddenly, the horizon and the sky burst open all around her and she entered another land entirely.

It was not what she had expected. Before her, as far as the eye could see, lay a vast tract of brown heath. The sun, still low on the horizon, was starting with a yellowish stare to disperse the trails of morning mist that stretched like strands of cobweb across the landscape. The bracken and heather-clad ridge on to which they had emerged swept down long slopes on each side into broad, shallow bottoms: a bog on the left; on the right, a gravelly stream with grass verges. All around, the heather was dotted with bushes and brakes of gorse in yellow flower. On another ridge, a mile away, a clump of holly trees stood out against the skyline. And, past that, the next ridge was covered by oak woodland, like the fringe behind her.

There was something else about the landscape too. As she glanced down at the peaty topsoil by her horse's hoofs, noticed the gravel stones there, which were an almost luminous white, and then looked up again and sniffed the air, she had a curious sense that, even though she could not see it, she was somewhere near the sea.

Were there human habitations in this great wild waste? Were there hamlets, isolated farmsteads or cottages? There must be, she supposed; but there were none in sight. All was empty, quiet, primitive.

So this was King William the Conqueror's New Forest.

Forest: a French term. It did not mean woodland, although huge woods lay within its borders, but rather an area set apart – a reservation – for the king's hunting. Its deer, in particular, were protected by savage forest laws. Kill one of the king's deer and you lost your hand, even your life. And since the Norman conqueror had only recently taken the region for his own, the New Forest – *Nova Foresta*, in the Latin of official documents – the place was now called.

Not that anything in the medieval world was supposed to be new. Ancient precedent was sought for every innovation. Certainly the Saxon kings had gone hunting in the area since time out of mind. So according to the Norman conqueror the place had already been under a stern forest law two generations earlier, in the good old days of King Canute, and he even produced a charter to prove it.

The area he took for his New Forest was a huge wedge: from west to east it stretched from the Avon valley almost twenty miles across to a great inlet that came in from the sea. From north to south it descended gently for over twenty miles in a series of gravelly shelves, from the chalk ridges east of Sarum all the way down to a tract of wild marshland on the coast of the English Channel. It was a mixed terrain, a great patchwork of heath and woodland, grassy lawn and bog, over which little bands of men had wandered, settled, made clearances and departed for so many thousands of years that it was no longer possible to decipher with certainty whether any patch of the landscape was fashioned by the design of God or the cruder hand of man. Most of the land was peaty and acidic, and therefore poor; but here and there were tracts of richer soil, which could be cultivated. The greatest oak woods lay in the southern basin, often by boggy ground, and had probably not been disturbed for over five thousand years.

And then there was the other feature of the New Forest that Adela had correctly sensed: the presence of the sea. Often the warm south-westerly breezes carried a faint hint of salt air even to the northern parts of the Forest. But the sea itself was nearly always hidden until one came out of the oak woods on to the coastal marshes. One visible sign there was, however. For opposite the eastern part of the Forest's shore and divided from it by a three-mile channel known as the Solent water, rose the friendly hump of the chalky Isle of Wight. And from numerous vantage points, even from the high downs below Sarum, one could look right across the whole basin of the Forest to see the island beyond, misty and purple across the sea.

"Stop daydreaming! You'll get left behind."

Walter was facing her, looking embarrassed, and she realised that, to take in the view, she had unconsciously pulled up and let the rest of the party draw ahead.

"Sorry," she said and they went forward, Walter trotting officiously at her side.

She looked at him critically. With his small, curling moustache and slightly stupid pale-blue eyes, how did Walter manage to insinuate himself everywhere? Probably because, even though he had no special talent, it was clear that he was doggedly determined to make himself useful to the powers that be. Even his powerful in-laws might feel pleased that, if he was on their side, he must think they were winning. Not a bad fellow to have in the family in these uncertain times.

There were always political intrigues going on in the Norman world. When King William the Conqueror had died a dozen years before, his inheritance had been divided between his sons: red-haired William, known as Rufus, had got England; Normandy had gone to Robert; a third son, Henry, received only an income. But as even Adela knew, the situation was always uneasy. Many of the great nobles had estates in both England and Normandy; but while Rufus was a competent ruler, Robert was not and it was often said that Rufus would take over Normandy one day. Yet Robert had his admirers. One great Norman family who held some of the lands along the New Forest coast was said to like him. And what of young Henry? He seemed contented with his lot, but was he? The situation was further complicated by the fact that so far, neither Rufus nor Robert had married and produced an heir.

But when she had innocently asked Walter when the King of England would marry, he had only shrugged. "Who knows?" he had answered. "He prefers young men."

Adela sighed to herself. Whatever turn events might take in the future, she supposed Walter would be sure to know which was the winning side.

The party was making swift progress across the heath. Here and there she noticed small groups of sturdy ponies eating grass or gorse. "They're all over the Forest," Walter explained. "They look wild but many of them belong to the peasants in the hamlets." They were pretty little creatures and, judging by the numbers she could see, there must be thousands of them in the Forest.

Cola and his sons led the way. If the king had reserved the New Forest for his deer, this was not only for his amusement. Of course, the sport was excellent. Not only deer, but wild boar could be hunted. There were a few wolves to be killed, too. When the king went hunting with his friends they normally used bows. But the underlying need for the Forest was much more practical. The king and his court, his men at arms, sometimes even his sailors, had to be fed. They needed meat. Deer breed and grow rapidly. The venison meat they produce is delicious and very lean. It could be salted – there were salt beds by the coast – and sent all over the kingdom. The New Forest was a deer farm.

It was a very professional one. Run by several foresters – some of them Saxons like Cola, left in place because of their intimate knowledge of the area – the Forest kept a stock of about seven thousand deer. When one of the royal huntsmen led a party out to kill deer for the king, as Cola was doing today, they would not rely on bows, but on a far more efficient method. Today would be a great drive, or drift, with this and other parties fanning out over a wide area and expertly driving the game before them towards a huge trap. The trap, which was being set up at the royal manor of Lyndhurst in the centre of the Forest, consisted of a long curving fence, which would funnel the deer down towards an inclosure where they could be shot with bows or caught in nets in large numbers. "It's like a spiral seashell in the middle of the Forest," Walter had told her. "There's no escape."

Though cruelly efficient, it conjured up an image in her mind that was magical and strangely mysterious.

They began to descend a slope towards a wood. On her right, she heard a skylark singing and looked up at the pale-blue sky to find it. As she did so, she realised Walter was speaking to her. "The trouble with you," she heard him start, before she closed her mind to the sound of his voice.

There was always so much the matter with her, according to Walter. "You should try to walk more elegantly," he would say. Or smile more. Or wear another gown. "You're not bad looking," he had been good enough to tell her the week before. "Even if some people would say you should be slimmer."

This was a new fault. "Do they say that?" she had gently asked.

"No," he had replied after consideration. "But I should think that they might."

Underlying all these criticisms, though, and the faint embarrassment her presence clearly caused him, was the one great shortcoming she was powerless to correct. I'm sure, she thought wryly, that if I had a huge dowry, he would think me beautiful.

She could see the lark now: a tiny speck high over the ridge, its voice descending, full-throated, clear as a bell. She smiled, then turned, as something else caught her eye.

The figure riding over the heath was catching up with them rapidly. He rode alone. He was wearing a hunting cap and was dressed in dark-green; but even before she could see more of him, it was clear from the magnificent bay he rode that this was no ordinary squire. With what an easy, powerful stride the big horse cantered towards them. It made her heart thrill to watch. And the rider, in a quiet way, seemed as impressive as his mount. As he drew closer she saw a tall, dark-haired man. His face was aquiline, Norman and somewhat stern. She guessed he might be thirty and he was obviously born to authority. As he passed them he lightly touched his cap in polite acknowledgement, but since he did not turn his head it was impossible to tell whether he had actually seen her. She saw him canter straight to the head of the party and salute Cola, who returned the greeting with evident respect. She wondered

who this latecomer might be and rather unwillingly turned to
Walter, who she found was watching her already.

"That's Hugh de Martell," he said. "Holds large estates west
of the Forest." And then, just as she had started to remark that
he looked a rather cold, disagreeable character, Walter gave an
irritating laugh. "You can't have him, little cousin." He
grinned. "He's already taken. Martell's married."

The morning sun was well up in the sky and, although everything was quiet, it still seemed to his wife that Godwin Pride
was taking a bit of a chance. Normally he finished soon after
dawn. "You know the law," she reminded him.

But Pride said nothing and went on. "They won't come
down this way," he finally said. "Not today."

There was a scent of sweet grass in the air. A fly nearly settled on Pride's neck, but then thought better of it. After another
minute or two, a small boy came and stood beside her to watch
his father.

"I can hear something," she suggested.

Pride paused, listened, gave her a quiet look. "No, you
can't," he said.

The hamlet of Oakley consisted of a small scattering of
thatched huts and homesteads by a green of close-cropped
moorland grass. Across the green was a shallow pond whose
surface at present was covered by a straggling carpet of little
white flowers. Two small oaks, an ash and several bushes of
bramble and yellow gorse overhung the water at various
points. Although the grass was short and coarse, three cows
and a couple of ponies were grazing on the green. Just behind
the hamlet, a gravel track led into woodland where it soon descended, between high banks, to a small river. At the eastern
end of the hamlet, set a little apart, was the homestead of
Godwin Pride.

Godwin Pride: the two names could hardly have been more
Saxon; yet a glance at their owner suggested a different ancestry. He was stooping over his work again now, but when he
had straightened up to answer his wife, what a fine figure he
had presented. Built long, with a straight back, hair falling in
rich chestnut curls to his shoulders, a full matching beard and

moustache, a beak of a nose, lustrous brown eyes – all these indicated that, like many of the people living in the Forest, he was, at least in part, a Celt.

Romans had come; Saxons had come. In particular that branch of the Saxon peoples known as Jutes had settled in the Isle of Wight and the eastern part of the Forest, which was known as Ytene – the land of the Jutes. But in that isolated region, whose deep woods, poor heaths and marshland did not invite much attention, a remnant of the old Celtic population had quietly lived on. Indeed, their life on their homesteads, modest but well adapted to their forest environment, had probably changed very little since the ancient and pleasant peace of the Bronze Age.

It was unusual in the reign of Rufus for a man, especially a peasant, to have a family name. But there were several cousins bearing the name of Pride in the Forest – *Pryde* in Old English signifying not so much arrogance, although there was some of that, as a sense of personal worth, an independence of spirit, a knowledge that the ancient Forest was theirs to live in as they pleased. As Cola the Saxon noble would still advise visiting Normans: "It's easier to coax these people than try to give them orders. *They won't be told.*"

Perhaps it was for this reason that even the mighty Conqueror, when he had created the New Forest, allowed some compromises. As far as the land was concerned, many of the Forest estates were already royal manors, so there was no need to kick anybody out. Some others he did take over; but many estates around the Forest edge lost only their woodland and heathland to the king's hunting. As for the people, several Saxon aristocrats like Cola found themselves left in place, so long as they made themselves useful: and whatever it may have cost his soul, Cola had played safe. Other lords did lose their land, as Saxon nobles had all over England; so did some of the peasants, either moving to new hamlets or, like Puckle, living off the Forest. Yet for all those remaining in the area there were compensations.

True, the Norman forest laws were harsh. There were two overall categories of offence: those called *vert* and those termed *venison*. The *vert* concerned vegetation – forbidding

the chopping down of trees, the making of inclosures, anything that could damage the habitat of the king's deer. These
were the lesser offences. The *venison* crimes concerned the
poaching of game and, most especially, deer. The Conqueror's
penalty for killing a deer had been blinding. Rufus had gone
even further: a peasant who killed a stag must suffer death.
The forest laws were hated.

But there were still the ancient common rights of the Forest
folk; and these the Conqueror left largely intact and even, in
places, extended. In Pride's hamlet, for instance, though a piece
of land beside his homestead had been taken under forest law
– which Pride regarded as an imposition – except during certain prohibited periods of the year, he could turn out as many
ponies and cattle as he pleased to graze all over the king's
Forest; in the autumn his pigs could forage on the rich crop of
fresh acorns; he also had the right to cut turves for his peat fire,
gather fallen wood, of which there was always plenty, and to
carry home bracken as bedding for his animals.

Technically, Godwin Pride was termed a copyholder. The
local noble who now held Oakley hamlet was his feudal lord.
Did this mean that he had to go out and plough the lord's land
three days a week and bow his head if his lord passed? Not at
all. There were no great manorial fields; this was the Forest.
True, he put marl on the lord's small field, paid some modest
feudal dues, such as a few pence for the pigs he kept, and
helped if there was wood to be carted. But these were more
like rents for his smallholding. He lived, in practice, just as his
ancestors had done, minding his holding, and earning useful
extra money in occasional labour connected with the king's
hunting and the maintenance of his forest. He was practically
a free man.

The forest smallholders did not live so badly. Were they
grateful? Of course not. Godwin Pride, faced with this foreign
interference, had done what people in such circumstances
have done through the ages. First he had raged; then grumbled; finally he had come to a resentful compromise laced with
contempt. And then he had settled down, quietly and method-
ically, to beat the system. This, watched nervously by his wife,
was what he was doing this morning.

He had been a child when the land by his family's homestead had been taken into the king's New Forest. Just beside their little barn, however, a small strip of about a quarter-acre had been left for them. This was used as a pen where the family's livestock could be kept and fed in the months when they were not allowed on the Forest. Around it was a fence. But the pen was really not big enough.

Every year, therefore, in the spring when the animals were back on the Forest, Godwin Pride enlarged it.

Not by much. He was very careful. Just a few feet at a time. First, during the night, he would move the fence. That was the easy part. Then, as the light came up, he would go over the ground minutely, filling in and masking the place where the fence had been before, and using turves he had secretly cut in advance, where necessary, returfing the area he had taken over. By early morning it was very hard to see what he had done. But, to be safe, he would immediately put the pigs on that section. A few weeks of the pigs using it and the ground would be too messy to see anything. The next year the same thing again: imperceptibly the pen was growing.

It was illegal, of course. Chopping down trees or stealing a piece of the king's land was a crime of *vert*. A tiny encroachment like this, termed a *purpresture*, was not a serious offence, but a punishable crime all the same. It was also, to Pride, a secret blow for freedom.

Normally he would have finished long before this time and the pigs would already have been moved in with as much general mess as possible. But today, because of the big deer drive, he saw no need to hurry. The king's servants would all be up at Lyndhurst where the deer would be caught.

There were several woodland settlements in the middle section of the Forest. First there was Lyndhurst with its deer trap. Since *hurst* in Anglo-Saxon meant "wood," the name probably signified that a grove of lime trees had once grown there. From Lyndhurst a track led south through ancient woodland until, after four miles, it reached the village in a break in the woods known as Brockenhurst, where there was a hunting lodge in which the king liked to stay. From there the track continued south beside a small river running down in a tiny, steep valley, past the village of Boldre, where there was a small church,

towards the coast. The little hamlet containing Pride's homestead lay over a mile to the east of this river and nearly four
miles south of Brockenhurst, at a point where the belt of ancient woodland gave on to a large heath. Even as the crow
flies, the hamlet was nearly seven miles away from Lyndhurst.

The huntsmen, he knew, were going to drift the deer down
from the north into the trap. Every one of the king's Forest servants would be up there; none of them would be coming down
his way that morning.

With an almost deliberate slowness, therefore, he was taking his time, inwardly chuckling to himself at his wife's anxiety and annoyance.

So he was more than surprised, a moment later, when he
heard his wife give a little cry of alarm and looked up to see
two riders approaching.

The morning had gone by quietly for the pale deer. For several
hours her little herd had remained feeding in the open as the
sun rose higher.

They were all does or fawns, since the adult males had
mostly begun by this season to dwell apart. A slight swelling
of their flanks indicated that a number of the does were pregnant; in another two months they would give birth. The fawns
who still accompanied them were weaned now. The male
fawns exhibited the bumps which later in the year would grow
into their first horns – the little spikes which, when they are
yearlings, give them the name of prickets. Very soon, now, the
prickets would forsake their mothers and move away.

Time passed. The birds' chorus subsided to a tuneful twittering, which was joined, in the increasing warmth, by the
quiet whirr, drone and buzz of the countless forest insects. It
was mid-morning before the senior doe who was the leader indicated by stalking into the trees that it was time to go to the
day rest.

Deer are creatures of habit. True, in spring, they might wander away in search of choice feeding – visiting the fields of
grain by the forest edge or, leaping his fences like silent shadows in the night, raiding the smallholdings of men like Pride.
But the old doe was a cautious leader. Only twice that spring
had she left the square mile that the herd usually inhabited;

and if some of the younger does, like the pale deer, had felt restless, she had showed no sign that she meant to satisfy them. They followed the same path, therefore, that they always used to reach the day rest – a pleasant and sheltered glade in the oak woods – where the does obediently sank down to their usual position, lying with legs tucked in and head erect, their backs to the faint breeze. Only some of the prickets, unable to contain themselves, moved about, playing in the glade under the old doe's watchful eye.

The pale deer had just lain down when she thought about her buck.

He was a handsome young fellow. She had noticed him at the time of the last rut in the autumn. She had been too young to take part then, although she had seen the fully grown does being serviced. He had been watching with the other junior bucks beside one of the lesser rutting stands; she had guessed from the size of his antlers that the next year he would be ready to claim a stand of his own.

The male fallow went through a series of growth stages, marked by the size of their antlers, which they cast each spring in order to grow a new and finer set for the next rutting season. After the spikes of the yearling pricket came the little antlers of the two-year-old, the sorel. The next year he became a sore, then a bare buck and then, at five, the proper antlers of the buck appeared. Even now, another two or three years would pass before he was fully grown and his antlers developed into the magnificent crowning set of the great buck.

Her buck was still young. She did not know where he had come from: for the bucks usually made their way to their rutting stands from home bases in other parts of the Forest. Would he be at the same stand this coming autumn, or would he perhaps be large and strong enough to dislodge the occupant of some more important stand? Why had she especially noticed him? She did not know. She had seen the great bucks with their mighty antlers, their powerful shoulders and swollen necks. Crowds of does clustered eagerly around their stands where the air was thick with the pungent odour they exuded and which made the pale deer almost dizzy. But when she had seen the young buck waiting modestly by the stand, she felt something else. This year his antlers would be bigger, his body thicker. But his scent would be the same: the sharp but, to her, sweet smell of him. It was to him, when the rutting season came, that she would go. She stared at the treetops in the morning sun and thought of him.

The terror began suddenly.

The sound of the hunters came from the west. They were travelling faster than the breeze, which might have carried their scent. They made no attempt to be quiet; they came loudly through the Forest, straight towards the glade.

The leading doe got up; the others followed her. She began to spring towards the trees. The prickets were still playing at the other side of the glade. For a moment they did not heed the calls of their mothers, but in another instant they, too, realised that something was amiss and began to spring.

The spring of the fallow deer is an extraordinary sight. It is known as a pronk. All four feet leave the ground while the legs appear to be hanging down straight. They seem to bounce, hover and fly forward through the air as if by magic. Normally they make several of these gravity-defying springs before running only at intervals, to spring again. With a beautiful, magical motion the whole group fled towards the covert. In seconds they had melted from the glade and were strung out in a line behind the senior doe who was leading them north towards the deepest part of the wood.

They had gone a quarter-mile when she abruptly halted. They did the same. She listened, ears flicking nervously. There was no mistaking it. There were horsemen in front of them. The leader turned, headed south-eastwards, away from both dangers.

The pale deer was frightened. There was something deliberate, sinister about this double approach. The leader obviously thought so too. They were at full gallop now, leaping over fallen trees, bushes, anything in their path. The dappled light through the leaves above seemed to flicker and flash with menace. Half a mile they went, came to a larger light, broke cover into a long grassy glade. And stopped dead.

There were about twenty riders, waiting only yards away. The pale deer had just time to notice them before the leading doe turned and made back towards the trees.

But she made only two springs before realising that there

were more hunters in the trees too. Checked, she turned again and started to run down the glade, darting this way and that, looking for a chance of safety. The rest of the deer, sensing that the leader had no idea what to do, followed her in an increasing state of panic. The hunters were racing behind them now, with whoops and cries. The doe veered right into a belt of trees.

The pale deer had gone about a hundred yards into the trees when she caught sight of yet more hunters – on their right flank this time, a little way ahead. She uttered a warning cry, which the others, in their panic, did not notice. She paused in her run. And then she saw the strangest thing.

From ahead of them a small party of bucks, half a dozen of them, suddenly ran into view from a thicket. Presumably there was a danger behind them. Seeing the does in panic, however, and the hunters on their flank, the bucks did not join the does but, after only a flicker of hesitation, dashed, leaping splendidly, straight towards the horsemen, flashing clean through their line and away through the trees before the startled hunters could even raise their bows. It was as quick and magical as it was unexpected.

And most astonishing of all, to her, was that her buck was one of them. There was no mistaking him. She spotted his antlers and his markings at once, as he passed like a leaping shadow in the trees. For a moment, just before their daring dash, he turned his face fully in her direction and she saw his large brown eyes staring straight towards her.

The leading doe had seen the bucks and their brave dash through the hunters, but she did not attempt to follow them. Instead, blindly, no longer knowing what to do, she led them in headlong flight; so that the pale deer found herself streaming eastwards; the only way left open, the way the hunters wanted.

Adela had watched the gathering at Lyndhurst with excitement. Parties from several estates had arrived, although they were all under the general direction of Cola. The royal manor was a small collection of wooden buildings with a fenced paddock sitting on a small rise in the oak forest. But a short distance away, on its south-eastern side, the trees were broken by a scrics of glades, before giving on to a large, long expanse of lawn, beyond which lay open moor. It was to this lawn that Cola had led them to inspect the great trap.

Adela had never seen anything like it. The thing was huge. At the entrance, surrounded by green lawn, was a small round knoll, like a mound for a miniature castle or lookout post. Two hundred yards south-east of the knoll a natural ridge rose and ran for half a mile in a straight line, with the green lawn on one side and the brown heath on the other. All this was impressive enough. But as the ridge slowly dipped at its south-eastern end, man had taken over and built a lower extension to the ridge. First, on the inner lawn side, was a deep ditch; then a large earthwork bank and, surmounting the bank, a stout fence. For a short distance this barrier stretched in a straight line. Then it began, very gently, to curve inwards, crossing the lawn where a rise in the ground made a natural line, then continuing on its way round towards the west, through wooded ground and glade, until it curved right round and ran back up towards the manor. This was the park pale of Lyndhurst.

"It's like a fortress in the Forest," she exclaimed. Once in this inclosure, the deer had no hope of leaping the pale as they were turned and driven, infallibly, towards the hunters' nets.

"We shall take about a hundred deer today." Cola's younger son, Edgar, had placed himself at her side during this inspection. The business within the park pale was always carefully managed, he explained. Of the huge number of game driven into the great trap, the pregnant does would not be killed, but the bucks and other does would be culled. When Cola had his hundred the rest would be released.

She was glad to have the handsome Saxon for company. Walter, as usual, had left her alone and as she saw him now, walking his horse beside Hugh de Martell and talking to him, she wondered if he would introduce the Norman to her and decided he probably would not. "Do you know the man my cousin is talking to?" she asked Edgar.

"Yes. Not well. He's from Dorset. Not the Forest." He hesitated for a moment. "My father has a high opinion of him."

"And you?" Her eyes were still on Martell.

"Oh." His voice sounded uncomfortable. "He's a big Norman lord."

She glanced across at him. What did that mean? That Edgar was a Saxon with no love for Normans? That he thought Martell arrogant? That he was even a little jealous of the knight, perhaps?

There was quite a crowd assembled on the lawn by the knoll. Besides the riders there were men with spare horses, others with carts for removing the carcasses and others who had simply come to watch. One figure particularly caught her attention. He was making his way across to a cart piled with sections of wattle fencing: a thickset man who, with his bushy eyebrows and forward stoop, seemed to Adela more like some stunted but sturdy old forest tree than a human being. She noticed, however, that Edgar saluted him as he passed and that the peasant returned the greeting by a slight nod. She wondered who he was.

There had been no time to think about this, however, for just then Cola had sounded his hunting horn and the great deer drive had begun.

It was actually a series of drives. The area around Lyndhurst was split into sectors; the hunters, organised into parties, were carefully co-ordinated to draw over a wide area in each sector, drifting as many deer as possible towards the centre. It was skilful work: the deer could prove elusive or, on the outer fringes, escape. When one sector had been drifted, the riders would be sent out on to the next and might go out several times until Cola decided they had enough.

Though deer might be missed out in the woods, as they approached the great trap their chances soon faded to nothing. Looking around, Adela observed that other, smaller earthworks and fences radiated out from the entrance so that as the deer from each sector approached they would find themselves in a kind of funnel that narrowed down towards the trap. It was hard not to admire the cleverness of the thing.

Having sounded the horn, Cola went up to the knoll from which vantage point, like a general, he could watch the whole proceedings. The riders all had their instructions. To her disappointment, Edgar left them before, with only Walter and four others for company, she rode out.

Their station was not an exciting one. The first drift was in the south-eastern sector. Here the heath beyond the park pale extended in a broad swathe about two miles across to the south-east, with long fingers of woodland pointing into it from the darker forest on the other side. While the riders drove the deer in from these various woods, their job was to fan out in a line from the pale to make sure that none of the animals made a dash down that way at the last minute. In all probability, she realised, there would be nothing to do at all. As the parties of riders disappeared into the distant woods, she prepared for a long wait.

It was more for the sake of having something to say that she asked Walter what he had been talking to Martell about. He made a face. "Nothing much." A long silence ensued before he added, "If you really want to know, he asked me why I'd brought a woman out on the hunt."

"He didn't approve?"

"Not much."

Was it true or was Walter making it up to annoy her? She allowed her eyes to rest calmly on his face for a moment or two and concluded that he might be telling the truth. A flash of resentment at the arrogant Norman went through her. He had noticed her then, damn him!

Time passed, but they did not speak any more. Once or twice she heard faint whoops and cries from the woods, then nothing. Until, at last, she saw something appear on the edge of the heath far away on her right.

A little group of deer had broken cover. There were eight of them. Even at that distance one could count them clearly. They advanced on to the heath and began to zigzag. A second later three riders came out behind them, then two more, at full gallop, moving to the right to outflank them; then another pair of riders, dashing down the other flank. Sensing both movements, the deer ran across the heath towards them.

It was astonishing how fast they came: the running deer, despite their pauses and sideways darts, covered the intervening ground, it seemed, in only a minute or two, with the riders behind them. Across the heath they raced, and swerved and ran in past the knoll so neatly that it was hard not to applaud. Minutes later a further group came, with a herd of two dozen this time; then another, and another. Only once did her own party have to shout and wave their arms to divert some deer

that had peeled away. The hunt could not have been more perfectly managed. By the time they were called in there were
over seventy deer in the great inclosure.

Soon after this, Cola had announced that they would draw
the woods above Lyndhurst next, and Adela was delighted
when a few moments later Edgar came up and, with a grin at
her, remarked: "You and Walter are riding with my party this
time."

She did not know for how long they had walked their horses
through the woods until they came to the glade where Edgar
had said they would wait. She had heard other parties making
sounds somewhere in the trees; she had noticed Edgar tense in
his saddle, but even so she had been completely taken aback
when suddenly, with a crashing sound, not thirty yards in front
of her, the small herd of does burst out from the trees into the
glade. For a second she was almost as startled as they were. As
they veered away she had just had time to notice that one of
the young does was paler than the rest. Then, with whoops and
cries, they were off in pursuit, driving the deer before them,
and moments later they had passed into a grove of trees.

It was because she had fallen a little behind that she had
such a perfect view of what happened next. A group of bucks
had abruptly appeared on the right, followed by another party
of hunters – in the forefront of whom, she saw, rode Hugh de
Martell. The bucks were young. They had hesitated.

But who in the world could have anticipated their next
move? How astonished the huntsmen looked as the bucks
wheeled round and dashed back straight through their line.
Even Martell was completely taken by surprise and stared,
open-mouthed. The proud Norman had been humbled by some
young bucks: she reined her horse and laughed aloud.

"Come on!" Walter, calling crossly, had brought her back to
her duty and she had quickly caught up. The two groups had
joined into a single party now; Edgar, Walter and Hugh de
Martell all riding together. They certainly managed everything
with wonderful precision. Though the deer tried to veer this
way and that, there was no hope of escape. Indeed, other
groups of deer driven by lines of huntsmen twice joined them
as they cantered and galloped towards Lyndhurst, so that in a
while she could only identify her own little herd by seeing

where the pale deer ran among the dozens of leaping forms. She was a pretty little doe, Adela thought. Perhaps it was just her imagination, but to her this deer seemed somehow different from the rest. And although she knew it made no sense, she couldn't help feeling sorry that such a lovely creature was about to be killed.

Several times she saw Edgar glance in her direction and once, she was pretty sure, Hugh de Martell looked at her too. Had he done so with disapproval, she wondered? But although she kept an eye on him when she could, he did not seem to be taking any further notice of her. Meanwhile the chase was gathering speed. The riders were breaking into a gallop. "You're doing well," Edgar called to her in encouragement.

The next few minutes were some of the most exciting of her life. Everything seemed to flash past. Hunters were crying out: she wasn't sure if she had joined in or not. She was scarcely conscious of time, or even where they were, as they dashed after the fleet-footed deer. Once or twice she caught sight of Edgar and Hugh de Martell, their faces tense, alert. Despite the loss of the bucks they must be pleased with themselves. This would surely be the biggest single group of deer brought in that day. How hard they looked, how suddenly fierce.

And she, too, shared in their glory. It might be harsh, this killing of deer, but it had to be. It was nature. Men must be fed. God had granted them animals for the purpose. It could be no other way.

Through the trees on the right now, she got a glimpse of the royal hunting lodge. She could hardly believe that they were at Lyndhurst already. The riders had been unable to prevent the herd from splitting and a group of does, including her pale one, had peeled left into a glade. Martell and some of the others galloped off to outflank them.

Just then, glancing to her left, she noticed Walter.

She must have got ahead of him without realising it. He was galloping hard, to be in front of her when they emerged into view by the trap. As he drew level she was granted a perfect view of his profile and, despite all her excitement, she suddenly experienced an inward shudder.

He was flushed and concentrated. Somehow – even now – his pug face still managed to look pompous and self-satisfied.

But it was something else that really struck her. His cruelty. It was not the hardness that Edgar's face had suddenly acquired; it was more like lust – lust for death. He looked gorged. For a strange moment it almost seemed to her as if his face in its keen desire, little moustache and all, had floated forward and was hanging, gloating, over the deer.

Oh, it was cruel – necessity or not. You couldn't get away from the truth of what was to come; Cola's perfectly organised drive, the huge trap ahead, the bleak wooden machinery of the walls in the woods, the nets, the culling – not one, not even ten, but deer after deer until they had a hundred. It was cruel to kill so many.

It was too late to think of that now. The trees opened out. She saw the high mound where Cola waited ahead. Just before it, a line of men were shouting and waving their arms, to make sure the deer turned right towards the entrance of the trap. The foremost deer were already up to them, with galloping riders only yards behind. From her left, now, came the does that had split off, driven by Martell. They streamed by her. She saw the pale doe. It was the last of them. Already they were all wheeling, coming past Cola's mound. Just after the mound, she noticed, on the grassy lawn between it and the start of the ridge there were only a few people standing. The deer, already turned, with the riders along their left flank, were streaming past them, oblivious. The pale doe had fallen a little behind. Having made the turn, she seemed, for just an instant, to hesitate before being drawn in to her death.

Then Adela did a strange thing.

She did not know why; she hardly even realised she was doing it. Putting spurs to her horse, she suddenly raced ahead of Walter, pulled her horse's head, cut clean across him and made straight towards the pale doe. She heard Walter shout a curse but she took no notice. Half a dozen strides and she was almost up with the deer; another second and she was between the pale doe and the herd. Voices were crying out behind her. She did not look. The doe, startled, tried to veer away from her. She urged her horse forward, pushing, willing the doe away from the great trap ahead. The park pale was only a hundred yards away. She must keep the deer to the left of it.

And then, with a single, frantic leap, the pale deer did what she wanted. A second later, to the astonishment of all the by-standers, they were racing together across the lawn between the mound and the ridge, and out on to the open heath.

"Go," she muttered, "go," as the pale doe fled out into the heather. "Go!" she cried, as she raced after her. "Get away!" For all she knew one of the hunters was already following with a bow. Too frightened and embarrassed to look back, she urged the little deer forward until at last it darted straight across the open ground and made for the nearest piece of woodland opposite. She cantered forward, watching the doe, until she finally saw her make the trees.

But what to do now? She was alone in the middle of the open heath. Looking back at last, she saw that no one had followed her. The line of the ridge and the park pale seemed deserted. All the people were on the other side. She could not even hear the cries of the huntsmen any more, only the faint hiss of the breeze. She turned her horse's head. Hardly knowing what she wanted, she began to ride down the heath with the park pale away on her right. When it curved westwards she started to do the same, walking her horse into the woods about a quarter of a mile below the wall. She entered a long glade. The ground was soft with grass and moss. She was still alone.

Or nearly. He was standing by the uprooted stump of a fallen tree. There was surely no mistaking him – the forward stoop, the bushy eyebrows. Unless these gnarled men grew identically in the Forest, it was the same strange figure she had seen earlier. But how had he got there? It was a mystery. He was quietly watching her as she went down the glade, although whether with approval or disapproval she could not guess.

Remembering what she had seen before, she raised her hand and saluted him as Edgar had done. But he did not answer with a nod this time and she remembered being told that the Forest people did not always care for strangers.

She had ridden, after that, for almost an hour. She still wouldn't go back to Lyndhurst. She could imagine her reception: Walter's furious face; the huntsmen – contemptuous she supposed. Hugh de Martell – who knew what he thought? It was all too much; she wasn't going back there.

She kept to the woods. She did not know exactly where she was although, judging by the sun, she was heading south. She guessed, after a while, that the hamlet of Brockenhurst must be somewhere on her right, but she did not particularly wish to be seen and kept to the woodland tracks. Later on, she thought, I'll head back towards Cola's manor. With luck she could sneak in before the hunters returned, without attracting too much attention.

So she hardly knew whether to be annoyed or relieved when, just as she was wondering which of two tracks to take, she heard a cheerful cry behind her and turned to see the handsome form and friendly face of Edgar, cantering towards her.

"Didn't they tell you," he said laughingly as he came up, "that you're not supposed to deer-hunt on your own?" And she realised she was glad that he had come.

His French was not very good, but passable. Thanks to a Saxon nurse in her childhood and a natural ear for languages, she had already discovered that she could make herself understood by these English. They could communicate well enough, therefore. Nor was it long before he had put her at her ease. "It was Puckle," he explained, when she asked how he had found her. "He told me you'd ridden south and no one saw you at Brockenhurst so I thought you'd be somewhere this way."

So Puckle was the name of the gnarled figure.

"He seems mysterious," she remarked.

"Yes." He smiled. "He is."

Next, when she confessed her fear of going back he assured her: "We pick and choose the deer. You'd only have had to ask my father and he'd gladly have spared your pretty deer." He grinned. "You are supposed to ask him, though." She smiled ruefully as she tried to imagine herself asking for a deer's life in front of the hunters, but, reading her thoughts, he gently added: "The deer have to be killed, of course, but even now, I hate doing it." He was silent for a moment. "It's the way they fall, so full of grace. You see their spirits leave them. Everyone who's ever killed a deer knows that." He said it so simply and honestly that she was touched. "It's sacred," he concluded, as if there were nothing to argue about.

"I wonder," she said, after a pause, "if Hugh de Martell feels the same."

"Who knows." He shrugged. "He doesn't think like that."

No. His way, she imagined, was more blunt. A proud Norman landholder had no time for such thoughts.

"He didn't think I should be hunting. I expect your father agrees."

"My mother and my father used to ride out hunting together," he said softly, "when she was alive." And instantly she had a vision of that handsome couple, sweeping beautifully through the forest glades. "One day," Edgar added gently, "I hope to do the same." And then with a laugh: "Come on. We'll ride back along the heath."

So it was, a little time afterwards, that the two riders cantering along the short turf at the heath's edge approached the hamlet of Oakley and came upon Godwin Pride, moving his fence, illegally, in broad daylight.

"Damn," muttered Edgar under his breath. But it was too late to avoid the fellow now. He had caught him in the act.

Godwin Pride drew himself up to his full height: with his broad chest and splendid beard, he looked like a Celtic chief facing a tax collector. And, like a good Celtic chief, he knew that when the game was up, the only thing to do was bluff. To Edgar's enquiry – "What are you doing, Godwin?" – he therefore replied imperturbably: "Repairing this fence, as you see."

It was so quietly outrageous that, for a moment, Edgar almost burst out laughing; but unfortunately this was not a laughing matter. "You've moved the fence."

Pride considered thoughtfully. "It used to be further out," he said coolly, "but we pulled it back years ago. Didn't need so much space."

The cheek of the man was breathtaking.

"Nonsense," Edgar said sharply. "You know the law. It's a *purpresture*. This can land you in court."

Pride gazed at him as he might have looked at a fly before swatting it. "Those are Norman words. I wouldn't know what they mean. I expect you would, though," he added.

The thrust went home. Edgar coloured. "It's the law," he said sadly.

Godwin Pride continued to stare him down. He didn't dislike Edgar personally, but the Saxon noble's co-operation

with the Normans seemed to him proof that Edgar was an outsider.

Not that Cola's family were strangers. But when had they
come to the Forest? Two hundred, three hundred years ago?
The Forest folk could not remember. However long they had
been there, anyway, it was not long enough. And Pride was reminding himself of this fact when, to his surprise, the Norman
girl spoke.

"But it wasn't the Normans who started it. This land was
under forest law back in the days of King Canute."

Adela's Anglo-Saxon had been good enough to follow most
of the conversation. She had not liked the surly way in which
this fellow had treated Edgar and, as she was a Norman noblewoman, she decided to put him in his place. Brutal though
he could be, William the Conqueror had been clever enough
always to show that he was following ancient customs in his
troublesome new kingdom. So it was no use this peasant com-
plaining. She stared at him defiantly.

To her surprise, however, he only nodded grimly. "You believe that?"

"There's a charter, fellow." She spoke with some importance.

"Oh. Written, is it?"

How dare the man use this tone of irony? "Yes, it is." She
was rather proud that she could read quite well and had a little
learning. If a clerk had taken her through a charter, she would
have been able to follow.

"Don't read, myself," he replied with an impertinent smile.
"No point." He was right, of course. A man could farm, operate a mill, run a great estate – why, even be a king – and have
no need to read and write. There were always poor clerks to
keep records. This intelligent smallholder had not the slightest
reason to read. But Pride had not finished. "I believe there's a
lot of thieves who do, though," he calmly added.

By God the man was insulting. She looked to Edgar, expecting him to defend her, but he seemed embarrassed.

It was Pride who now addressed him. "I don't remember
hearing of any charter, do you, Edgar?" He stared straight at
his head.

"Before my time," the Saxon answered quietly.

"Yes. You'd better ask your father. He'd know about that, I should think."

There was a pause.

Adela began to get the point. "Are you saying," she asked slowly, "that King William lied about Canute's forest law? That the charter's a fake?"

Pride pretended surprise. "Really? They can do that, can they?"

She was silent herself, now. Then she nodded slowly. "I'm sorry," she said simply. "I didn't know." She looked away from him and her eyes rested upon the strip of ground he had just appropriated. She understood now. No wonder he was surly when they had caught him trying, legally or not, to claw back a few feet of the inheritance he considered had been stolen from him.

She turned to Edgar. Then she grinned. "I won't tell if you don't." She spoke in French, but she suspected that Pride, observing them, had guessed what she had said.

Edgar looked awkward. Pride was watching him. Then Edgar shook his head. "I can't," he muttered in French. And to Pride, in his native tongue: "Put it back, Godwin. Today. I'll be looking out for you." He motioned to her that they must leave.

She would have liked to say something to Pride, but realised she must not. A few minutes later, as the smallholder and his family were lost to sight, she spoke. "I can't go back to Lyndhurst, Edgar. I can't face all those huntsmen. Can we return to your father's house?"

"There's a quiet track," he said with a nod. And after a couple of miles he led her down through a wood to a little ford, quite soon after which they came up to heathland over which they walked their horses, picking up a track that led westwards until, late in the afternoon, they descended from the Forest into the lush quiet of the Avon valley.

It was some time before they reached the forest edge that Puckle, on some errand of his own, had happened to pass by Pride's hamlet and hear his tale.

"Who's the Norman girl?" the smallholder asked. Puckle was able to tell him and to relate the incident of the pale deer.

"Saved a deer?" Pride grinned ruefully. "She could have

brought it to me." He sighed to himself. "Are we going to see her again, do you think?" he asked Puckle.

"Maybe."

Pride shrugged. "She's not bad, I suppose," he said without much feeling, "for a Norman."

Adela's fate, however, was to be decided by a much harsher court than that of Pride and Puckle, as she discovered when dusk fell that day.

"A disgrace. There's no other word for you," Walter stormed. In the light from the evening sky there seemed to be purple shadows under his slightly bulging eyes. "You've made a fool of yourself in front of the whole hunt. You've ruined your reputation. You've embarrassed *me*! If you think I can find you a husband when you behave like this . . ."

For a moment words apparently failed him.

She felt herself go pale, both with shock and with anger. "Perhaps," she said icily, "you do not feel you can find me a husband."

"Let's just say that your presence will not help." His little moustache and his dark eyebrows seemed clenched, now, in quiet rage, menacing. "I think you'd better stay out of sight for a while," he went on, "until we're ready to try again somewhere else. I feel that would be best, don't you? In the meantime, might I suggest that you think rather carefully about how you conduct yourself."

"Out of sight?" She felt alarmed. "What do you mean?"

"You'll see," he promised. "Tomorrow."

The great, sunbathed silence of a midsummer afternoon: it was the season known as the "fence" month when, to ensure that the deer could give birth in peace, all the peasants' grazing livestock were removed from the Forest; after which, more than ever, the area seemed to return to those ancient days when only scattered bands of hunters had roamed the wastes. It was a season of quiet, of huge light on the open heaths and of shade, deep green as river weed, under the oaks.

The buck moved stealthily, keeping to the dappled shadows, his head held carefully back. His summer coat, a creamy beige with white spots, made a perfect camouflage. It was also handsome. But he did not feel handsome. He felt awkward and ashamed.

The change in the psychology of the male deer in summer has been observed down the ages. In spring, first the red deer and then, about a month later, the fallow males cast their antlers. First one antler, then the other breaks off, leaving a raw and usually bleeding stump, or pedicel. In the days after this, the fallow buck is a sickly fellow and may even be bullied by other bucks; such is the nature of animals. Like new teeth, his next antlers are already growing, but it will be three months before they are complete again. And so, though his fine new summer coat is on him, he is robbed of his adornment, as the antlers are known, naked, defenceless, ashamed.

No wonder he wanders alone in the woods.

Not that he is inactive. The first thing nature silently instructs him to do is to find the chemicals he will need to manufacture his new antlers. That means calcium. And the obvious place to find that is in the old antlers he has cast. Using his corner incisor teeth, the buck gnaws at them, therefore. Then, feeding on the rich summer vegetation and living in seclusion, he has to wait patiently as new bone tissue, drawing nutrients up through blood vessels from the pedicels, slowly grows, branches out and spreads. The growing antlers, however, are delicate; to supply blood they also grow a covering of soft veined skin, which has a velvety texture, so that during these months the buck is said to be "in velvet." Supremely conscious that he must not allow the precious antlers to get damaged, the reclusive deer will walk through the woods with his head raised and held back, the velvet antlers on his shoulders, lest they should get caught in branches – a magical attitude in which he has often been depicted, from cave paintings to medieval tapestries, down the centuries.

The buck paused. Though still shy of being seen, he knew that the worst of his yearly humiliation was over. His velvet antlers were already half grown and he was conscious of the first faint stirrings, the beginning of the chemical and hormonal changes that, in another two months, would transform him into the magnificent, swollen-necked hero of the rut.

He paused because he saw something. From the tree line where he was walking, a stretch of heath extended, about half a mile across to a gentle slope scattered with silver birch where the violet heather gave way to green lawn backed by a line of woodland. On the lawn he could see several does, resting in the sun. One of them was paler than the others.

He had noticed the pale doe at the last rutting season. He had caught sight of her again that spring when he had escaped from the hunters. He had supposed they might have killed her; then he had glimpsed her in the distance once more, not long afterwards, and the knowledge that she was alive had pleased him strangely. Now, therefore, he paused and watched.

She would come to him at the rut. He knew it as surely as he could feel the sun in the huge open sky; he knew it with the same instinct by which he knew that his antlers would grow and his body change in readiness. It was inevitable. For several long moments he watched the little pale shape on the distant green. Then he moved on.

He did not know that other eyes were watching her also.

When Godwin Pride had set off that morning his wife, seeing his face, had tried to stop him. She had used several excuses – the roof of the cow stall needed repairing, she thought she had seen a fox near the chicken coop – but it was no good. By midmorning he was gone, without even taking his dog with him. Not that he had told her what he was up to. Had she known that, she would probably have called the neighbours to restrain him. Nor did she see that, a few moments after leaving, he took a bow from a hiding place in a tree.

He had been waiting two months for this. Ever since his encounter with Edgar he had been careful to be a model of good behaviour. He had retracted his fence to its proper place. His cows were brought in from the Forest two days before the fence month. When Cola only glanced suspiciously at his dog, he had turned up at the royal hunting lodge at Lyndhurst the very next day. This was where they kept the metal hoop known as the stirrup – if a dog was not small enough to crawl through it, then his front claws were "lawed," cut off, so that he could not be a threat to the king's deer. Pride had insisted they took his dog to the stirrup, "Just to make sure he's all legal, like," he assured them with a charming smile as the dog wriggled safely through. He had been careful. He had also had to wait for the right weather conditions; and those had come today when the faint breeze had blown from an unusual quarter.

He might not be able to get his field, but he was going to get something back from those Norman thieves. He would strike a little personal blow for freedom: or for his own obstinacy, as his wife would have said. As secretly pleased with himself as a boy on some forbidden adventure, the tall man with the swinging gait had made his way through the woods. If he was caught the consequences would be terrible: the loss of a limb, even his life. But he wouldn't be caught. He chuckled to himself. He had thought it all out.

It had been noon when he had taken up his position. This had been carefully chosen – a little vantage point by the edge of some trees with a hidden depression where he could easily lie concealed while watching out to see if anyone was approaching. He had studied the habits of his quarry carefully.

Soon after noon, as he had expected, they had appeared and, thanks to the change in the direction of the breeze, he was downwind of them.

He had made no move. For over an hour he had patiently watched. Then, as he had expected, he had seen one of Cola's men walk his horse silently across the open ground about half a mile away. He had let another hour pass. No one had come.

He had already selected his target. He needed a small doe – one that he could carry swiftly on his broad back up to his place of concealment. He would return for it that night with a handcart. There would be just enough moon tonight to allow him to see his way through the dark forest tracks. There were several small does in this little herd. One was paler than the rest.

He took aim.

For the first few days Adela could not believe that Walter had done it to her.

If the villages of Fordingbridge and Ringwood, which lay on the River Avon as it flowed down the Forest's western edge, were scarcely more than hamlets, the settlement at the river's southern estuary was more substantial. Here the Avon, joined by another river from the west, ran into a large, sheltered harbour – an ancient place where men had fished and traded for more than a thousand years. Twyneham, the Saxons had first called the settlement and the great sweep of meadow, marsh, woodland and heath that extended for miles along the south-western edge of the Forest from there, had long been a royal manor. In the last two centuries, thanks to a series of modest religious foundations endowed there by the Saxon kings, the village was more often referred to as Christchurch. It had grown into a small town and been fortified with a rampart. Five years ago, Christchurch had been given a further boost when the king's chancellor decided to rebuild the priory church there on a grander scale and work on the riverside site had already begun.

But that was all it was: a quiet little borough by the sea, with a building site for a church.

And he had left her there. Not with a knight – there was no castle nor even a manor house. Not even with a person of the slightest consequence – only four of the most decrepit priory canons had remained in residence while the building went on. He had left her with a common merchant whose son made flour at the priory mill.

"I had to pay him, you know," Walter had explained crossly.

"But how long am I to stay here?" she had cried.

"Until I come for you. A month or two, I should think."

Then he had ridden away.

Her quarters could have been worse. The merchant's household consisted of several wooden buildings around a small yard, and she was given a chamber of her own over a store-room beside the stable. It was perfectly clean and she had to admit that she would not have been any better housed in a manor.

Her host was not a bad man. Nicholas of Totton – he had come from a village of that name that lay fifteen miles away on the eastern edge of the Forest – was a burgess of the borough, where he owned three houses, some fields, an orchard and a salmon fishery. Though he must have been over fifty, he retained a slim, almost youthful build. His mild grey eyes only looked disapproving if he thought someone had said something cruel or boastful. He spoke sparingly, yet Adela noticed that, with his younger children, he seemed to have a quiet, even playful sense of humour. There were seven or eight of these.

Adela supposed that it must be dull to be married to such a man, but his busy wife seemed to be perfectly contented. Either way, the Totton family were hardly relevant to her.

There was no one to talk to and nothing to do. The site where the new priory church was to be built, beautifully set by the river, was a mess. The old church had been pulled down and soon dozens of masons would be hard at work there, she was told. But at present it was deserted. One day she rode around to the headland, which protected the harbour. It was very peaceful. Swans glided on the waters; wild horses grazed in the marshes beyond. On the other side of the headland a huge bay swept round to the west, while to the east the low gravel cliffs of the New Forest shore extended for miles until they receded up the Solent channel from which there interposed the high chalk cliffs of the Isle of Wight. It was a lovely sight but it did not please her. On other days she walked about, or sat by the river. There was nothing to do. Nothing. A week passed.

Then Edgar came. She was surprised he had known she was there.

"Walter told my father you were staying here," he said. He did not tell her that already, all the way up the Avon valley as far as Fordingbridge, people were calling her "the deserted lady."

Things got better after that. He would come to see her at least once a week and they would ride out together. The first time they rode up the Avon valley a couple of miles to where a modest gravel ridge known as St Catherine's Hill gave a splendid view over the valley and the southern part of the Forest.

"They nearly built the new priory up here," he told her. "Next time I come," he pointed to one area of the Forest, "I'll take you there. And the time after that, over there."

He was as good as his word. Sometimes they rode up the Avon valley; or they might wander along the Forest's coastline with its numerous tiny inlets, as far as the village of Hordle, where there were salt beds. Wherever they went he would tell her things: stopping by some tiny dark stream, hardly more than a trickle: "The sea-trout come to spawn up here. You'd never think it, would you, but they do. Right into the Forest."

On their third trip she had met him near Ringwood and he

had conducted her across the heath to a dark little hamlet in a woodland dell called Burley.

"There's something strange about this place," she had remarked.

"They say there's witchcraft in the area," he observed. "But then people always say that about a forest."

"Why, do you know any witches?" she had asked with a laugh.

"They say Puckle's wife is a witch of some kind," he replied. She glanced at him to see if he was joking, but he didn't seem to be. Then he grinned. "A very good rule in the Forest is: if in doubt, don't ask." And he had nudged his horse into a trot.

Often on these rides he would question her about herself, whether she meant to stay in England, what sort of man she expected Walter to find for her. She was guarded in her replies. Her position, after all, was a difficult one. But once she did allow herself, with a trace of condescension, to confess: "My main attraction for a Norman knight, you see, is that I am a Norman too." She was sorry if he looked a little crestfallen, but she wanted to maintain her status.

Two months had passed and still no word from Walter.

If she had not felt confident after all these excursions into the Forest, Adela might not have gone so far by herself that midsummer day. Having ridden into the central section of the Forest, she had let her mind wander and for some time her horse had taken his own course along the woodland tracks, at a gentle walk. Then she had dismounted and rested for a little while in a tiny glade while the animal cropped the grass. The sound of a herd of deer suddenly crashing through the undergrowth somewhere ahead had woken her from her reverie. Curious, she had quickly mounted and trotted forward to see what had disturbed them. Coming out abruptly on to open ground, and seeing a figure she thought she recognised ahead, she cantered towards him, hardly thinking what she was doing. He turned. She saw. And it was already too late.

"Good day, Godwin Pride," she said.

Pride stared. Just for once, he lost his usual composure. His mouth sagged open. He couldn't believe it: how could he have failed to hear her coming? It had only taken him a few moments to run across the open ground and a few more to hoist the fallen doe on to his shoulders. Obviously it had been long enough. The bad luck of the thing was past belief.

And, of all people, this girl. A Norman. Worse still, all the Forest knew she had been riding out with Edgar.

Worst of all, he was caught, as the forest law termed it, "redhanded:" the deer and its blood on his hands. There was no escape. He was for it. Mutilation: they'd cut off one of his limbs. They might even hang him. You couldn't be sure.

He glanced about. They were alone. Just for a moment he wondered if he should kill her. But he put the thought out of his mind. The doe slipped from his back as he stood up straight, brave as a lion before her. If he was frightened at facing death he wasn't going to show it.

And then he thought of his family. What were they going to do if he swung? Suddenly they came before his mind's eye: the four children, his daughter only three, his wife, and the bitter words she would say. She'd be right. How could he explain it to his children? He could hear his own voice. "I did a foolish thing." Without even realising he was doing it, he gave a short gasp.

But what could he do? Plead with this Norman girl? Why should she help him? She'd be bound to tell Edgar.

"A fine day, isn't it?"

He blinked. What was she saying?

"I rode out early this morning," she went on calmly. "I hadn't meant to come so far, but the weather was so good. I suppose if I go that way" – she pointed – "I should get to Brockenhurst."

He nodded, slightly bemused. She was talking on, as though there were nothing the matter in the world. What the devil was she at?

And then he got the message. *She had not looked at the deer.*

She was looking straight at his face. Dear God, she was asking after his children. He tried to mumble some reply. *She had not seen the deer.* Now he comprehended: she was chattering quietly on so that he would understand clearly. There was to be no complicity, no shared guilt, no embarrassment, no favours owed – she was too clever for that. She was better than that. *The deer did not exist.*

She went on a little more, asked him the best route by which she should return and, still without a single glance at the deer on the ground in front of her, she announced: "Well, Godwin Pride, I must be on my way." Then she turned the horse's head and with a wave of her hand she was gone.

Pride took a deep breath.

Now that, he considered, was style.

Moments later, the deer was safely hidden and he was ready to go home. As he started off one further thought occurred to him and he smiled a little grimly.

Just as well, he mused, it wasn't the pale doe he had shot.

Adela was surprised, returning in the evening to Christchurch, to find Walter Tyrrell crossly awaiting her.

"If you hadn't come back so late, we could have left today," he rebuked her. The fact that she had no idea he was arriving did not seem to matter. "Tomorrow morning, first thing. Be ready," he ordered.

"But where are we going?" she asked.

"To Winchester," he informed her, as though it were obvious.

Winchester. At last – a place of real importance. There would be royal officials there, knights, people of consequence.

"Except," he added as an afterthought, "we're to stay a few days, first, at a manor west of here. Down in Dorset."

"Whose manor?"

"Hugh de Martell's."

There was a change in the weather the next morning. As they rode westward into the sweeping ridges of Dorset, a great, grey cloud had risen up from the horizon, blocking the sun, its shining edges imparting a dull, luminous glow to objects in the landscape below.

Walter had maintained his usual grumpy silence for most of the way, but as they came over the last, long ridge he remarked to her gloomily: "I didn't want to bring you here, but I thought I might as well before you go to Winchester. Give you a day or two to smarten up your manners. In particular," he went on, "you should observe Martell's wife, the Lady Maud. She knows how to behave. Try to copy her."

The village lay in a long valley. It was very different country from the Forest. On each side huge fields of wheat and barley, neatly divided into strips, swept up the slopes until they rolled over the valley's crests. At the near end a small stone Saxon church rested on a green by a pond. The cottages were neatly fenced, more ordered than most such places. Even the village street looked tidy, as though swept by some unseen controlling hand. And finally the long lane led to the gatehouse to the manor itself. The house was set some distance back. Perhaps it was a trick of the light but as they rode through the entrance the close-cropped grass lawns, which lay on each side of them, seemed to Adela to be a darker green than the grass they had passed before. Ahead to the left was a large, square range of farm buildings, timber frame over stone, and to the right, set apart behind a large, well-swept open courtyard, stood the handsome hall with its accompanying buildings, all in knapped flintstone and topped with high, thatched roofs with not a straw out of place. This was no ordinary squire's house. It was the base of a large territorial holding. Its calm, rather dark order said quietly, but just as clearly as any castle: "This land is the feudal lord's. Bow down."

A groom and his boy came out to take their horses. The door of the hall opened, and Hugh de Martell stepped out alone and came swiftly towards them.

She had not seen him smile before. It was warmer than she had expected. It made him more handsome than ever. He extended his long arm and held out his hand to help her down. She took it, noticing for a moment the dark hairs on his wrist, and stepped down beside him.

He quietly moved back and, before Walter could say anything remarked: "Just as well you came today, Walter. I was called away to Tarrant all day yesterday." Then he led the way, with an easy stride, towards the hall, holding the door for her as she went in.

The hall was large, as high as a barn with great oak-beamed rafters and woven rush matting on the floor. Two large oak tables, both gleaming, flanked the big open hearth in the centre. The wooden shutters were pulled back; the high windows let in a pleasant, airy light. She looked around for her hostess and almost at once, from a smaller doorway at the far end, the lady came in and went straight to Tyrrell.

"You are welcome, Walter," she said softly, as he took her hand. "We are glad you could come." After only a short pause, she turned to Adela also. "You too, of course." She smiled, although with just a trace of doubt, as if faintly uncertain as to the younger woman's social status.

"My kinswoman, Adela de la Roche," said Walter without enthusiasm.

But it was not the cool reception that claimed Adela's attention. What really struck her was the other woman's appearance.

What had she expected Hugh de Martell's wife to look like? More like him, she supposed – tall, handsome, nearer his age, perhaps. Yet this woman was only a little older than herself. She was short. And she wasn't handsome at all. Her face, it seemed to Adela, was not exactly bad-looking but it was irregular; certainly her lips, which were small, weren't straight – as if they had been slightly pulled up on one side. Her gown, although good, was too pale a shade of green and made her look even more pasty-faced than she was. A poor choice. She looked meagre, insignificant. That, Adela decided, was what she thought.

She had no chance to observe more just then. The manor house boasted two chambers where guests might sleep, one for men, another for women, and after her hostess had shown her the women's chamber she left Adela to her own devices. But a little later, returning to the hall and finding Walter alone there, she quietly asked him: "When did Martell marry?"

"Just three years ago." He glanced round and went on in a low voice: "He lost his first wife, you know." She had no idea. "Lost her and their only child. Heartbroken. Didn't marry again for a long time, then thought he'd better try once more, I suppose. Needs an heir."

"But why the Lady Maud?"

"She's an heiress, you know." He gave her a quick, hard look. "He had two manors, this one and Tarrant. She brought him three more, same county. One of them marches with his land at Tarrant. Consolidates the holdings. Martell knows what he's doing."

She understood the bleak reminder of her own lack of manors. "And has he got an heir now?"

"No children yet."

Shortly after this the Lady Maud appeared and conducted her to the solar, a pleasant room up a flight of steps at one end of the hall. Here she found an old nurse, who greeted her courteously, and she sat and made polite conversation while the two women worked on their needlepoint.

Their talk was friendly enough. Dutifully following Walter's earlier advice, she paid close attention to all that her hostess said and did. Certainly the lady of the manor seemed quite easy company in this setting. She clearly had a complete grasp of everything relating to the household. The kitchen where the beef was already on the spit, the larder where she was making preserves, her herb garden, her needlework, of which both she and the old nurse were quite rightly proud – all these things she spoke about with a quiet warmth that was pleasing. But if Adela asked her about anything outside these boundaries – about the estate or the politics of the county – she would only give a slightly twisted smile and answer: "Oh, I leave all that to my husband. That's for the men, don't you think?"

Yet at the same time she obviously knew all the landholders of the area well and Adela found it hard to believe that she did not have some idea of their affairs. Evidently, however, she did not believe it was her role to admit to such knowledge. She has decided what she wants to be and what she ought to think, Adela realised. She does so because she believes it's to her advantage. No doubt, behind her mincing little smile, she thinks me a fool if I don't play the same game. She also noticed that as she quietly stitched, the Lady Maud asked her almost nothing about herself – although whether it was because she was not interested or because she did not wish to embarrass Walter's obviously poor relation, it was impossible to tell.

In the afternoon they all went for a ride round the estate. With its huge fields, its neatly kept orchards, its well-stocked fish ponds, it was the perfect model of what such a manor should be. There could be no doubt that Hugh de Martell knew his business well. When they came to a long slope that led up to the crest of the ridge, the two men cantered up it and Adela would have liked to follow at the same pace.

But the Lady Maud was firm: "I think we should walk the horses. Let the men canter." So Adela was obliged to keep her company and they only got halfway up the ridge before the return of the men caused them to turn round again.

"Fine view," Walter remarked as they did so.

On their return from the ride they found that the servants had set out trestle tables in the hall, spread them with cloths and soon afterwards they were seated for a meal. Since they had not eaten yet that day a full dinner was now served. Everything was quietly but handsomely done. A small procession brought bread and broth, salmon and trout, three meats. Hugh de Martell carved himself; the Lady Maud served Walter from her own plate. The wine – this was rare indeed – was clear and good, lightly spiced. Fresh fruits, cheeses and nuts rounded off their meal. Tyrrell politely complimented the Lady Maud upon each course and Martell took the trouble to amuse Adela by telling her a funny story about a merchant from Normandy who spoke no English. And perhaps she drank just a little too much.

Yet how could she possibly have known she was making a mistake when she mentioned the Forest? Since, in Walter's eyes, she had made such a fool of herself there, he might have assumed she would not bring up the subject of the deer drift. It was hard to know. All she did at first, in any case, was to ask her hostess if she ever ventured into the New Forest.

"The New Forest?" The Lady Maud looked faintly startled. "I don't think I'd want to go there." She gave Walter one of her little smiles, as if Adela had said something socially inappropriate. "The people who live there are very strange. Have you been there, Walter?"

"Only once or twice. With the royal hunt."

"Ah. Well that's rather different."

Adela saw that Walter had just given her a disapproving frown. Obviously he wanted her to change the subject. But it also irritated her. Why should she be treated like an idiot all the time? He was going to despise her anyway. "I ride in the Forest alone," she said blithely. "I've even hunted there." She paused to let that sink in. "With your husband." And she gave Walter a smile of cheerful defiance.

But whatever reaction she might have expected, it was not the one she got.

"Hugh?" The Lady Maud frowned, then went a little pale. "Went hunting in the Forest?" She looked at him questioningly. "Did you, my dear?" she asked in a strangely small voice.

"Yes, yes," he said quickly, with a frown. "With Walter here. And Cola. Back in the spring."

"I don't think I knew that." She was looking at him with a silent reproach.

"I'm sure you did," he said in a firm tone.

"Oh. Well," she replied softly, "I do now." And she gave Adela her twisted smile before adding with a forced playfulness: "Men will go off hunting in the Forest."

Walter was gazing down at his food. As for Martell, was there a hint of impatience in his manner? A slight shrug of the shoulder? Why would he not have told her? Was there some other reason for his visit to the Forest? Were there other absences, perhaps? Adela wondered. If he escaped from his wife from time to time, she was not sure she blamed him, whatever he got up to.

It was Walter who came to the rescue. "Speaking of things royal," he calmly remarked, as though nothing awkward had occurred, "have you heard . . ." And a moment later he was relating one of the latest scandals from the royal court. As they so often did, this concerned the king's shocking words to some monks. Impatient of religion himself, Rufus could seldom resist baiting churchmen. As usual also, the Norman king had contrived to be both rude and funny. Shocked though she felt she must be, the Lady Maud was soon laughing as much as her husband.

"Where did you learn this?" Martell enquired.

"Why, from the Archbishop of Canterbury himself," Walter confessed, which made them laugh all the more. For it was a fact, quite amusing to Adela, that Tyrrell had somehow managed to ingratiate himself with the saintly Archbishop Anselm, too.

And then, having got into his stride, Walter started to entertain them. First one, then another, the stories rolled out. Witty, amusing, mostly about the great figures of the day, frequently accompanied by the admonition "Don't repeat this," Walter told his stories well. No one could have failed to be delighted, flattered, fascinated by such an amusing courtier. For Adela it was a revelation. She had never seen Walter being charming before. He certainly never is to me, she thought. But you had to admit he had the skill. Despite herself she was impressed.

And it occurred to her, too – if he was impatient with her, could she entirely blame him? This clever Walter Tyrrell, who had married into the mighty Clares, was a friend of the great – could she really complain if he was ashamed of her as she did one gauche thing after another?

When, some time later, the contented party broke up and prepared to retire early to bed, she went to his side and murmured: "I'm sorry. I keep doing the wrong thing, don't I?"

To her surprise, in reply, he smiled at her quite kindly. "My fault too, Adela. I haven't been very nice to you."

"True. But I can't have been a burden you wanted much."

"Well, let's see if we can do something for you in Winchester," he said. "Goodnight."

She woke early the next morning feeling wonderfully refreshed. She opened the shutters. The day was beginning, the pink of dawn already fading from a clear blue sky. The damp cool air tingled on her face. Apart from the gentle twittering of the birds, everything was quiet. Some way off a cock crowed. She thought she detected the faint smell of barley in the air. No one was stirring yet in the house, but across the ridge she saw a single peasant making his way along a path. She took a breath.

She couldn't wait in the chamber until the household started to appear. The day was too inviting. She felt too excited. Pulling on her chemise and a linen overshirt, tying her girdle, sweeping back her loose hair with both hands and with only slippers on her feet, she went quickly out of the house. If she looked a little wild, she thought, it didn't matter. No one would see her.

Just beyond the house was a walled garden entered by a gate. She went in. It would be some time before the sun invaded that silent space. Herbs and honeysuckle grew there. Three apple trees occupied a patch of lawn, their half-ripened apples still hard, although they had put on their first blush of colour. Wild strawberries showed among the grass, too, spangling the green with tiny specks of red. There were cobwebs in the corners of the wall. Everything was drenched in dew. Her mouth widened with delight. Why, she might have been in some castle or monastery garden in her native Normandy.

She remained there, drinking in the peace of the place for some time.

There still did not seem to be anyone about when she came out. She considered walking across to the stables, which were in the big square of outbuildings, or perhaps the field beyond where some of the horses had been put out for the night. But as she came along the side of the manor house her attention was caught by a small door set low in the side wall, with three stone steps leading down to it. She assumed this must lead to an undercroft and that it would be locked. But as it was her nature to do so, she went down to try it and, to her surprise, it opened.

The undercroft was large; the low cellar extended the whole length of the building. Its ceiling was supported by three thick stone pillars down the centre, which divided the area into bays. The light from the door, which she left open, was supplemented by a small barred window set high in the opposite wall.

Her eyes took a few moments to accustom themselves to the shadows but she soon saw that it contained the sort of items she would have expected – although unlike the jumble one often found in such storage places, everything here was stacked in an orderly fashion. There were chests and sacks; one bay was taken up by barrels of wine and ale; in another hung some archery targets, unstrung bows, arrows, half a dozen fishing nets, collars for hounds, falconing gloves and hoods. Only as she came to the furthest bay on the left, where there were wood shavings on the floor, did she see something strange – gleaming faintly, a tall form in the shadows so like a man that it made her jump.

It was a wooden dummy. The reason it shone softly was that it was wearing a long coat of chain mail and a metal helmet. Behind it, she now saw, was a second dummy wearing the leather shirt that went under the chain mail. On a stand was a high-pommelled saddle, against which rested a long studded shield; on a frame next to this, a huge broadsword, two spears and a mace. She gave a little intake of breath. This must be Hugh de Martell's armour.

She knew better than to touch anything. The chain mail and the weapons had all been carefully oiled to keep them from rusting; in the faint light she could see that everything was in perfect readiness. Not a link in the armour was out of place. There was a mingled smell of oil and leather, metal and resinous wood shaving that she found strangely exciting. Instinctively, she moved close to the armoured figure, smelling it, almost touching.

"My grandfather used a battleaxe."

The voice came so unexpectedly, not an inch from her ear, that she almost screamed. Her slippered feet left the stone floor. She whirled round, all but brushing against his chest as she did so.

Hugh de Martell did not move but he chuckled. "Did I startle you?"

"I . . ." She tried to get her breath. She could feel herself blush wildly. Her heart was palpitating. "Oh, *mon Dieu*. Yes."

"My apologies. I can move softly. I thought you were a thief at first, in this light." He still had not shifted. The space between them seemed only enough for a shadow.

She realised suddenly that she was only half dressed. What could she say? Her mind would not focus. "A battleaxe?" It was the last word she seemed able to remember.

"Yes. We Normans are all Vikings, after all. He was a big, red-headed man." He smiled. "I get my dark hair from my mother. She was from Brittany."

"Oh. I see." She saw nothing, except his leather jerkin and the sleeve of his long arm. She was aware, only, that there was a pause before he spoke.

"You're always exploring, aren't you? First the Forest, now here. You have an adventurous spirit. That's very Norman."

She turned her face up towards his. He was smiling down at her. "Aren't you adventurous?" she asked. "Or perhaps you don't need to be."

His smile went, but he did not look angry, only thoughtful. He had understood her, of course: the settled manors, the rich wife; her little challenge to suggest he had lost his Viking ancestors' spirit. "I've plenty to do, as you see," he answered quietly. There was a sense of calm authority, of power that emanated from him as he spoke the words.

"I am put in my place," she replied.

"I wonder where your place is." His look of amusement had returned. "Normandy? England?"

"Here, I think."

"You are going to Winchester. That's a good place to find a husband. So many people go there. Perhaps we shall see you again in this part of the country."

"Perhaps. Do you go to Winchester?"

"Sometimes."

He took a step back now. His eyes, she realised, had automatically taken all of her in. He was about to turn away. She wanted to say something, anything to keep him there. But what could she say? That he had married a rich woman unworthy of him? That he'd have been better with her? Where, where on God's earth could anything between them possibly lead?

"Come." He was offering to escort her out. Of course, she should go and dress herself properly. She did as he indicated, walking in front of him towards the light at the door. Only just before she reached it did she feel him take her hand, firmly raise it and brush it softly with his lips.

A courtly gesture in the shadow. Unexpected. She turned to him. Something like a pain seemed to stun her across the chest. For just a second she could not breathe. He bowed his head. Like a sleepwalker she went through the door into the bright world outside, almost blinded by the light. He had turned to lock the door. She walked on, not looking back, into the manor house.

The rest of the day passed quietly. Most of it she spent in the company of the Lady Maud. When she saw Hugh de Martell, he seemed polite but somewhat cold and aloof.

And when she and Walter parted from him the next morning to make their way to Winchester he remained formal and unapproachable. But at the top of the ridge she glanced back and saw his tall, dark figure, still watching after them until they passed out of sight.

• • • •

Autumn comes with kindness to the Forest. The long light of summer slides into September; the spreading oaks are still green; the peaty humus of the heath retains a soft, seaside warmth; the air smells sweet and tangy.

In the world outside it is a mellow time. The harvest is done, the apples are ready to fall, the mists on the bare fields a damp reminder to men to gather in all they can as the sun begins its gradual recession towards the ending of the year.

But in the Forest nature takes a different form. This is the season when the oaks shed their green acorns and the forest floor is covered with their falling. Men like Pride turn out their pigs to eat the acorns and beech nuts – the mast, as this feed is called. It is an ancient right, which even the Norman Conqueror had no wish to stop. "If the deer eat too many acorns when they're green," his foresters reminded him, "they get sick. But the pigs love them." As the days pass, the beech trees begin to yellow; yet, just as this sign of gentle decay is seen, another almost contradictory transformation also takes place. The holly tree is either male or female and it is now, as though to welcome the future coming of winter, that the female holly bursts into berries whose thick, crimson clusters gleam against the crystal-blue September sky.

As the equinox passes and all nature becomes aware that the nights are starting to be just a little longer than the days, further changes are seen. The heather flowers having turned into a haze of tiny white dots, the heathland goes from its summer purple to autumn brown. The brown of the bracken stem climbs into the drying ferny leaves until, in certain clumps, they catch the autumn sunlight like polished bronze. The acorns lying in the fallen leaves have rolled free from their cups and they, too, are brown. The evening mist brings a damp chill. The cold dawn has a bracing bite. Yet in the Forest, these signs mark not an end but a beginning. If the sun is now departing, it is only to cede his place to a yet more ancient deity. Winter is on the way: it is the time of the silver moon.

It is the time for the rutting of the deer.

The buck stalked down the centre of the rutting stand. It was dawn. There was a light frost on the ground. Around the edge of the stand, on ground marked by their slots, as the tracks of the deer's cleft feet are called, eight or nine does were waiting to be serviced. Some of them were moving about making a wickering sound. There was tense excitement in the air. The pale doe was also there. She was waiting quietly.

The buck's antlers were splendid and he knew it. Their heavy, burnished blades spread out some two and a half feet from his head and they were fearsome to behold. They had been fully grown since August when their velvet covering had begun to peel off. For many days he had scraped and rubbed the new antlers against small trees and saplings, leaving scour marks on their bark. It had felt good when the strong saplings braced and bent against their weight; he had felt his growing power. This honing served a dual purpose: not only did it clean off the last vestiges of peeling velvet, but the bone of the antlers, creamy white when they emerged, became coated, polished, hardened to a gleaming brown.

By September he was getting restless. His neck swelled. His Adam's apple enlarged; the tingling sensation of power seemed to be filling his whole body, from his hindquarters to his thickening shoulders. He began to strut and stamp the ground; he had an urge to exercise, to prove his power. He moved about the woods alone at night, wandering here and there like some knight in search of adventure. Gradually, however, he began to move towards that part of the Forest where the pale doe had seen him the year before – for bucks instinctively move away from their original home when they are going to mate, so that the genetic stock of the deer will be constantly mixed. By late September he was ready to mark out his rutting stand. But before that, one other ancient ceremony had to begin.

Who knew when the red deer first came to the Forest? They had been there since time immemorial. Bigger than the fallow interlopers, men had designated them by different names: The male red was a stag, the female a hind; the young red was not a fawn, like the fallow, but a calf. While the fallow buck's antlers rose in broad blades, the stag's still larger crown rose in spiky branches. The red deer's numbers were never large. Lacking the fleetness and cleverness of the fallow, they were easier to kill and already the fallow far outnumbered them. While the fallow liked the wooded glades, the red remained on the moor where, as they lay in the heather, they seemed, even in full daylight, to blend into the land itself. Primeval and Nordic, compared with the elegant French arrivals, it seemed appropriate, as the autumn rut approached, that even the fallow great bucks should yield precedence to these ancient figures who had endured in the empty silences of the heath since, very likely, the age of ice.

It is normally a few days after the autumn equinox, when he has taken charge of the group of hinds who will form his exclusive harem, that the red stag raises his mighty head and utters the haunting call, a few notes higher than the bellow of cattle, which echoes over the heather at twilight and causes men to listen and say: "The stags have started to roar."

And more days will pass before, in the woodland glades, the fallow bucks add their own, different call to the sounds of autumn.

The buck's stand was not one of the most important – older and more powerful great bucks held those – for this was still his first rut. It was about sixty yards long and nearly forty wide. He had prepared it carefully for days. First, working his way around the perimeter of the stand, he had used his antlers to thrash the saplings and bushes. As he did so, a strong scent exuded from glands below his eyes, marking the bushes as his territory. He anointed the trees along the perimeter too. Then, as the moment came closer, he had made scrapes with his forefeet, which also contained glands, upon the ground, even tearing it up in places with his antlers. He urinated in the scrapes, then rolled in the wetted dirt. This created the pungent smell of the rutting buck, thrilling to does: for unlike the red deer, it is the females who come to the male in the fallow rut.

And so, as if for some magical knightly tournament that was to take place in the forest glade, the handsome young buck was ready to challenge all comers on his rutting stand. His rut would last many days, during which time he would not eat, living on the energy provided by a phenomenal production of testosterone. Gradually he would grow less alert; by the end he would be exhausted. The watching does would guard him, therefore, patrolling the outer edges of the stand, looking out and listening. And indeed, all nature participated: for the birds would call out at the approach of danger and even the forest ponics, usually silent, would whinny in warning if they saw human intruders come near the dappled forms in their secret ceremony.

The buck had been pacing the stand for hours. Trampled grass, crushed bracken and nutty brown acorns lay underfoot. As well as the does, two prickets and a sore, who was trying to look as if he might step into the ring, were watching. A faint light was filtering through the trees. From time to time he would pause in his pacing to give the rutting call.

The rutting call of the fallow buck is known as a groan. Stretching his head slightly downwards, he then raises his swollen throat to emit this call. Its sound can hardly be described – a strange, grunting, belching trumpet. Once heard, it can never be forgotten.

Three times he groaned, handsome, powerful, from the centre of the stand.

But now a new figure was approaching through the trees. There was a rustle as the does scampered out of his path. He emerged and crossed the line quietly into the stand, walking calmly towards the buck as though he had not a care in the world.

It was another buck and, judging by his antlers, the two were perfectly matched.

The pale doe trembled. Her buck was going to fight.

The interloper moved slowly across the stand. He was darker than her buck. She could smell his scent, pungent, sour, like the mud from brackish water. He looked strong. He walked past her buck who fell into step – this was the ritual of the fight – just behind. The two males kept walking, almost casually; she saw the muscles flexing in their powerful shoulders, their antlers waving slowly up and down as they went along. She noticed that one of the two little curved horns just in front of the base of the antler blades on the dark buck's head was broken, leaving a jagged spike. A sudden twist of the head and he could gouge out her buck's eye. The other does were watching silently. Even the birds in the trees seemed to have quietened. She was aware only of the slow swish of the feet of the two males on the fallen leaves and bracken.

All nature knew her buck's fate was about to be decided. A

buck might challenge one of the mighty great bucks and lose with honour. Perhaps the interloper had broken his horn that way. But when two matched bucks come head to head, one must be defeated. He may be wounded, sometimes killed; but most important he has lost, his pride is shattered. The does know it, the whole forest has seen. He slinks away, and the stand and the does belong to the victor.

The pale doe watched as the two males reached the end of the stand, turned and started back again. Was it, after all her waiting, to be the darker, sour-smelling buck with the vicious spike who destroyed her chosen mate and then possessed her? She had come to the rutting stand. She belonged to the winner by right. That was the way of it. Then she saw her buck give the sign.

A nudge. That was the signal. Her buck moved forward just a little so that his shoulder nudged the hindquarter of the interloper.

The dark buck wheeled. For just a second there was a pause as the two bucks braced back on their hind legs; then, with a crack that echoed through the woods, the two huge antlers crashed together.

Two full-grown bucks fighting is a fearsome thing to behold. As the powerful bodies with their swollen necks strained, grunting, against each other, the pale doe involuntarily backed away. They suddenly seemed so huge, so dangerous. If one of them broke loose, if they came charging towards her . . . They were evenly matched. For long seconds they inched back and forth, their antlers locked low, their hind legs digging into the ground, muscles bulging as if they might snap. Her buck seemed to be gaining.

Then she saw his hind legs slip. The interloper pushed forward, a foot, a yard. Her buck was clawing the ground, but slipping in the damp leaves. He was about to go down. She saw him lock his legs. He was sliding back, his body rigid, locked in position. The interloper gave a final shove; he seemed about to lunge forward and grind her buck down.

But something had changed. Her buck had hit firmer ground. His feet suddenly got their purchase on grass. His hindquarters shivering, he dug in. She saw his shoulders rise and his neck bear down. And now the interloper was slipping on the wet leaves. Slowly, cautiously, their antlers locked, the two straining bucks began to turn. Now they were both on grass. Suddenly the interloper disengaged. He gave his head a twist. The jagged spike was aiming at her buck's eye. He lunged. She saw her buck rock back, then smash forward. His whole weight came down on the interloper's antlers. There was a rasping crackle. The interloper, because of his vicious manoeuvre, was not quite straight. His neck was twisting. He was giving ground.

And then, in a rush, it was all over. Her buck was shoving him back, foot after foot. The interloper was off balance; he struggled, turned and was caught on the flank. Her buck was in full spate now, butting, tossing his head, driving his opponent before him. There was blood on the interloper's side. Her buck's head rammed again into his antlers with a tremendous blow. The interloper cried out, turned, stumbling, and limped off the stand. He had lost.

Having strutted magnificently down the stand of which he was now the undisputed master, her buck turned his face towards her.

Why did he suddenly look strange? His huge antlers, his triangle of a face, the two eyes like black holes, staring blankly towards her: it was as if her buck had vanished, been transmogrified into some other entity named only "deer" – an image, a spirit, swift and terrible. He bounded towards her.

She turned. It was expected of her; it was instinctive; but she was also afraid. All year she had waited. Now it was her turn. She began to run, away from the stand, through the trees, the bushes brushing against her. All year she had waited, yet now, knowing him so large, so powerful, so strange and terrible, she was trembling with fear. Would he hurt her? Yes. Surely. Yet it must be so. She knew it must. She had a strange sensation, as though all the warmth, all the blood in her body was rushing backwards, into the base of her spine and her hindquarters, which were trembling as she ran. He was coming. He was just behind, she could hear him, sense him. Suddenly she could smell him. Hardly knowing what she did, she stopped abruptly.

He was there. He was upon her. She felt him mount her; her body staggered under the weight. She had to fight to stand up.

His scent was all over her like a cloud. Her head involuntarily snapped back. His antlers appeared, hovering above, terrible, absolute. And then she felt him enter. A searing red pain and then, something full, urgent, tremendous, filling her like a flood.

Adela liked Winchester. Lying in the chalk downs, due north of the great Solent inlet, it had once been a Roman provincial town. For centuries after it had been the chief seat of the West Saxon kings, who had finally become kings of all England. And though, during the last few decades, it was London that had become the effective capital of the kingdom, the old royal treasury remained at Winchester and the king would still from time to time hold court at his royal palace there.

It was not far from the New Forest. A road led south-west for eight miles to the small town of Romsey, where there was a religious house for nuns. Four miles more and one was in the Forest. Yet, as Adela quickly found, it seemed a world away.

Set on a slope, overlooking a river and surrounded by sweeping ridges topped with woods of oak and beech, Winchester was essentially a walled city of about a hundred and forty acres, with four ancient gates. The southern end contained a fine new Norman cathedral, the bishop's palace, St Swithun's priory, the treasure house and William the Conqueror's royal residence, together with several other handsome buildings of stone. The rest of the town was on a fitting scale, with a market place, several merchant halls, houses with gardens and dovecotes, and busy streets of craftsmen and tradesmen. By one of the gates there was a hospice for poor folk. The views over the downs were broad, the air bracing.

The city had retained much of its ancient character. The streets all had their Saxon names, from Gold Street and Tanners Street even to the Germanic-sounding Fleshmongers Street. But the court of Wessex had been an educated place. Even before the Norman Conquest, the city had bustled with priests, monks, royal officials, rich merchants and gentlemen, and one would have heard Latin and even French spoken, as well as Saxon, in Winchester's halls.

The arrangements Walter had made for her were certainly an improvement upon the merchant at Christchurch. Adela's hostess was a widow in her fifties, the daughter of a Saxon noble by birth, who had been married to one of the Norman keepers of the Winchester treasury and who now lived in pleasant stone-built lodgings beside the western gate. Walter had been closeted with her for a long time when they first arrived and after he had gone the lady had given Adela an encouraging smile and told her: "I'm sure we can do something for you."

Certainly, she hadn't lacked company. The first day they walked through the streets, to St Swithuns and back through the market, her hostess was greeted by priests, royal officials and merchants alike. "My husband had many friends and they remember me for his sake," the lady remarked; but after a day or two's experience of the other woman's kindness and common sense, Adela concluded that they liked the widow for herself.

Her own position was made easy.

"This is a cousin of Walter Tyrrell's, from Normandy," her hostess would explain; and Adela could see from their respectful reaction that this immediately placed her as a young noblewoman with powerful connections. Within a day, the prior of St Swithuns had requested that the two women would dine with him.

In private her new friend was reassuring, but down-to-earth. "You are a handsome girl. Any noble would feel proud to have you at his side. As to your lack of inheritance . . ."

"I'm not penniless."

"No, of course not," said her friend, although perhaps with more kindness than conviction. "One should never claim anything that isn't true," she went on, "but equally there's no need to put people off. So I think it would be best if we just . . . say nothing." Her voice trailed away. She gazed into space. "Anyway," she added brightly, "if you make yourself agreeable to your cousin Walter, perhaps he might provide something for you."

Adela looked surprised. "You mean . . . money?"

"Well, he isn't poor. If he thinks you might be useful . . ."

"I hadn't thought of that," Adela confessed.

"Oh, my dear child." The widow took a moment to recover herself. "From now on," she said firmly, "we must both work to ensure that your cousin feels you will be a *great* credit to him."

If her hostess encouraged her to be a little wiser about her own situation, the society of Winchester also made her more aware of what was passing in the outer world. She had known, for instance, that the king had his differences with the Church, but she was quite shocked when a senior churchman, talking casually to them in the cathedral yard, referred to him openly as "that red devil."

"Yet think of what Rufus has done," her friend said afterwards. "First he has a flaming row with the Archbishop of Canterbury. The Archbishop goes to see the Pope and Rufus refuses to let him re-enter England. Then, here in Winchester, the bishop dies and Rufus refuses to install a new one. You know what that means, don't you? All the revenues of the Winchester diocese, which is hugely rich, are paid to the king instead of the Church. And now, to add insult to injury, he's just made his best friend, who is an absolute rogue, into the bishop of Durham. The churchmen don't just hate the king. Many of them would like to see him dead."

Another subject she soon encountered concerned her native land. Several times, when they learned that she had come from Normandy, people had remarked: "Ah, I dare say we shall all be under one king again soon." She had known that when Duke Robert of Normandy had gone on crusade three years before, he had raised the money for the expedition by a huge loan from his brother Rufus, offering Normandy itself as security. What she had not realised, but everyone in Winchester knew, was that Rufus hadn't the slightest intention of seeing his brother return to his duchy. "If he isn't killed on crusade," he had apparently told his friends gleefully, "he'll come back penniless. He'll never be able to repay. Then I'll get Normandy and be as great a man as my father the Conqueror was."

"He's probably right," the widow told Adela, "but there is a danger. Some of Robert's friends tried to kill Rufus a few years ago. Some of the Clares, actually. Mind you, they're all afraid of Rufus. But you never know . . ."

"What about the third brother, young Henry?" Adela ventured. "He's got nothing to rule."

"That's true. You may see him, by the way. He comes through here from time to time." Her friend considered for a few moments. "I think he's probably clever," she said finally.

"I don't think he'd take sides with either brother because you only get caught in the middle. I think he keeps his head down and gives no trouble. That's probably the wisest thing to do. Don't you think?"

Whenever there was any entertaining to be done in Winchester – if a party of knights came through, or some royal official and his retinue were to be given a feast by the keeper of the treasury – the widow and Adela were sure to be of the company. Within a few weeks she had met a dozen eligible young fellows who, if they were not necessarily interested themselves, might mention her to others.

It was at one of these feasts that she met Sir Fulk.

He was a middle-aged man, but quite agreeable. She was sorry to hear that he had just lost his fourth wife – he did not seem to say quite how. He had estates in Normandy and in Hampshire, quite near Winchester. He thought he had once met her father. She could not help wishing that, with his little moustache and round face, he did not remind her so much of Walter, but she tried to put the thought from her. He spoke affectionately of all his wives.

"All my wives," he told her kindly, "have been very amiable, very docile. I've been very fortunate. The second," he added by way of encouragement, "looked like you."

"You mean to marry again, Sir Fulk?"

"Yes."

"You are not looking for an heiress?"

"Not at all," he assured her. "I'm all right as I am. Not ambitious. And you know" – he said this with a sincerity which was obviously meant to touch her – "the trouble with these heiresses is that they often have rather a high idea of the importance of their own opinions."

"They should be guided."

"Quite."

When they left the feast, her hostess was briefly delayed, but as soon as she joined Adela she told her: "You have made a conquest."

"Sir Fulk?"

"He says he has received encouragement."

"He's the most plodding man I ever met in my life."

"Perhaps, but he's sound. He'll give you no trouble."

"But I'll give him trouble," Adela cried.

"You mustn't. Control yourself. At least get safely married first."

"But," Adela said in exasperation, "he looks just like Walter!"

Her companion took a little breath and gave her a tiny glance, which Adela failed to see. "Your cousin is not so bad looking."

"He is to me."

"You mean to refuse Sir Fulk if he asks for your hand? Your family could insist. Walter, that is."

"Oh, just tell him my true nature and he'll go away at once."

"I'm afraid you're being foolish."

"You don't sympathise?"

"I didn't say that."

"You think I have to make a sacrifice of myself?" She looked accusingly at the older woman. "Did *you* make a sacrifice when you married?"

For a moment her companion paused. "Well, I'll tell you this," she said quietly. "If I did, my dear late husband never knew it."

Adela digested this in silence, then nodded ruefully. "Am I clever enough to be married?"

"No," the older woman replied. "But very few girls are."

The proposal came the next day. Adela rejected it. Walter Tyrrell arrived a week later, and went straight to see the widow.

"She has refused Sir Fulk?"

"He may not be the right one," the widow suggested kindly.

"Without my permission? What's wrong with him? He has two good estates."

"Perhaps it was something else."

"He's a very handsome man."

"No doubt."

"I take this rejection personally. It's an outrage."

"She's young, Walter. I like her."

"You speak to her, then. I won't. But tell her this," continued the infuriated knight. "If she refuses one more good man I'll take her to Romsey Abbey and she can live the rest of her life as a nun. You tell her that." And with only a perfunctory kiss of his old friend's hand he left.

"So you see," the widow told Adela an hour later, "he's threatening you with Romsey Abbey."

Adela had to admit that she was shaken. "What sort of place is it? Do you know anyone there?" she asked in alarm.

"It's rather grand. Mostly noblewomen. And yes, I do know a nun there. She's a Saxon princess called Edith – one of the last of our old royal house. I knew her mother very well. Edith's about your age."

"Does she like it?"

"When the abbess isn't looking, she takes off her habit and jumps on it."

"Oh."

"I shouldn't go there unless you want to be a nun."

"I don't."

"I think you'd better make sure you do marry, but we can take a little time. Just be careful not to encourage any more Sir Fulks." Then, taking pity on her, the widow added: "I think, actually, that Walter isn't very likely to carry out that particular threat."

"Why?"

"Because, Romsey Abbey being what it is, to get you in there he'd probably have to pay."

However, the autumn season had brought few visitors to Winchester after that. November came, the leaves had all fallen, the sky was grey and the wind that blew over the bare downs was often bitter cold. There were no suitors now. She thought of the Forest sometimes and could almost wish herself back in Christchurch, riding out with Edgar. She thought, many times, of Hugh de Martell. But she never mentioned this, even to her kindly hostess. December arrived. Soon, they said, there would be snow.

She could hardly have been more surprised, coming out of the cathedral one cold December day, to see her cousin Walter, wearing a jaunty hunting cap with a feather in it, standing beside a handsome covered wagon from which, taking his outstretched hand, a lady wrapped in a cloak with a fur trim was carefully alighting.

It was the Lady Maud.

She hurried forward and called out to them. They both turned.

Walter looked slightly annoyed. She supposed he thought

she was interrupting the Lady Maud. He had sent no word that he would be in Winchester, but that was not so surprising. He surely could not have been meaning to pass through the place without coming to see her? The nod he gave her seemed to indicate that she might join them and so she went in with them as they entered the royal residence where the porter and servants evidently knew her cousin.

Lady Maud, she thought, might have been more friendly or showed more recognition, but Adela supposed she must be tired from her journey. While the Lady Maud left them for a short while, Walter explained that they were only breaking the journey. Lady Maud was to visit a cousin of hers who lived beyond Winchester and Hugh de Martell, with whom Walter had just been staying, had asked him to accompany her there. "Then I return to Normandy," Walter said. He was pacing moodily, which did not make conversation easy.

It was only a short while before the Lady Maud rejoined them, apparently in better humour. As usual, she looked slightly wan, but her manner was civil even if it contained the hint of caution that Adela had experienced before. When Adela asked if she was well, she acknowledged that she was.

"Your husband is also well, I trust," she forced herself to say. She hoped it sounded polite but unconcerned.

"Yes."

"You are travelling to one of your relations, Walter said."

"Yes." She seemed to consider for a moment. "Richard Fitzwilliam. Perhaps you have seen him."

"No. I have heard of him, of course." She had heard often. Thirty years old with one of the finest estates in the county, he lived not five miles away. He was unmarried. "I understand he is very handsome," she added politely.

"Yes."

"I did not know he was your kinsman."

"My cousin. We're very close."

No word of this connection, Adela was well aware, had been made during her stay with the lady in the summer. She wondered if Lady Maud would suggest that they might meet now.

She didn't. Walter said nothing.

There was a pause.

"Perhaps you'd like to rest a little before we go on," Walter suggested.

"Yes."

He turned to Adela and gave her a little nod. A courtier's sign that it was time for her to retire.

She could take the hint, but it would have been nice if Walter had come with her to the door. "Shall I see you again before long, Walter?" she asked as she turned.

He nodded, but in a way to indicate that her retiring was more important; and before she could even ·collect her thoughts she found herself outside in the cold streets of Winchester.

She did not want to go back to her lodgings. She walked about. After a little, she went out of the gateway and stared across the open countryside. The sky was grey. The bare brown woods on the ridge opposite seemed to mock her. I am scorned, she thought; she might be poor, but why should her own cousin treat her like that, dismissing her like a lackey? She felt a hot surge of anger. Damn him. Damn them both.

She paced up and down in front of the gate. Would they come out that way? Could she say something to them? No. What a fool she'd look standing impotently by the roadside. She felt crushed.

And yet something in her still rebelled. I'm better than that, she decided. I won't let them put me down. She needed to see them again, put them in a position where they would be forced to be polite. But how? What excuse could there be for going back?

Then it suddenly occurred to her. Of course: her hostess and Walter were friends. What could be more natural than for her to return with the older woman who might wish to greet him as he was passing through. The widow was a noblewoman. Lady Maud would have to recognise her. And if by chance she were to tell them that Adela was a great favourite with everybody there and a credit to her cousin . . . The beauty of the idea was no sooner growing in her mind than she turned and ran back as fast as she could to her lodgings.

Her friend was there. Without dwelling on the more humiliating features of the interview, it was only the work of a few moments to explain the situation and the widow readily agreed to come, so long as Adela gave her a brief space to prepare herself, which she did with all speed.

She was still arranging her hair, though, when another thought occurred to Adela. What if Walter and the lady should leave before they got there? She had better make sure they didn't. Walter could hardly go if she told him the widow was on her way.

"I'll meet you by the royal palace entrance," she cried and hurried back through the street, praying she was not already too late.

All was well, however. The porter assured her they were still inside. She waited by the doorway, but then, as it was cold and she felt a little foolish, she asked the porter if she might step inside. Having seen her do so before, he made no objection, and agreed to send the widow in the moment she arrived.

"She is an old friend of my cousin Tyrrell's," Adela explained, feeling much happier now.

Between the outer door and the great hall there was a smaller hall or vestibule. Here Adela waited. She had carefully prepared herself. If they suddenly left the great hall and came upon her she would smile easily and say that she had only returned because the widow was on her way. She was sure she could carry it off. She rehearsed it repeatedly. But they did not come. She began to grow restless. Was it possible that they could have gone out some other way? She listened at the heavy door to the hall but heard nothing. She paced, listened again, hesitated. And cautiously began to open the door.

They were standing together. Both were already wrapped in their cloaks and Walter had on his feathered cap – evidently they were on the point of leaving. But they had paused in front of a wall hanging depicting a hunting scene.

Walter was just behind her shoulder, leaning over her, pointing to something in the scene. His cheek was near to hers, but that was not so strange. He drew away from her, just a little and she leaned towards him. There was something teasing and familiar in the gesture. His hand lowered, she half turned. And, there could be no possible mistaking it, his hand rested, just for a moment or two, holding her breast. The Lady Maud smiled. Then she saw Adela.

They sprang apart. The lady, turning away to pull her cloak more tightly around herself, took a step or two towards the wall hanging. Walter, looking straight at Adela, glowered as though he fully expected her to be swallowed up by the ground.

What did it mean? Were they lovers or was this just the sort of flirtation which, she knew, happened all the time in courtly circles? What did this imply about the lady's feelings for her husband? It was this thought, suddenly arising in her mind, that caused her to remain there motionless, staring at them stupidly.

"What the devil are you doing in the king's hall?" Walter was far too clever to show anything but anger. Even in her dazed confusion she noticed how quickly he had managed to make her the criminal – a trespasser on the king's property.

She blurted out that the widow wanted to see him, that they had come together. Somehow it sounded foolish, especially when Walter asked "Well, where is she?" and she wasn't there.

"The Lady Maud is leaving now," he said curtly. Whether he even believed the widow was coming Adela could not tell.

The Lady Maud, repossessed of her dignity, walked straight towards the door as though Adela did not exist. But suddenly, struck by a thought, she stopped and looked at Adela. "The whole county knows you're looking for a husband," she said sweetly. "But I don't think you'll have much luck. I wonder why."

It was too much. First their contemptuous treatment of her, then the little scene of infidelity, and now this brazen insult. Well, let them discover she could hit back. "If I do marry," she replied with a calm tone she was proud of, "I'm sure I shall honour my husband. And give him a child." It was a devastating counter-blow. She knew it and she didn't care. She watched the other woman's face for a reaction.

But to her surprise the Lady Maud only drew her two red lips into a bow and glanced at Walter with a small look of triumph. "I'm afraid you will soon get a reputation for having a vicious tongue," she remarked. "An untruthful one, too," she added carefully. Then she continued on her way to the door, which Walter held open for her. Adela expected him to turn his back and leave at this point, but instead he remained there, holding the door open for her, too, and indicating that she should walk out with him. Slightly dazed, a few moments later, she found herself walking after the Lady Maud, with Walter following, into the cold air outside. The lady was helped into the wagon and Walter prepared to mount his horse.

But before he did so, he gestured that Adela should draw close to him. "I think you should know," he said in a low voice, "that when I arrived at Hugh de Martell's the other day, he told me some good news. The Lady Maud has recently discovered she is expecting a child." He looked her bleakly in the eye. "You've just made two more enemies – her and her husband. For you can be sure she'll speak to him against you. I should take care if I were you." He swung up into the saddle and they moved off.

They had passed out through the gate when the widow appeared, hurrying towards her, too late.

There was a frost that night. Adela did not sleep well. She had made a fool of herself again. She had secured the undying hatred of the Lady Maud and probably the enmity of Hugh de Martell as well. Walter must finally be sick of her. She was alone in the world without any friend. But even all these troubles might at last have faded as she passed into unconsciousness, had it not been for one stark fact, which arose, again and again, driving away the clouds of sleep before it. His wife was going to give Martell a child.

In the morning a wind from the north came down from the ridges and dusted the city with snow; and it seemed to Adela that the world had grown very cold.

Edgar usually enjoyed the winter months. They were hard of course. The grasses shrank down to tiny, pale tussocks. Frost came, and snow. The deer fed mostly on holly and ivy, and heather. In the worst conditions they would even gnaw tree bark for nutrients. The sturdy wild ponies, who would munch almost anything, would feed on the spiky gorse. By the end of January many of the animals were becoming gaunt; the ponies moved about less, conserving energy. It was nature's testing time and some animals would not survive.

Yet many did. Even when the birds skimmed low and in vain over the bleak, snowy heath and the solitary owl flapped on his quest through the bare trees and saw no prey, still it seemed to Edgar that the peaty earth below retained its warmth. The frosts covering its surface were broken by the slotting footfalls of the delicate deer. The larks and warblers somehow found food, and foxes stole from farms. Squirrels, jays, magpies all had their own stores; the smallholders fed their cattle. And at various places in the Forest the foresters, when necessary, put out food for the deer to ensure their survival.

Once, riding across the Forest, he had seen the pale doe feeding and this had reminded him once again of Adela.

He had wanted to go and see her in Winchester. It was his father who had always stopped him. "Leave her alone. She wants a Norman," he had advised. Then Cola had told him she already had an offer of marriage. In November he had informed his son that Adela had almost no dowry and in December he had told him rather brutally: "No point in marrying a woman who will always look down on you because you're only a Saxon huntsman." But even these arguments might not have kept Edgar away, if it had not been for one other consideration.

Edgar had never fathomed exactly how his father came by his information. Was it the friends he had made on the royal hunts who kept him informed? Strange people with messages would appear from time to time. Or was it his monthly visits to an old friend up at the castle of Sarum? Or other sources encountered on his occasional unexplained absences? Who knew? "Maybe it's the forest owls talking to him," Edgar's brother had once suggested. Whatever it was, the old man heard things and during that winter Edgar could see that he was becoming worried. In November he had sent his older son to London to attend to a matter of business, which was to keep him there some months. To Edgar the old man had grunted: "You stay here. I need you with me."

When Edgar had ventured, once or twice, to ask his father what was on his mind, Cola had been evasive, but when he had frankly asked, "You fear another plot against the king?" his father had not denied it. "Dangerous times, Edgar," he had muttered and refused to be drawn any further.

The possibilities for intrigue were so many that Edgar could hardly guess from which quarter the danger might be coming now. There were the supporters of Robert, of course; and one of these held the lands on the forest's southern coast. But further behind might be the King of France, fearful of an attack on his own territory if aggressive Rufus became his neighbour in Normandy. Or it could be something less obvious. Only four years before there had been a plot to assassinate Rufus and put his sister's husband, the French Count of Blois, on the throne. Tyrrell's relations, the powerful family of Clare, had been involved in that before they suddenly changed sides and warned Rufus of his danger. And as they had already been involved in other plots in the past it seemed clear to Edgar that the Clares, including their henchmen like Tyrrell, were not to be trusted. The Church, with no reason to love Rufus, would hardly be sorry to see him fall either.

But why should these great affairs worry his father so much? Whoever the next king was, he would probably be glad of the services of the expert forester and Cola had always been good at staying out of trouble. Why, then, should he be so concerned? Was he implicated? It remained a puzzle.

Edgar was a dutiful son. He did not go to Winchester. He stayed at his father's side, patrolled the Forest and made sure that most of the deer came safely through the winter.

Towards the end of the season another rumour reached England. Robert of Normandy, on his way back from crusade – where he had fought rather well – had stopped in southern Italy. Not only was he given a crusading hero's welcome there, but it seemed he had found a bride who would bring him a fabulous dowry. "Enough to pay off the loan and get back Normandy," Cola remarked. For some reason the Italians were also calling Robert the King of England. "God knows what that means," Cola continued, "but even if he pays off the loan, Rufus isn't going to let him back into Normandy. He'll use force. And then Robert's friends will be after Rufus's blood."

"I still don't see why this need affect us in the Forest," Edgar commented. But his father only shook his head and refused to say more.

Another month passed and there was no more news from any quarter. Except, of course, the worrying news from Hugh de Martell.

• • •

When Adela saw Hugh de Martell standing at the door of her lodgings, for a moment she could hardly believe it.

There had been a shower, which had cleared, leaving the streets glistening in the watery sun. A sharp, early spring breeze had given her cheeks a flush and made them slightly numb, as she went for a quick walk round the cathedral precincts and the market.

She gave a little involuntary gasp. His tall, handsome form was so exactly as she always saw him in her mind's eye. She thought she would have known him even if he were halfway across the Forest. Yet he also looked different and as he turned towards her she was even more struck by the change.

"They told me you would be back soon." He seemed almost relieved to see her.

What could this mean? Why had he come? Walter had assured her that the Lady Maud would turn Martell against her; but it did not seem so.

He smiled, but it was clear that there was strain on his face. "May we walk?"

"Certainly." She indicated the way towards St Swithuns and he fell into step beside her. "Are you in Winchester for long?"

"Only an hour or two, I think." He glanced down at her. "You have not heard. But of course, why should you? My wife is ill." He shook his head. "Very ill."

"Oh. I'm sorry."

"Perhaps it is because she is with child, I do not know. No one knows." He made a gesture of helplessness.

"And so you are here . . . ?"

"There is a doctor. A skilful Jew. He has attended the king. They told me he was to be found here in Winchester."

She had heard of this personage, even seen him once – a rather magnificent, black-bearded man who had been staying for the last week as a guest of the keeper at the royal treasury.

"He is out riding with some of his king's men," Martell continued. "But they are expected back in an hour or two. I hope you did not mind my coming to your lodgings. I know no one in Winchester."

"No." She was not sure what to say. He was pacing beside her, his long strides, so full of nervous energy, carefully kept slow so that she should not need to hurry. "I am glad to see you."

Why had he come to her? Glancing up at his face, so full of worry and concern, she suddenly realised. Of course, this strong man was also an ordinary man, with feelings like any other. He was in anguish. He was lonely. He had come to her to be comforted. A wave of tenderness passed through her. "They say the Jewish doctors have great skill," she suggested. The Normans had a high regard for the learning of the Jews, which went back to classical times. It had been the Conqueror who established the Jewish community in England and his son Rufus particularly favoured them at his court. "I'm sure he will cure her."

"Yes." He stared ahead absently. "Let us hope so." They walked on together in silence for a short distance. The cathedral loomed ahead. "Winchester is a fine city," he remarked, in a brave effort to make conversation. "Do you like it?"

She told him she did. She talked about recent small events in the city, of people who had passed through – anything that might distract his mind from his worries for a while. And she could see that he was grateful. But she also saw, after a time, that he wanted to return to his thoughts and so she said no more and they continued in silence together round St Swithuns.

"The child is due at the start of summer," he said suddenly. "We have waited so long."

"Yes."

"My wife is a wonderful woman," he added. "Brave, gentle, kind." Adela nodded quietly to this also. What could she say? That she knew his wife to be timid, small-minded and vicious? "She is devoted. She is loyal."

The memory of the lady standing close to Tyrrell, the sight of his hand moving to her breast and remaining there, came into Adela's mind with terrible vividness. "Of course." How good he was. A thousand times too good for the Lady Maud, she thought. Yet here she was, because she must, quietly acquiescing in his self-deception.

They said little more as they made their way back towards her lodgings and were getting near the city gate when they saw a party of horsemen ride in among whom, unmistakably, was the impressive figure of the Jew.

Martell started forward, checked himself and turned. "My dear Lady Adela." He took her two hands in his. "Thank you for keeping me company at such a time." He looked into her eyes with real tenderness. "Your kindness means so much to me."

"It was nothing."

"Well . . ." He hesitated. "I know you only a little, but I feel that I can talk to you."

Talk to her – as she looked up into his manly, troubled face, how she wished she could respond truthfully. How she wished she could say: "You are grieving over a woman completely unworthy of you." Dear heaven, she thought, if I were in the Lady Maud's place I should love you, I should honour you. She could have screamed it. "I should always be glad to be of help to you at any time," she said simply.

"Thank you." He smiled, bowed his head respectfully and turned away, striding purposefully towards the horsemen.

She did not see him again in the days that followed. The Jewish doctor departed with him and returned a week later due to stay at Winchester, she learned, until Easter when the king was expected there. She made enquiries and learned that though the Lady Maud was still alive and, miraculously, had not lost the child so far, the Jew could not answer for whether she would survive or not.

More days passed. It grew a little warmer. Adela reflected. She pondered.

Then, early one morning, leaving only a message for her hostess, she rode out of Winchester alone. In the message, which was deliberately vague, she begged her friend to say nothing and promised to return by nightfall the following day. She did not say where she was going.

Godwin Pride, it was plain to see, felt rather pleased with himself. He was standing outside his cottage holding a rope. At the other end of the rope was a brown cow. His wife and three of his children were looking at it. A robin on the fence was also watching with interest.

Godwin Pride had come through the winter well enough. At the end of the autumn he had killed most of the pigs he had turned out on the acorn mast and salted them. He had eggs from his chickens, milk from his few cows; there were preserves from his apple trees and dried vegetables. As a commoner of the Forest he also had his right of Turbary, which gave him turf fuel. He had stayed snug in his cottage, kept his small stock alive and emerged into the Forest's spring in good humour.

He had also bought a new cow. "It was a bargain," he declared. He had walked with it from Brockenhurst.

"Oh? What did you pay?" asked his wife.

"Never you mind. It was a bargain."

"We don't need another cow."

"She's a good milker."

"And I'm the one who'll have to look after her. Where did you get the money, anyway?"

"Never you mind about that."

She looked suspicious. The children watched silently. The robin on the fence looked a bit quizzical too.

"And where are we going to put her?" By which she meant, in winter. Was he going to build another cow stall? There really wasn't space for one more beast in the little cattle pen. Surely he wasn't intending to try to enlarge that again after being caught out last year. "You can't enlarge the pen," she said.

"Don't you worry. I've got something else in mind. It's all planned, that is. All planned." And, although he refused to be drawn, he looked more pleased with himself than ever. Even the robin seemed impressed.

And the fact that he had bought the cow on impulse, that there was no plan, that he hadn't the faintest idea how he was going to accommodate it next winter, did not unduly trouble him. There was the whole long Forest spring and summer to think about that. Sometimes, as his wife knew so well, he could be like a little boy. But if she was thinking of arguing any more she never got the chance.

For it was at this moment that Adela appeared, walking her horse towards them.

"Now what the devil can she want?" Godwin Pride exclaimed.

It was late afternoon when the two figures came down from the plateau of Wilverley Plain – a huge level heath almost two miles in extent where the Forest ponies grazed with nothing around them but the open sky. Adela was walking her horse; just ahead of her, on a sturdy pony, Godwin Pride led the way. He did so very unwillingly.

The clouds were clearing from the sky to reveal, against the blue, the silver crescent of a waxing moon. There was a hint of spring warmth in the air. Adela was glad to be back in the Forest, even if she was a little afraid of what she was doing.

They had taken the track westwards from the central section of the Forest, up across the heathland of Wilverley, and were now about four miles west of Brockenhurst. Ahead of them lay a stretch of oak wood. To continue straight would lead down into the large dell where the dark little village of Burley lay. Instead, therefore, they cut right, through some woods and down a slope known as Burley Rocks. Crossing a big empty area of marshy lawn, they took a little track that led along the edge of some moorland. "That's Burley moor on our right," Pride told her. "White Moor lies ahead. And that" – he indicated a tummock on top of which a single tree seemed to be waving its arms distractedly – "is Black Hill." The track suddenly turned left, leading down to a stream, running swiftly as it made a sharp turn, like a crook in a man's arm. "Narrow Water," he said. On the right, along the stream was a boggy area infested with stunted oaks, holly, birch and a tangled mass of saplings and bushes. And just past this, quite alone, stood an untidy collection of huts and a mud cabin with a roof made of branches, twigs and moss through which wisps of smoke were seeping.

They had come to Puckle's place.

Pride had not wanted to take her, but she had insisted. "I don't know where he lives and I don't want to ask. People mustn't know I went there. I think," she added, looking at him hard, "that you owe me a favour." The deer. He couldn't deny it. "Besides," she continued with a smile, "if you ask her, she's more likely to agree to talk to me."

And there was the rub, the real reason why he had been unwilling to take her. For it was not Puckle she wanted to see, but his wife. The witch.

Adela waited by the stream while Pride rode up to the cabin and went in. After a while she saw Puckle and various children and grandchildren emerge and busy themselves outside.

Then Pride appeared and made his way over to her. "She's waiting for you," he said briefly. "You'd best go in." A few moments later Adela found herself stooping her head as she went through the small doorway into the witch's little house.

It was rather shadowy inside. The cabin consisted of a single room, such light as there was coming from a window whose shutters were only partly open. In the centre of the floor a circle of stones served as a hearth in which a small turf fire was glowing. On the other side of the fire sat a figure in a low wooden chair. By her feet, warming itself, was a grey cat. There was a three-legged stool, also by the fire, to which the other woman motioned.

"Sit down, my dear."

Although Adela had not formed any precise image in her mind, Puckle's wife was not what she had expected. Before her, as she got used to the light, she saw a comfortable middle-aged woman with a broad face, a rather snub nose and grey eyes spaced wide apart.

She was observing Adela with mild curiosity. "A fine young lady," she now continued quietly. "And you've come all the way from Winchester?"

"Yes."

"Fancy that. And what can I do for you?"

"I understand," Adela said bluntly, "that you're a witch."

"Oh?"

"They say you are."

"They do, do they?" The older woman seemed to receive this information with quiet amusement. Not that the accusation was so shocking: although witchcraft was certainly frowned upon by the Church, systematic persecution was rare in Norman England, especially in the depths of the country where ancient folk magic had always persisted. "And what if I were?" she went on. "What would a fine young lady like you be looking for? A cure for a sickness? A love potion perhaps?"

"No."

"You want your future told. A lot of young girls want to know the future."

"Not exactly."

"What is it then, my dear?"

"I need to kill someone," said Adela.

It was a moment or two before the other woman spoke after that. "I'm afraid I can't help you," she replied.

"Have you ever?"

"No."

"Could you?"

"I wouldn't even try." She shook her head. "These things only happen if they're meant to be." She looked at Adela severely. "You should be careful. Wish someone good or wish someone evil, it will return to you three times."

"Is that what the witches say?"

"Yes." After waiting for that to sink in, the older woman continued more kindly, "I can see you are troubled, though. Would you like to tell me about it?"

So Adela did. She explained about Martell and the Lady Maud. She told the woman all she had seen, the lady's terrible faults of character, her unfaithfulness, the way Hugh de Martell was being misled.

"And you think you'd make him a much better wife?"

"Oh, yes. So you see, if his wife, who's very sick anyway, were to die, it would really only be for the best."

"So you say, my dear. I see you've thought about it."

"I'm sure I'm right, you see," she said.

Puckle's wife sighed, but she made no comment. Instead, she rocked to and fro in her chair while her cat raised its head enough to give Adela a long stare before apparently going to sleep again. "I think," she said at last, "I can help you."

"You could make something happen? You could foretell?"

"Perhaps." She paused. "But it may not be what you want."

"I've nothing to lose," Adela said simply.

After nodding her head thoughtfully, Puckle's wife rose and went outside. She was gone for a few moments, then returned, although not to sit down. "Witchcraft, as you call it," she said quietly, "is not about casting spells. It's not just that. So" – she nodded to the chair where she had been sitting – "you go and sit down in that chair and relax." With that, she went over to a chest in one corner of the little room and busied herself with certain articles inside it, humming to herself as she did so. Her cat, meanwhile, moved away from its former position, settling down near the chest where, after one more meaningful look at Adela, it went back to sleep.

After a while, Puckle's wife began to place some objects on the floor near the chair. Adela noticed a little chalice, a tiny bowl of salt, another of water, a dish containing, by the look of it, some oatcakes, a wand, a small dagger and one or two other items she did not recognise. While she was doing this, Puckle appeared in the doorway for a moment and handed her a sprig from an oak tree, which she took with a nod and placed beside the other articles. When all was ready she came and sat quietly on the stool for a time, apparently thinking to herself. The room became very quiet.

Reaching forward, she picked up the dish of oatcakes and offered them to Adela. "Take one."

"Are they special? Is there a magic ingredient in them?" Adela asked with a smile.

"Ergot," the witch replied simply. "It comes from grain. Some use an extract from mushrooms, or from toads. They all make the same sort of potion. But ergot is the best."

Adela ate the little cake, which tasted of nothing very special. She felt both nervous and rather excited.

"Now my dear," Puckle's wife said at last, "I want you to sit quite still and rest your feet flat on the floor. Put your hands in your lap, push your back straight against the back of the chair." Adela did so. "Now," the witch continued gently, "I want you to take three breaths, very slowly, and when you let them out, taking your time, I want you to relax as completely as you can. Will you do that for me?"

Adela did so. The feeling of relaxation, coupled with her nervousness, made her give a little laugh. "Are you going to take me away to a magic kingdom – another world?" she asked.

The witch only looked down quietly at the floor. "As above, so below," she said quietly. "The magical kingdom is the world between the worlds." Looking up again she continued: "Now I want you to imagine you're like a tree. There are roots growing down from your feet into the earth. Can you imagine that?"

"Yes, I think so."

"Good." She paused a moment. "Now there's a root growing down from your spine, right through the chair and down into the ground. Deep into the ground."

"Yes. I can feel it."

The witch nodded slowly. It seemed to Adela that she was

indeed rooted like a tree, in that space. At first it felt strange, then immensely relaxing. Only then did the witch get up and slowly begin to move about.

First she picked up the little dagger and, pointing it, she made a circle in the air that seemed to contain them both and all the articles on the ground. The cat remained outside the circle.

Then she touched the water in the bowl with the tip of the dagger, murmuring something; next she did the same to the salt. After this she transferred three tips of salt on the dagger point into the bowl of water and stirred, still murmuring softly.

Next she took the bowl of water and performed sprinklings, three times each, in four places round the imaginary circle, which Adela realised must be the four points of the compass. She took a tiny glowing shard from the fire, whispered something and snuffed it out, watching wisps of smoke drift upwards. Then once again she went round the four points, making curious signs at each.

"Do you always move round the same way, from north to east to south?" Adela ventured to ask.

"Yes," came the reply. "If you go the other way we call it moving widdershins. Don't talk."

Now, a third time, she was going to the compass points around the circle, holding the dagger, and at each one she made a curious casting in the air. At the first Adela thought it was a random sign, but she realised that the second was identical. At the third she understood: the witch was drawing a pentagram, the five-pointed star whose structural lines have no break or ending, in the air. And though the fourth casting took place behind her head, she had no doubt it was the same. Finally the witch made a pentagram at the centre of the circle. "Air, Fire, Water, Earth," she said quietly. "The circle is made."

Picking up the wand, she went round once more, repeating the pentagrams. Then, satisfied, she stood in the centre of the circle, not looking at Adela but apparently at the points on the circle's edge, speaking softly to each before at last sitting down on the stool and quietly waiting, like a householder expecting visitors.

Adela, too, sat quietly waiting – she was not sure for how long. Not long, she thought.

At first, when Puckle's wife had told her to imagine herself a tree, she had experienced a vague downward pressure on her body. After a little, to her surprise, she found she could not only imagine herself in this transformed state, she could actually feel the roots extending out of the soles of her feet and then from her spine, seeking their way down into the dark earth. She could feel the earth, as though she had acquired several new sets of hands and fingers: it was cool and damp, musty but nourishing. This downward sense continued. If she wanted to move, she realised, the roots would hold her down, keeping her in this single place. At first this seemed a little irksome. I'm not a free animal any more, she thought, I'm a tree, I'm trapped, a prisoner of the earth.

But gradually she began to get used to it. Although her body might be rooted in the earth, her mind seemed to have gained a new freedom. It was a peaceful, pleasant feeling. She felt as if she were floating.

Some time passed. She was aware of the shadowy room, the gentle glow of the fire, the witch's quietness. But then one or two strange things happened. The grey cat began to grow. It roughly doubled its size and then started to change into a pig. Adela thought this rather funny and laughed. Then the pig floated out of the window, which seemed sensible enough, since a pig obviously belonged outside.

A little later she realised something else. It had grown dark outside, but she could see the sky and the stars through the cabin roof. This was remarkable. The branches, the twigs and moss were still there, but she found she could see straight through them. Better yet, it seemed that she herself, being a tree, was growing up through the roof now, opening out her canopy of leaves to the night.

And now she was flying. It was so simple. She was flying in the night sky under the crescent moon. Her clothes were no longer on her, nor did she want them. She could feel the cool air with a hint of dew on her skin. She was high over the Forest and the stars in the sky were clustering round her, tapping on her skin like diamonds. For a short, wonderful time she flew around over the woodlands, which rippled gently like waves. Finally, seeing an oak, larger than the others, she flew towards

it and reached its branches, vaguely realising as she did so that
this tree was herself.

She floated down, comfortably, to the mossy ground. Once
there, she could see numerous pathways leading away under
the arching oak trees; but one in particular caught her attention
because it was like a long, almost endless tunnel that glowed
with a greenish light. In the distance down this tunnel she also
became aware of something, some swift creature, coming in
her direction. It seemed very far away, but in no time at all it
drew much closer. Indeed, it was bounding towards her.

It was a stag, a magnificent red stag with branching antlers.
Closer and closer it came. It was coming for her. She was
frightened. She was glad.

Silence. Blankness. Maybe she had dozed for a short while.
She was in the little room again. The grey cat was in the corner. Puckle's wife was making the sign of the pentagram, although her hand was moving in the opposite direction from the
way she had done it before. After finishing, the older woman
looked at her and remarked quietly: "It's completed."

Adela remained still for a moment or two, then moved her
hands and feet. She felt rather light. "Did something happen?"

"Oh, yes."

"What?"

Puckle's wife did not answer. The faint glow of the turf fire
threw a soft light around the room.

Glancing at the window, Adela saw that there was now only
a faint hint of light outside. She wondered vaguely how long
she had been there. An hour or more if it was already dusk.
She had planned spending the night with the Prides at their
cottage; she supposed Pride could still take her back there
after dusk. "I must go. It will be night soon," she said.

"Night?" Puckle's wife smiled. "You've been here all night.
That's dawn you see out there."

"Oh." How extraordinary. Adela tried to collect her
thoughts. "You said something happened. Can you tell me?
Will the Lady Maud . . .?"

"I saw a little of your future."

"And?"

"I saw a death, which will bring you peace. Happiness too."

"So. It is going to happen, then."

"Don't you be sure. It may not be what you think."

"But a death . . ." Adela looked at her but the other woman would not say more. Instead, she went to the door and summoned Pride.

Adela rose. Obviously Puckle's wife expected her to leave now. She went to the doorway. She wasn't sure if she should give her money or just thank her for the visit. She felt in a pouch in her belt and brought out two pennies. Puckle's wife took them with a quiet nod. Evidently she felt this was her due. The figure of Pride, leading her horse, came looming out of the pale darkness.

"Thank you," she said. "Perhaps we shall meet again."

"Perhaps." Puckle's wife looked at her thoughtfully, not unkindly. "Remember," she admonished, "things are not always what they seem in the Forest." Then she went back inside.

Dawn was breaking as they rode out onto the huge lawn below Burley Rocks. The moon had departed. The stars were fading gently in the clear sky and a golden light shimmered along the eastern horizon.

A skylark started singing, high above – a starburst of sound against the withdrawing night. Did he, also, know she was going to marry Martell?

Adela felt pleased with herself as she rode into Winchester that afternoon. She and Pride had travelled at a leisurely pace across the Forest, passing north of Lyndhurst, and he had refused to leave her until, just short of Romsey, they had encountered a respectable merchant who was going her way.

She had wondered whether, upon her return, she should tell her friend the widow where she had really been and concluded that she should not. Instead, she had concocted a story about a Forest friend being in trouble and asking for help, and even persuaded a reluctant Pride to back it up if necessary. Altogether she thought she had handled things quite well.

So she was surprised, upon her return, as she began her tale, when the widow raised her hand to stop her. "I'm sorry, Adela, but I don't want to hear." Her face was calm, but cold. "I am only relieved that you are not harmed. I would have sent people out to look for you but you gave me no idea which way you had gone."

"There was no need. I said I'd be back."

"I am responsible for you, Adela. Your going off like that was unforgivable. Anyway," she continued, "I'm afraid you'll have to go. I can't have you here any more. I'm sorry, because it's nearly Easter." At Easter the king and his court would be there. The perfect opportunity to find a husband. "But I won't take responsibility for you. You'll have to go back to your cousin Walter."

"But he's in Normandy."

"The keeper of the treasury has a messenger crossing to Normandy in a few days. He will accompany you. It's all arranged."

"But I can't go to Normandy," Adela cried. "Not now."

"Oh?" The widow looked at her sharply, then shrugged. "Who will take you in? Have you other arrangements in mind?"

Adela was silent, thinking furiously. "Perhaps," she said hesitantly. "I may have."

Edgar would often ride out past Burley, where the forester was a friend of his. He had ridden over to the dark dell where the village lay, that spring morning, and finding him out had continued eastwards across the great lawn and into the woods when he caught sight of his friend standing in a clearing, talking to Puckle. Seeing Edgar, the forester waved and signalled him to dismount. Edgar did so and walked over.

"What is it?"

The forester looked excited. It was evident that Puckle must have brought him some piece of news as the two men were obviously about to go off together. In answer, his friend just put his finger to his lips and motioned Edgar to accompany them. "You'll see."

Together the three men went quietly through the trees, saying nothing and taking care not to step on any twigs that might crack. Once the forester licked his finger and held it up to check the direction of the breeze. They went on in this manner for nearly half a mile. Then, Puckle and the forester began to move slowly, crouching and using the bushes for cover. Edgar did the same. They edged forward another hundred yards or so. Then Puckle nodded and pointed to a place not far ahead in the trees.

It was a small clearing, only twenty paces across, with an ancient tree stump and a small holly bush in the middle. If it had not been for a dark ring of tracks in the fallen leaves, not even Puckle would have given the place a second glance. But today it was occupied.

There were five of them, all bucks, ready to rut the next season, if they had not the last. They all still had their antlers. They looked very handsome. And they were dancing in a ring.

There really was no other way to describe it. Round they processed, kicking their heels in the air. Every so often one, then another, would stand up on their hind legs, turn and spar with each other just like boxers. It was not in earnest, though, but in play. This was one of the rarest and most lovely of the Forest's many ceremonies. Edgar smiled with pleasure. It was ten years since he had seen a dancing of the deer in a play ring.

And why should the bucks dance in a circle? Why did humans do the same? The three men watched for a long time, experiencing the joy and reverence that is special to the Forest people, before creeping silently away.

Edgar's heart was singing as he rode down into the Avon valley. He was looking forward to telling his father all about it.

On his arrival home, however, he found his father had other things on his mind. The old man looked grim. "We've received a messenger," Cola told his son as he led him into the hall. Edgar noticed a young fellow waiting with his horse by the barn. "From Winchester."

"Oh?" This meant nothing to Edgar, although he realised that his father was watching him carefully.

"That girl. Tyrrell's kinswoman. She wants to come here. Some problem in Winchester. She doesn't say what."

"I see."

"You know nothing about this?"

"No, Father." He didn't. But his mind was working fast.

"I don't like it." Cola paused, glanced at Edgar again. "She has powerful kin."

"Hmm . . . I'm not sure they care about her. But you're right.

I wouldn't want to offend Tyrrell. And the Clares . . ." He became silent, thoughtful. As so often happened, Edgar had the feeling that his father knew more than he was saying. "I think this girl's trouble," he said finally. "I'm sure that's why she's leaving Winchester. She's got into mischief of some sort. And I don't need that here. Also . . ." He looked glumly at Edgar.

"Also?"

"I seem to remember you took an interest in her."

"I remember."

"Could that happen again?"

"Perhaps."

"That's what worries me." The old man shook his head. "She'd be no help to you, you know," he growled. "Or me," he added in a mutter.

"Do you think she's bad?"

"No. Not exactly. But . . ." Cola shrugged. "She's not what we need."

Edgar nodded. He understood. They needed someone rich. Someone who would give no offence. But whether it was the sight of the dancing deer, the spring air, or the memory of his rides with her, he felt impelled to say: "We ought to give her shelter, Father."

Cola nodded. "I was afraid you'd say that." He sighed. "Well, she can stay here until I can get word to Tyrrell. I'll ask him what he wants me to do with her. I just hope to God that as soon as he knows she's here, he takes her away.

She was nearer to Martell. It was fated to happen. Her position, admittedly, might have been awkward, but luckily the widow in Winchester had at least relented enough to give her a cover story. Adela was being harassed, Cola was told, by an unwanted suitor and she needed to escape from Winchester for a time. She was not sure the old man believed it, but it was the best she could do. She thanked him for his kindness, murmured how grateful Tyrrell and her Norman relations would be, kept her head held high and did her best to make herself agreeable.

It was clear to her after a day or two that Edgar, although he treated her with a polite caution, was still attracted to her; and since she liked the handsome young Saxon this made her life easier.

When he asked her if she would like to ride out with him, she gladly accepted. She did not lead him on. She was sure she didn't. But it was nice to be admired.

And it was easy to get news of the Lady Maud. She told Cola how she met Martell in Winchester. It seemed natural that she should be concerned about the health of a lady with whom she had stayed. The huntsman heard about Martell from time to time and so it was that Adela knew that the Lady Maud continued to be very sickly and that some said she would never survive the birth. Adela therefore waited patiently.

Tyrrell's response did not come for nearly a month. When it did, it was a minor masterpiece.

It arrived in the form of a letter, written in Norman French. Cola took it to one of the old monks at Christchurch to make sure he had the sense correctly. It ran:

> *Walter Tyrrell, Lord of Poix, sends greetings to Cola the Huntsman.*
>
> *I thank you, my friend, and so would her family, for your kindness to the Lady Adela. Your care for even such a distant kinswoman of mine will not be forgotten.*
>
> *I come into England again in the late summer and will collect her from you at that time, and settle any expenses you may have incurred.*

"The cunning devil," Cola grunted. "He makes sure I have to keep her for three months. And if she gives trouble, she's only a 'distant kinswoman.' He can't be held responsible."

Meanwhile he watched Adela and his son with growing concern. It was not as if he hadn't got other things on his mind to worry about.

When King William II, called Rufus, had spent Easter in Winchester his mood had been notably good. As the weeks followed, it had only grown better.

The conduct of his brother Robert had been everything that he could wish. Having married his heiress in Italy, the obvious move for the Duke of Normandy would have been to hasten back with his bride and her cash, and pay off the mortgage on Normandy. Not a bit of it. After a rather heroic spell on crusade, he was reverting to his usual lackadaisical form. The duke and his bride proceeded at a leisurely pace, stopping everywhere, spending freely as they went. They were not likely to reach Normandy until the end of summer.

"Give him time," Rufus laughed to his court. "He'll spend the whole dowry. You'll see." Meanwhile he himself not only held Normandy, but never ceased his plans to steal any other bits of neighbouring France that he could.

At the start of the summer, however, came an even more agreeable development. Inspired by the sight of so many other Christian rulers winning glory on crusade, the Duke of Aquitaine, the huge, sunlit, wine-growing region south-west of Normandy, decided that he must be a holy crusader too. And what should he do but ask Rufus for a massive loan, just as Robert of Normandy had done, to finance the campaign?

"He's offering to mortgage the whole of Aquitaine," his emissaries announced. Rufus, who probably held no religious beliefs at all, only laughed: "It's enough to restore one's faith in God!" he commented.

And soon the rumour was running round Europe: "Rufus means to have not only Normandy but Aquitaine as well." To those who disliked or feared him, it was not welcome news.

Edgar loved to show her the Forest. It was, after all, the thing he knew best. And with his brother still in London, he had her all to himself.

He showed her how to read the spoor of the fallow deer. "You see, the deer has a cleft foot. When the deer walk, the two cleaves of the foot are together and so the track looks like a little hoof print on the ground. When they trot, the foot opens out and you see a cleft. When they gallop, the foot opens right out and you see a V in the ground." He smiled happily. "Here's something else. See these tracks, with the feet turned out-wards? That's the male deer. The footprints of a female deer point straight ahead."

On another occasion, after they had ridden right across from Burley to Lyndhurst in some of the deepest woods, he asked her: "Do you know how you can tell what direction you are headed in the Forest?"

"By the sun?"

"What if it's cloudy?"

"I don't know."

"Find an exposed, upright tree," he told her. "The lichen, you see, always grows on the damp side of the tree. That's where the prevailing wind carries the moisture to them from the sea. In this part of England it is from the south-west. Look for the lichen and that's south-west." He grinned. "So if you get lost, the trees will be telling you where I live."

She knew he was falling in love with her and by June her conscience was beginning to trouble her. She was aware that she should hold herself a little distant from him, but this was difficult when she found him such pleasant company. They rode, they laughed, they walked together.

Some days she would refuse to go out. She had begun a large and handsome piece of needlework as a present for his father. It seemed the least that she could do. It was like the hunting scene she had seen in the king's hall at Winchester, but she hoped it would be even better. It depicted the forest trees, the deer, hounds, birds and hunters. One of the hunters was clearly Cola himself. She had wanted to place the handsome, golden-haired form of Edgar in one corner also, but had thought better of it. This great work was a good excuse for avoiding Edgar's company some days, without giving offence. And quite often, on these occasions, Cola himself would come in and watch her at work with apparent approval. As the weeks went by, although his quiet manner never changed, it seemed to her that despite himself the old man was getting to like her too.

It was on just such a day, in the second week of June, as she was busy at her needlework in the slanting light under the open window of the hall, that Cola came in to her, smiling. "I have news that will please you."

"Oh?"

"Hugh de Martell has a son. A healthy boy. He was born yesterday."

She felt her heart beat wildly. "And the Lady Maud?" She held her needle, watching it gleam in the falling sunlight.

"She survived. Remarkably, it seems she is rather well."

• • •

There was another birth in the Forest that day.

For some time now the pale doe, heavy with her fawn, had been searching the Forest alone. It is the habit of the fallow deer to give birth in solitude, almost always to a single fawn. She had searched with care, finally deciding on a small space in a thicket, screened from view by holly bushes. Here she made a bed in the long grass.

It was necessary to be careful. In the first days of its life her fawn would be completely defenceless. If a dog or fox found it alone, the fawn would surely die. This was the handicap that nature, in her bleak wisdom, had placed upon the deer. The foxes tended to live at the edge of the Forest, however, near the farms. She sniffled about carefully but could detect no scent that would tell her a fox had passed that way.

And there, in deep green shadow, in the great warm silence of June, she gave birth to her fawn – a little, sticky, bony mass in the grass – and licked it clean and lay beside it. The fawn was a male; it would be coloured like its father. They lay together and the pale doe hoped that the huge Forest would be kind to them.

Towards the end of June two developments took place. Neither was unexpected.

Cola announced the first. "Rufus is going to invade Normandy."

His brother Robert was now expected to reach his duchy in September. Rufus intended to be waiting for him.

"Will it be a big invasion?" Edgar asked.

"Yes. Huge." Edgar's brother had sent word from London of the preparations there. Large sums were being raised to pay mercenaries. Cartloads of bullion were being withdrawn from the treasury at Winchester. Knights were being summoned from all over the country. "And he's demanding transport vessels from most of the harbours along the southern coasts," Cola explained. "Robert will arrive to pay off his mortgage and find himself locked out of his house. Rufus has all the resources. If Robert gives battle he'll lose. It's a bad business."

"But didn't everyone expect it?" Adela asked.

"Yes. I think they did. But it's one thing to foresee an event, to say it's likely, and another when it actually starts to happen." He sighed. "In a way, of course, Rufus is right. Robert really isn't fit to govern. But to act like this . . ."

"I don't think the Normans will all welcome this," said Adela.

"No, my dear lady, they won't. Robert's friends, in particular, are . . ." He paused before choosing the word, "perturbed." The old man shook his head. "And if he does this to his own brother in Normandy, what do you imagine he'll do to Aquitaine? It will be just the same. The Duke of Aquitaine goes on crusade. Rufus lends him the money and waves him God speed. Then steals his lands while he's gone. How do you think people feel about that? How do you suppose the Church feels about it? I can tell you," he growled, "the tension in Christendom is rising."

"Thank heaven these things don't affect us down in the Forest," Edgar remarked.

His father only stared at him grimly. "This is a royal forest," he muttered. "Everything affects us." Then he left them.

A week after this a man dressed in black, whom Adela had never seen before, rode up and spent some time alone with Cola. After he had gone, the old man looked furious. She had never seen him like this before. Nor, in the days that followed, did he look any less angry. She could see that Edgar was concerned about him too, but when she asked him if he knew what the matter was he only shook his head.

"He won't say."

The second development came a few days later while they were out riding. Edgar asked her if she would marry him.

On the western edge of the dark dell of Burley the ground rises to a substantial wooded ridge, which achieves its highest point about a mile northwards of the village on a promontory known as Castle Hill. Not that there was any Norman castle there, but only the outline, under the scattered ash and holly trees, and the clusters of bracken, of a modest earthwork inclosure – although whether these low earth walls and ditches were the remains of a stock pen, a lookout post or a small fort, and whether the folk who had used it were distant ancestors of the Forest people or some other dwellers from unrecorded time, nobody could say. But whatever spirits might be resting there, it was a pleasant, peaceful place from which, looking westwards, one was granted a panorama that began with the brownish heather sweep down the Forest's edge to the Avon valley and, over that, to the blue-green ridges of Dorset in the distance.

It was a charming spot to choose, on a sparkling summer morning. The sun was catching his golden hair. He asked her quietly, yet almost gaily and he looked so noble. What woman could have wanted to refuse? She wished she could have been transformed into someone else.

And indeed, why should she refuse? Did it make any sense? It was not as if the conquering Normans never married members of the defeated Saxon noble class. They still did. She would lose a little face, but not too much. He was delightful. She was charmed.

But in front of her, out in that western distance, lay the manor of Hugh de Martell. It was down in one of the valleys between the ridges over which she was looking. And behind her, only a mile or so away, she realised, was the narrow stream where Puckle's wife had seen what was to come.

She would marry Martell. She still believed it. After the shock of hearing that the Lady Maud had safely given birth she had wondered for a while what it could mean. But the witch's cautious words had come back to her: "Things are not always what they seem." She had been promised happiness and she had faith. Something would happen. She knew it would. It seemed clear to her that in some unforeseen way the Lady Maud would depart.

If so, she would be a mother to his son. An excellent one. That would be her good deed, her justification for what must happen.

So what should she say to Edgar? She certainly did not want to be unkind. "I am grateful," she said slowly. "I think I could be happy as your wife. But I am not sure. I cannot say yes at present."

"I shall ask you again at the end of summer," he said with a smile. "Shall we ride on?"

Hugh de Martell gazed at his wife and child. They were in the sunny solar chamber. His son was sleeping peacefully in a wicker cradle on the floor. With his wisp of dark hair, everyone said he looked like his father already. Martell looked at the baby with satisfaction. Then he transferred his eyes to the Lady Maud.

She was propped up, almost in sitting position, on a small bed they had set up for her. She liked to sit in there with her baby, which she did for hours each day. She was rather pale but now she managed a small wan smile for her husband. "How is the proud father today?"

"Well, I think," he replied.

The pause turned into a little silence in the sunlit room.

"I think I shall be better soon."

"I'm sure you will."

"I'm sorry. It must be difficult for you that I have been sick so long. I'm not much of a wife for you."

"Nonsense. We must get you well again. That's the main thing."

"I want to be a good wife to you."

He smiled rather automatically, then looked away to the open window, staring out thoughtfully.

He no longer loved her. He did not altogether blame himself. No one could reproach him for his behaviour during the months of her sickness. He had been solicitous, loving, nursed her himself. He had been with her, held her hand, given all the comfort a husband can, on the two occasions when she thought she was dying. In all this, his conscience was clear.

But he did not love her any more. He did not desire her intimacy. It was not even her fault, he thought. He knew her too well. The mouth he had kissed, which had even breathed words of passion, was still, in repose, small and mean. He could not share the petty confines of her affections, the neatly tidied chamber of her imagination. She was so timid. Yet she was not weak. Had she been so, the need to protect her, however irksome, might have held him. But she was astonishingly strong. She might be sick, but if she lived, her will would remain unchanged, as constant as ever. Sometimes her will seemed to him like a little thread that ran through the innermost recesses of her soul — thin enough to pass through the eye of a needle, yet as strong as steel and quite unbreakable.

In what did her love for him consist? Necessity, pure and simple. Understandable, of course. She had determined how her life was to be, and had the means to make it so. The modest fortress of her proprieties was complete. And for this she needed him. Could marriage be any other way?

It was hardly surprising, therefore, that his thoughts at such a time should have turned to Adela.

They had done so quite often in the last year. The lone girl, the free spirit: she had intrigued him from the first. More than that. Why else should he have sought her out in Winchester? And since then, quite often, almost as though some influence was working on his mind, she had made her appearance or seemed invisibly to be beside him in his thoughts. He had met Cola a little while ago, and the huntsman had told him where she was and that she had asked after him and his family. At the last full moon he had experienced a sudden yearning for her. Three nights ago she had come to him in his dreams.

He gazed for some time, now, out of the window, then abruptly announced: "I'm going for a ride."

It was early afternoon when he arrived at Cola's manor. The old man was out, but his son Edgar was there. So was Adela.

He left his horse with Edgar, and he and Adela walked down the lane towards the Avon where the swans glided and the long, green river weeds waved gently in the current. They talked – they scarcely knew of what – and after a time he suggested that, if he sent word, they should meet again, in private.

She assented.

On their return to Edgar he was careful to thank her, rather formally, for her interest in his family during their time of trouble and then, with a courteous nod to the young man, he rode away.

As he did so he felt a tingling excitement he had not known for a long time. He had no doubt that he would be successful in this romantic adventure. It was not as if he had never done such a thing before.

The letter from Walter arrived one week later. It was brief and to the point. He was on his way to England. He was to meet some of his wife's family, then join the king. By early August he expected to be free to come and collect her. The letter ended with one other item of information:

By the way, I have found you a husband.

Three weeks had passed. No message had come from Martell. Although she tried to conceal her agitation, Adela was pale and tense. What did it mean?

Why had he not come? Had the Lady Maud fallen ill again? She tried to find out. The only report she could obtain said that the lady was getting stronger every day.

She was not sure what would come of it when she and Martell met. Would she give herself to him? She did not know, she hardly cared. She wanted only to see him. She longed to ride over to his manor, but knew she could not. She wanted to write, but did not dare.

The news from Walter made the situation even more urgent. He would take her away and marry her off. Could she refuse to go with him? Could she turn down another suitor? Nothing seemed to make sense.

Meanwhile, the king had arrived in Winchester. The army and fleet would soon be ready. More money, it was said, was coming into the Winchester treasury. Rufus was so occupied that he had not even had time to hunt.

Whether Walter had reached Winchester yet she did not know. Nor had she any wish to communicate with him if he had.

In the last week of July she went to see Puckle's wife. She found her in her little cabin, just as she had been before; but when she asked for help and advice the witch refused to give it.

"Couldn't we cast a spell again?" she asked.

The woman only shook her head calmly. "Wait. Be patient. What will be, will be," she answered.

So Adela went back, discouraged.

The atmosphere at Cola's manor was not made easier by the fact that Edgar seemed moody. No further word had been spoken about his proposal – and she could not imagine that he had any inkling of her secret feelings for Martell – but the news that Walter was coming to take her away could hardly have pleased him. Superficially their relationship continued the same, but there was distress in his eyes.

Cola, too, continued to be darkly silent. She did not know

whether Edgar had told his father of his proposal or not. If he did know, did he approve or disapprove? She had no wish to ask, or bring up the subject at all. But she wondered if his sombre mood was connected with this, or with the dangerous events of the outside world.

In the closing days of July the tension in the household seemed to grow. Walter's visit could not be far away. Cola looked black and Edgar was becoming visibly agitated. Once or twice he seemed on the point of raising the subject of their marriage again, but he held back. The tension, Adela sensed, could not continue much longer.

Matters were finally brought to a head on the last day of July when Cola called them together. "I've received word that the king and a party of companions are arriving at Brockenhurst tomorrow," he announced. "He wishes to hunt in the Forest the following day. I am to attend on him." He glanced at Adela. "Your cousin Walter is one of the party. So no doubt we shall see him here soon." Then he went out to see to some business, leaving her alone with Edgar.

The silence did not last long.

"You will be leaving with Tyrrell," Edgar said quietly.

"I don't know."

"Oh? Does that mean that I may hope?"

"I don't know." It was a stupid answer, but she was too flustered at that moment to make much sense.

"Then what does it mean?" he suddenly burst out. "Has Walter found a suitor? Have you accepted him?"

"No. No, I haven't."

"Then what? Is there someone else?"

"Someone else? Whom do you mean?"

"I don't know." He seemed to hesitate. Then he said in a tone of exasperation: "The man in the moon, for all I know." Turning on his heel furiously, he strode away. And Adela, knowing she was treating him badly, could only comfort herself that her own exasperation and suffering were probably worse than even his. She avoided him for the rest of the day.

The following morning she was left to herself. Cola was busy making arrangements. He went to see Puckle for some reason; there were spare horses to be ready at Brockenhurst where the local forester was preparing to receive the king.

Edgar was sent on several errands and she was glad he was not there.

In the afternoon, having nothing better to do, she went for a walk down the lane by the river. She had just turned back towards the manor when a fellow dressed like a servant stepped out in front of her and held out something in his hand. "You are the Lady Adela? I am to give you this." She felt something slipped into her hand, but before she could say another word to him, he had run off.

His delivery was a small piece of parchment, folded over and sealed. Breaking the seal, she saw a short message, neatly written in French.

> *I shall be at Burley Castle in the morning.*
> *Hugh.*

Her heart leaped. For a moment the world, even the flowing river, seemed to have stopped. Then, clasping the parchment tightly in her hand, she walked back to Cola's manor.

Taken up though she was with her own affairs, she was intrigued to notice on her return that the huntsman had received a visitor that day. This was hardly unusual and she would scarcely have bothered to think about it, except that she recognised him as the black-cloaked stranger she had seen once before, after whose visit the old man had become so distressed. The man was deep in conversation with Cola when she arrived, but not long afterwards she saw him depart. From that time until they gathered for their evening meal she did not see Cola.

But when she did the change was extraordinary. It was terrible to see. If he had looked angry before, now he looked like thunder. But even that, she quickly perceived, was a mask for something else. For the first time since she had known him it seemed to her that the old man might be afraid.

As she served him the venison stew that had been prepared, he only nodded to her absently. When he poured her a goblet of wine she noticed that his hand shook. What in the world could the messenger have said to him to produce so unusual an effect? Edgar, too, whatever else he had on his mind, was looking at his father with alarm.

At the end of their brief meal, Cola spoke: "You are both to remain here at the manor tomorrow. Nobody is to leave."

"But Father . . ." Edgar looked startled. "Surely I am to accompany you on the king's hunt?"

"No. You'll remain here. You are not to leave Adela."

They both stared in horror. Whether Edgar wanted her company at present Adela did not know. She certainly knew what it meant for a young man in his position to hunt with the king. As for herself, the last thing she needed was to be confined there with him tomorrow. "May he not accompany you?" she ventured. "He would see the king."

But if she hoped to help matters, she only provoked a storm. "He will do no such thing, Madam," the old man roared. "He will obey his father. And you will do as you are told, too!" He banged his hand on the table and rose to his feet. "Those are my orders and you, Sir" – he glared at Edgar with blazing blue eyes – "will obey them."

He stood there, bristling, a magnificent old man who could still be frightening and the two young people wisely remained silent.

As she retired, later that evening, Adela could only wonder how she was going to get away in the morning. For disobey him she must.

The noise that woke her, a little before dawn, was of human voices. They were not loud, though it seemed to her that in her dreams she might have heard the sound of quarrelling.

Softly she got up and stole towards them. She came to the doorway of the hall. She looked in.

Cola and Edgar were sitting at the table upon which a taper gave just enough light to see their faces. The old man was already fully dressed to go hunting; Edgar was wearing only a long undershirt. It was evident that they had been in conversation for some time and at this moment Edgar was looking questioningly at his father who in turn was staring down at the table. He looked tired.

Finally, without looking up, the old man spoke: "Don't you think that if I tell you not to come into the Forest, I might have a reason?"

"Yes, but I think you should tell me what it is."

"It might be safer, don't you see, if you didn't know."

"I think you should trust me."

The old man was thoughtful for a while. "If anything happens to me," he said slowly, "I suppose it might be better if you understood a little more. The world is a dangerous place and perhaps I shouldn't shelter you. You're a grown man."

"I think so."

"Tell me, have you ever thought how many people would like to see Rufus disappear?"

"Many."

"Yes. In a good few quarters. And never more than at present." He paused. "And so if Rufus were to have an accident in the Forest, those people, whoever they are, would think it convenient."

"An accident to the king?"

"You forget. The royal family are rather prone to accidents in the Forest."

It was true. Years ago a fourth son of the Conqueror, Richard, had been killed as a young man by riding into a tree in the New Forest. And one of Rufus's nephews, a bastard son of his brother Robert, had been killed by a stray arrow in the Forest even more recently.

Even so. A king! Edgar was thunderstruck. "You mean Rufus is to have an accident?"

"Perhaps."

"When?"

"Perhaps this afternoon."

"And you know?"

"Perhaps."

"And if you know, you must have some part in it."

"I did not say that."

"You could not refuse? To know, I mean."

"These are powerful people, Edgar. Very powerful. Our position – mine, one day yours – is difficult."

"But you know who is behind it?"

"No. I'm not sure that I do. Powerful people have spoken to me. But things are not always what they seem."

"It's to happen today?"

"Perhaps. But perhaps not. Remember, Rufus was to be killed in a wood once before, but one of the Clares changed his mind at the last moment. Nothing is ever certain. It may happen. It may not."

"But Father . . ." Edgar was gazing at him with concern now. "I won't ask you what your part in this may be, but are you sure that, whatever happens, they won't blame you? You're only a Saxon huntsman."

"True. But I don't think so. I know too much and" – he smiled – "through your brother in London I've taken certain precautions. I think I'll be safe."

"Won't they need someone to blame, then?"

"Good. I see you've got a head on your shoulders. They will. He's already been chosen, as a matter of fact. That I know. And they've chosen very well. A clever fool, who thinks he's part of the charmed circle, but who actually knows very little."

"Who's that?"

"Walter Tyrrell."

"Tyrrell?" Edgar gave a tiny whistle. "You mean his own family, the Clares, would sacrifice him?"

"Did I say the Clares were involved?"

"No, Father." He smiled. "You said nothing."

Tyrrell. Adela felt herself go cold. Her cousin Walter was being set up, just like a target. God knows what danger he was in. Her throat went dry at the thought that she, too, was witness to such a terrible secret. Trembling, afraid that the sound of her own thumping heartbeat might give her away, she stole back.

What should she do? Her mind was in a whirl. But in the cool grey darkness her duties began to loom like ghosts before her. They were planning to kill the king. It was a crime before God. There was none more terrible. Yet was he her king? She did not think so. Her loyalty was actually to Robert until such time as she married a vassal of the English king. But Walter was her kinsman. She might not like him; he might not be very loyal to her. But he was her kinsman and she had to save him.

Very quietly she began to get dressed. After a little while, through her open window, she saw Cola ride out alone in the half-darkness. He had a bow and a quiver on his back.

She waited until he was out of sight. The house was quiet. Cautiously, she climbed out of her window and let herself down to the ground.

She had not realised, in her nervousness, that as she went to the window Martell's letter had fallen to the floor.

Dawn was just breaking when Puckle set off with his cart. Cola had told him to go to the lodge at Brockenhurst where there would be further instructions, and to be prepared to carry any deer killed to wherever he was directed.

His wife saw him off. As they parted she remarked: "You won't be back tonight."

"I won't?"

"No."

He gave her a curious look, then went upon his way.

Adela had been careful. Saddling her horse in the darkness, she had not mounted but led him carefully out, keeping on the grassy verge beside the path to minimise the sound until she was well away from Cola's manor. Then she rode slowly across the valley and up into the Forest.

It was terrible to her that she should miss Martell, yet what could she do? She could not send word to him. Neither could she abandon Walter to his fate. When she reached the castle at Burley she waited as long as she dared, until the sun was well over the horizon, in the hope that he might come early. But he did not. Then it occurred to her to ask Puckle or one of his family to wait there with a message and she rode down to the narrow stream in the hope of finding them. But, unaccountably, none of them was there, and she did not dare go into Burley and start gossip by asking some stranger from the dark village to deliver her message.

So she gave up. Perhaps, she prayed, if she could find Walter quickly, she might even be able to return to Castle Hill while Martell was still there. She rode on quickly, therefore, anxious not to be late.

As it happened, she need not have hurried.

The movements of King William II, known as Rufus, at the start of August in the Year of Our Lord 1100, are tolerably well known. On the first of the month he issued a charter, from the lodge at Brockenhurst. He ate with his friends and later went to bed.

But then he slept badly. As a result, instead of leaving at dawn, the sun was well over the horizon and glistening on the treetops by Brockenhurst before he finally stirred to join his waiting courtiers.

They were a small, select company. There was Robert FitzHamon, an old friend; William, the keeper of the treasury of Winchester; two other Norman barons. There were three of the powerful family of Clare, who had once nearly betrayed him. And there was his younger brother Henry – dark-haired, energetic, yet self-contained. Ruthless, some said, like his father. And lastly there was Walter Tyrrell.

As the red-headed king sat down on a bench and started to pull on his boots, an armourer appeared with half a dozen newly forged arrows to present to the king.

Rufus took them, inspected them and smiled. "Beautifully made. Perfect weight. Supple shaft. Well done," he congratulated the armourer. Then, looking over to Tyrrell, he remarked: "You take two of them, Walter. You're the best marksman." And as Tyrrell accepted them, beaming, he added with his harsh laugh: "You'd better not miss!"

There followed some of the usual courtly banter, to keep the king amused. Then a monk appeared. This did not particularly please Rufus, who barely tolerated churchmen, at best. But since the lugubrious fellow insisted on delivering an urgent letter from his abbot, the king shrugged and took it.

After he had read it he laughed. "Now, Walter, don't you forget what I told you. You'd better not miss with my arrows," he remarked to Tyrrell; then, turning to the general company: "Can you believe what this Gloucestershire abbot writes? One of his monks has had a dream. He saw an apparition. Of me, if you please. Suffering hellfire, no doubt." He grinned. "I should think half the monks in England dream of me in torment." He waved the letter. "So he sits down and writes a letter to let me know and sends it halfway across England to warn me to be careful. And this man, God help us, is an abbot! You'd have thought he'd have more sense."

"Let's go hunting, Sire," somebody said.

It was well into the morning before Hugh de Martell set off from his manor. For some reason his wife had chosen that

morning, of all mornings, to delay him with one small matter
after another so that finally he had been forced to leave her
quite abruptly. It had made him feel guilty and bad-tempered.
He pushed his horse along at a canter down the long lane that
led over the chalk ridge.

He was not unduly worried, though. He felt sure Adela
would wait.

Edgar was quite astonished when one of the servants said that
Adela's horse was missing. It was mid-morning and he had
kept himself busy; he had not noticed Adela but had assumed
that she was somewhere about the place. It seemed odd that he
had not seen her go out for a ride. When someone else assured
him that her horse had gone before dawn, he went straight to
her chamber. There he found Martell's message.

He did not need to read Norman French to understand it. He
could make out the letters: "Burley Castle" and "Hugh."
Minutes later he was riding out.

She had disobeyed his father and he was supposed to look
after her. That was the first thing. But then there was the matter of Martell. For that was what the letter and her absence
must mean. She had gone out to meet him.

He had been suspicious when Martell had called to see her,
but to say anything would have been insulting. That Martell had
an eye for women, that he had indulged in love affairs on the
Forest borders from time to time, was something Cola had told
him long ago. It had not shocked him. The lords of the feudal
world were as used to getting their way as the powerful are in
any generation. He had supposed that with the dangerous condition of his wife, Martell would desist for a bit. Seeing Adela at a
loose end, he supposed the rich landlord was unable to let such a
chance slip. The fact that he, Edgar, wanted to marry her, if he
knew it, would certainly not deter him. Probably spur him on,
Edgar thought, to prove his superiority.

But what did he mean to do? He hardly knew. Observe them
first, he thought. Try to discover what was going on. Confront
them? Fight? He was not sure.

It was not long before he had left the valley. He only had to
make a small detour of about a mile to pass unseen to the
north of their meeting place and then approach it quietly

from behind, through the trees. Feeling like a spy, he tethered his horse to a tree when he got near and advanced on foot.

There was no trace of them. Their horses were not there. He looked out, scanning the heath below and saw no sign of any movement. Were they somewhere nearby, hidden from view in the bracken or the long grass? He searched about, but found nothing.

They had been and gone. They had ridden off together. And then? He knew he must not imagine too much, but it was impossible. With a sick feeling in his stomach, it seemed to him that he knew it. They were together.

His nerves strung taut, his pulse beating fast, he rode about, asking in Burley if they had been seen and looking out over various nearby high points. There was nothing. He returned slowly to the valley, thinking to check back at his home. Perhaps, he told himself, he had been mistaken. But if not he would come back to the Forest and try again.

Adela had been cautious as she approached Brockenhurst. On the one hand she had to find Walter, but on the other she must avoid Cola. She certainly could not tell the old man why she had disobeyed his orders and he would probably send her home before she could accomplish her mission.

As she came close to the royal hunting lodge, however, she had what seemed to be a piece of luck. She saw Puckle, standing alone by his cart. When she asked him where the king's party were, he looked thoughtful, then said that they had gone northwards, somewhere above Lyndhurst.

This was good news indeed. The area was wooded. Perhaps she could intercept Walter without being spotted. Asking Puckle to say nothing of having seen her she set off, with a lighter heart, towards the north.

Not until some time after her husband had left did the Lady Maud stir from her usual position of resting in the solar. But when she did she astonished the entire household by demanding not only her outdoor clothes but that her horse should be saddled as well.

"You do not mean to ride, My Lady?" her maidservant enquired anxiously.

"Yes. I do."

"But My Lady, you are so weak."

It was true that, after so much inactivity, the Lady Maud was hardly steady on her feet. But despite all the woman's remonstrances she insisted: "I shall ride." There was nothing they could do about it. One brave servant ventured to say that the master would not like it, but was cut with such a mean little look that he shrivelled back against the wall.

"That is between me and him, not you," she said coldly and told them to bring the horse round to the door.

Moments later, while the groom held the bridle, they were helping her to mount.

"Please, My Lady, you could fall," the groom now begged. "Let me at least accompany you."

"No." Abruptly she turned her horse's head away and started off at a walk. So she proceeded, wobbling once or twice, pale-faced, looking straight ahead, all the way down the long village street, while the cottagers came out to watch her pass. She started up the track that her husband had taken. She swayed, seemed about to fall, but pressed on.

She was following him. Her journey was instinctive. Did she know that she had lost his love? She sensed it. Did she know he had gone to another woman? She guessed it. And something in her, an animal knowledge, told her she must get well, and ride and take him back. So that August day she rode out in front of them all, kept in the saddle by her will alone. At the top of the rise she urged her horse into a canter, and those who saw it below gasped and muttered: "Dear God, she will be killed."

The king's hunting party had set out gaily from Brockenhurst, accompanied by Cola.

"My faithful huntsman. I can always trust you to do everything perfectly." Rufus was in a good humour. His sharp eyes bored into the old huntsman; then he laughed. "I don't want to drive the deer into your great trap today, my friend. I want to hunt the woods."

Hounds had been produced. There were two kinds: the tufters, agile scenting hounds, whose job was to sniff out the deer and spring them from the dense covert; and the running hounds, which, today, would only be used to bring down any deer who, having been wounded, escaped into the open.

They proceeded first into the woods below Brockenhurst; but after hunting there a while the king insisted on going eastwards, across a huge expanse of open heath, despite the fact that Cola warned him: "You'll find some red deer, Sire, but few fallow."

At noon the king decided to stop and rest, and demanded some refreshment. Then, some way into the afternoon, he agreed to let Cola lead them to a better hunting ground, although even now he seemed to be in no hurry. "Come on, Tyrrell," he cried. "We shall all be watching you."

The pale deer started. She trembled for a moment, then listened.

The huge silence of the August afternoon seemed to lie like an endless covering over the warm blue sky. By her side, her little fawn could walk a few steps now. Gangling, delicate, feeding from her, precious to her, he had survived the first dangerous days of life. But was he old enough to run, if the hounds came?

She turned her head. She was sure she could hear them now. She looked at her fawn, her heart full of fear. Were the hunters coming this way?

Hugh de Martell had waited long enough. He was not used to being kept waiting. He knew from the messenger that Adela had received his letter. Could something have prevented her coming? Perhaps. But he doubted it. Had she arrived and waited for him and then left? Possibly. But his message had only said that they should meet in the morning and it had not been noon when he arrived. She would have stayed, he was sure of it. And now he had been kept waiting. Two hours, he guessed.

No. She had changed her mind and thought better of it. He was sorry. He had liked her.

He wondered what to do. Should he go down to Cola's manor? He thought not. Too risky. Should he turn back and go home? It irked him to do so because it seemed an admission of failure. Anyway, it was a fine day. He might as well enjoy it. Leaving Castle Hill, he skirted Burley and idly walked his horse up on to the high heath. After a mile or two there would be a magnificent view eastwards and down to the sea. He had once had a girl, the daughter of a fisherman, down on the coast there. He had soon grown tired of her, but today the memory seemed a pleasant one.

His temper improved by the time he reached this high place. It could be that Adela had been prevented from coming after all. He would make enquiries. She might be his yet.

Godwin Pride had finished his new fence just after dawn that morning and he was proud of it. Not that the area enclosed was so much larger. He had actually extended it less than one yard. But – here was the cleverness of it – he had done so on two sides instead of one. As a result, the proportions of the pen were exactly as they had been before. Unless a person inspected the ground, he would never notice that there had been any alteration.

"But what's the point?" his wife had asked. "There still isn't enough space for that extra cow."

"Never you mind about that," he had replied. It was the principle of the thing. And he had been surveying his work for perhaps the fifth time that afternoon when he had looked up and seen a curious sight.

It was Adela. But he had never seen her like this before. She seemed exhausted, almost crushed. Her horse was on his last legs, his mouth foaming, his flanks drenched. She gave Pride a look of desperation. "Have you seen them? The king's party?" He hadn't. "I've got to find them." She didn't say why. It was lucky that he was close enough to catch her as she swayed and fell from her horse.

She had spent hours searching around Lyndhurst before finally concluding that the royal party had gone some other way. Retracing her steps down to Brockenhurst she had been told by a servant which way they had gone and so she had searched the woods to the south. Casting about this way and that, riding down tracks, through glades, listening for some faint echo in the endlessly receding trees, she had encountered nothing except a huge silence broken occasionally by the flapping of a bird in the leaves.

She had searched in a state of near panic, lost heart, almost despaired. Yet she could not give up. She had asked in the few hamlets but nobody knew where they were. By now she knew that her horse was giving out and that brought her to a kind of nervous hopelessness too. Then finally she had thought of Pride.

It took a while to revive her. When they had, she was determined to go on. "Not on that horse, you won't," Pride had to tell her.

"I'll walk if I have to," she said.

He led her outside with a smile. "Do you think," he asked, "you could ride one of these?"

Adela could feel the warmth of the late afternoon sun on her back as its golden rays fell, in great slanting shafts, over the forest wastes.

The sturdy little New Forest pony she rode was surprisingly fast. She had not realised how sure-footed these animals were, compared with her high-bred gelding. Born to the heather, he seemed to dance through it.

Pride was riding beside her. At first they had intended to try the woods near Brockenhurst again; but they had met a peasant who told them he had seen horsemen out on the heath to the east. And so it was, in the late afternoon, that Adela found herself passing on to the one huge tract of the Forest where she had never been before.

It was open country – a broad, low, gently undulating coastal plain. To the south, not seven miles away, the long, looming, blue-green hills of the Isle of Wight told her that she was near the Solent water, with its promise of the open sea. In front of her the heath, violet and purple in August, with fewer gorse brakes than on the western side of the Forest, stretched from Pride's hamlet all the way down to the belt of wooded marsh and meadowland that masked the line of the coast. Ytene, as they had anciently called it: the land where the Jutes from the Isle of Wight had come to farm.

She was glad to have Pride with her. She could not tell him

what they were doing, of course, but his calm presence gave her heart again. After all, she reminded herself, if the king's party were still out hunting then nothing had happened yet. Walter was probably still safe. Perhaps the whole thing had been called off. As long as there was light, though, she must try to find him and deliver her message; and there were still hours to go before the sun would sink over the Forest.

Perhaps it was because she was tired, perhaps it was the heat, but as they went over the heath the great silence of the August afternoon seemed to take on an air of unreality. The occasional birds hovering overhead seemed to lose their substance as if at any moment they might recede upwards into the endless blue heavens, or dissolve down into the purple heather sea, becoming nothingness.

But where were the hunters? She and Pride travelled a mile, then another, crossed some marshy ground, rose up again on to dry heath, saw clumps of holly trees and oaks in the distance, but no riders. Only the same blue sky and purple heather.

"There are two places they could be," Pride said at last. "They could be over there." He pointed eastwards to where she could see a line of woodland. "Or they might be down in the marshes." His arm made a sweeping gesture towards the south. "It's your choice."

Adela considered. She hardly cared, now, whether she encountered Cola, or even the king himself; but if she was going to deliver her message that day it would need to be done soon. "We'd better split up," she said.

Since the tracks in the coastal oak woods were treacherous, they quickly agreed that Pride would go down there while she went east.

"And what am I to say if I find your cousin?" he asked.

"Tell him . . ." She paused. What could the forester say? If she saw Walter herself, little though he respected her, she thought she could draw him to one side and tell him enough, at least, of what she knew to make him realise his danger. But what message could she possibly send by Pride that might make him take notice? She searched her mind. And then she had an inspiration. "Tell him," she said, "that you come from the Lady Maud. Tell him she will explain all, but that, on any excuse he can think of, he must flee at once for his life." That, she thought, should do it. Moments later they went their separate ways. As they parted she called after him: "What's the name of the place you're going to?"

"There's a farm down there," he called back, "known as Througham." Then he trotted away.

For nearly another hour she wandered all along the line of the eastern woods but found no sign of them. Time and again she glanced back across the heath and saw nothing. She finally concluded that, if they were still in this part of the Forest at all, they must be somewhere in the woods where Pride was riding and had started back across the heath in that direction, when suddenly in the distance she caught sight of the strangest vision.

An animal was moving, with extraordinary speed, across the heath towards the woods at Througham. The sun in the west was shining, fiery gold, in her eyes and she raised her hand to shield them. But even in that reddening glare it seemed to her she could make out the creature well enough; and she realised with a start that she recognised it.

The pale doe. The pale doe was racing like a darting speck of light across the purple glow of the heather. There were two horsemen, hunters, behind her. Two hounds as well, she was almost sure. The deer was quite alone. Were there other deer nearby, a fawn perhaps, trembling by a thicket, watching its mother being chased by the hunters? The pale doe was going faster than they, running, almost flying for her life towards the shelter of the woods and marshes.

Hardly thinking what she was doing, almost forgetting Walter, she found herself urging her pony forward, following the deer. She waved at the hunters, but they did not seem to see her. The pale deer was already near the trees. The two hunters were at a gallop now. Try as she might, she could not cut them off and she was still half a mile behind them when they followed the pale doe into the woods.

Nor did she even see them again. When she reached the trees herself she encountered nothing but silence. The pale doe, the riders, the hounds might have been so many phantoms. All she found as she rode down one track after another, was a succession of oak woods, open glades and marshy meadows.

She had just tried a track through the woods that led south when, to her left, she heard hoof-beats rapidly approaching her. She stopped. Was it Pride? One of the hunting party? A moment later the horseman came into sight. She gave a little cry of relief. But it died in her.

For it was Walter as she had never seen him before. He was gasping, his eyes were wild and he was pale, almost green as though he were about to vomit. Seeing her, he scarcely even had the emotion left, it appeared, to register surprise. But as he came up, he cried out hoarsely: "Flee. Flee for your life."

"You got my message, then?" she cried back. "About the king?"

"Message? I had no message. The king is dead."

Hugh de Martell awoke. Foolishly, perhaps, after enjoying the view over the Forest, he had returned to Castle Hill and stayed up there. He must have fallen asleep in the sun. He blinked. It was late afternoon. And perhaps he might even have stayed there a little longer if he had not noticed, just then, coming over the ridge from the northerly Ringwood direction, a single horseman whom he recognised to be Edgar.

He muttered a curse. On the one hand the young fellow could probably tell him what had happened to Adela, but he was not sure he wanted to ask him. There was also the possibility, he supposed, that Cola and his family might have discovered about the assignation, might even have stopped Adela meeting him. Edgar could be coming to Castle Hill to look for him. Either way, he had no wish to encounter him.

There was a track from the bottom of the hill that led due west across open heath before entering a wood at a small promontory known as Crow Hill, from where it descended steeply into the Avon valley. It was less than a mile to the cover of Crow Hill. On his powerful horse he could be across it in no time. Moments later he was in the saddle.

He put his horse into a canter. The firm, peaty track was easy going. Ahead of him, in the west, the sun was starting to sink over the Avon valley, bathing the place in a pinkish, golden light. On each side the heather was like a shimmering purple lake. The moment was so magical that, despite himself, he almost laughed aloud at the sheer beauty of it.

He was a third of the way over when he realised to his irritation that Edgar had taken a path that led diagonally across
the little heath. The tiresome young fellow meant to cut him
off. He smiled to himself nonetheless. The Saxon might find
that harder than he thought. His splendid stallion was bounding along. He measured the distance with his eye, bided his
time.

Halfway across he went into a gallop. Glancing right, he
saw that Edgar was doing the same. He chuckled to himself.
The young Saxon hadn't a chance. His stallion was thundering
along, eating up the ground, making sparks when his shoes
struck against the white gravel stones in the peaty turf.

But to his surprise he realised that Edgar was keeping pace.
The fellow was going to meet him before he got to the wood.
Ahead to his left, however, a little spur of wood came out, just
in front of which, like a marker, was a solitary ash tree.

Suddenly, therefore, he veered left. His stallion plunged
through the heather. Just ahead he noticed that some Forest
fool had made piles of logs. He was almost level with the ash
tree, which would screen him from the Saxon's view, damn
him. He urged his horse forward, forgetting that the surface of
the Forest is not firm and true, like the sweeping chalk downs
around his manor, but soft, shifting and treacherous to those
who try to impose upon it. So he had no warning at all when
his mighty beast's leg plunged into a hidden pocket of boggy
ground, throwing him head first towards the woodpile.

"But what happened?" She had never seen Walter at a loss before.

He gazed at her almost as if she were not there. "It was an
accident."

"But who? How?"

"An accident." He stared straight ahead.

She looked at him carefully. Was he just in a state of shock?
Was he describing what he saw, or what someone had told
him? They were trotting briskly, now, on to the heath.

"Where are you going?" she asked.

"West. I have to go west. Away from Winchester. I have to
find a boat. Further along the coast."

"A boat?"

"Don't you understand? I have to get away. Flee the realm. I wish to God I knew the way through this cursed forest."

"I do," she said. "I'll guide you."

It was astonishing how quickly the time seemed to pass. But then she was no longer searching and wandering; she was going straight for a point in the terrain whose position she knew: the little deserted ford north of Pride's hamlet. The heath was empty. They saw no one. They did not speak. Avoiding the tiny hamlet, they found the long path that led down to the ford, crossed below Brockenhurst and came out on to the rolling heathland of the western Forest.

"Do you want to try to get a boat at Christchurch?" she asked.

"No. It's too near. I might have to wait a day or two and by then" – he sighed – "they could arrest me. I have to go much further west."

"You'll have to cross the River Avon. I know the Avon valley." Thank God for her rides with Edgar. "There's a cattle ford about halfway between Christchurch and Ringwood. After that you cross the meadows and it's open heathland for miles and miles."

"Good. I'll go that way, then," Tyrrell said.

The sun was sinking in the west, a huge deep red; here and there a solitary tree stood out like a strange indigo flower against the red sky, casting a long shadow towards them like a cautionary finger. They had to walk their horses, but apart from the Forest ponies and the occasional cattle they had the place to themselves.

Tyrrell seemed to have recovered a bit now. "You said you were looking for me, that you sent a message," he said quietly. "What was that?"

She told him the whole story, the behaviour of Cola, what she had heard and how she had searched, with Pride's help.

He listened carefully, then was silent for a few moments. "Did you realise that you might have been risking your life for me, my dear cousin?" he said at last. He had never called her his dear cousin before.

"I didn't really think of it," she replied honestly.

"This Pride – he knows nothing except the message you gave him, from the Lady Maud?"

"Nothing."

"Let's hope he is discreet, then." He stayed lost in thought for a while. Then, gazing ahead he said quietly: "You must forget everything you heard, everything you saw. If anyone asks, if Cola asks, you went for a ride in the Forest. Is there any reason why you should have done so?"

"Actually," she confessed, "I had an assignation with Hugh de Martell. But I missed it."

"Aha!" Despite everything, he laughed out loud. "He's incorrigible, you know. Be warned. But it couldn't be better. Stick to that if you must. Say you panicked and fled to find me if further pressed. But," he became very serious, "if you value your life, Adela, forget everything else."

"What really happened?" she asked.

He paused for some time before he spoke and, when he did, he chose his words carefully. "I don't know. We'd split up. One of my Clare kinsmen came racing up to me and said there'd been an accident. 'And as you were alone with the king,' he said, 'you'll take the blame.' I told him I hadn't been with the king, but I got the message, if you see what I mean. He promised me they'd keep the hue and cry off my trail for a day or two if I made myself scarce and got across the sea. No point in arguing."

"Was it an accident?"

"Who knows? Accidents happen."

She wondered if he were telling the truth, and realised she could not know. She also realised that it was irrelevant. What mattered most – a hidden truth or a series of fleeting appearances? Or what men chose to say, or chose to believe?

"I'm afraid, my poor little cousin, there's nothing much I can do for you at present. I did have a possible suitor for you, but nobody will be wanting an alliance with a poor cousin of mine for a while. And you certainly can't come with me to Normandy now. What's to be done?"

"I'll go back to Cola's first," she replied. "Then we'll see. They tell me" – she smiled – "that I'm going to be very happy."

"You are slightly mad," he replied, "but I begin to love you."

Just then they came to the top of a low ridge. The sunset was in all its glory now, ahead of them, a vast red glow on the horizon over the Avon valley. And then Adela turned round to look back and saw all the purple heather of the heath suddenly transformed into a vast, magnificent, crimson fire, so that it seemed as if the whole Forest floor were molten, like the mouth of a secret volcano.

Then she and Tyrrell continued on their way, and when they could see the darkening river and the broad meadows by the cattle ford, she turned northwards and left him to take his flight towards the west.

A single arrow from a bow had killed Rufus. The red-headed monarch had died instantly. His companions had gathered and taken counsel quickly. It was his silent, thoughtful younger brother Henry who, after only moments of persuading, had announced: "We must go to Winchester at once." The treasury was there.

It was fortunate indeed that, no doubt thanks to the efficiency of Cola, Puckle and his cart should have been near at hand. They wrapped the body of the king, put it in Puckle's cart and all set out for the ancient capital. All, that is, save Cola who, his work done, returned slowly home.

He reached his manor some time after dark, at just the same time as, in another, larger manor further west, they woke the Lady Maud, sleeping after her ride, to tell her that her husband, out riding in the Forest, had fallen from his horse, broken his neck on a pile of wood and was dead. She slept no more that night.

Another mother and child, deep in the Forest, did rest quietly that warm summer night: the pale doe and her fawn were at peace with the world, as they had been during most of the day. For, having briefly heard riders nearby and thought they were hunters, the pale deer had heard no more and settled down with her fawn once again. She lived in a part of the forest far distant from that in which King Rufus fatally hunted that day. So that whether Adela had seen another pale deer as she came across the heath, or whether the deer's colour was only a trick of the light, or whether there was some other cause of her mistake, it was impossible to say.

Nor have men ever been able to say with certainty what really passed in the Forest that strange and magical day. The hunting companions of the king were known. Tyrrell, it was said, had taken aim at a stag, missed and struck the king. No one, or very few, asserted that he had done it deliberately, nor was there any clear reason why he should.

Who benefited from his death? Not his brother Robert, as it happened, nor the Clare family, as far as is known. But his younger brother – loyal, silent Henry with his fringe of black hair – took over the Winchester treasury by dawn and was crowned in London within two days. In time he took Normandy from Robert, just as Rufus had planned to do. But if he had any hand in the death of Rufus – and many have whispered that he must have done – not a trace of evidence remains.

Indeed, so completely did the Forest hold its secret, that even the place where it happened became forgotten until, centuries later, a stone was put up to mark the spot – in the wrong part of the Forest entirely.

There was, however, one other beneficiary of the mystery. A few days after it, Cola happened to come across Godwin Pride, who politely approached to have a private word with him. It seemed, he assured the surprised huntsman, that he had reason to believe that he had, in all honesty, a right to a large pen, far bigger than the one he had illegally made, next to his smallholding.

"What possible proof have you, man?" Cola enquired.

"I think you could be satisfied," Pride replied carefully. "And if you'd be satisfied, I'd be satisfied."

"Meaning?"

"I happened to be down Througham way the other day."

"Oh?"

"Yes. Funny what you see sometimes."

"Funny?" Cola was watchful now. Very. "Care to tell me what you saw?"

"Shouldn't care to tell anyone."

"Dangerous."

"Shouldn't wonder."

"Well, I've no idea what you think you saw." Cola looked at him thoughtfully. "And I don't think I want to know either."

"No. I shouldn't say you did."

"Talk can be dangerous."

"See what I mean about that pen?"

"See? I don't suppose I see any better than you do, Godwin Pride."

"All right, then," said Pride cheerfully and walked off.

And when, the next summer, a splendid new pen, almost an extra acre, with a small bank and a ditch and a fence appeared by Pride's homestead at the heath's edge, neither Cola, nor his elder son, nor his younger son Edgar, nor Edgar's wife Adela – who had received a nice little dowry upon her marriage from Tyrrell in Normandy – nor any of the royal foresters, ever seemed to see it or take any notice of it at all.

For in such ways life is arranged in the Forest.

Beaulieu

1294

He ran along the edge of the field, bending low, hugging the hedgerow. He was red in the face, panting. He could still hear the shouts of rage from the grange behind him.

The mud-splattered habit he wore marked him as belonging to the monastery; but his thick hair was not shaved in the choir monk's tonsure. A lay brother, then.

He reached the corner of the field and looked back. There was no one behind him. Not yet. *Laudate Dominum.* Praise the Lord.

The field he was in was full of sheep. But there was a bull in the next field. He didn't care. Hoisting his habit, he swung his long legs over the stile.

The bull was not far off. It was brown and shaggy, and like a small haystack. Its two red eyes looked at him from under the thatch between its long, curling horns. He almost raised his hand to make the sign of the cross in benediction, but thought better of it.

Tauri Basan cingunt me . . . The bulls of Bashan have beset me round: the Latin words of the twenty-second psalm. He had sung them only last week. A kindly monk had told him what they meant. *Domine, ad juvandum me festina.* O Lord, make haste to help me.

He started off as fast as he dared along the side of the field, keeping one eye on the bull.

There were just three questions in his mind. Was he being

117

followed? Would the bull charge? And the man he had left bleeding on the ground at the grange: had he killed him?

The abbey of Beaulieu was at peace in the warm autumn afternoon. The shouts at the grange were far out of hearing. Only the occasional beating of swans' wings on the neighbouring water broke the pleasant silence by the grey riverside inclosure.

In his private office, secure behind a bolted door, the abbot stared thoughtfully at the book he had been inspecting.

Every abbey had its secrets. Usually they were written down and kept in a safe place, handed down from abbot to abbot, for his eyes only. Sometimes they were of historical importance, concerning matters of royal statecraft or even the secret burial place of a saint. More often they were scandals, hidden or forgotten, in which the monastery was involved. Some, in retrospect, seemed trivial; others rose from the page like shrieks over which history had clapped a stifling hand. And lastly came the recent entries, concerning those still in the monastery – things which, in the view of the previous abbot, his successor needed to know.

Not that the entire Beaulieu record was so long. For the abbey was still a newcomer to the Forest.

Since the killing of Rufus the Forest had seen little drama. When, after a long reign, Henry had died, his daughter and his nephew had disputed the throne for years. But they did not fight in the Forest. When the daughter's son, ruthless Henry Plantagenet, had come to the throne, he had quarrelled with his Archbishop, Thomas Becket, and some said he had had him murdered. All Christendom had been shocked. There had been another flurry of excitement when Henry's heroic son, Richard the Lionheart, had gathered up his knights at Sarum to go on crusade.

But the truth was that the Forest folk cared little about any of these great events. The hunting of deer went on. Despite the numerous attempts of the barons and the Church to reduce the vast areas of the royal forests, the rapacious Plantagenet kings had actually enlarged them so that the boundaries of the New Forest were now even wider than they had been in the Conqueror's time; though the forest laws, mercifully, had grown less harsh. The king no longer made Brockenhurst his main hunting base but usually stayed at the royal manor of Lyndhurst, where the old deer park pale had been greatly enlarged.

One national event had got their attention, though. When Lionheart's brother, bad King John, had been forced by his barons to grant the humiliating Magna Carta, that great charter of English liberties had set out the limits to his oppressions in the Forest. And the matter had been even more clearly stated in a separate Charter of the Forest two years later. This was not a parochial business, either, given that almost a third of England had become royal forest by that date.

And then there had been Beaulieu.

If King John was called bad, it was not only because he lost all his wars and quarrelled with his barons. Worse still, he had insulted the Pope and caused England to be placed under a Papal Interdict. For years there were no church services in the land. No wonder the churchmen and monks hated him – and the monks wrote all the history. As far as they were concerned he had only done one good deed in his life: he had founded Beaulieu.

It was his sole religious foundation. Why did he do it? A good act by a bad man? In monkish chronicles such complexity was usually frowned upon. You were either good or bad. It was generally agreed that he must have done it to pay for some particularly awful deed. One legend even had it that he had ordered some monks to be trampled under his horses' feet and had been haunted afterwards by a dream.

Whatever the reason, in the Year of Our Lord 1204, King John founded Beaulieu, a monastery of the order of Cistercians, or white monks as they were known, endowing it first with a rich manor in Oxfordshire and then with a great tract of land down in the eastern half of the New Forest – which included, by chance, the very place where his great-great-uncle Rufus had been slain a century before. In the ninety years since its foundation, the abbey had received further grants both from John's pious son, Henry III, and the present king, mighty King Edward I, who had also been a loyal friend. Thanks to all this beneficence, the abbey was not only rich: small groups of its expanding body of monks had even gone out to start up little daughter houses in other places; one, Newenham, even lay seventy miles away, down the south-west coast in Devon. The abbey was both blessed and successful.

The abbot sighed, closed the book, carried it over to a large strong box in which he placed it and carefully locked the box.

He had made a mistake. The last abbot's judgement, which he had so foolishly ignored, was right. The man's character was clear: he was flawed and possibly dangerous.

"So why did I appoint him?" he murmured. Had he done it as a sort of penance? Perhaps. He had told himself that the man deserved a chance, that he had earned the position, that it was up to him as abbot – with prayer and the grace of God, of course – to make it work. As for his crime? It was in the book. It was long ago. God is merciful.

He glanced out through the open window. It was a beautiful day. Then his eyes fell on a pair of figures, walking quietly together in conversation. At the sight of these his face relaxed.

Brother Adam. There was a very different type. One of the best. He smiled. It was time to go outside. He unbolted the door.

Brother Adam was in a playful mood. As he sometimes did when he was pacing, he had pulled out the little wooden crucifix that hung on a cord round his neck, under his hair shirt, and was thoughtfully fingering it. His mother had given it to him when he first entered the order. She said she had got it from a man who had been to the Holy Land. It was carved from the wood of a cedar of Lebanon. He was enjoying the fact that the afternoon sun was gently warming his bald head. He had gone bald, and grey, by the time he was thirty. But this had not made him look old. Thirty-five, now, his finely cut, even features gave him a look of almost youthful intelligence, while one could sense that, under the monk's habit, his thick, muscular body exuded a sense of physical power.

He was also quietly enjoying the business in hand, which was, as they paced up and down between two beds of vegetables, to inculcate, in the kindest way, some much-needed common sense into the young novice who walked respectfully beside him.

People often came to Brother Adam for advice, because he

was calm and clever, yet always approachable. He never offered advice unless asked – he was far too shrewd to do that – but it might have been noticed that whatever the problem, after a troubled person had discussed it with Brother Adam for a while, that person nearly always started to laugh, and usually went away smiling.

"Don't you ever rebuke people?" the abbot had once asked him.

"Oh, no," he had replied with a twinkle. "That's what abbots are for."

The present talk, however, was not entirely comforting. Nor was it meant to be. Brother Adam had given it before. He called it his "Truth about Monks" catechism.

"Why," he had asked the novice, "do men come to live in a monastery?"

"To serve God, Brother Adam."

"But why in a monastery?"

"To escape from the sinful world."

"Ah." Brother Adam gazed around the abbey precincts. "A safe haven. Like the Garden of Eden?"

In a way it was. The site the monks had chosen was delightful. Parallel to the great inlet from the Solent water that lay to the east of the Forest a small river ran down, forming a small coastal inlet, about three miles long, of its own. At the head of this inlet, where King John had kept a modest hunting lodge, the monks had laid out their great walled inclosure. It was modelled on the order's parent house in Burgundy. Dominating everything was the abbey church – a large, early Gothic structure with a squat, square tower over the central crossing. Though simple, the building was handsome, and made of stone. There was no stone in the Forest; some of it had been brought across the Solent water from the Isle of Wight; some, like the best stone in the Tower of London, from Normandy; and the pillars were made of the same dark Purbeck marble, from along the south coast, as had been used in the huge new cathedral up at Sarum. The monks were particularly proud of their church's floor, paved with decorative tiles they had painstakingly made themselves. Beside the church was the cloister; on its southern side the various quarters of the choir monks; along the whole of its western side the

huge, barn-like *domus conversorum* – the house where the lay
brothers ate and slept.

The walled inclosure also contained the abbot's house, numerous workshops, a pair of fish ponds and an outer gatehouse
where the poor were fed. A new and grander inner gatehouse
had also just been begun.

Outside the wall lay the inlet and a small mill. Above the
mill-race was a large pond surrounded by banks of silvery
rushes. Beyond that, on the western side, some fields sloped up
a small rise, from which there opened out a magnificent
panorama: to the north mostly wood and heath; and to the south
the rich, marshy land, which the monks had already partly
drained to produce several fine farms, and which stretched
down to the Solent water, with the long hump of the Isle of
Wight lying like a friendly guardian just beyond. The entire estate, woodland, open heath and farmland, extended to some
eight thousand acres; and since the boundary was marked by an
earthwork ditch and fence, the monks referred not to the walled
abbey inclosure, but to the eight-thousand-acre estate itself as
the "Great Close."

Bellus Locus, the abbey was called in Latin – the Beautiful
Place; in Norman French: *Beau Lieu.* But the forest people did
not speak French, so they pronounced it Boolee, or Bewley.
And before long the monks were doing so, too. Rich, tranquil
haven that it was, the Great Close of Beaulieu might well have
been mistaken for the Garden of Eden.

"One is secure here, of course," Brother Adam remarked
pleasantly. "We are clothed and fed. We have few cares. So tell
me" – he suddenly rounded on the novice – "now that you have
had the chance to observe us for several months, what do you
think is the most important quality for a monk to possess?"

"A desire to serve God. I think," the boy said. "A great religious passion."

"Really? Oh, dear. I don't agree at all."

"You don't?" The boy looked confused.

"Let me tell you something," Brother Adam cheerfully explained. "The first day you pass from your novitiate and become a monk, you will take your place as the most junior
among us, next to the monk who was the last to arrive before
you. After a time there will be another new monk, who will be

placed below you. For every meal and every service you will always sit in the same position between those two monks – every day, every night, year in, year out; and unless one of you leaves for another monastery, or becomes abbot or prior, you will stay together, like that, for the rest of your lives.

"Think about it. One of your companions has an irritating habit of scratching himself or sings out of tune, always; the other dribbles when he eats; he also has bad breath. And there they are, one each side of you. Forever." He paused and beamed at the novice. "That's monastic life," he said amiably.

"But monks live for God," the novice protested.

"And they are also ordinary human beings – no more, no less. That," Brother Adam added gently, "is why we need God's grace."

"I thought," the novice said honestly, "you were going to be more inspiring."

"I know."

The novice was silent. He was twenty.

"The most important qualities a monk needs," Brother Adam went on, "are tolerance and a sense of humour." He watched the young man. "But these are both gifts of God," he added, to comfort him.

The last part of this conversation had been quietly observed. The abbot had actually intended to join them, since he always enjoyed Brother Adam's company; and he had been secretly irritated when, just as he got outside, the prior had appeared at his elbow. Courtesies must be observed, though. As the prior murmured at his side, the abbot eyed him from time to time, bleakly.

John of Grockleton had been prior for a year now. Like most of his ilk, he was going nowhere.

The position of prior in a monastery is not without honour. This is, after all, the monk whom the abbot has chosen to be his deputy. But that is all. If the abbot is away he is in charge – but only on a day-to-day basis. All major decisions, even the assignment of the monks' tasks, must await the abbot's return. The prior is the workhorse, the abbot is the leader. Abbots have charisma; their deputies do not. Abbots solve problems; priors report them. Priors seldom become abbots.

John of Grockleton: properly speaking, he was just Brother

John, but somehow his original name, Grockleton, had always been appended. Where the devil was Grockleton anyway? The abbot couldn't remember. In the north, perhaps. He didn't really care. Prior John of Grockleton was nothing much to look at. He must have been quite tall once, before the curving of his spine caused him to stoop. His thin black hair had once been thick. But despite these infirmities, the prior still had plenty of life left in him. He'll outlive me I'm sure, the abbot thought.

If only it weren't for those hands. It always seemed to the abbot that they were like claws. He tried to correct himself. They were just hands. A bit bony, perhaps, a bit curved. But no worse than any other pair of hands belonging to one of God's creatures. Except they *were* like claws.

"I'm glad to see that our young novice is seeking instruction from Brother Adam," he remarked to the prior. "*Beatus vir, qui non sequitur . . .*" Psalm One: Blessed is the man that walketh not in the counsel of the ungodly . . . Verse One.

"*Sed in lege Domine . . .*" the prior quietly murmured. But his delight is in the law of the Lord. Verse Two.

It was quite natural, this reference to the psalms in ordinary conversation. Even the lay brothers, who attended fewer services, did it. For in the constant monastic offices in the church that punctuated the daily life of every monk, from matins to vespers and compline, and even the night office for which you were wakened long after midnight, it was the psalms, in Latin of course, that the brothers chanted. They could get through all hundred and fifty in a week.

And all human life was in the Psalms. There was a phrase apposite to every occasion. Just as simple village folk would often converse in local sayings and proverbs, so it was natural for the monks to speak the psalms. These were the words they heard all the time.

"Yes. The law of the Lord." The abbot nodded. "He has studied, of course, hasn't he? At Oxford." Their order was not an intellectual one, but a dozen years ago there had been a move to send a few of the brightest monks to Oxford. Brother Adam had gone from Beaulieu.

"Oxford." John of Grockleton said it with distaste. The abbot might approve of Oxford, but he didn't. He knew the psalms by rote: that was enough. People like Brother Adam might think themselves superior. But although the monks at Oxford had been quartered well away from the university city itself, they were still sharing the worldly corruption of the place. They weren't better than he was, they were worse.

"One of these days, when I have gone," the abbot remarked, "Brother Adam would make a good abbot – don't you think?" And he looked at the prior as though he expected him to agree.

"That will be after my time," Grockleton answered sourly.

"Nonsense, my dear Brother John," the abbot said happily. "You'll outlive us all."

Why did he taunt the prior like this? With an inward sigh, the abbot awarded himself a penance. It's the man's stubborn refusal to recognise his own limitations that brings out the worst in me, he thought, and now it's made me guilty of cruelty.

These reflections were abruptly cut short, however, by a series of cries from the outer gate. A moment later a figure came running towards them, followed by several anxious monks.

"Father Abbot. Come quickly," cried the man, half out of breath.

"Where, my son?"

"To Sowley grange. There has been a murder."

No one had followed him. Luke rested by a gorse brake, wondering what to do next. A mile away one of the abbey shepherds was tending his flock of sheep on the open heath, but the shepherd had not seen him.

Why had he done it? God knows he hadn't meant to. It would never have happened if Brother Matthew hadn't come. But that was no excuse. Especially when it was Brother Matthew – he winced to think of it, poor Brother Matthew lying in a pool of blood – who had put him, a humble lay brother, in charge of the grange in his absence.

The Cistercians were different from other monks. Nearly all monastic orders were based on the ancient Rule of St Benedict. And St Benedict's model was clear: monks were to lead a communal life of constant prayer balanced by physical labour; and they must take vows of poverty, chastity and obedience. Obedience and even chastity, more or less, had usually been achieved. But poverty was always a problem. No matter how simply they began, monasteries always finished up rich. Their churches became grand, their life easy. Time and again there had been reformers. The most notable was the huge French order centred upon Cluny; but even the Cluniacs, eventually, had gone the same way and their place had been taken by a new order, spreading out from their parent house of Citeaux in Burgundy: the Cistercians.

There was no mistaking them. Known as the white monks, because they wore habits of simple, undyed wool, the Cistercians avoided the sinful world by choosing wild and lonely places for their monasteries. Operating through farmsteads, called granges, often miles out from the monastery, they were especially known for raising sheep. The Beaulieu monks raised thousands, grazing them not only over the Great Close but the open Forest too, where they were given grazing rights. And to ensure that they could devote the majority of their time to prayer they had a subsidiary category of lesser monks – the lay brothers – who took monastic vows and attended some of the services, but whose main occupation was to tend the sheep and work in the fields. Usually these were quite rustic, local fellows who, for one reason or another, were drawn to the religious atmosphere of the monastery or its security. Men such as Luke.

They had come the night before. Eight of them. With bows and hounds. There had been Roger Martell, a wild young aristocrat, and four of his friends; but the other three had been local men, ordinary fellows like himself. One of these had been his kinsman, Will atte Wood. He sighed. The trouble was, everyone was your cousin in the Forest.

If only he hadn't been put in charge. Brother Matthew had been doing him a favour, of course. Sowley grange was an important place. As well as the usual livestock and arable farming, the monks there had charge of a huge pond stocked with fish. There was a deer park belonging to the abbey, too, at nearby Througham.

Brother Matthew had known the prior didn't like Luke. By putting him in charge of the grange he had been giving Luke a chance to prove to the prior that he was reliable. But when young Martell and his friends arrived, demanding shelter for the night, it hadn't been so easy for a simple man like Luke to refuse.

He knew they'd been poaching, of course. They even had a deer with them. It was a serious offence. The king no longer demanded your life or limb for killing his precious deer, but the fines could be heavy. By giving them shelter he was guilty of a crime too. So why had he done it? Had they threatened him? Martell had certainly cursed him and given him a look that frightened him. But the real reason, he knew in his heart, was when Will had nudged him and whispered: "Come on, Luke. I told them you were my cousin. Are you going to embarrass me?"

They'd eaten all the bread and a whole cheese. They didn't think much of the beer. The best beer and the wine for guests was all at the abbey, not out there at a humble grange. In the morning they had gone.

There were only half a dozen lay brothers at the grange besides himself and as many hired labourers. But there was no need to say anything. They had all understood. The illegal visit would never be mentioned to anyone.

"What shall we do about the missing cheese and beer?" one of the lay brothers had ventured.

"We'll open the tap a fraction, spill some beer on the floor under it and say nothing. When someone notices they'll think it leaked away. As for the cheese, I'll say it must have been stolen."

Perhaps it might have worked if Brother Matthew had not been so sharp-eyed and if he hadn't decided to call at the grange only two days after his last visit. Bustling in shortly after midday, he quickly inspected the premises, noticed the leaking barrel of beer at once and summoned Luke.

"It must have leaked since yesterday," Luke had begun, but got no further.

"Nonsense. It was full. The tap was only just dripping. Anyway, it was sealed tight when I left. Someone's been drinking it." He looked about. "There's a whole cheese missing."

"It must have been stolen." It was no good. Luke needed to prepare himself for a lie and Brother Matthew had caught him

off balance. The monk looked at him severely. And who knew
what stupid story he might have started next if there had not
begun, just then, a furious knocking at the door.

It was Martell. He nodded to the lay brethren. "We're back,
Luke. Need your help again." Then, glancing at Brother
Matthew whom he had not yet deigned to notice, he casually
asked: "And who the devil are you?"

Luke buried his face in his hands as he remembered the rest:
the fury of Brother Matthew; his own humiliation; the terse order
to the poachers to leave and their arrogant refusal. And then . . .

If only Brother Matthew had not lost his temper. First he
had cursed him for being in league with the criminals. God
knows, it was only natural that he should have thought so. He
had threatened to tell the prior and have him thrown out of
the monastery. In front of the other lay brothers. Witnesses.
The two of them had been outside by then, confronting the
poachers. Then Brother Matthew had told the others to bar the
entrance. Martell had insolently put his foot in the door and
the monk had lost his temper. Seeing a staff leaning against the
wall, he had rushed to it, seized it and turned.

He had not meant to hurt Brother Matthew. Quite the reverse. There had been only one thought in his mind. If the
monk struck Martell the young blood might kill him. There
had been no time to think of more than that. Beside the staff
there was a spade – a heavy wooden implement with a metal
rim. Grabbing the spade he had swung it to break the blow just
as Brother Matthew's staff came down.

He had swung too hard. With a crash, the staff snapped
back, the blade of the spade smashed through and bit into the
monk's head with an awful jarring thud. Then all hell seemed
to break loose. The other lay brothers hurled themselves forward to tackle him, Martell and Will had gone for the lay
brothers, and in the mêlée he had dropped the spade and run
for his life.

One thing was certain. However the matter was explained,
he would be blamed. He had let the poachers in; he had struck
Brother Matthew; the prior hated him. If he wanted to keep his
life he would have to run, or at least hide. It couldn't be long
before they came after him.

He wondered where to go.

Mary paused from scrubbing the pot for long enough to shake her head.

The problem, in essence, was simple enough. Or so she told herself. The problem was the pony.

John Pride reckoned it was his. And Tom Furzey said it wasn't. That was it, really. You could say other things about it. By the time a week had passed, a lot of people had said a lot of things. But that didn't alter the fact: Pride reckoned it was his and Furzey said it wasn't.

To an impartial observer there was room for honest doubt. A pony would foal out on the Forest. As long as the foal was with its mother, you knew where you were; but if the mare died or the foal strayed – and such things happened – then you might find a spare foal wandering about and not know its owner. That was what had happened in this case. The foal had been found by Pride. At least, that was what he said. There was room for doubt.

It was a pretty thing, too. That was half the trouble. Though it was a typical New Forest pony – short and sturdy with a thick neck – there was something finely drawn, almost delicate in its face and it moved so daintily on its feet. The pony's coat was an even chestnut brown all over, with a darker mane and tail.

"Prettiest little pony I ever saw," her brother had told her and she didn't disagree.

Mary and John Pride were born only a year apart. They had played together all their childhood. Dark, well-made, slim, free and independent spirits, no one could keep up with them when they went racing through the Forest. They would only slow down for their dreamy little brother. John had been a bit contemptuous when she had married Tom Furzey. Chubby Tom, with his round face and curly brown hair, had always seemed a bit dull. But they had known him all their lives; they all lived in Oakley. They didn't mind him. Her marriage was just an extension of the family, really.

And she had been happy enough. Five pregnancies later, with three healthy young children living, she had grown plumper herself; but her dark-blue eyes were as striking as ever. If her thickset husband was sometimes surly and always unexciting, what did that matter when you were living with all your family in the Forest?

Until the pony. It was three weeks, now, since John Pride and Tom Furzey had stopped speaking. And it wasn't only them. A thing like that couldn't just be left. Things had been said and repeated. None of the Prides – and there were many – was speaking to any of the Furzeys – and there were no less – anywhere in the Forest. God knows how long it might go on. The pony was kept in John Pride's cowshed. He couldn't put it out on the Forest, of course, because one of the Furzeys would have captured it. So the little creature was kept there, like a knight awaiting ransom, and all the Forest watched to see what would happen next.

But for Mary the real trouble lay at home.

She wasn't allowed to see her brother. John lived only a quarter of a mile away in the same hamlet, but it was now forbidden territory. A few days after the dispute began she had gone over, hardly thinking about it. By the time her surly husband came home, though, he had already been told. And he hadn't liked it. Oh, he had made that very clear. From that day on, she wasn't to speak to John: not as long as he had that pony.

What could she do? Tom Furzey was her husband. Even if she ignored his wishes and sneaked round to see John, Tom's sister lived between them and she'd be sure to spot her and tell. Then there'd be another violent row and the children would see. It wasn't worth the trouble. She had stayed away and John, of course, could not come to their house.

She went outside. The autumn afternoon was still warm. She glanced up, bleakly, at the blue sky. It looked metallic, threatening. She had never lived alone with her husband before.

She was still staring up at the woods nearby when she heard a whistle from the trees. She frowned. It was repeated. She went towards the sound and was greatly surprised, a few moments later, to see a familiar figure emerge from behind a tree.

It was her little brother Luke, from Beaulieu Abbey. And he looked frightened.

• • •

In the early morning mist Brother Adam did not notice the woman at first. Besides, his mind was elsewhere.

The events of the previous day had shaken the whole community. By the evening office of vespers everyone knew what had happened. It was not often that the monks wanted to talk. The Cistercians, although not a silent order, restrict the hours when conversation is permitted, but time expands in the long silences of a monastery and there is seldom any sense of urgency: one day is as good as another to exchange a piece of news. By the evening, however, everyone was dying to talk.

Brother Adam knew it must be discouraged. Excitement of this kind was not just a distraction: it was like a screen between oneself and God, filtering out the Holy Spirit. God was best heard in silence, seen in darkness. So he was glad when, after the night office of compline, the *summum silencium*, the rule of total silence, interposed itself until breakfast.

The night was a special time for Brother Adam. It always brought him solace. Occasionally he regretted what he had missed by entering the religious life, or yearned for the more bracing intellects he had known at Oxford. And, of course, there were times when he cursed the bell that tolled in the middle of the night, when one pulled on felt slippers and went down the cold stone steps into the shadowy abbey church. Yet even then, singing the psalms in the candlelight, knowing that outside the huge starry universe hung watchfully over the monastery, it seemed to Adam that he could feel the palpable presence of God. And the life of continuous prayer, he would reflect, built up a protective wall as solid as that of any cloister, making a quiet, empty space within oneself in which to receive the silent voice of the universe. So, for many years, Brother Adam had lived within his prayer walls and felt the presence of God in the night.

The mornings had been especially pleasant for him recently. A few months ago, feeling the need for a period of contemplation, he had asked the abbot to assign him light duties for a while and his request had been granted. After the dawn service of prime, and breakfast, which the choir monks ate in their *frater* and the lay brothers in their separate *domus*, he usually went for a solitary walk.

This morning had been delightful. An autumn mist shrouded the river. On the opposite bank the oak leaves in the trees looked golden. The swans seemed to liquify out of the mist, as though miraculously engendered by the surface of the water. And he had still, on his return, been so entranced by this image of God's creation that he scarcely noticed the woman until he had almost reached the collection of poor folk waiting to receive their daily alms at the abbey gate.

She was a rather pleasant-looking woman: broad-faced, blue-eyed, Celtic, intelligent he guessed – obviously one of the Forest people. Perhaps he'd seen her before? She seemed to be hoping to talk to someone, although her eyes watched him cautiously. Fine eyes.

"Yes, my child?"

"Oh, Brother. They say Brother Matthew has been killed. My husband works for the abbey at harvest. Brother Matthew was always so kind. We wondered . . ." She trailed off, looking anxious.

Brother Adam frowned. Probably the whole Forest would have heard something about yesterday by now. Besides the lay brothers, the abbey gave casual employment to many Forest people. No doubt kindly Brother Matthew was well liked. His frown was caused only by the memory of the incident imping-ing on his peace. How selfish of him. He smiled instead. "Brother Matthew lives, my child." The first reports of the in-cident, as usual, had been garbled. Brother Matthew had taken a very nasty knock and lost much blood, but thank God he was alive, in the abbey's infirmary and had already taken a little broth.

Her relief was so palpable that he was touched. How blessed that this peasant woman should care so deeply about the monk.

"And those who did this?"

Ah. He understood. The religious houses had a name for protecting their own people from justice and it was resented. Well, he could reassure her on that score.

The abbot had been furious. There had been an incident like this before, about fifteen years ago: a huge party of poachers; a strong suspicion that the lay brothers in one of the granges had been party to the business. That, together with the prior's bad report of Luke, had done it. "The lay brother who struck him will get no protection from the abbey," he assured her. "The Forest courts will deal with him."

She nodded quietly, then looked thoughtful. "Yet might it have been an accident?" she asked. "If the lay brother repents, wouldn't they show mercy?"

"You are right to be cautious in judging," he said. "And mercy is God's grace." What a good woman she was. She feared for the monk, yet thought with compassion of his assailant. "But we must all accept righteous punishment for our transgressions." He looked stern. "You know the fellow has run away?" She seemed to shake her head. "He will be caught." The steward of the Forest had been informed by the abbot that morning. "I believe they are taking out the hounds."

With a kindly nod he left her. And poor Mary, her heart pounding, ran all the way back across the heath to the place where, last night, she had hidden her brother Luke.

Tom Furzey clenched his fists. They'd get what was coming to them now. Already he could hear the hounds in the distance. He was not a bad man. But bad things had been happening to him recently. Sometimes he hardly knew what to think.

The Prides had always thought he was a bit slow. He knew that. But everything had been so friendly and easy before. They were all part of the Forest: all family, so to speak. That pony, though – that had been a shock. If John Pride could just casually take a pony foaled by his, Tom Furzey's, own mare, with not so much as a by-your-leave: what sort of brother-in-law was that? He despises me, Tom thought, and now I know it.

It was strange. The first day he couldn't quite believe it had happened, even with the foal in Pride's pen, before his very eyes. Then, when challenged, Pride had just laughed at him.

And then Tom had called him a thief. In front of the others. Well, he was, wasn't he? Things had snowballed after that.

But Mary: that was another matter. That first day, after she *knew* what had passed between him and her brother, she had gone round to Pride's house as friendly as you like. "Didn't you tell him to give the pony back?" he had stormed. But she had just looked blank. Never even thought of it. "So whose

side are you on, then?" he had cried. The fact was, after years
of marriage, she hadn't really given him a thought. That was
the hurtful truth of it. Poor old Tom, a useful husband for
Mary: that's all I am to the Prides, he reckoned.

But whatever she thought of him, she owed him respect as
head of their family. What sort of example did it set the children if she let all the Forest see how little regard she had for
him? He wasn't going to be made to look a fool. He had put
his foot down; forbidden her to go to John Pride's. Wasn't that
right? His sister said it was. So did a lot of others. Not everyone in the Forest thought so well of the Prides and their high
and mighty ways.

It hadn't been easy, though, watching his wife, day by day,
growing colder towards him.

Well, the Prides were going to be put in their place today.
And after that . . . He wasn't sure what. But something, any-
how.

His mind was full of these thoughts when he caught sight,
nearly a mile away, of Puckle riding a Forest pony. He seemed
to be dragging something behind him.

There were ten riders. The hounds were in full cry. The prior
had given them a scent of Brother Luke's bedding and they had
been following it all the way from the grange. The steward of
the Forest himself was leading them. Two of the other riders
were gentlemen foresters, two more were under-foresters, the
rest servants.

Since its inception, the New Forest had always been divided
into administrative areas, known as bailiwicks, each in the
charge of a forester, usually from a gentry family. Down the
western side ran the bailiwicks of Godshill, Linwood and
Burley. A big tract just west of the centre was known as
Battramsley bailiwick. Recently, however, the largest bailiwick of all, the central royal bailiwick of Lyndhurst, which ran
right across the heath to Beaulieu, had been subdivided, the
hamlet of Oakley where Pride and Furzey lived falling within
the southern section. Over all these presided the warden of the
forest, a friend of the king, whose steward supervised the
Forest for him day-to-day.

They were surprised, as they came to the hamlet, to see Tom Furzey in front of them, waving his arms and crying out: "I know where he is."

The party pulled up. The steward looked stern. "You've seen him?"

"Don't need to. I know where he is."

The steward frowned, then glanced at the fair, handsome young man riding beside him. "Alban?"

Philip le Alban was a lucky young gentleman. Two centuries before, his ancestor Alban, born to Norman Adela and her Saxon husband Edgar, had not quite maintained his position in the increasingly French society of Plantagenet England; but his descendants, who had taken his name for several generations, had continued as under-foresters for various bailiwicks and, as a reward for this long service and because he had married well, young Philip le Alban had been promoted to forester of the new Southern bailiwick. No one knew the Forest or its inhabitants better. "Where is he, then, Tom?" he asked pleasantly enough.

"At John Pride's house, of course," Tom cried and, without another word, turned and started leading them in that direction.

"The runaway and John Pride are brothers," Alban explained. And since the hounds, it was true, were going in that general direction, the steward nodded brusquely as they followed Tom.

Pride was out, but his family were there. They stood silently while two of the men searched their cottage without result. The rest of the little farmstead yielded nothing.

But it was the cowshed at which Furzey was gesticulating wildly. "In there," he cried. "Look in there."

He was so excited that this time the entire party, even the steward, crowded into the shed. But it took only moments to see that nobody was lurking there.

Tom looked crestfallen. But he wasn't prepared to let it go at that. "He was here," he insisted; then, seeing their disbelieving faces, he burst out: "Where do you think John Pride is now? Making fools of you! Hiding his brother somewhere." They were starting to move out. This wouldn't do. "And look at this pony," he cried. "What are you going to do about that?" The foal was tethered in one corner, blinking its frightened eyes at him. "This pony's stolen. From me!"

They were already outside again. His plan was dissolving. He had quite persuaded himself that they were going to find Luke, lead John Pride away in chains and restore his pony to him. He rushed after them. "You don't understand," he shouted. "They're all the same, these Prides. They're all criminals."

Two of the men started to chuckle.

"That include your wife, then, Tom?" one of them asked. Even Alban had to repress a smile. To the steward, who had looked up sharply, he explained that Tom's wife also had the runaway for a brother.

"God save us!" the steward exclaimed irritably. "Isn't that just like the Forest?" Turning to Tom, he exploded: "How the devil do I know *you* aren't hiding him? You're probably the biggest criminal of the lot. Where does this man live?" They told him. "Search his cottage at once."

"But . . ." Tom could hardly believe this turn of events. "What about my pony?" he wailed.

"Damn your pony," cursed the steward, as he started to ride towards Tom's cottage.

They found nothing there either. Mary had seen to that. But a short while later the hounds picked up Luke's scent in the trees nearby and followed it for many a mile.

Indeed, as time went by, the route they took became quite curious, winding about until at last it went in a huge circle round Lyndhurst where, so to speak, it continued for ever.

There had been no one to see, a couple of hours before, the lone figure of Puckle on his pony, dragging the bundle of Luke's clothing Mary had provided.

"Damn waste of time," the steward remarked to Alban. "I suppose that idiot was right this morning. The Prides are hiding him."

"Perhaps." Alban smiled. "But no one can hide in the Forest for ever."

When the summons to the abbot came, one November morning, Brother Adam was well prepared. He had done what the abbot had asked a month before and reached his conclusions.

Strangely enough, given the worldly and political nature of the business, he had found that his continuing period of meditation and private study had given him strength and certainty. His mind was at peace.

So, he was glad to say, was the abbey. October had passed quietly. The migratory birds had wheeled and headed southwards across the sea. Then November's greying clouds, like the sails of an ageing ship, had drawn eastwards across the sky; the yellowed oak leaves had fallen by the river bank and nothing had disturbed the abbey's silence. At Martinmass in November, at the Forest's minor court, the Court of Attachments, the verderers had sent the incident at the grange forward to the senior court, which would be held at the good pleasure of the king's justices, when they visited the Forest the following spring. Young Martell and his friends had wisely turned themselves in to the sheriffs of their counties, who would produce them at the spring court. Luke, the lay brother, had not yet been found. Kindly Brother Matthew had wanted to forgive him, but the abbot had been firm.

"Justice must be seen to be done, for our good name."

As he walked towards the abbot's quarters Brother Adam looked with pleasure at the scene around him. Punctuated by the clanging bell that, every three hours or so, summoned the monks to prayer, the monastery was always a hive of quiet activity. There were the weaving and cloth-making workshops, and the fulling mill by the river at which the estate's huge clip of wool was cleaned. The skins of the sheep and cattle provided numerous departments: a tannery – smelly, so outside the gate; a skinner's shop for making hoods and leather blankets; a shoemaker's – very busy since every monk and lay brother needed two pairs of boots or shoes every year. By the cloisters was the parchment and bookbinding department. There was a flour mill, a bakery, a brewery, two stable ranges, a piggery and a slaughterhouse. With its forge, carpenter's, candlemaker's, two infirmaries and a hospice providing accommodation for visitors – the abbey was like a little walled town. Or perhaps, with its Latin books and services, and the monks' habits resembling the Roman dress of a thousand years before, it was more like a huge Roman villa.

Nothing, Adam reflected, was wasted; everything was used.

Between the various buildings, for instance, the ground was carefully arranged in beds for vegetables and herbs. Fruits grew on trellises by sheltered walls, grapes on vines. There was honeysuckle for the bees whose hives, scattered about the inclosure, yielded honey and wax.

"We are worker bees ourselves," he had once joked to a visiting knight. "But the queen we serve is the Queen of Heaven." He had been rather pleased with this conceit, although chiding himself afterwards for falling so easily into the sin of vanity.

Above all, the abbey was self-sufficient. "All nature," he delighted to point out, "flows through the abbey. Everything is in balance, everything complete. The monastery can endure, like nature itself, to the end of days." It was a perfect machine for contemplating God's wondrous creation.

And it was precisely this truth that was in his mind when he entered the abbot's office, sat down beside the prior and gazed steadily forward, as the abbot turned to him and bluntly demanded: "Well, Adam, what are we to do about these wretched churches?"

It was a curious fact, born out of the experience of centuries, that if one thing brought trouble and strife to any monastery, it was, above all others, the possession of a parish church.

Why should this be? Wasn't a church by its very nature a place of peace? In theory, yes. But in practice, churches had vicars, parishioners and local squires; and they all had one thing to argue about: money.

The church tithes – about a tenth of the parish's production, usually – were paid by the parish to support the church and its priest. But if the church came into a monastery's possession then the monastery took the tithe and paid the vicar. That frequently meant a dispute with the vicar. Even worse, if a Cistercian house had land in a parish it would normally refuse to pay any tithes itself – an ancient exemption granted the order when it was mostly clearing wasteland for its sheep, but hardly fair when it took over existing productive land. This would infuriate the vicar, squire and parishioners, and often led to litigation.

It was the threat of just such a dispute that had caused the abbot to ask Brother Adam to go through the abbey's entire cartulary record and make a recommendation. The church in question lay a hundred miles away, beyond even the abbey's little daughter house of Newenham, in still more westerly Cornwall and had been given to the abbey by a royal prince several decades earlier.

The abbot was particularly anxious to have everything settled because he had soon to depart, as abbots often did, to attend the king's council and Parliament – a duty which might keep him away for some time.

"I have two recommendations to make, Abbot," Brother Adam replied. "The first is very simple. This Cornish vicar hasn't got a case. The yearly income he is to receive was agreed with his predecessor and there's no reason to change it. Tell him we'll see him in court."

"Quite right." John of Grockleton might be jealous of Adam, but he approved of this kind of talk.

"You're sure of your legal ground?" the abbot asked.

"Certain."

"Very well. Let it be done." The abbot sighed. "Send him a pair of shoes." The abbot had a rather touching faith that anyone who needed placating could be rendered happy by a gift of a pair of the abbey's well-made shoes. He gave away over a hundred pairs a year. "You said you had a second recommendation?"

Brother Adam paused a moment. He had no illusions about the reception he was about to get. "You asked me to go over the entire record of our dealings with churches," he began carefully, "and I did. Outside Beaulieu itself, we have holdings in Oxfordshire, Berkshire, Wiltshire and Cornwall – where we also receive a large income from the tin mines. All these have parish churches. We also own a chapel elsewhere.

"And in every single case we have been involved in disputes. In the nine decades since Beaulieu's founding I can't find one free from legal disputes over churches. Some have dragged on for twenty years. They'll still be fighting us down in Cornwall, I can promise you, long after we're all underground."

"But the abbey has always managed to deal with these problems, hasn't it?" the abbot asked.

"Yes. Our order has become highly skilful at it. A compromise is found. Our interests are always protected."

"There we are, then," Grockleton interjected. "We always win."

"But," Brother Adam gently went on, "at what cost? In Cornwall, for instance, do we do any good works? No. Are we respected? I doubt it. Hated? Certainly. Are we legally in the right in these matters? Probably. But morally?" He spread out his hands. "We are amply endowed with Beaulieu alone. We don't actually need these churches and their income." He paused. "I dare to say, Abbot, in this respect, that we are scarcely different from the Cluniacs."

"Cluniacs?" Grockleton almost jumped out of his seat. "We are not in the least like the Cluniacs."

"Our order was set up precisely to avoid their mistakes," Adam agreed. "And after performing the task you set me, Abbot, I read the founding charter of our order again. The *Carta Caritatis*."

The *Carta Caritatis* – the Charter of Love – of the Cistercians was a remarkable document. Written by the first effective head of the new order, an Englishman as it happened, it was a code of rules designed to ensure that the white monks would stick, without deviating, to the original intent of the ancient rule of St Benedict. His point was, exactly, that the Cistercian houses should be modest, plain and self-sufficient, so as to avoid the distractions of worldly entanglements. And one of his sternest injunctions was that on no account were Cistercian houses to own parish churches.

"No parish churches," the abbot nodded sadly.

"Would it not be possible," Adam asked gently, "for Beaulieu to exchange these churches for other properties?"

"They were royal gifts, Adam," the abbot pointed out.

"Given long ago. Perhaps the king would not mind."

King Edward I, that mighty legislator and warrior, had spent much of his reign subduing the Welsh and was planning to do the same to the Scots. He might not be interested in what the abbey did with its royal endowments. But you never knew.

"I'd hate to ask him," the abbot confessed.

"Well," said Brother Adam with a smile, "I have satisfied my conscience by bringing the matter before you. I can do no more."

"Quite. Thank you, Adam." The abbot indicated that he could retire.

For some time after he had gone, the abbot remained gazing silently into space, while John of Grockleton, his claw-like hand resting on the edge of the table, sat watching him. At last the abbot sighed.

"He's right, of course."

Grockleton's claw clenched just a little, but he did not interrupt.

"The trouble is," the abbot went on, "many of the other Cistercian houses own churches too. If we make a fuss, the other abbots might not take it very kindly."

Grockleton continued to watch. Privately he couldn't have cared less if the abbey owned a dozen churches and hammered half the vicars in Christendom.

"As abbot," the abbot mused on, "one has to be careful."

"Very." Grockleton nodded.

"His first recommendation is clearly right. This Cornish vicar must be squashed." He sat up briskly. "What else have we to deal with?"

"The assignment of duties, Abbot, while you are away. There were two appointments you mentioned: the novice master and the new supervisor of the granges."

After the recent violent episode involving Luke at the grange the abbot had decided that, for a year at least, a trusted monk ought to act as a permanent supervisor, visiting the granges continuously. "I want them to feel," he had said, "an iron hand." It was not a pleasant task for any monk; he would miss many of the daily offices in church. "But it must be done," the abbot had decreed.

"Novice master," the abbot began. "Brother Stephen needs a rest, we all agree. I was thinking, therefore, of Brother Adam. He's awfully good with the novices." He nodded contentedly.

Grockleton's claw remained at rest upon the table. When he spoke, it was quietly. "I have a request, Abbot. While you are away and I am in charge, I should like you not to put Brother Adam in charge of the novices."

"Oh?" The abbot frowned. "Why?"

"Because this matter of the churches is in his mind. I do not doubt his loyalty to the order . . ."

"Certainly not."

"But if, for instance, a young novice should ask, while

reading the *Carta Caritatis* . . ." He paused conscientiously. "Brother Adam might find it hard not to criticise us . . ." He stopped, then added meaningfully: "That would leave me in a very difficult position. I don't think I'd be adequate . . ."

The abbot gazed at him. He wasn't deceived. He could just imagine the care with which Grockleton would ensure that Brother Adam was embarrassed. On the other hand he couldn't deny that there was an element of truth in what the prior said. "What do you propose?" he asked coldly.

"Brother Matthew is still shaken. But he would make a perfectly adequate novice master. Why not let Brother Adam supervise the granges? His period of meditation, I believe, will have strengthened him for the task."

The sly dog, the abbot thought. That last was a dig at him for favouring Adam with light assignments. The message was clear: I'm your deputy, making a reasonable request. If you don't give your favourite an unpleasant task I'll make trouble for him.

And then an unworthy thought occurred to him: if I can put up with the prior, then Adam can put up with the granges for a while. He smiled at Grockleton sweetly. "You are right, John. And if, as I suspect, Adam may one day be abbot, a *reforming* abbot, perhaps" – he enjoyed watching Grockleton wince when he said that – "then this experience will be very useful to him."

So, before the abbot left the monastery at the ending of the year, Brother Adam was assigned to the granges.

On a wintry December afternoon Mary walked hurriedly towards Beaulieu.

A cold wind was blowing into her back, pushing her along the tiny track as the heather scraped her legs. To the north the distant tree line had sunk beneath the slow swell of the ground so that the landscape resembled the bare tundra it must have been thousands of years before. Behind her, over the expanse of brownish heather and dark-green gorse, banks of cloud with a faint orange glow were moving steadily along the coastline, threatening to overtake and smother her as she went eastwards, across the great waste between the Forest centre and the abbey, which was now called Beaulieu Heath.

She had no wish to be there; she was only doing it to please her husband.

Tom did not work for the abbey in winter, but this year the monks had called him in for a special task. They wanted a cart.

Tom was not usually a carpenter. It was difficult to persuade him to make anything in the house. But for some reason, all his life his imagination had been fired by the idea of making carts. A cart made by Tom Furzey was a formidable affair, with a framework base and four framework sides, each of which could be removed. Every beam was neatly jointed into its fellow. Tom's carts were always the same and they would last until doomsday. But he would never make the wheels. "That's wheelwright's work," he would say. "I make the cart and he makes it go. That's the way I look at it." He seemed to like to dwell upon this thought.

Once, when they were still on speaking terms, John Pride had got him to confess that he disliked the thought of making wheels because they were curved. "You'd make wheels if they could be square, wouldn't you Tom?" he had genially asked.

And Tom, to Pride's delight had answered, thoughtfully: "Reckon I might."

So Tom had gone to work on the cart for the monks. That had been ten days ago. It would take him at least six weeks to complete and while he did so he was staying at St Leonards Grange. Every few days Mary would visit him there. Today, she had promised to bring him some cakes. She was especially anxious to do so because she felt guilty for the fact that she was glad he was away – firstly because of Tom's moods; secondly because of Luke.

In his strange, dreamy way, Luke had seemed almost happy living out in the Forest. Even as the weather grew cold he had always managed to make himself a snug lair somehow. "I'm just a forest animal," he had told her contentedly. He always claimed he could feed himself. But as she pointed out: "Even the deer get fed in midwinter." So as soon as Tom had departed for St Leonards she had brought Luke into their little barn. No one, neither her brother nor her children, knew he was being fed and sleeping there. She didn't know how long it could last; it frightened her. But what else was she to do?

By the time she reached the edge of the farmlands that lay around the grange the wind had strengthened. There was a cold dampness around the back of her neck. Looking behind her, she saw that the yellowish clouds were barrelling on to Beaulieu Heath, bringing flurries of snow to the western edge. For a moment she wondered if she should turn back, but decided to continue, having come so far.

Brother Adam looked gratefully at the door of the grange. The flurries of snow, although they seemed so soft, had started to sting his face.

There were five granges south-west of the abbey: Beufre, the main centre for the plough oxen; Bergerie, where all the sheep were sheared; Sowley, down by the coast, where the monks had built the huge fish pond; Beck and, nearest to the mouth of the river estuary, St Leonards. He had been to Bergerie that day and intended to walk back from St Leonards to the abbey that evening.

The last two weeks had been exhausting. Within the Great Close, apart from the five in the south-west, there were ten more granges north of the abbey and another three on the eastern side of the Beaulieu estuary. Then there were the string of little holdings over in the Avon valley west of the Forest, which supplied the abbey with hay from their rich meadows. And there were other outliers he'd hardly considered yet. He had had no rest. The prior had seen to that. The period of contemplation he had been enjoying was completely shattered.

He pushed open the door of the grange. The half-dozen lay brothers looked startled to see him. Good. He had already learned to turn up suddenly, like a schoolmaster. He hardly paused to shake off the snow. "First," he said sternly, "I will inspect the food stores."

The grange at St Leonards was a typical Cistercian affair. The dwelling house was a long, single-storey structure with an oak door in the middle. Here the lay brothers lived in spartan conditions, returning to the abbey *domus* for the main saints days and festivals, and being relieved from the centre from time to time. About thirty of the roughly seventy lay brothers were to be found out at the granges, usually.

"So far, so good," Adam told them, as soon as he had checked for signs of pilfering or illicit drinking. "Now I will see the barn."

It was strange, he reflected, that although, for years, he had seen the lay brothers every day, he had never really known them. The huge *domus conversorum* of the lay brothers might take up the whole western side of the cloister, but it was also completely separated even from the cloister wall by a narrow lane. One had to go right round the outside to reach the *domus*. In church the monks sang in the choir, the lay brothers in the nave. They ate apart.

Until now, he had never realised that he looked down upon them. It was true that he had found it necessary to treat them a little like children, to ensure discipline in the granges. Yet they were also men. Their commitment to the abbey was no less than his. They think less intensely than I do, he considered: each day I measure my life by what I have thought, about God, or my fellow men, or the world around the abbey. Yet their way is to feel these things and they remember the days by how they felt upon them. It may even be that, by thinking less, and feeling more, they remember more than I do.

If the dwelling house was modest, the rest of the farm buildings were not. There were cattle yards and cowsheds – even St Leonards often had a hundred oxen and seventy cows to take care of. There were sheepcotes and piggeries. But towering over everything was the huge barn. It was the size of a church, built of stone, with massive oak rafters. The wheat and oats they harvested were stored there in huge piles of sacks; so was all the farm equipment. On one side was a mountain of bracken, used for bedding. There was even a threshing floor. And at the moment, in the middle of its cavernous space, lit dimly by some lamps, stood Tom Furzey's recently started cart.

Peering across the shadows, however, it was something else that caught Adam's eye: a figure beside the peasant in the half-light. Unless he was mistaken, it was a woman.

Women were not allowed in the abbey. A great lady might visit, of course, but she was not supposed to stay the night even in the quarters reserved for royal guests. The womenfolk of the hired hands might visit them at the granges but, as the abbot had particularly stressed to him, "They're not to hang about. And never, on any account, to stay the night."

He went over to them at once, therefore.

She was sitting beside Furzey on the floor. As he approached, they both got up respectfully. The woman had a shawl of some kind over her head and as she was looking down modestly he could not see her face very well.

"This is my wife," the peasant said. "She brought me some cakes."

"I see." He did not want to offend Furzey, but he thought it best to be firm. "I'm afraid she must leave before dusk, you know, and it's already getting dark." The fellow looked sulky, but although she did not look up, it seemed to him that the woman did not mind. "Your husband's cart will be magnificent," he said in a friendly tone, before turning back to the others.

He spent some time in conversation while he went round the barn, so he was not surprised to see, when he finished, that the woman had left. Intending to trudge back to the abbey himself, now, he went to the small door in the huge barn entrance and opened it.

The blizzard hit him like a blow. He could scarcely believe it. The thick walls of the barn had completely muffled the sound of the wind as it had grown: in the little while that he had been inside the flurries had turned into gusts and the gusts into a howling storm. Even by the shelter of the barn the snowflakes lashed his face. Turning into the wind, he had to blink to see. To go even the three miles to the abbey seemed a foolish idea. He'd better remain at the grange.

Then he remembered the woman. Dear heaven, he'd sent her out in this. And how far did she have to go? Five miles? Nearer six. Across the open heath into the mouth of the blizzard. It was outrageous; he felt a sense of shame. What would her husband think of him and of the abbey? Ducking back into the barn, he summoned Tom and two of the lay brothers. "Wrap yourselves quickly. Bring a leather blanket." Only pausing long enough to find out which path she would have taken, he dashed out into the snow, leaving them to catch up with him.

According to the hour, it was still afternoon. Somewhere

above, the darkness had not fallen. But here below the light had been expunged. Before him, as he plunged forward, there was nothing but a blinding whitish fury, attacking his face as though God had summoned up some new plague of locusts for the northern lands. The snow came almost horizontally, enveloping everything so that, only yards ahead, the world seemed to vanish into a grey opacity.

Dear Lord, how was he to find her? Would she die? Would she join the deer and ponies who, several dozen to be sure, would be found, stiff on the ground, after a night like this?

He was quite astonished, therefore, having left the last hedgerow behind, to see just in front of him a dark shape, like a bundle of clothing, struggling forward into the blizzard. He cried out, taking a dozen snowflakes into his mouth; but she did not hear him. Only when he came up with her and put his arm protectively round her shoulders did she realise his presence as, feeling her start with fright, he turned her away from the driving fury of the storm.

"Come."

"I can't. I must go home." She was even trying to push him gently away and resume her impossible journey.

Almost surprised at himself, however, he held her firmly. "Your husband is here," he said, although they could not see him. And guiding her path, he led her back.

The blizzard that night was the worst that anyone in the Forest could remember. Down by the coast the snowstorm seemed to have become one with the churning sea. Around St Leonards Grange huge snowdrifts piled up along the hedgerows, covering them right over. The wind over Beaulieu Heath was either a searing whistle or a great white moan. And even when a faint greying in the darkness indicated that morning must have come, the blizzard continued, blocking out the light.

To Brother Adam his duty was clear. He wasn't returning to the abbey; he must stay in the grange and give what spiritual leadership he could.

On the way back to the barn he had recognised the woman as the one he had spoken to about Brother Matthew. He was glad it should turn out to be such a good soul that he had saved from the storm.

The arrangements were simple enough. He had them set up a brazier filled with charcoal in the barn. Furzey and his wife could spend the night there well enough, while he and the others remained in the dwelling house. And in order that there should be no misunderstanding of the situation he called everyone together in the barn after the evening meal and, having said some prayers, he made them a little sermon.

On this cold night close to Christmas, he told them, as they found shelter, like the Holy Family, in a humble barn, he wished to remind them that everyone had a proper and honourable place in God's plan. The two categories of monks in the abbey, he told them, were like Mary and Martha. Mary, the prayerful, had perhaps the better part, like the choir monks. But Martha, the loyal worker, was necessary too. For how would the abbey keep up its life of prayer without the hard work of the lay brothers? And did not they, too, need help, from the good peasants who lived outside the religious order? Of course they did. And last of all, did not the good peasant Tom need the support of his wife, humbler still but equally beloved of God?

"You may wonder," he said, "why this woman is allowed to remain here this night. For the abbot's rule is not to be ignored. No women in the Great Close." He looked at them severely. "But," he went on, "Our Lord also enjoins us to show mercy. Did not he himself save the woman taken in adultery from being stoned? And so it is, on my authority given me by the abbot, that we allow this good woman to remain here this terrible night and seek shelter from the storm." Then he blessed them and retired.

When the next day the blizzard continued unabated – at times it almost knocked him off his feet when he opened the door – the poor woman grew very agitated about her children. But Furzey assured him that his sister and the other villagers would be taking care of them, so he forbade the woman to leave. And thus, with the brazier providing heat and Tom at work on his cart, she remained while, three times during the day, Brother Adam led them all in simple prayers.

How she longed to go back. She didn't really want to be with Tom. Her eldest girl would see the younger children were safe, but they would all be frightened that something had happened to her. Above all, there was Luke.

What would he do? He'd have wondered where she was when she failed to appear in the evening. Would he try to investigate the cottage? What if the children saw him? All day she waited anxiously for the blizzard to abate.

There was nothing much to do. Now and then Brother Adam would appear and she found herself watching him with interest. The lay brothers, she could see, found him distant. Tom just remarked, with a shrug: "He's a cold fish." But then Tom never thought much about people if they didn't belong to the Forest.

The monk came from another world, certainly. Yet, as she thought of the way he had brought her in from the blizzard, she didn't think he was cold. She said nothing, though. When he led them in prayer, in the half-light of the great barn, his soft voice carried such quiet conviction that she was impressed. She supposed he must be so much more intelligent than simple folk like her; yet perhaps, deep inside her, a small voice might have suggested: you, also, could read and write, and know what he knows too. If so, however, she could only answer with a sigh: in another life. Until then, the monk had something she did not. She did not say it to Tom, but she thought Brother Adam, in his way of course, was rather fine.

She was entirely caught off guard late in the afternoon, when the small door of the barn opened with a brief moan from the wind and closed fast again behind the monk who, advancing to within a few feet of the brazier, beckoned to her. She went to him obediently. There was nothing else she could do.

For a moment he stood there, looking at her curiously. He was stoutly built, like Tom, she realised, but a little taller. In the glow from the brazier behind them that warmed her back, his eyes looked strangely dark. Tom, working a few yards away by the lamplight, seemed separated from them, in another world.

"I did not realise, when you spoke to me at the abbey gate . . ." He remembered her then. "I have just been told that Luke, the runaway, is your brother." She noticed that he spoke quietly, so that Tom could not hear them.

A stab of fear went through her. She could not meet his eye. Her relationship was common knowledge, of course, but in the hands of this clever man it seemed more dangerous. She hung her head. "Yes, Brother. Poor Luke."

"Poor Luke? Perhaps." A pause. Then, very quietly: "Do you know where he is?"

Now she looked him straight in the eye. "If we knew that, Brother, you'd already know. You see, I think he shouldn't have run away, being innocent. And my husband would turn him in anyway." She could look him in the eye because, technically, she had just told the truth. She had said "we."

"*You* might know, though, mightn't you?"

She was conscious of the smell of his habit. There was a scent of wax candles in the damp wool. She could smell him, too. A nice smell.

"He could be the other end of England by now." She sighed. This, too, was true. He could have been.

Adam looked thoughtful. When he asked a question the lines on his broad forehead wrinkled. But when he was thinking he tilted his head slightly back and the lines smoothed in a way that was pleasing.

"You said to me that morning at the abbey," he said carefully, "that it might have been an accident – that he might not have meant to strike Brother Matthew." She was silent. "If so, I think he should come and say so."

"He'll never return here, I think," she answered sadly. "He'll have to walk to the ends of the earth." She wasn't sure this satisfied the monk.

And then she did something she had never done before.

How does a woman let a man know that she desires him? It can be done with a smile, a look, a gesture. But these outward and visible signs would have been off-putting to a monk like Brother Adam. So she just stood in front of him and sent out that simple, primitive signal: the heat from her body. And Brother Adam felt it – how could he not? – that invisible, unmistakable, radiating warmth that came from her stomach to his. Then she smiled and he turned away, confused.

Why did she do it? She was an honest woman. She didn't flirt. She acted from a primordial instinct. She wanted to suggest an intimacy and attraction that, even if it shocked him, would divert the monk's attention. She had to lay a false trail to protect her little brother.

Moments later, Brother Adam left the barn.

The storm did not abate. They put charcoal on the brazier for a second night. Once again, after the evening meal, Brother Adam led them all in prayer. But some hours later, alone with her husband and only the glow from the charcoal showing in the great barn's cavernous dark, she allowed herself a faintly ironic smile when, as Tom raised his stocky haunches over her, she closed her eyes and thought secretly of Brother Adam.

It was deep in the night, about the time of the night office, when Brother Adam awoke from a fitful sleep and became aware that the moaning of the wind outside had ceased and that all around the grange was quiet.

Rising from the bench on which he had been sleeping, he went through the psalm and prayers by himself in a whisper. Then, still not satisfied, he whispered a Pater Noster. *Pater Noster, qui es in coelis*: Our Father, who art in Heaven . . . Amen. The night. The time when the silent voice of God's universe descended upon him. Why, then, should he feel so disquieted? He got up, wanted to pace about but could hardly do so without waking the lay brothers. He lay down again.

The woman. She was asleep, no doubt, with her husband in the barn. A good woman, probably, in her way. Like all the peasant women, she had slightly red cheeks and smelled of the farm. He closed his eyes. Her warmth. He had never felt such a thing before. He tried to sleep. The Furzey fellow. Had he made love to her in the barn this night? Might they, possibly, be doing so now, even as he lay there in the silence? Was the cart maker enveloped in that warmth?

He opened his eyes. Dear God, what was he thinking? And why? Why should his mind be dwelling on her? Then he sighed. He should have known better. It was just the devil, up to his usual tricks: a little test of faith; a new one.

Was the devil in this woman, then? Of course. The devil had been in all women from the first. When she had stood in front of him like that this afternoon he should perhaps have spoken severely to her. But it was the devil who was using her, really; just as he was using her image now to distract him. He closed his eyes again.

He did not sleep.

The morning was sparkling. The wind had passed away. It was utterly still. The sky was blue. Beaulieu, its abbey, its fields, its granges were all carpeted and coated by a soft white mantle.

When he came out of the grange, Brother Adam saw by the footprints from the barn door that the woman had already left. And for several moments, before he corrected himself, he thought of her, walking alone across the dazzling white heath.

In late February Luke disappeared and Mary hardly knew whether she was relieved or sad.

As soon as the snow had melted in late January he had started going out before dawn, returning only after dusk. Her terror had been that he might make tell-tale tracks in the frost, but somehow he didn't, and every day she would leave a little food hidden in the loft where he slept.

All through January, while Tom was working at St Leonards, she would sneak out after the children were asleep and then, sitting together just as they had when they were children themselves, they would talk. Several times they had discussed what he should do. The full Forest Court was not meeting until April. The verderer's court had only forwarded the case to them, so until then it wouldn't be clear how serious a view they took of the Beaulieu matter. They discussed Brother Adam's suggestion that Luke should give himself up, but Luke always shook his head.

"That's easy for him to say. But with the abbot and the prior disowning me, you don't know what's going to happen. At least this way I'm free."

For her, it was a joy to have one of her family to talk to. And what talks they had had. He would describe the abbey, the prior with his stooping walk and claw-like hands, every lay brother and monk, until she laughed so hard she was afraid of waking the children. Yet there was something so gentle and simple about Luke that he never seemed to hate anyone, even Grockleton. She asked him about Brother Adam.

"The lay brothers don't quite know what to make of him. The monks all love him, though."

In a way, because of his dreamy, gentle nature, Mary had never been surprised when Luke joined the lay brothers; but she couldn't resist asking him once: "Didn't you ever want a woman, Luke?"

"I don't know, really," he said easily. "I've never had one."

"Doesn't that bother you?"

"No." He laughed quite contentedly. "There's always so much else to do in the Forest, isn't there?"

She smiled, but didn't bring up the subject again. With him in hiding, there wasn't much point.

They also discussed the quarrel between Furzey and Pride over the pony. He sympathised with her, of course, but here he showed the irresponsible, rather childish side of his nature, she thought. "Poor old Tom'll never get his pony back. That's for sure."

"So how long will this quarrel last?"

"A year or two, I should think."

When Tom returned at the end of January, their meetings had to be curtailed – a snatched conversation now and then. And since there was certainly no sign of the quarrel ending she felt almost like a prisoner herself. Luke would be gone before dawn and come back after dark, with only the empty wooden bowl of food to show that he'd been there.

Then he had told her he was going.

"Where?"

"Can't say. Better you don't know."

"Are you leaving the Forest?"

"Maybe. Probably best."

So she kissed him and let him go. What else could she do? So long as he was safe, that was all that mattered. But she felt very much alone.

On the Thursday after the feast of St Mark the Evangelist, in the twenty-third year of the reign of King Edward – that is, on a wet April day in the Year of Our Lord 1295 – in the great hall of the royal manor of Lyndhurst, the court of the New Forest met in solemn session.

It was an impressive scene. From the walls of the hall, alternating with splendid hangings, hung the antlers of great bucks and stags. Presiding over all, in a blackened oak chair set on a dais at the front, the Forest justice was resplendent in a green tunic and crimson cloak. Assisting him, also in oak chairs, were the four gentlemen verderers, who acted as magistrates and coroners and ran the lower Court of Attachments. The foresters and the agisters, who were responsible for all the stock pastured on the Forest, were also present. From each of the villages, or vills as they were called, came representatives to render account for any crimes committed there. The court was also assisted by a jury of twelve gentlemen of standing in the region. Any man accused of a serious offence could, if he chose, ask that this jury should decide his innocence or guilt. The king liked juries and encouraged their use. Though not obligatory, many chose a jury trial.

Today the prior of Beaulieu had also appeared, the abbot being still away on the king's business. Two sheriffs from neighbouring counties had come with young Martell and his friends. It was a long time since there had been such a gathering and the hall was packed with spectators.

"Oyez, Oyez, Oyez," the clerk called out. "All manner of persons who have any presentments to make, this court is now in session."

There were a number of cases to be heard, concerning the usual matters. Some were forest offences. All venison cases automatically went to the Forest court. So did crimes against the king's peace. Civil cases between parties often came up too.

All through the morning the business went on. A fellow had stolen wood from the Forest. Another had made an illegal *assart* of land. One of the vills had failed to report a dead buck within its boundaries. Life in the Forest did not change much. But had a forester from Rufus's time been brought there, he would have observed one difference. For whereas the Norman forest law had been designed, with its mutilations and killings, to punish and frighten the people, the accommodation between the monarch and his Forest folk had long ago been reached, even in the most formal court. There was no mutilation. Only the most habitual felons were hung. The penalty for almost all offences was a fine. The guilty party was "in mercy" or "amerced" a sum. And even this varied according to the wealth of the offender. A poor man amerced sixpence at the last court, who had been unable to pay, was let off. Many of the fines for encroachments on crown land were repeated so automatically in the records of court after court that they were, in effect, rents paid for illegal tenancy. Pledges were taken from the better-off that their neighbours would pay their fines, or behave themselves in future. The law in the Forest, as elsewhere in Plantagenet England, was a common-sense and communal affair.

Finally, some time after noon, they came to the Beaulieu business.

It is presented that on the Friday before the Feast of St Matthew last, Roger Martell, Henry de Damerham and others did enter the Forest with bows and arrows, dogs and greyhounds, to harm the venison . . .

The charge, which would be inserted in the court record in Latin, was read out by the clerk. It gave exact details of what the poachers did and was not contested. All threw themselves on the mercy of the court. The justice looked at them severely while the forest folk in the hall listened carefully.

"This is a venison offence, carried out in open contempt of the law, by those who, by reason of their position, should know better. It will not be tolerated. You are amerced as follows: Will atte Wood, half a mark." Poor Will. A stiff fine. Two of his cousins stood surety and he was given a year to pay it. The other local men in the party all got the same.

Next came the turn of the young gentlemen: five pounds each – fifteen times the amount of the Forest men. This was only just. Finally, the justice came to Martell.

"Roger Martell. You were, without question, the leader of these malefactors. You led them to the grange. You took deer. You are also a young man of substance." He paused. "The king himself was not amused to hear about this matter. You are amerced the sum of one hundred pounds."

A collective gasp. The two sheriffs looked shattered. It was a stupendous fine, even for a rich landowner; and it was also very clear that King Edward himself had approved it beforehand. Royal disfavour. Martell went white as a sheet. He would either be selling land or losing his income for many a year. Manly though he was, he visibly shook.

The court had only just started to buzz, however, when the justice said sharply to the clerk: "Now then, what about this lay brother?"

And again, the courtroom grew quiet. Luke was one of the Prides. There was a lot of interest. Near the back of the court Mary strained to hear every word.

The case against Luke was less clear.

"First," the clerk announced, "that he gave shelter to the malefactors at the grange. Second, that he was in league with them. Third that he attacked an abbey monk, Brother Matthew, who sought to prevent the poachers from entering the grange."

"Is the abbey represented?" the justice demanded.

John of Grockleton raised his claw, and a moment later Brother Matthew and three of the lay brothers stood with him before the justice.

The justice, naturally, was well acquainted with the facts from the steward, but there were aspects of the business he did not like.

"You refuse to take responsibility for this lay brother?"

"We disown him utterly," said the prior.

"The charge says he was in league with these poachers. Presumably because he let them into the grange?"

"What other explanation is possible?" said Grockleton.

"I should think he might have been frightened of them."

"They offered no violence," remarked the clerk.

"That's true. Now what about this attack?" He turned to Brother Matthew.

"Well." Brother Matthew's kindly face was a little embarrassed. "When Martell refused to take his wounded companion away, I'm afraid I attacked him with a staff. Brother Luke grabbed a spade and swung it, and broke the staff. Then the spade hit me on the head."

"I see. Was this lay brother your enemy?"

"Oh no. Quite the reverse."

Grockleton's claw shot up. "Which proves that he must have been in league with Martell."

"Or was trying to prevent this monk from starting a fight."

"I must confess," Brother Matthew said mildly, "I did wonder that myself, afterwards."

"Brother Matthew is too kind, Justice," the prior cut in. "His judgement is too forgiving."

It was at this point that the justice decided he really did not like Grockleton. "So he ran?" he continued.

"He ran," chimed Grockleton definitively.

"Why the devil isn't the abbot trying him over his assault of this monk?"

"He is expelled from the order. We are here to prosecute him," said Grockleton.

"He's not here, I suppose?" Heads were shaken. "Very well, then." He eyed the prior with distaste. "Since he belonged to the abbey at the time of this crime, if such it was, and was within the Great Close, you do realise that you are responsible for producing him, don't you?"

"I?"

"You. The abbey. Of course. For his non-appearance, therefore, the abbey is amerced. Two pounds."

The prior went bright red. All round the court there were smiles.

"I'm sorry he isn't here to defend himself," the justice went on, "but there it is. The law takes its course. As the offence seems to be a felony and he's not here, I have no option. Let him be exacted and, if he doesn't appear at the next court, outlawed."

From her position at the back, Mary listened with a heavy heart. Exacted: that just meant he must be produced. And outlawed? Technically it signified he was outside the law. You couldn't be harboured by anyone; you could even be killed with impunity. You had no rights. A powerful sanction.

If only Luke had turned up. Brother Adam, the clever monk, had been right. Luke had underestimated the good sense of the court. It was obvious that the justice was inclined to give him the benefit of the doubt. But what could she do? Luke had gone and no one even knew where he was. She could have wept.

"That's it, I think." The justice was looking at the clerk. People were preparing to move. "Is there any other business?"

"Yes."

Mary started. Tom had left her at the beginning of the proceedings to stand with some of the other men and she had not been able to see him over the crowd of heads. Yet this was his voice and she could see him now, elbowing his way to the front. Whatever was he doing? At the same time, over on her left, she was conscious of a small movement by the door.

Now Tom was standing, squared off, in front of the justice, with his tousled hair and leather jerkin, as if he was ready to fight him.

"We've had no notice. This hasn't been forwarded from the Court of Attachments," said the clerk crossly.

"Well, as we're here, we may as well hear it," the justice replied. He fixed Tom sternly with his eye. "What's your business?"

"Theft, my lord," Tom bellowed in a voice that shook the rafters. "Damnable theft."

The hall fell silent. The clerk, having almost jumped off his bench at the shout, took up his quill.

The justice, a little taken aback, gazed at Tom curiously. "Theft? Of what?"

"My pony!" Tom shouted again, as if to call the heavens themselves to witness.

It took a second or two for the titters around the court to begin. The justice frowned. "Your pony. Stolen from where?"

"The Forest," Tom cried.

Chuckles were breaking out now. Even the foresters were starting to grin. The justice glanced across at the steward, who shook his head and smiled.

The justice liked the Forest. He enjoyed its peasants and secretly relished their modest crimes. After the business of Martell, which had truly annoyed him, he had no objection to ending the day with a little light relief. "You mean your pony was depastured on the Forest? Was it marked?"

"No. It was born there."

"A foal, you mean? How do you know it was yours?"

"I know."

"And where is it now?"

"In John Pride's cowshed," Tom cried in rage and despair. "That's where."

It was too much. The whole courtroom began to laugh. Even his Furzey kinsmen couldn't help seeing the joke. Mary had to look down at the floor. The justice turned to the agisters for illumination and Alban, in whose bailiwick this lay, stepped over and whispered in his ear, while Tom scowled.

"And where is John Pride?" the justice demanded.

"He's here," Tom shouted, swinging round and pointing triumphantly to the back of the crowd.

Everybody turned. The justice stared. There was a brief silence.

And then, from beside the door, came a deep voice: "He's gone."

It was no good. The hall dissolved. The Forest people howled. They wept with laughter. The foresters, the solemn verderers, even the gentlemen of the jury couldn't help themselves. The justice, watching, shook his head and bit his lip.

"You may laugh," Tom yelled. And they did. But he wasn't done. Looking right and left, red-faced, he turned back to the justice and, pointing at Alban, he shouted: "It's him, and the likes of him, that lets Pride get away with it. And you know why? Because he pays them!"

The justice's face changed. Several of the foresters stopped laughing. At the back, Mary groaned.

"Silence!" the justice roared and the laughter in the hall began to die. "You are not" – he glared at Furzey – "to be impertinent."

The trouble was, there was some truth in it. Young Alban probably was innocent, as yet. But there was inevitably a certain traffic between the Forest people and those in authority in the bailiwicks. A nice pie, a cheese, a fence mended without charge – it might be hard after such kindnesses for the steward not to overlook some minor infraction of the law. Everyone knew it. The king himself had once remarked to the justice, not wholly in jest, that one day he would have to set up a commission to investigate the whole Forest administration. If Furzey wanted to be a troublemaker this was neither the time nor the place to be watched.

"You are to go through the proper channels," the justice told him curtly. "Your case will only be heard here after it comes through the Court of Attachments. Clerk," he ordered, "enter that in the record. The court," he announced, "is closed."

So while Tom stood there in his impotent rage and the crowd, chuckling again, started to make for the door, the clerk dipped his quill in the ink and wrote in the parchment the record that would be preserved, as the true voice of the Forest, down the long centuries:

Thomas Furzey complains of John Pride theft of a pony. John Pride did not come. Therefore to next court, etc.

Luke loved to walk through the Forest. He would stride for miles. When he was a child he had learned to move fast to keep up with John and Mary; so that now, anyone who tried to walk beside him would be astonished at his speed.

People thought him dreamy, yet his eyes were always sharper than theirs. There wasn't a stream in the whole Forest he didn't know. The most ancient oaks, every great ivy-covered hulk, were like his personal friends.

His appearance had altered since leaving the abbey. Dressed in a woodman's smock and jerkin, with woollen leggings and a thick leather belt, his hair and beard now grown long and shaggy, he looked exactly like a score of other such fellows and no one seeing him trudging along a forest path would have given him a second thought.

But he was on the run – about to be outlawed. What did that mean? In theory, that every man's hand was against you. And in practice? It depended on whether you had friends and whether the authorities really wanted to find you.

As things stood at present, if one of the foresters met him face to face and recognised him, they'd take him into custody. No question. But if young Alban, say, caught sight of a shaggy figure in the distance that just might be Luke, would he ride up to challenge him? Possibly. But he was far more likely to turn his horse's head and ride another way.

What should he do, though? He couldn't go on like this for ever. The court at Lyndhurst had made its feelings pretty clear. He might do well to turn himself in and hope for mercy.

The trouble was – perhaps it was in his blood – Luke had an instinctive distrust of authority.

That might seem strange for a man who had chosen to live under the monastic rule of Beaulieu. Yet in reality it was not. For Luke, the abbey was a sanctuary in the middle of a huge estate where he enjoyed working and which gave him the freedom of the Forest. He liked the services in the abbey church. He would listen, enraptured, to the singing. His natural curiosity had led him to learn many of the Latin psalms and their meaning even if he could not read. But he wouldn't have wished to go to services all the time like the choir monks. He wanted to get back out in the fields, or to help the shepherds as they went from grange to grange. The abbey fed him and clothed him, and left him free of responsibilities, without a care in the world. What more could you ask?

Above all, in his mind the abbey worked because it was tied to the natural order. Nature was what he understood. The trees, the plants, the forest creatures: they had their own rhythm. You could never know it all, but it worked; and the abbey estate made sense only because it had made itself part of the process.

So if outsiders, men like Grockleton or the king's justices who didn't really understand the Forest, came along and tried to impose a lot of stupid rules, if they claimed to be authority, the only thing to do was to avoid them. In his heart, the only laws he respected were the laws of nature.

"The rest don't amount to anything, really," he would say. And the authorities who set such store by these laws were certainly not to be trusted. "They may speak you fair one day, but they'll get you the next. The only thing they truly care about is their power."

It was a simple peasant's view of authority and entirely accurate.

So he didn't intend to trust the justice and his court, especially with Grockleton still around. The best thing to do, he reckoned, was to stay out of sight and wait for something to turn up. You never knew what might.

He had friends. He'd be all right until the next winter. In the meantime he had found plenty to keep him busy. Every few days, although she had no idea of it, he had gone to keep an

eye on his sister Mary. He liked to observe her going about her
tasks by the cottage, or running after the children as they
played outside, even if he never spoke to her. It was as if he
were a guardian angel, secretly watching over her. "I'm closer
than you think, girl," he would mutter with satisfaction. He
found this exercise in invisibility so pleasing that he took to
watching his brother John as well. The pony was allowed to
run in the field now, but there was always one of John's children guarding it.

And then, of course, he would walk the Forest.

His route that day had taken him from near Burley over to
the north of Lyndhurst. The woods were quiet. Huge oaks
spread all around. Here and there, a small clearing appeared
where some ancient tree, brought down by a storm, lay across
the forest floor, leaving a patch of open sky in the canopy
above. As he walked, he would pause occasionally to inspect
some lichen-covered trunk, or turn over a fallen branch to see
what creatures were dwelling under it. And he had just passed
above the village of Minstead and come to a section of the
Forest that bordered a high open heath, when he paused and
looked down at something with interest.

It was such a tiny object: just an acorn from last year's fall,
which had escaped the hungry pigs and, nestling in the damp
brown leaf mould, had cracked open and struck roots into the
ground.

Luke smiled. He liked to see things grow. The tiny white
roots looked so vulnerable. A little green shoot was emerging.
How astonishing to think that this was the beginning of a
mighty oak. Then he gently shook his head. "You'll never
make it there," he said.

How many of the acorns that fall ever become oak trees?
Who knows? One in a hundred thousand? Surely not. Less
than one in a hundred times that number, perhaps. This is the
vast strength, the massive, numberless oversupply of nature in
the forest silence. The chances of an acorn living were almost
infinitesimally small. The pigs turned out for the autumn mast,
or any of the other forest animals might eat them. Ponies or
cattle might crush them underfoot. If an acorn survived that
first season and happened to be on ground where it could
strike root, it could only grow into a tree if there was a break

in the canopy above to give it light. But even for those few that grew to be saplings, there was still an ever present danger.

It is not only man who destroys. Other animals, too, left to themselves, will destroy grasslands, woods, whole habitats with a stupidity as great as, perhaps even greater than, that shown by humans. The deer loved to eat oak shoots. The only way for one to survive was to have a protector. Nature provided several. Holly, although the deer ate holly, might screen an oak. Butcher's-broom, the little evergreen shrub with the razor-sharp spikes – the deer avoided that. For some reason they seldom cared to eat bracken either.

Very carefully, scooping out the soil around the seedling with his hands, Luke carried it in a cradle of earth, without disturbing its tiny life. A few yards away there was a small ring of holly surrounded by butcher's-broom. Entering this, ignoring the scratches on his arms, he planted the seedling in the patch of earth in the centre. He glanced up. There was clear blue sky above. "Grow there," he said happily, and went on his way.

Brother Adam knew Beaulieu Abbey so well that sometimes he thought he could have walked around it blindfold.

Of all its pleasant places none, he thought, was more delightful than the series of arched recesses, known as the carrels, that lay along the north side of the great cloister, opposite the *frater* where the choir monks ate their meals. They were perfectly sheltered from the breeze; facing southwards, they caught and trapped the sun. Sitting, book in hand, on a bench in one of the carrels, gazing across the quiet green square of the cloister, smelling the sweet aroma of cut grass laced with the sharper scent of daisies – this, it seemed to Adam, was as close to heaven as anything knowable by man on earth.

His favourite carrel lay near the middle. Down the stone steps from the doorway to the church: that was five steps down. Turn right. Twelve paces. If it was a sunny afternoon you felt the warmth through the open arches by the seventh step. Turn right after the twelfth pace and you were there.

There had been few opportunities in the last weeks to enjoy this pleasure. His work in the granges had changed all that. But he had managed to do so one warm May afternoon and he was sitting quietly with his hood up – the monk's sign that he does not want to be disturbed – rather idly reading a life of St Wilfrid, when his reverie was interrupted by a novice hurrying round the cloister and calling softly: "Brother Adam! Come quickly. Salvation is here. And everyone's going to see."

Naturally, therefore, Adam arose at once. "Salvation," as the ignorant novice had rather sweetly called it, was *Salvata*, the abbey's ship, a squat, square-rigged vessel in frequent use. After leaving the Beaulieu estuary her first port of call was nearby; at the head of the great inlet from the Solent water, which ran up the eastern side of the Forest, a flourishing little port had grown up in the last few centuries, known as Southampton. By its quay the Beaulieu monks had their own house to store the wool clip that was to be exported. Later, the returning *Salvata* would pick up all kinds of goods at Southampton, including the French wine the abbot's guests enjoyed. From Southampton she might proceed along the coast to the county of Kent and thence across the English Channel. Or she might continue round, into the Thames estuary, to London or more likely up England's eastern coast as far as the port of Yarmouth, where she would collect a large cargo of salted herrings for the abbey. *Salvata's* return to the jetty below the abbey was always a source of excitement.

Sure enough, by the time Brother Adam arrived, most of the community at the abbey – over fifty monks and about forty lay brothers – had gathered to watch, and the prior, who loved this kind of thing, was calling out unnecessary orders: "Steady. Watch that mooring rope."

Adam observed the scene with affection. There were times, it had to be admitted, when even the most devout of the monks became almost like children.

The cargo was salted herrings. As soon as the gangplank was in place, they all seemed to want to roll out one of the barrels.

"Two to each cask," the prior called out. "Roll them up to the store."

Twenty barrels were already on their way up. The monks were joking to each other; there was a festive atmosphere about the place, and Brother Adam was just about to return to the peace of his cloister when he noticed the ship's master go over to the prior and say something. He saw the man point downstream and John of Grockleton start violently.

Then the shouting began.

If there was one thing in the world that would put Grockleton in a rage it was an attack on the abbey's earthly rights. He had invested his life in protecting them. Among these many rights were those over the fishing on the Beaulieu river. "Villainy!" he shouted. "Sacrilege." The monks rolling their barrels stopped and turned. "Brother Mark," the prior called, "Brother Benedict . . ." He started pointing at one brother after another. "Fetch the skiff. Come with me."

One did not need inspiration to guess what had happened. A party of men had been seen fishing – openly casting nets from a boat – further down the river. Worse, one of them was a merchant from Southampton, where the burgesses had stoutly maintained that they, too, had fishing rights, older than the abbey's, on the river. This was just the kind of battle, Grockleton believed, that God had intended him to fight.

It is not every day that God calls those who have forsworn all worldly delights to the excitement of the chase. In, it seemed, the twinkling of an eye, a skiff containing three monks was skimming downstream while two parties, each of a dozen monks and lay brothers, were hurrying down the river banks. Leading the one down the western bank, his staff in his hand, his bent back causing him to lean forward like an attacking goose, was Grockleton. Brother Adam attached himself, unasked, to his party.

They kept up a remarkable pace. Using his staff as though it were an extra leg, the prior punted himself forward so fast that some of the monks had to lift their habits and almost run as they bustled along at his heels. Two of the lay brothers were allowed to run ahead to scout. For over a mile the path led through oak woods before emerging on to a big marshy bend of the river; and no sooner had they appeared than they heard a cry from the skiff on their left and at the same moment saw their quarry ahead of them, just below the bend.

The Southampton men had a big, clinker-built boat with a single mast and eight oars. As there was no sign of a sail, they presumably intended to row themselves round the coast back to Southampton. Their nets were still out in the river but, with infernal cheek, three of them had built a little fire on the river bank and were in the act of cooking themselves a meal. From the quality of his dress, Adam guessed that one of these was a merchant of some position. This was confirmed when the prior hissed: "Henry Totton." The man even owned the warehouses next to their own woolhouse near the quay.

"Trespassers!" Grockleton's voice honked across the marsh. "Villains. Desist at once."

Totton looked up, surprised. It seemed to Adam that he muttered something, then shrugged. His two companions seemed uncertain what to do. But there could certainly be no doubt about the attitude of the people in the boat.

There were five of them. One, in the bow, was a curious-looking fellow. Though at least two hundred yards off, there was no mistaking him because, apart from his black hair, which was pulled back and tied behind his neck, his straggly beard could not conceal the fact that, once it had descended past his mouth, his face had decided to cut down straight into his neck, dispensing almost completely with the boring necessity of a chin. There was a certain cheerfulness in his face, which suggested he was pleased with this arrangement. And it was this fellow who now, turning slowly, with no particular malice but more as a general salutation, looked straight at the prior and, raising his arm, lifted a solitary finger.

To Grockleton, it might have been an arrow from a bow. "Impious dog!" he screamed. "Seize them," he shouted, pointing at the men on the bank. "Beat them," he cried, waving his staff.

For just an instant his followers hesitated. Some looked round for sticks to use as weapons. Others clenched their fists in preparation before dashing upon the men by the campfire.

It was only an instant, but Brother Adam used it. "Stop!" he shouted, in a voice of authority. He knew he was cutting across the prior, but he had to. Moving swiftly to Grockleton's side, he murmured quickly: "Prior, if we use violence, I think the men in the boat might attack us." He pointed, as if he were drawing something to his attention that Grockleton had not seen before. "Even with right on our side," he added with deference, "after the trouble at the grange . . ."

The sense was clear. The reputation of the abbey would hardly be enhanced if the prior started a brawl.

"If we have their names," Adam added, "we can bring them to justice." He paused and held his breath.

Grockleton's reaction was curious. He gave a little start, as if he had been awoken from a dream. He stared at Adam for a moment, apparently uncomprehending. The brethren were all watching him. "Brother Adam," he suddenly said loudly, "take their names and identify them. If any show resistance we shall overpower them."

"Yes, Prior." Adam bowed his head and went forward promptly. After a few steps he turned and requested respectfully: "May I take two brothers with me, Prior?"

Grockleton nodded. Adam indicated two of the monks, then hurried about his task.

He had done all he could to save the prior's face. He hoped it had worked. So he was dismayed when, as soon as they were out of Grockleton's hearing, one of his companions muttered: "You really showed the prior up then, Brother Adam."

For he knew that Grockleton would never forgive him now.

A week later, in a secluded part of the western forest, two men rested quietly by their little campfire and waited.

A few yards away, adding to the shadowy mystery of the scene, stood a huge, turf-covered mound and, from holes here and there in its sides, wisps of smoke were issuing. Puckle and Luke were making charcoal.

The charcoal burner's craft is very ancient and requires much skill. During the winter Puckle would cut the huge quantity of sticks and logs – the billets as they are called. All the main forest woods – oak and ash, beech, birch and holly – were good for charcoal. Then, late in the spring, he would construct his first fire.

The charcoal burner's fire is unlike any other. It is huge. Slowly and carefully, Puckle would begin by laying out logs in a great circle, about fifteen feet in diameter. By the time he finally completed it, the mountain of wood stood over eight feet high. Then, climbing up a curved ladder on to his mighty construction, Puckle would coat the entire pile with a skin of soil and turf, so that when it was done it resembled a mysterious grassy kiln. He lit it from the top. "Charcoal fire burns downwards," he explained. "Now we just wait."

"How long?" Luke had asked.

"Three, four days."

The charcoal cone is a wonderful machine. Its object is to convert the moist and resinous wood within to a material which is, as near as possible, pure carbon. To do this it is necessary to char the wood without allowing it to burn away and oxidise to useless ash, and this is achieved by restricting the oxygen within the cone to a minimum, hence the turf sides. The process is also slowed and controlled by burning the material downwards, which is more gradual. The resulting charcoal is light, easy to transport and, once heated in a brazier to a point when it ignites, will burn slowly, without a flame and giving off a heat far more intense than does the wood from which it is derived.

By the end of a day, the first time they had done this, Luke noticed that the smoke from the holes was steamy and that the upper sides of the cone were moist.

"That's called sweating," Puckle said. "Water's coming out of the wood."

On the third day, towards the completion of the process, Luke noticed that tarry waste was coming out through the run-offs at the base. At the end of that day Puckle announced: "It's done. All we have to do now is wait for it to cool."

"How long's that?"

"Couple of days."

They would fill their little cart many times with the charcoal from that cone.

Luke was happy as a charcoal burner. These men lived out in the Forest mostly; seldom seen, hardly noticed. It was a perfect role for him, especially as the area around Burley where Puckle operated was far from the abbey, and the forest officials in that bailiwick did not know him. The work was undemanding. While the fire was burning he could wander off to roam the woods or watch Mary whenever he liked.

Puckle was quite content to shelter him. The woodman had always been a law unto himself. His family was extended, what with his own children, his dead brother's and various other family progeny whose origins no one ever bothered to enquire about. So when a forester had once asked him who his assistant was, and he had casually replied "one of my nephews," the man had just nodded and thought no more about it.

He could remain out in the Forest with Puckle, Luke reckoned, at least for some months. Only Puckle's family knew about him. They didn't talk.

"Fewer people that know the better," Puckle had said. "You'll be safe that way."

Even so, Luke could not suppress a small shudder of alarm that May afternoon when Puckle, suddenly glancing up, remarked: "Hello. Look who's coming." And then added quietly: "Do as I told you, now."

Brother Adam rode his pony slowly. He was feeling rather listless. He thought he knew why. He even muttered the word to himself: *"Acedia."* Every monk knew the state. *Acedia* – the Latin word had no real equivalent in the English tongue. A falling away, into boredom, depression, listlessness; one's feelings seemed to have died; a sense of nothingness; a numbness, as when a tolling bell is heard but never answered. It came to him some afternoons, like a drowsiness, or at certain times of year – midwinter, when nothing was happening, or late summer, after the harvest was done. One had to fight it, of course. It was only the devil, trying to sap one's spirit and weaken the faith. Hard work was the best way.

He had certainly been doing that. He had been over in the Avon valley in the last few days. Great cartloads of hay would wend across the Forest from there when the meadows were mown. Lodging at Ringwood, he had gone up and down the river inspecting every meadow. He had practically inspected the peasants' scythes. Three lay brothers would be despatched to oversee operations and he would be supervising them himself. Not even Grockleton could suggest that he had been neglecting his duty.

For once, he had to confess, he had been glad to be away from the abbey. The days after the incident on the river had been strained. It was the duty of every monk to put all evil thoughts and intentions away from him and to be charitable to all his brothers, and, like him or not, Grockleton had probably tried in all sincerity to do this. But Adam's presence just then

could not fail to be irritating to him, and so Adam was glad
to go.

But now he had to return, and he didn't want to. By the time
he reached Burley he was already depressed; hardly aware that
he was doing so, he had let his pony take a wrong track and he
was cutting across the woods to the proper path, a little
guiltily, when he saw the charcoal burners at their work.

A year ago he would probably have ridden by without more
than a quick salutation, but now it seemed natural to pause and
speak with them. And if it was also an excuse to delay his return a little, he did so all the same.

The woodman was standing beside the small campfire; the
second fellow had moved away a little, to the other side of the
smoking charcoal cone. Brother Adam thought he had seen
Puckle before, delivering stakes for the abbey's vines the previous year. The younger man had also looked vaguely familiar, but as all these Forest folk were related that wasn't
surprising. Looking down at Puckle, he asked in a friendly
tone if the charcoal fire was nearly done.

"Another day," Puckle replied.

Adam asked a few more obvious questions – where Puckle
came from, who the charcoal would be sold to. An easy topic
of conversation with any of the forest folk, better even than the
weather, was the movement of the deer.

"I thought I might see the red deer over by Stag Brake," he
remarked.

"No, they'll be nearer Hinchelsea now, most likely."

Adam nodded. Then his eyes went over to the charcoal cone
behind which the other fellow was lurking. "You've only the
one helper?" he asked.

"Just one today," Puckle replied. Then, quite casually, he
called out: "Peter. Come here, boy." And Brother Adam looked
curiously as the young man came towards him.

He seemed shy as he shuffled forward. His head was bowed,
his eyes were cast down. His jaw appeared to be hanging
slackly. A rather pathetic specimen, really, the monk thought.
But not wishing to be unkind he enquired: "So, Peter, have you
ever been to Beaulieu?"

The young man seemed to start but then mumbled something incoherent.

"He's my nephew," Puckle remarked. "Doesn't talk much."

Brother Adam stared at the shaggy head before him. "We use your charcoal to heat the church," he said encouragingly, but couldn't think of anything else to add.

"That's all right, boy," Puckle said quietly, waving the young man away. "Actually," he confided to the monk, as his nephew withdrew, "he's a bit simple in the head."

As if to give living proof of this fact, as he reached the great smoking cone, the fellow paused, half turned, pointed at the charcoal cone and in a voice of perfect imbecility uttered a single word: "Fire." Then he sat down.

Adam should have moved on, but for some reason he didn't. Instead, he remained a while with the charcoal burner and his nephew, sharing the quiet of the scene. What a strange sight it was, that huge turf cone. Who knew what mighty heat, what ardent fire was contained, quite hidden, in that great green mound? Then there was its smoke, issuing silently from the crevices in its sides, as though from Tartarus, or the infernal region itself, deep below. An amusing thought suddenly struck him. What if Puckle, here, deep in the New Forest, was really guarding the entrance to hell? The thought caused him to observe the charcoal burner once again.

He had not noticed before what a curious figure Puckle really was. Perhaps it was the shadowy setting, or the reddish gleam from the embers of the campfire, but suddenly his gnarled form looked as if he were a gnome, his weathered, oaken face seemed to take on a mysterious glow. Was it devilish? He chided himself for his foolishness. Puckle was just a harmless peasant. And yet there was something about him that was unknowable. There was a heat, deep, hidden, strong – a heat he himself did not seem to possess. At last, with a nod, he gave his pony a light kick and moved off.

"Dear God," Luke laughed, as soon as he was out of sight. "I thought he was never going."

He should not have taken the way he did. After passing the little church at Brockenhurst, Brother Adam had followed a track that led southwards through the woods and brought him to the quiet ford in the river. The place was as deserted as when Adela and Tyrrell had used it. On the other side of the ford however, at the top of the long path that led up from it through the woods, the broad shelf of land had been cleared into several large fields, which the monks supervised.

Ahead, over the lip of this cleared land under the open sky, lay Beaulieu Heath and the track that led eastwards towards the abbey. That was the path he should have taken. But instead he turned south. He told himself it made no difference, but that wasn't true.

He kept to the edge of the woods. After a time he came to a track on the right. Down there, he knew, set alone on a dark knoll looking over the river valley, was the old parish church of Boldre. He did not go there, though. He continued southwards. Soon he came to a small cow station, a vaccary as they were called, with pasture for thirty cows and a bull, and a few cottages: Pilley. He hardly noticed it.

Why had the woman come into his mind – the peasant woman who had stood in front of him in the barn? There was no reason he could think of. He was bored. It was nothing. He went on, nearly another mile. Then he came to the hamlet. Oakley it was named.

He could go across the heath just as well from there.

The villages of the New Forest were the same as ever. They seldom had a centre. They straggled, sometimes by a stream, or along the edge of open heathland. No manorial lord had coerced them into a tidy shape. The same thatched cottages, homesteads with small wooden barns, smallholdings all, rather than farms, declared that these were the communities of equals that had nestled in the Forest since ancient times.

The track through Oakley ran east–west and had the usual forest surface of peaty mud and gravel. Instead of turning east, Adam turned west and walked his pony along. There were several cottages, but after less than a quarter of a mile these ended and the track then started to descend, between deep banks, into the river valley. He noticed that the last place, which lay on the northern side of the track, was a homestead with several outbuildings including a small barn. Behind it lay a paddock, some open ground dotted with gorse and beyond that woodland.

He wondered if this was where the woman lived. If she appeared, he supposed he would stop and ask politely after her husband. There could be no harm in that. He took his time turning his pony, to see if anyone came out, but nobody did. He paused, surveying the other cottages, then went slowly back. At the point where he had started he saw a peasant and asked him who lived at the homestead he had passed.

"Tom Furzey, Brother," the fellow replied.

He was aware of a little leaping sensation in his stomach. He nodded calmly at the peasant and glanced back. So that was where she lived. He suddenly wanted to turn. But with what excuse? He exchanged a word or two more with the peasant, remarked casually that he had never looked at this village but then, fearing he might look foolish, went on.

At its eastern end, the hamlet gave on to a green with a pond at the side. The last homestead here, somewhat larger than the others and with a field beside it, belonged, he knew, to Pride. There were some stunted oak, small-ash and willows dotted along the edges of the pond, which was covered with white water crowfoot.

The track went past Pride's, then out on to the heath.

He rode slowly across. It was marshy in places. Had he crossed further to the north it would have been drier.

He was sorry he had not seen the woman.

When he was halfway across, he saw the dull light catching the pale mud walls of a sheepcote out on the heath. Beyond, lay the fields of Beufre grange.

Soon he would be back at the abbey.

Acedia.

Tom Furzey was so pleased with himself that when he was alone he would sit there silently hugging himself with joy. He was honestly astonished that he'd been able to think of it all. The plan was so subtle, so full of irony, it had such perfect symmetry; Tom might not know such words as these, but he would have understood them, every one.

The thing had come out of the blue sky. John Pride's wife had a brother who had gone to Ringwood and now he was getting married there; a good marriage, to a butcher's daughter with money. The whole Pride family were going. Better yet, Tom's sister had informed him: "They'll be staying late at Ringwood. Won't come back till next day at dawn."

"All of them?" he'd asked.

"Except young John." This was Pride's eldest son, a boy of twelve. "He's got to look after the animals. And the pony." She had given him a little look when she said that.

"Set me thinking, that did," he had said to her proudly, later, when he told her his plan.

She was the only one who knew, because he needed her help. She had been impressed by it, too. "I reckon you've thought of everything, Tom," she said.

Sure enough, on the day, the Prides departed early to Ringwood in their cart. The morning was warm and sunny. Tom went about his business as usual. In the middle of the day he mended the door of the chicken house. It wasn't until late afternoon that he told Mary: "We're going to get my pony back today."

He had been looking forward to her reaction and it was just as he had foreseen.

"You can't, Tom. It'll never work."

"It'll work."

"But John. He'll . . ."

"Nothing he can do."

"But he'll be angry, Tom . . ."

"Really? Seem to remember I was, too." He paused while she digested this. The best was yet to come. "There's one other thing," he added placidly. "You're the one that's going to take it."

"No!" She was horrified. "He's my brother, Tom."

"It's part of the plan. Vital, you might say." He took his time now, before delivering the final blow. "There's something else you've got to do." And then he told her the rest of the plan.

She didn't look at him, after he was done, as he had guessed she wouldn't. She just looked down at the ground. She could refuse, of course. But if she did her life would hardly be worth living. It was no good pleading, pointing out how humiliating it would be for her. He didn't care. He wanted it to be so. It was his revenge against them all. She wondered, when it was all over, where this would leave her. He'll be cock of the walk, she thought. But he doesn't really love me. And with this proof of his feelings she bowed her head. She would do it, to keep the family peace. But she would despise him. That would be her defence.

"It'll work," she heard him say quietly.

As the sun began to set, young John Pride felt quite pleased with himself. Of course, he'd fed the chickens and the pigs, cleaned out the cowshed and done every other job about the place a thousand times before. But he'd never been left in charge for a whole day and he'd been understandably nervous. Now all he had to do was bring the pony in from the field.

He'd been careful of the pony, exactly as his father had told him. Never let it out of his sight all day. Just to be really sure, he was going to sleep in the shed that night.

The scream that cut the evening air came from close by. Tom Furzey's sister only lived across the green. She and John Pride didn't speak much since the pony business, but their children saw one another most days. You couldn't do much about that. And the scream came from Harry, a boy his own age.

"Help!"

He ran out of the yard and across the green, skirting the edge of the pond. The sight that met his eyes was shocking. Harry's mother was lying face down on the ground. She seemed to have slipped by the gate and maybe banged her head against the post. She was lying very still. Harry was trying to lift her, without success. Just as he got there her husband and Tom Furzey came out of their cottage. Tom must have been visiting. The rest of her children came as well.

Tom was all action, knelt down beside his sister, felt her neck for a pulse, turned her over, glanced up. "She's not dead. Hit her head, I reckon. You boys" – he gave young John a quick nod – "take her legs, then." He and her husband each lifted under her arms, and they carried her into the cottage. "You better go out now," Tom told the children. He was gently patting his sister's cheek as they left.

John hung about there for a few minutes. Another neighbour came by. He didn't notice anyone over by the Pride farmstead, though.

After only a few moments Tom came out and gave them all

a smile. "She's coming round. Nothing to worry about." Then he went back in.

A few moments later John thought he'd better go back to his home. He walked round the pond and into the small yard. He glanced into the paddock and didn't immediately see the pony. He frowned, looked again. Then, rushing round, with an awful, sinking sense of panic, young John Pride saw that the field was empty. The pony had gone.

But how? The gate was shut. The field was bordered by an earth wall and fence: surely it could not have jumped that. He ran to check the shed. It was empty. He dashed round on to the green and started running round it. Halfway, he saw Harry, who called to ask him what was up. "Pony's gone," he cried.

"Hasn't been here," the boy replied. "I'll come with you." And he ran with John back to the Pride farmstead. "Let's try the heath," he shouted. So together they ran out on to Beaulieu Heath.

The sun was sinking now. A reddish glaze was covering the heather and the gorse cast dark shadows. Here and there, sure enough, were the dark forms of ponies by the brakes. Young Pride looked out desperately.

Then his companion nudged him and pointed. "Look there." It was the pony. He was sure of it. The little creature was standing by a gorse brake over half a mile away. The two boys started running towards it. But, as though it had seen them, the pony suddenly seemed to dart away, and vanished behind a dip in the ground.

Harry stopped. "We'll never get him this way," he gasped. "We'd better ride after him. You can ride my pony. I'll take my father's. Come on."

They hurried back. Young Pride was so anxious that he wouldn"t even wait to saddle up. So a short while later the two boys set off, with the red glow of the sunset behind them.

"I reckon they'll be out all night," Tom chuckled.

He had planned it all exactly and it had worked.

Some time after dark, Mary had led the pony through the woods behind their farmstead and he had helped her bring it into the little barn. There, with the door closed, they had inspected it by lamplight. It was even prettier than he had remembered. He could see, although she said nothing, that Mary was thinking the same thing. It was well into the night when they finally left, bolting the door behind them.

When Tom woke it was already past dawn and the sun could be seen above the horizon. He leaped up. "Feed the pony," he whispered. "I'll send word when you're to come." And without pausing, he hurried out of the cottage and along the track towards John Pride's. He didn't want to miss Pride's face when he returned.

All was well. Pride was not yet back.

But his son was. Poor young John was sitting on the edge of the green with Harry beside him. He looked pale and miserable. They'd been out all night, said Harry, who'd followed his uncle's instructions and never left the boy's side. Now John would have to tell his father he'd let the pony escape.

Tom even felt a little sorry for the boy. But this was his day and all Prides must suffer.

He had rehearsed everything. People were starting to gather: his sister, tactfully wearing a bandage over her head, some of the other hamlet folk, a gaggle of children, all waiting to see the Prides' return. Tom knew exactly what he was going to say.

"That pony get out, then, John? I dunno how he did that." Hadn't he been with young Pride just when it happened? Hadn't his sister's son pointed it out on the heath? "Out on the Forest, is he?" That's what he was going to say next. "You'd better go look for him, John. I reckon you're good at finding ponies, John."

But the best bit of all was going to come next. As soon as Pride appeared, young Harry was to run and fetch Mary. And now Mary would come up the track and call out: "Oh, Tom, guess what. I just found that pony of ours wandering on the heath."

"Better put it in the barn, Mary," he'd reply.

"I have, Tom," she'd say.

And what was John Pride going to do when his sister said that? What was he going to do about that, then?

"Oh, sorry about that, John," he'd cry. "I reckon he just wanted to come home."

It was going to be the best moment of his entire life.

Minutes passed. People chatted quietly. The sun was a watery yellow, just over the trees. The dew was still thick on the ground.

"Here they come," a child called. And Tom made an imperceptible nod to young Harry, who slipped away.

Mary had stood for a while in the little barn after she had gone in to feed the pony. At first she had been so surprised that she had just stared. Then she had frowned. Finally, after glancing up at the loft where she had spent so many happy hours that winter, she nodded.

That must be it. She couldn't see any other explanation. She even whispered, "Are you there?" But this was met only by silence. Then she sighed. "I suppose," she murmured, "that's your idea of a joke." She hardly knew whether to laugh or cry.

She walked outside after that, and went over to the fence and looked across the open ground to the trees. She half expected a signal, but there was none. Forgetting even the pony for a few moments, she stood gazing out, as if in a dream.

This was his way of letting her know he was there, watching over her. She felt a warm rush of happiness. Then she shook her head. "But what have you done now, Luke?" she muttered.

Then young Harry appeared.

It had all gone to plan. Tom was almost chortling to himself with pleasure and excitement. The words had all been said, John Pride was looking at his son like thunder; the boy was close to tears. The whole hamlet was enjoying the joke as the Prides got out of their cart looking uncomfortable.

"Better check none of your other animals is missing," he called out. "Maybe they all walked off! Eh?" He had only just thought of that one. He was so pleased with it, and the laughs it produced, that he went even further. "Something about your place they don't like, then, is it, John? Something they don't like?"

Oh, they were laughing now. He glanced at the track. Mary should be arriving any moment. The final surprise. The triumph. She'd better hurry up, though. While everyone was there.

One of Pride's younger children had run round to the cowshed, just to see for herself. She returned now, looking puzzled. She was tugging at Pride's jerkin, saying something. He saw Pride frown and then walk round to the cowshed himself. Oh, this was rich! Now Pride was returning, looking straight at him. "I don't know what you're on about, Tom Furzey," he called out. "That pony's in the cowshed."

Silence. Tom stared. Pride shrugged, contemptuous now, after his shock. Still Tom stared. It was impossible.

He couldn't help himself. He ran forward. He ran straight past Pride, through the yard to the cowshed. He looked in. The pony was tethered there. One look was enough. You couldn't mistake it. For just an instant the thought flashed through his mind to take it, seize the rope and lead it out with him. But it would never work. In any case, the pony itself was hardly the point now. He turned and came back.

"Whoah, Tom. Something wrong there, Tom?" The joke was on him now. The little crowd was having its fun.

"Run back home and lock himself in, did he, Tom?" "Where did you think he was, Tom?" "We know you was worried about him." "Don't you worry, Tom. That pony's safe now."

John Pride was looking at him, too; but not exactly laughing. He was still puzzled. You could see that.

Tom walked past him. He walked past the crowd. He didn't even look at his own sister. He went along the edge of the pond and down the lane.

How? It was impossible. Had somebody tipped Pride off? No. There wasn't time. Pride hadn't known. You could see that. Had his son guessed what had happened and stolen the pony back? Couldn't have. Young Harry was with him all night. Who even knew? His sister and her family. Had one of them been talking? He doubted it. Anyway, he didn't think anyone in the hamlet was going to do John Pride's work for him.

Mary. The only link left. Could she have gone out in the night while he slept? Or got someone else to do it? He couldn't believe it. But then, he thought, he couldn't believe the way she'd behaved over the pony in the first place.

He didn't know. He supposed he'd never know. One thing was sure: if he'd been made to look a fool before, he looked twice as big a fool now. It doesn't matter where I walk, he thought, the ground is always going to be shifting under my feet.

She was standing in the yard alone when he got back. Just looking at him. Not saying anything. But you could see she knew there'd be trouble. Well, if that was what she wanted she could have it.

As he reached her, therefore, he didn't say anything. He wasn't going to, either. But suddenly swinging, with an open hand, he struck her across the face as hard as he liked and she crashed to the ground.

He didn't care.

Harvest time. Long summer days. Lines of men in smocks, with long scythes, working their way slowly, rhythmically across golden fields. Lay brothers in white habits and black aprons, following behind with scythes and sickles. The air thick with dust; fieldmice and other tiny creatures patter and scuttle to the droning hedgerows; flies in summer swarms, everywhere.

The sky was cloudless, deep blue; the heavy heat of the sun was oppressive. But already showing itself in one quarter of the sky, a huge full moon was gently rising.

Brother Adam sat calmly on his horse. He had been to Beufre; now he was at St Leonards. He was going across the heath after that, to the fields above the little ford. He was being vigilant.

The abbot had come back the week before, then gone again, to London. Before going he had given Adam particular directions. "Be especially careful at harvest time, Adam. That's when we have the most hired hands. Take care they don't drink or get into trouble."

A cart was coming up the track, pulled by a great affer, as the Beaulieu men called a carthorse. In it were loaves of bread from the abbey bakery, made from the coarser "family" flour for the workers, and barrels of beer.

"They're to have only Wilkin le Naket," Adam had firmly instructed. This was the weakest of the several abbey beers. It would quench their thirst, but no one would get drunk or sleepy. He glanced up at the sun. When the cart arrived, he would declare a rest period. He looked across the other way in the direction of the heath. The wheat in the next field had been harvested the day before.

And there he saw the woman, Mary, dressed in a simple kirtle, tied at the waist, coming towards him across the stubble.

Mary took her time. Tom was not expecting her. That was the point. She was carrying a little basket of wild strawberries she had picked for him.

What does a woman do when she is forced to live with a man? When there is no escape; when there are children to share? What does she do when she lives in a farmstead where a marriage is over and yet is not?

They had been cold to each other for so long and, even though she did not love him, she couldn't bear it any more. What did it take, then, to save a marriage? A little gift, a show of love. Perhaps, if she were determined, if love were returned, she might even somehow manage to feel love again herself. Or near enough to get by. This was her hope.

The pony was never mentioned now. Tom didn't want to think about it, probably didn't even want it back, she guessed. Once or twice, on some pretext like, "I just need to drop this at John's" she had been to her brother's, and Tom had made no comment. She had been careful always to come straight back. Perhaps, in time, she could stay a little longer. Luke she had not seen or heard from. A few times Tom had mentioned him. He might have suspected he was in the Forest somewhere. It was hard to tell.

To outward appearances they seemed tranquil enough. But never once, since the incident in May, had there been any intimacy between them. Tom had been quiet, but cold – or evasive, which was the same thing. When the harvest had come, at which time the hired men often slept out at the granges or in the fields, he had seemed glad of the chance to go, and made no attempt to return home at nights.

She entered the field just as Brother Adam gave the order for the men to rest.

Tom was surprised to see her. He even looked a shade embarrassed as she came towards him and gave him the basket, explaining: "I picked them for you."

"Oh." He didn't, it seemed, want to show feelings in front of the other men, so he turned up his scythe and started to sharpen it with a small whetstone.

The men were moving over towards the cart where a lay brother was dispensing beer. Tom had his own wooden mug tied with a thong to his belt. She untied it and went to fetch some beer, then stood quietly by while he drank.

"You came a long way," he said at last.

"It's nothing," she answered and smiled. "The children are all well," she added. "They'll be glad when you're back."

"Oh yes. I dare say."

"So will I."

He took another gulp of the thin beer, muttered, "Oh, yes," and non-committally went back to sharpening the scythe again.

Some of the other men were coming over now. There were nods to Mary, an inspection of the basket, some appreciative murmurs: "That's nice." "Nice strawberries your missus brought you there, Tom." "Be sharing them will you, then?" The mood of the little group was rather jolly. Tom, still a little cautious, went so far as to say: "Maybe I will, and maybe I won't." Mary, relieved by the light-hearted mood, was anxious to laugh.

So the conversation went on, as it often does when people really have nothing to say, each person feeling obliged to keep the little stream of laughter going at the centre while, at the edges, those of a different humour form eddies, their muttered jokes and darker comments sometimes curling away and sometimes re-entering the stream.

"Them Prides look after you," came now from the centre. "Here's Tom with strawberries and the rest of us got nothing."

Mary laughed gladly at this friendly comment and smiled at Tom.

"I 'spect Tom gets everything he wants, eh, Tom?" from the edges. Though a bit cheeky and sadly inaccurate, Mary laughed at this, too, and Tom, a little flummoxed, looked down at the ground.

But then some evil spirit caused one of the younger men at the edge of the group to cry out in a raucous voice: "If you'd married her brother, Tom, you could have got a pony!"

And again Mary laughed. She laughed because they were

laughing. She laughed because she was anxious to please. She laughed because she was caught, for a moment, by surprise. She laughed only for an instant before, realising what had been said, and seeing Tom's stunned face, she checked herself. Too late.

Tom saw something different. Tom saw her laughing at him. Tom saw her gift for what he'd suspected it was, a ploy like giving an apple to a pony to keep him happy. These Prides were all the same. They thought they could just hoodwink you and you'd be so stupid you wouldn't notice. They'd even do it in front of other people to make a bigger fool out of you. Tom saw her openly laughing at him and then check herself as if she'd suddenly thought: oh dear, he's noticed. He saw even greater mockery and contempt in that. And all the pent-up resentment and rage of that spring and summer rose up inside him again.

His round face flushed. With his boot he kicked the little basket, scattering the tiny strawberries in a red spray across the stubble. "You can get out of here," he told Mary. Then he swung his arm so that the back of his hand caught her across the face. "That's right. Go on," he called.

So, choking, Mary turned and walked away. She heard their murmurs, some voices raised in remonstrance with Tom, but she didn't look back and she didn't want to. It wasn't the blow that stunned her. She could understand it. But it was the tone of his voice which, it seemed to her, said plainly, in front of them all, that he did not care about her any more.

Brother Adam had been some way off when this happened, but he had seen it all and he could hardly let it pass. Walking across to the group, he told Furzey sharply: "You are on abbey lands. This sort of behaviour is not tolerated here. And you should not treat your wife in such a way."

"Oh?" Tom looked at him defiantly. "You never had a wife, so what do you know, monk?" There were looks all round at this. What would the monk do?

"Control yourself," Adam said and turned away.

But Tom had worked himself up too far. "I can say what I like to you! And you just keep your nose out of business that don't concern you," he shouted.

Brother Adam stopped. He knew he couldn't let it go at that;

and he was about to turn and order Furzey off the field when he thought of the woman. Fortunately, the lay brother in charge was standing close by. He turned to him instead. "Take no notice and leave him be," he ordered calmly. "There's no point in his going after his wife when he's in this state." He said it just loudly enough for a couple of the other hired men to hear. Retribution would have to follow, of course, but not now.

Then he went across to his horse and rode away. It was time to inspect the fields across the heath.

He had paused to talk to the shepherds near Bergerie, so it was not until he reached the open heath that he caught sight of her. He did not know whether he had supposed he might see her or not.

He hesitated, watching her for a little while as she walked through the heather. He saw her almost stumble. Then he urged his horse towards her.

As he drew close, she must have heard him, for she turned. There was a red mark across her face and it was clear that she had been crying. She still had almost three miles to go, across rough terrain.

"Come." He leaned down, stretching out his arm to her. "Your village is on my way." She didn't argue and a moment later, surprised at the monk's strength, she found herself lifted up and placed easily astride the big horse's withers in front of him.

They went at a slow pace over the heath, taking care to skirt the marshy ground. Far away on the right they saw a flock of the abbey sheep moving across the landscape.

The sun beat down heavily; the heather was a purple haze, its sweet scent heady as honeysuckle. The full moon added its strange silver presence to the azure sky.

They rode in silence, Brother Adam's arms holding the reins around her body, and neither spoke until they were ascending the slope from a little stream in the middle of the heath, when she asked: "You are going up to the fields above the ford?"

"Yes, but I can take you to the village." It only meant a detour of a mile or so.

"I'd sooner walk down from where you're going. There's a

back way through the woods. I don't want them all to see me with my face like this."

"What about your children, though?"

"At my brother's. I'll collect them this evening."

Brother Adam said nothing. There was a stretch of flat open heath in front of them, beyond that, about a half a mile away, a screen of trees, which hid the vaccary of Pilley beyond. There was not a soul to be seen, only a few cattle and ponies.

He felt hot, and observed that little beads of sweat had formed at the nape of Mary's neck and the back of her shoulders, which had become exposed under her kirtle. He could smell her salty skin – it seemed to him like wheat with a faint tang of warm leather from her soft shoes. He noticed the way her dark hair grew from the paler skin of her neck. Her breasts, not large but full, were only just above his wrists, almost touching. Her legs, strong peasant's legs, but nicely shaped, had become exposed from the knees down as they rode.

And suddenly it came to him, with a rush, a vivid urgency that he had never experienced before: that foolish peasant Furzey could hold this woman, become intimate with this body, any time that he wished. In his head he had always known it, of course. It was obvious. But now, suddenly, for the first time in his life, the simple physical reality hit him like a wave. Dear God, he almost cried out, this is the daily life, the world of such simple fellows. And I have never known it. Had he missed life – had he missed it all? Was there another voice in the universe, warm, blinding like the sun, echoing, racing in his veins, that he had never heard in those star-filled silences in his cloister? And, taking him utterly by surprise, he felt a sudden sense of jealousy against Furzey and the whole world. All the world has known it, he thought, but not I.

They still did not speak as they entered the screen of trees that reached out like a curving arm on to the heath. The woods were empty, the dappled light falling softly through the summer leaves. It was quiet as a church.

Once or twice he caught a glimpse, across the fields, of one of the thatched roofs of the hamlet cottages, golden in the sun. Then, as the wood curved southwards, the track went deeper into the trees, along the crest of the little gulf that led down to the river. They had gone some way, making an arc round the hamlet, when she pointed to the left and he turned the big horse off the path and rode through the trees.

After a short while she nodded. "Here."

He saw now that they were only twenty paces from where the trees gave way to some gorse bushes and a small paddock. Dismounting, he reached up and lifted her gently to the ground.

She turned. "You must be hot," she said simply. "I will give you water."

He hesitated, took a moment to reply. "Thank you." He tethered his horse to a tree and rejoined her. He was curious, he supposed, to see more closely the farmstead where she passed her days.

They could not be seen from the next cottage as they crossed the paddock. The gate in the paddock fence gave on to the small yard. The cottage was on the left, the barn on the right. By the barn was a rick of cut bracken, like a miniature haystack. She disappeared into the cottage for a moment, then came out with a wooden cup and a pitcher of water. She poured the water into the cup, placed the pitcher on the ground and then, without a word, went back into the cottage.

He drank. Then refilled the cup. The water was delightfully cool. The hamlet's water, like that from many of the forest streams, had a fresh, sharp taste, like fern. She did not reappear at once, but he decided it would be impolite to leave without thanking her; so he waited.

When she returned he saw that she had bathed her face. The cold water had already lessened the redness of the mark on her cheek. Her hair had been brushed; her kirtle somewhat pulled down so that the tops of her breasts were slightly exposed – from the act of washing he imagined.

"I hope you feel better."

"Yes." Her dark-blue eyes surveyed him thoughtfully, it seemed to Adam. Then she gave a faint smile. "You must see my animals," she said. "I'm very proud of them."

So he followed her, attentive as a knight upon a lady, as she led him round her domain.

She took her time. She fed the chickens and told him their

names. They inspected the pigs. The cat had just had kittens; they duly admired them.

But most of all he admired the woman who was leading him. It was remarkable to him how well she had recovered her equanimity. Her face was calm; she looked refreshed. When she told him the chickens' names she had a faintly ironic smile. They seemed so apposite – one or two were rather witty – that he asked her if she had thought of them all.

"Yes." She gave him a wry look. "My husband goes to the fields. I name the chickens." She gave a little shrug and he thought of the scene in the field that he had witnessed. "That's my life," she said.

He felt a tenderness as well as admiration. He felt protective; he hovered beside her, watching all that she did. How gracefully she moved. He had not realised before. Although quite sturdily built, she was light on her feet and she walked with a delightful swinging motion. Once or twice, as she knelt down to tend her animals, he observed the firm line of her thighs and the lovely curves of her body. When she reached up, almost on tiptoe, to pull down an apple from the tree and the sunlight caught her, he saw her breasts in perfect silhouette.

The afternoon sun was warm upon him. As well as the faint smells of the yard, he detected honeysuckle. It was strange: in her presence, now, everything – the animals, the apple tree, even the blue sky above – suddenly seemed more real, more actual than they usually did.

"Come," she said. "I have one more creature to visit. It's in the barn." And she led the way past the rick, which scented the air with bracken.

He followed her, but at the door of the barn, instead of entering, she paused and glanced up at him. "I'm afraid this must be boring for you."

"No." He was taken aback. "I'm not bored at all."

"Well." She smiled. "A farm can't be very interesting to you."

"When I was a child," he said simply, "I lived on a farm. Some of the time." It was quite true. His father had been a merchant, but his uncle had possessed a farm and he had spent part of his childhood there.

"Well, well." She seemed amused. "A farm boy. Once upon a time." She gave a soft laugh. "A very long time ago."

Then she reached up and gently touched his cheek. "Come," she said.

When had the idea taken shape in her mind? Mary was not quite certain herself. Was it out on the heath, when the handsome monk had rescued her, like a knight rescuing a damsel in distress? Was it the soothing motion of the horse, the feel of his strong arms around her?

Yes. Perhaps then. Or if not then exactly . . . It was probably when they had taken the track through the woods and she had thought: we are unseen. The village, her sister-in-law, even her brother – all unaware that she was passing close by with this stranger. Oh, yes, her heart had been pounding then.

And even if she had not been certain what she wanted before she arrived back, then surely she had known it when she washed her face. The tingling cold of the water on her brow and on her cheeks; she had pulled her kirtle down and some drops had fallen on her breasts; she had gasped and given a tiny shudder. And there, through the half-open door, she had seen him, waiting for her.

They entered the barn together. The creature to which Mary had referred was not part of the farmstead's livestock. Instead, going into one corner and kneeling down, she showed him a small, straw-filled box. "I found him two days ago," she said.

It was just a blackbird, which had broken its wing. Mary had rescued it and made a tiny splint for the wing, and she was keeping it in the barn for safety until it was healed. "The cat can't get at it here," she explained.

He knelt down beside her and, as she gently stroked the bird, he did the same, so that their hands lightly touched. Then he leaned back, watching her, while she continued to bend over the bird on its bed of straw.

She did not look at the monk. She was aware only of his presence.

It was strange: until today he had been just that for her – a presence, almost a spirit. Someone unobtainable, above her, forbidden, protected by his vows and reserved from the touch of all women. And yet, now she knew, he was also like other men.

And obtainable. She knew it was so. Her instinct told her. Although her husband might choose to humiliate her it was in her power to attract, to have this man, so infinitely superior to poor Tom Furzey.

Suddenly she was overcome by desire. She, modest Mary on her farmstead, had the power – here, now – to turn this innocent into a man. It was a thrilling, heady sensation.

"See." She lifted the bird's wing so that he would lean forward to touch it. As he did so, she half turned, so that her breasts brushed lightly against his chest. She slowly rose and stepped past him. Her leg touched his arm. Then she moved to the door of the barn, which was ajar, and stood gazing out at the bright sunlight. Her heart was beating faster.

For a moment she thought of her husband. But only for a moment. Tom Furzey did not value her. She owed him nothing more. She closed him out of her mind.

She was conscious of the sunlight upon her, of the tingling in her breasts and of a fluttering sensation that seemed to be spreading like a blush down her whole body. She closed the door of the barn and turned round. "I don't want the cat to get in." She smiled.

She moved quietly towards him. The barn was shadowy but here and there the slivers of bright sunlight came in through cracks in the wooden walls. And as she came towards him he slowly rose, so that in a moment they were standing face to face, she looking up, almost touching.

And Brother Adam, who loved the voice of God in the great panoply of the stars at night, knew only that his universe had been invaded by a warmer, larger brightness that had caused the stars to vanish.

She reached up her arm, curving it behind his neck.

The summer afternoon was quiet. Far away, on the Beaulieu grange, the reapers had resumed their work and the faint drone of the hedgerows had been joined by the rhythmic hiss of scythes upon the stalks of golden wheat. By the little farmstead all seemed quiet. Now and then a bird fluttered in the trees. On the grassy verges the forest ponies moved occasionally as they grazed upon their shades or drank from the tiny streams and rivulets that still flowed in the summer dryness.

Across the wide open heath the sun, watched by the pale moon, bore down upon the purple glow of the heather and the bursting yellow flower of the spiky gorse. And to the south, in the Solent channel, the sea tide ran and its healing waters washed the New Forest shore.

The morning service. The unchanging forms. The eternal words.

Laudate Dominum . . . Et in terra pax . . .

Prayer. *Pater Noster, qui es in coelis . . .*

Sixty monks, thirty each side of the aisle, each in his place, which only death can change. White habits, tonsured heads, voices all raised together in the nasal chanting of the unchanging psalms. The Cistercians had a precise, clipped form of Gregorian chant, which he had always found particularly satisfying. *Laudate Dominum:* Praise the Lord. Voices rising in strength, in joy, from the very fact that these psalms and prayers were the same five hundred years ago, and today, and for ever. The joy and comfort of the certain marriage, the knowledge that your fellowship is with the one order that has no end.

There they all were: the sacristan who was responsible for the church, the tall precentor leading the chant, the cellarer who looked after the brewery and the sub-cellarer who controlled all the fish. Dear Brother Matthew, now novice master, Brother James the almoner, Grockleton, his claw hooked round the end of his stall – grey-haired, fair-haired, tall or short, thin or fat, busy with their chant, yet watchful, the sixty or so monks of Beaulieu Abbey, joined by about thirty lay brothers down in the nave, were at their morning service all together and Brother Adam, too, was in his proper place among them.

There were no candles on the choir stalls this morning. The sacristan saw no need. The summer sun was already falling softly through the windows on to the gleaming oak stalls and forming little pools of light on the tiled floor.

Brother Adam looked around him. What was he singing? He'd forgotten. He tried to concentrate.

Then a terrible thought occurred to him. He was seized with

a sense of panic. What if he had blurted something out? What if he had said her name? Or worse. Hadn't his mind just been dwelling upon her body? The innermost recesses. The taste, the smell, the touch. Dear God, had he shouted something out? Was he doing so now, unaware of it?

They all sank down to pray. But Brother Adam did not murmur the words. He closed his mouth, clamped his tongue between his teeth just to make sure. He blushed with his sense of guilt and stole a look at the faces opposite. Had he said anything? Had they heard? Did they all know his secret?

It did not seem so. The tonsured heads were bowed in prayer. Was anyone stealing a furtive glance in his direction? Was Grockleton's eye about to stare at him in terrible judgement?

It was not so much guilt that afflicted him; it was the terror that he might have blurted it out in that enclosed space. The morning service, instead of refreshing him, brought him only a nervous torture that day. He was relieved, when it ended, to get outside.

After breakfast, somewhat calmer, he went to see the prior.

The time of morning business in the prior's office was normally given over to routine administration. But there were other matters that could come up. If, for the sake of the community's well-being, it was necessary, as it was your duty to do, to make any personal reports – "I am afraid I saw Brother Benedict eating a double helping of herrings," or "Brother Mark went to sleep instead of doing his tasks yesterday" – then that was when you did it.

Wondering whether anyone was going to report on him, he waited until the end before he went in. If he had been caught, he thought he'd sooner know now. When he finally joined Grockleton, however, the prior gave no sign of having such information.

"I'm afraid," he explained, "it's Tom Furzey." He gave Grockleton a precise account of what had taken place in the field and the prior nodded thoughtfully.

"You did quite right not to send the man home at that moment," Grockleton said. "He would probably have struck his poor wife again."

"He must go now, though," Adam pointed out. "We can't have indiscipline." He knew the prior would heartily agree with that.

Yet instead, Grockleton paused. He eyed Adam thoughtfully. "I wonder," he said, pushing himself gently back in his chair with his claw, "if that is right."

"Surely, if a hired worker insults the monk in charge . . ."

"Reprehensible, of course." Grockleton pursed his lips. "Yet perhaps, Brother Adam, we need to take a larger view."

"A larger view?" This was indeed a new departure for the prior.

"Perhaps it is better if this man and his wife are apart. He will miss her. Let us hope he will repent. In time one of us may speak to him, quietly."

"Doesn't that leave me in an awkward position, Prior? He will feel – all the men may think – that they can speak to me rudely with impunity."

"Really? Do you think so?" Grockleton looked down at the table where his claw was now very comfortably resting. "Yet sometimes, Brother Adam, we must work hard not to consider our own feelings, but the greater good of others. I have no doubt, if we leave Furzey where he is, that the work will still be done and well done. You will see to that. Perhaps you may imagine you look foolish – even feel humiliated. But we must all learn to live with that. It is part of our vocation. Don't you agree?" He smiled quite sweetly.

"So Furzey must stay? Even if he is rude to me again?"

"Yes."

Brother Adam nodded. He's paid me out nicely for humiliating him at the river, he thought, although that was really his fault and not mine. But it was not so much his public humiliation that he was thinking of, as he now bowed his head before the happy prior.

By sending Furzey away, he would have ensured that he returned home to his wife. That would make any further relations with her on his own part almost impossible. But now she would be alone. He wondered what would happen.

How little you know, John of Grockleton, he thought, what you may just have done.

• • •

Luke crept forward in the darkness. There was only a sliver left of the silver moon, but he could see well enough by the starlight. The horse was tethered to a tree about a hundred yards off. This was the third time he had seen it there.

He lay down at the edge of the tree line. He could see the little barn from there, the barn where he had spent so many winter nights. Behind him, in the woods that rose up from the small river valley by Boldre, an owl hooted. He waited patiently.

It was still some time before dawn when he saw the figure slip out from the barn and make its way silently along the edge of the paddock to the trees. It passed fifty yards away from him, but he had no doubt about the stranger's identity. It was only a few moments before he heard the horse moving through the trees behind him.

Luke waited a little, then started to make his way towards the barn.

The abbot had still not returned when the news came that the Forest court would meet again just before Michaelmas and John of Grockleton thought for two days before deciding to take his own initiative. Before announcing it, however, he sent for Brother Adam.

There was no doubt, he thought, as the monk stood before him, that Adam looked uncommonly well. The weeks out in the fields had left him rather suntanned. He looked fitter, even taller. Since he knew that Adam would rather have been in the cloister, and as this almost muscular bearing was not really appropriate for a choir monk, Grockleton did not begrudge him his well-being. He only wanted to know one thing anyway. "Have any of the hired men heard anything of that runaway, Brother Luke?"

"If they have," Adam answered with perfect truth, "they've said nothing to me."

"Do you think anyone knows where he is?"

Brother Adam paused. Mary had twice spoken to him of Luke. She had told him Luke's version of events and, although he had never asked her directly, he assumed she knew that her brother was in the Forest somewhere. "I believe most of our hired hands think he's left the Forest."

"The court is going to meet again. If he's in the Forest, I want him found," said Grockleton. "What do you advise?"

Adam shrugged. "You know," he replied carefully, "there is a feeling that he may have been trying to prevent an affray. The justice himself did indicate that such a view could be taken. I wonder if it wouldn't be better to let sleeping dogs lie."

"The court may take any view it likes," Grockleton snapped. "I'm supposed to produce him and I intend to. So I'm going to offer a reward. A price on his head."

"I see."

"Two pounds to anyone who can bring him in. I think that should concentrate the Forest people's minds, don't you?"

"Two pounds?" It was a small fortune to men like Pride and Furzey. His face fell as he thought of Mary and how worried she would be.

"Something wrong?" Grockleton was eyeing him sharply.

"No. Not really, Prior." He recovered himself quickly. "It seems a lot."

"I know," said Grockleton, with a smile.

Sometimes, when Adam lay with Mary, he was overcome by a sense of wonder that such a thing should have happened at all.

They did not use any light. They did not dare. She would come out to the small barn late at night when the children were asleep – thank God they took so much exercise that they always slept soundly – and he, watching from the trees, would sneak across to meet her. He was getting good at that.

Once, the third time they had met, she had stood in a shaft of moonlight that came through a crack in the door and silently undressed before him. He had watched, entranced, as she took off her rough gown and stood, barefoot, in only her linen kirtle. With a little shake of her head she had let her dark hair fall loose over her shoulders. Then she had pulled down the kirtle, slowly exposing her full, pale breasts and, letting it drop to the floor, stepped out, turning her naked body towards him while he gasped.

It was all a revelation: the touch, the smell of her flesh as he explored her body without shame. When they were apart in the first days, her presence would come into his mind like a spirit, but soon he found his imagination dwelling on her body. He would tense with desire and lust as he thought of some new way to approach and possess her.

But it was more than that: her whole physical presence, her life, the way she thought; now that he had entered this new world, he wanted to know it all. Dear heaven, he thought, I had known God's universe, yet missed His whole creation. Nor did he really feel guilty: that was the strangest thing. He was far too honest a man to deceive himself about it. He was proud of himself. Even the danger of the business only added to his pride and excitement. God knows, he considered, I have never done anything dangerous before.

And the threat to his immortal soul? Sometimes, when he was within her, in the full power of his passion, it seemed to him as though he had entered another landscape, as simple, as full of God's echoing presence as the ancient desert was, before these ideas of celibacy were born. And at such times, whatever vows he had taken, it felt to Brother Adam as if his innermost soul had not been lost but found.

How long could it go on? He did not know. Furzey had made only brief visits to his home. He didn't seem to want to spend time there, so it was easy enough to ensure he was kept busy at the granges. Adam had already thought of tasks to keep the peasant busy until late September. As for his own absences, they were easy to explain. Many nights he was at the abbey; but if he muttered one evening that he was leaving one grange to visit another, no one even thought twice about it. As for the prior, he was only too glad to think of Adam being forced to spend a night out. So all this could last into the autumn. After that he did not know.

He and Mary were lying together drowsily, late in the night, when he told her about the prior's plan to put a price on the head of her brother. As he had imagined it possible that she might know Luke's whereabouts, in common kindness, he had thought of warning her. But even so, he had not quite expected the reaction he got when he gave her the news.

She sat bolt upright in the straw. "Oh, God. Two pounds?" She seemed to be staring straight ahead. "Puckle won't give him away. Not even for that." She paused, then turned towards him. "So." She sighed. "Now you know."

"He's with Puckle, the charcoal burner?"

"Yes. Over Burley way."

"Well, I'm not going to tell anyone."

"You'd better not."

"Actually." He chuckled to himself. "That's rather funny."

"Why?"

"I think I must have seen him."

"Oh." She was silent for a moment. "There's something else you may as well know. He came here the other morning. Early."

"And?"

"He knows about us. He saw you."

"Oh." This opened up new vistas for the monk. The runaway lay brother had information on him now – a new kind of danger. "What did he say about it?"

"Nothing much."

"I should think," Adam reflected, "he's as safe with Puckle as anywhere. But if I hear anything I'll tell you."

They passed another three hours together and the first light of dawn was already spreading when Adam slipped out, after agreeing to return in two nights' time. As usual, he made his way cautiously out to the trees and then rode quietly through the woods towards the ford.

This time, however, his departure from the barn had been seen by a watchful pair of eyes. And they did not belong to Luke.

The news of John of Grockleton's two pound reward was known the next day. By evening it had reached Burley. Puckle himself was at home that evening, having left Luke out watching a new charcoal fire in the woods. His extended family was gathered round in front of the cottage.

"It's two pounds," said his son.

"Two pounds of nothing," said Puckle.

"Still, two pounds . . ." echoed one of his nephews.

Puckle looked round them all. He looked also at his wife, who wisely kept silent.

He was roasting a hare on a spit over a small fire he had built outside. Its skin lay on the ground by his feet. He did not speak for a little while, then he pointed. "Ever seen me skin a hare?" he asked quietly. They all nodded. Then he gestured to the hare roasting on the spit. "If any one of you opens his mouth about Luke." He looked quite calmly both at his son and his nephew, then allowed his eyes to move round the rest of the circle. "That's what I'll do to him."

There was silence. It was wise, if an old Forest man like Puckle said a thing like that, to pay attention.

Early the next morning Puckle talked to Luke. "Two pounds is a lot," he said sadly.

"Your lot won't talk, will they?"

"Better not. But people are going to start looking now. They see you they'll think: 'Now which one of his nephews is that?' I reckon someone'll put two and two together."

"I told Mary."

"That was stupid." Puckle shrugged. "Still, I don't reckon she'll talk."

"So what'll I do?"

"Don't know." He looked thoughtful. Then suddenly his gnarled face broke into a grin. "I reckon I do, though." He nodded his shaggy head. "How'd you like to help me build another charcoal fire?"

Tom Furzey's sister had always been puzzled about the pony, but now, she thought, as she walked across Beaulieu Heath towards St Leonards, she probably had the answer.

And best of all, it was worth a fortune.

It had been chance that she should have been up so early the day before. Her husband had set two rabbit snares in the woods in the valley and she had decided to walk down that way to see if he'd caught anything. She'd been just about to go down the slope when she had caught sight of a muffled figure running, stooped over, from Tom's place into the trees.

For some time she'd stood there, wondering who it could possibly be. Even when she had found a rabbit and brought it home, she had kept the thing to herself. Then, that very day, had come news of the prior's reward and the suspicion had grown into a certainty. It was Luke. It had to be.

That probably explained the pony, too. Luke Pride was hanging about at Tom's place, sneaking in and out at night. He must have been the one who replaced the pony like that, then. Cheeky devil.

She smiled now, though. The Prides were going to get their come-uppance after all. She and Tom could enjoy it equally. "A pound for him and a pound for me," she muttered.

It was near the end of the working day when she reached St Leonards. She found Tom easily enough and took him to one side.

When she had finished her tale, his round face broke into a happy smile. "Got 'em," he said.

"It's Luke, isn't it?"

"'Course it is. Has to be."

"Two pounds, Tom. Equal shares. We can start watching tonight."

He frowned. "Trouble is, I'm supposed to stay here tonight. We start at dawn, see?" Brother Adam had come past only a short while before to ensure himself that everyone was accounted for.

"You could slip away, couldn't you? After dark?"

"I suppose so."

"I'll be waiting, then. Two pounds, Tom. I'll take it all if you don't turn up."

It was long past dark when Brother Adam quietly tethered his horse and began to creep towards the edge of the paddock. It was very black so that once or twice he even had to feel his way. At the edge he paused. Slowly he began to make his way towards the vague shape of the barn.

When something threw him to the ground.

It was like a huge double blow to his back. He had no idea what it was, but he hit the ground so hard he was winded. An instant later his two assailants had his arms and were trying to turn him over. He still couldn't speak, but he kicked out violently. He heard a man's voice curse. Then one of the two wrapped his arms round his legs while the other punched him, very effectively in the solar plexus. It seemed to Adam that neither of his assailants was very large, but both were strong.

Were they robbers? Here? His mind was just starting to work again when, with a sinking heart, he heard the voice of Tom Furzey.

"Caught you."

What in the world could he say? He could think of nothing.

Was this peasant going to haul him back to the abbey for fornicating with his wife? What would become of him?

One of the two was fumbling with something. Then suddenly a lantern was being shone in his face.

"Brother Adam!"

Thank the Lord he still had his wits about him. Tom Furzey's voice expressed such total astonishment, such confusion: whatever it meant, it was not him they had expected. His legs were let go. Another sign that they felt at a disadvantage. He struggled and sat up. He must bluff. "Furzey? I know your voice. What's the meaning of this? Why aren't you at St Leonards?"

"But . . . What are you doing here, Brother Adam?"

"Never mind that. Why are you here and why have you attacked me?"

There was a pause. "Thought you might be someone else," Furzey's voice replied sullenly.

"He isn't worth two pounds anyway." A woman's voice, but not Mary's.

And then, of course, he realised. "I see. You thought Luke might come this way."

"My sister reckons she seen him."

"Ah." Thank God. He knew what to say now. "Well, Furzey," he said slowly, "you should not have left the grange without permission, but that is why I am here too. I had an idea he might be coming here and if so he'll be taken."

"Then we won't get our two pounds but you will, I suppose," said Tom.

"You forget, I have no use for two pounds. Monks have no worldly goods."

"You mean we can catch him?"

"I suppose so," Adam said drily.

"Oh." Furzey audibly brightened. "Maybe we can all watch for him then."

What could he do? Adam gazed towards the barn. What if Mary, wondering what had become of him, were to come out looking for him? Worse still, call his name? Could he tell them he was going to inspect the barn and try to warn her? He decided that was too risky. They'd think his presence might alert Mary to the fact that they were watching for her brother.

Worse yet, what if Tom went in and Mary, seeing him, mistook him for her lover and called out the wrong name?

Fortunately, he soon realised, Tom was far more eager to catch Luke than to encounter his wife. But there was still the possibility that poor Luke would come to visit his sister at dawn. He wondered if there were some way he could head him off, but could not see how, in the dark.

So they waited. There was no sound from the barn, nor did Luke appear. When light came, they agreed to give up. Might he come and watch again? Furzey asked him.

"I suppose so," Brother Adam replied. Then he rode away.

He had much to do.

The sun was well up when he reached the site where he had encountered the charcoal burner near Burley. It did not take him long to find Puckle, who had evidently seen him coming.

There were two great charcoal cones he was tending now. The burning process of one was almost completed, by the look of it; the other had just started. Puckle was alone. There was no sign of Luke.

Brother Adam did not waste time. "I've a message for Luke."

"For who?"

"I know. You haven't seen him. Just give him a message." He told Puckle briefly about Tom's vigil. "He'd better not go there. Now." He took a deep breath – he'd thought about trying to give her the message himself but decided the risk was too great – "I need to ask a favour of you. Please tell Mary the house is being watched. You can tell her I told you. She'll understand."

And how much, he wondered, would Puckle understand? Might he wonder why he was doing Mary and Luke a favour or might he guess the whole truth? Staring at that oaken face it was impossible to know. He looked Puckle in the eye. "Silence buys silence, I hope."

Puckle just looked at him, then gazed down at his fire. Only as the monk rode away did he mutter: "Always has done in the Forest."

Dear God, thought Adam, as he went back towards the abbey lands, I'm even in league, criminally, with Puckle now.

Yet, as he listened to the morning birdsong, he found only a strange sense of exhilaration at his fall from grace.

He would have been most surprised, once he was out of sight, to see what happened to the second charcoal fire. A small door opened in its turf side from which, not at all burned or even heated, Luke emerged.

The hiding place Puckle had contrived was the neatest thing imaginable. The top half of the huge cone was constructed internally more or less as an ordinary charcoal fire, except that by using damp materials Puckle could produce a great deal of smoke with very little heat. But below this, with a thick turf inner roof, was a hollow space in which Luke could remain, quite comfortably, with air holes providing ventilation, for as long as he liked. Each day at dawn Puckle intended to remake the fire at the top and no one passing by, even the sharpest-eyed, would ever guess its secret.

The next week was a busy one in the Forest.

On two successive days, because of the insistence of the prior, the foresters had the hounds out. The steward was so bored by the business that he gave the whole responsibility to young Alban. The first day they drew in the woods near Pride's and went all the way across almost to Burley. But there the scent became so confused that they did nothing but go round in circles. The next day they tried over towards Minstead. But mysteriously the scent seemed to lead straight to the house of the forester, who was not at all amused.

Half the Forest, either openly or secretly, was on the look-out. The foresters and their stewards rode about in groups. Cottages were visited, every woodsman stopped. It all came to nothing, but as Puckle remarked sadly to Luke one night: "It's going to be difficult for you to come out."

Mary waited for ten days before she set off to her appointment. During this time she did not see Brother Adam once. But he was seldom out of her thoughts.

What does a woman feel when she seduces a monk? She smiled now, a little, to think that even on that first afternoon, although she had been distressed and he protective, he was still unaware that it was she, really, who had seduced him. It was his innocence that she instinctively wanted, this strong, manly man who had never known a woman. And she, the peasant wife of a humble labourer, had it in her power to teach him to know life. He had taken a step, even half a step towards her. He had asked without even knowing he was asking – or certainly for what he was asking.

I have taken a man of God, a man forbidden, and I have made him blaze like the sun: at moments she had been almost heady with the sense of her womanly triumph. Not that she had let him see it. Not at first, anyway. She had brought him along, she thought with a smile, very nicely.

Was that all, then? Just a seduction? Oh, no. There was the reason that she had been drawn to him in the first place: his fineness, his intelligence; her sense that he had what she did not; her certainty that, even if she wasn't quite sure what these things were, she wanted to have them.

At first, when they talked in the night, she would ask him: "What are you thinking?" And he would reply something that he thought she would understand. But soon, when she made clear she wanted more, he would make an effort and try to explain his nightly musings. "There was a great philosopher, you see, called Abelard, and he thought . . ." he might explain. Or he would speak of far-off lands, or great events, a world that was far beyond anything she had known, yet which, dimly, as though seeing light coming through a church window, she could discern. And he was in that other world. She knew it. "Your mind is in the stars," she once whispered, but not in mockery. And when another time, after he had told her some wonderful idea, she laughed – "And being inside me made you think of that?" – she was, in truth, more pleased than she had ever been in her life.

But recently there had been more to worry about.

Her appointment with Luke, made when Puckle brought her the message, was in a quiet place in the woods north of Brockenhurst. She took care she was not followed.

He was already waiting for her there, by a huge old oak tree, thick with moss and ivy. She was glad to see he was looking well and he seemed quite cheerful. Yet the news he had was less so. "Puckle thinks I ought to leave the Forest. The prior's never going to give up."

"After the Michaelmas court he might."

"No." Luke sighed. "You don't know him."

"I still think you should turn yourself in. They aren't going to hang you."

"Probably not. But you can't trust them."

"Where'd you go?"

"On pilgrimage, maybe. Compostella. Thousands of people go there."

Compostella. Spain. You could beg along the way, they said. She doubted it. She shook her head. "You've never been out of the Forest."

"I like walking, though."

For a while they were silent.

"What's happening with Brother Adam, then?" he asked.

Now it was her turn to announce worrying news. "I think I'm pregnant."

"Oh. You sure?"

"Almost. I think so. It feels like it."

"Couldn't be Tom?" She shook her head. "What'll you do?" She only shrugged. Luke was thoughtful. "Reckon you and Tom . . . You'd better give him a chance to think it's his, hadn't you?"

She took a long breath. "I know." Her voice was flat. He'd never heard it quite like that before.

"You've been with him a lot of years. Can't be so bad."

"You don't understand." He didn't. They were all just forest creatures to him.

"You going to tell Brother Adam?"

"Maybe."

"You know, Mary, this can't go on. I mean, it'll be winter. Tom'll be home. You've a family and Brother Adam's a monk."

"There'll be next spring and summer, Luke."

"But Mary . . ."

How could he understand? He was a simple boy. She might lie with Tom. She'd have to. There was no way out of that, really. But Adam was there too. She'd heard women talk about lovers. Such things occurred in some villages, especially around harvest time. Perhaps when she'd started with Brother Adam she'd thought that, being a monk, he'd be safe: back in Beaulieu Abbey where he belonged when it was over. The trouble was, she had known a finer kind of man now. The fact of Brother Adam could never be taken from her. She could not step back into the same stream. The landscape had subtly changed.

"Beaulieu's not far, Luke. I'm not going back to only Tom."

"You have to."

"No."

Luke and Puckle talked for a long time that night.

In the end Puckle said: "I think you've got to do it."

"Will you help me?" Luke asked.

"Of course."

If one walked along the eastern side of the cloister at Beaulieu from the church one came first to the big locked cupboard – for that was all it was – known as the bookcase, where the abbey's stock of books was mostly kept. Then came the vestry; after that the larger chapter house where every Monday morning, while the abbot was away, Grockleton would read out the abbey's rules to the assembled monks. Then the scriptorium where Brother Adam liked to spend his time studying, then the monks' dormitory and just round the corner, next to the big *frater*, was the warming house, a spacious room with a fire.

John of Grockleton had just emerged from the warming house when the message came and he hurried to the gate.

The messenger was a servant, from Alban, who desired to speak with him privately. His message caused the prior's face to crease into a smile: "We think we have Brother Luke, Prior."

The problem was that he wasn't talking. Alban, it seemed, was reluctant to turn up at the abbey with him unless he was quite sure who he was. Otherwise, he felt, they'd all be made to look like fools again. So he was holding the fellow secretly at his house. Would the prior come, discreetly, and identify the lay brother? "I am to conduct you, if you are willing," the servant explained.

"I shall come at once," Grockleton said and sent to the stables for his horse.

It was all the prior could do, as they rode across the heath, to contain his enthusiasm. They proceeded at a trot or a canter. He would happily have galloped. At the far edge of the heath, they entered the woods west of Brockenhurst and started to canter along a track. The prior was smiling. He had hardly been happier in his life.

"This way, Sir," called the servant again, taking a track to the left. "Short cut." The track was narrower. Once or twice he was smacked in the face by overhanging branches, but he didn't care. "This way, Sir," called the servant, veering right. He followed eagerly, then frowned. Where the devil had the fellow gone? He pulled up. Called out.

And was greatly astonished when a pair of hands seized him from behind, pulling him off his horse and, before he even had time to struggle, slipped a rope round him which a second later was made fast to a tree.

He was about to cry out "Murder! Thieves!" when another figure appeared miraculously in front of him. A shaggy, forest figure whom he recognised, after only a moment: Brother Luke.

"You!" His natural posture was to lean forward. Now the prior strained towards him so hard it seemed as if he meant to bite him.

"It's all right," the insolent fellow replied. "I only wanted a talk. I'd have come to the abbey, but . . ." He smiled and shrugged.

"What do you want?"

"To return to the abbey."

"Are you mad?"

"No, Prior. I hope not." He sat down on the ground in front of Grockleton. "Can I talk?"

It was not, Grockleton had to admit, what he would have expected. Firstly, Luke spoke of the abbey and its granges and his years there. He did so quite simply and with such feeling that, like it or not, Grockleton could see that he genuinely loved the place. Then he explained what had happened that day at the grange. He made no excuses about letting the poachers in, but explained how he had tried to stop Brother Matthew striking Martell and how he had panicked and fled. Little as he liked this either, the prior secretly guessed that it was true.

"You should have returned then."

"I was afraid. Afraid of you."

It did not wholly displease Grockleton that this peasant should be afraid of him. "And why should I do anything for you now?" he demanded.

"If I told you something important, for the good of the abbey, something nobody knows, might you see your way . . . ?"

"It's possible." Grockleton considered.

"It would be bad for one of the monks, though."

Grockleton frowned. "Which monk?"

"Brother Adam. It'd be very bad for him."

"What is it?" The prior could not conceal the glint in his eye.

Luke saw it. This was what he needed. "You've got to send him away. No scandal. That'd be bad for the abbey anyway. He's got to go away. And I've got to come back, with no more Forest court or anything. You can arrange that. I need your word."

Grockleton hesitated. He understood deals and his word was his word. But there was an obvious difficulty. "Priors don't bargain with lay brothers," he said frankly.

"You'll never hear another sound from me afterwards. That's my word."

Grockleton pondered. He put it all in the balance. He thought also of the reaction of the court and the foresters, who he knew very well were sick of him, if they heard this honest fellow speak as eloquently in court as he had just done now. He might be better off with Luke on his side. And then . . . Luke said he had something on Brother Adam. "If it's good, you have my word," he heard himself saying.

So Luke betrayed Brother Adam and his sister Mary.

Except, Grockleton thought as he listened to the peasant, that it was not really a betrayal. Seen from Luke's point of view there was something profoundly natural about it. He saw his sister's family about to be blasted by a storm; so he was protecting them. A sudden blow, the shedding of blood; it was just nature.

Nor did the perfect balance of the thing escape the prior. Once Adam was gone, Mary would have no choice but to live in peace with her husband. The child would be treated as

Tom's. It was in nobody's interest to say a word. Except his own, of course, if he wanted entirely to destroy Brother Adam. But even that made no sense. For if he exposed Adam, he'd damage the abbey's reputation. And what would the abbot say about that? No, the peasant's judgement was good. Besides. He thought of something else, something in the secret book, known only to the abbot. He had to be a little careful himself.

What of Luke, though? Could he be trusted to behave himself? Probably. He had no wish to hurt his sister by making trouble, though he continued to hold the threat of his knowledge about the monk as a sort of protection. In any case, I'm better off with him safely inside the abbey than outside, the prior considered.

And so, for the first time in his life, Grockleton started to think like an abbot.

With what joy, a few days later, the monks of Beaulieu learned that their abbot had returned and that, so far as he knew, there were no plans for him to depart from them again in the foreseeable future.

Brother Adam, too, was glad. His only concern was lest the abbot, out of a now mistaken sense of kindness, should decide to relieve him of his duties at the granges. He had prepared for this carefully, however. His record was excellent. It would take anyone else a year to learn what he now knew. Who else would want the job? For the good of the abbey he should certainly keep it another year or two. All in all, he hoped he was well prepared.

As for his guilty secret, he had learned to get through the offices now without the terror of giving himself away. He had already, he confessed to himself, become hardened in his sin. He was just glad the abbot knew nothing, that was all.

When he received a summons to present himself before the abbot and the prior one morning he was prepared for everything except what awaited him.

The abbot looked friendly, if somewhat thoughtful, when he entered. Grockleton was sitting there, leaning forward with his claw on the table as usual. But Adam was too glad to be looking at the abbot again to take much notice of the prior. And it was the abbot, not Grockleton, who spoke. "Now, Adam, we know all about your love affair with Mary Furzey. Fortunately neither her husband nor the brethren in the abbey do. So I'd just like you to tell us about it in your own words."

Grockleton had wanted to ask him whether he had anything to confess and give him the chance to perjure himself, but the abbot had overruled him.

It did not take long. If his humiliation was complete, the abbot did nothing to prolong it. "This will remain a secret," he told Adam, "for the sake of the abbey and, I may add, for that of the woman and her family. You must leave here at once. Today. But I want no one to know why."

"Where am I to go?"

"I'm sending you to our daughter house down in Devon. To Newenham. Nobody will think that strange. They've been struggling a bit down there and you are – or were – one of our best monks."

Adam bowed his head. "May I say farewell to Mary Furzey?"

"Certainly not. You are to have no communication with her whatsoever."

"I am surprised" – it was Grockleton now, he couldn't resist it – "that you should even think of such a thing."

"Well." Adam sighed. Then he looked at Grockleton sadly, though without malice. "You have never done such a thing."

There was silence in the room. The claw did not move. Perhaps the prior might have stooped forward a little lower over the dark old table. The abbot's face was a mask as he gazed carefully into the middle distance. So Brother Adam did not guess that in the abbot's secret book there was a notation concerning John of Grockleton and a woman, and a child. But that had been in another monastery, far away in the north, a long time ago.

After he had gone the abbot asked: "He doesn't know she's pregnant, does he?"

"No."

"Better he shouldn't."

"Quite." Grockleton nodded.

"Oh dear." The abbot sighed. "We are none of us safe from falling, as you know," he added meaningfully.

"I know."

"I want him given two pairs of new shoes," the abbot added firmly, "before he goes."

It was not quite noon when Brother Adam and John of Grockleton, accompanied by one lay brother, rode slowly out of the abbey and up the track that led to Beaulieu Heath.

As he rode, Adam noticed the small trees that crowned the slope opposite the abbey. The salt sea breeze from the south-west had not bent them, but shaped the tops so that they all looked as if they had been shaved down that side; and they flowered towards the north-east. It was a common sight in the coastal parts of the Forest.

White clouds were scudding over the tranquil, sunlit abbey behind them and, as they crested the little ridge, Adam felt the sharp salt breeze full upon his face.

Brother Luke returned quietly to St Leonards Grange a week later. His case did not come up before the justice at the Michaelmas court.

At about the time of the court, Mary told her husband that he might be going to be a father again.

"Oh." He frowned, then grinned, a little puzzled. "That was a lucky one."

"I know." She shrugged. "These things happen."

He might have thought about it more, except that, a short time later, John Pride – who had suffered two hours of his brother Luke's urging – turned up to suggest that their quarrel should be over. With him he brought the pony.

1300

On a December afternoon, when a yellow wintry sun, low on the horizon, was sending its parting rays across the frozen landscape of Beaulieu Heath, which was covered in snow, two riders, muffled against the cold, made their way slowly east-wards towards the abbey.

The snow had fallen days before; and right across the heath, now, there was a thin layer of icy crust, which broke as the horses' hoofs stepped on it. A light, chill breeze came from the east, sweeping little particles of snow and ice dust across the surface. The branches of the snow-covered bushes cast long shadows, fingering eastwards towards Beaulieu.

Five years had passed since Brother Adam had left the abbey to go down to the bleak little daughter house of Newenham, so far along the western coast – five years with only a dozen other brothers in the little wilderness. It might have seemed a cheerless scene that greeted him now, this icy landscape lit by the sulphurous yellow glow of a falling winter sun, but he was not aware of it. He was only aware, as if by a homing instinct, that the grey buildings by the river lay less than an hour away.

It is a curious fact, never fully explained, that at around this time in history a number of the monks belonging to the little house of Newenham in Devon started suffering from a particular affliction. The abbey records of Beaulieu make this very clear, but whether it was the water, the diet, something in the earth or the buildings themselves, nobody has ever been able to discover. Several, however, suffered so acutely that there was nothing to do for them but bring them back to Beaulieu where they could be looked after.

This was what had happened to Brother Adam. He was unaware of the yellowish light around him because he was blind.

It was often remarked with wonder by the monks of Beaulieu, from that time on, how Brother Adam could find his way about unaided. Not only in the cloister. Even in the middle of the night, when the monks came down the passageway and the stairs to perform the night office in the church, he would walk down with them quite unaided and turn into his choir stall at exactly the right place. Outside, too, he would pace about in the abbey precincts without, it seemed, ever getting lost.

He seemed to find all manner of tasks he could perform without the use of his eyes, from planting vegetables to making candles.

He was still a handsome, well-made man. He conversed little and liked to be alone, but there was always about him an air of quiet serenity.

Only once, for a matter of a few days some eighteen months

after his return, did something occur within him that seemed to distract his mind. Several times he became lost, or bumped into things. After a week, during which the abbot was rather worried about him, he seemed to recover his equanimity and balance, and never bumped into anything again. No one knew why this brief interlude had occurred. Except Brother Luke.

It had been a warm summer afternoon when the lay brother had offered to escort him along his favourite path down along the river.

"I shall not see the river, but I shall smell it," Adam had replied. "By all means, then."

It had been necessary, in this instance, for Luke to take his arm, but with an occasional warning about any small obstacles along the path, they had been able to stride along quite easily through the woods, emerging finally on to the open marsh by the river bend where, to his delight, the monk had heard the sound of a party of swans, rising off the water on the wing.

And they had been standing in the afternoon silence for a little while, feeling the sun on their faces very pleasantly, when Brother Adam heard light footsteps on the path. "Who's that?" he asked Luke.

"Someone to see you," the lay brother replied. "I'm walking off a little way now," he added. And it was with a slight shock of surprise, a moment or two later, that Adam realised who it must be.

She was standing in front of him. He could smell her. He was, as only the blind can be, aware of her whole presence. He wanted to reach out to touch her, but hesitated. It seemed to him that she was not alone.

"Brother Adam." Her voice. She spoke calmly, softly. "I have brought someone to see you."

"Oh. Who is that?"

"My youngest child. A little boy."

"I see."

"Will you give him your blessing?"

"My blessing?" He was almost surprised. It was a natural thing to ask of a monk, but, knowing what she did about him . . . "For what my blessing is worth," he said. "How old is the boy?"

"He is five."

"Ah. A nice age." He smiled. "His name?"

"I called him Adam."

"Oh. My name."

He felt her move very close, her body almost touching, but so that she could whisper, close in his ear. "He is your son."

"My son?" The revelation hit him so that he almost staggered back. It was as if, in his world of darkness, there had been a great flash of golden light.

"He doesn't know."

"You . . ." His voice was hoarse. "You are sure?"

"Yes." She was standing back now.

For a moment he stood there in the sunlight, quite still, though he felt as if he might be swaying. "Come, little Adam," he said quietly. And when the small boy approached, he reached down with his hands and felt his head, then his face. He would have liked to lift him, feel him, press him to him. But he could not do this. "So, Adam," he said gently, "be a good boy, do as your mother tells you and accept another Adam's blessing." Resting his hand on the boy's head, he recited a brief prayer.

He wanted so much to give the boy something. He wondered what. Then, suddenly remembering, he drew out the cedarwood crucifix that, so long ago, his mother had given him and, with a single pull, broke the leather string that secured it round his neck and handed it to the boy. "My mother gave me this, Adam," he said. "They say a crusader brought it from the Holy Land. Keep it always." He turned to Mary with a shrug. "It is all that I have."

They went, then, and soon afterwards he and Luke made their way back towards the abbey.

They did not speak, except once, halfway along the path through the woods.

"Does the boy look like me?"

"Yes."

Of all the times, during the long years of his blind existence, it was on those sunny afternoons as he sat quietly meditating in the carrels in the sheltered north wall of the abbey cloister, that Brother Adam appeared most serene. It seemed to the younger monks that, being obviously very close to God, Brother Adam was in a silent communion that it would be impious to interrupt. And sometimes he was. But sometimes, also, as he smelled the grass and the daisies in the cloister, and felt the warm sun coming from over the *frater*, it was another thought that filled his mind with a joy and delight which, if it led him down even to perdition, he could not help.

I have a son. Dear God, I have a son.

One afternoon, when he was all alone with no one to see, he even took out a small knife he had been using earlier in the day, and discreetly carved a little letter A in the stone beside him.

A for Adam. And sometimes, he thought, if his punishment was to be cast out of God's garden into some darker place, then still, perhaps, for the sake of his son, he would do it all again.

So, for many years, Brother Adam lived with his secret, in the abbey of Beaulieu.

Lymington

1480

Friday. Fish market day in Lymington. On Wednesdays and Fridays, at eight o'clock in the morning, for one hour, the fishermen set out their stalls.

A warm early April morning. The smell of fresh fish was delicious. Many of them had been landed down at the little wharf that dawn. There were eels and oysters from the estuary; hake, cod and other white fish from the sea; there were goldfish also, as they called the yellow gurnard then. Most of the women in the small borough went to the fish market: the merchants' wives in their big-sleeved gowns with wimples covering their heads, the poorer sorts and the servants, some in back-laced bodices, all with aprons and little hoods on their heads to make them look respectable.

The bailiff had just rung a bell to close the market as, from the direction of the wharf, two figures appeared.

Even a glance, as the lean figure made his way up the street that warm April morning, and you felt you knew him. It was just the way he walked. It was so obvious he didn't give a damn what anyone thought. The loose linen leggings he favoured flapped cheerfully on his calves, leaving his bare ankles exposed. On his feet he wore only sandals secured with leather thongs. His jerkin was made of ray – striped cloth – blue and yellow, none too clean. On his head was a leather cap he had stitched together himself.

Young Jonathan Totton could not remember ever seeing Alan Seagull without this item of headgear.

If Alan Scagull's cheerful face took a short cut from his mouth to his chest, if his sparse black beard went from his mouth down to his Adam's apple pretty much without pausing for such an ornament as a chin, you could be sure it was because he and his forebears had reckoned they could do perfectly well without one. And there was something about his cheerful, canny grin that told you they were right. "We've cut a corner, there," the Seagull smile seemed to say about their chin, "and we could probably cut a few more too, that you don't need to know about."

He smelled of tar and of fish, and of the salty sea. As he often did, he was humming a tune. Young Jonathan Totton was enchanted by him and, walking proudly beside the mariner, he had just reached the point on the sloping street where the squat little town hall stood when a voice, calm but authoritative, summoned him: "Jonathan. Come here."

Regretfully, he left Seagull's side and went over to the tall-gabled timbered house outside which his father was standing.

A moment later, with the older man's hand resting on his shoulder, he found himself inside and listening to his father's quiet voice. "I should prefer, Jonathan, that you should not spend so much time with that man."

"Why, Father?"

"Because there is better company to keep in Lymington."

Now that, Jonathan thought, was going to be a problem.

Lymington, lying as it did by the mouth of the river that ran down from Brockenhurst and Boldre to the sea, was geographically at the centre of the Forest's coastline – although, strictly speaking, on its small wedge of coastal farmland and marsh, it had not been included in the legal jurisdiction of the Conqueror's hunting forest.

It was a thriving little harbour town nowadays. From the cluster of boathouses, stores and fishermen's cottages down by the small quay, the broad High Street ran up quite a steep slope fronted by two-storey timber-and-plaster houses with overhanging upper floors and gabled roofs. The town hall at the crest of the hill on the left-hand side, typical of its kind at that date, was built of stone and consisted of a small dark chamber surrounded by open arches in which various sellers offered their wares; above which, reached by an outside staircase, a spacious overhanging penthouse served as a courtroom for discussing the town's affairs. In front of the town hall stood the town cross; across the street, the Angel Inn. About two hundred yards further along the crest of the slope, a church marked the end of the borough. There were two other streets, at right angles, a church, a market cross – for Lymington had the right to hold an annual three-day fair each September. There was a stocks and a tiny prison house for malefactors, a ducking-stool and whipping post. There was a town well: all this to serve a community of, perhaps, four hundred souls.

From the High Street you could look down over the wharf and the little estuary water to the high slope of the river bank beyond. From behind the town hall, you could see the long line of the Isle of Wight on the other side of the Solent.

This was the Lymington that contained better company than Alan Seagull.

It was hard to say when Lymington had first begun. Four centuries before, when the Conqueror's clerks had compiled his Domesday Book, they had recorded the little settlement near the coast known now as Old Lymington, with land for just one plough, four acres of meadow and inhabitants to the number of six families and a couple of slaves.

Technically, small though it was, Lymington was a manor held along with many others, by a succession of feudal lords who first began to develop the place. Its original use, as far as they were concerned, was as a harbour from which boats could cross the narrow straits to the lands they also held on the Isle of Wight. Even this choice was not inevitable. The feudal lords also held the manor of Christchurch where, soon after the death of Rufus, they had built a pleasant castle beside the new priory and the shallow harbour. At first sight that seemed the natural port. The trouble was, however, that between Christchurch and the Isle of Wight there were some awkward shoals and currents to navigate, whereas the approach to the Lymington hamlet was discovered to have a deep and easy channel.

"The crossing's shorter, too," they observed. So Lymington it was.

It was still only a hamlet; but around 1200 the manor lord

had taken a further step. Between the hamlet and the river, on an area of sloping ground, he had laid out a single dirt street with thirty-four modest plots beside it. Fishermen, mariners and even traders, like the Tottons, from other local ports were encouraged to come and settle there. And to induce them still further, the development, known as New Lymington, was given a new status.

It became a borough.

What did that mean in feudal England? That it had a charter from the monarch to operate as a town? Not quite. The charter was granted by the feudal lord. Sometimes this might be the king himself; in the new cathedral cities springing up at this time – places like Salisbury – the charter would come from the bishop. In the case of Lymington, however, it was granted by the great feudal lord who held Christchurch and many other lands besides.

The deal was simple. The humble freemen of Lymington – they would be called burgesses now – were to form themselves into a corporation, which was to pay the lord a fee of thirty shillings a year. In return, they were recognised as free from any labour service to the lord, and he also threw in the concession that they could operate anywhere on his wide domains free of all tolls and customs dues. Confirmed half a century later by a second charter, the Lymington burgesses could run the borough's daily affairs and elect their own reeve – a sort of cross between a small-time mayor and a landlord's steward to answer for them.

Know ye all men present and to come that I, Baldwin de Redvers, Earl of Devon, have granted and by this my present charter have confirmed to my burgesses of Lymington all liberties and free customs . . . by land and by sea, at bridges, ferries and gates, at fairs and markets, in selling and buying . . . in all places and in all things . . .

So began the stirring words of the charter, typical of its kind, by which the lord's small harbour graduated into a little town.

But the feudal lord was nonetheless the borough's lord and its burgesses and mayor, as the reeve was called nowadays, though free, were still his tenants. They still owed him the rents on the plots of land – the burgages – and tenements they occupied. If they made rules, he had the right to approve them. In day-to-day matters of law and order they and their borough were subject to his manor court. And even though, as time went on, the king's courts took over more and more of local justice, the feudal manor of Old Lymington, based on the rural land holding outside the borough, still continued as legal custodian of the place.

For about a century the great events of English history barely touched the place. Around 1300, when King Edward I asked why this borough had failed to supply a vessel for his campaign against the Scots, his commissioners reported back: "It's a poor little harbour – only a village, really" and they were excused. But the next century saw a dramatic change.

When the terrible Black Death swept across Europe in the years following 1346 it altered the face of England for ever. A third of the population died. Farms, whole villages, were left empty; labour was so scarce that serfs and poor peasants could sell their labour and acquire their own free land. In the great deer forests, with their small populations of woodsmen and huntsmen, there was little to change; but in the eastern half of the New Forest, on the Beaulieu estate, a muted form of the great agricultural revolution did occur. There were no longer enough lay brothers to run the granges. The abbey continued its life of prayer, therefore; its monks actually lived rather well. But instead of running the granges on their huge estates, they mostly let them out, sometimes subdivided, to tenant farmers. Young Jonathan was taken out to one of the granges from time to time to visit his mother's family, who had lived there very comfortably for three generations. When his father pointed eastwards along the coast, he did not say to Jonathan: "Those are Cistercian lands" but "that's where your mother's farm lies." The Beaulieu monks were no longer a special case. They were just another feudal landlord, now.

And if the abbey retreated, the little port advanced. Soon after the great Death, when the third King Edward and his glamorous son the Black Prince were conducting their brilliant campaigns – in the so-called Hundred Years War – against the French, the Lymington men were already able to supply several vessels and mariners. Better yet, this proved to be one of the few wars that were actually profitable for England. Plunder and ransom money flowed in. The English took land and valuable ports from their French cousins. Modest though it was, the port of Lymington found itself trading wines, spices, all sorts of minor luxuries from the rich and sunlit territories of the French. Its merchants grew in confidence. By the time, in 1415, that heroic King Henry V won the final English triumph over France at Agincourt they felt very pleased with themselves indeed.

And if, in recent times, things had not been going so well, their attitude was: "There's still money to be made."

There were times when Henry Totton worried about his son. "I'm not sure he really takes in what I say to him," he once complained to his friend.

"All ten-year-olds are the same," the other assured him. But this was not quite good enough for Totton and, as he looked at his son now, he felt an uncertainty and disappointment he tried not to show.

Henry Totton was of rather less than medium height and he had an unassuming manner; but his dress informed you at once that he meant you to take him seriously. When he was a young man, his father had given him clothes suitable for his station; and this was important. The old Sumptuary Laws had long ago set out what each class in the richly varied medieval world might wear. Nor were these laws an imposition. If the aldermen of London wore crimson cloaks and the lord mayor his chain, the whole community felt honoured. The master from Oxford University had earned his solemn gown; his pupils as yet had not. There was honour in order. The Lymington merchant did not dress as a nobleman and would have been mocked if he had; but he did not dress like the peasant or the humble mariner either. Henry Totton wore a long *houppelande* – a sleeved coat, buttoned from neck to ankle. He wore it loose, without a belt and, although plain, the material was the best brown burnet cloth. He had another, made of velvet, with a silken belt for special occasions. He was clean-shaven and his quiet grey eyes did not quite conceal the fact that, within the precise limits belonging to his station in life, he was ambitious for his family.

There had been Totton merchants in Southampton and Christchurch for centuries; he did not intend the Lymington branch to lag behind their many cousins.

He tried not to worry about Jonathan. It wasn't fair to the boy. And God knows he loved him. Since the death of his wife the previous year, young Jonathan was all he had.

As for Jonathan, looking at his father, he knew he disappointed him even if he did not quite know why. Some days he tried so hard to please him, but on others he forgot. If only his father would understand about the Seagulls.

It was the year his mother died that he had taken to wandering down to the quay alone. At the bottom end of the High Street, where the old burgage plots came to an end, there was a steep slope down to the water. It was a sharp drop in every sense. The old borough stopped at the top of it; so, as far as people like the Tottons were concerned, did respectability. Down that steep social slope clustered the untidy cottages of the fishermen. "And the other flotsam and jetsam," as his father put it, that drifted in from the sea or the Forest.

But to Jonathan it was a little heaven: the clinker boats with their heavy sails, the upturned boats on the quay, the seagull cries, the smell of tar and salt and drying seaweed, the piles of fish traps and nets – he loved to wander among all these. The Seagulls' cottage – if you could call it that – lay at the seaward end. For it was not so much a cottage as a collection of articles, each more fascinating than the last, which had gathered themselves together into a cheerful heap. It must have happened by magic – perhaps the sea one stormy night had deposited them there – for it was impossible to imagine Alan Seagull going to such trouble to build anything that was not meant to float.

Perhaps, though, the Seagulls' cottage would have floated. Along one wall the remains of a large rowing boat, hung lengthwise, its sides turned outwards, formed a sort of arbour where Seagull's wife would often sit, nursing one of her younger children. The roof, which tracked this way and that, was made from all manner of planks, spars, areas of sailcloth, exhibiting here and there ridges and bumps that might be an oar, the keel of a boat, or an old chest. Smoke issued at one place from what looked like a lobster pot. Both roof and the outer plank walls were mostly black with tar. Here and there a tatty shutter suggested the existence of windows. By the doorway stood two large painted scallop shells. On the seaward side of the cottage a boat stood and fishing nets hung out to dry, with numerous floats. Beyond that lay a large area of reed beds, which sometimes smelled rank. In brief, to a boy it was a place of magical wonder.

Nor was the owner of this maritime hovel a pauper. Far from it: Alan Seagull owned his own vessel – a single-masted, clinker-built craft, bigger than a fishing boat and with enough hold to carry small cargoes, not only along the coastal waters but even across to France. And although nothing was ever polished or showy, every part of that ship was in perfect working order. To the ship's crew he was the master. Indeed, it was widely believed that Alan Seagull had a bit of money hidden away somewhere. Not like Totton, of course. But if ever he wanted something, it was noticed that he could always pay for it with cash. His family ate well.

Young Jonathan had often hung around the Seagull place, observing the seven or eight children who, like fish in an underwater grotto, would continually dart in and out of it. Watching them with their mother, he sensed a family warmth and happiness that had been missing from his own life. He was walking alone near their cottage one day, when one of them, a boy of about his age, had slipped after him and asked: "Do you want to play?"

Willie Seagull – he was such a funny little boy. He was so skinny you might have thought he was weak; but he was just wiry, and he was ready for anything. Jonathan, like the other sons of the better-off merchants, had to attend a small school run by a schoolmaster whom Burrard and Totton had hired. But on days when he was free, he and Willie would play together and every day had been an adventure. Sometimes they would play in the woods or go up the Forest streams to fish. Willie had taught him to tickle trout. Or they would go down to the mud flats by the sea, or along the coast to where there was a beach.

"Can you swim?" Willie asked.

"I'm not sure," Jonathan replied and soon discovered his new friend could swim like a fish.

"Don't worry. I'll teach you," Willie promised.

On level ground Jonathan could run faster than Willie; but if he tried to catch the smaller boy, Willie could dodge him every time. Willie also brought him into games with the other fishermen's children down by the quay, which made him very proud.

And when, encountering Alan Seagull by the waterfront one afternoon, Willie had said to that magical personage, "This is Jonathan; he's my friend," young Jonathan Totton had known true happiness. "Willie Seagull says I'm his friend," he had told his father proudly that evening. But Henry Totton had said nothing.

Sometimes Willie was taken by his father on his ship and would be gone for a day or two. How Jonathan envied him then. He had not even dared to ask if he could go too; but he was sure the answer would be no.

"Come, Jonathan," the merchant now said, "there is something I want to show you."

The room in which they were standing was not large. At the front, it gave on to the street. In the middle stood a heavy table and around the walls were several oak cupboards and chests, the latter with impressive locks. There was also a large hourglass, of which the merchant was very proud and by which he could tell the precise time. This was the counting house where Henry Totton conducted his business. On the table, Jonathan could see, his father had arranged a number of items and, guessing at once that these were intended for his instruction, he gave an inward sigh. He hated these sessions with his father. He knew they were meant for his own good; but that was just the trouble.

To Henry Totton the world was simple: all things of interest were shapes and numbers. If he saw a shape he understood it. He would make shapes for Jonathan out of parchment or paper. "See," he would show him, "if you turn it this way, it looks different. Or spin it and you produce this figure." He would rotate triangles into cones, build squares into cubes. "Fold it," he would say of a square, "and you have a triangle, or a rectangle, or a little tent." He would invent games for his son with numbers, too, assuming these would delight him. And all poor Jonathan could do, to whom such things seemed dull, was yearn for the long grass in the fields, or the sound of the birds in the woods, or the salty smells down by the wharf.

He would try so hard to be good at these things, to please his father. And just because he was so anxious, his mind would seize up and nothing would make sense and, red-faced, he would say foolish things and see his father try to hide his despair.

Today's lesson, he could see at once, was meant to be straightforward and practical. Spread out on the table were a series of coins.

"Can you tell me," Totton asked quietly, "what they are?"

The first was a penny. That was easy. Then a half-groat: twopence; and a groat: four pence. Standard English coinage. There was a shilling: twelve pence; a ryal, worth more than ten shillings. But the next – a splendid gold coin with the figure of the Archangel Michael killing a dragon on it – Jonathan had not seen before.

"That's an angel," Totton said. "Valuable and rare. But now" – he produced another coin – "what's this?"

Jonathan had no idea. It was a French crown. Then came a ducat and a double ducat. "That's the best coin of all, for sea trade," Totton explained. "Spanish, Italians, Flemings – they'll all take a ducat." He smiled. "Now let me explain the relative value of each. For you will have to learn to use them all."

The use of European currency was not only for the merchant who traded overseas. Foreign coins were found at inland market towns, too. The reason, very simply, was that they were often better value.

The fifteenth century had not been a happy period for the English. Their triumph over the French at Agincourt had not lasted long before that extraordinary figure Joan of Arc, with her mystical visions, had inspired the French to kick the English out again. By the middle of the century when the long drawn-out conflict of the Hundred Years War finally ended, the conflict had become costly and trade had suffered. Then had followed the generation of dispute between the two branches of the royal house, York and Lancaster. If these so-called Wars of the Roses were a series of feudal battles rather than a civil war, they did nothing to promote law and order in the countryside. With civil disorder and land rents falling, it was not surprising if the royal mints, as they have always done when the treasury is empty, clipped the coinage. And although some efforts had been made in recent years to improve its value, Henry Totton was quite right in saying that good English coinage was hard to find. Trade therefore, whenever possible, was carried on in the strongest currency, which was usually foreign.

Henry Totton quietly explained all this to his son. "Those ducats, Jonathan," he concluded, "are what we really need. Do you understand?" And Jonathan nodded his head, even though he was not truly sure whether he did or not.

"Good," the merchant said and gave the boy an encouraging smile. Perhaps, he thought, since Jonathan was in a receptive mood, he would touch upon the question of ports.

Few subjects were dearer to his heart. For a start, there was the whole question of the great Staple port of Calais and its huge financial dealings. And then, of course, there was the vexed question of Southampton. Perhaps, he considered, he would explain Calais first, today.

"Father?"

"Yes, Jonathan?"

"I was thinking. If I stay away from Alan Seagull, I can still play with Willie, can't I?"

Henry Totton stared at him. For a moment he scarcely knew what he could say. Then he shrugged in disgust. He couldn't help it.

"I'm sorry, Father." The boy looked crestfallen. "Shall we go on?"

"No. I think not." Totton looked down at the coins he had spread on the table, then out of the window at the street. "Play with whom you like, Jonathan," he said quietly, and waved him away.

"You should see it, Dad!" Willie Seagull's face was shining as he helped his father, who was mending a fishing net.

It had been the very next morning after Totton had had his conversation with his son that Jonathan had taken Willie Seagull into his house for the first time.

"Was Henry Totton there?" the mariner broke off his humming to enquire.

"No. Just Jonathan and me. And the servants, Dad. They have a cook and a scullion, and a stable boy and two other women . . ."

"Totton's got money, son."

"And I never knew, Dad – those houses, they don't look so wide at the front, but they go back so far. Behind the counting house, there's this great big hall, two floors high, with a gallery down the side. Then there's more rooms at the back."

"I know, son." Totton's was a very typical merchant's house, but young Willie had never been in one before.

"There's this huge cellar. Whole length of the house. He's got all sorts of stuff down there. Barrels of wine, bales of cloth. He's got sacks of wool, too. There's boatloads of it. And then," Willie went on eagerly, "there's this attic under the roof, big as the cellar. He's got sacks of flour and malt, and God knows what up there."

"He would have, Willie."

"And outside, Dad. I never realised how long those gardens are. They go from the street all the way to the lane at the back of the town."

The layout of the Lymington burgage plots followed a pattern very typical in English medieval towns. The street frontage was sixteen and a half feet wide – the measure known as the rod, pole or perch. This was chosen because it was the standard width of the basic ploughing strip of the English common field. A strip two hundred and twenty yards long was called a furlong and four furlongs made an acre. The burgage plots were long and thin, therefore, just like a ploughed field. Henry Totton had two plots together, the second forming a yard with a rented workshop and his own stables. Behind this, his double garden, thirty-three feet wide, stretched back almost half a furlong.

Alan Seagull nodded. He wondered if Willie hankered after this sort of thing himself but, as far as he could see, his son was quite happy just to observe the merchant's way of life. All the same, there were two warnings he decided it was time to give his son. "You know, Willie," he said quietly, "you mustn't think that Jonathan will always be your friend."

"Why, Dad? He's all right."

"I know. But one day things will change. It'll just happen."

"I should mind that."

"Maybe you will, maybe you won't. And there's something else." Alan Seagull looked at his son carefully now.

"Yes, Dad?"

"There's things you mustn't tell him, even if he is your friend."

"You mean . . . ?"

"About our business, son. You know what I mean."

"Oh, that."

"You keep your mouth shut, don't you?"

"'Course I do."

"You mustn't ever talk about that. Not to any Totton. You understand?"

"I know," Willie said. "I won't."

The bet was made that night. It was Geoffrey Burrard who made it, in the Angel Inn.

But Henry Totton took it. He calculated and then he took it. Half of Lymington was witness.

The Angel Inn was a friendly establishment at the top of the High Street; all the classes of Lymington folk used the place, so it was no surprise that Burrard and Totton should have chanced to meet there that evening. The family of both men belonged to the class known as yeomen: free farmers owning their own land, or prosperous local merchants. Both were important figures in the little town – men of worship, as the saying was. Both lived in gabled houses with overhanging upper floors; each owned shares in two or three ships and exported wool through the great Staple entrepôt at Calais. If the Burrards had been in Lymington longer than the Tottons, the Tottons were no less devoted to the interests of the borough. In particular, the two men were united by a common cause.

The big port of Southampton had been a significant town when Lymington was only a hamlet. Centuries before, Southampton had been granted jurisdiction over all the smaller harbours along that part of the southern coast, and the rights to collect any royal customs and taxes on cargoes shipped in and out. The mayor of Southampton was even called "Admiral" in royal documents. But by the time of the Hundred Years War, when Lymington was supplying the king with vessels of its own, this overlordship of the bigger port seemed an offence to Lymington's pride. "We'll collect the customs for ourselves," the Lymington burgesses declared. "We've got our own borough to support." Indeed, there had been sporadic disputes and court cases, now, for over a hundred and sixty years.

The fact that several of the burgesses of Southampton were his kinsmen in no way diluted Totton's commitment to this cause. After all, his own interests lay in Lymington. With his precise mind he went into the whole matter thoroughly and advised his fellow burgesses: "The issue of royal customs is still in Southampton's favour, but if we limit our claims to keelage and wharfage tolls, I'm sure we can win." He was right.

"Where would we be without you, Henry?" Burrard would say approvingly.

He was a big, handsome, florid-faced man, some years older than Totton. Exuberant, where Totton was quiet, impetuous where Totton was careful, the two friends had one other rather surprising passion in common.

Burrard and Totton loved to bet. They frequently bet against each other. Burrard would bet on a hunch and was quite successful. Henry Totton bet on probabilities.

In a way, for Totton, everything was a wager. You calculated the odds. It was what he did with every business transaction; even the great tides of history, it seemed to him, were just a series of bets that had gone one way or the other. Look at the history of Lymington. Back in the days of Rufus the lords of the manor were a mighty Norman family; but when Rufus had been killed in the New Forest and his young brother Henry had taken the throne, they had foolishly supported Henry's other brother, Robert of Normandy. The result? Henry took Lymington and most of their other estates, and granted them to a different family. Since then, for three and a half centuries, the lordship had passed down by family descent until the Wars of the Roses, when they had supported the Lancastrian side. Well enough; until 1461 when the Lancastrians had lost a great battle and the new Yorkist king had beheaded the lord of the manor. So another family held Lymington now.

Even his own modest family had taken part in that dangerous game of fortune. Totton had secretly been rather proud when his favourite uncle had become a follower of that most aristocratic adventurer of all, the Earl of Warwick who, because of his power to change the fortune of whichever side he joined, was known as the Kingmaker. "I'm a yeoman now," he had told Henry before setting off, "but I'll come back a gentleman." Serving the mighty Kingmaker a man might indeed advance to a fortune. Nine years ago, however, just after Easter, the Forest had echoed with the news: "There's been another battle. The Kingmaker's slain. His widow's come to Beaulieu seeking sanctuary." Henry's favourite uncle had been killed, too, and Henry had been sorry. But he did not feel it as a tragedy, nor even as cruel fate. His uncle had made a bet and lost. That was all.

It was a cast of mind that kept him calm and even-tempered in adversity: a strength, on the whole, though his wife had sometimes thought it made him cold.

So when Burrard had proposed the wager, he had calculated carefully.

"I bet you, Henry," his friend had exclaimed, "that the next time you have a vessel going across, fully laden, to the Isle of Wight, I can run a laden boat against you and get back first."

"At least one of your ships is faster than anything I've got," Totton had stated.

"I won't run one of my own."

"Whose, then?"

Burrard considered a moment, then grinned. "I'll run Seagull against you." He watched Totton, eyes gleaming.

"Seagull?" Totton frowned. He thought of his son and the mariner. He preferred to keep some distance between them. "I don't want to have wagers with Seagull, Geoffrey."

"You aren't. You know Seagull never bets anyway." Strangely enough, this was true. The sailor might have a devil-may-care attitude in most of his dealings with the world, but for some reason known only to himself he would never bet. "The wager's with me, Henry. Just you and me." Burrard beamed. "Come on, Henry," he boomed affectionately.

Totton considered. Why was Burrard betting on Seagull? Did he know the relative speeds of the boats? Unlikely. Almost certainly he just had a hunch that Seagull was a cunning rascal who would somehow pull it off. He, on the other hand, had obscrved Scagull's boat many times and had also taken careful note of the speed of a neat little vessel at Southampton in which he had recently acquired a quarter share. The Southampton vessel was definitely a little faster.

"The bet is against Seagull's vessel," he stated. "You have to persuade Seagull to make the crossing for you or the bet's off."

"Agreed," his friend confirmed.

Totton nodded slowly. He was just weighing up the factors when young Jonathan appeared in the doorway. It might not be such a bad thing, he thought, for his son to see his hero the mariner lose a race. "Very well. Five pounds," he said.

"Oh-ho! Henry!" Burrard whooped, causing other faces in the place to turn in their direction. "That's a big one." Five pounds was a large wager indeed.

"Too rich for you?" Totton asked.

"No. No. I didn't say that." Even Burrard's cheerful face was looking a bit taken aback, though.

"If you'd prefer not . . ."

"Done. Five pounds!" Burrard cried. "But you can buy me a drink, Henry, by God, for that."

As young Jonathan advanced, it was obvious to the boy from all the faces round that, whatever it was, his father had just done something that had impressed the men of Lymington.

It was perhaps to hide a trace of nervousness that Geoffrey Burrard, catching sight of young Jonathan, greeted him with unusual bluster. "Ho! Sirrah!" he cried, "What adventures have you been having?"

"None, Sir." Jonathan was not quite sure how to respond, but he knew that Burrard was a man to treat with respect.

"Why, I supposed you'd been out slaying dragons." Burrard smiled at Jonathan and, seeing the boy look doubtful, added: "When I was your age, you know, there was a dragon in the Forest."

"Indeed," Totton nodded. "The Bisterne dragon, no less."

Jonathan looked at them both. He knew the story of the Bisterne dragon. All the Forest children did. But because it concerned a knight and such an antique beast, he had just assumed it was an ancient tale like that of King Arthur. "I thought that was in olden times," he said.

"Actually not." Totton shook his head. "It's quite true," he explained seriously. "There really was a dragon – or so it was called – when I was young. And the knight at Bisterne killed it."

Looking at his face, Jonathan could see that his father was telling the truth. He never teased him anyway. "Oh," Jonathan said, "I didn't know."

"What's more," Burrard continued in a serious tone and with a wink to the company that the boy did not see, "there was another dragon seen over at Bisterne the other day. Probably descended from the first one, I should think. They're going to hunt it, I believe, so you'd better be quick if you want to see it."

"Really?" Jonathan stared at him. "Isn't it dangerous?"

"Yes. But they killed the last one, didn't they? Quite a sight, I should think, when it's flying."

Henry Totton smiled and shook his head. "You'd better get home," he said kindly and kissed his son. So Jonathan obediently left.

By the time Henry Totton came home himself, he'd forgotten about the dragon.

They set out soon after dawn. Willie would have been ready to go the day before, as soon as he heard about it, but as Jonathan pointed out, they needed a full day, starting at dawn. For it was a twelve-mile walk each way to Bisterne, where the dragon was.

"I'll be with Willie until dusk," he had said to the cook as he slipped out quickly, before anyone could ask him where he was going.

The journey, although quite long, was a very easy one. The manor of Bisterne lay in the southern portion of the Avon valley below Ringwood near the place called Tyrrell's Ford. So they had to cross only the western half of the Forest, move along its southern edge and then descend into the valley beyond. Leaving early, even at a walk, they could be there by mid-morning, with no need to return until late afternoon.

Willie was waiting for him at the top of the street. Anxious to get well away before anyone stopped them, they went quickly along the lane that led through the fields and meadows of Old Lymington, crossed a stream by a small mill and within half an hour were passing the manor of Arnewood, which lay between the villages of Hordle and Sway.

It was a clear, bright morning, promising a warm day. The countryside west of Lymington was one of intimate little fields with hedgerows and small oaks in rolling dips and dells. The pale-green leaves were starting to break out on the bare branches; white blossom from the hedges was being scattered on the lane by the light breeze. They passed a ploughed field whose furrows were receiving a visit from a flapping mass of seagulls.

To anyone familiar with the inhabitants of Lymington, the two boys passing Arnewood manor would have been easy to identify, since each was a perfect miniature of his father: the serious face of the merchant on the one boy, the cheerful chinlessness of the mariner on the other, were almost comical. Within an hour, however, they were leaving the world of Lymington well behind. They came to a wood through which there was a narrow track. And then, passing through a belt of stunted ash and birch, they emerged on to the wide open world of the Forest heath.

"Do you think," Willie asked nervously, "the dragon comes here?"

"No," said Jonathan. "He doesn't come over this way." He had never seen his friend hesitant before. He felt rather proud of himself.

It was a five-mile walk along the southern edge of the heath, but the going was easy on the close-cropped, peaty forest turf. The morning sun was behind them, catching the sparkling sheen of the dew on the grass. The great sweep of the heath was sprinkled with the sharp yellow stare of the gorse brakes. Here and there, on the little hillocks away on their right, small round clumps of holly trees could be seen. Holly holms the English had anciently called them. But more recently they had acquired another name. For since the deer and ponies ate their overhanging branches as far up as they could – to the browse line as it was termed – the trees had each acquired a mushroom shape and, taken together, a clump of holly trees on a hillock appeared to have a sort of hanging brim.Therefore the Forest folk nowadays referred to them as holly hats.

They walked for an hour and a half on the springy turf. They had walked nearly five miles along the edge of the heath when they came to the big rise known as Shirley Common. And then, as they reached the crest, they stopped.

The Avon valley lay below.

It was a richer world. First a small field, where bracken had been cut and heaped and some goats were now browsing; then groves of oak and beech and further fields swept gracefully down the slopes, until they reached the parkland and lush meadows along the wide banks of the Avon, of whose silver waters, here and there through the trees, they caught a tanta-lising glimpse. Then, beyond the valley, the low ridges of Dorset stretched into a bluish haze. You could see at once that this was a landscape fit for knights and ladies, and courtly love. And dragons.

To the north, however, two miles away across a broad sweep of brown and open heath, the wooded ridge rose up, behind which lay the dark forest village of Burley.

"I think," said Jonathan, "we might see the dragon now." He looked at Willie. "Are you afraid?"

"Are you?"

"No."

"Where does the dragon live?" asked Willie.

"There." Jonathan pointed to the long Burley ridge with its northern promontory of Castle Hill. The ridge at this time was known as Burley Beacon.

"Oh." Willie looked at the place. "It's quite close," he said.

It had probably been a solitary wild boar. There were not many left in England, now. They had all been hunted away. There were pigs that ran in the Forest, of course, in the mast season every autumn; and occasionally one of these might turn wild and be mistaken for a boar. But the real wild boar, with its grizzled hair, powerful shoulders and flashing tusks, was a ter-rible creature. Even the bravest Norman or Plantagenet noble, with his hounds and his huntsmen, might know fear when this huge ball of fury charged out of his cover towards him. It was the most exciting chase, though. All over Europe the boar hunt was the noblest aristocratic sport, after the joust. The boar's head was the centrepiece of any great feast.

But the island kingdom of England, though graced with many forests, lacked the vast empty tracts of France or the German lands. If a wild boar lived, his presence would be known and noblemen would hunt him. Four centuries after the Norman Conqueror came, few English boars remained in the south. Now and then, however, one would appear. For some reason it might not be caught. And over the years, perhaps living in isolation, it could grow to a huge size.

It seems likely that this is what occurred in the Avon valley some time around 1460.

The manor of Bisterne lay in a beautiful setting on the broad valley floor, on the forest side of the Avon a little way north of Tyrrell's Ford. Bede's Thorn it had been called in Saxon times, which had evolved in stages to Bisterne. Kept by its Saxon owner after the Conquest, it had passed by inheritance to the noble family of Berkeley from the western county of Gloucestershire; and it was Sir Maurice Berkeley, married to the niece of no less a personage than mighty Warwick the Kingmaker, who, just before the start of the Wars of the Roses, had often delighted to stay at his Bisterne manor and hunt in the Avon valley with his hounds.

The boar, it seems, had a lair somewhere up on Burley Beacon, overlooking the valley, and had been known to raid the farms there. Some time around Martinmass, when most of the livestock were slaughtered, it had come down to Bisterne, following the streams that led down from Castle Hill, until, near the manor house, it had come to Bunny Brook. By the manor farm it had found milk pails cooling in the stream, taken the milk, and then killed one of the farm's remaining cows.

Its appearance at this time would have been terrifying indeed. It was not only the black beast's blazing eyes, frothing mouth and tusks. If thwarted, the wild boar has a hideous scream; its breath in the cold November air would have steamed; boars also move across the ground with the strangest silence. As it ran across the Bisterne fields by the pale light of dawn it would have seemed an unearthly creature.

And no wonder, one cold November night, the brave Sir Maurice Berkeley went out to fight the monster. The encounter took place in the valley and it was bloody. The knight's two favourite hounds died in the mêlée and Sir Maurice, having killed the beast himself, received wounds that became infected. By Christmas he was dead.

Some legends are invented later, from half-forgotten events; others spring to life at once. Within a year, the whole county knew of Sir Maurice Berkeley's battle with the Bisterne dragon. They knew the dragon flew over the fields from Burley Beacon. They knew the knight had killed him single-handed and died of the dragon's poison. And if the wider world was soon distracted by the knightly dramas of the Wars of the Roses, in the New Forest and the Avon valley, as the years passed, men remembered: "We had a dragon not so long ago."

It was another two miles from the crest of Shirley Common to Bisterne manor, and the boys took their time descending. Sometimes they could see the spur of Burley Beacon, at others it was hidden; but they kept an eye out in that direction in case the dragon should take wing from its hill and come flying towards them.

"What'll we do if we see it coming?" asked Willie.

"Hide," said Jonathan.

On the lower part of the slope the track led through woodland. The slanting morning sunshine made a pale-green light in the undergrowth. Mosses gathered by the bases of the trees, ivy on the trunks. They heard a pigeon cooing. The path veered left out of the trees and led down the side of the wood. A grey hen scuttled across in front of them from the long grass. And they had only descended another hundred yards when suddenly on their right there was a flapping sound and, in a flash of dark metallic blue, a blackcock with his lyre tail, disturbed by something, burst over their heads out of the trees.

"That made you jump, Willie," said Jonathan.

"So did you."

Soon after this they came down on to the open valley floor and saw at once that they had entered a world where a dragon might appear at any time.

The world of Bisterne was very flat. Its large fields stretched over two miles westwards to the Avon's silver waters which, as they often did in spring, had spread out over the lush water meadows in a magical, liquid sheen. The manor house – it was more of a hunting lodge for the Berkeley knights, really – was a single timber-and-plaster hall with a stable yard attached, standing by itself in the middle of open parkland where cattle grazed and rabbits in an enclosed warren bobbed on the close-cropped grass. Away in the distance were the slopes behind which Burley Beacon lay; and dotting the landscape from hedgerow and field, single oaks or elms were holding out their bare arms as though expecting the winged monster to fly down from the Beacon and perch upon them.

It was quiet. Occasionally, they heard the lowing of cattle; once, the sawing sound of swans' wings, beating over the distant water. And now and then a hoarse cawing and sudden flapping would come from the crows in the trees. But most of the time Bisterne lay in silence, as though all nature were awaiting a visitation.

Not many folk were about in the fields. A few hundred yards south of the manor hall lay a small thatched farmhouse with a slip of ash trees by the brook nearby. Coming down the cattle drove beside it they met a cowherd who, when they asked him politely where the dragon had been slain, smiled and pointed to a field behind the farm. "That's Dragon's Field," he told them. "By Bunny Brook."

They wandered about for an hour or more along the paths and down to the river. They could see by the sun that it must be noon when Willie announced that he was hungry.

Just down river, at the old cattle crossing of Tyrrell's Ford, there were some cottages and an old forge. Saying they had come from nearby Ringwood, so as not to draw any suspicion on to themselves, Jonathan begged some bread and cheese, which a woman in one of the cottages gave them readily enough. He asked her also about the dragon.

"Twenty years or more since he was killed," she said.

"Yes. But what about the new one?"

"I haven't seen that myself," she said, with a smile.

"Perhaps it isn't there," said Willie to Jonathan, as they ate their bread and cheese by the river.

"She only said she hadn't seen it," Jonathan replied.

After they had eaten they slept for a while in the warm sun. It was past mid-afternoon when they went back up the drove by the farmhouse. If they felt daunted by the long walk home, they tried not to show it. They knew they needed to step out now to be safely back at dusk.

They were halfway up the drove when they encountered the cows, about half a dozen of them, being driven to the farmhouse by a boy. He was older than they were, perhaps twelve, and eyed them curiously. "Where d'you come from?"

"Never mind."

"Want a fight?"

"No."

"Well, I got to drive these cows anyway. What're you doing here?"

"Came to see the dragon."

"Dragon's Field's over there."

'We know. They told us there was another dragon now, but there isn't."

The boy looked at them thoughtfully. His eyes narrowed. "Yes there is. That's why I have to get these cows in." He paused and nodded. "Comes over every evening, just like the last one did. From Burley Beacon."

"Really?" Jonathan searched his face. "You're making it up. Nobody'd stay here."

"No, it's true. Honest. Sometimes he don't do much. But he's killed dogs and calves. You can see him flying at sunset. Breathes fire, too. Horrible-looking thing, really."

"Where does he go?"

"Always the same place. Down into Dragon's Field. So we stay away from there, that's all."

He turned away then, tapping the nearest cow with his stick, while the two boys went on. They didn't speak for a moment or two.

"I think he was lying," said Willie.

"Maybe."

Now they were returning, it did not seem to take long to get back up to the crest of Shirley Common. Although the sun was not yet sinking in the afternoon sky, there was just a hint of chill in the April breeze and a tinge of orange in the golden haze to the west. Once again the whole valley from the Avon river up to the ridge of Burley Beacon was stretched out before them in a panorama.

"We'd get a good view from here," said Jonathan.

"We'll get back late," said Willie.

"Depends when it comes. It might come now."

Willie didn't reply.

Jonathan knew his companion hadn't been as keen to go as he was. Willie had done it for friendship's sake. Not that he was afraid – or no more afraid than he was, anyway. In most of their games, especially playing by the river or anything to do with water, it was Willie with his funny chinless face who was the dare-devil and Jonathan who was cautious. And he knew that he wouldn't have dared to come there alone. But as the long day wore on Jonathan had also discovered something else in himself that he hadn't known about before: a quiet, driving determination rather different from his friend's free nature.

"If we get back after curfew," Willie said, "we'll get whipped."

Even in the villages, the curfew – the *couvre-feu* when the fires were damped down for the night and all men were supposed to be indoors – was generally observed. After all, there was nothing much you could do in the deep darkness of the countryside anyway, unless it was some poaching or an illicit affair. In Lymington, men like Totton might cross to their houses from the Angel after dark, but generally the streets were empty. The curfew bell sounding from the church signalled a long silence.

Jonathan had never been whipped before. Most boys were, from time to time, by parents or schoolmasters but, perhaps because of his nature and the muted atmosphere that his mother's illness had brought to the house, he had escaped this normal punishment. "I don't care," he said. "But you can go back if you want, Willie."

"And leave you alone?"

"It's all right. You go on. You've got time."

Willie sighed. "No. I'll stay."

Jonathan gave his friend a smile and realised for the first time that he himself was capable of being ruthless.

"What if there isn't a dragon any more, Jonathan?"

"Then we won't see it."

But what if there was? They waited an hour. The sun was

sinking across the valley now. A faint mist rose from the distant water-meadows. The heath that swept down to the north of them a burnished, orange tint. But the line of Burley Beacon, catching the sun's full rays, was gleaming gold as though it might ignite.

"Watch the Beacon, Willie," Jonathan said and ran off down the slope.

It was only two hundred yards to the edge of the field. For some reason the bracken had been cut there and raked into heaps by the hedgerow, yet never carted away. It was easy enough to build a compact little shelter with a good, thick bed of bracken to lie on. If bracken made bedding for animals, he reasoned, it would for humans, too. When he was done he went back to Willie.

"We won't get home tonight. It's too late."

"I guessed that."

"I've made us a shelter."

"All right."

"Did you see anything?"

"No."

Sunset came and Burley Beacon turned fiery red, and it was easy to imagine a dragon, like a phoenix, arising from its embers into the evening sky. Then the sun sank and the western sky turned crimson, and the fire on Burley Beacon went out. Above, the first stars appeared.

"I think it may come now," said Jonathan. He had quite a clear picture of what it would be like: about the size of a cow, he supposed, with a large wingspan. It would be green and scaly. The wings would sound like a huge swan when they beat and there would be a hissing noise from the fire coming out of its mouth. That was the main thing you'd see in the dark. He estimated it would fly across about a mile in front of them on its way down to Bisterne.

The sun was gone. The stars were brightening in the sapphire sky. The line of Burley Beacon looked dark and dangerous as the boys both waited, their eyes fixed upon it.

When, at dusk, there was still no sign of Jonathan, Henry Totton had reluctantly walked down to the quay and approached the disreputable dwelling of Alan Seagull. Had he seen his son? No, the mariner replied, a little perplexed; both boys had been missing since dawn and he had no idea where they were.

At first Totton had been afraid they might have gone out in a boat, but Seagull was soon able to discover that no boat was missing. Could they have fallen into the river somewhere?

"My boy's a strong swimmer," Seagull said. "What about yours?"

And Totton realised to his shame that he did not know.

Then word came that someone had seen them leave the top end of the town in the early morning. Could they have encountered danger in the Forest? It seemed unlikely. There had been no wolves reported for years. It was early for snakes.

"I suppose," said Alan Seagull glumly, "they could have fallen in a mill-race."

By curfew time the mayor and bailiff had been consulted, and two search parties had been equipped with torches. One had gone to the mills of Old Lymington; the other through the woods above the town. They were prepared to search, if necessary, all night.

The shelter was quite effective. By packing the bracken close, they kept most of the moisture out. The night was not chilly, fortunately, and by lying together they kept warm. They had discovered a bramble and some stinging nettles in the dark, but apart from that, and the fact that they were extremely hungry, their sufferings were not great.

There was no moon that night. The stars, peeping from behind shrouds of cloud, were very bright. They had waited for a long time for the dragon, but by the time their eyes were drooping they had decided that, if it was residing at Burley, it was not coming over tonight.

"You'll wake me if you see it," Jonathan made Willie promise.

"And you wake me."

But once they were settled down, perhaps because of the dew forming on their faces, or through fear of animals disturbing them, neither boy slept for a while. And it was as they were gazing up at the night sky that Willie raised a subject they had discussed the day before. "You really think your dad's boat from Southampton will beat my dad's?"

"I don't know," said Jonathan truthfully. The huge bet had been the talk of Lymington the previous day. After a short pause, however, thinking he owed it to his friend and his family to give them the best information he could, he added: "I think if my father's bet so much on the race he must be sure he's going to win. He's very careful. I don't think your father ought to bet on winning, Willie."

"He never bets."

"Why's that?"

"Says he takes enough risks anyway without betting as well."

"What sort of risks?"

"Never mind. I can't tell you."

"Oh." Jonathan thought. "What can't you tell me?" It sounded interesting.

Willie said nothing for a bit. "I'll tell you something," he said finally.

"What?"

"My dad's boat can go faster than your father thinks. But you mustn't tell him."

"Why?"

Willie was silent. Jonathan asked him why again, but got no answer. He gently kicked him. Willie said nothing.

"I'll pinch you," Jonathan offered.

"Don't."

"All right. But tell me."

Willie took a deep breath. "Do you promise not to tell?" he began.

All Lymington was buzzing when Jonathan Totton and Willie Seagull returned safely in the morning, which they were able to do quite early since they had hurried along the Forest edge as soon as the first hint of dawn had allowed them to see their way.

All Lymington rejoiced, all Lymington was curious. And when all Lymington discovered that they had been up all night and worried themselves half to death because the two boys had gone looking for a dragon, all Lymington was outraged.

At least, they claimed they were. The women all said that the boys should be soundly whipped. The men, remembering their own boyhoods, agreed, but were more or less lenient. The mayor told the fathers firmly that if they didn't deal with their sons he would take them to the whipping post himself. Everyone privately blamed Burrard for telling them foolish stories about dragons in the first place. So Burrard hid in his house.

Henry Totton, before delivering sentence on his son, explained to him carefully that this showed the dangers of mixing with people like Willie Seagull, who had obviously led him astray; and was astonished when his son stoutly assured him that the whole expedition had been his idea and that it was he who had made Willie stay the night. At first he was unable to believe it, but when finally he did, his grief and disappointment were very great. For once, however, Jonathan really didn't care.

Alan Seagull took his son by the ear and hauled him away to the quay and along to their strange house into which they disappeared together. There he took down a strap from the wall and hit Willie twice, after which he was laughing so much that his wife had to finish the job for him.

The punishment of Jonathan, however, was a sadder affair. Nobody laughed. Henry Totton did what he knew he must do. He did it not only with a sense of mystification at the whole episode but also with the belief that it could only make this strange boy hate him. So that Jonathan, although the whipping hurt, was rather proud of the whole affair; while his poor father ended the session in a far greater agony than any his son felt.

He is all I have, the merchant thought, and now I have lost him. Because of a dragon. Nor – so little did the poor man know of childhood – had he any idea what to do with Jonathan next.

It was a source of complete amazement to him therefore, the next day, when his son quite cheerfully asked him: "Will you take me to the salterns with you when you go there next time, Father?"

And anxious not to lose the chance of a reconciliation he answered quickly: "I'm going there this very afternoon."

The unusual warmth of the last few days had changed to more typical April weather. Small white and grey clouds crossed the washed blue sky. The breeze was damp; occasional gusts brought a light spotting of rain, as Henry Totton and Jonathan, having walked to the church at the top of the High Street, turned left and descended the long lane that led down towards the sea.

The coastal strip below the borough was a bare and windswept place. From Lymington quay, the river's small estuary continued south for about a mile until it emerged fully into the Solent. On the right side, below the small ridge on which the borough stood, and extending south-west for two and a half miles to the little inlet and hamlet of Keyhaven, lay the wide, watery flats of Pennington Marshes.

It was an empty-seeming place: green wastes of tufted marsh grass, little gorses soaked with salty mist, small thorn trees stunted and warped by the sea breeze dotted the landscape. Beyond, the long line of the Isle of Wight hovered across the Solent, its blue-green slopes turning into chalk cliffs away on the right. You might have thought the place was habitation only for the gulls and curlews and wild duck upon the marshes. But you would have been wrong.

For down near the shore a string of small buildings and a score or more of what looked like tiny windmills, their sails at present motionless, told a different story, reminding you that it was this marshland that provided the most important commodity the merchants of Lymington shipped: salt.

There had been salt pans there since Saxon times. The need for salt was huge. There was no other way of preserving flesh or fish. When the farmers killed their pigs and cattle in November, the meat had all to be salted so it could be used during the winter. If the king wanted venison from the Forest for his court or to feed his troops, it must be salted. England produced vast quantities and it all came from the sea.

Henry Totton owned a saltern on Pennington Marshes. They could see its boiling house and wind pumps as soon as they started along the gravelly path across the levels. It was one of a group down by the shoreline. It did not take them long to reach the place.

Jonathan liked the salterns; perhaps it was because of where they were, so close to the sea. The first thing needed for making salt was a large feeder pond, set just in from the shoreline, into which the sea water could flow at high tide. Jonathan loved to watch the sea come rippling in down the curving channels. He and Willie had once made a similar construction of their own when they were playing on a sandy beach along the coast.

The salt pans that came next were carefully built. They were, in fact, a huge single basin – shallow and dead level – divided into small ponds, about twenty feet square, by mud banks six inches high and just wide enough for a man to walk on. Water from the feeder pond was baled into these with wooden scoops; but they were only filled about three inches deep. From here, the salt-making began.

It was very simple. The water had to evaporate. This would work only in the summer and, the warmer the weather and hotter the sun, the more salt you could produce. The season usually began at the very end of April. In a good year it might last sixteen weeks. Once, in a very bad year, it had lasted only two.

The idea was not to leave the water to evaporate in a single pan.

"Evaporation takes time, Jonathan," his father had told him long ago, "and we need a continuous supply."

So the method was to move the water up a line of pans, so that it gradually evaporated and achieved a higher salt concentration as it went. To keep it moving along the pans, they used wind pumps.

They were very simple; they had probably been used on the marshes below the New Forest in Saxon times and were hardly different from those known in the Middle East two thousand years before. They were about ten feet high, with a simple cross carrying four little sails like a windmill. As the sails went round they drove a cam, which operated a rudimentary water pump below. From shallow pan to shallow pan the water was pumped along, until it reached the final part of the process at the boiling house.

Totton's reason for going out today was to make a thorough inspection so that any repairs needed after the winter could be made in good time. He and Jonathan went over it together.

"The channel to the feeder pond needs dredging," remarked the boy.

"Yes." Henry nodded. Several of the mud walls in the salt pans needed mending, too.

Here Jonathan made himself particularly useful, walking lightly over every one of the narrow barriers, marking each crack he found with a splash of whitewash. "Don't we have to clean out all the bottoms, too?" he asked.

"We do," his father said.

The final process was the actual salt-making. By the time the evaporated sea water reached the last salt pan it was a highly concentrated brine. Now the salt-maker would place a lead-weighted ball into the pan. When it floated, he would know the brine was thick enough. Opening a sluice, he would allow the brine to flow down into the boiling house.

This was just a shed, with strengthened walls. In here was the boiling pan, a huge vat over eight feet across, under which there was a furnace, usually heated by charcoal or wood. Here the vat gradually boiled away all the water, leaving a great piecrust of salt.

The boiling was almost continuous during the salt-making season. Each boiling, or turn, took eight hours. Starting on Sunday night and ending on Saturday morning, this allowed sixteen turns a week. At this rate Henry Totton's boiling pan was able to produce almost three tons of salt each week. It was crusty and not very pure, but it was pure enough.

"We burn nineteen bushels for each ton of salt produced," Totton remarked. "So," he started to calculate for the boy, "if the cost of fuel per bushel is . . ."

It was only moments before Jonathan's concentration had started to wander. He didn't enjoy the boiling house as much as the rest. When the boiling was going on, the clouds of steam, impregnated with salt, were blinding. His throat would feel on fire after a while. The area all round the boiling house would grow hot and cloudy. He would run away whenever he could to the fresh sea breeze, the curlews and seagulls along the shore by the feeder pond.

His father had just finished explaining how to calculate the total profit achievable if the weather held good for the full sixteen-week season when he noticed that Jonathan was looking at him thoughtfully.

"Father, can I ask you something?"

"Of course, Jonathan."

"Only" – he hesitated – "it's about secrets."

Totton stared. Secrets? It was nothing to do with salt, then. Nothing to do with anything he had been trying to teach the boy in the last half-hour. Had Jonathan taken in anything he'd said? The all too familiar wave of disappointment and irritation started to sweep over him. He fought to control himself, not to let it appear in his face. He wished he could bring himself to smile, but he couldn't. "What sort of secrets, Jonathan?"

"Well . . . It's like this. If someone tells you something important, but they make you promise not to tell anyone, because it's a secret; and if you wanted to tell someone, because it might be important; should you keep it a secret?"

"Did you promise to keep a secret?"

"Yes."

"And is the secret something bad? Something criminal?"

"Well." Jonathan had to consider. Was the secret that his friend Willie Seagull had told him so bad?

It concerned Alan Seagull and his boat. The secret was that it could run faster than Totton thought. And the reason for that was that Seagull was in the habit of making some very swift and illicit voyages indeed.

His cargo on these occasions was wool. Despite the increasing cloth trade, it was still wool that was the backbone of England's export trade and her wealth. In order to ensure his treasury profited from it, the king insisted, as his predecessors had done, that the entire trade was funnelled through the great entrepôt, known as the Staple, of Calais. On all Staple wool duty was paid. When the monks of Beaulieu sent their vast clip abroad – mostly through Southampton, a little through Lymington – or when Totton bought wool from Sarum merchants, it all went through the Staple and was duly taxed.

When Alan Seagull made his illicit runs for other, less honourable exporters, he did so at night, slipping across from coast to coast, paying neither duty nor heed, for which he was well paid. Others did the same all along the coast. It was known as owling. It was illegal but every child in every harbour knew that such things took place.

"It could get someone in trouble," Jonathan said carefully. "But I don't think it's very bad."

"Like poaching," his father guessed.

"Like that."

"If you gave your word, you should keep it," said Totton. "No one will ever trust you if you don't."

"Only . . ." Still Jonathan was uncertain. "What if you wanted to tell someone to help them?"

"How help them?"

"If you had a friend and it would save them money."

"To break your word and betray a confidence? Certainly not, Jonathan."

"Oh."

"Does that answer your question?"

"Yes. I think so." Although Jonathan still frowned a little. He wished there were some way of warning his father that he was going to lose his bet.

There were times during the next two weeks when Alan Seagull found it hard not to laugh.

The whole of Lymington was placing bets. Most were small, a few pence usually; but several merchants had a mark or even more on the race. Why were they betting? Often, the mariner guessed, it was just because they didn't want to be left out. Some reckoned Seagull's small craft would outsail the bigger ship because of the shortness of the crossing; others made elaborate calculations based on the likely weather. Others again put their trust in the soundness of Totton's judgement and followed him.

"The more they talk the less they know," Seagull pointed out to his son. "And none of 'em really knows anything."

Then there were the bribes. Hardly a day passed without someone coming to the mariner with an offer. "I've got half a mark on your boat, Alan. There'll be a shilling in it for you if you win." More interesting were the people who offered him money to lose. "I don't know the Southampton men," one merchant told him frankly. "And besides, the only way to be sure of the result is if you promise to lose."

"It's funny," Seagull remarked to Willie. "All these people come at you like waves and you can just sail across them. The way things are now, if I win I get paid and if I lose I get paid." He grinned. "Makes no difference, see? You remember that, son," he added seriously. "Let them do the betting. You just say nothing and take the money."

More impressive was Burrard. At the end of the first week he told Alan: "A mark to you if you win." At the end of the second: "I'm in deeper now. Two marks."

"Is he stupid?" Willie asked.

"No, son. He ain't stupid. Just rich."

Totton, meanwhile, remained as calm and quiet as usual. This Seagull respected. "I don't like him, son," he confessed. "But he knows when to keep his mouth shut."

"So are you going to win, Dad?" Willie asked. But to this, infuriatingly, his father would only reply by humming a little sea ditty to himself.

Willie did better, however, when he asked his father if he could go with him for the race, for after a pause, and looking at him with amusement, his father, to Willie's great surprise agreed.

This was a great prize. He shared it with his friends, who were duly envious. Jonathan's eyes opened wide and every day asked Willie again: "Is it really true you're sailing? I know," he would add confidentially, "that you're going to win." It was heaven.

But was his father going to win? Willie had boasted to Jonathan that he would, that night out at Bisterne, and he certainly wasn't going to take it back. But he wished he knew what his father was really up to.

The truth of the matter was that Alan Seagull didn't know himself. Certainly, he hadn't the least intention of publicly disclosing his vessel's speed. If that were needed to win, he would cheerfully lose. But you never knew with the sea. Something might happen to the other boat. The sea itself would decide, and chance, and his own free will. He hadn't a care in the world. Until one evening, three days before the race.

He knew something was up the moment he saw young Willie, and the sheepish way he was approaching; but even so, he was completely taken aback by the boy's question.

"Dad, for the race, can Jonathan come in the boat, too?"

Jonathan? Jonathan Totton? When his father was betting on the other boat? The mariner stared in amazement.

"If his father says yes, that is," Willie added.

Which he certainly won't, thought Alan.

"I said I thought you might let him. He isn't heavy," Willie explained.

"Let him go in the other boat, then."

"He doesn't want to. He wants to come with me. And anyway . . ."

"Anyway what?"

Willie hesitated, then said quietly: "Dad, the Southampton boat's going to lose isn't it?"

"So you say, my son." Alan started to smile, but then a thought hit him. "Willie?" He looked at his son carefully. "You think I'm going to win?"

"'Course I do, Dad."

"Is that why he wants to come with us, then? Because you told him we'd win?"

"I don't know, Dad." Willie looked awkward. "Maybe."

"Did you tell him about our business?"

"No, Dad. I mean, not really." There was a pause. "I may have said something." He looked down, then raised his eyes hopefully to his father again. "He won't tell, Dad. I swear."

Alan Seagull said nothing. He was thinking.

There were quite a few people in Lymington who knew Alan Seagull's business. His crew for a start. One or two merchants also – for the obvious reason that they gave him the illicit wool to carry. But Totton wasn't one of them and never would be. And the rule in the business was very simple: you didn't talk to people like Totton. For sooner or later, if people like him knew, things would get out; boats would be stopped, men fined, business disrupted and, strangely intangible but perhaps most important of all, freedom would be limited.

Did Totton know? Perhaps not yet. What he really needed, Seagull thought, was some time alone with Jonathan. He'd be able to tell, he guessed, if the boy had told his father. If he had, there was nothing to be done. If not . . . he mused. If the boy were out at sea, some men in his situation would quietly tip him overboard. He shrugged to himself. There was no chance of Totton allowing him to come anyway. "Don't say any more about our business. Just keep your mouth shut," he ordered his son, and waved him away. He needed to think some more.

Jonathan found his father sitting in an upright chair in the hall, under the gallery. Totton was asleep.

The gallery passage that ran from the front to the back of the bigger Lymington houses was quite an impressive feature, but it was not handsome. Although two storeys high, the central hall was quite narrow, so that the gallery seemed to overlook a rather cramped covered area. Since the death of his wife, instead of going at the end of his workday to the pleasant parlour at the back of the house, which looked over the garden, and where his wife had liked to sit, Totton had taken to sitting in a chair in the rather awkward space of the hall. There he would remain until it was time to eat dinner, which he punctiliously did with his son. Sometimes he just sat staring quietly ahead; sometimes he dozed a little. He was dozing when Jonathan approached him.

Jonathan, after standing in front of him for several moments, touched his wrist and gently asked: "Father?"

Totton woke with a perceptible start and stared at the boy. He had not been sleeping deeply but it took him a moment to focus his mind. Jonathan had that slightly doubtful look on his face, which suggests a child is hoping for a permission he expects to be refused.

"Yes, Jonathan."

"Can I ask you something?"

Totton prepared himself. He was fully awake now. He sat up straight and tried to smile. Perhaps, if the request were not too foolish, he would surprise the boy and grant it. He would like to please him. "You may."

"Well. The thing is . . ." Jonathan took a deep breath. "You know the race between your ship from Southampton and Seagull's boat?"

"I do indeed."

"Well. I don't think he'll say yes anyway, but I was

wondering: if Alan Seagull said I could, do you think it would be all right if I sailed with him?"

"In Seagull's boat?" Totton gazed at him. It was a few moments before he could quite take it in. "For the race?"

"Yes. It's only to the Isle of Wight," Jonathan added helpfully. "I mean, we don't go out to sea, do we?"

Totton did not answer. He couldn't. He stared away from Jonathan, towards the door of the parlour where his wife used to sit. "Do you not know," he enquired at last, "that my bet is against Seagull's boat? You want to sail with my opponents? With a man I had asked you to avoid?"

Jonathan was silent. He was really only thinking that he wanted to sail with Willie; but he wasn't sure if he should say so.

"How will that look to people, do you suppose?" Totton quietly asked him.

"I don't know." Jonathan felt crestfallen. He had not thought about what other people might think. He did not know.

Henry Totton continued to stare away. He felt a sense of mortification and of rage. He could hardly bring himself to look at his only son, but finally he did. "I am sorry, Jonathan," he said softly, "that you do not feel any sense of loyalty to me, or to your family." Which, God help me, he thought, is only me now, anyway.

And suddenly Jonathan understood that he had hurt his father. And he was sorry for him. But he did not know what to do.

Then Henry Totton, overcome with the uselessness, the utter hopelessness of achieving love between himself and his son, shrugged his shoulders in despair and exclaimed: "Do what you like, Jonathan. Sail with whom you wish."

And then there was a struggle inside the boy, between his love and his desire. He knew he should say he would not go, or at least offer to sail in the other ship. This was the only way to tell his father he loved him; although he was not sure, even then, that the cold merchant would believe it. But his desire was to go with Willie and the carefree mariner, and to sail the sea in their little craft with its secret speed. And as he was only ten, desire won. "Oh, thank you, Father," he said and kissed him, and ran out to tell Willie.

• • •

Willie appeared the next morning. "My dad says you can come," he reported gleefully. Henry Totton was out, so he did not hear these good tidings.

There had been a brief April shower, but now the sun was shining. The news was far too exciting to contemplate indoors, so it was not long before the two boys set off together to find amusement. Their first plan was to walk a couple of miles northwards and play in the woods at Boldre; but they had not gone a mile when, as the lane dipped down a gentle incline, their attention was caught by something on the lip of higher ground just ahead.

"Let's go into the rings," said Jonathan.

The place that had attracted them was a curious feature of the Lymington landscape; it was a small earthwork inclosure set on a low knoll from which it overlooked the nearby river. Buckland Rings it was known as – although its low, grassy walls formed a rectangle rather than a circle. Dating from Celtic times, before the Romans came, it might have been a fort to guard the river, or a cattle pen, or both; but while the borough of Lymington might well contain descendants of the folk who built it, even the memory of this earlier settlement had probably been forgotten over a thousand years before. Animals grazed on the sweet grass within and children played on its banks.

It was a good place to play. The earlier rain had made the grassy banks slippery and Jonathan had just defended the fortress from assault by Willie for the third time when they saw a handsome figure riding down the lane who, when he caught sight of them, gave a cheerful wave, dismounted and strode towards them.

"So," he said genially, "today you battle by land and soon your fathers will battle by sea."

Richard Albion was a very pleasant gentleman. His ancestors had been called Alban, but somehow, over the last two centuries, like some forest stream that gradually alters its course, the pronunciation of the name had shifted from Alban to the more comfortable Albion within whose banks, so to speak, it had been flowing very easily for several generations. As foresters, they had maintained a position among the gentry

of the area and married accordingly. Albion's own wife was
one of the Button family who held estates near Lymington. In
late middle-age now, with his grey hair and bright-blue eyes,
Richard Albion bore a striking resemblance to his ancestor
Cola the Huntsman of four centuries before. A naturally generous man, he would often stop to give some child a farthing;
he was familiar with most of the inhabitants of Lymington by
sight; and so he knew at once who the two boys playing on
Buckland Rings must be. He chatted to them very amiably,
therefore, and discussed the coming race.

"Will you watch it, Sir?" asked Jonathan.

"Indeed I shall. Wouldn't miss it for the world. Why, the
whole area will be there, I should think. As a matter of fact,"
he added, "I was just in Lymington, trying to place a bet on the
race myself. But I couldn't find any takers." He laughed. "The
whole town's so deep in already that nobody dares bet any
more. See what your father's done to the place, Jonathan
Totton!"

"Which way were you betting, Sir?" asked Willie.

"Well," the gentleman answered him honestly, "I'm afraid I
was betting on the Southampton ship, not because I have any
idea who will win, but because I like to be on the same side as
Henry Totton."

"And" – Jonathan was not sure if it was proper to ask, but
Albion was not a man to take offence – "how much would you
bet, Sir?"

"Five pounds, I offered," Albion replied with a chuckle.
"And no one would take my money!" He grinned at them.
"Either of you interested?"

Jonathan shook his head and Willie answered seriously:
"My dad told me never to bet. He says only fools bet."

"Quite right," cried Albion, in high good humour. "And
mind you do what he tells you." And he got on his horse and
rode away.

"Five pounds!" said Jonathan to Willie. "That's a lot to lose."
Then they resumed their play.

Although Alan Seagull had not yet forgiven his son for his
stupidity in telling the Totton boy his secret, he was in a tolerably good mood when he caught sight of Willie that afternoon.

He had just counted up all the money he had been promised
and, even if he lost the race, he would be paid more for this run
then he had made in the last half-year. If he won, then with
Burrard's money he'd do better still. Student of human nature
though he was, the mariner confessed himself astonished by
the whole business. But he wasn't expecting any more sur-
prises, when Willie came up to him and enquired: "You know
Richard Albion, Dad?"

"Yes, son. I do."

"We met him at Buckland Rings today. He wants to bet on
the race. Against you. But he can't find no takers. All the
Lymington money's already been bet."

"Oh." Alan shrugged.

"Guess how much he was going to bet, Dad."

"I don't know, son. Tell me."

"Five pounds."

Five pounds. Another five-pound bet! Seagull shook his head
in wonderment. Someone else was actually prepared to wager
that amount of money that he would lose. Nothing to Albion,
perhaps. A small fortune to him. For a long time after his son had
run inside the mariner sat staring out at the water, thinking.

Darkness had just fallen when Jonathan heard his father coming along the gallery passage.

Until the last few days of her life, when she could not move,
his mother had always come to kiss Jonathan goodnight.
Sometimes she would stay awhile and tell him a story. Always,
just before going, she would say a little prayer. She had been
dead only a few days when Jonathan had asked his father: "Are
you going to come to say goodnight to me?"

"Why, Jonathan?" Totton had asked. "You are not afraid of
the dark, are you?"

"No, Father." He had paused uncertainly. "Mother used to."

Since then, Totton had come to say goodnight to his son
most evenings. On his way up the stairs the merchant would
try to think of something to say. Perhaps he might ask the boy
what he had learned that day; or mention something of interest that had happened in the town. He would enter the room
and stand quietly by the door looking down to where his son
lay on his little bed.

And if Totton could think of nothing to say, Jonathan would just lie still for a moment and then murmur: "Thank you for coming to see me, Father. Goodnight."

This evening, however, it was Jonathan who had been preparing something to say. He had been thinking about it all afternoon. So when his father's quiet shadow appeared in the doorway and looked towards him without speaking, it was he who broke the silence. "Father."

"Yes, Jonathan."

"I don't have to race with Seagull. I could go in your boat, if you prefer."

His father did not reply for a little while. "It is not a question of what I prefer, Jonathan," Totton said at last. "You have made your choice."

"But I could change, Father."

"Really? I don't think so." There was just a hint of coldness in the voice. "Besides, you have already promised your friend to go with him."

The boy understood. He perceived that he had hurt his father, that now his father was hitting back with this quiet rejection. He was so sorry, now, that he had wounded him, and afraid, too, of losing his love; for his father was all he had. If only he did not make it so difficult.

"He would understand, Father. I'd rather go in your boat."

Not true, thought the merchant, but aloud he said: "You gave your word, Jonathan. You must keep it."

And now came the other matter that had been on the boy's mind. "Father, you remember at the salterns you told me that if I knew a secret I promised not to tell, that I must keep my promise?"

"Yes."

"Well . . . If I tell you something and ask you to keep it a secret, but I don't exactly tell you everything, because if I did, that would be giving away the other secret . . . Would that be all right?"

"You want to tell me something?"

"Yes."

"A secret?"

"Between us, Father. Because you're my father," he added hopefully.

"I see. Very well."

"Well . . ." Jonathan paused. "Father, I think you're going to lose this race."

"Why?"

"I can't tell you."

"But you are sure of it?"

"Pretty sure."

"There is nothing further you wish to say, Jonathan?"

"No, Father."

Totton was silent for a little while. Then his shadow began to recede and the door slowly closed.

"Goodnight, Father," said Jonathan. But there was no reply.

The morning of the race was overcast. During the night the wind had turned and was now coming down from the north; but it seemed to Alan Seagull that it might yet change again. His canny eyes glanced out at the waters of the estuary. He wasn't sure he liked the weather. One thing was certain: they would have a fast crossing to the island.

And after that? His eyes scanned the crowded quay. He was looking for someone.

Yesterday had been strange indeed. He had made bargains before, but never one so unexpected. Surprising though the business was, many things had been resolved.

One of these was the fate of young Jonathan.

The scene at the quay was lively. The whole of Lymington had gathered there. The two boats, moored by the waterside, were clearly contrasted. The Southampton vessel was not a full-size merchant ship but the more modest short sea-trader known as a hoy. Its size was forty tuns – which meant that in theory it could carry forty of the huge, two-hundred-and-fifty-gallon casks of wine that were then in use for the big shipments from the Continent. Broad, clinker-built of oak, with only a single mast and a large, square sail, the hoy looked primitive when compared with the great three-masted ships, six times its size, which the English merchants usually imported from the shipbuilders of the Continent. But it served its purpose well enough in coastal waters and could easily make the Channel crossing to Normandy. It carried a crew of twenty.

Seagull's boat, although of similar construction, was only

half its size. Besides the two boys, it had a hand-picked crew of ten, plus Seagull himself.

The cargo carried by each vessel was typical for the run across to the Isle of Wight: sacks of wool, fardels of finished cloth, casks of wine, some bales of silk. For extra ballast the Southampton boat also carried ten hundredweight of iron. Both boats had been inspected by the mayor and declared fully laden.

The terms of the race had been carefully worked out between the parties and it was the mayor who now called the two ship's masters together on the quay and rehearsed them.

"You cross to Yarmouth fully laden. You unload on to the quay there. You return unladen, but with the same crew. The first back is the winner." He looked at them both severely. Seagull he knew; the big, black-bearded master from Southampton he did not. "On my orders you will cast off and row out to midstream. When I wave the flag, you may hoist sail or row forward as you wish. But if you foul the other boat then or at any time during the race, you will be judged the loser. I will decide who is first back and my decision on all matters is final."

The two-way crossings, laden and unladen, the unloading, the opportunity to use oar and sail and the changeability of the weather – all these had added enough uncertainty, the mayor had judged, to make the race worth watching; although personally he couldn't see how the bigger boat could fail to win and had placed his own bet accordingly.

The Southampton man nodded, scowled at Seagull, but held out his hand nonetheless. Seagull took it briefly. But his eyes were hardly on the other mariner. He was still scanning the crowd.

And now he saw who he was looking for. As he turned back to his boat, he called Willie over to him. "You see Richard Albion, son?" He pointed to the gentleman. "Run quickly and ask him if he still wants to bet five pounds against me winning the race."

Willie did as he was told and a minute later returned. "He said yes, Dad."

"Good." Seagull nodded to himself. "Now just you run back

to him and tell him I'll take his bet, if he cares to lay it with a working man."

"You, Dad? You're betting?"

"That's right, son."

"Five pounds? Have you got five pounds, Dad?" The boy gazed at him in astonishment.

"Maybe I have, maybe I haven't."

"But Dad, you never bet!"

"Are you arguing with me, boy?"

"No, Dad. But . . ."

"Off you go, then."

So Willie ran back to Richard Albion who received the offer with almost as much surprise as the boy. Without hesitation, however, he came striding across to Seagull's boat. "Do I hear you'll really take a bet on this race?" he enquired.

"That's right."

"Well." He smiled broadly. "I never thought I'd live to see the day that Alan Seagull took a bet. What'll it be, then?" His sparkling blue eyes gave just a hint of concern on the mariner's behalf. "No one will take my five pounds, so name your figure and I'll be honoured."

"Five pounds is all right with me."

"Are you sure?" The rich gentlemen had no wish to ruin the mariner. "I'm getting a bit nervous about five pounds myself. Couldn't we make it a mark? Two if you like."

"No. Five pounds you offered, five pounds I took."

Albion hesitated only another second, then decided that to question the mariner any further would be to insult him. "Done, then," he cried and gave Alan his hand, before striding back to the watching crowd. "You'll never guess," he announced to them, "what's just happened."

It took only a couple of minutes for the whole of Lymington to be buzzing with this unexpected news – and scarcely a couple more before there were theories about what it meant. Why was Seagull suddenly abandoning the habit of a lifetime? Had he lost his head? Had he got five pounds anyway, or had he found someone to stake him? One thing seemed clear: if he was betting, then he must know something they didn't.

"He knows we're going to win," cried Burrard, cock-a-hoop.

Was it so? Those who had bet against the mariner began to look uncomfortable. Some of them, standing near Totton, turned to him nervously. What was going on, they demanded? "We were following you," they reminded him.

Henry Totton had already endured some chaff when it had been noticed that his son was in Seagull's boat. "Your son's sailing with the opposition?" his friends had cried. He had treated the question with perfect equanimity. "He's still friends with the little Seagull boy," he had replied calmly. "He wanted to go with him."

"I would have stopped him," one merchant remarked grumpily.

"Why?" Totton had given a quiet smile. "My son's extra weight and will undoubtedly get in the way. I think he'll cost Seagull a furlong at least." This shrewdness had drawn some appreciative laughs.

So now, as they looked at him accusingly, he only shrugged. "Seagull has made a bet, like the rest of us."

"Yes. But he never bets."

"And he is probably wise." He looked round their faces. "Has it not occurred to any of you that he may have made a mistake? He may lose." And faced with this further piece of common sense, there wasn't much anyone could say. There was a feeling, all the same, that there was something fishy about the business.

Nor was this suspicion confined to the spectators. Down in the boat, Willie Seagull was looking at his father curiously, while the mariner, his leather hat squashed at a jaunty angle on his head, leaned very comfortably against a cask of wine. "What are you up to, Dad?" he whispered.

But all Seagull did was murmur a short sea-shanty:

> Hot or cold, by land or sea
> Things are not always what they seem to be.

And that was all Willie could get out of him until the mayor's voice cried: "Cast off."

Jonathan Totton was happy. To be with his friend Willie, and the mariner on their boat – and for such an event – it did not seem to him that heaven itself could be much better.

It was a bracing scene. The little river between the high green slopes on its banks had a silvery tinge. The sky was grey but luminous, the ribs of the clouds spreading southwards. Pale seagulls wheeled round the masts and dipped over the reeds, the waterside echoing with their cries. The two boats were out in midstream now, the Southampton boat nearer the eastern bank. At the quay it had looked larger, but to Jonathan, now, down on the water, the hoy with its built-up platforms fore and aft seemed to tower over the fishing boat.

The crew were all ready. There were four men on the oars, but only to keep the boat steady in the stream. The rest were in position to raise the sail. Seagull was on the tiller, the two boys, for the time being, crouched down in front of him. As Jonathan looked up at the mariner's face, with its dark wisps of beard against the gleaming grey sky, it looked, for a moment, strangely sinister. But he put that thought from him as being foolish. And just then, on the shore, the mayor must have waved his flag, for Seagull nodded and said: "Now." The boys looked forward as the square sail went up with a flap and the four men on the oars gave a few good pulls, and in a few moments they were moving down the stream with the north wind pressing behind them.

Looking across to the quay, Jonathan could see his father's face watching them. He wanted to get up and wave to him, but he did not because he was not sure his father would like it. Soon the borough on its sloping crest was falling behind. A shaft of light through a break in the cloud lit up the town's roofs for a few brief, rather eerie moments; then the clouds closed and greyness descended. They were slipping downstream fast. The trees on the river bank intervened and the borough was lost to sight.

The smaller craft was able to pick up speed more quickly so that they had moved just ahead of the Southampton boat for the moment. They were in a long reach, now. To the right lay the open wastes of Pennington Marshes; to the left a strip of muddy marsh; and ahead, past a broad tract of mud banks that the high tide had submerged, the choppy waters of the Solent.

For sailors, the Solent harbours had some remarkable benefits. At first sight, the entrance to the Lymington river might have seemed unpromising. Across the river mouth, stretching from below Beaulieu in the east to beyond Pennington Marshes in the west – some seven miles in all and over a mile wide in places – lay vast mudflats, through which various streams cut narrow channels. Rich in nutrients, growing eel-grass and algae, this large feeding area produced molluscs, snails and worms in their billions, which in turn supported a huge population, some year round, some migrant, of waders, ducks, geese, cormorants, herons, terns and gulls. A paradise for birds but not, one might suppose, for mariners. Its virtue for shipping, however, lay in two features. One was the obvi-ous fact that the whole twenty-mile stretch of water was shel-tered by the comfortable mass of the Isle of Wight, at whose eastern and western ends one entered the sea. But the real key was not the shelter. It was the tides.

The tidal system of the English Channel operates rather like a see-saw, oscillating about a fulcrum, or node line. At each end of England's south coast, the waters rise and fall consid-erably. At the central node, although much water washes back and forth, the water level remains relatively constant. Because the Solent lies quite near the node its tidal rise and fall is mod-est. But the barrier of the Isle of Wight adds another factor. For as the tide in the English Channel rises, it fills the Solent from both ends, thereby setting up a complex set of internal tides. In the western Solent, where Lymington lies, the tide usually rises with a gentle current for seven hours. There is then a long stand – sometimes, in fact, there are two high waters a couple of hours apart. Then there is a short, fast ebb tide, which scours out a deep channel in the narrows by the western end of the Isle of Wight. All this is perfect for the shipping using the big port of Southampton.

And even modest Lymington was amply favoured. By high water, the huge mudflats were all submerged. The little river channel was easy to see and deep enough for the draught of any of the merchant vessels then in use.

As they entered the Solent now, the boat began to pitch against the dark and choppy waves that the wind had raised; but it was quite a light motion and Jonathan enjoyed it. Ahead lay the broad slopes of the Isle of Wight, only four miles away. Their destination, the small harbour of Yarmouth, was almost directly opposite. Looking east, he could see the great funnel of the Solent, rolling away for fifteen miles, a huge grey corridor of sky and water. On the west side, past the marshes and Keyhaven, a long sand and gravel spit with a hooked end came out for a mile from the coast towards the chalk cliffs of the island and, through the narrow channel between, Jonathan could see the open sea. The salt spray stung his face. He felt exhilarated.

With the wind directly behind them, there was nothing to do except run before it. Coming back, however, would be more difficult. Although the boat had a large, centred rudder, the primitive square sail was not well adapted for tacking. They might need to use their oars then. Perhaps, he supposed, this might turn out to the smaller vessel's advantage. It would need to be so, for already he could see that the Southampton boat was closer. Before they were halfway across, he suspected, the heavier ship would overtake them.

Jonathan might be contented enough, but as he looked across at Willie he noticed that his friend was not. The two boys had shifted forward a little to a position just below the small deck on which Seagull was standing at the tiller. While Jonathan had been gazing eagerly out at the seascape, the other boy, sitting a few feet away, had been frowning and shaking his head to himself.

Jonathan slid over to him. "What's the matter?" he enquired.

At first Willie did not reply, then, lowering his head he muttered: "I can't understand it."

"What?"

"Why my dad hasn't raised the big sail."

"What big sail?"

"In there." Willie nodded towards the space under the aft deck. "He's got a big sail. Hidden. He can outrun almost anyone." He jerked his thumb back towards the Southampton boat, which was now visibly gaining on them. "With a following wind like this they'd never catch us."

"Perhaps he will raise it."

Willie shook his head. "Not now. And he's bet on the race. Five pounds. I don't know what he's doing."

Jonathan stared at his friend's small, chinless face, so perfect a replica of his father's, saw his worried frown and suddenly realised that the funny little boy who ran through the woods and played in the streams with him was also a miniature adult, in a way that he was not. The children of farmers and fishermen went to work alongside their parents, while the child of a well-to-do merchant did not. The poorer children had responsibilities and, to an extent, their parents treated them as equals. "He must know what he's doing," he suggested.

"Then why hasn't he told me?"

"My father never tells me anything," said Jonathan, then suddenly realised that this was not true. The merchant was always trying to tell him things, but he never wanted to listen.

"He doesn't trust me," Willie said sadly. "He knows I told you about his secret." He glanced at Jonathan. "You never told anyone, did you?"

"No," said Jonathan. It was nearly true.

For a little while, however, Seagull's boat managed to keep just ahead of the other as the coast of the island drew closer.

They were halfway across when the Southampton boat passed in front. Jonathan heard a cheer from her men but Seagull and his crew ignored it. Nor did the bigger boat, as they drew nearer to Yarmouth, establish more than a half-mile lead.

The port of Yarmouth was smaller than Lymington and protected from the Solent waters by a sand bar that acted as a harbour wall. They were still about a mile out from the harbour entrance when Jonathan noticed something strange: the sail was flapping.

He heard Seagull call out an order and two of the men leaped to loosen one of the sheets while two more tightened the other, altering the angle of the sail. Seagull leaned on the tiller.

"Wind's changing," cried Willie. "Nor'-east."

"That'll make it a bit easier to get back," ventured Jonathan. "Maybe."

The Southampton boat was having to employ the same tactic, but was already nearer the harbour entrance, so had the advantage. Before long they saw it turn and make for the narrow channel by the sand bar, dropping its sail as it passed into the protection of the harbour; but it was some time before they could do the same. Just before they made their run in he saw Alan Seagull gazing up at the sky, watching the clouds. The half-smile that was usually on his face had gone and it seemed to Jonathan that he looked worried.

As they came in, the Southampton boat was already tied up and its crew busy unloading.

The town of Yarmouth had also been founded by Lymington's feudal lord. In this case he had laid out his borough as a little grid of lanes on the eastern side of the harbour water. Though small, it was a busy place, for the greater part of the Isle of Wight's trade flowed through it. During the last hundred years, the quay had been built and lifting equipment set up, so that ships could unload directly on to the dock instead of into lighters.

The boat had no sooner tied up than the crew sprang into action. While gangplanks were pushed out from the quay and a beam moved out, the mariners raced to raise a block and tackle from the masthead by which the heaviest items, like the casks, could be swung outboard from the yardarm. Everybody was busy. Even the two boys rushed up and down the gangplanks with bales of silk, boxes of spices and any other cargo they could carry. Jonathan had hardly a moment to look, but he knew that, with their smaller cargo, this was where they should be able to make up some time against the Southampton boat. He was so busy that he scarcely noticed that over the harbour the sky was getting darker.

Alan Seagull had noticed, though. For a while he had helped his men unload; but as the last of the wine casks was safely lowered he moved along the quay to where the master of the other boat was directing operations. Standing beside him for a moment, he pointed up at the sky.

The burly Southampton man glanced, too, then shrugged. "I've seen worse," he growled.

"Maybe you have."

"We'll be back before it gets bad."

"I don't think so."

As if to make his point, a gust of wind suddenly came with a whistle over the rooftops of the Yarmouth houses, wetting their faces with a spattering of raindrops.

"Swing that cask. Hurry now!" the big man shouted to his crew. "That's it!" He turned to Seagull. "We'll be gone first. If you haven't the stomach for the crossing, then be damned to you." And turning his back on the other master, he went across the gangplank into his ship.

He was wrong in his assessment about their departure, however. For it was actually Seagull's boat that cast off first and made for the harbour entrance. Under his direction the crew were rowing out. Before leaving, they had already reefed the sail, so that its shape, when it was raised, would be a narrow triangle rather than a square. To Jonathan, their leaving ahead of the big boat seemed a cause for rejoicing, but he could see from the tense faces of the crew and the concentrated look on Seagull's face that they were anything but happy.

"This is going to be rough," said Willie.

Moments later, they passed the sand spit and encountered the open water.

The one thing in the Solent that the sailor truly has to fear is the big easterly gale. It is not a regular occurrence, but when it does come it can be sudden and terrible. Its favoured month is April.

When the big easterly comes down the English Channel, the Isle of Wight offers no protection. Far from it. Sweeping in at the Solent's wider eastern end, the wind barrels down its narrowing funnel and whips its waters to a frenzy. The peaceful paradise becomes a raging brownish cauldron. The island disappears behind great grey sheets of moving vapour. Over the salt marshes the gale howls as though it means to tear out the quivering vegetation and hurl it – thorn trees, gorse bushes and all – high over Keyhaven and into the frothing Channel beyond. Sailors who see the big easterly coming hurry to shelter as fast as they can.

Alan Seagull reckoned they just had time.

The wind came at them sharply the moment they cleared the sand bar. The choppy waves were developing already into a rolling swell, but being higher in the water now, the boat could ride this well enough. All ten of the crew were rowing: five a side, all skilled. His plan was to row well clear of the shore, heading a little upwind, then hoist a small sail and try, with a combination of sail, tiller and oar, to get as near to the Lymington river entrance as possible. Since Lymington was almost opposite they would almost certainly be carried too far west. But at least that would bring them to the comparative safety of the shallows over the mudflats and, with their shallow draught, they could row round the coastline of the marshes. If the worst came, they could beach the boat on the salt marshes and walk safely home. One thing was certain: it was anybody's race now, if you could just get home.

The wind, although growing stronger, was still only gusting. Using the tiller, the mariner was able to keep the boat's prow pointing north-east, roughly in the direction of Beaulieu as his men strained on the long sea oars. For perhaps a dozen strokes he would feel the wind blowing evenly in his face and the boat would make solid progress. Then a gust would catch them, roll the vessel, heaving the bow round, while a cascade of salt spray came flying off the crest of the swell, almost blinding him as he fought the tiller to bring the boat round again. To the east, up the Solent, he could see a brownish veil of rain above the waters. He tried to calculate where they would be when the rain got to them. Halfway across. Perhaps.

They made slow progress: a hundred yards; another hundred. They had gone about a quarter-mile when they saw the Southampton boat emerge behind them.

The larger boat took a different course. Laying its prow directly into the wind, staying close to the shore, its crew began to row lustily eastwards. Their plan was evidently to get as far up the coast as they could before the wind got stronger, and then make the whole crossing by sail, dashing with the wind half behind them straight for the Lymington entrance. The Southampton master's bet was no doubt that Seagull would be blown too far west and be unable to get back in the increasingly bad weather. He might well be right.

"We'll raise the sail now," called Alan Seagull.

At first it seemed to be working. Using a minimum of canvas, with the boat nearly athwart the wind but aiming for the eastern edge of the Lymington estuary, he was able to supplement the oars. Every so often a squall would catch the sail and roll the boat so strongly that the oarsmen lost their stroke, but they pressed on. There was more and more spray, but from his occasional glances back to the island Seagull knew they were making progress. He could see the Southampton boat, following its steady path along the coast. Meanwhile, he was nearly a mile out and still in line with the harbour entrance. He scanned the clouds. The veil of rain was approaching quicker than he had expected.

"Ship oars." The men, surprised, started to pull the oars in. Willie looked at him questioningly. In reply, he only shook his head. "More sail," he called out. The crew obeyed. The boat lurched. "All hands to starboard." They would need as much weight as possible to counterbalance the sail. "Here we go, then," he muttered to himself.

The effect was dramatic. The boat shuddered, creaked, and plunged forward. There was nothing else for it. The storm was coming in too fast to do anything now but try to run across, as far as they could, before it really struck. As the prow rose and dipped he watched the northern shoreline. He was going to be driven west, of course; the question was, how far? Rolling and pitching, fighting to keep his line, the mariner guided his vessel out towards the middle of the Solent.

And then the storm struck. It came with a roar and a cascade of rain, and a terrible engulfing darkness, as though it meant to deny the existence of everything but itself to those it had swallowed in its maw. The island vanished; the mainland vanished; the clouds above vanished; everything vanished except the spray and the sweeping sheets of rain and the billowing swell, which soon grew so high that the waves towered over the boat, which sank into troughs so deep it seemed a miracle it ever rose again. Frantically the crew trimmed the sail and Seagull eased the tiller. There was nothing to do but to run before the wind with a small sail and hope it would bring them swiftly to the edge of this watery abyss.

The two boys, holding fast to the rail at its edge, were sitting just in front of him on the deck. He wondered if either would be sick and whether to send them into the body of the ship. And thinking of his decision about what to do with Jonathan, the boy who knew his secret, it occurred to him that the circumstances could never be better than now. A shove with his foot when no one was looking and he'd be overboard in a trice. The chances of saving him in that sea? Minimal.

He could not see the shore, but he estimated that since the gale must now blow them almost due west, it should take them either to Keyhaven or the long spit of gravel and sand that came out across the Solent's entrance. Either way, this would drive them on to a shore where they could safely beach the boat. Thank God there were no rocks.

He did not know how much time passed after this. It seemed a little eternity, but he was too busy on the tiller, as the boat rode and plunged in the swell, to think of anything much except that it could not, surely, be long before they came close to the spit. And he had finally reached the conclusion that they must be near indeed when suddenly a divide in the clouds hurtling overhead caused a short break in the blinding rain. Over the whipping spray, as the wind howled, it was possible to see forward a quarter, then half a mile, then further, as if he were looking into a huge grey tunnel. And then, as the little boat rose up from a trough, he saw a vision that made him gasp.

It was a phantom – a huge, narrow, three-masted vessel, a hundred and sixty feet long, appearing ghost-like through the receding curtain of rain. He knew at once what it was, for there could only be one ship of this kind in those waters. It was a great galley from Venice, making its entry into the Solent on its way to Southampton. They were magnificent ships, these galleys, or galleasses as they were often called. Little changed from the great ships of classical times, they carried three lateen sails, but could manoeuvre in almost any waters with their three mighty banks of oars. A hundred and seventy oarsmen they carried, galley slaves sometimes, just as in Roman times. Although their cargo space was not huge, the value of the cargo was: cinnamon, ginger, nutmegs, cloves and other oriental spices; costly perfumes like frankincense; drugs for the apothecaries; silks and satins, carpets and tapestries, furniture and Venetian glass. It was a floating treasure house.

But it was not just the sight of the phantom galleass that made Seagull stare in shock. It was the ship's position. For the Venetian vessel, directly in front of them, was in the narrow channel that led out of the Solent. He let out a cry. How could he have been so stupid? In the rage of the gale he had forgotten one crucial factor. The tide.

The ebb tide had begun. They were not heading for the sand spit and safety. The gale was blowing them right into the current that, in moments, would sweep them inexorably through the Solent's exit and out into the boiling wrath of the open sea.

"Oars!" he cried. "Port side." He threw himself against the tiller. The boat rolled violently.

And he just had time to see the two boys, caught unawares, tumbling across the deck towards the water.

By the time evening began to fall in Lymington, many people had secretly given up hope.

Not that you could really call it evening: the doors and shutters had already been closed against the howling wind and the lashing rain for hours; the only change was that the enveloping darkness of the storm had grown blacker until at last you could see nothing at all. Only Totton, with his hourglass, could tell the time with precision and know, as the grains of sand fell, that it was now eight hours since his son had disappeared.

At first, when the Southampton boat had arrived, there had been celebrations. In the Angel Inn, where most of those with money on the race had gathered, some people had started collecting their bets. But questions were also being asked. Had the other boat attempted the crossing? Yes. They had got out of Yarmouth first. What course had they taken? Straight across.

"They've been blown west, then," Burrard concluded. "They'll have to row round. We shan't see them for a while." But behind his bluffness some detected a hint of concern and it was noticed that he made no effort to collect any of his own winnings. Totton, soon after this, went down to the quay and not long afterwards Burrard had followed him. The conversation in the Angel had grown quieter after that, the jokes less frequent.

Down on the quay it had been impossible to see anything past the waving reeds. Totton, after visiting the Seagull family, had insisted on going down the path across the marshes towards the rivermouth where Burrard had accompanied him. There he had gazed uselessly into the rain and the raging sea for half an hour before Burrard had gently told him, "Come, Henry, we can do nothing here" and led him home.

After that, Burrard had set in motion enquiries of his own and returned in the evening to keep his friend company.

"I owe you our bet," Totton said absently.

"So you do, Henry," Burrard agreed cheerfully, understanding his friend's need. "We can settle up tomorrow."

"I must go out and look for them," Totton suddenly declared a few moments later.

"Henry, I beg you." Burrard laid a hand on his shoulder. "The best thing you can do is wait here. It's impossible to see anything out there. But when your son comes back soaked to the skin after walking halfway along the coast, the best thing is for him to find you here. I've already got four men out looking in the likely places." The fact that two of them had already returned all the way from Keyhaven and reported no sighting of Seagull's boat was a piece of information he did not share with Totton for the moment. "Come, tell that pretty servant girl of yours" – this was a description of the poor girl that would have surprised most people – "to bring us a pie and a pitcher of red wine. I'm starving."

So while he thus ensured that Totton ate something, Burrard sat with his friend in the empty hall, saying little, while Totton stared ahead as if in a trance.

Yet even Burrard would have been most astonished had he known what his friend was thinking of.

It had been the day before the race when Henry Totton had gone to see Alan Seagull.

The mariner had been alone, mending his nets, when he had seen the quiet merchant approaching and had been surprised when he stopped in front of him.

"I have some business with you," Totton had begun, and as Seagull had looked up enquiringly, he had proceeded: "There's a great deal of money on tomorrow's race."

"So they say."

"You don't bet, though."

"Nope."

"You're wise. Wiser than me, I dare say."

If Seagull agreed he did not say so. It was an unexpected thing for Totton to admit, but not half so unexpected as what came next.

"I hear you're going to win."

"Oh?" The mariner's eyes narrowed. "Where'd you hear that?"

"My son. Told me last night."

"And why" – Seagull looked down at his nets again – "would he think that?"

"He won't say."

If that was true, Seagull thought, then young Jonathan had kept his secret better than his own son. But was it true, or had this merchant come to threaten him in some way? "I expect it'll depend on the weather," he said.

"Perhaps. But you see," Totton went on quietly, "the reason I bet against you originally was because I didn't think you'd care to win."

There was a long pause.

Seagull stopped mending his net and gazed at his feet. "Oh?"

"No." And then, speaking softly, the merchant mentioned two illegal owling runs Seagull had made, one for a Lymington merchant, another for a wool dealer from Sarum. The first had been five years ago, the second more recent. But here was the interesting thing: young Willie could not possibly have known about either. Wherever Totton had got his information, it wasn't from the boys. "So you see," Totton concluded, "when I bet Burrard five pounds on the Southampton boat, it was because I reckoned that even if you could outsail it, you wouldn't want everyone to know. At least, the probability lay that way."

Seagull considered. The merchant's reasoning, of course, was quite right. As for his information, it seemed a waste of time to dissemble. "How long've you known?" he asked simply.

"Years." Totton paused. "Each man's business is his own. That's my rule."

Seagull looked up at the merchant with a new respect. Knowing when to keep your mouth shut was the highest virtue for the fishermen, just as it was for the forest folk. "You had business with me?"

"Yes." Totton had smiled. "Not that sort. It's about the race. If my boy's right and you are planning to win, then that alters the probabilities. And I'm in for five pounds." He paused. "I've heard that Albion wants to bet five pounds that you lose. So I'm asking you to take his bet. You won't really be betting – I'll provide the money. And I'll pay you one pound whichever way it goes."

"You're betting against yourself?"

"Hedging."

"If you pay me either way, you'll still be down a pound, won't you?"

"I've laid some other bets. I break even either way, if you'll help me."

"But I might lose."

"Yes. But I can't calculate the probabilities. When I can't do that, I don't bet."

Seagull chuckled. The coolness of the merchant amused him. And to think he'd been wondering whether to drown young Jonathan. Not only was that pointless now but the lad, by confusing Totton's calculations, was actually making him another pound. "All right, then," he'd said. "I'll do it."

But as Henry Totton sat in his hall now, staring ahead and remembering this transaction, he could only curse himself. He had settled his stupid bet. But what about his son? Why had he let him go with the mariner? Because the boy had hurt him and he was angry. Angry with a mere child who had only been thinking of the adventure of going with his friend. He had let him go; he had acted coldly towards him. And now he had probably sent him to his death.

"Don't despair yet, Henry," he heard Burrard's gruff voice. "They'll probably turn up in the morning."

If the men Burrard sent out had failed to find any sign of Seagull and his boat it was not surprising. At the moment when they reached Keyhaven in the late afternoon he was just over a mile away at the end of the long gravel spit and had been there for some time. But he had made no attempt to get to Keyhaven, nor did he particularly want anyone to see him.

He had been lucky not to lose the boys. It had been very close. At the instant when he saw them rolling towards the side, he had let go of the tiller and lunged after them, grabbing one with each hand as the boat yawed. They had almost gone over, all three of them. "Hold him," he had cried to Willie as he released his grip on Jonathan and grabbed the rail with his free hand; and if Willie hadn't clung on to his friend like a limpet, young Jonathan would surely have been lost.

The next quarter of an hour had been like a nightmare. They

had dropped the sail and rowed; but each time they had
seemed to make progress the current, with an awful dreamlike
logic, had carried them further towards the long shadow of the
galleass, which mysteriously hovered, sometimes hidden in the
shrouds of the storm, sometimes glimpsed, yet never moving.
At last, pulling for all they were worth, the men had managed,
as the tide still swept them remorselessly, to touch the gravel
edge of the spit and get the boat grounded almost on the very
lip of the channel that rushed by, out to sea.

But now Seagull had other things on his mind. He cupped
his hands over his eyes and stared intently across the water.

The storm had not slackened; but seen from the shore the
downpour had resolved itself into trailing curtains of grey
clouds that swept past remorselessly. Through these, nothing
could be seen at more than a hundred yards; but in the brief intervals between, Seagull could see some way into the foaming
channel.

At last he turned. The crew and the boys were doing their
best to shelter from the rain in the lee of the boat, which they
had pulled up on to the beach.

"What are we going to do, Alan?" one of them called now.
"We going to Keyhaven?"

"Nope."

"Why?"

"Because of that." And as he turned and pointed they saw
once more the long, tall shape of the galleass appear faintly
out in the channel. "She ain't moved," he said. "Know what
that means?" The man nodded. "I don't reckon anyone but us
has seen her," Seagull continued.

"She may get off all right."

"And then she may not. So we'll wait and see."

And with that he returned to his position, watching.

The gravel banks in the west mouth of the Solent were not
usually a hazard. Firstly, they were well known. Every pilot
knew how to approach them. Secondly, the channel between
them was deep and necessitated only a single turn as one came
near the tip of the Isle of Wight. In spring storms, however, it
was not unknown for vessels to run aground and shipwrecks to
occur.

Clearly the galleass had run aground. With the tide running

out, she would be left stranded, buffeted by the gale. She might even be blown over on to her side and broken up. It was hard to be sure but it seemed to Seagull that the crew of the stricken vessel were trying to work her free with the oars. Once, when he caught a glimpse of her, she was clearly listing. He could make out nothing. Long minutes passed.

But then, just for a moment, he saw her through the veil of rain again. She was half off the gravel bank now. But something else had happened. Somehow she had veered round; she was still veering as he watched. She was going athwart the tide, exposing her whole side to the wrath of the storm. She was keeling over. Then a great barrage of rain roared past and he could see no more.

Long minutes passed. Still nothing. Nothing but the howl of the storm. Poor devils, he thought. What frantic efforts would they be making now? Had the galley capsized? He stared, as if his eyes could bore through the rain.

And then, as though in answer to a prayer, the rain thinned. It almost stopped. Suddenly, ahead of him, he could see the centre of the channel where the gravel banks were and even further. He could make out the faint white shape of the island's cliffs, over a mile away opposite. He stared at the gravel banks. The galleass wasn't there.

Without even waiting to explain, he started running across the spit, to the seaward side. The curtain of rain was drawing back. By the time he had covered the few hundred yards to the beach looking out to the English Channel, he could see right out to the tip of the island. He saw the galley then.

At the westernmost tip of the Isle of Wight, where the old chalk cliffs had collapsed at some time, long ago, into the sea, there remained four spikes of chalk, like teeth, just off the white cliff's high edge, as an indicator that the spine of land did not, in fact, end with the island but continued for some way, under the water. These sturdy outcrops, rising over fifty feet above the water, were known as the Needles. They were chalk, but they were hard and sharp.

The galley had listed badly. One of its masts had broken and was hanging over the side. The oars on the upturned side were either drooping or pointing erratically at the stormy sky. Even as he watched, she spun round helplessly. Then he saw her crash into one of the Needles. She drew back, after which, as if she meant to, the galley thumped into the rock once more.

A renewed cascade of rain interrupted his view. At first he could still see the nearer cliffs, but in a while they also vanished. And though he remained there on watch until it grew dark, he did not see the galleass again.

That night was not a comfortable one for Jonathan. Fortunately there were some blankets stored under the deck. The two boys, at least, were able to get tolerably dry and shelter in the hold during the night. The men pulled sailcloth out from the side of the boat and remained under that. Alan Seagull stayed out on the beach. He didn't care.

It was somewhere in the early hours of the morning that the storm began to abate. By first light Seagull was waking them.

There was no sign of the galley as they rowed round the spit into the sea in the grey dawn. The sky was still overcast, the water choppy. It was not long, however, before Seagull called out and pointed to something floating in the water. It was a long oar. A few minutes later he steered the boat towards something else. A small cask this time. They hauled it aboard.

"Cinnamon," the mariner announced. And it was not long before they found more. "Cloves," said Alan Seagull this time.

The galley had obviously sunk; but how much of its precious cargo was floating or had been washed ashore would depend very much on how badly it had been broken up before sinking. Judging by the number of spars they saw the galley had considerably disintegrated before going down.

"Dad knows the currents," Willie explained. "He knows where to find the stuff."

To Jonathan's surprise, however, the mariner did not stay out long, but instead headed for the shore. "Why are we going in now?" he asked Willie, who gave him a funny look.

"Got to check for survivors," he said obliquely. The white cliffs by the Needles would have smashed any man who came up against them in the storm. The nearest safe beach, even if you could find it in the darkness, would have been three miles away and, strangely perhaps, few mariners could swim in those times. If the galley had gone down out in the sea that night, the chances were that its crew were drowned. But you never knew. Some might have floated to shore on a piece of wreckage.

They brought the boat in about two and a half miles along the coast from the sand spit, where there was a tiny inlet from which a stream descended. Dragging the boat into the mouth of the inlet, where it could not be seen, Seagull and his crew prepared to scour the area. The beaches were empty. Along the shore was mostly scrub and heathland. Ordering the boys to guard the boat, Seagull disappeared with the men.

Jonathan noticed that the mariner carried a small spar which he held like a club. "Where are they going?" he asked after they had left.

"Along the coast. They'll fan out."

"Do you think there'll be any survivors?"

Again, Willie looked at him a little strangely. "No,' he said.

And at last Jonathan understood. The law of the sea in England was simple but bleak. The cargo of wrecks belonged to whoever found it, unless there were survivors from the ship to claim it. Which of course is why there very seldom were.

The two boys waited; it grew a little lighter.

It was during this time that Henry Totton reached the end of the spit at the Solent entrance and stared across the sea.

He had been out since first light. After a quick look down the estuary he had cut across Pennington Marshes, past the salterns to Keyhaven. From there he had a good view of the Isle of Wight and the shoreline nearby. There was no sign of anything. Then he had walked out along the spit in the hope that they might have been blown there. But there was not a trace of Seagull and his crew.

He gazed across the end of the spit at the narrow channel, then walked round to where he could see the Needles and scanned the sea and the long shoreline of the Forest's western coast. And since by this time Seagull's boat was concealed in its little inlet, he did not see it. But in the water nearby he did see some bits of wreckage and, knowing nothing of the Venetian galley, he assumed it was probably Seagull's boat and that his son was drowned; so he wandered down the western length of the spit to see if the boy's body was there. But there were no bodies on the spit, for the currents had carried what bodies there were to another place entirely.

Just then he saw his friend Burrard coming towards him and that gruff worthy, who had been out looking for him since not long after dawn himself, put his arm round him and took him home.

It was boring waiting by the boat. They did not dare to leave it in case Seagull returned suddenly, but the two boys took turns to walk along the beach a little way to see what they could find.

The current was starting to bring things in now: another oar, some rigging, a shattered barrel.

And bodies.

Jonathan had been inspecting the remains of a sea chest, wondering what it had contained, when he saw the corpse. It was about ten yards out and the waves were bringing it gradually towards him. The body was drifting face downwards in the water. He stared at it, a little frightened, yet curious.

He would probably have edged away from it if he had not noticed one thing: the tunic the man wore was of a rich brocade, threaded with gold. His shirt was bordered with the finest lace. This was a rich man: a merchant or perhaps even an aristocrat accompanying the ship on its northern voyage. Gingerly he went towards it.

Jonathan had never seen a drowned man before, but he had heard what they looked like: the bluish skin, the swollen face. He waded out until the corpse was beside him. The water was up to his waist. He touched it. It felt heavy, waterlogged. He did not look at the head but felt around the waist. The corpse was wearing a belt. It was not made of leather but gold thread. His fingers worked round it. He had to pull the body close to him to steady it.

Suddenly the dead man's arm floated round with a bump, as if, in return, he was trying to grab the boy round the waist. For a terrifying moment Jonathan imagined the corpse might wrap its arm around him, press him close and pull him down under the surface to join his watery death. In a panic he threw himself backwards, lost his balance and rolled under. For a second, under the water, he caught sight of the corpse's ghastly face, staring down, fish-like, at the bottom.

He stood up, steeled himself and went back. He pushed the dead man's arm firmly away, got hold of the belt, took a deep breath and searched with his fingers under water until he found what he was looking for.

The leather pouch was fastened to the belt with thongs, but they were tied in a simple knot. It took him a little time, moving beside the corpse as the waves brought it in, but the water was still up to his knees when he got it loose. The purse was heavy. He did not trouble to open it, but glanced about to see if he was observed. He wasn't. Willie was still by the boat in the creek. The thongs were just long enough to tie round his waist under his clothing. He did so, adjusted his sodden shirt and tunic over the purse and went back.

"You're wet," said Willie. "D'you find anything?"

"There's a body," he replied. "I'm afraid to touch him."

"Oh," said Willie and ran off. A short while later he returned. "He was washed up on the beach. I got this." He was holding the belt. "Must be worth something."

Jonathan nodded and said nothing.

They waited some time, until Seagull returned. He gave them a glance, saw the belt but made no comment.

"Anyone out there, Dad?" Willie asked.

"No, son. There's no one. The bodies'll be coming in on the beach now, I reckon." He thought for a moment. "We'll be taking the boat out. See what we can find. Be out all day, I shouldn't wonder." If there was anything of value on the beaches or in the Channel waters for miles around, Alan Seagull would be sure to find it. "You boys cut home. Tell your mother where we are," he instructed his son. "Your father'll be worried about you," he remarked to Jonathan. "You make sure you go straight home. All right?"

So the two boys obediently set off. It was only a five-mile walk back if they crossed directly above Pennington Marshes. They went along at a good pace.

There was a break in the clouds and pale sunlight was filtering on to Lymington as the two boys came down the High Street from the little church towards Totton's house. They realised that people were looking at them. One woman ran out and seized Jonathan's arm and started to bless God that he was alive, but he managed to shake her off politely and, not wanting to be further delayed, he broke into a trot.

When he reached his house he went to the street door that gave into his father's counting house thinking, if his father was at home, to surprise him. But the room was empty, so he went through it into the galleried hall, which was silent also.

For a moment he assumed that it, too, was empty. None of the servants was there. The light came in through the high window and fell into its pale, vacant spaces; it seemed like a yard that had been swept clean before its owners had departed for another place. Only when he had taken a couple of steps into the hall did he realise that the upright wooden chair under the gallery passage was occupied.

It was turned slightly away from him so that the first thing he noticed was his father's ear. But the merchant had not heard him. He was sitting in his usual posture, but staring so straight ahead that it seemed as if he were in a trance. Saying nothing, the boy tiptoed forward, watching his father's face.

He had not seen grief before. When his wife had died, believing he was protecting the boy, Totton had hidden his distress beneath a calm exterior. But now, thinking himself alone, he was staring in silent misery at the images his mind presented before him: the baby he had loved, but left, as was proper, to be cared for by his mother; the toddler he had watched and for whom he had done nothing but make plans; the child he did not know how to comfort; the boy who only wanted to sail away from him; the son he had lost.

Jonathan had never witnessed anguish, but he did now. "Father."

Totton turned.

"It's all right. We're all safe." The boy took a step forward. "We were blown down the coast." Totton was still staring at him as though he were a ghost. "There was a shipwreck in the storm. Alan Seagull is still out there."

"Jonathan?"

"I'm quite all right, Father."

"Jonathan?"

"Did your boat get home?"

His father was still in a daze. "Oh. Yes."

"So you won your bet."

"My bet?" The merchant stared. "My bet?" He blinked. "Dear God, what's that when I have you?"

So Jonathan ran to him.

And then Henry Totton suddenly burst into tears.

It was some minutes, as he lay in his father's arms, before Jonathan gently disengaged himself and reached for the purse around his waist. "I brought you something, Father," he said. "Look." And he opened it and took out the contents. They were golden coins. "Ducats," he said.

"So they are, Jonathan."

"Do you know what they're worth, Father?"

"Yes, I do."

"So do I." And, to his father's astonishment, he repeated, entirely correctly, the values the merchant had told him in their lesson three weeks before.

"That's exactly right," said Totton with delight.

"You see, Father," the boy said happily. "I remember some of what you tell me."

"The ducats are yours, Jonathan." He smiled.

"I got them for you," said his son. He paused a moment. "Can we share them?"

"Why not?" said Henry Totton.

The Armada Tree

1587

"**Y**ou will go with me, a little way, upon my journey?"
The moment she had spoken he had felt his heart sinking. It was an order, of course. "Willingly," he had lied, feeling almost like a schoolboy.

He was forty and she was his mother.

The road from Sarum towards the south-east – it was a wide, grassy track, really – made a gentle progress across the broad meadows in which the city lay and then rose slowly, in stages, on to the higher ground. The cathedral was more than three miles behind them before they started the long drag up and over the high ridge, which was the south-eastern lip of the broad basin where Sarum's five rivers met. Although there was a hint of sharpness in the breeze, that September morning, the weather was fine.

It was no light matter when Albion's mother took to the road. Only upon the bridegroom's thrice repeated promise of the best room in the house of Salisbury's richest merchant had she consented to come to the wedding festivities without bringing her own furniture. Even so, as well as the carriage in which she travelled with coachman, groom and outrider, there was the wagon behind, groaning under the weight of two manservants, two maids and such a prodigious quantity of chests containing her dresses, gowns, shoes and formidable collection of toiletries – the coachman swore that one of the chests had a Roman priest in it, too – that one could only thank God the autumn weather was still dry for otherwise it must surely have stuck in the mud. But then his mother had firm views about how things should be done and, Albion reflected a little sadly as he rode beside the carriage, she did not stint herself. So the horses, at least, were glad when, cresting the ridge, the lady abruptly called a halt and ordered her litter.

The groom and the manservants silently assembled it, slotted in the poles and brought it to the carriage door. As his mother stepped out, Albion observed that she was already wearing wooden pattens on her feet to protect them from the mud. She had planned this halt, therefore. He should have guessed. She pointed, now, to the path along the ridge. Evidently she wished to go up there and expected him to accompany her. Dismounting, he walked up behind as the four men carried the litter and so, a curious little procession silhouetted against the sky, they made their way along the chalk rim as the small white clouds hurried over them.

At the high point she ordered the litter put down and stepped out of it. The men were told to wait at a distance. Then she turned towards her son, and beckoned. "Now, Clement," she said with a smile – the name had been her particular choice, not his father's – "I want to talk to you."

"Gladly, Mother," he said.

At least she had chosen a fine place to do it. The view from the ridge below Sarum was one of the finest in southern England. Looking back the way they had come, the long slope now appeared as a beautiful sweep down into the lush green basin from which, four miles away, Salisbury Cathedral rose like a grey swan from the Avon valley floor, its graceful spire soaring so high that you might have supposed the surrounding ridges had been spun out from it, like clay on a lathe, driven by an ancient spirit. To the north lay the bump of Old Sarum's castle mound and the sea of chalk ridges beyond. Eastwards, the rich, undulating countryside of Wessex rolled away into the distance.

But it was turning south, in the direction of their journey, that one saw the longest sweep of all. For there, shelving gradually down, mile after mile, lay the whole vast expanse of the New Forest – wild oak wood, gravel ridges, sweeping gorse and heather heath, all the way to Southampton and the misty blue slopes of the Isle of Wight, plainly visible, twenty miles away in the sea.

Clement Albion stood before his mother on the bare ridge and wondered what she wanted.

Her opening words were not encouraging. "We should not fear death, Clement." She smiled at him in quite a friendly way. "I have never been afraid to die."

The Lady Albion – for although her husband had not been a knight, so she was always called – was a tall, slim woman. Her face was powdered white; her lips were, as God had graciously made them, red. Her eyes were dark and tragic unless she was annoyed, when they became adamantine. Her teeth were very fine – for she despised all things sweet – and long, and the colour of ancient ivory.

To the casual observer it might have seemed that she had continued to dress in the fashion of her heyday because, being neither at court nor in London, and proud no doubt of the finery of her best years, she had quietly slid, as older women often did, a decade or two behind the times. Instead of the large ruff now in fashion, she maintained a simple high, open collar; her long heavy gown had large slit puffs on the shoulders and her arms were encased in the close-fitting sleeves of an earlier time. She wore a richly embroidered underskirt. On her head she usually carried a heavy veil held with a linen hood; but today, for her journey, she had put on a jaunty man's cap with a plume. From a chain around her waist hung a fur-lined muff. To the casual observer it might have seemed a picture of dated charm. But her son was not deceived. He knew better.

Her clothes were all black: black cap, black gown, black underskirt. She had dressed in this way ever since the death of Queen Mary Tudor, thirty years before; there being, she would say, no reason to leave off mourning. Yet what made this attire so truly startling was the fact that the embroidery of the underskirt and the whole inside of her stiff, high collar were bright crimson: red as the blood of the martyrs. She had trimmed her widow's black with crimson, now, for half a year. She was a walking emblem.

He looked at her cautiously. "Why do you speak of death, Mother? I hope you are in good health."

"I am, by God's grace. But I was speaking of yours."

"Mine? I am well, I think."

"Before you, Clement, may lie great earthly glory. I pray it may be so. But if not, we should equally rejoice to wear the martyr's crown."

"I have done nothing, Mother, to cause me to be martyred," he said uneasily.

"I know." She smiled at him almost gaily. "So I have done it for you."

When the Wars of the Roses had ended, a century before, with a final royal bloodletting, the new Tudor dynasty had picked up England's crown. Descended only from an obscure branch of the royal Plantagenets, and on the female side, the Tudors had been anxious to prove their right to rule and, with this in mind, had been the most pious supporters of the Holy Roman Church. But when the second Tudor had needed a marriage annulled to get a male heir and secure the dynasty, politics had taken pride of place over religion.

And when King Henry VIII of England quarrelled with the Pope, divorced his royal Spanish wife and made himself head of the Church of England, he had acted with a terrifying ruthlessness. Sir Thomas More, saintly old Bishop Fisher, the brave monks of the London Charterhouse and several others all suffered martyrdom. Most of Henry's subjects were either cowed, or indifferent. But not all. In the north of England a huge Catholic uprising – the Pilgrimage of Grace – had made even the king tremble before it was put down. The English people, especially in the countryside, by no means accepted the break with the old religious ways.

Yet as long as King Harry lived, good Catholics could still hope that the true Church might be restored. Other rulers might be impressed by the doctrines of Martin Luther and the new generation of Protestant leaders who were shaking all Europe with their clamour for change. But King Harry of England certainly believed he was a good Catholic. True, he had denied the authority of the Pope; true, he had closed down all the monasteries and stolen all their vast lands. But in all this he claimed he was only reforming papal abuses. His English Church was still in doctrine Catholic; he continued to execute troublesome Protestants as long as he reigned.

It was only when his poor, sickly son, the boy-king Edward

VI and his Protestant guardians came to power that the new Protestant religion was forced upon England. The Mass was outlawed, the churches stripped of popish ornament. Protestants – they were mostly merchants and craftsmen in the towns – might have liked it, but honest Catholic folk in the countryside were horrified.

Hope returned for loyal Catholics when, after six years of this enforced Protestantism, the boy-king died and Henry's daughter Mary came to the throne: child of the long-suffering Spanish princess – whom even Protestant Englishmen agreed Henry had treated shamefully when he divorced her – Mary wanted passionately to restore her mother's true faith to her now heretic island kingdom and, given time, she might have succeeded.

The trouble was, the English didn't like her. She was a sad woman. Deeply marked by her father's treatment of her mother, passionate for her faith, all she longed for was a good Catholic husband and the blessing of children. But she had no charm; she was dictatorial; she wasn't her father. When she decided to marry the most Catholic king of mighty Spain – which was sure to put Englishmen under Spanish rule – and the English Parliament protested, she told them it was none of their business. And then, of course, she burned several hundred English Protestants.

By the standards of the age the burnings were not so terrible. By the time of the later Middle Ages, although there was nothing in the scriptures to support such a thing, the Christian community had developed an extraordinary appetite for burning human beings alive and it was a fashion that lasted for several centuries. Nor did it seem, in England, to make much difference which side of the denominational divide you were on. Catholics burned Protestants and Protestants burned Catholics. The Protestant Bishop Latimer had personally presided over what can only be described as the sadistic ritual murder of an elderly Catholic priest – a burning carried out in so disgusting a manner that even the crowd who had come to watch it broke down the barriers and intervened. Now, under Mary, it was Latimer's turn to be burned, although with less sadism, thereby to earn the reputation of a martyr for his faith. But there were others – simple townsmen, innocent of po-

litical connivance but humbly seeking God – who were
burned; and there were too many of them. Before long, the
English were calling their Catholic queen "Bloody Mary."

The King of Spain came and went, and there was no child;
the burnings continued. Then Mary tried to fight a little war
and lost Calais, the last English possession in France. And by
the time the poor woman died, after five miserable years upon
the throne, the English were sick of her and welcomed good
Queen Bess.

Clement Albion stared at his mother in horror.

Did she deceive herself or was she really so fearless?
Perhaps she herself did not know. One thing he was sure of:
she had woven herself so closely into the part she played, and
for so long, that she had become as stiff as the brocade of her
dress.

Old King Harry had still been alive when she had married
Albion. She was a Pitts – a notable family in the county of
Southampton, as Hampshire was often called – and due, from
a cousin, to receive a great inheritance. It was a marriage that
had seemed to promise Albion great advancement. Nor, at
first, had it seemed a difficulty that, like all her Pitts family,
she was devout.

The crisis of Henry VIII's reign had caused great shock in
the county of Southampton. Bishop Gardiner of Winchester, in
whose great diocese the region lay, was a loyal Catholic who
had only with difficulty been persuaded to acknowledge
Henry's supremacy over the Church. He had nearly gone to execution like Fisher and More. When Henry had dissolved the
monasteries huge tracts of the county had changed hands. In
the New Forest, in particular, the great monastery of Beaulieu,
the lands of Christchurch priory to the south-west, the smaller
house of Breamore in the Avon valley and the great abbey of
Romsey just above the Forest – these were all stolen, their
buildings stripped and left to fall into ruin. For a family like
the Pitts this was terrible indeed.

But the Protestant years of the boy-king that followed were
almost beyond enduring. Bishop Gardiner was taken to the
Fleet prison – a London common gaol – and then to the Tower,
before being left under house arrest. In his place as bishop the

king's Protestant council sent a man who had been married three times, who held two bishoprics at the same time and who cheerfully sold part of Winchester's endowment to pay off the family of the Duke of Somerset who had appointed him. "See," a Pitt remarked drily, "how these Protestants purify the Church." And certainly, in the years of the boy-king that followed, the diocese of Winchester was well and truly purified. The churches of Hampshire and the Isle of Wight had been particularly well furnished. With what boundless joy, therefore, the Protestant reformers now fell upon them. Silver plate and candlesticks, vestments, hangings, even the bells were taken down. Some of this huge haul simply disappeared, stolen. Some was sold, although for whose account it was not always easy to say. Thus the English Church was liberated from popery.

Clement had no memory of his mother during these years. He had been born early in the boy-king's reign, but he was not yet three when his mother had left. He could only guess at what strains these events had put upon his parents' marriage, but it was apparently his father's purchase of some property that had belonged to Beaulieu Abbey that made his pious mother realise she could no longer dwell in her husband's house. She had returned to her family, the other side of Winchester. His father had always told him that he had refused to let her take her little child with her, so Clement supposed it must be so.

With the accession of Queen Mary to the throne and the return of Bishop Gardiner to the diocese his mother, also, had returned to her marital home and Clement had come to know her. She was a strikingly handsome woman. He had felt so proud of her. And indeed, it seemed to him that these were happy years. He would never forget his parents' gorgeous apparel when he was allowed to accompany them to Southampton to greet the King of Spain when he landed there to marry Mary Tudor. His mother's strong faith was well known, and she and her husband had been well received at the royal court.

There had even been a child born, Clement's sister Catherine. She was a pretty little girl. He had pushed her about in a small cart and she had loved him. But then Queen Mary had died and Elizabeth had come to the throne; and not long after, his mother had gone again, taking his sister with her.

His father would never say why she had left; nor, when they met, did his mother ever tell him much. But he supposed he could imagine.

"The Whore's Daughter." That was how his mother always referred to the queen. To good Catholics, of course, King Henry's Spanish wife had been his only wife until she died. The charade of the divorce and remarriage, sanctioned by Henry's breakaway English Church, was nothing but a fraud. So Queen Anne Boleyn had never been married and her daughter Elizabeth was a bastard. Nor, for Clement's mother, could Queen Elizabeth's Church be of any interest. The Church that Elizabeth and her counsellor Cecil tried to create was a compromise. The queen did not claim to be its spiritual head but only its governor. Its doctrines were a sort of re-formist Catholicism and on the vexed question of the Mass – whether or not a miracle took place and the bread and wine of the Eucharist actually became the body and blood of Christ – the English Church maintained a formula whose ambiguity was little short of genius.

But what was ambiguity to her? The Lady Albion knew she was right. And this, Clement assumed, was the reason for her departure. His father was kindly and, in his way, devout. But the Albion family had been making accommodations ever since the days of Cola the Huntsman, five hundred years be-fore and Clement's mother despised compromise. She also de-spised her husband so she left. Perhaps, Clement thought, his father had been relieved to see her go.

Queen Elizabeth's cunning compromise had not been enough to preserve her island kingdom's peace. The terrible religious forces that the Reformation unleashed had now di-vided all Europe into two armed camps who would war with each other, at a huge cost in human life, for more than a cen-tury. Whichever way the Queen of England turned, she found herself beset with danger. She deplored the extremes of the Catholic Inquisition. She shared the horror of her Puritan sub-jects when, one terrible St Bartholomew's Day, the conserva-tive Catholics of France massacred thousands of peaceful Protestants. Yet she could not sanction the growing Puritan

party in England who wanted, through an increasingly radical
Parliament, to destroy her compromise Church and dictate to
the queen herself. Even if her natural inclination was to move
towards the ordered world offered by traditional Catholicism,
that did her no good either. For since she couldn't deliver her
country to Rome, the Pope had not only excommunicated her
but absolved all Catholics from allegiance to the heretic
queen. Elizabeth couldn't tolerate that: the Roman Church was
outlawed in her realm.

The English Catholics did not rise in revolt, but they took
all the steps they could to preserve their religion. And few
places in southern England contained more loyal Catholics
than the Winchester diocese. Even at the start of the reign,
thirty priests there had resigned sooner than put up with
Elizabeth's compromise Church. Many of the better sort, as
the gentry and merchant class were called, quite openly maintained their Catholic faith. One of the Pitts women was put in
the Clink prison by the bishop for defying him and the queen's
secretary Cecil himself sent word to Albion to keep his wife
quiet.

"I cannot control her; she does not live in my house," Albion
sent word back. "Although I couldn't curb your mother's
tongue," he privately confessed to Clement, "even if she did
live with me." His father had died not long after and it seemed
the authorities had decided to ignore the Lady Albion since
then.

But Clement always lived in dread. He strongly suspected
that she harboured Catholic priests. The Isle of Wight and the
inlets on the Southampton stretch of the southern coast were
natural places to land Roman priests, and the loyal Catholic
gentry, the recusants as they were already being called, were
ready to give them shelter. These priests were strictly illegal
now; no less than four had been discovered in the Winchester
diocese recently and taken away for burning. Any day,
Clement expected to hear of his mother's arrest for harbouring
priests. She would not even exercise caution. The crimson she
was wearing, he thought, was a typical case in point.

When, twenty years before, the Catholic Mary Queen of
Scots had been thrown out of her own kingdom by the Scottish
Presbyterians, she had soon become the focus of every

Catholic plot to overthrow her heretic English cousin. Held under house arrest in England, the wilful exile schemed endlessly until at last, at the start of 1587, Elizabeth had been practically forced by her own council to execute her.

"She is a Catholic martyr," the Lady Albion had immediately declared and within a week she had come to visit her son, wearing the martyr's crimson for all to see.

"But must you openly defy the queen's council and the bishop in this way?" he had asked in a plaintive tone.

"Yes," she had answered simply. "We must."

We. That was the trouble. Whenever his mother spoke to him of the necessity of dangerous acts, she always spoke of "we" – to let him know that in her mind he was infallibly included.

Ten years ago his mother had finally come into her cousin's large inheritance. She became, therefore, a very rich woman, free to leave her fortune where and how she pleased. She never spoke of it. Neither did he. The idea that he could be loyal to the sacred cause in order to inherit her money was as unthinkable as to imagine that he would see a penny of it if he wasn't. The nearest hint she had ever given of her position was once, when he had mentioned that his father had been short of money before his death, to remark: "I could not help your father, Clement. He was a broken reed." And in those words he thought he could hear, like a soft snap, the sentence of poverty for those who disappointed her.

"We," therefore, it was. The fact that she had yet to give him anything, that he now had a wife and three children and that, if he displeased the queen's council he could count upon losing the several posts in the Forest that provided his modest income – these considerations, of course, must mean nothing if he were to keep her good opinion as they both stood before the most high God.

"What do you desire of me, Mother?" he managed to say at last.

"To speak a word or two alone. I could not do it at the wedding." The celebration at Salisbury had been a large affair: one of her nieces had been marrying into a prominent Sarum family. To talk without risk of being overheard would have been difficult.

"I have received a letter, Clement." She paused, looking at him solemnly. He wondered uneasily what was coming next. "From your sister. From Spain."

Spain. Why had his mother insisted on marrying his sister to a Spaniard? A foolish question, really. Even the French, in her eyes, were not truly reliable in matters of religion compared with the Spanish. Back in Mary Tudor's reign, when King Philip of Spain and his courtiers were in England, she had lost no time in making friends among the Spanish nobility. And sure enough, as soon as his sister Catherine reached the age of fifteen, his mother had boarded a merchant ship at Southampton and departed without so much as a by-your-leave for Spain. Once there, the whole business had been arranged in a trice. With the promise, no doubt, of a handsome dowry, Catherine had been betrothed to a Spaniard of impoverished but impeccable family – he was even related, distantly, to the powerful Duke of Medina Sidonia.

He had not seen her since then. Was she happy? He hoped so. He tried to visualise her. He had his father's fair hair, but she was dark like her mother. She had probably turned into a completely Spanish lady by now. In which case, he thought glumly, you could be sure what her views were about the present crisis.

When King Philip of Spain had married Catholic Mary Tudor he had naturally supposed that he was adding England to his vast Hapsburg family domains. He had been disappointed when, at her death, the English council had politely but firmly told him he wasn't wanted. Not that you could fault his persistence: he had offered repeatedly to marry Elizabeth, who had played him along for years. But the King of Spain was not to be trifled with. Not only had this English queen spurned him; she made friends and flirted marriage with his rivals the French. Her seafaring buccaneers – they were legalised pirates, really – raided his shipping; she aided the Protestants who rebelled against Spanish rule in the Netherlands. She had proved to be a heretic and the Pope wanted her deposed. When, at the start of 1587, she had executed the Catholic Mary Queen of Scots it was the final excuse he needed. With the Pope's blessing he prepared a huge fleet.

The Spanish attack upon England would have taken place

that very summer if that boldest of English buccaneers, Sir Francis Drake, had not sent fire ships into Cadiz and destroyed half the Spanish fleet. By the end of the summer, as Clement and his mother were contemplating the family wedding in Salisbury, though the danger seemed to be past that year, few people imagined that Philip of Spain had given up. He would surely try again. It was his nature.

"We shall soon be delivered, Clement." It was "delivered" as far as his mother was concerned; not "invaded."

"You have definite news?"

"Don Diego" – this was Catherine's husband – "has risen far. He is to be a great captain in the army that will come." She smiled with satisfaction. "It will come, Clement, with the banner of the true Church. And then the faithful of England will rise."

He had no doubt that she believed it. Encouraged largely by contact with people like the Lady Albion, the Spanish Ambassador had assured his royal master that at least twenty-five thousand Englishmen under arms would flock to join the Catholic army as soon as it set foot on English soil. It had to be so. Wasn't it God's will? And Queen Elizabeth herself, whatever she might say, was by no means confident of the loyalty of her Catholic subjects. The fact that some of the southern shore defences might be in the hands of Catholic sympathisers had already caused her loyal Secretary Cecil some alarm.

Yet would they rise? Albion's own estimate was different. English Catholics might not like Queen Elizabeth much, but they had lived under her rule for thirty years, now. Few of them wanted to be subjects of Spain. "English Catholics long for the return of their religion, Mother," he said. "But few of them want to be traitors."

"Traitors? We cannot be traitors if we serve the true God. They are afraid."

"Doubtless."

"So they must be given heart. They must be led."

He said nothing.

"You lead part of the muster in the Forest, Clement. Is it not so?" All along the southern coastal regions, musters of men had been raised in every parish – a local militia to resist the

Spanish if they landed. "And the muster point for the Forest is down by the shore battery?"

"Yes." He had been quite proud of his work with the muster that spring, even if they were still poorly armed.

"But you do not mean, of course, to oppose the Spanish when they land?"

"I?" He stared at her. Did she imagine he was going to act the traitor – join the Spanish – for the faith?

But now she smiled. "Clement, I have news that will bring you joy. I have a letter for you." She reached into her black gown and from some secret recess drew out a little roll of parchment which she handed to him in quiet triumph. "It is a letter, Clement – a warrant – from your brother-in-law, Don Diego. He gives you your instructions. There may be more in the spring. They are coming next summer, without fail. God's will be done."

He took the letter from her in a daze. "How came you by this?" he asked hoarsely.

"Through your sister, of course. There is a merchant who carries me her letters. And other things."

"But, Mother. If this should ever be discovered. Cecil and the council have spies . . ." And very good ones; it was well known. "Such a letter . . ." He trailed off. Such a letter, intercepted, meant death.

She observed him silently for a moment or two; but when she spoke, her voice was surprisingly gentle. "Even the most faithful may be afraid," she said quietly. "This is how God tests us. And yet," she continued, "it is the very fear of God that also gives us courage. For you see, Clement, we cannot escape Him. He is everywhere. He knows all, judges all. We have no choice but to obey Him, if we believe. So it is only lack of faith that holds us back, that keeps us from rushing to His arms."

"Faith is not always easy, Mother, even for the faithful."

"And it is for that, Clement," she went on earnestly, "that He sends us signs. Our Blessed Lord performed miracles; the saints, their very relics, cause wonders even now. Why, here in the Forest, does not God send us a marvellous miracle every year?"

"You speak of the oak trees?"

"Of course, what else?"

It had been remarked upon for many generations now that there were three magical, or miraculous trees in the New Forest. They were all to be found in the area to the north of Lyndhurst; all three were old. And unlike any other oak trees in the Forest, or anywhere else in Christendom for all that Clement knew, they burst all three into green leaf for a mysterious midwinter week, at the feast of Christmas when everything else was bare. The Christmas Green Oaks, or the Green Trees they were called.

No one knew how and why it happened. Their breaking into leaf was against all nature. No wonder, then, if to pious Lady Albion and many like her, this reminder of Our Lord's crucifixion, of the three crosses upon Calvary and of the resurrection of the dead, was seen as a sign that the divine message is everywhere and that the Holy Church sends forth new shoots in any season of the year.

"Oh, Clement." Her eyes now grew suddenly misty. "God's signs are everywhere. There is nothing to fear." She was looking at him with such emotion. It was the nearest thing to maternal affection he could ever remember seeing. "When we are delivered from heresy and King Philip rules, this will only lead to your glory." She smiled so tenderly. "But if – which I cannot think – it should be God's will that this business fall out otherwise, I had rather see you, my dearest son, raised on a scaffold, even torn limb from limb, than that you should forsake your God, your Heavenly King."

He knew she meant it, every word. "You know what my instructions are?"

"To lead your muster, Clement, silence the shore battery and help the Spanish to land."

"Where?"

"Between Southampton and Lymington. The Forest shore will not be easy to defend."

"You expect me to reply to this letter?"

"There is no need." She beamed. "It is already done. I sent a letter to your sister, and Don Diego will convey it to the King of Spain himself. I have told them that you may be relied upon. Even unto death."

He gazed southwards, over the Forest, towards Southampton

and the distant blue haze by the coast. Was her letter, perhaps, already in the hands of Cecil's spies? Would he live to see Christmas? "Thank you, Mother," he murmured, drily.

But his mother did not hear him. For she was already signalling to the servants to bring her litter.

The oak tree stood just apart from the wood.

The afternoon was warm.

In the wood, smooth, stately beech trees soared up to share the canopy with crusted oaks. The ground was mossy. All was quiet except for the faint rustle of the leaves and the tiny popping sound as, now and then, a green acorn fell to the ground.

Behind the tree, on a slight incline dotted with young oaks, lay a green glade down which the shadows stole at sunset.

Albion was alone as he rode towards the tree.

Oak: the genus *Quercus*, sacred since ancient times. There are five hundred species of oak tree upon the planet, but the island of Britain since the ending of the Ice Age contained mainly two: *quercus robur*, the common or pedunculate oak, whose acorns grow upon little stalks; and *quercus petraea*, the sessile oak, whose leaves have fewer lobes and whose acorns grow side by side with the leaf. Both kinds grew on the sandy New Forest soil. The common oak produced more acorns.

Albion gazed at the tree with pleasure. He had a particular interest in trees.

The New Forest and its administration had not changed greatly in the last four hundred years. The royal deer were still protected; the midsummer fence month still in force; the verderers still held courts and the foresters their bailiwicks. From time to time, also, gentlemen regarders – knights of the county often as not – would survey and check the Forest boundaries, although a steady trickle of small land grants to private individuals down the generations had made this a more complex task than it had been in olden times. But one change had been taking place. It was subtle, sometimes vague, yet increasingly present.

No one could say exactly when it had begun, but there had been an informal management of the trees in the Forest for centuries. The woodland crop was important: rods, poles, branches for wattle fencing, brushwood, fuel for fires and for charcoal.

The trees supplied so many of man's needs. Most of the supply came from the smaller trees and bushes like the hazel and holly. To obtain straight poles from a hazel, for instance, it would be cut just above the ground, causing it to send up multiple shoots which could be harvested every few years. This process was known as coppicing. More rarely, with oak trees, a similar cutting took place about six feet up, causing a mass of spreading shoots to emerge. This was termed pollarding, and the resulting tree with its stocky trunk and fan of branches was known as a pollard oak.

The only trouble with coppicing was that, when you had cut the underwood, the deer and other forest stock would come and eat up all the new shoots, destroying the whole process. And so the practice had grown up of inclosing small areas, usually with a low earth wall and a fence, to keep the animals out for three years or so, until the new shoots were too sturdy to be eaten. These inclosures were known as coppices.

A century earlier, just before the Tudors came to the English throne, an act of parliament had finally regulated the coppices. Inclosures could be made under licence and fenced for three years to allow regeneration. Since then the period had been extended to a generous nine years. These coppices were valuable and were leased out.

But beyond this activity there was the question of timber – of the felling of whole trees for the construction of large buildings, ships or other of the king's works. In ages past there had been little need for timber from the New Forest, although huge trees might be provided for a cathedral church or other great project from time to time. But as building activity slowly rose in the Tudor period, the royal treasury began to look more carefully to see what income could be derived from its timber. In 1540, King Henry VIII had appointed a surveyor general to oversee the income, including that from timber, from all the royal woodlands, with a woodward for each county where the royal woodlands lay. The New Forest was not only, nowadays, a preserve for the king's deer; very gradually the faint consciousness was stealing through the glades that it might also be a huge store of royal trees.

A few years earlier, Albion had managed to get himself appointed as the woodward for the New Forest. This had brought him some extra income; it had also caused him to learn a good deal more than he had ever known about trees. He had even become quite interested in them for their own sake. He looked with approval and even admiration, therefore, at the stately old oak.

It was a great, spreading oak; although its spread came naturally, and not from any pollarding. It was also famous. The first reason for its fame was that, situated some three miles or so north of Lyndhurst, it was one of the three curious trees that broke into leaf for a week at Christmas. But even this magical fact was not all for, somewhere in its long life, it had acquired a second reputation.

"That was the oak tree that Walter Tyrrell's arrow glanced off before it killed King William Rufus." So people said, and for all Albion's life, at least, the forest folk had called it the Rufus tree.

Could it be so, Albion wondered? Did oak trees really live so long in the rather poor soil of the Forest?

"The life of an oak is seven times the life of a man," his father had long ago told him. His own guess was that few of the great rotting, ivy-encrusted hulks with their twenty-foot girths were above four centuries old; and in this estimate he was roughly correct. The Rufus oak did not look five hundred years old to him.

Yet there was certainly something wonderful, even magical about the mighty tree.

The tree knew many things.

It was nearly three hundred years since Luke the runaway lay brother had planted it in a place of safety. Since then the wood had moved a little, as woods may do; deer and other grazing animals had eaten up the new shoots in the grassy glade and in this way the tree had been granted an open space of its own in which to grow. While its brethren in the wood, therefore, had grown up tall and narrow beside their neighbours, as oaks in natural woodland usually do, the branches of the Rufus oak had been free to spread outwards as well as upwards, seeking the light.

Despite the name that men had foolishly given it, the Rufus oak had begun its life two centuries too late to play any role in the dramatic death of the red-haired king – which had anyway taken place in quite another part of the Forest. But its life was already old, and complex.

The tree knew that winter was coming. The thousands of leaves, which had gathered in the light, would soon become a burden in the winter frosts. Already, therefore, it had begun to shut down this part of its huge system. The vessels that took the sap to and from the leaves were gradually closing. The remaining moisture in them was evaporating in the September sun, causing them to grow dry and yellow. Just as, in its different season, the male deer seals off the supply of blood to its antlers so that they dry out and are shed, so the tree in a similar fashion would shed its golden leaves.

Before the leaves, however, there would be two other fallings.

The acorns were already dropping in their green thousands. The crop of acorns for any oak will vary, depending mostly on the weather, from year to year; but unlike most other species, the oak as it grows older increases its production of seed, reaching the height of its fecundity in late middle age. Already the pigs were feeding upon the acorns as they pattered down below the spreading branches and scurrying mice would nibble them at night; and others would be taken further away by squirrels, or by jays who might fly some distance before burying them for safekeeping in the ground. Thus the oak was dispersing its seed for future generations.

The other falling was subtler and scarcely noticed. For during the spring the tiny gall wasp, which more resembles a flying ant than the common wasp, had laid its spangle-galls on the underside of the oak leaves. Now these galls, like little red warts, were detaching themselves and flittering down so that they could lie for the winter, hidden and insulated by the leaves that were about to fall on top of them.

Meanwhile, in the bark of the tree, the sap containing the essential sugar was sinking down to its roots, deep underground, to be stored there through the frosts.

Yet if it seemed that this was a season only of closure, it was not so. True, the falling of the leaves would see some of the oak tree's companions of the spring and summer depart: the various warblers, the blackcaps and redstarts, would leave for warmer climes. But the hardy year rounders, the robins and wrens, the chaffinches, blackbirds and bluetits, although they might diminish or end their song, would still remain. The tawny owl had no thought of leaving the ancient oak; weeks had yet to pass before the myriad bats settled down into their winter sleep within its crevices. Others, thrushes and redwings, were just arriving in the Forest on their way from much harsher habitats. And the ivy that crept along its lower branches would actually use this season to flower, thus attracting the insects who would have been too busy, before now, to pollinate its flowers.

Indeed, the oak tree was about to supply the Forest with a prodigious quantity of food. It was not only the acorns. Upon the tree itself, its bark presented a continent of cracks and crevices in which countless tiny insects and other invertebrates moved about. In autumn the tits would descend upon this territory in flocks to feast upon them. Nuthatches would walk down while tree creepers went up, so that nothing was missed. But most important of all were the dropping leaves.

Death is not final in the Forest, but only a transformation. A rotting tree trunk lying on the ground provides home and food for a thousand tiny invertebrates; the falling leaves, as they decompose, are broken down by many organisms, especially woodlice and worms – although because of its acid soil, the Forest has few if any snails. But the greatest breakdown of material takes place afterwards and at a deeper level. For then it is the turn of the fungi.

Fungus – pale, loathsome, connected with mildew and rot, and poison, and death. And yet it is not. Is it a plant? Of a kind, although it is seldom green like the plants that sustain themselves, for the fungus contains no chlorophyll. Its cell walls, strangely, are made not of cellulose but of chitin, which also forms the walls of an insect's body. It lives upon other organisms, like a parasite. The ancients, uncertain how to classify the fungus, said that it belonged to chaos.

And in the Forest the fungi are everywhere. Mostly they exist as strings of fungal matter, almost like bootlaces, called hyphae. Under the tree bark, under the rotting leaves, under the ground, they spread into a tangled web known as mycelium. And it is this hidden mass of mycelium that converts the rotted leaf mould, returning the nutrients – nitrogen, potassium, phosphorus – to the soil to nourish the forest's future life.

It is only the fruit of the fungus that is normally seen and at no time did so much appear as at the autumn season in the oak woods. In the vicinity of the Rufus oak there were hundreds of species: the beefsteak fungus, like a raw steak on the base of an ancient oak bole; edible mushrooms and the poisonous death caps that mimicked them; red-and-white-spotted toadstools; the friendly penny bun, which is edible and whose mycelium draws sugar from the oak roots and gives them minerals in return; and the evil-smelling stinkhorn which, growing from a round underground pod called a witch's egg, bursts into the upper world in a single day, with a slimy cap that draws the flies, before collapsing and shrivelling back only a day or two after its appearance.

These and many others shared the forest floor beneath the oak with tufted grass and moss, and yellow pimpernel.

When Albion reached the tree he dismounted. He had taken his time. After his mother had turned eastwards towards Romsey and Winchester, he had come slowly down into the Forest, pausing at hamlets here and there, hoping that the wood's great quietness might calm his spirits. But it had not worked. Not only had his mother terrified him, but after her revelation, the business he must conduct the next day made him still more apprehensive. He was glad, therefore, to come and rest under the spreading oak. Perhaps that would bring him peace.

Why was it, he wondered, that the great oak had this power to revive him? What was its magic? Was it just the huge, gnarled strength of the tree? The fact that it remained there, a living thing yet unchanging, like an ancient rock? Both these things, he thought; and the falling acorns, and the rustling leaves. There was, however, something else – something he had often felt when he stood by the trunk of some full-grown spreading oak. It was almost as if the tree were enclosing him within an invisible sphere of strength and power. It was a strange feeling, yet palpable. He was sure of it, even if he could not say why.

In a way, his sense of the tree was accurate. For it is a fact

that the roots of a tree mirror the spreading crown of its
branches. As the branches spread out, so do the roots in pro-
portion. If the tree's branches die back, the roots do too. As
above, so below. In this respect the system of the tree as a
whole rather resembles, at top and bottom, the magnetic
field of a bar magnet, or indeed of the Earth itself. And who
knows what force fields, as yet unmeasured by man, may
surround the physical manifestation of a tree?

After a little time, therefore, somewhat strengthened, Albion
emerged from the oak to face the dangers of the coming days.

Jane Furzey was happy because she was with Nick Pride who
was tall and handsome, and going to marry her when she said
yes. She was going to say yes, but not until she had made him
wait; that was what every girl did if she could.

"Make him wait a year, Jane," her mother had told her. "If
he loves you truly, he'll want you all the more."

She wasn't going to give herself to him until they married
either. She was going to get married in style. And in this exciting state they went about together often.

It had been kind of Clement Albion to allow her to come
with the men this morning. There were just three men including Nick, and herself, bumping along in the little cart, while
Albion rode his horse beside them. She was proud that Albion
should have selected Nick for such special duties. She dangled
her sturdy legs over the back of the cart. She had taken off her
sandals. The sun was warm on her legs; the cool, salty air on
her bare toes was delicious.

This expedition was rather an adventure and she looked
about her with interest. They had already passed Lymington;
she had never been down here before.

Jane was sixteen, Nick Pride eighteen. He lived in the village of Minstead, a couple of miles north of Lyndhurst, she in
the hamlet of Brook, a mile and a half north of that. Their parents who, like most parents, were wise in these matters,
thought they were perfect for each other; and so they were.

During the centuries the Prides had settled in many parts of
the Forest, but the Furzeys had mostly stayed down in the
south. Except for Jane's family. For some reason – no one could
remember when – the descendants of Adam Furzey had moved

up to the Minstead area. "The Furzeys up at Minstead don't get along with the other Furzeys," the Forest people would remark. And although in that region, where all the smallholding families intermarried, such differences usually got ironed out, it remained true that the Minstead Furzeys were a bit unusual. During the Wars of the Roses one of them had become a priest; and in the reign of old King Harry another had gone to Southampton. "He became a merchant," Nick's father had told him. "Did very well, they say." The other Furzeys might mutter that the Minstead family thought too much of themselves, but this was no problem for the Prides, who thought well of themselves too. Nick Pride's father and Jane's father had always got along well and on the day, ten years ago, when Jane's father had moved up to Brook, Nick's father had remarked: "I reckon your Jane and my boy Nick would make a nice pair." And Jane's father had agreed and told his wife, who knew it anyway. So there it was.

There was nothing very remarkable about Jane. She had a broad brow, brown hair parted in the middle, deep-blue eyes; she was short, with wide, well-shaped hips. Men were drawn to her. She cooked and baked and sewed; she looked after her little brothers and sisters; she had a dog called Jack who liked to chase squirrels; and there was nothing about the family's smallholding she didn't know.

She could also read, which was unusual. No one else in the family could, nor in any of the families like hers in Minstead or Brook. Had her father lived in a city like London as a small merchant or craftsman at this date, he would probably have been able to read. But in the country there was still little need. A rich yeoman with a big farm of his own might be a man of considerable substance but still mark his name with a cross, while the penniless clerk wrote it out in full.

No one had taught her to read. She had just, somehow, picked it up herself, from a Bible she had pored over in Minstead church, and from other written material she had found in visits to local markets. She did not prize this knowledge highly, since it was of little practical use; but it had amused her to learn something new. Nick Pride was rather pleased, though. "My wife can read," he could hear himself saying. It was an accomplishment, enough to show the world that he had married a superior woman. These things were important to a man.

When they married Jane would not be bringing any gold or jewellery or silken clothes with her: there was no need for such things in the Forest. But there was one small and humble ornament which she had begged and she had been promised for her wedding day.

It was a strange little wooden cross that hung on a string round her mother's neck. Jane's father had given it to her when they married.

"I don't know where it comes from, but it's always been in the family," he had told her. "Hundreds of years, they say." He had shaken his head. "Funny old thing, really, but my grandfather told me: 'You keep hold of that. That's your birthright.'"

The cedarwood cross with its curious carving had been worn on the skin of so many generations now that it was almost black. But there was something about this family talisman that had always fascinated Jane since she was a little girl. She loved to touch it and hold it in her hand. She would try to decipher its carving as though it might hold some secret meaning. For she felt that it must, even if she could have no idea of the message that had been sent her, by a monkish ancestor, nearly three hundred years before.

She was going to wear it at her wedding.

The cart bumped down the lane and came on to a gravel strand.

"Look," she cried in delight. "We're at the sea."

Albion looked irritably at the fortress ahead. Why the devil had his good friend Gorges insisted that he bring these men out here, anyway? It was a waste of his time, in his opinion. But behind this bravado lay a deeper apprehensiveness. After his talk with his mother yesterday – he couldn't help it – he secretly viewed the fortress with a kind of panic.

"Halloa," he cried to the sentry, "Albion's muster."

"Pass, Sir," came the reply.

They had crossed Pennington Marshes, passed the inlet of Keyhaven and now they had started along the track that led out to the end of the mile-long gravel spit opposite the Isle of Wight. On their right was the open sea. Above the sky was blue and seagulls were crying. And just visible at the end of the spit, glinting palely in the sun, lay their destination.

Hurst Castle. It would probably never have been built if it hadn't been for Henry VIII's marital troubles. England's coasts had been threatened with raids, on and off, for over a thousand years. But when the Pope, at one point in his quarrel with Henry, had urged both Spain and her rival France to join forces and attack the heretic island, the king had decided he had better prepare himself and sent commissioners to inspect the coastal defences; and few places were more important than the port of Southampton and the Solent. When they got there, however, and saw the defences, their conclusion was simple: useless.

The most intelligent course was obviously to defend the two entrances to the Solent system so that enemy ships could not enter its huge shelter at all. At the western end this meant a pair of batteries, one on the Isle of Wight near the Needles, the other on the mainland. On the island there was already a ramshackle tower which could be put into service.

And on the mainland coast: "God has provided for us."

The long, curving gravel spit that ran out from below Keyhaven was indeed a perfect God-given site. It ended with a broad platform; it commanded the narrowest part of the channel leading in and out of the Solent. Immediately they ordered an earthwork with gun emplacements – a bulwark. But King Henry wanted something more and soon an ambitious building was going up.

Hurst Castle was a small, squat, stone-built fort. It was an unusual structure, though. For it was neither round nor square but built in the shape of a triangle. At each of its three corners was a stout, semicircular bastion. In the western wall there was an entrance with a portcullis and a drawbridge over a small moat. Over the middle of the triangular fort stood a two-storey tower. Bastions, walls and tower all bristled with cannon. The Spanish, who knew all about it, considered Hurst a formidable obstacle.

And this was the place Albion's mother expected him to betray. To her, of course, it was not only an obstacle to the true religion; its very stones were an offence.

When King Harry had sold off all the Church's monastic

lands to his friends, Beaulieu had passed into the hands of the noble family of Wriothesley. But many others in the area were keen to benefit from the opportunities of the age and none more so than a prominent Southampton merchant named Mill. An able man, he had already acted as steward of the old Beaulieu estate and was eager to please the king and acquire monastic lands of his own. As it was usual practice for the crown to subcontract important projects like building ships or forts to local entrepreneurs, it was not surprising that, when it came to the new Solent defences, the business should have been put in the capable hands of Mill. He had done an excellent job. The king was delighted. And when asked where he had got so much stone – there being little in the region – he affably replied: "From Beaulieu Abbey, of course."

"That impious Mill!" the Lady Albion had exploded. To use the sacred abbey stones to defend the shoreline against the Pope! The fact that plenty of others had been busy dismantling the abbey and even its church, was not something that her son had cared to point out to her.

As they reached the end of the promontory, Albion saw that the drawbridge was lowered and the gate open; and he had no sooner ordered the three men down from the cart than a familiar figure, a man of about his own age with a broad intelligent face, fine grey eyes and thinning hair, which did not detract from his handsomeness, came striding towards him.

"Clement."

"Thomas."

"Welcome."

Thomas Gorges was of ancient lineage and, Albion thought, it showed. He had friends at court. But above all, Cecil and the council trusted him. For that reason he had been chosen to escort Mary Queen of Scots to her final imprisonment. He had also been knighted. And for some years he had been captain at Hurst Castle where, with the threat of invasion imminent, he had been spending a good deal of time. "These are your men?" he enquired. Albion nodded. "Good. My master gunner will show them round." Apart from Gorges himself and his deputy, there was a considerable garrison at Hurst, headed by the master gunner. "I always think," Gorges went on quietly, "that the more you show the men how things are done, the better you fire their loyalty. Come, Clement," he continued pleasantly, "let us talk."

As he glanced around him, Albion considered, it would be hard not to be impressed. Two tiers of cannon protruded from embrasures in the bastions and the walls on the seaward sides. There were cannon in the central tower as well. No ship entering the Solent could escape this battery and, as for its defences, not only were the walls thick, but they had been built slightly convex to deflect cannonballs. Even under heavy bombardment, Hurst Castle would be a tough nut to crack.

Gorges grinned. "I hope you find everything in good order, Clement." There was no question that Gorges had been an excellent custodian. He had added more cannon, had the central tower rebuilt and greatly strengthened, trained the garrison admirably. He was so highly regarded by the council now that, although the lord-lieutenant of the country was nominally in charge of the county's musters, if Gorges wanted anything – arms, materials or men, he got them at once. "So tell me, Woodward," he enquired genially, "when am I getting my elms?"

It was a curious thing, Albion reflected, that although you built ships of oak, if you used it in a place like Hurst, open to the salty sea breeze, oak timber soon rotted. When Gorges needed new mountings for the cannon, therefore, he had advised him to use elm, which lasted better. "I marked the trees last week. They'll be cut and timber delivered in ten days."

"Thank you. Now tell me about these men you've brought."

"I'm putting Pride in charge. He's young but trustworthy. Intelligent. Pleased with the responsibility and anxious to prove himself. He'll be on his mettle. The other two are good fellows. They'll be all right."

"How wise you are. I shall speak with them at once. By the way," he added casually, "did I tell you that Helena is here?" Helena: his wife. Albion felt a glow of pleasure. He was fond of Helena. "She's been waiting for you. Why don't you talk to her while I see the men?"

Albion paused. The suggestion was so charmingly made that he might not have given it a second thought. Instead, he frowned. He had never been quite sure why it was necessary to bring these men down here at all when he could perfectly well have told them their duties up at Minstead. "Surely, Thomas, if you are seeing my men, you wish me to be present?"

A slight blush. A look of embarrassment, quickly covered, but not quite quickly enough. What did it mean? "Look, here she comes. Do walk with her a little, Clement. She has been so anxious to see you." And before Albion could argue, his friend had gone, leaving him alone.

Nick Pride felt pretty pleased with himself. They were standing in the master gunner's chamber, which had a fine view over the Solent, when Thomas Gorges came in. The aristocrat had spoken to them very civilly for a few minutes, explaining the importance of their duties and Nick had observed him with interest.

He was impressed. If Albion was a gentleman, he sensed that this man was something more. He came from another world, even if Nick did not quite know what that world might be. Putting the two men side by side in his mind, he decided that Albion needed Gorges, but Gorges didn't need Albion. I reckon that's what it is, he thought.

"So, Nicholas Pride," Gorges now said. "I hear you are the guardian of the beacon."

"Yes, Sir," he cried, swelling out his chest. "I am."

The idea of planting beacons of fire on hilltops to alert the countryside of an enemy approaching went back to classical times; but it was the Tudors who had developed them into a regular system in England. A beacon lit at the south-western tip of England could start a chain reaction of coastal fires that would warn London within a couple of hours. At the same time as the message was passed along the coast, however, a network of secondary beacons, radiating inland, picked up the message and alerted the musters in the local settlements to assemble and go to their muster places to defend the coast.

There were two big coastal beacons for the Solent area, one at each end of the Isle of Wight. The hinterland of the New Forest was mainly served by three inland beacons: one up on Burley Beacon, a second on a hill towards the Forest's centre and a third, to summon the northern hamlets, upon an old earthwork at the top of the hill above Minstead village.

"Come and stand by me now, Nicholas Pride," the captain

commanded and he drew apart from the others. "Now then," he said softly, so that only he and the young man could hear each other, "recite to me the duties of your watch."

Nick Pride reckoned he did all right. Albion had coached him thoroughly. There was a precise sequence of signals the Isle of Wight beacon would send, culminating in the one that told him to light his own. He recited them all correctly. He gave the details of how it was to be manned, who would keep watch and when, how it was set up and lit. Gorges questioned him, quietly but thoroughly, and seemed to be satisfied. To Nick's surprise, though, when this was over, the officer did not immediately end their conversation. He seemed to want to know more about him; asked about his family, his brothers and sisters, their smallholding. He even talked about his own family and made Nick laugh. Nick felt surprisingly relaxed. Gorges asked Nick what he thought of the Spaniards and Nick told him they were cursed foreigners. Gorges told him that their King Philip was nonetheless said to be very pious and Nick said that might be so but he was a foreigner anyway and any good Englishman should be glad to cut off his head. "Francis Drake singed his beard for him at Cadiz, Sir, didn't he? With those fire ships. That taught him a lesson I should think." Gorges said he hoped it had.

The aristocrat had been listening and watching him carefully and now knew him better than he knew himself, but young Nick Pride was entirely unaware of it. "I see, Nicholas Pride, that I may trust you," he said at last. "And if the queen herself asks me – and she may – who keeps the watch at our inland beacon, I shall remember your name and tell her you are her loyal man."

"Indeed, Sir, you can," cried Pride, more delighted with himself than ever.

Jane was sitting on a sandy bank, gazing across the Solent when the strange couple came along.

It was warm; there was a hint of haze across the waters so that the Isle of Wight was a sleepy blue. Sandpipers and waders skimmed over the mudflats in front of her and around the fort the fork-tailed swallows darted and sped, although soon they would be leaving for warmer climes.

The man and woman were driving a large wagon with high-boarded sides. It was carrying charcoal.

Jane had already noticed that just below the fort on the Solent side there was a small lime kiln. It had been there, in fact, for some time, a solid business – not on the scale of the nearby salt pans, of course, but profitable – the lime being shipped mostly across the English Channel to the island of Guernsey near the French coast. The charcoal would be needed as fuel for the kiln's furnace.

The wagon turned off the track just before reaching the fort and went down to the kiln. Moments later she saw the man, aided by two others from the kiln, start to unload the sacks from the back of the wagon. She watched him with interest.

He was somewhat shorter than the other men, but he looked very muscular. His hair was thick and black, but his beard was short and neatly trimmed. His eyes were set wide apart and watchful – hunter's eyes, she thought. She felt sure he had already taken her in as he unloaded the sacks of charcoal. So why did he seem strange? She wasn't sure. She had lived with the Forest folk all her life; but this man looked different from the Prides and Furzeys, as if he belonged to some other, more ancient race, inhabitants of a deeper woodland than they knew. Was it her imagination or had his face been burnished by the charcoal fires to a darker hue? Was there something oaken, almost tree-like about him?

It was not hard to guess his family. She had seen several men like him before, at local fairs or at the court at Lyndhurst. "That's Perkin Puckle," her father would point out. Or: "I think that's Dan Puckle, but it may be John." And always the litany continued: "The Puckles live over Burley way." No one had anything to say against them. "They're good friends, long as you keep on the right side of them," her father had told her. But, even if nobody said so, Jane had understood that there was something vaguely mysterious about the family. "They're old," her mother had once remarked, "like the trees." Jane watched the man curiously.

She did not at first realise that she was being watched herself. She had not noticed the woman leave the wagon; but there she was, sitting not far off by a tuft of marsh grass, gazing at Jane thoughtfully. Not wishing to seem unfriendly, Jane nodded to her. Unexpectedly, the woman moved across and sat down only a few feet away from her. For several moments they both watched the men at their work.

"That's my husband." The woman turned to look at her.

She was small and dark-haired – cat-like, Jane thought. She supposed the woman might be about thirty-five, like her husband. Her eyes were dark, almond-shaped; her face looked pale.

"Is he one of the Puckles, from Burley?" Jane ventured.

"That's right." It seemed to her that the woman's eyes were measuring her in some way. "You married?"

"Not yet."

"Considering it?"

"I think so."

"Your man: he's here?"

"In there." Jane indicated the fort.

Puckle's dark-haired wife did not say anything for a little while. She seemed to be staring across the water. Only when she spoke again did she transfer her gaze to her husband. "He's a good man, John Puckle," she said.

"I'm sure."

"Good worker."

"He looks it."

"Lusty. Keep any woman happy."

"Oh." Jane was not sure what to say.

"Your man. He good? He knows how to halleck?" A coarse word.

Jane blushed. "I expect so. But we are not yet married."

The woman's silence conveyed that she was not impressed with this information. "He made himself a bed." She nodded towards her husband. "All oak. Carved it, too. At the four corners. I never saw such carving." She smiled. "Carved his bed so he might lie in it. Once you lie in his oak bed with John Puckle, you'll not want any other bed, nor other man."

Jane stared. She had heard the village women talk at Minstead, but although they would joke quite crudely about the men sometimes, there was a directness about this strange person that both repelled yet fascinated her.

"You like my husband?"

"I . . . ? I do not know him."

"You like to halleck with him?"

What did this mean? Was it some kind of trap? She had no idea but the woman was making her nervous. She rose. "He is your husband, not mine," she said and began to move away. But when, from a safe distance, she stole a glance back, her companion was still sitting quietly, apparently quite unperturbed, and gazing thoughtfully out towards the island.

Helena had suggested they walk along the beach together. Beside them lay the broad open waters of the English Channel. The thrift and sea-campion were no longer in flower but their green shoots extended like a haze all along the strand. Their words as they conversed were accompanied by the quiet hiss and the deep-drawing rattle of sea on shingle, and the cries of the white gulls rising from the foam.

Clement Albion was very fond of Helena Gorges, even if she sometimes made him smile. She was Swedish by birth, very fair, beautiful. "You are as kind as you are beautiful," he would tell her with perfect truth. Although he could have added: "And not a little vain."

It is a universal law that no woman, once she has acquired a title, is ever willing to give it up. Or so it seemed to Albion. When Helena the Swedish beauty had been brought to Queen Elizabeth's English court it had not been long before she had been snapped up as a bride by no less a person than the Marquis of Northampton. She had also become a great favourite of the queen. Sadly, her noble husband had died after only a year, leaving her glamorous, lonely, but a marchioness.

There were very few peerages in Queen Elizabeth's England. The Wars of the Roses had killed off many of the great titles and the Tudors had no wish to make more feudal lords. But one title they had brought into use in England was that of marquis. There were scarcely a handful of them. They ranked only below the haughty dukes. In the order of precedence, therefore, the young Marchioness of Northampton walked through the door before even countesses, let alone ladies and gentlewomen.

So when she had met and fallen in love with aristocratic Thomas Gorges, who was then not even a humble knight, she had married him, but still insisted on calling herself the Marchioness of Northampton.

"And she's still doing it," Albion would say to his wife with a laugh. "Thank God Thomas just thinks it's funny."

Certainly she and Thomas were very happy together. She was a good wife. With her striking looks, her golden hair, her dazzling eyes, she would come on foot along the spit to the fort – she had a wonderful, elegant stride – and charm the garrison. If she was at court she never lost a chance to advance her husband's career. At present, Albion knew, she had a particular project in hand and so, after they had asked the usual tender questions about each other's families, he gently enquired: "And what of your house?"

The fact was, he knew very well, that his friend Gorges for once in his life had overreached himself. He had recently acquired a fine estate just south of Sarum – indeed, Albion had looked over the land the day before, during the interview with his mother. On this estate, known as Longford, Gorges had intended to build a great house. But some time had passed and not a stone had been laid.

"Oh, Clement." She had a charming way of taking your arm to share a confidence. "Do not tell Thomas I have told you, but we are" – she made a little grimace – "in difficulty."

"Can you not build a smaller house?"

"*Very* small, Clement." She smiled conspiratorially.

"A cottage?" He meant it as a jest, but she shook her head and looked serious.

"A small cottage, Clement. Perhaps not even that."

Could things really be so bad? Thomas must have overspent more than he had guessed. "Thomas's fortunes have always risen," he offered. He had no doubt his friend's career would continue to be brilliant.

"Let us hope they rise further, then, Clement." She smiled again, but ruefully this time. "No new dresses for me this year, I fear."

"Perhaps the queen . . ."

"I've been at court." She shrugged. "The queen hasn't a

penny herself. This Spanish business" – she waved towards the horizon – "has emptied the treasury."

Albion nodded thoughtfully.

"Speaking of this Spanish business." He hesitated a moment, but decided to go on. "I brought some of my men down, as you know. Thomas wanted to see them." He gave her a sidelong glance. It was as he had suspected. He could see that she knew something. "Then Thomas insisted he see them alone, without me. Why did he do that, Helena?"

They had both stopped.

Helena was looking down at the shingle at her feet. A wave broke up the beach towards them, then ebbed away. When she answered, she did not look at him. "Thomas is only following his orders, Clement," she said quietly. "That is all."

"It is thought that I . . . ?"

"There are many Catholics in the county, Clement. Everyone knows it. Why, even the Carews . . ." Thomas Carew had been the previous captain of Hurst Castle. His family, good Catholics all of them, still lived at the village of Hordle at the Forest's edge, only a few miles away.

"One can be a Catholic without being a traitor, Helena."

"Of course. And you are still left in command of part of the muster, Clement, are you not? Consider that."

"But your husband nonetheless has to make sure that I and my men are loyal."

"The council is watching everyone, Clement. They have no choice."

"The council? Cecil? They distrust me?"

"Your mother, Clement. Remember, even Cecil has heard of your mother."

"My mother." A wave of panic suddenly seized him. He thought of their interview the day before, and felt himself blushing. "What" – he tried to sound unconcerned – "has my foolish mother been saying now?"

"Who knows, Clement? I am not privy to all these things, but I told the queen . . ."

"The queen? The queen knows of my mother? Dear God!"

"I told her – forgive me, Clement – that she was a foolish woman. Her opinions are not yours."

"God forbid!"

"So, dear Clement, you should not be alarmed. Concern yourself with my house instead. Find me a way to build more than a cowshed at Longford."

He laughed, relieved, and they turned to go back towards the fort. The sea was edging a little higher up the shingle. Ahead, across the water, the four chalk Needles of the Isle of Wight were gleaming. To Albion, at that moment, they seemed phantom-like, unreal. Some gulls rose, ghostly white, cried, then flew away, out to sea.

"Clement." She had stopped. She was facing him. "You know we love you. You're not a traitor, are you?"

"I . . . ?"

Her eyes were searching his face. "Clement? Tell me?"

"Dear God, no."

"Swear it."

"I swear. Upon my honour. Upon all that is sacred." Their eyes met. Hers were troubled. "Don't you believe me?"

"Of course I do." She smiled. "Come on." She linked her arm in his. "Let's go back."

But she was lying. He knew it. She wasn't sure. And if she and Thomas Gorges didn't trust him, then neither did the council nor the queen herself. The months ahead suddenly looked bleaker than ever.

And wasn't it ironic when, whatever his mother might demand, he had just told Helena the truth.

Hadn't he?

When winter came, it was icy cold. But the tree was used to that. For even as the tree had reached middle age, a century before, England had been entering the period, which lasted through the Tudor and Stuart dynasties, known to history as the little Ice Age. Temperatures throughout the year, on average, were several degrees cooler. In summer the difference was not so noticeable. But winters were often cruel. Rivers froze. In great trees cut during this time the yearly growth rings are close together. ·

By early December the oak tree was sealed off for the winter. Its branches were bare and grey; the tight little buds on their twigs were protected from the frosts by waxy brown scales. Deep underground the sugar in the sap would ensure that the moisture in the tree did not freeze.

On St Lucy's Day, the thirteenth, the traditional day of the winter solstice, sleet fell at dawn, then froze by noon so that when a pale sun shone during the brief hours before the grey day's ending, the oak tree's crown was all hung with icicles as though some ancient silver-haired dweller of the forests had stopped there and become rooted to the spot. And even as the faint sun lent a shining to the greyness, the wind hissed through the icicles to freeze them further still.

Some way up, in a fork in the tree, where once a pigeon had made her nest, a large owl perched silently. A visitor from the deep-frozen forests of Scandinavia, it had come for the winter months to the more temperate island. Its eyes gazed blankly at the snow, but when dusk fell its astonishing asymetric ears would guide it, on soundless wings, infallibly down upon any little creature that ventured out into the darkness. Had anyone looked carefully at the ground by the oak tree's base the remains of a thrush would have told them of the owl's last meal. Slowly the silent bird turned its head. It could do so, if it chose, through more than three hundred and sixty degrees.

Above the owl's perch, in a blackened fissure, a little colony of bats hung, like webbed pellets, in their winter hibernation. All over the tree, on branch and twig, tiny larvae, like that of the winter moth, were tight-wrapped in their cocoons. Down the tree's great trunk spiders crouched in crevices behind windows of ice. Around its foot the brown bracken, bent and broken, lay flattened in the fallen leaves, ice-frosted.

Below the ground worms and slugs, and all manner of earth creatures, were insulated by the frozen leaves above from the bitter cold. But in the bushes, although the robin, like a puffball in its downy winter feathers, would probably survive, the song thrushes and blackbirds were ragged and gaunt. Two weeks of deep frost or snow, and many would reach a point of weight-loss and weakness from which there would be no return.

But if these little creatures dwelt always perilously at the brink of life and death during their few brief seasons of consciousness the tree, with its massively larger system, was also massively stronger. It was still less than three hundred years old. Yet nature imposed limitations upon the mighty oak as well. For of its vast fall of acorns that autumn thousands had been eaten by the pigs and other grazers; others trampled; others stored by squirrels or birds, others yet destined, as saplings, to be eaten by the deer. Of all that inundation of acorns, not a single new oak tree would result; nor would one for another five or ten or even twenty years.

She was feeling very weak now. She had sensed that something was wrong back at summer's end, been sure of it before she had gone with Puckle, that autumn day, to deliver the charcoal to Hurst. She had been thinking of the future by then.

She had used all the remedies she knew. She had tried to shield herself. Each month, as the moon waxed from maiden to mother and waned back to crone, she secretly prayed. Three times she drew down the moon. But as winter came she knew: nothing can change the wheel of life; there would be no healing and she must pass from this life to another.

Nature is cruel, yet also merciful. The canker that was eating away the life of Puckle's wife caused other changes in her body. She became pale; her blood changed its composition; she began to be drowsy, thus ensuring that, before the canker grew into its final monstrous life and racked her body with pain, she would instead slip sleepily towards an earlier closing.

She and Puckle had three children. She loved the woodsman. She knew very well that, after her passing, life must go on. And so it was, in secret, that she made her prayers and did what she thought best.

And now it was the year's midnight, when scarcely seven hours of sunlight is seen and all the world seems to withdraw into the deep blackness under the ground.

Two weeks later, just after Christmas, Clement Albion rode by.

The hard frost had broken just before the sacred festival. Although the ground was still crisp underfoot, he saw a clique of birds fighting over a worm in the ground leaves. A squirrel, a blur of red, dashed across into a cover of hawthorn bushes.

But it was the oak he had come to see.

In the wood beside it the soaring grey and silver branches

were bare, save for encrustations, here and there, of dark ivy or lichen, white as death. The oaks that dotted the glade were all bare too.

But the oak that stood apart was a stranger sight entirely. It had shed its icicles. Its tiny, tight-wrapped buds had broken out into sprigs of leaves. The midwinter tree was green. Albion stared in silence. Nothing stirred.

Why did this New Forest tree, which is well recorded, behave in this way? Possibly some accident had occurred during its growth – a lightning strike, for instance – which had somehow reset the internal clock, whose operation is not fully understood, by which a tree regulates its flowering. Perhaps more likely was some genetic peculiarity. One such trait, in which there is a failure in the autumnal sealing-off process, causes certain oaks to retain their leaves right through winter into spring. The Christmas leafing might have been another such genetic condition and the recorded existence of three such oaks in the same area further suggests that it could be so. But nobody knows.

Albion sighed. Was it a miracle, as his mother insisted? Was the tree speaking to him, reminding him of his duty and his religion? Was this marvellous tree a living emblem, like one of those haunting signs on the road to the Holy Grail in the tales of knightly romance?

He hoped not. Since the autumn there had been no whisper from the council to suggest he was further suspected. He had encountered Gorges twice, and each time his friend had been warm and natural towards him. The truth was that he just wanted a quiet life. Was that so wrong? Didn't most people? A tree that flowers at midwinter: the promise of life in death. Three flowering trees, three crosses: the crucifixion upon Calvary. Whichever way you looked at it, if the green trees were a sign from God they suggested death and sacrifice.

If only the Spanish invasion did not come. His mother could leave him her fortune believing that he would have joined the invaders; Gorges, the council, the queen herself would have nothing with which to reproach him. He heartily prayed that he would not be put to the test.

He had not heard from his mother for some time. He should

have gone to see her at the Christmas season but had found an excuse not to. He wondered for how long he could avoid her.

A second later he saw her.

She was in the green tree, high in the branches. She was all in black, as usual, but the entire lining of her cloak was bright red. She was flapping it and flying from branch to branch like a huge, angry bird. She turned her head to look at him. Dear heaven, she seemed about to take wing towards him.

He shook his head and told himself not to be so foolish. He glanced at the tree again and it was normal. But his hands were trembling. Not a little shaken by this maternal hallucination, he turned his horse's head and made away for Lyndhurst.

Young Nick Pride bided his time all through winter. Early April saw drenching rains but then a gentle warmth spread through the Forest. The world became green again; blossoms broke out. He knew that the time had now come, that Jane was waiting for him to declare himself; but he, too, had his part to play.

All through April he came courting. Sometimes they might not see each other for a day or two, but if they did not find some other reason, they were sure to meet at Minstead church on Sunday. Nor were there any lovers' quarrels; they had, it seemed, no need for that. She was sensible Jane Furzey and he was handsome young Nick Pride, and that was all there was to it.

All the same, Nick Pride thought as the time approached, perhaps it was better if she were not quite sure of him – just for a day or two; so she didn't take him for granted. He planned it very carefully.

Towards the end of April Albion assembled a muster at Minstead. Nick Pride was called, of course; so were Jane's brother and two other men from Brook. They were going to stage a small parade and John knew that Jane and her family would be coming down to watch. He chose the evening two days in advance of the muster, therefore, to make his opening move.

The village of Minstead lay on the slope of a high rise that ran westwards across the central section of the Forest. The

Minstead cottages mostly straggled along the lower half of the lane that climbed up to the crest of the rise, at the top of which the lane passed round a curious feature.

Castle Malwood, they called it, although there was never any castle there. It was just another of the small earthwork rings, like those at Burley and Lymington, which demonstrated that iron-age folk had used the Forest once, before the Romans came. Occupying the ridge's highest local point, however, it had obviously been chosen because it offered commanding views of the area and, since Albion had ordered a thinning of the trees that had grown up below its modest banks, the site's ancient pre-eminence had been partly re-established. From the top of its earth wall, now, one could see clean across the southern half of the Forest to the Isle of Wight: which was why it had been chosen as the perfect place to build the inland beacon, of which Nick was the guardian.

He was feeling quite proud of himself, therefore, as he led Jane, with her little dog Jack, up on to the grassy rampart of Malwood that evening and pointed out the view. "That's where the big beacon will be." He pointed to the Isle of Wight. "And here" – he indicated – "the very spot you're standing on, Jane, is where we'll be putting up our beacon next week."

He was pleased to see that she looked suitably impressed.

"What do you think will happen, Nick, if the Spanish come?" She was looking at him with a trace of concern.

"I'll light my beacon and we'll all muster, and then we'll go down and fight them. That's what'll happen." He watched her and saw the thoughtful look on her face. "Afraid something might happen to me, are you?" he asked, secretly delighted.

"I? No," she lied and shrugged. "I was thinking of my brother."

"Ah." He smiled to himself. "You shouldn't fear," he said handsomely. "When the Spanish see the whole muster I doubt they'll dare to land."

They talked, after this, of smaller matters. The sun slowly sank towards the horizon. The Forest before them was bathed in a golden haze, while the Isle of Wight in the distance began to turn blue-grey. It was very quiet. She gave a small shiver; he put his arm round her and then they gazed together towards the south in silence.

"I love to look over the Forest," she said after a while.

"So do I." He let some more time pass.

"Well, Nick." She smiled up into his face now. "If the Spaniards have not killed us, I suppose there will be rejoicings at summer's end." Then she stared out towards the island again.

It was his cue and he knew it. But he said nothing. Long moments passed.

"I'd best get home," she said at last.

He heard her disappointment and let some more time pass. Then he nodded. "I'll walk with you," he answered quietly. Then, briskly, "There's much to think of this summer, isn't there?" And, secretly chuckling at his cleverness, he walked her back to Brook.

Let her wait. Let her be uncertain, he thought, just for a day.

A fine day it was, when it came.

Minstead was a curious place. Technically it was a feudal liberty: which was to say that, although lying completely surrounded by the royal forest, it had its own private lord with his own manor court. In practice this did not make a huge difference to anybody. The lord rented out some fields and received some modest feudal dues. Neither the manor peasants nor the lord could break the forest law of the territory all around the manor's few hundred acres. Both the lord and his peasants, however, derived benefit from the manor's common rights of fuel and pasture on the Forest, and this was quite valuable. Since time out of mind, the manor had belonged to the same feudal family as Bisterne in the Avon valley, which had now passed, by marriage, from the male line of Berkeley the dragon-slayer to the equally mighty family of Compton. But the lord of the manor had no house at Minstead. His steward came and took the rents, held court, gave what management was needed. The feudal liberty of Minstead was just a quiet village in the Forest.

It did, however, have one building of significance. Beside the lane, near the bottom, was the small village green. On one side, in a shallow dell, lay the nearest thing to a manor house the village possessed, which was the vicar's rectory with its four acres of glebe. On the other, set upon a little knoll only two hundred yards from the green, was the parish church –

significant because it was the only one in this part of the
Forest. Not that the structure itself was large; although its
walls were stone, the thatched roof made it seem more like a
big cottage. Inside, the nave was not thirty feet wide and had
a homely gallery you could reach up and touch. But it was a
parish church. Even the chapel used by kings and queens at
Lyndhurst came under its aegis. And it was Minstead church
where the men of Minstead and Brook were meeting for their
muster.

As Nick Pride looked around he felt delighted. The afternoon sky was a fresh light-blue; white puffs of cloud sailed
over the church on its knoll. The muster consisted of the chosen men of the parish together with its outlying hamlets,
known as tithings. There were a dozen men, including the
three from Brook and a fellow from Lyndhurst, and it seemed
to Nick that they were quite an impressive fighting force.

Of the twelve men, eight had bows and, thanks to Albion's
strict command, every one of these now possessed a full dozen
arrows. Six of the men had long bills in their hands, sharpened
and gleaming. God help the Spaniard, he thought, who came
within reach of these terrifying spears. Three of the men had
short-brimmed metal helmets. And he, from his father, had a
breastplate of armour, a sword and metal splints to protect his
forearm. One of the men had complained that since Nick was
minding the beacon he had no need of these arms and should
give them to someone else. But he had protested: "Once the
beacon's lit, I'll be fighting too." And Albion had ruled that he
should keep everything. Nobody had an arquebus, but that was
not surprising: few English villagers had guns.

The orders for the day were straightforward: they would
train for an hour or two up by the church; then they would
march down to the green to give a demonstration of their fighting skills to the village; after which they would break up and
there would be refreshments. And then, he thought cheerfully,
he would carry out his plan. He looked at the weapons glinting in the sun and smiled to himself.

Clement Albion looked at them too. He had done his best.
Indeed, he was actually rather a good commander. His men
were probably as well armed as they could be. He had put
heart into them, and taught them how to stand firm and thrust

with their long bills. Trained bowmen they would never be, but at least four of them were accomplished poachers and could probably shoot better than most.

And how long would these good fellows last against four fully trained, fully armed Spaniards? He didn't know; a few moments, perhaps. Then they would all be dead; shot and hacked to pieces every one. Thank God they didn't know it. So it would be, he knew very well, for every parish muster in the county.

In the spring of 1588 the defending forces in the all-important central section of England's southern coast were in a state of complete shambles.

The musters of raw village recruits with their ancient bills and hunting bows were all but useless. Often the bowmen had only three or four arrows. Many of the men had no weapons at all. When the county knights and squires had come to a big review at Winchester, it was found that only one in four was fit for any kind of service. Worst of all, the business was in the hands not of one, but two great noblemen, who constantly quarrelled with each other and not even the commissioners sent down by the council had been able to bring order to the business. Neither Winchester, the all-important port of Southampton, nor the harbour of Portsmouth, a little further along the coast, where old King Harry had started to build up a naval dockyard, was properly defended with troops. Three thousand men, the best of what there was, were being stationed on the Isle of Wight, but the mainland was, for all practical purposes, undefended. This was England's state of readiness as it awaited the great invasion of the most highly trained army in Christendom. In the words of one of the reports back to Queen Elizabeth's council: "All thinges here is unperfect."

All this, although he kept it from his men, Clement Albion knew very well. He had visited Southampton and the naval yards at Portsmouth. He had attended meetings at Winchester. Not only was there no effective army to oppose the Spaniards, but the council was even afraid that some of the peasantry who longed for a return to the old religion might help the invaders. And while he personally rather doubted this, as Clement gazed at his poor, doomed little troop of men, he found himself wondering: was his mother right, after all? Would it be wiser, if the Spanish came, to join them? As a loyal son of the true Church, connected through his sister to the grandees of Spain, they'd be sure to welcome him. But if so, when? As the ships approached? After the troops landed? Could he, should he, really attempt something at Hurst Castle?

"Well done, Nicholas Pride," he called out, as the young fellow attempted to parry and thrust with his sword. "We'll show those Spaniards what Englishmen can do."

By late afternoon it was time to show the village. They lined up in a column two abreast and, because he had armour, Albion put Nick in the front row. Then they gave three cheers, so that everyone would know they were coming, and sent a boy down to make sure; and Nick secretly wished they had a drum to beat, but they didn't. Then they marched, almost in step, down the short track, shaded by overhanging trees and came down on to the green and there was everybody waiting, including Jane, who was wearing a red shawl round her shoulders. So they marched to the middle of the green, which was only thirty yards from end to end anyway, and took up their positions. And then they gave a display.

It was a brave show, no question about it. The men with their long bills stood in a line and raised and lowered and thrust with their weapons all together, so that you could hardly imagine any Spanish troops getting past such an awesome phalanx. Next they set up targets and the bowmen shot their arrows, hitting somewhere on the target every time. But the finest show of all, surely, was when Nick Pride and Albion himself unsheathed their swords and had a mock fight. Back and forth on the green they went, with a display of skill such as, very likely, Minstead had never seen before, until at last Albion, who was taking the part of the Spaniard, let Nick win and gamely surrendered. And there was laughing and cheering on the echoing green, and Jane watching, half smiling, while Nick raised his sword high in the air and the afternoon sun glinted on his armour, just as he had hoped it would. For now his moment had come. Striding across the green to where Jane was standing, he stood in front of her and stuck his sword into the ground – she looked a bit surprised – and then he went down on one knee and her eyes opened very wide as he said: "Jane Furzey, will you marry me?" Everyone heard it. She started to blush and a voice from somewhere called out: "That's a fine offer, Jane." Other voices joined in, but they were listening, too.

He guessed she might say no just because he had taken her by surprise like that, so he looked straight up into her eyes to let her see that he loved her truly, and then he began to look just a little bit afraid himself, which worked very well because after only a moment's more pausing, which was probably just for show, really, she said: "Well, I suppose I might."

Then everybody cheered.

"Name the day," he cried.

But now it was her turn to put him in his place, so she pursed her lips and looked around, and glanced at Albion and started to laugh. "When you've fought a real Spaniard, Nick Pride," she cried, "and not before!"

Which Albion told her was a very good answer.

The following morning Jane Furzey walked across to Burley. She hardly ever went over that way but her mother had heard there was a woman there who made lace, and she asked Jane to go and see if there might be work for one of her younger sisters. So Jane set off, taking her little dog Jack with her.

The morning was sunny. Passing by the Rufus tree she went westwards for a time, which quite soon led her across high heath, before turning down through woodland in the direction of Burley.

Jack was in his element. If he spotted a blackbird after a worm, he chased it. If he saw a patch of mud, or a pile of leaves, he rolled in them. Three red squirrels, in his opinion at least, were lucky to escape with their lives. By the time they came towards Burley his brown-and-white coat was black with mud and Jane was ashamed of him. She didn't want to arrive at the lace maker's cottage with her dog in this condition. "You'd better have a bath," she told him.

There were several ways to approach Burley from the Minstead direction, but the most pleasant, and also the cleanest, was along the great lawn from due east. For here there ran a clean, gravelly stream and, on each side of it, several hundred yards across and almost two miles in extent, stretched the broad, delightful swathe of close-cropped grass.

It was one of the largest of the forest's great lawns. Partly dry, part marsh, it was grazed by cattle and ponies, and continued up to the edge of the village. Burley Lawn, it was called at the village end; but a few hundred yards further east a small mill had stood for a couple of generations and, from there, in its long eastward extension, it was known as Mill Lawn.

Having held a protesting Jack in the clear stream until he was clean, Jane had let him scamper along the short grass of Mill Lawn. Once or twice, out of bravado, he had made as if to chase a pony, but he was still clean as they passed the mill and came on to Burley Lawn. The ground was soggier here, so she made him keep to the dry path beside her; and confident that all was in good order she continued very cheerfully. There were clumps of small trees and gorse brakes dotting the lawn now. The woodland to right and left, with its small oaks and bushes of hazel, seemed to be edging closer. They passed a dark, gnarled little ash tree.

Then Jack saw the cat.

Jane saw it also, but a moment too late. "Jack!" she shouted, but it was no good. He was off in a flash and there was no stopping him. A yelp, a hiss, a blur of bodies as they raced away to her right. She saw the cat leap and Jack splash through a puddle of mud, watched and groaned as his filthy, dripping form tore away through the bushes. She was surprised the cat didn't race up a tree, but obviously it had some other cover in mind for she could hear Jack still in hot pursuit, barking wildly. And then there was silence.

She waited, then called. Nothing happened. There was no sound. She called again, several times. Still nothing. Had the cat finally taken refuge somewhere? She would have expected to hear Jack barking. She waited a little more and then, with a sigh, followed in the direction the two animals had gone.

She had walked perhaps fifty yards into the trees when she saw the cottage. It was a fairly typical white-walled, thatched Forest cottage, although better than many since a window under the roof on one side indicated that there was at least one room upstairs. In the clearing round it were a small yard and some outbuildings. There was no sign of the cat, or of Jack and she was wondering if they had veered off somewhere else when she heard the dog's bark. It came, unmistakably, from inside the cottage.

She went to the door, found it ajar and knocked. No reply. She called out. Surely there must be someone about. Still nothing. She called to Jack and heard him bark again, somewhere within; but he did not come. She wondered if he might have got trapped in there, yet still hesitated. She did not want to go in without permission. At the same time, she did not like to think of her dog wreaking havoc in a stranger's house.

She pushed open the door and entered.

It was a cottage like many others. The door gave into the main low-ceilinged room, which had a fire and hanging pots at one end. In one corner were a scrubbed table, some benches and a cot where, by the look of it, a small child slept. To the right, behind a door, which she did not like to open, was another room. Ahead, a narrow staircase, hardly more than a ladder, led up to the loft room above.

"Jack?" she called softly. "Jack?" A small bark came in answer, from upstairs. "Jack," she called, "come down." Was somebody holding the dog up there? She looked round to see if anyone was watching her from outside. They did not seem to be. She stepped forward and started to go up the stairs.

There were two rooms up there: on the left, an open loft; on the right an oak door, which the wind, presumably, had blown shut. Slowly, she pushed it open.

The room was only a small one. The light came from a low window at knee height, on her left, just below the eaves. On her right, against the wall, was an old chest upon which, to her surprise, the cat was now lying, comfortably curled and watching her as if her presence were awaited. But strangest of all was the sight in front of her.

Taking up most of the wall was an oak four-poster bed. Across the top of the four posts was a simple cloth canopy whose edges just touched the sloping thatch of the bare roof above. It was not a huge bed. It had been built, perhaps, in that very room she guessed, to take two people, neither very large. The oak was dark, almost black, and gleamed.

And it was carved. She had never seen such carving. Animals, stags' heads, grotesque human faces, oak leaves and acorns, fungi, squirrels and even snakes – all climbed up or looked out from the four dark, gleaming posts of that strange bed. And suddenly remembering where she had heard such a bed described, she murmured aloud: "This must be Puckle's place."

Yet almost stranger than the bed itself was the behaviour of Jack.

The bed was covered with a simple linen counterpane. He was sitting on it. His black paw marks were clearly visible where he had jumped up. Yet he sat there now, wagging his tail, showing no sign of wanting to come to her nor, apparently, of chasing the cat. He seemed to expect her to come and sit there beside him.

"Oh, Jack! What have you done? Come off that bed at once," she cried. And she went to pull him off. But he resisted, crouching down, although still wagging his tail. "You naughty dog," she scolded. "Come." And she had just started to lift him off when a gruff voice behind her made her jump and almost scream, as she whirled round.

"He seems to like it there."

Puckle was standing in the narrow doorway. There was no mistaking him. His black beard was still close-cropped; she had not realised that his eyes were so bright. He did not move. He just watched her.

"Oh." She gave a little gasp of fear. Then, as he remained where he was, giving no sign of anger, she began to blush. "I am so sorry. He ran after your cat."

"Yes." He nodded slowly. "He looks like he would." Did he believe her? Something in his manner suggested he thought this was not the whole truth.

"He's made such a mess." She indicated the counterpane. "I am sorry."

"Doesn't matter."

She stared at him. He had clearly been out working in the Forest somewhere. She could see the tiny beads of sweat still on the black hairs that curled at his open neck. When she had seen him before, at the end of summer, his face had seemed dark, almost oaken; but now, like a snake that has shed its old skin, or a tree that has put on its fresh leaves for the spring,

John Puckle's colouring seemed quite light. He made her think of an alert, handsome fox.

"I must clean it," she said.

He did not reply, but he turned his eyes to the dog. Jack looked back at him happily and wagged his tail. Jane began to relax a little. Nobody moved.

"Did you carve all this?" She indicated the bed.

"Yes." His gaze returned to her face, watchful. "You like it?"

She looked again at the strange, dark faces, the gnarled and curling oaken forms. Did they repel her or attract her? She wasn't sure. But the skill of the carver's hand was astonishing. "It's wonderful," she blurted out. He did not reply but only nodded quietly, so after a small pause, she added: "Your wife told me about the bed."

"She did?"

"At Hurst Castle. September last. You were delivering charcoal."

"That's right."

"Is she here?" Jane asked, not certain whether she would care to see the strange woman or not.

"She's dead. Died this winter."

"Oh. I'm sorry." She hardly knew what to say. She stared at Jack and the counterpane. He had made an awful mess of it. She scooped him up now, and turned. "Let me take the counterpane and wash it."

"It'll brush off," he pointed out.

But somehow her trespass made her feel so guilty that she wanted to do more to make amends. "Let me take it," she said. "I'll bring it back."

"As you like."

So she took the counterpane off the bed, gave the pillows a good shake, smoothed everything down and departed with Jack, feeling a little less guilty now than she had before.

The oak tree put on its leaves slowly in the spring. After its miraculous midwinter greening it had drawn its systems down again like any other oak; the Christmas leaves had frozen and fallen; and there it had remained through the rest of the winter, grey and bare. By March, however, the sap was rising. The oak trees in the wood did not all break into leaf at the same time but over a period of about a month, so that the canopy in early spring varied greatly, from bare brown buds, or the palest leaves, to a fresh green rustling crown.

Colour came to the oak, however, in many forms. Ivy fruits in spring, providing pleasant feeding for the blackbirds; but on its lower part the deer in winter had eaten away the ivy leaves up to the browse line, leaving the space clear for the lichen to grow. Oaks carry more lichens than other trees. Some were already yellow but, since they contain algae with green chlorophyll, others were growing grey-green beards. Most dramatic were the big, furry lichens sprouting out from the trunk and known as "lungs of oak."

Scarcely had the oak's buds begun to open into leaf when the green woodpecker, flashing green, gold and scarlet, came through the woods with its undulating flight and found a cavity, high up in a dying branch, in which to make its nest. Chaffinches with grey heads and pink breasts began trilling in the branches. By April, with fresh leaves coming out all over and the birds of summer beginning to return from southern climes, the cuckoo's call was echoing through the woods; the bracken, everywhere, was springing up in stiff stalks and its tightly curled ferns beginning to unfurl; the gorse was in luminous yellow flower and hawthorn bushes breaking out into thick white blossom. Only one feature of oak woods was notably missing. For in the open Forest, although there are wood sorrel, yellow pimpernel, primrose and dog violet to add their pretty colours to the ground, there are no carpets of bluebells – because the deer and grazing livestock eat up any they can find.

And now, as its leaves unfolded, it was time for the oak to begin the huge process of spreading its seed. Each mighty oak brings forth both male and female seed when, in the spring, it breaks into flower. The male pollen, which must be carried down the wind, is in the form of hanging strings, like golden catkins, with tiny flowers. As spring progresses, the oak becomes so thickly bearded that it is as if it has grown a golden fleece.

The female flowers – it is these, when pollinated, which will grow into acorns – are as yet less visible. Like little opening buds, close inspection reveals that they have three tiny red styles which will collect the pollen as it is blown by.

By late April, therefore, the oak, green-leaved, bearded with golden strings, like some hoary old figure from the days of the classical myths when the gods played games with men by the oak groves, was ready to spread its seed. The pollen could be carried great distances across the thick woodland canopy, encountering and intermingling with the pollen of a hundred other trees along the way. It would be hard to say, therefore, which oak was the father of any single acorn grown; for the female buds of any oak tree might receive the passing pollen of dozens of other oaks so that an acorn on a single branch might have been fathered by one oak while the acorn next to it could be the result of pollination from another. So the oak tree would fructify, communally, with perhaps a hundred brother and sister oaks, and children, too, who made its old community.

They had set up a maypole at Minstead on May Day. The vicar, who wisely allowed such harmless pagan practices, had organised a modest feast on the village green. The people from Brook had come down, too.

The children had danced round the maypole very prettily; there had been some drinking; and in the evening when it was all over, Nick Pride had walked Jane Furzey home.

They walked up the rise above Minstead and then, drifting idly together, took the path that led past the Rufus oak.

There had been several days of rain recently. Indeed, although nearly a week had passed since Jane's strange encounter in Burley, she had still not found a good day to return Puckle's counterpane. But today the sun had shone with scarcely a cloud to interrupt it and the evening was still deliciously warm. She walked beside Nick contentedly.

It was only natural, it seemed to Nick, that they should have paused by the Rufus tree and kissed.

Nick had never kissed for as long as this before. As the minutes went by, his lips and tongue exploring, time seemed to cease in the womb-like space under the spreading tree. The turquoise sky at the end of the glade was turning to orange. Somewhere in the wood behind, a faint rustling told him that a deer was making its delicate way between the trees. He clasped Jane tightly, his hands searching, trying to draw her evermore completely to him. With slowly mounting excitement he wanted to possess her entirely. He must. It was time.

"Now," he murmured. They were betrothed. They would be married. There was no prohibition any more. All nature told his body this was the moment. "Now."

She pulled back. "No. Not now."

He moved forward, took her in his arms again. "Jane. Now."

"No." She pushed him gently but firmly back and shook her head. "I cannot, now."

He was trembling with passion. "Jane." But she turned away from him, staring down the glade. He stood there, breathing rapidly. Just for a moment, it occurred to him to take her, there and then, by force. But he knew that would not do. Was she really so determined that she would not give herself to him until they were married? Or perhaps she had only meant that her monthly curse was upon her. He did not know. "As you like," he said with a sigh and, gently putting his arm round her, began to walk her home.

She said little on the way back. Indeed, it was all she could do to hide her feelings. For how could she tell him what was really in her mind? How could she admit that her refusal came from another cause entirely? She did not understand it herself. All she knew, that warm May evening, was that something had come between them: that despite her intentions, her feelings for him, despite everything, as she had felt him holding her fast, pressing against her, some invisible barrier had suddenly interposed itself, so that she could not let him possess her. Was it her fear, because she was a virgin? Was it panic at the thought she was about to lose her freedom? She did not know. It was mystifying, troubling. He was the man she was to marry and suddenly she did not want him. What did it mean?

Three miles away, when Nick and Jane were leaving the maypole on the green, Clement Albion had been engaged in that exercise so necessary to busy men. He had been assuring himself that his conscience was clear. He even muttered aloud: "I have done all I can. God knows."

The trained bands he had mustered were as ready as they were ever likely to be. The beacons were prepared. For all the fearsome reputation of the council's spy system, nobody knew exactly when or how the great Spanish invasion fleet was coming; but those like Gorges with any pretence to information assured him that it would, and soon. Had he, then, anything with which to reproach himself? If the council were to summon him tomorrow and demand whether he were a loyal servant of his queen, could he look Cecil in the eye and declare fearlessly that he was?

"My conscience is clear." Nobody was listening. He tried it again. "Her Majesty has no cause for complaint against me. I have deceived her about nothing. Nothing."

Well, almost nothing.

The position of woodward was a profitable one. In return for acting as guardian of the trees in Her Majesty's forest he received a salary and valuable perquisites. The bark, for instance, from felled or fallen oaks was his; and he would arrange for cartloads to be taken across to Fordingbridge, to the tanning pits there, where the tanners would pay well for this useful ingredient in the preparation of leather. Then there were the leases to see to.

The coppice in front of him was a well-made thirty-acre inclosure, near a track that ran west from Lyndhurst. It had an earth bank and a stout fence in good repair. It was the woodward's responsibility to let this coppice on the usual thirty-one-year lease and this he had done. To be precise, he had let it to himself. By the terms of the lease, he had the right to sell off the underwood, which was mostly thorn and hazel; but at the same time he was obliged to conserve the more valuable timber wood, keeping at least twelve untouched standards, as the young timber trees were called, to the acre. Albion's coppices, therefore, should have contained not less than three hundred and sixty standards of timber and, when the lease had begun, so it had. But somehow a hundred and fifty of them had disappeared, leaving two hundred and ten. The profits from these timber sales had been a useful addition to his income.

It was the sort of thing Her Majesty's woodward was supposed to notice and report, to ensure that the leaseholder was fined. But as he was the leaseholder, too, this dereliction had miraculously escaped his notice.

More serious, perhaps, had been the sale of a much larger

coppice, not long ago, for the benefit of the crown. He had arranged the sale efficiently enough and fowarded the money to Her Majesty's treasury. A large quantity of underwood had been sold and was fully accounted for with a written record. What the record did not show, however, was that much of this underwood was actually timber, of far higher value. The difference between the real and the recorded sale had gone into Albion's purse.

This error still might be found out by the regarders when they next made their inspection of the Forest, as they did every few years. But then, as he was also one of Her Majesty's regarders, Albion thought it unlikely that the issue would be raised.

Yet again, the crown had been known to set up a commission of inquiry to investigate even the regarders as well, and the woodwards and the gentleman leaseholders of the Forest. But so serious a matter was this, that the last time such a thing had been done, the said regarders, woodwards and gentlemen had found it necessary to arrange that the members of the said commission should consist entirely of – themselves.

For a time, during the months after his conversation with Helena Gorges at Hurst Castle, Albion had lived in some discomfort. To be an undisturbed woodward was one thing; but if the council ever started to take steps against him; if neighbours should understand he was a marked man; if Cecil's servants came down to the Forest seeking crimes with which to charge him, who knew what might come to the surface? Even if no treason was found, the prospect of disgrace and ruin grew uncomfortably large.

But winter and spring had passed, and now it was May. The cuckoo was sounding in the woods. In the manner of every good man who thinks it unlikely he will be found out, Albion's conscience was clear. Although the sun was sinking in the west, the huge canopy of sky over the Forest was still azure, with thin ribs of high cloud gleaming pink and silver overhead, as Albion rode southwards. Having passed Brockenhurst and gone south another mile, he then turned east to cross the Forest's modest central river by the quiet ford below which his house lay.

He was rather surprised, therefore, as he came in sight of the ford, to see two wagons, one richly curtained, the other groaning under a stupendous load of boxes and furniture of every kind, crossing the river just ahead of him. Across the ford, one either continued up to Beaulieu Heath or turned south along a track that led to Boldre. The Albion house, a timber gabled manor, lay in a wooded clearing about half a mile down the track that led to Boldre.

They turned south. He rode after them. But the second wagon took up so much of the path that he had to wait behind it; and so, a little while later, he saw with astonishment that the first was turning up the track that led to his house. It had already rumbled up to his door, and the servants were coming out and a groom was holding back the wagon's curtains to allow its occupant to descend, before he could ride up to the door himself.

The figure descending was dressed all in black, except for the inside and trimming of her gown, which was crimson. Her face was powdered a thick, ghostly white.

"Dear God!" he cried, scarcely thinking. "Mother, why have you come?"

She gave him a brilliant smile in return, although her eyes were as keen as those of a bird after a worm. "I have news, Clement," she said. And a moment later, finding his ear close to her red mouth as he entered her unavoidable embrace, he heard her whisper as to a fellow conspirator: "A letter from your sister. The Spanish are coming. I have come here so that we may welcome them, my dearest son, together."

May passed and most of June, and still the Spanish fleet – the Armada, they called it – did not come. The weather was unusual. One day there would be blue sky and summer sun over the Forest; but time and again, the dark, lowering clouds had returned, sweeping up from the south-west with gales of rain or hail; few could remember a summer like it in years. Late in June, news came that a storm had dispersed the preparing Spanish fleet to several ports. "Drake will be up and at them," people said. But although Sir Francis was urging the council to let him go, the Queen was hesitant. The trouble with England's favourite pirate was that as soon as he attacked the enemy successfully, he'd go running off trying to capture prizes instead of attending to duty. For the great explorer and patriot still loved money, she well knew, more than anything.

As Jane Furzey came on to the long stretch of Mill Lawn she felt rather guilty. Had she really let two months pass before returning to Burley? What with the weather and so much going on, she told herself, she really hadn't had time to return Puckle's counterpane. With luck, she thought, he won't be there. Then she could leave it and hurry away.

Today the weather was fine. Across the big Forest lawn the gorse was all green now, but the short turf was brightly spangled with daisies and white clover, yellow buttercup and hawkweed. Pressing close to the turf, tiny sprigs of self-heal added purple tints to the green; and on the banks of the little gravel streamlet that ran down the lawn, blue forget-me-not grew out of the weeds.

Jane reached the thatched cottage just before noon. Puckle was not at home, but his children were. There were three of them. The eldest was a girl of about ten; obviously going through a skinny stage, she was thin as a spindle, dark-haired, rather solemn and had clearly been left in charge of the other two. A younger girl, also dark, was playing on the patch of grass in front of the cottage door.

But it was the youngest child who really caught her attention. He was a chubby, cheerful little boy of three. He had evidently been playing with a toy horse his father must have made for him; but the moment he saw Jane he toddled happily up to her, his round face wearing a big smile, his bright eyes full of trust and apparently sure that she would amuse him. He was wearing a nicely embroidered smock and not much else and, taking her hand he asked: "I'm Tom. Would you like to play?"

"I'm sure I should," she said. But first she explained her errand to the older girl.

The child was naturally a little suspicious at first, but when she inspected the counterpane she nodded. "My father said a person would come with it," she remarked, "but that was a long time ago." It seemed that Puckle was not expected back for a while and so Jane talked with the girl. It was soon clear from her manner and the things she said that she had had to take on the role of mother to the family, and Jane began to feel rather sorry for her. She needs a mother herself, she thought.

As for Tom, the toddler was enchanting. He produced a ball and demanded that she kick it to him, which she did, to his great delight, for some time. He is such a pretty little boy, she considered, I wish he could be mine. Finally, however, if she was not to run the risk of meeting Puckle, she thought she had better go.

"I had best put this back on your father's bed," she said to the girl, picking up the counterpane. The child assured her there was no need, but she insisted and went alone up the stairs to the little room where Puckle's oak bed stood.

There it was: dark, almost black, and gleaming. It was certainly curious, every bit as strange as she remembered it from her encounter before. The oaken faces, like gargoyles in a church, stared out at her as though she were a friend they were welcoming back. Hardly meaning to, she ran her hand over some of the carved figures – the squirrel, the snake. They were so perfect it was as if they were alive, about to move under her hand at any instant. She even felt a trace of fright and, as if to reassure herself, tightened her grip, squeezing the gnarled oak wood under her hand to prove to herself that that was all it was. For an instant she felt almost giddy.

Carefully she spread the counterpane, made sure that everything was tidy, then stood back to survey her handiwork. This was where Puckle had lain with his wife. "Keep any woman happy." The strange woman's words came back to her. "Once you lie in his oak bed with John Puckle, you'll not want any other bed." Jane's eyes went round the room. There was a linen shirt of Puckle's on the chest where the cat had been lying the first time she came in there. Glancing behind her to make sure she was not observed, she went over and picked it up. He had worn it, but not much, she thought. It smelled only a little of sweat, more of woodsmoke. A good smell. A little salty. She laid it carefully down again.

She looked once more at the bed. It was so strange: the bed seemed to look back at her, as though it and Puckle were one and the same. As in a way they were, she realised, given how much of himself he had put into the carving. Puckle turned into oak, she thought with a smile, and laughed to herself. If all this carving, this astonishing strength and richness were within the soul and body of the man, too, no wonder his wife had had good things to say of him. But why to her? Perhaps she had said such things to everybody. But then again, perhaps not.

She turned and, with a last look at the gleaming four-poster, went down the stairs and out of the cottage door into the bright sunlight. Just before she reached it she heard the little boy cry out in pleasure and, blinking for a moment in the sudden light, she looked at the figure now scooping the toddler up in his arms.

Puckle was black – as black as one of the oaken faces on his bed. He turned, catching sight of her, looked straight at her, and she felt herself give an involuntary shudder. She understood, of course. He had been out at one of his charcoal fires and was covered with black dust. But he looked so like one of the strange, almost devilish faces on the bed that she couldn't help herself.

"Bring me water," he said to the girl, who reappeared in a moment with a wooden pail. He stooped, scooping the water quickly on to his face and head, then washed his arms. He stood up straight again, his face now clean, while from his head the water was dripping down, and laughed.

"Do you recognise me now?" he asked Jane, who nodded and laughed as well. "You have met Tom?" he enquired.

"I played ball with him." She smiled.

"Will you stay a while?" he asked, cheerfully.

"No. No, I must go." She started to turn, and was astonished to discover that she wanted to stay. "I must go," she repeated, disconcerted with herself.

"Ah." He came over to her now. His hand reached out and took her elbow. She was aware, suddenly, of the muscles on his thick, powerful forearm. "The children like you," he said quietly.

"Oh. How do you know?"

"I know." He smiled. "I am glad you came," he said gently.

She nodded. She hardly knew what to say. It was as if, as soon as he had touched her, they had shared something. She felt a flood of strength coming from him, while her own knees went weak. "I must go," she stammered.

His hand was still on her arm. She did not want him to take it away.

"Come, sit." He indicated a bench near the door.

So she sat in the sun with him, and talked and played with the children until, after an hour, she left.

"You must come again, for the children," he said. And she promised that, when she could, she would.

By July, Albion often rode out into the Forest simply to be alone. The last two months had not been easy.

Perhaps his wife had summed it up best. "I can't see the Spanish invasion will make any difference to us, Clement," she had said at the end of May. "This house has already been occupied."

His mother and her occupying forces appeared to be everywhere. There never seemed to be less than three of her servants crowding into the kitchen. Within two weeks her groom had seduced his wife's young maid. At meals, at family prayers, morning, noon and night, his mother's brooding presence seemed to fill the house.

Why was she there? Albion had no doubt. She was going to make sure he fulfilled his obligations when the Armada came.

For three weeks his wife had suffered. She understood very well that his mother had a large fortune to leave, and she was a good daughter-in-law; but she was a mother first and she wanted a quiet life for her family. He had not dared tell her about his mother's insane offer of his services to the King of Spain and had begged his mother not to, for fear of frightening her. Meekly therefore, his wife had done her family duty. But finally even she could take no more. "This occupation has gone on too long," she told him. "My house is no longer my own. I don't care if your mother has ten fortunes to leave. We can live without. They must all go."

It was with no small fear that he went to his mother to explain the problem. Her reaction astonished him.

"Of course, Clement. She is quite right. Your household is not large. My poor manservant has been sleeping in the barn. Leave everything to me."

And the very next morning, to his astonishment, the whole cortège – the wagons piled high, the servants all on board – had been ready to depart. He and his family had stood and watched in wonder as the order was given to move off. There had been only one puzzling feature.

"Shouldn't you be in your carriage now, Mother?" he asked. "It is about to move."

"I?" His mother looked surprised. "I, Clement? I am not going." She raised her hand and waved as the two wagons began to rumble past them. "Do not worry, Clement." She gave him a brilliant smile. "I shall be quiet as a mouse."

And from that day, with just a few chests of clothes and her prayer book, she had kept to herself in her chamber. "Like a good nun," as she put it. That is, when she was not sitting in the parlour, or instructing the children in their prayers, or giving the servants little commissions to do, or letting his wife know that the roast beef could have been cooked a little less. "You see," she would observe, every day at dinner, "how I live like a hermit in your house. You must scarcely know I am here."

If her continued presence was a nuisance for his wife, to Albion himself it grew daily more alarming. Her private conversations with him left no room for doubt: the Spanish were going to triumph. "I wrote to your sister long ago about the strength of the musters," she declared. "The Spanish troops will smash them easily. As for our ships, they are all rotten." The first statement was true, the second false. But she had entirely made up her mind about it.

The problem was, how could he deal with the suspicions that must attach to him from her presence in his house? He decided that the best defence was attack.

"My mother is now completely out of her wits," he told one or two gentlemen who he knew would repeat the information, "and there's an end of it." When a number of recusants were interned by the council in case they proved dangerous, he remarked wryly to Gorges: "I have interned my mother myself. I am now her gaoler." When Gorges reminded him that he personally had had charge of Mary Queen of Scots, Albion riposted: "My mother is the more dangerous." And when Helena asked if he actually kept her under lock and key, he replied morosely: "I wish I had a dungeon."

Were they convinced? He hoped so. But two incidents soon told him better. The first occurred just after news came that Drake had been refused permission to attack the Spanish in their ports again. The orders that the queen had wanted to give had caused some wry amusement among her commanders. Albion had been down at Hurst Castle just afterwards.

"Do you know, Clement," Helena had remarked, "the queen wanted the fleet to go back and forth like men on sentry duty?" She laughed. "It seems that Her Majesty, although she sends her buccaneers across the seas, did not know that their ships cannot change directions just as they please, ignoring the wind. Now the fleet is going to . . ." But she suddenly checked herself and added sheepishly: "To do something else. I do not know what." And Albion had turned and seen Gorges standing behind him, quickly removing a warning finger from his lips.

The second incident came early in July.

The fact was that, despite its fearsome reputation at home, the royal spy system in England had been unable, with the Spanish Armada almost daily expected, to discover anything about its plan of action. There were, in fact, two threats to consider. One came from the great fleet itself; the other from the Spanish forces already just across the sea in the Netherlands, where they had been busy putting down the Protestant revolts against Catholic Spanish rule. The Spanish troops in the Netherlands numbered tens of thousands, they were battle hardened and their commander, the Duke of Parma, was a fine general. It was assumed that they would attack England's eastern coast, probably near the Thames estuary, at the same time as the Armada arrived. If so, that would stretch England's defences in two directions. But was this correct? Was one attack a diversion? Did the Armada mean to destroy the English fleet at sea, take the first English port it came to, Plymouth probably, and use that as a base; or would it sail up the English Channel to capture Southampton, the Isle of Wight, or Portsmouth? Nobody knew.

"I have had another letter from Spain," his mother said quite calmly, one evening, when he returned from a visit to Southampton.

"Today? How?" Who could possibly have brought such a thing to his house in that quiet corner of the Forest?

She waved the question aside as if it were irrelevant. "You must be ready, now, Clement. The time is close."

"When? When are they coming?"

"I have told you. Very soon. No doubt the beacons will be lit. You will know. Then you must do your duty."

"What other news did you receive? What is their intention? Do they make for the Isle of Wight? For Portsmouth?"

"I cannot say, Clement."

"Let me see the letter, Mother."

"No, Clement. I have told you all you need to know."

He stared at her. Did she not trust him? Of course she didn't. She suspects, he thought, that if I learn anything more about the Spanish movements, I might tell Gorges or the lord-lieutenant. And she is right. I probably would. He wondered where the letter was. Should he search her chamber? Was there any way – during her sleep, maybe – that he could search her clothing? No hope, he considered.

And then another thought came to him. Could this be a ruse, a cunning contrivance? Was it possible that there was no letter, that she had invented it to test him, to see what he would do? Was she as devious as that? Perhaps.

"I am sorry you keep secrets from me, Mother," he said stiffly; but this had no effect upon her at all.

It was the sequel the next day, however, that was truly frightening. He had chanced to meet Thomas Gorges in Lymington and Gorges, after they had talked a few moments, had given him a keen look and remarked: "We are still trying to discover the Spanish intentions, Clement. We suspect that letters may be coming to recusants in England which might contain information of value."

"That is possible, I suppose." Albion tried to keep calm.

"People like your mother."

He could not help it. He felt himself go white. "My mother?"

"Has she received any letters, any messengers, any strange visitors? You surely must know."

"I . . ." He thought furiously. Did Gorges know she had received a letter? If so, hadn't he better tell him? Let the authorities search his mother, since he didn't dare, and uncover her secret. But in that case what would they find? God knew what such a letter might contain to incriminate him. He dare not risk it. "I do not know of any such letter," he said hesitantly. "But I will question her." And then, in a flash of inspiration: "Do you suspect her, Thomas? God knows what her madness may lead her to."

"No, Clement. I ask in a general way only."

Albion studied his face. He could be lying. Gorges was far too discreet to give himself away. And then a horrible thought occurred to him. What if Gorges, or those above him not only knew of the letter but had already read its contents? In that case Gorges knew more about it than he did. God knew what sort of trap this might be. "If my mother received a letter from the King of Spain himself, Thomas," he said, "mad as she is, she very likely would not tell me because she knows very well that I am loyal to my queen. That's the truth of it."

"I know you can be trusted, Clement," Gorges said and moved off. But when a man says he knows he can trust you, Albion thought sadly, it usually means that he does not.

Nick Pride had certainly proved himself so far.

"Who keeps the watch and ward at Malwood?" Albion would cry as he came to make his inspection – almost daily by mid-July. He had discovered that the young man loved to be hailed in this manner.

"Nicholas Pride, Sir," the youth would answer. "And all is in good order, may it please you."

It certainly was, but for form's sake Albion would inspect everything, starting with the beacon.

The beacons that would warn England of the coming of the Spanish Armada are often imagined as bonfires. But it was not so at all. Nick Pride's up at Malwood was typical of its kind.

It had been placed at the highest point on the old earth wall from which, thanks to Albion's tree thinning, it was visible for many miles. It consisted of a stout pole, about twenty feet high, which had been securely planted several feet into the ground and was also held firm by four supporting stakes, called spurs, angled up like guy ropes to its apex. On top of the pole was fixed a large metal barrel filled with a mixture of pitch, tar and flax, which would burn with a bright flame for hours.

You reached the tar barrel up a ladder – a single beam fitted with cross bars – and you lit it with a flaming torch. In order to have a flame to ignite the torch, Nick and his companions kept a small charcoal brazier alight, day and night, just below.

Nick always shared the watch with one other man, the one not on duty resting in a tiny wooden hut just inside the earth wall. In recent days Nick had been up on Malwood all the time, the other two men taking it turn and turn about. People would drift up from the village from time to time to keep them company; but for some reason the council had ordained that no dogs were permitted at any of the beacons. Perhaps it was feared they would be a distraction.

There was only one eventuality where the beacons would not be useful: if there was fog or extreme bad weather – and given the repeated storms this last was a distinct possibility. In that case, a chain of staging posts had been organised across the country. Light horsemen would race from one to another, carrying the news. The horse they rode was called a hobby, and so each man, with his single message that he must deliver, would ride his hobby horse from post to post.

The beacons on the Isle of Wight were more complex. At each end of the island there were a set of three. If one was fired it indicated either that a signal had been received from down the coast, or that the watchers on the island had seen the invading fleet on the horizon themselves. This served to alert the next county whose watch would light their beacon in turn. If the enemy was approaching the coast, a second was lit. This signalled the beacons of the coastal defences to be ignited and summoned the musters. If three beacons were lit, however, it meant that the coastal defences needed reinforcements from further inland, and then the inland beacons were lit and the trained bands were to go quickly to their meeting points and march down to the coast. Malwood was counted as an inland beacon. "However," Albion had instructed Nick Pride, "as we're short of men, you are to light your beacon if you see a two-beacon alert on the island and then we'll march down to Hurst."

Most days Jane would come and spend an hour or two with him. She would bring him a pie that she had cooked, or cakes, or a jug of some cool drink made from fruit and flowers that she and her mother had prepared. And they would sit together up on Malwood's grassy walls and gaze over the green forest towards the blue haze of the sea. In the evenings, sometimes, she would remain with him until long after dark, keeping watch together.

So Nick Pride waited for the Spanish Armada in company with the girl he was to marry; when he saw her coming, his heart would dance; when he looked down at her and put his arm round her waist as they viewed the Forest at twilight, he felt a great surge of warmth and thanked the faint evening stars that he had been blessed with her.

Obsession. She did not know the word, but everything belonging to it she had learned to understand. Disquiet, melancholy, distraction – all the long litany – Jane was sixteen and in three weeks she had experienced it all.

She had been back to see him several times already. The first time she had walked by, seen the children and played with the little boy until he came. The next time she had come, knowing Puckle would be there. They had talked; she had sat and watched as he played with Tom, or quietly carved a piece of wood. She realised that she already knew every sinew in his hands.

She had felt his hand upon her arm and upon her shoulder; she longed, now, to feel it around her waist. She could not help it. Nor was this all. Strong though he was, when she watched his daughter preparing the food, or saw him rather helplessly set out to wash the children's dirty clothes, he suddenly seemed vulnerable. He needs me, she thought.

Twice she had gone to where she knew he would be working in the woods and watched him from a distance, although he did not know it. Once, unexpectedly, she had seen him go by in his cart, along the track up from Lyndhurst. She had felt her heart jump, but stood quite still, just staring after him as he passed, unaware of her presence.

Obsession. She had to conceal it. Her family knew nothing of her walks to Burley since she had always made some excuse for her absence. Nick Pride, of course, had no idea of it. But what did it mean? Why was she suffering? Why was it, night and day, that she longed to be only there, in the woodman's presence?

Each time she went to Burley she passed the Rufus tree and each time she came back, she would pause there, trying to make sense of her thoughts and prepare herself, before returning to her family and to Nick.

How aware one became of the forest sounds, resting under the great oak's shade in the late afternoon. The woods were full of birds – chiff-chaffs and tits, redstarts and nuthatches – but their mating and nesting was all done now, their young were mostly grown and flying. Their song was muted and occasional, therefore, and only the cooing of the pigeons came regularly through the woods. It was the ceaseless sound of the wood crickets, the drone of myriad insects, the humming of the bees as they visited the honeysuckle scenting the forest air – this was the sleepy summer music Jane listened to, all around.

But the shady space in which she rested was not still. Far from it. For summer was the time when the vast, hidden population that the tree's huge system had housed came out to make an appearance. The space under the tree was teeming with life.

It would have been impossible to say how many species there were – perhaps ten thousand; probably more. There were the ticks and mites, so small you could hardly see them, which had made their way from the ground up the swaying bracken so that they could be brushed off on to the bodies of passing warm-blooded animals, like humans, sucking the blood and causing the skin to itch. More irritating still were the horseflies, who had spent the winter as maggots by the oak tree's roots and now attacked, clumsily but constantly. There were spiders and bugs by the hundred, crawling over the warm bark, caterpillars – blue, yellow, green, orange – making their fantastic, furry progress to feed upon the leaves; there were weevils and ladybirds and moths. Butterflies were rarer in the Forest, but the handsome red admiral could be seen and, high in the canopy, the gorgeous purple emperor would feed on the sugar-rich trails left by the tiny aphids as those minute insects made their way across the leaves.

Jane would remain for an hour under the tree. She would look at the bright caterpillars, or gaze out at the green shadows of the other oaks in the glade. Sometimes her thoughts would

turn to the coming Armada and to young Nick up by his beacon; sometimes she would think of Puckle. Before she left, she
would appear to be calm. But she was not.

Above her, the huge system of the great tree was in a high state
of activity. It knew nothing of the Armada, or of Jane. The
myriad leaves of its spreading canopy, upturned to the sun,
were daily converting the heavy carbon dioxide in the air to
carbon, which was transmitted to its bark, while the oxygen
was released back into the air. In this manner, through the
great tree, the planet itself was breathing.

And also growing. As the carbon passed into the oak tree's
bark, which in turn would be added, as a yearly ring, to the
thick wood beneath, so eventually when the oak and its fellows
crashed to the ground and their successors did the same, century after century, a thin carbon layer would be added to Earth
which, imperceptibly, would grow down the aeons.

His mother had vanished.

It was a late afternoon in the third week in July when Albion
returned to his house to find that she had taken a horse, ridden
out and not been seen for hours. For a few moments – he
couldn't help it – he devoutly prayed that she might have
fallen, or struck an overhanging bough in the woods, and broken her neck. "She said nothing of where she was going?" he
asked his wife.

"Nothing."

"You couldn't stop her?" His wife only replied with a look
that told him the question was foolish. "No." He sighed. "Of
course not."

Alive or dead, he would have to go out and search for her.
There were still long hours of daylight left. But he dreaded
what he might find. A rendezvous with the Spanish army itself
hardly seemed too unlikely. "God save us," he muttered.

As the Lady Albion came towards the Rufus tree she was feeling very pleased with herself. Indeed, she thought, she really
should have done this before.

She had ridden in quite a large arc. Coming up from
Albion's quiet house by the ford, she had taken the road up to

Brockenhurst, inspected the little church there and spoken to several of the villagers. Although few of them had seen her before, word of the strange lady at Albion's house had gone round Brockenhurst long ago, so when they saw the odd figure in black and red come riding by they guessed who it was. The rumours about her were mixed, however. If the gentry knew all about the Pitts family and Albion's troubles, the local forest folk were less clear. It was thirty years since she had lived in the Forest herself. Few remembered her and those memories were vague. They knew she was devout and a recusant, but that did not shock them. Word was that she was rich, which was always impressive. She might be liberal with her money, too, if you got on the right side of her. Some said she had gone mad. This could be interesting. They politely doffed their hats or put knuckle to forehead and gathered round in hopeful anticipation.

In fact, she was rather good with them. She was not a Pitts for nothing. She had an easy, proud style that impressed them and she spoke them fair.

She told them she had inspected their church and was sorry to see it had been somewhat damaged by carelessness, not malice, she hoped. At once, several long faces in the group told her she had sympathisers. She had not said more but bade them a courteous good day and proceeded on her way towards Lyndhurst, leaving behind the impression that she was surely not mad, but a fine lady.

At Lyndhurst she had encountered a cottager and had a similar conversation. Then she had swung up, round Minstead and come down through Brook, where she had done the same thing.

Now, as she approached the miraculous tree, she saw a girl, standing alone looking thoughtful, under its branches. The girl had an intelligent face. She drew up in front of her. "Good day, my child," she said kindly. "I see you are standing under a tree which, they tell me, is miraculous."

Indeed, Jane politely replied, it was so. And she told the strange lady about the tree's midwinter leafing and the Rufus legend.

"Perhaps," the Lady Albion pointed out, "this is a sign from God." She mentioned the two other trees. "Did not Our Lord hang on the cross with two thieves?"

"And there are three persons also, My Lady," the girl suggested, "in the Trinity."

"Indeed you are right, my child," said Albion's mother approvingly. "And is this not a sign to us that we should be faithful to the true Church?"

"I suppose, My Lady, it may be so. I had not thought of it," Jane answered truthfully.

"Think on it now, then," the Lady Albion commanded firmly. And then more gently: "Are you faithful, child, to Our Holy Church?"

Jane Furzey knew nothing of Albion's mother. Brook was ten miles from Albion's house; the lady had departed from the Forest almost fifteen years before Jane had been born. She had no idea who this impressive person with her air of splendid authority might be; but as she gazed at her now a thought occurred to her.

Jane had never seen the queen. Each summer, Queen Elizabeth would make a royal progress through some part of her kingdom. Several times she had come into other parts of the county, although not into the Forest. Was it possible that Her Majesty was coming down here now to see the shore defences? Would the queen ride about without a retinue? It seemed odd; but perhaps her gentlemen were nearby and would come up in a moment. The lady's rich clothes, her haughty bearing and kindly words certainly matched every description she had ever heard of the queen. If it isn't her, she thought, it's somebody very important. "Oh, yes, My Lady," she said and attempted a rustic curtsy. She wasn't sure what the queenly figure had meant, but she was certainly going to agree.

Albion's mother smiled. It had been clear to her in all the three places she had visited that many of the peasants, perhaps most, were still faithful to the old religious ways. In this assessment she was perfectly correct. Now here was this intelligent girl, quite alone, confirming everything.

Another thought occurred to her. "They say, child, that the Spanish will soon be here. What will happen when they come?"

"They will be met by the muster, My Lady. My brother," Jane added eagerly, "and my betrothed" – she hesitated only a moment when she said this last word – "are both in the muster."

"They are both steadfast to the true Faith?"

"Oh, yes."

"And brave men both, I am sure," the lady continued warmly. "Who is their captain?"

"A noble gentleman, My Lady," Jane hoped this was the way to talk to a queen. "His name is Albion."

"Albion?" This was exactly what she wanted. "And will they follow him obediently?"

"Why yes, My Lady."

"Let me put you a question, child. If it should chance that the Spanish upon our shores are truly our friends and not our foes, what will your brother do?"

Jane looked perplexed. How was she meant to answer?

"If this good captain, Albion, should instruct him so?"

Jane's brow cleared. "He will obey, loyally, I promise you, My Lady, whatever Albion commands."

"Well said, my child," the lady cried. "I see you are truly loyal." And with a wave that might, indeed, have been given by a queen, she rode off towards Brockenhurst.

When she met her unhappy son just north of that village she greeted him gaily with words that made him quake even further: "I have been speaking with the good people of the Forest, Clement. All is well. You are loved and trusted, my son." She beamed at him approvingly. "You have only to give the word and they are ready to rise."

Two more days passed and the weather over the Forest continued fine. It was said that the Spanish had definitely set sail, yet no one knew their whereabouts. The English fleet was down in the west, at Plymouth. The beacons were ready, but still no message came. Up at Malwood young Nick Pride wailed in high excitement. Each evening Jane visited him, and this evening she had promised to stay and keep him company as he took the night watch. "I may fall asleep, Nick," she had warned.

"You may." He had smiled confidently. "I shall not."

So when evening fell she told her parents she would remain up at Malwood with him and took her usual path down from Brook past the Rufus tree. The shadows were lengthening as she reached the old oak and she was walking by, not intending to pause, when suddenly she realised she was not alone. Under the trees nearby stood a small cart. In the cart sat Puckle.

She gave a little start. He was watching her calmly. She wondered if he had been there long and why he was waiting. He seemed to expect her to approach and so, conscious that her heart was beating faster than she wanted it to, she went over.

"What brings you here?" she asked with a smile.

When she had drawn near his eyes had dropped as though studying his hands. Now he slowly raised them. They were very clear, large and bright as they looked straight into hers. "You do."

She gasped. She didn't mean to. She couldn't help it. She remembered telling him she usually came this way to Malwood. So he had been waiting for her. She did her best to stay calm. "And what can I do for you?"

He continued to look at her coolly. "You could get into the cart for a start."

She felt her breath suddenly short above the heart. A tiny tremble went through her body. "Oh?" She managed another smile. "And where are we going?"

"Home."

Her home? She frowned, glanced at his face, then looked down at the ground. He meant his home: the cottage at Burley with the carved bed. The nerve of his offer was almost shocking. She could not look up. She had not expected this. Yet his manner suggested he thought it was inevitable. He had come for her. It was shocking, but simple. She ought to turn and walk away. Yet, against all reason, she experienced an unexpected sense of hidden, deep relief.

She knew she had to walk away, but did not move.

"I have to spend the watch at the beacon with Nick," she said at last.

"Leave him." His voice was quiet as the dusk.

She shook her head, paused, frowned. "I must see him."

"I'll wait."

She turned and began to walk towards Malwood. The light catching the leaves was crimson gold. She glanced back, once, towards the Rufus oak, standing in a pool of orange light. Puckle had not moved. She walked on.

What did she mean to do? She didn't know. Did she know? No, she urged herself, she didn't. She needed to see Nick Pride. She had to look at him.

It did not take long to reach the old earthwork. As she entered it the fire of the Forest sunset was making a bright crescent around the dark-green shadow within its walls.

Nick was standing by the hut and he came towards her, looking excited. "It's time to go up. You're late."

How young he seemed. How sweet – she felt a wave of affection for him – but how young.

She let him lead her up on to the earth wall beside the beacon. He was talking eagerly about the day he had passed, how one of his men had almost missed his watch. He sounded so proud of himself. She was glad for him.

After a while, she said: "I have to go back to Brook for a while, Nick. But I'll try and come by later."

"Oh." He frowned. "Something wrong?"

"Some things I have to do. Nothing much."

"But you won't come after dark."

"'Course I will. If I can. I know the way."

"There'll be a bit of moon tonight," he agreed. "You could see your way, I suppose."

"I'll try to come." Why was it that this lie gave her such pleasure, such excitement? She had never behaved like this before. The delight of deception was quite new to her. With an extraordinary sense of lightness she kissed him and left him, and made her way back towards the Rufus tree.

She was trembling, nonetheless, when she got into the cart. Without a word, Puckle took up the reins, touched the pony with his whip and they moved off. What was she doing? Did she mean to go with Puckle in secret and return to Nick? Was this a sudden severance from her family, her former life and her betrothed, to become Puckle's woman? She did not know herself.

The sunset was glowing deep red ahead of them as the cart came out on to the open heath. The red shafts caught Puckle's face so that it looked strangely ochre, almost demonic, as they rolled towards the west. Seeing it, she gave a little laugh. Then the great orb of the sun sank and the heath grew dark, and she leaned over so that, for the first time, he put his arm round her to comfort her as she journeyed with him towards the mystery of the forbidden.

The cottage was silent in the pale moonlight when they arrived. The children were not there. Presumably they were with some other member of the Puckle clan that night. He lit a candle from the embers when they got inside and, carrying it upstairs, set it on the chest so that its soft light made the strange oak bed glow in an intimate and friendly manner. The counterpane was off.

When he took off his shirt, she put her hands on the thick dark hairs of his chest, feeling them wonderingly. His face, with his short pointed beard, suddenly looked triangular, like some forest animal's in the candlelight. She was not quite certain what she should do next, but he gently lifted her up and laid her on the bed, and when she felt his powerful arms around her she almost swooned. As he came on to the bed with her she was soon aware that he was as hard and firm as the oak bed itself, but for a long time he stroked and caressed her so that it seemed to her as if, in some miraculous way, she had become one of the creatures he had so expertly carved, nestling, peeping out, or writhing upon the bedposts. And if, once, she cried out for a moment in pain, she could scarcely afterwards remember quite when or how it was, during that night when, as though by magic, she became at one with the Forest.

She was not aware, as she slept, that just before dawn the coastal beacons had sprung into flame to announce that the Armada had been sighted.

Don Diego yawned. Then he bit his knuckle. He must not fall asleep. He must complete his task. His honour was at stake.

He was tired, though, very tired. Six days had passed since the Spanish Armada had been sighted entering the English Channel and the beacons had been lit. Six days of action. Six days of exhaustion. And yet he had been lucky. His relationship, distant though it was, with the Duke of Medina Sidonia, who had now been given command of the whole Armada, had secured him a place in the flagship itself. And from this privileged vantage point he had witnessed it all.

The first days had been promising. As they passed the south-western tip of the island kingdom a cheeky English fishing vessel had come out to look at them, circled the whole fleet counting numbers, then vanished. Although one of the Spanish boats had chased it unsuccessfully, the Duke had only smiled. "Let it go and tell the English how strong we are, gentlemen," he declared. "The more terrified they are the better."

The next day, as they sailed slowly towards Plymouth, they learned that the English fleet was trapped by the wind in Plymouth harbour. A council of war was called on the flagship and it was not long before Don Diego knew what was being said.

"Smash them now. Take the port and use it as our base," the bolder commanders urged. And it seemed to Don Diego that this was good advice.

But his noble kinsman thought otherwise. "King Philip's instructions to me are very clear," he told them. "Unless we have to, we are to take no unnecessary risks." So the mighty Armada had sailed slowly on.

But that very night the English ships had rowed out of Plymouth and stolen the advantage of the wind. And they had been on the Spanish fleet's heels, like a pack of hounds, ever since.

The English attack had been almost continuous. The Spanish galleons, with their high castles fore and aft, and their huge complement of soldiers, were certain to win any encounter if the English came close enough to grapple. So the English circled, darted in and out, and poured in volley after volley of cannon fire, while the Spanish responded. "But the English seem to fire much more often," Don Diego had observed to the captain.

"They do. Our crews are used to firing only once or twice before we come alongside and grapple. But the English ships are organised as gun platforms. So they just keep firing. They've got more heavy cannon, too," the captain added morosely.

But what Don Diego particularly noticed was the relative speed of the English and Spanish ships. It was not, as he had supposed, that the English vessels were smaller – some of the biggest English vessels were actually larger than the Spanish galleons. But their masts were set differently; they dispensed with the cumbersome castles; they were built not for coming to grips and grappling with the enemy, but for speed. The traditional medieval sea battle had been an extension of an infantry attack; the English navy was almost entirely artillery. When the Spanish ships tried to catch them and board them, as they did several times, the English ships sailed easily away.

But the Spanish were not an easy prey. The Armada had entered the Channel in a single formation – a huge crescent seven miles across with the most heavily armed ships forming a protective screen all round its leading edge and the most vulnerable transports huddled in the centre. The English, harrying them from the rear, had scored some successes. On Sunday, three days before, they had inflicted horrible damage on some ships that had fallen behind and the next day they had taken several of these while the commander of one galleon, Don Pedro de Valdez, which had damaged its rigging by fouling another vessel, ignobly surrendered to Sir Francis Drake without even putting up a fight. But after that the Duke had ordered the wings of the great crescent to fold in behind and from then on the mighty fleet had proceeded up the Channel like a huge moving stockade.

In this new formation the Armada was almost impregnable. If the Spanish could not catch the English, the English could not dent the Spanish. Again and again they tried.

"Take care," the Spanish captains had been warned. "The English gunners aim for the waterline." And on Tuesday, off the southern promontory of Portland, the English had given the Spanish everything they had. Yet although there had been a number of casualties, remarkably little damage had been done. This was partly because the English did not dare come too close. As a result, even the cannon balls from their largest cannon had lost much of their velocity before they struck the huge galleons and many of them just bounced off. The other reason, which would never be reported in the island kingdom, was plain. As Don Diego remarked to one of his companions: "I'm glad these English fellows aren't terribly good shots."

The Armada was almost impregnable, but not quite. And it was a minor success on the part of the English gunners that gave Don Diego his opportunity for glory now.

When Albion's mother had told her son that his brother-in-law was an important captain in the Spanish army she had, as usual, overstated the case. What Catherine had actually written to her mother was that her husband Don Diego hoped to gain a command. Only in the celestial world of the Lady Albion's imagination had this hope already been translated into a brilliant existence.

In truth, Don Diego had never had a career at all. He was a good man. He had elegant manners. He loved his wife, his children and his farms. And if, like every true aristocrat, he longed to add lustre to his family name, his happiness with his domestic life had always held him back. But now, in middle age, when a man knows that if he is ever to do anything with his existence he had better do it now, Don Diego had seen the prospect of the great expedition in England as a lifetime's chance. His kinship with the Duke of Medina Sidonia, although distant, was real and had secured him a place on the flagship. And so this middle-aged man, whose marriage had saved his estate, and whose children loved him, went out to risk death so that he could bequeath them a little of the military glory that had so far been lacking in his homely life.

But what exactly was his position in this great enterprise? Why the same, exactly, as that of all the other gentlemen like him who were travelling with the Armada. There were scores of them in the fleet: rich gentlemen, poor nobles, royal princelings from all over Europe; there were bastard sons of Italian dukes in search of fame and plunder, plus, almost certainly, a natural son of the pious King of Spain himself. Some knew how to fight, some came to watch, some, like Don Diego, were vague about why they came. It was, after all, a crusade. But tonight, at last, Don Diego's chance had come.

It was in the nature of the defensive formation the Armada had adopted that the great convoy could only move at the speed of its slowest vessel. If one of the ships were disabled, then every ship would have to slow down – and they were moving slowly enough already. Crippled vessels, therefore, had to be ruthlessly left behind.

The ship that had been damaged was a common hulk – a slow, blundering vessel with only a few guns but a contingent of troops and a hold full of ammunition and supplies. Yesterday's pounding from the English had damaged one of her masts and holed her, as well as killing the captain. All day today the hulk had limped along, but by evening it was clear she couldn't keep up. And it was in early evening that the duke, who had been wondering if he could find something for his harmless kinsman to do, suddenly summoned him and enquired whether he could deal with it.

Don Diego had been working, now, for hours. He had laboured hard and intelligently. The first thing he had done was to get the troops off on to other vessels. Next he had turned his attention to the all-important ammunition. Unlike the English, the Spanish ships had no means of getting fresh supplies. Everything they needed had to be carried with them. They had been returning the English fire for four days now and some of the ships were getting short of powder. Using what smaller boats he could, Don Diego and the remains of the hulk's crew had unloaded barrel after barrel of powder and conveyed them to other ships. Then he had done the same with the cannon balls. That had been a slow and difficult process. Half a dozen had fallen into the water. One had almost gone through the bottom of the boat they were loading. Darkness had fallen and they were still at it. The crew were beginning to get a little grumpy, but he gave them no rest. Towards eleven o'clock the job was done.

As he had been awake since before dawn that day and had taken no siesta, Don Diego was starting to get very tired. Despite the fact that they had been lightening the hulk for hours, she was going slower and settling in the water all the time. A message came from the duke: he thanked Diego for his good work, but now the hulk must be left behind. The crew, it was clear, were ready to leave.

Yet Don Diego hesitated. There was still one thing he wanted to do.

He had made the discovery when he went down to check the hold. Although there were still all sorts of things down there, the gunpowder, which had been in the upper part, and the shot below had all been cleared. In the lowest part of the hold, against the bottom of the ship, he could hear the water sloshing about as the hulk wallowed lower. Holding the lantern over the water, he had peered down to see how deep it was. And then he had seen a faint, silvery glow and realised.

The entire bottom of the hulk was lined with bullion: silver bars; thousands of them. They gleamed mysteriously under the watery light as he gazed at them.

Such treasure, of course, was of no great importance to the Armada, for the fleet as a whole was carrying a prodigious quantity of gold and silver. In the present circumstances the powder and shot was of far more value. But if the hulk was just left to drift, the English would have the silver and this idea irked him. It's my operation, he thought, and it's going to be perfect.

The solution was quite easily arranged. Half the crew he put off straight away. The rest, just enough to do what was needed, he ordered to remain. He also kept two pinnaces, one on each side.

"We shall allow this ship to fall behind," he told them, "taking care not to foul any others as we do so. Then we shall scuttle her."

The men looked at him sullenly. They had to obey this gentleman, who knew nothing of ships and who had been foisted upon them; but they didn't like it.

"What do we do after that?" one of the men asked, with a hint of insolence in his voice.

"Get into the pinnaces," Don Diego replied. "No doubt," he added coolly, "if you row hard we can catch up."

The night was dark. Clouds covered the moon. Very slowly, yard by yard, the hulk was falling back through the fleet. To right and left, as the minutes passed, great shapes loomed up at them, hovered, showing lights here and there, then drew mysteriously away. The process of falling back might take half an hour, he guessed.

He went down into the captain's big cabin in the stern. There was a large chair there and he sat in it. He was tired, but he felt a sense of satisfaction at what he had done. Well, nearly done. He was exhausted, but he smiled. For a moment, a wave of sleepiness almost overcame him, but he shook his head to drive it off. It would be time, he thought, in a little while, he'd go back on deck again.

Don Diego's head sank on to his chest.

· · ·

Albion inwardly groaned. It was the middle of the night and still, God help them, his mother had not gone to bed.

The oak-panelled parlour was brightly lit: she had ordered fresh candles an hour ago. And now, for perhaps the fourth time – he had lost the will to keep count – she had worked herself up to a climax of fervour again.

"Now is the time, Clement. Now. Saddle your horse. The game's afoot. Summon your men."

"It is the middle of the night, Mother."

"Go up to Malwood," she cried. "Light the beacon. Call the muster."

"All I have asked, Mother," he said patiently, "is that we wait until dawn. Then we shall know."

"Know? Know what?" Her voice rose now to a pitch that might have pleased any preacher. "Have we not seen, Clement? Have we not *seen* them coming?"

"Perhaps," he said flatly.

"Oh!" She threw up her hands in exasperation. "You are weak. Weak. All of you. If only I were a man."

If you were a man, thought Albion privately, you would have been locked up long ago.

It had been late afternoon when the Armada had been sighted. The two of them, with a party of other gentlemen and ladies, had gathered at the top of the ridge by Lymington from which there was a fine view over Pennington Marshes down the English Channel. As soon as the distant ships had come in sight his mother had started to become highly agitated and he had been forced to take her horse's bridle, pull her to one side and whisper urgently: "You must dissemble, Mother. If you cry for the Spanish now, you will ruin everything."

"Dissemble. Yes. Ha-ha," she had cried. Then, in a whisper which, surely, must have reached well beyond Hurst Castle. "You are right. We must be wise. We shall be cunning. *God save the queen!*" she had suddenly shouted, so that the ladies and gentlemen turned in surprise. "The heretic," she hissed with delighted venom.

For three nerve-wracking hours they had continued to watch as the Armada came eastwards. The wind had been dropping and its progress seemed slower and slower. The English fleet, drawn up in tidy squadrons now, was visible not far behind. Before long, several small, swift vessels could be seen detaching themselves from their squadrons and making their way swiftly across the waters towards the Solent entrance. In less than an hour, two had navigated the entrance and anchored in the lea of Hurst Castle, while two more had pressed on towards Southampton. Soon they could see the men from Hurst Castle going out in lighters laden with powder and shot, and as soon as the two vessels had taken on all that could be spared they sped off again towards the fleet, from which tiny puffs of smoke and fire could be seen from time to time, accompanied, after a long pause, by a faint roar like receding thunder.

The Armada, so far, showed no sign of making towards the English shore. The ships remained in silhouette, a mass of tiny spikes like cut-outs, inching along the horizon line. On the Isle of Wight the garrison still had not lit the second or third beacons. But as darkness began to fall and the distant show resolved itself into a few sporadic flashes, Albion's mother remained as committed as ever to her former belief. "They will turn and approach us under cover of darkness, Clement," she assured him confidently. "They'll be in the Solent by morning." And so she had been saying ever since.

Albion glanced across at his wife. She was dressed in her nightclothes, prepared for bed. Her fair hair, only lightly streaked with silver, hung loose. She had gathered a shawl around her and was sitting quietly in a corner, saying nothing. If she took no part in the conversation, however, Albion knew quite well what she was doing. She was watching. As long as he could control his mother, well and good. But if not, she had already warned him she had given the servants their orders, which even he did not dare to countermand.

"We shall lose our inheritance," he had cautioned.

"And keep our lives. If she commits us to treason we shall lock her up."

He did not blame her. She was probably right; but the thought of losing all that money was very hard for him; which was why even now – for his children's sake, he told himself – he was temporising with his mother, playing for time. "I sent a servant up to Malwood, Mother," he pointed out for the third time. "If the beacons signal any approach, I shall be told at once."

"The beacons." She said it with disgust.

"They work very well, Mother," he said firmly. "Where do you think I should be? Down at the coast with my men already? Ready to silence the guns at Hurst Castle?" He regretted it even before he finished speaking.

Her face lit up. "Yes, Clement. Yes. Do that, I beg you. Be ready, at least, to strike quickly. Why do you hesitate? Go at once."

Albion stared thoughtfully at the gleaming candles. If he went out upon this errand, would it pacify her? Was that the sensible thing to do? Perhaps. But at the same time, another idea was in his mind. He was quite sure the Armada was not heading into the western Solent. They had been too far out to sea. But what if they came in at Portsmouth, just past the Isle of Wight? Or at any of the havens along the southern coast? There was Parma to consider, too. What about his great army in the Netherlands? That could be landing by the Thames even as they spoke. His mother might be dangerous; she might be mad. But was she wrong? It was the calculation he had never shared even with his wife. The time was very close. If the Spanish landed they might win. If they won, shouldn't he be on their side? How could he discover who was winning? There were probably not a few Englishmen who were thinking such thoughts that night.

And surely, he considered, when there was a strong chance his mother's cause might triumph it would be foolish indeed to make of her, his greatest advocate, an enemy.

"Very well, Mother. You may be right." He turned to his wife. "You and my mother should remain here and tell no one I have gone. There are some good men I can trust." This was pure invention. "I shall gather them now and we shall go down to the shore. If the Spanish show signs of landing . . ." He hadn't, in truth, any idea what he would do, but his mother was beaming.

"Thank God, Clement. At last. God will reward you."

Not long afterwards Albion rode out of his house in the wood and made his way southwards towards Lymington. If he was going to stay out all night, he considered, he might as well be down at the shore. Who knew? Something might happen.

Behind him his wife and his mother sat quietly in the

parlour. Some of the candles had been snuffed. The room was bathed in a soft, pleasant glow.

After a while the older woman yawned. "I think," she said, "I may rest for a little while. Will you promise to wake me as soon as there is any news?"

"Of course."

The Lady Albion went over, kissed her daughter-in-law on the forehead and yawned again. "Very well, then," she said and, taking a candle, left the room. A few moments later Albion's wife heard her enter her chamber. Then there was silence. She waited, snuffing out all but one of the candles, after which she went up to her own bed, got in as quickly as she could and laid down her head. As far as she was concerned her mother-in-law could sleep until doomsday.

And she was fast asleep herself, half an hour later, when the Lady Albion quietly stole out of the house.

Everything was pitch-black when Don Diego awoke. For a few moments he stared about him, trying to remember where he was. Then, feeling the arms of the chair and dimly seeing the big cabin around him, he remembered. He rose with a start. How long had he been sleeping? He staggered out and went up on to the deck, calling to his men.

Silence. He ran to the side to look for the pinnace. It had gone. He crossed to the other. That had vanished too. He was alone. He stared forward into the darkness. The sky was cloudy; only a few stars peeped through, but he could see the waters all around. And he saw no ships. He frowned. How was it possible? If so much time had passed the hulk should have sunk. What had happened?

Had he known the sailors better he might have guessed quite easily. Anxious to lose as little time as possible, they had made only the smallest attempt to scuttle the ship, then taken to the pinnaces as soon as they could. Afterwards the men on each pinnace, having gone to different ships, would claim they thought Don Diego was in the other. As for the hulk, it had continued to sail slowly forward but, one of the departing sailors having thoughtfully turned its rudder, it had peeled off to port. By the time the English boats saw it distantly in the darkness they had mistaken it for a ship of their own. And so for several hours, the hulk had been wallowing gracelessly forward, on an increasingly north-easterly course.

It was now, peering forward, that Don Diego suddenly realised something else. Ahead of him in the blackness, perhaps two miles off, was a faint, pale shape. At first he had thought it was a cloud, but it wasn't. He realised it was part of a larger, darker shape. It was a line of white cliffs. He could make them out, now. He looked to port. Yes. There was a low, dark coastline there, running for many miles. His mind was working clearly. He realised where he must be. The dark line must be the south coast of England. The white cliffs must belong to the Isle of Wight.

He was drifting into the western mouth of the Solent. For long moments he gazed ahead, awestruck but thinking. Then he slowly nodded his head.

Suddenly he laughed aloud.

For see, he realised, what God's providence had done. He had just been granted an opportunity far greater than any he had dared to hope for. It was quite beyond his dreams. Truly God granted miracles.

He was still marvelling at his good fortune when the hulk struck a sandbank, lurched and stuck fast.

Nick Pride heard the horse as soon as it entered the place, but he kept his eyes on the distant beacon. There was still only a single pinpoint of light out there in the blackness.

Nick was alone on the wall. His relief was asleep in the hut. He had been on his own since dusk when, after watching the distant Armada on the horizon for an hour or so, Jane had left. This was the critical night. If the Spanish started to make for the coast, the Isle of Wight beacons would certainly go to three. He had not taken his eyes off the signal for even a minute since nightfall.

Yet even so, his mind had several times wandered to other matters.

What was the matter with Jane? Three nights in a row, now, when she had come to see him she had kept him company for a little while but refused to stay. Each time, in some way, there had been a strangeness in her manner. One night she had seemed preoccupied and elusive, on another she had suddenly criticised him and seemed cross for no reason. A third time she had seemed good-humoured, yet almost motherly, kissing him on the forehead as if he were a child. Tonight, when she had said she must go, he had looked at her strangely and asked her what was wrong. She had pointed out towards the ships of the Armada on the horizon and asked him: "Isn't that enough to be worried about, Nick? What is to become of us all?" Then she had abruptly left him.

He supposed this must be the reason for her agitation. Yet each time he turned the matter over in his mind it still did not seem quite right.

A snort from the horse behind him told him it was almost at the wall. He had not expected Albion, but it was typical of his captain to take the trouble to visit even at this time of night. He awaited the familiar salute.

"You. Fellow. Watchman."

A woman's voice. What could this mean?

Whatever he was supposed to say in challenge he forgot. Instead, like a village rustic he enquired: "Who's that, then?"

There was a brief pause, then the same person called out in a tone of authority: "Light your beacon, fellow, summon the muster."

This was too much.

"The beacon gets lit only when there be three on the island. Well, two, anyway. Those are my orders from Captain Albion." That sounded definitive.

"But I come from Albion, good fellow. It is he who bids you light the beacon."

"And who might you be?"

"I am the Lady Albion. He sent me." Some practical joker, obviously.

"So you say. I only light this beacon when I see two down there," Nick said firmly. "And that's that."

"Must I force you?"

"You can try." He drew out his sword.

"The Spanish are coming, fool."

For a moment Nick Pride hesitated. Then he had an inspiration. "Tell me the password, then."

There was a pause. "He told it me, good fellow, but alas I have forgotten it."

"He told you?"

"Yes. Upon my life."

"Was it" – he searched his mind – "Rufus oak?"

"Yes. Yes, I believe it was." The miraculous tree.

"Well, then, I'll tell you something."

"Yes?"

"There ain't no password. Now be off with you, you trollop."

"You shall pay for this." The voice was furious, but disappointed – you could hear that in the dark.

"Be off, I say." He laughed. And a moment later the strange rider retreated into the shadow again. He wondered who she was. At least it gave him something else to think about as he gazed down, once more, at the single light in the distance.

As for the Lady Albion, she turned her horse southwards. If necessary, she was going to seize the guns at Hurst Castle herself.

The short night was already well advanced by the time Albion came on to the high ground at Lymington. The clouds were still obscuring the stars. Looking out to sea past the faint paleness of the Isle of Wight's chalk cliffs and the Needles, he could see nothing in the deep gloom. Wherever the Armada was, he did not think it was approaching the shore. In all probability it had vanished behind the Isle of Wight by now. Perhaps, at first light, he thought, he would ride westwards a few miles along the coast to see if he could get a view of the fleets behind the island. For the time being he dismounted and sat on the ground.

He had been there some time when he thought he saw a dark shape out in the water. For a moment he felt he'd imagined it. But no: it was there. A ship was approaching. He stood up, his heart suddenly pounding. Was it possible that the Armada had slipped in unnoticed? Or perhaps a squadron had been sent in under cover of night to seize the Solent? He turned and swung himself into the saddle. He must race to Hurst Castle and alert them.

But then he paused. Must he? Was he going to help Gorges or let the Spanish take him by surprise? Nobody could blame him. Nobody knew he was there. He suddenly realised, with a horrible force, that his moment of decision had come. What side was he on?

He had no idea.

He had spent so much time telling his mother one thing and the world another that he truly couldn't remember where he stood. He stared helplessly out to sea.

The ship was still approaching, but very slowly. He searched in the darkness, trying to see others, but could not find them. He waited. Still nothing. Then the dark shape seemed to stop. It had. He smiled. It must have hit a sandbank. He continued to watch. It would be perfectly possible for half a dozen Spanish ships to run aground out there. But although he waited no other shapes appeared. Whatever it was, the ship was alone.

He gave a sigh of relief. He needn't make a decision after all. Not yet.

Another hour later the first hint of light appeared in the east. The clouds were thinning, too. In the greyness the horizon line appeared unbroken. The Armada was no longer in sight.

He could see the hulk clearly, now. He looked for any sign of life upon it, but there didn't seem to be. The wind had dropped to the lightest of breezes; the water around the ship was calm. There might be survivors. If so, they would probably be on the beaches past Keyhaven.

He wondered whether to go and see. It could be dangerous if there was a boatload of them. On the other hand he was mounted. He had a sword. He considered, then shrugged.

His curiosity had got the better of him.

Don Diego watched cautiously. He was still rather wet, but he counted himself fortunate. The hulk had run aground only a mile or so out from the shore. The sea was calm. It had been quite easy, in the ship's hold, to find all he needed to make a simple, buoyant raft and fashion a broad-bladed paddle. The tide had helped him reach the sandy beach well before dawn broke. He had concealed the raft, climbed the sandy little cliff and started to walk along the heath. One precaution he had taken. Like most of the gentlemen travelling with the Armada, he wore a long gold chain round his neck. Its links were as good as any currency. For the time being he had concealed this inside his shirt and doublet. He also made himself as presentable as he could. He cleaned his shoes and stockings, brushed his breeches and doublet as far as possible. He understood the English fashions followed the Spanish. He was not sure how well he spoke English. He had gone to great trouble to do so and his wife assured him he did. Perhaps he could pass for an English gentleman who had been robbed rather than a Spaniard who had been shipwrecked. He would find out soon enough.

He walked along cautiously, ready to dive for cover in an instant if necessary. He knew from the maps on the duke's flagship what the lie of the land was around the mouth of the Solent. He knew where Hurst Castle stood. He wished he knew where Brockenhurst was, but he didn't.

His mission now, in any case, was wonderfully simple. He had to avoid being robbed, or killed by any overeager musters. He had, as soon as possible, to find one man; then all his troubles would be over.

He saw the lone horseman coming towards him from some way off. He leaped behind a gorse bush and waited, preparing himself carefully.

As he approached the gorse bush Albion slowed his horse to a walk and then stopped. He had seen the lonely figure walking along, apparently by himself, and watched him dart behind the bush. Now, with his hand on his sword, he waited for the next move.

He did not have to wait long.

The dishevelled Spaniard – for it was quite obvious that this was what he was – stepped out and, to his surprise, addressed him, despite his Spanish accent, in passable English. "Sir, I ask your help."

"Indeed?"

"I have been waylaid and robbed, Sir, on my journey to a kinsman who lives not far from here, I believe."

"I see." Clement kept his hand on his sword, but decided to play out this charade to see where it would lead. "You come from where, Sir?"

"From Plymouth." It was true, in a way.

"A long journey. May I know your name?"

"You may, Sir." The Spaniard smiled. "My name is David Albion."

"Albion?"

"Yes, Sir." Don Diego watched as the Englishman's face registered complete astonishment. I have impressed him, he thought and, emboldened, continued: "My kinsman is no less a person than the great captain, Clement Albion himself."

To say that this information impressed the Englishman would be an understatement. He looked stupefied. "Is he so great a man?" he asked weakly.

"Why, I think so, Sir. Is he not captain of all the trained bands and shore defences from here to Portsmouth?"

For several terrible seconds Albion was silent. Was this his reputation with the invading Spanish? Had the entire Spanish Armada heard of him? Would any captured Spaniard cry out his name? How, unless England fell into Spanish hands within days, was he to explain this to the council? Appalled though he was, he collected his wits enough to realise he had better find out more. "You are not David Albion, Sir. Firstly, because I perceive that you are Spanish." He quietly drew his sword. "And secondly because Albion has no such kinsman." He looked at him severely. "I know this, Sir, because I am Albion."

For a moment the Spaniard broke into a delighted smile, then checked himself. "How do I know that you are Albion?" he asked.

"I don't know," Clement replied calmly.

But the Spaniard was looking thoughtful. "There is a way," he said quietly. And then he told Clement his name.

"But what luck – I should say what a sign of God's providence – my dear brother, that of all the people in England I might have encountered" – Don Diego looked so delighted, so touched – "I should have come straight upon you." He looked at Albion happily but seriously. "It's wonderful, you know."

They were sitting, at Albion's suggestion, in a pleasant hollow near the cliff where they would not be disturbed. It had only taken a few moments to verify who they were. Albion had asked tenderly after his sister Catherine and Don Diego had been equally anxious to know the good health of the mother-in-law whom he described as: "That wonder, that saint." When Albion had politely congratulated him on his own high command, however, Don Diego had looked mystified.

"My command? I have no command at all. I am merely a private gentleman travelling with the Armada. It is you, my dear brother" – he inclined his head – "who have achieved such a high and honourable state. Your mother wrote to us about it long ago."

Albion nodded slowly. He began to understand. He saw his mother's fantastic hand in all this now. But this did not seem the moment to disillusion the well-meaning Spaniard. There were so many things he needed to find out. Was the King of Spain himself expecting him to deliver Hurst Castle to the invaders?

"Ah, my plan!" Don Diego's face lit up. "Your mother's plan, of course, I should say. What a woman!" But then his face fell. "I tried, my dear brother. God knows I tried. I wrote a long memorandum to my kinsman the Duke of Medina Sidonia. But . . ." His hand indicated a falling motion. "Nothing."

"I see." Things were looking up.

But what exactly, Albion ventured to ask, was the Spanish plan of invasion?

"Ah. What indeed?" Don Diego shook his head. "We all supposed, all the commanders of the ships supposed, that we should take a port as a base. Plymouth. Southampton. Portsmouth. One of them. From there our ships could be supplied."

"That seems wise."

"But His Majesty King Philip insisted the Armada go straight to meet Parma. In the Netherlands."

"The Armada will transport Parma's troops across, you mean?"

"No. It seems the waters by Parma's army are too shallow for our galleons. The Armada will rest at Calais."

"That's only a day's sailing away."

"And then?"

"Then Parma will cross to England. He's a great general, you know. Some say" – he dropped his voice as though he could be overheard – "that it's Parma who will make himself king of England, instead of King Philip. Not that he would be so disloyal, of course." Don Diego still looked doubtful.

"So how will Parma cross? Has he a fleet?"

"Flat-bottomed boats only. So he'll need fine weather."

"But the English ships would blast any such transport vessels out of the water," Albion objected.

"No, no, brother you forget. Our Armada will be only a day's sailing away. And our galleons are bristling with troops. The English won't dare come near enough to attack them."

"Then why are they doing so now?"

As if to underline the question a faint rumble was heard from the sea beyond the Isle of Wight. The English attack on the Armada had just begun again.

Don Diego looked troubled. "Actually, my kinsman the Duke of Medina Sidonia did seem to hint that he . . . thought the king's plan was imperfect." He shook his head. "We were told your ships were all rotten and that they'd run away."

"Did my mother tell you that too?"

"Oh, most certainly." But now Don Diego brightened. "However, my dear brother, we must never forget one all-important thing."

"Which is?"

"That God is with us. It is His will that we should succeed. Of this we are certain." He smiled. "So all will be well. And of course, the moment the English know we are on land, even if only half Parma's men get across . . ."

"What then?"

"They will rise." He beamed. "They will understand that we have come to liberate them from the witch Elizabeth, that murderess who has them in thrall."

Albion thought of the simple men of the musters, who had just been told that the main cargo of the Spanish galleons was the torture instruments of the Spanish Inquisition. "They may not all rise," he said cautiously.

"Oh, a handful of Protestants. I know."

Albion did not reply. One thing was becoming clear to him. If his brother-in-law was even half correct about the Spanish strategy the dreaded invasion was unlikely to succeed. And he was considering this, and its implications for him personally, when he realised that his brother-in-law was speaking excitedly.

". . . such an opportunity. You and I together. The moment Parma lands we can lead the trained bands from here and sweep up to London to join him."

"You want us to put ourselves at the head of a great rising?"

"It will bring you even further glory, brother. And as for me." Don Diego shrugged. "Even to ride with you would be a great thing for me."

Albion nodded slowly. It was a piece of glorious insanity worthy even of his mother. "Raising a great force," he said tactfully, "is not so easy in England. Even if the Faith were stronger . . ."

"Ah." Don Diego looked at him gleefully. "That is just the wonder of what has occurred. That is where God's providence is so clearly seen. Our own Spanish troops," he added reassuringly, "are no better. They have all been promised huge plunder in England. But this, my brother, is just the point. God has placed in our hands all that is needed to do His will. We can pay the troops." And seeing Albion's look of astonishment he waved towards the sea. "When I was shipwrecked, all alone, I supposed it was a punishment. But it was not. That ship out there. Under the waterline, the whole hull is filled with silver!" And he laughed with joy at the wonder of the thing.

"You had no companions at all?"

"No. You and I alone, brother, are in possession of this silver. It has been placed in our hands."

Albion became very thoughtful again.

Motioning the Spaniard to remain where he was, he stood up and moved to the edge of the cliff. The ship had settled down. It would not budge. Not even the high tide would float it off now. As he gazed at the stranded hulk the silver morning sun started to break over the Forest horizon in the east.

He turned to look down at Don Diego. What a strange thing fate was. That he should have encountered the Spaniard in such circumstances, after so many years, and find, moreover, that he liked him. For there was not the least question: this well-meaning, middle-aged Spaniard was a very nice man. Albion sighed.

His mind was going over the ground carefully. He thought of his sister, he thought of himself; he thought of Don Diego with his belief in the Catholic cause and of his mother. He thought of the council, of Gorges, of their suspicions about him. And he thought, very carefully, about the silver. That, he realised, made the situation very interesting. After a while he began to form a plan. As he considered its several aspects it seemed to him that it would work. Meditatively he glanced back, towards the rising sun.

Then he saw her. She was riding alone across the ridge by Lymington. Her cloak was flapping behind her, black and crimson. Her hat was at a mad angle. She looked like some wild apparition, a mounted witch who might canter clean off the ridge and sail up into the air. At the same instant the thought struck him, with a sudden, cold panic: what if she saw him and found Don Diego now?

He threw himself to the ground in terror, realised that the Spaniard was looking at him in astonishment, waved him to be silent and peeped over the tussock in front of him. The Lady Albion was still up there. She had not seen him. She had halted and was staring out to sea. He continued to observe her for a moment or two, then slid back into the hollow to join the Spaniard.

"Is everything all right?" Don Diego asked, puzzled.

"Yes. All is well." Albion looked at his new-found brother-in-law with affection. It really was an infernal pity that things could not have been otherwise. "There is something I must show you, brother," he said quietly and drew his sword. "On the blade. See."

Don Diego leaned forward to look.

Then, very suddenly, Albion ran him through.

Or nearly. For the sword point struck the golden chain under the Spaniard's shirt. And while Don Diego offered a cry and stared in wide-eyed astonishment, Albion, wincing, had to lunge again, several times, until he was successful. It was a messy business.

He waited until the body had finished shuddering, then removed the gold chain, which weighed nearly four pounds, and covered Don Diego as well as he could with sandy soil, before going to his horse. Mercifully his mother had vanished again. She's probably trying to raise a rebellion in Lymington, he thought grimly.

He glanced back at the place where Don Diego lay. He felt guilt, of course. But sometimes, it seemed to him, you could hardly say whether a thing was good or bad. It was a question of survival.

But now he must hurry. There were things to do.

• • •

"Silver? You are sure?"

Gorges and Helena were alone with him in the big chamber in Hurst Castle. They had kept him waiting there some time while he gazed over the Solent, but now they had both come to join him.

"I questioned him closely. At sword point. I think he was telling the truth."

"And this Spaniard – he was alone?" Gorges enquired.

"He said he was. He was trying to scuttle the vessel and got left on board by mistake. I saw no others," Albion continued, "so I think he was. No one," he said carefully, "knows about this silver except ourselves. I came straight to you."

"But you killed the Spaniard." Gorges was looking thoughtful.

"He suddenly drew on me. I had no choice."

"Shouldn't we get the body?" Helena asked.

There was a long pause. Gorges looked carefully at Albion and Albion looked back.

"Perhaps not," said Albion helpfully.

"The wreck," Gorges said firmly, "belongs to the queen. There's no question about that. I shall hold it in her name."

"I was wondering," Albion suggested. "The queen is very fond of you, Helena. She might grant you the wreck. I mean, she's granted prizes to Drake and Hawkins, and Thomas has held Hurst for her even if he hasn't been to sea."

"But Clement." Helena looked doubtful. "I don't think she'd part with all that silver."

Gorges was looking at her silently.

"What silver?" said Albion very softly.

"Oh." She got the point at last. "I see."

"I shall report the wreck to her at once. You could write a letter, too. Ask her if we may have the salvage. Say it's only a hulk. Any ammunition will go to the fort, but if there's anything else of value, may we have it. You know the sort of thing. She knows," Gorges confessed drily, "that I am somewhat in need at present."

"But what'll she say when we find all the silver?" Helena asked.

"Luck," said Gorges firmly.

"We don't *know* that there is any silver," Albion added. "Even my information may be incorrect. Your conscience should be quite clear. There *may* be something, that's all."

"And the Spaniard?"

"What Spaniard?"

"I will go and write the letter at once, Clement." She gave her husband a glance. "We are grateful."

There was silence in the room for a few moments after she had gone.

Then Gorges spoke. "Did you know that just before you arrived here your mother was arrested in Lymington?"

"No."

"We had a message from the mayor. It seems she was trying to persuade the people there to rise. For the Spanish."

Albion went pale, but kept his composure. "I wish I could say I was surprised. She went mad last night. But I didn't know she'd got out."

"That's rather what I thought. She said that you would lead the rising, Clement."

"Really?" Albion shook his head. "Last night she told me that since I didn't seem to want to, she'd do it herself." He smiled ironically. "I'm grateful for her new faith in me."

"She said you always planned to join the Spanish."

"Is that so? The only Spaniard I've seen so far I killed."

"Quite." Gorges nodded slowly.

"You know," Albion proceeded quietly, "even if my mother were not entirely out of her wits – and she has been talking like this for years – it would have been completely impossible for me to do any of these things she speaks of. I have heard it all a hundred times. She dreams of risings every day. She places me at their head whatever I tell her." He sighed. "What can I do?"

Gorges was silent. "It's quite true," he said after a few moments. "You couldn't have anyway."

"I wouldn't have, Thomas. I am loyal." He looked Gorges in the eye. "I hope you know that, Thomas. Don't you?"

Gorges stared straight back. "Yes," he said slowly. "I know."

From dawn until ten that morning, in a near calm, out on the horizon behind the Isle of Wight the English ships pounded the Armada. By afternoon both fleets were on their way again up the English Channel and for two days they continued, until the Duke of Medina Sidonia anchored off Calais and sent urgent messages to the Duke of Parma asking that general to come at once and cross to England.

Parma said: "No." With irritation he explained that a crossing in his flat-bottomed boats was quite impossible if enemy ships were anywhere in sight. Unless the Armada could come and fetch him – which, in the shallow waters off the Netherlands, they couldn't – he wasn't coming. All this, it turned out, he had been telling the King of Spain for weeks – a fact which the king, preferring to trust in providence, had not seen fit to tell the Duke of Medina Sidonia.

So the Spanish Armada lay off Calais, sending ever more baffled messages to Parma, and Parma stayed in the Netherlands, a day's journey away, despatching even crosser messages back. And the English waited by the Thames, expecting an invasion at any moment because the one thing that had never occurred to them was that the King of Spain had sent his Armada without any co-ordinated battle plan at all.

The Armada spent two fruitless days like this. Then, in the dead of night, the English sent in eight fire ships, coated with tar, blazing as brightly as a thousand beacons and the Spanish captains, in panic, cut their cables and scattered. The next day the English fell upon them. The Spanish were driven towards the shore, some wrecked, some taken; but the majority were still intact.

Then, on the following day came God's wind.

The Protestant wind, they called it. Nobody, on either side could ever deny that, whatever their valour or their piety, it was the weather that truly destroyed the mighty Armada. Day after day, week after week it blew, turning the seas to heaving froth. Ships lost sight of each other; galleons were scattered all over the northern waters, some were driven on to the rocks in northern Scotland or even Ireland. Less than half reached home. And whether it was to reward the Protestants for their faith or punish the Catholics for their shortcomings, both Queen Elizabeth of England and King Philip of Spain could agree that such winds could only come from God.

• • •

For the Lady Albion the weeks of gales were a time of trial indeed. For a start, she was kept, on Gorges's strict instructions, in the tiny gaol in Lymington. And although the mayor of Lymington petitioned many times for her to be taken to another place – or beheaded, or set free, or anything so long as the indefatigable lady could be removed from *his* charge – it was not until October that the council agreed that, although a traitor, the lady represented no actual danger to the state. After her release, while Albion had never ceased to profess his personal loyalty to her, she never felt quite the same about him. And the following year she had taken ship and gone to visit her daughter Catherine whose husband Don Diego had been lost – no one knew exactly how – in the great disaster of the Armada. That poor Don Diego had been safely buried by her son, the first night she had been in gaol, deep in the Forest where he would never be found, was something she never imagined.

It was hardly surprising that she remained with her daughter in Spain; and if, after failing to answer her summons that he join her there, Clement Albion forfeited any hope of inheriting her fortune, he was philosophical about it. "I really think," he once confessed, "that I'd give up one of my coppices just to make sure she never returned."

Albion's own fortune remained modest, however, but that of his friends Thomas and Helena Gorges enjoyed a spectacular increase. For Queen Elizabeth looked kindly upon their request and granted them the hulk. By the time they had quietly emptied its contents, Sir Thomas Gorges and his wife the marchioness realised that they had one of the greatest fortunes in the south of England.

"And now," Helena joyfully declared, "you can build your house at Longford, Thomas."

It was not until nearly two years later that Albion was invited to accompany them up to the big estate below Sarum. "The house isn't quite finished yet, Clement," his host told him, "but I'd like you to see it."

They had certainly chosen a beautiful site, Albion thought, as they came to the lush parkland down by the Avon. But what no one had prepared him for, and which caused him first to gasp and then to burst out laughing, was the design.

For there, in the tranquil peace of an inland Wiltshire valley, built on a huge scale, with handsome windows instead of embrasures, was a massive triangular fortress. "By all the saints, Thomas," he cried, "it's Hurst!"

It was indeed. The great country house, which Gorges called Longford Castle, was an almost exact replica of the triangular coastal fortress by the Forest. In memory of the Spanish hulk and its cargo of silver he had even had carved, high over the entrance, a depiction of Neptune reclining cheerfully in a ship with his trident sloped over his shoulder, on each side of which was a caryatid, one with his face and the other with his wife's carved upon them. You had to admire his cheerful humour.

"Helena insists that Swedish castles are all triangular and that the carving depicts her Viking ancestors," he said with a wink.

Swedish castle or gunnery fort, whatever you thought it was, the great triangular mansion would long remain one of the most eccentric country houses in England.

And if perhaps thereafter, Albion felt an occasional pang of jealousy at his aristocratic friends' good fortune, he had to confess that, thanks to Gorges and Helena, his loyalty was never questioned again. He was even able, with a good conscience, to expropriate a considerable quantity of Her Majesty's timber in the course of his subsequent career.

Jane married Puckle.

Nick Pride was completely astonished and so was everyone else. "If I hadn't been stuck up at Malwood at the beacon, it would never have happened," he said.

"If she was going to do a thing like that," said his mother, "you're better off without her."

"I don't know," said Nick. "It's like she was under a spell, I reckon." Which didn't make much sense.

Jane's parents weren't too pleased about it either. In fact, when they got married Jane's mother didn't want to give her the little wooden cross she'd always promised her. But in the end, not wanting to quarrel with her, she did. And Jane wore it like a talisman.

The great Armada storm did not only change the lives of men; here and there it made small alterations in the greater life of the Forest, too.

It was deep on a night, when the Spanish galleons were tossing helplessly in the northern seas, that the wind chose to race
with a particular urgency through the glade by the miraculous
Rufus tree. The branches of the great tree bent and shook. The
myriad life forms in its crevices clung or crouched deeper into
their shelters. Tiny organisms, minute particularities, flew off
into the moving darkness of the wind, carried into chaos. All
around, tall trees swayed, bent, oak leaves and acorns rattling
in the furious tearing and buffeting of the wind, which howled
and gusted and whooshed in the blackness.

But the roots of the miraculous tree were as wide as its
branches and even though, on this wild Armada night, the
upper world might have succumbed to madness, the lower
world of the tree was silent, still, unmoved by the frantic waving of its branches.

Nearby, however, just inside the neighbouring wood, a different oak, only two centuries old, had grown up in close company with other oaks and beech trees, tall and straight. Its
canopy was therefore very much smaller; its roots smaller in
like measure.

And so it was, in the great turning and wrenching of the
howling wind, that suddenly, dragged clean out of the ground
by nature's blind forces, this tall oak crashed down through its
neighbours and smashed, a falling giant, to the Forest floor.

It is an awesome thing when an oak tree is torn down, but
also beneficial. For the broken sections of the tree's canopy, its
great network of branches, lie like so many protective cages
upon the ground. Within these cages for a year or two a new
shoot may grow because the deer and other creatures that prey
upon saplings cannot reach it.

Two cages of this kind fell upon that stormy night. And in
the coming acorn fall, after so many years in which its children all had been wasted, two acorns from the miraculous tree
would lie in the leaf mould within these oaken cages and take
root, and grow.

Alice

1635

What's a life? Not a continuum, certainly. A collection of memories, perhaps; only a few.

She could just recollect old Clement Albion. She had been only four when he died, but she still remembered her grandfather. Not a face, exactly, but a quiet, benign presence in a Tudor house with big timber-framed gables. That must have been the old Albion House, she realised; not her Albion House.

Her Albion House began on a summer day.

It was very warm. It must have been late morning; perhaps it was a Saturday. She did not know. But they had walked down, just the two of them, from the old church at Boldre – just she and her father. She was eight at the time. They walked along the lane on the east side of the river and turned down the track into the wood. There were a number of young beech trees, saplings mostly, mixed with the oak and ash. The sun was slanting through the light-green lattice of the canopy; the saplings spread their leaves like trails of vapour through the underwood; birds were singing. She was so pleased that she had started to skip; her father was holding her hand.

They saw the house when they came round the bend in the track. The red-brick walls were nearly up. One of the two gables had already been refaced; the old oak roof timbers exposed their bare framework to the blue sky. The dusty site looked peaceful in the warm sun. A few men were quietly working on the upper storey; the clink of bricks being tapped into place was the only sound that disturbed the quiet.

They had stopped and stood there together, looking at the scene for a little while; then her father had said: "I'm building this house for you, Alice. This will be your very own and no one shall take it away from you." Then he had looked down and smiled, and squeezed her hand.

She had looked up and thought that her father must love her very much if he was building a whole house for her. And she experienced a moment – perhaps there are just one or two in a lifetime – of perfect happiness.

It wasn't a big house. It was only a little larger than the old Tudor house of her grandfather and his father before him. Built in red brick, in a simple Jacobean style, it certainly qualified as a small manor house; yet hidden away, in a modest clearing in the middle of the woods, it had almost the air of an isolated grange or hunting lodge. To Alice it was magical. It was her house; because her father loved her.

Of course, he had hoped to have a son. She understood that now; but ten years had passed since that summer's day.

Of Clement Albion's two sons, William and Francis, it was her father William, the elder, who had done better. In fact, he had done brilliantly. As a young man, in the last years of Queen Elizabeth's reign, he had gone up to London to study law. William had worked hard. It was a litigious age; a clever lawyer could do well. And when, fifteen years after the great Armada, the old queen had died and been succeeded by her cousin, King James of Scotland, the opportunities for amassing money had grown even greater.

For if James Stuart had one idea when, as a middle-aged man, he became King James of England, it was to have a good time. He'd never had any fun before. Son of the ill-fated Mary Queen of Scots – whom he'd scarcely even known – the dour Scots Presbyterians who had thrown out his mother brought him up to rule according to their way of thinking and kept him on a tight rein. So when at last he got the throne of England as well, he was anxious to make up for lost time.

The liberated Scottish king's ideas of fun turned out to be curious. A taste for pedantic scholarship – he was really quite learned and could be witty – led him to develop a full-blown theory that kings had a God-given right to do whatever they liked. Whether he truly came to believe this piece of startling nonsensc or whether he was just amusing himself, no one has ever been sure. Another taste of this father of several children, which now became increasingly obvious, was his embarrassing, sentimental and even tearful passion for pretty young men. By his last years, court functions were apt to degenerate into a shambles of kissing and fondling these "sweet boys." His third taste, which God knows he'd never been able to enjoy in the north, was a love of extravagance. Not the great displays and festivities in which (for someone else was always paying) Queen Bess had taken such delight: King James's court favoured simple, gross excess. The feasts were often just a competition to see how much food could be conspicuously wasted. But even this was nothing compared with the licence given to the king's friends to make free of the public purse. Old nobility like the Howards, or new like the family of the pretty boy Villiers, it was all the same: sales of offices and contracts, bribery, outright embezzlement. Everyone was at it.

Where rogues are stealing and fools spending, a wise man can surely make a fortune. William Albion had done so. By the time James's small, shy son Charles had come to the throne in 1625, Albion had returned to the Forest a rich man. He had also married well – a modest heiress a dozen years his junior. His seat was a handsome estate in the Avon valley called Moyles Court – which contained, as it happened, the lands of his distant ancestor, Cola the Huntsman. Then he had Albion House, in the centre of the Forest, from his father; there were further holdings on Pennington Marshes; he also owned most of the village of Oakley.

Albion House he had rebuilt for Alice. The rest, he had hoped, would go to his son. But although his young wife had given him several more children, all had died in infancy. Time had passed. Then it was too late. Last year his wife had died, but William Albion had no wish to start anothcr family at the age of sixty.

Alice was eighteen now. She was to inherit it all.

William had paused before making this decision. After all, there was his younger brother to consider.

Technically, by title, all the land he had was William's to dispose as he wished. Old Clement, he felt sure, would have wanted him to give something to Francis; and if he hadn't

always promised Albion House to Alice he might have let
Francis have that. But there was a further consideration.

What had Francis ever done to deserve it? For years, despite
his father's help and encouragement, he had drifted, never
really worked. He was in London still. He had become a merchant, but not a very successful one. William was fond of
Francis, but he could not quite restrain the impatience of the
successful man for an unsuccessful brother. He gave, without
even knowing it, a tiny shrug when Francis's name was mentioned. So it seldom was. With the logic typical of the man
who had made money, he reasoned that it was a waste of time
to give it to someone who had not. Or, to put it more kindly,
should his desire to keep the family name in the Forest cause
him to dispossess the daughter he loved? No. Francis must
fend for himself. Alice was the sole heiress.

It had come as rather a surprise to her that a few months before, when discussing in a general way the men she might
marry, her father had mentioned one name with particular
favour: John Lisle.

They had met him at a gathering of a number of local gentry families in the Buttons' fine house near Lymington. He was
a few years older than she and recently a widower. He had
children. He had struck her as a sensible, intelligent man, although perhaps a little too earnest. Her father had talked to
him more than she had.

"But Father," she had reminded him, "his family . . ."

"An ancient family." The Lisles were indeed a family of
some antiquity who had for a long time possessed lands on the
Isle of Wight.

"Yes, but his father . . ." The whole county knew about John
Lisle's father. Inheriting a good estate, he had squandered both
it and his reputation. His wife had left him; he had taken to
drink; in the end, he had even been arrested for debt. "Isn't
there bad blood . . . ?"

Bad blood: that expression so beloved of the landed classes.
A notorious brigand or two gave a certain patina to the ances-
tral furniture. But you had to be careful. Bad blood meant danger, uncertainty, unsoundness, blighted harvests, diseased
trees. The gentry, who were still partly farmers, had their feet
on the ground. Breeding people, after all, was no different

from breeding livestock. Bad blood will out. It had to be avoided.

But to her surprise, her father only smiled. "Ah," he said, "now let me advise you on that." And giving her that look of his that announced, "I speak with a lifetime of experience as a lawyer," he proceeded: "When a man has a father who has lost his substance there are two things he can do. He can accept a lowly condition, or he can fight back and make his fortune."

"Isn't that what younger sons are meant to do?"

"Yes." A cloud crossed his face as he reflected that this was just what his own younger brother had failed to do. "But when a father has dishonoured his family as well then the case is even sharper. The son of such a man faces not only poverty but shame, ridicule. Every step he takes down the street is dogged by shadows. Some men hide. They seek a life of obscurity. But the bravest souls outface the world. They hold their heads high; their ambition is not like a fire of hope, but a sword of steel. They seek fame twice: once for themselves and once to erase the shame of their fathers. That memory is always with them, like a thorn, driving them on." He paused and smiled. "John Lisle, I think, is such a one. He is a good man, an honest man. I'm sure he is kind. But he has that in him." He looked at her with affection. "When a father has an heiress as a daughter he looks, if he is wise, for a husband who will know how to use that fortune: a man of ambition."

"Not another heir, Father? The ambitious man, surely, might care only for her money."

"You must trust my judgement." He sighed. "The trouble is that most of the heirs of fine estates are either soft, or lazy, or both." And then, suddenly and unexpectedly, he laughed.

"Why are you laughing?" she asked.

"I was just thinking, Alicia." He sometimes called her that. "With your strong character I wouldn't inflict you on some unsuspecting heir to a great estate. You'd destroy the poor boy entirely."

"I?" She looked at him in genuine astonishment. "I have no thought of being a strong character, Father," she replied, which only caused him to smile at her the more fondly.

"I know, my child. I know." He tapped his finger lightly on

her arm. "Consider John Lisle, though. I only ask that. You will find him worthy of respect."

When, two days later, Stephen Pride stopped at the cottage of Gabriel Furzey on the way to the green, he reckoned he was doing him a favour. "Shouldn't you be going?" he enquired.

"No," said Gabriel, which, thought Pride, was typical.

If, in the three hundred years since they had quarrelled about a pony, the Prides and the Furzeys had remained in Oakley, it was for the very good reason that there were few more pleasant places to live. If they had had other quarrels about Forest matters down the generations – as they surely must have done – these were buried and forgotten. The Prides, by and large, still thought the Furzeys a little slow and the Furzeys still considered the Prides a bit pleased with themselves; although whether, after centuries of intermarriage, these perceptions had any validity it would be hard to say. One thing, however, which Stephen Pride and anyone else could have agreed upon was that Gabriel Furzey was an obstinate man.

"Suit yourself," said Pride and went on his way.

The reason for his visit to the green was that young Alice Albion was there.

If there was one thing that had changed scarcely at all in the New Forest since the days of the Conqueror it was the common rights of the forest folk. Given their smallholdings and the poverty of much of the soil, this continuity was natural: the exercise of common rights was still the only way in which the local economy could work.

There were chiefly four, by name. The right of Pasture – of turning out animals to graze in the king's forest; of Turbary – an allowance of turves, cut for fuel; of Mast – the turning out of pigs in September to eat the green acorns; and of Estovers – the taking of underwood for fuel. These were the four; although there were also some customary rights to marl, for enriching your land, and of cutting bracken as bedding for livestock.

The system by which these ancient rights were allocated, like ancient common law, was often complex and they might attach to an individual cottage; but it had been the custom to consider them as belonging to each landowner, who would claim them on behalf of himself and his tenants. The estate under which both Stephen Pride and Gabriel Furzey came belonged to the Albions. And since it would all, one day, belong to her, it was Alice, that morning, whom her father had sent, together with his steward, to collect some important information.

As he came up, Pride saw that she was sitting in the shade at the edge of the green. They had provided a table and a bench for her. The steward was standing at her side. On the table a large sheet of parchment paper was spread. She sat very upright. She wore a green riding dress and a wide-brimmed hat with a feather in it. In colouring she took after her mother. Her fair hair had a reddish tint, her eyes were more grey than blue. He smiled, thinking she looked rather fetching. He had seen this Albion girl around the place ever since she was a child. He was only seven years her senior. When she was twelve, he remembered, she hadn't been too proud to race him on her pony. She had spirit. The Forest people liked that.

"Stephen Pride." She needed no prompting from the steward and gave him a bright look. "What shall I write down for you?"

It was the first time, as far as anybody knew, that a complete list of all the common rights had ever been written down. They had always existed. They were in people's memories. Any dispute in the Swainmote, as the old Venderers' Court was often called, could always be solved by reference to the local jury, advised by the representatives of the vills. So why would anyone want to write down all this mass of local information?

As Stephen Pride enumerated the commoning rights to which his smallholding was entitled, he knew the reason very well. "It is," as he had remarked to his wife the day before, "for our sovereign lord, the cursed king." And as he looked young Alice Albion in the eye now, he knew equally well, although neither of them said it, that her opinion was just the same.

If the evidence of history is anything to go by it seems clear that members of the royal house of Stuart only make good monarchs if they have been properly broken in first.

King James had. His miserable years in Scotland, where by tradition the knife was never far from any monarch's throat, had taught him to be canny. Whatever he might believe about the divine right of kings, he never in practice pushed his English Parliament too far. He was also quite flexible. His dream was to act as a broker between the two religious camps, marrying his children to both Protestant and Catholic royal houses, and seeking toleration for both religions in England. It was a dream largely unrealised; Europe was not ready for toleration yet. But, for all his faults, he tried. His son Charles, however, had received no such apprenticeship and displayed the Stuart inflexibility at its worst.

Sometimes it is a very great mistake to give a large idea, even a good one, to a small mind. And the idea of the divine right of kings was a very bad idea indeed. If one strips away the duplicity with which he tried to accomplish his aims, there is something naive and almost childish about the lectures that Charles I used to give his subjects. Although not without talent – his eye for the arts was remarkable – this belief in his rights blinded his intelligence to even the simplest political realities. No English king, not even mighty Harry when he kicked the Pope out of his Church, had ever made such claims to divine authority. No ruler, not even the Conqueror himself, had thought you could ignore ancient law and custom. Charles wanted to rule absolutely, as the French king was starting to do; but that wasn't the English way.

It had not been long, therefore, before King Charles and the English Parliament were at loggerheads. The Puritans suspected that he wanted to bring back Catholicism – after all, his French wife was Catholic. Merchants disliked his habit of raising forced loans. Members of Parliament were furious to be told that he considered them, in effect, nothing more than his servants. By 1629 Charles had dissolved Parliament and decided to rule without it if he could.

The only problem was, what was he to do for money? Charles wasn't desperate. As long as he didn't get involved in any wars – that was always a huge expense – he could just about get by. There were customs and other dues, and the profits from the crown lands. But still he always needed more. One thing he did was sell titles. The new order of baronets was a nice little earner. And as he and his advisers looked about for other assets to exploit someone had suggested: "What about the royal forests?"

What were they good for? No one was quite sure. There were the deer, of course. The only time the royal court usually bothered about the deer was for a coronation or some other huge feast, when they provided a large supply of venison. There was timber. That needed more looking into. And there ought to be some income from the fines levied by the royal forest courts.

It was then that a clever official suggested: "Why not have a Forest Eyre?"

It was an ingenious suggestion because, once it had been explained to him, nothing could have been better calculated to appeal to King Charles. The Forest Eyre went back to Plantagenet times. Every so often – years might pass between these visitations – the king's special justices would go down to inspect the whole system, correct any maladministration, clear up any outstanding cases and, you could be sure, levy some handsome fines. As far as anyone could remember, there hadn't been an Eyre in generations. Old King Harry had held one a century ago. Since then, everyone had forgotten about them. It was just what King Charles loved: an ancient royal prerogative his naughty people had forgotten. In 1635, to everyone's great annoyance, there had been an Eyre in the New Forest.

The results had been quite encouraging. The regular Forest court had been galvanised. Three huge thefts of timber – a thousand trees at a time – had come to light and elicited three stupendous fines of a thousand, two thousand and three thousand pounds. This was an enormous haul. But it was not these great fines that had infuriated the Forest. It was the attack on the ordinary folk.

That summer of 1635 there had been no less than two hundred and sixty-eight prosecutions brought before the Forest court. The average had usually been about a dozen. The Forest had never seen anything like it. Every inch of land they had discreetly taken in the last generation, every cottage quietly erected, all were exposed, all fined. There was not a village or family in the entire Forest that hadn't been caught. None of the fines were lenient; some were vicious. Labourers occupying illegal cottages were fined three pounds. You could buy a dozen sheep, or a couple of precious cows for that, when most smallholders had milk from only one. A yeoman was fined a hundred pounds for poaching. A few yards of ground taken for some beehives, a troublesome dog, some illegally grazed sheep – all resulted in abrupt fines. As always, when King Charles set out to assert himself, he was thorough.

Was he within his rights? Not a doubt of it. But with his typical lack of tact, the Stuart king had managed to find an entire population that was naturally well disposed towards him and alienate them at a single stroke.

When the political quarrels of the seventeenth century have finally died away – which as yet, in England, they have not – Charles Stuart will surely emerge on to history's page, once and for all, neither as a villain nor a martyr, but as a very silly man.

And now every cottager's right to his ancient common rights was to be listed. To Pride it seemed interference for its own sake. Alice had other ideas.

"The word in London," her father had told her the day before, "is that the king wants to make an inventory of the whole area. And do you know why? He wants to offer the New Forest and Sherwood Forest together, as security for a loan! Imagine it," he continued with a shake of the head, "the whole Forest could be sold off to pay the king's creditors. That's what's behind all this, in my opinion."

When Pride had finished his brief account she thanked him pleasantly and then enquired: "Where's Gabriel Furzey? Shouldn't he be here?"

"Probably," Pride answered truthfully.

"Well." Alice might be only eighteen, but she knew she wasn't standing any nonsense from Gabriel. "You tell him from me, if you please, that if he wants his rights recorded he'd better come now. Otherwise they won't be."

So, grinning quietly to himself, Pride went off and delivered the message.

When one looked at Gabriel Furzey and Stephen Pride, it was not hard to guess what the attitude of each might be to the inquiry. Pride – lean, keen-eyed – was every inch an independent inhabitant of the Forest. But he had his relationship with authority, too. His ancestors might have grumbled about the existence of any outside order in the Forest, but natural intelligence and self-interest had led the Prides, for a long time now, into a calculated relationship with the powers that be. When the representatives of the vills attended the Forest courts there was sure to be a Pride or two among them. Occasionally one would even take a junior position in the Forest hierarchy – an under-forester, for instance, or one of the agisters who collected the fees. Here and there a Pride had graduated from the tenant into the yeoman class, owning land in his own name; and as often as not, when the local gentlemen chose some yeomen to sit with them on juries they'd be glad enough to choose a Pride. Their reason was very simple: these Prides were intelligent, and, even in a disagreement, men in authority know that it is always easier to deal with an intelligent man than a slow-witted one. A gentleman forester felt on firm ground if he said, "Pride thinks he can take care of that," or "Pride says it won't work."

And if some well-meaning person were to suggest that Pride might have been doing a little discreet poaching on the side, the informer was more likely to be met with a quiet smile and a murmured, "I dare say he has," than any thanks – there being always a sporting chance that the gentleman receiving this information had been doing a little of the same himself.

But Gabriel Furzey, short, adipose – Alice used to think, rather harshly, that he resembled an irritable turnip – had not reached an accommodation with anyone and, as far as Pride knew, had no plans for doing so.

When Stephen told him that Alice was waiting for him, therefore, he just shook his head.

"What's the point of writing things down? I know my rights. Always had 'em, haven't we?"

"That's true. But . . ."

"Well, then. Waste of time, isn't it?"

"All the same, Gabriel, you'd better go, I reckon."

"No, I ain't goin'." He gave a snort. "I don't need that girl to tell me what rights I got. I know. See?"

"She's not bad, Gabriel. It isn't like that anyway."

"She tell me to come, didn't she?"

"Well, in a manner of speaking."

"Well, I won't then."

"But Gabriel . . ."

"An' you can go along too," Furzey suddenly shouted. "Go on . . ." This last was a sort of bray: "Goo . . . oon."

So Stephen Pride left and, shortly after, so did Alice. And nobody wrote anything down about Gabriel and his rights.

It didn't seem to matter.

1648

December. A cold breeze in a grey dawning.

A single man on a grey horse – in his forties; good-looking; dark hair greying, grey eyes watching – stared from the ridge by Lymington across the salt marshes to the small grey castle of Hurst in the distance.

Grey sea, grey sky, grey foam by a grey shore, soundless because distant. From that fort by the winter sea very soon would issue, under close guard, the small wreck of a captured king.

John Lisle pursed his lips and waited. He had thought of riding down to join the cavalcade, but then decided against it. It is not, after all, an easy thing to meet a king whose head, very soon, you plan to cut off. Conversation is difficult.

But it was not the fate of King Charles that concerned him so much. He cared nothing for him. It was the quarrel he had just had with his wife that worried him – the first serious crisis in the twelve happy years of their marriage. The trouble was, he couldn't see a way out.

"Don't go to London, John. I beg you." Again and again she had pleaded through the night. "No good will come of this. I can feel it. This will be the death of you." How could she know such a thing? It didn't make sense, anyway. It was not like her to be so timid. "Stay down here, John. Or go abroad. Make any excuse, but don't go. Cromwell will use you."

"No man uses me, Alice," he had responded irritably.

But it hadn't stopped her. And finally, some time before daybreak she had turned on him in bitter reproach. "I think you must choose, John, between your family and your ambition."

The absurd unfairness of this had struck him with such

force and so hurtfully that he could not speak. He had got up and ridden out of Albion House before dawn.

His eyes remained fixed on the distant fort. Like it or not, the thought kept nagging at him: what if she were right?

Although, two years after their marriage, her father's death had left Alice the mistress of large estates, it had never occurred to John Lisle to retire to the Forest and give up his career. Nor had Alice ever suggested it. However much she loved him, she probably would have scorned a husband who only lived off her wealth. Besides, he had two sons from his first marriage to provide for, as well as the children that he and Alice had soon started to have together. He had been a hard-working lawyer and a good one. He had risen in his profession. And when, after eleven years of personal rule, King Charles had finally been forced to call a Parliament in 1640, John Lisle had been chosen, as a man of wealth and stature, to represent the city of Winchester.

Did that make him too ambitious? It was easy for Alice to say such a thing. She had never known anything but security. Disgrace, failure, ruin – she had never felt their keen bite. There had been times as a student, with no allowance from his drunken father and too proud to beg from friends, when John had gone without food. For Alice a career was a pleasant matter, something to be taken for granted, but from which one could always choose to retire. For him it was life or death. William Albion had been right. There was steel in John Lisle's soul. And his ambition told him he must go to London.

They were coming out of Hurst Castle now, a party of horsemen. They started to ride along the narrow strand with the gunmetal sea behind them. King Charles was easy to spot because he was the smallest.

The party was taking a strange route. Instead of passing straight up the Forest centre through Lyndhurst, they were skirting its edge, riding westwards to Ringwood and then over the top to Romsey on their way, in stages, to Windsor Castle. Did they imagine anyone would try to rescue Charles in the Forest? It seemed unlikely.

Since King Charles had plunged the country into civil war, the New Forest had remained quiet. The nearby ports of Southampton and Portsmouth, like most of the English ports and the city of London, were for Parliament. Sentiment in Lymington had run with the bigger ports. Royalist gentry had tried to secure the Isle of Wight and Winchester for the king, but they couldn't keep it up. The Forest itself, however, containing no strongholds of any kind, had been left undisturbed. The only difference from normal life was that, since the royal government had broken down nobody had paid any of the forest officers. So they had paid themselves, from the gentleman foresters down to the humblest cottager, in timber and deer and anything else the place provided. It wasn't as if they didn't know how.

"The king can't exactly argue about it, can he?" Stephen Pride had remarked genially to Alice one day. Lisle wondered whether the new government, whatever form it finally assumed, would take an interest in the Forest.

Then he transferred his gaze back to the distant figures riding along the strand. How was it possible, he asked himself for the hundredth time, for that small person down there to have made so much trouble?

Perhaps, given the king's views about his rights, the war had always been inevitable, from the day when Charles came to the throne. He just could not accept the notion of political compromise. He had kept councillors his Parliament detested, raised new taxes, favoured the Catholic powers his people hated and finally tried to force his bishops, who were so "High Church" they could almost be taken for papists, on to the stern Calvinistic Scots. This last act of madness had brought the Scots out in armed rebellion and given Parliament the chance to impose its will. Strafford, his hated minister, had been executed; the Archbishop of Canterbury imprisoned in the Tower of London. But it had been no good. The two sides had been too far apart by then. They had drifted into civil war; thanks, in the end, to Oliver Cromwell and his "Roundheads," the king had lost.

Yet even in defeat, King Charles would not deal honestly with his opponents. For Lisle, the last straw had been after the defeat of the king at the final battle of Naseby. Captured documents had proved beyond a doubt that, if he could, Charles would bring an army from Ireland or from Catholic France to subdue his people. "How can we believe he wouldn't allow papism back into England, too?" Lisle had asked. And when he had been sent with other commissioners to negotiate with Charles on the Isle of Wight, where the king had been held before his transfer to Hurst Castle, he had perceived exactly what kind of man he had to deal with. "He will say anything; he will play for time, because he thinks he rules by divine right and therefore he owes us nothing at all. He has the same character as his grandmother Mary Queen of Scots: he will go on plotting until the day his head is off."

But this, of course, was just the trouble. It was what worried Alice and many others like her. It was why, now, there was a split between the many in Parliament who wanted a compromise and the sterner souls in the army, led by Cromwell, who believed that the king must die. How could you try to execute a king, the Lord's anointed? Such a thing had never been done. What did it mean? Where would it lead?

Strangely enough, it was precisely because he was a lawyer that John Lisle saw that a legal solution to the problem of the king was impossible.

The constitution of England was actually rather vague. Ancient common law, custom, precedent, and the relative wealth and strength of the people concerned had governed the politics of each generation. When Parliament declared that it had been consulted since the reign of Edward I, nearly four centuries before, Parliament was right. When the king said he could call or dismiss Parliament as he liked he was also right. When Parliament, looking for written authority, appealed to Magna Carta they were not quite right, because that document was an agreement between King John and some rebel barons in 1215, which the Pope had ruled was illegal. On the other hand the implication of Magna Carta, which no one had ever denied before, was that kings must govern according to custom and law. Even bad King John never invoked the idea of divine right and would have thought it very funny. When Parliament rediscovered the medieval form of impeachment, which everyone had forgotten for centuries, to attack Charles's ministers, they had law on their side. When they claimed, shortly before the Civil War began, that Parliament had the right to veto the king's choice of ministers and to control the army they hadn't a legal leg to stand on.

But at the end of the day, it seemed to Lisle, none of it mattered. "Don't you see," he had explained to Alice, "he has chosen a position from which, legally, he cannot be budged. He says he is the divinely appointed fount of law. Therefore, whatever his Parliament does, if he does not like it, will be illegal. Cromwell wants to try him. Very well, he will say the court is illegal. And many will hesitate and be confused." His incisive legal mind saw it all with complete clarity. "The thing is a perfect circle. He can continue thus until the Second Coming. It's endless."

But to break with law and custom: that was dangerous too. Defeating an impossible king was one thing, but destroy him entirely and what would arise in his place? Many of the Parliament men were gentlemen of property. They wanted order; they favoured Protestantism, preferably without King Charles's bishops; but order, social and religious. Many of the army, and smaller townsmen however, were starting to talk of something else. These Independents wanted complete freedom for each parish to choose its own form of religion – so long as it was Protestant, of course. Even more alarming, the party of Levellers in the army wanted a general democracy, votes for all men and perhaps even the abolition of private property. No wonder, then, if gentlemen in Parliament had hesitated and hoped to reach a settlement with the king.

Until two weeks ago. For then, finally, the army had struck. Colonel Thomas Pride had marched into Parliament and arrested any members who wouldn't co-operate with the army. It was a simple coup, done while Cromwell was tactfully absent. Pride's Purge, it was called.

"Do you suppose," Alice had asked with a smile, "that Colonel Pride has any relationship with our Prides here in the Forest?"

"Perhaps."

"I can see Stephen Pride arresting the Members of Parliament." She had chuckled. "He'd do it very well."

But that had been the last time she had been able to see the funny side of the business. As the December days wore on, and the time for Charles's removal from the little fort on the Forest shore drew closer she had become more and more gloomy.

"Anyone would think it was you or I who was going to trial," Lisle had remarked testily. But this did no good at all.

What made it worse was that he himself had heard that several of the prominent lawyers on the Parliamentary side were discreetly withdrawing from the process. When she said, "Cromwell needs lawyers, that's why he wants you," he knew, in fact, that she was right.

So what if he didn't go up to London? What if he pleaded sickness and stayed down in the Forest? Was Cromwell going to come and arrest him? No. Nothing would happen. He'd be left alone. But if he ever wanted any appointment or favour from the new regime he could forget it.

Ambition, then. She was right. It was his ambition drawing him to the trial of the king.

And his conscience, too, damn it, he thought angrily. He was going because he knew the thing had to be done and he was man enough to do it. His conscience, too.

And ambition.

The little king was turning off the end of the strand now. A few moments more and the party disappeared from sight. Slowly, reluctantly, John Lisle also turned and rode back towards his house. He and Alice had had several homes in the last ten years. They had been in London and Winchester, on the Isle of Wight, where he was busy repairing his own family estates, at Moyles Court in the Avon valley or at Alice's favourite Albion House. As it was almost Christmas now they were in Albion House.

What was he going to say to her on his return?

He had thought she might be asleep when he got back, but she was waiting for him, still in her nightclothes, although wrapped up, thank God, in the chilly air by the open door. Had she been waiting there since he left? A pang of pain and a rush of tenderness passed through him. Her eyes were red. He dismounted and went to her. "I'll stay until after Christmas," he said. "Then, after that, we'll think again." He told himself that this last bit was true, as if he had not already made up his mind.

"The king has gone?"

"Yes. On his way."

She nodded sadly. "John," she said suddenly, "whatever God tells you must be done, we are with you, I and your children. You must do what you must do. I am your wife."

Dear heaven, he thought, what a fine one. He embraced her and entered the house with a new joy in his heart.

1655

Thomas Penruddock would never forget the first time he saw Alice Lisle. He had been ten. That was two years ago.

They had set off from Compton Chamberlayne early in the morning. The village and manor of Compton Chamberlayne lay in the valley of the River Nadder, about seven miles west of Sarum, and the journey into the old cathedral city was easy and pleasant. After a rest and a brief visit to the ancient cathedral with its soaring spire, they had proceeded south, following the River Avon's course, past the Gorges family's great estate of Longford Castle and then, crossing the river a few miles further down, they had made their way up on to the plateau of wooded ground that is the northernmost corner of the huge New Forest.

The village of Hale lay just at this corner. From the manor house, set right on the edge of the ridge, there was a lovely view westward over the Avon valley floor. Two generations ago the Penruddocks had bought the manor for a younger son, and the Penruddocks of Hale and their cousins had always been on friendly terms. On this occasion his parents had taken Thomas to stay at Hale for a few days.

As it happened, Thomas had never been to Hale before. Their cousins welcomed them warmly, the young ones took him to play, and his first evening only seemed likely to be spoiled for a moment when an elderly aunt, looking at him intently, suddenly declared: "Dear heaven, John, that child looks exactly like his grandmother, Anne Martell."

It was from his mother's side, from her mother's family the Martells of Dorset, that Thomas had taken his dark, rather brooding good looks. The light-haired Penruddocks were a handsome family, too. His father, whom Thomas idolised, was thought especially so and it had always saddened the boy that they did not look exactly alike. So his saturnine face broke into a smile when the elderly aunt continued: "I hope you're proud of him, John" and his father replied: "Yes, I think I am."

Colonel John Penruddock. To Thomas he was the perfect man. With his brown beard and laughing eyes, hadn't he been one of the most dashing commanders on the royalist side? He had lost a brother in the war; a cousin had been exiled. His own gallant loyalty to the king had cost him dear – both in money and offices – when Cromwell and his wretched crew had triumphed; but Thomas would rather the Penruddocks lost every acre of their land than have his father any different, any less splendid than he was.

The next morning, to his great pleasure, he was allowed to join the men when they went for a ride.

"I think," their host said, "we'll start across Hale Purlieu. Do you know," he asked kindly, "what a purlieu is, Thomas?" And, when Thomas shook his head: "No reason why you should. A purlieu is an area at the edge of a royal forest that used to be under forest law but isn't any more. There are several places along this edge of the Forest that have been in and out, as the boundaries change down the centuries."

The Penruddocks had ridden across Hale Purlieu and had started up over a high, wide tract of New Forest heath when they saw the two riders coming from their right on a track that ran directly across their path a little below them. Thomas heard his father mutter a curse and saw his cousins pull up sharply. He was about to ask what it meant, but his father looked so grim that he did not dare. So the Penruddocks watched silently as the figures, a man and a woman, passed two hundred yards in front of them without a sign or a word and continued across the heath.

He had a good look at them as they rode by. The man, quietly dressed, was wearing a high-crowned, broad-rimmed black hat of the kind favoured by Cromwell's Puritans. The woman was equally quietly dressed, in dark brown with a small lace collar. Her head was bare, her hair reddish. They might be simple Puritans, but the quality of their clothes and their splendid horses indicated clearly that they were people of considerable wealth. Nobody moved until they were almost out of sight.

"Who were they, Father?" he at last ventured to ask.

"Lisle and his wife," came the bleak answer.

"They've got Moyles Court," his cousin remarked, "but they don't come up here much." He sniffed contemptuously. "We never speak to them." His eyes rested upon the two figures as they finally disappeared. "Damned regicides."

Regicides: the people who had killed the king. Not all the Roundheads had been for it. Fairfax, Cromwell's fellow commander, had refused to take part in the trial of the king. Several of the leading men were unwilling to sign the death warrant. But John Lisle had shown no qualms. He'd been at the trial, helped draw up the documents, argued for execution, shown no remorse when the king's head was cut off. He was a king-killer, a regicide.

"And profited by it handsomely," his cousin added angrily. When royalist estates were confiscated by Parliament, Cromwell had given Lisle the chance to buy up land cheap. "His wife's no better," Penruddock of Hale went on. "She's in it as deep as he is. Regicides both."

"Those people," his father said quietly, "are your family's mortal enemies, Thomas. Remember that."

"They have the power, John," his cousin remarked. "That's the trouble. And there's not much to do about it."

"Oh," Colonel John Penruddock said thoughtfully, "I wouldn't be sure of that, cousin. You never know." And Thomas saw the two men look at each other, but no further word was spoken.

He had wondered what it meant.

And now he knew. It was a Monday morning. They had been out all that damp March night, gathering parties of horsemen around Sarum; but Tom didn't feel tired for he was too excited. He was riding with his father. It was still dark, an hour to go before dawn, when the cavalcade – almost two hundred strong – rode in beside the old Close wall, under the high shadow of the cathedral spire. At the head rode his father, another local gentleman named Grove and General Wagstaff, a stranger who had come with messages and instructions from the royal court in exile.

Passing the corner where the cathedral's walled precincts

met the town, they rode up the short street that brought them into the broad open ground of Salisbury market place. As puzzled heads popped out from shuttered windows, awakened by this unexpected clatter in the dark, the men-at-arms went quickly about their work.

"Two men to each door," he heard his father order briskly. Moments later they had set guards by the entrance of each of the market place's several inns. Next, his father sent patrols down the streets and to the gates of the cathedral Close.

It was only a few minutes before a young officer rode up and reported: "The town is secured."

"Good." His father turned to his friend Grove. "Would you go door to door? Let's see how many of the good citizens of Salisbury are ready to serve their king." As Grove went off, Penruddock turned back to the young officer. "See how many horses you can find. Commandeer them, no matter whom they belong to, in the king's name." He glanced across at his fellow commander. General Wagstaff, a rather hot-headed man, had served valiantly in the Civil War. With a trace of irritation Penruddock asked him now: "Where's Hertford?"

The Marquis of Hertford, a mighty magnate, had pledged to join them with a large troop, perhaps a whole regiment of horse.

"He'll come. Have no fear."

"He'd better. Well, shall we look at the gaol? Wait here, Thomas," he instructed and, taking twenty men with them, the two commanders rode off into the darkness towards the city prison.

The Sealed Knot. Young Thomas looked around him at the shadowy horsemen in the market place. Here and there he could see the faint glow of a clay pipe that had been lit. There were soft chinks as a horse chewed its bit or a sword tapped against a breastplate of armour. The Sealed Knot – for two years the loyal gentlemen of this secret group had prepared to strike the blow that would restore England to its proper ruler. Even now, across the sea, the rightful heir, the eldest son of the murdered king, was waiting eagerly to cross. At strategic points all over the country, towns and strongholds were being seized. And his own gallant father was leading them in the west. He felt so proud of him that he could almost die.

It was not long before the two cavalier commanders returned.

His father was chuckling. "I found it hard to tell, Wagstaff, whether those men were more pleased to be let out of gaol or sorry to be made into soldiers." He turned as the young officer he had sent off came back to report on the horses. "We've just acquired about a hundred and twenty gaolbirds who are fit for service. Have we mounts for them?"

"Yes, Sir. The stables at all the inns are full. So many people in town for the assizes." The judges from London had just arrived in Salisbury to hold the periodic sessions there. The place was packed with people who had business with the courts.

"Ah, yes," Colonel Penruddock continued, "that reminds me. We've got the justices and the sheriff to deal with." He nodded to the officer. "Find them, if you please, and bring them here at once."

Thomas found it hard not to laugh a few minutes later when the gentlemen in question appeared. For the officer had taken his father's words quite literally. There were three men, two judges and the sheriff, all taken straight from their beds, still in their nightshirts and shivering in the early morning cold. A faint light was appearing in the sky. The expressions of angry dismay on the pale faces of the three could be clearly seen.

Up to now, Wagstaff had been content to confer quietly with Penruddock. After all, he had only come there as the representative of the king, whereas Penruddock carried all the weight of local respect. But for some reason the sight of these three important persons in their night attire seemed to stir him into a sudden access of irritation. He was a short, peppery soldier with a small beard and a long moustache. This last seemed to quiver with disgust as he glared at them.

"What is the meaning of this?" asked one of the judges with as much dignity as he could muster.

"It means, Sir," replied Wagstaff furiously, "that you are arrested in the king's name."

"I think not," replied the judge with a composure admirable for a man standing in a public place in only his nightshirt.

"It also means" – Wagstaff's person bristled until his small body seemed to turn into a shout – "that you are about to be hanged."

"That isn't quite the plan, Wagstaff," Penruddock gently interposed.

But for the moment it seemed Wagstaff wasn't listening. He turned upon the sheriff now. "You, Sir," he barked.

"Me, Sir?"

"Yes, Sir. You, Sir. Damn you, Sir. You are a sheriff?"

"I am."

"Then you will swear your oath of loyalty to the king, Sir. Now, Sir!"

The sheriff in question had previously fought as a colonel in Cromwell's army and, whatever his situation, he was not going to be browbeaten. "I will not," he replied stoutly.

"God's blood!" Wagstaff cried. "Hang them now, Penruddock. God's blood," he added again for good measure.

"That is blasphemy, Sir," observed one of the judges. It was a frequent complaint of the Puritan opponents of the loose-living royalist cavaliers that their language was blasphemous.

"Damn your snivelling cant, you flat-faced Bible thumper, I'm going to hang you. Bring ropes," Wagstaff cried, casting about in the dawning for a promising point of suspension.

And it was several minutes before Penruddock could persuade him that this was not their best course. In the end, the judges had their official commission documents burned in front of them and the sheriff was put on a horse, still in his nightshirt, to be taken with them as a hostage. "We can always hang him later," a rather grumpy Wagstaff muttered with a small revival of hope.

It was getting quite light now and the enlarged forces had gathered in the market. There were nearly four hundred in all. To Thomas they seemed a huge army. But he saw his father purse his lips and quietly enquire of Grove: "How many citizens did you get?"

"Not many," Grove murmured.

"Mostly the gaolbirds, then." He looked grim. "Where's Hertford?"

"He'll join us. Along the way," Wagstaff grunted. "Depend on it."

"I do." Colonel John Penruddock beckoned Thomas to draw close. "Thomas, you are to go to your mother and give her a full report of all that has passed. You are to remain at home until you receive my word to join me. Do you understand?"

"But, Father. You said I could ride with you."

"You will obey me, Thomas. You will give me your word as a gentleman to do exactly as I say. Remain guarding your mother, your brothers and sisters, until I send for you."

Thomas felt his eyes growing hot. His father had never asked for his word as a gentleman before, but even this tiny thrill of pleasure was swamped by the great wave of disappointment and misery that had just broken over him. "Oh, Father." He choked back the tears. He felt a huge sense of loss. He had been going to ride with his father, a fellow soldier at his side. Would the chance ever come again? He felt his father's hand on his arm. The hand squeezed.

"We rode together all this night. I was glad to have you at my side, my brave boy. The proudest, best night of my life. Always remember that." He smiled. "Now promise me."

"I promise, Father."

"Time to ride," said Wagstaff.

"Yes," said Colonel John Penruddock.

Monday passed quietly at Compton Chamberlayne. Thomas slept in the afternoon. Just before dusk a horseman on his way up the road from the west towards Sarum brought news to Mrs Penruddock that her husband and his men had been at Shaftesbury, only a dozen miles away; but fearing that it might tempt Thomas to ride out there she did not tell him. On Tuesday a party of Cromwell's horse arrived in Sarum. Within hours, they had ridden on, westward. When asked what their mission was they replied: "To hunt down Penruddock."

Wednesday passed. There was no news. Somewhere over the big chalk ridges that swept towards the west, Penruddock was collecting troops, perhaps fighting. But although young Thomas stopped every horseman coming from the west and his mother sent three times a day to Sarum for news, there was none. Only silence. Nobody even knew where they were. Penruddock's Rising had rolled away out of sight.

• • •

Why was it happening? Why had the members of the Sealed Knot decided they could strike now and why was level-headed Colonel John Penruddock involved in this perilous business?

Whatever the king's faults, the shock at the execution of Charles I had been widespread. Tracts describing him as a martyr had sold in such huge numbers that there were almost as many in circulation as Bibles. Nor was it long before the Scots – who had no more wish to be ruled by Cromwell and his English army than they had to be subject to Charles I and his bishops – had crowned his son as Charles II on condition that in Scotland, at least, whether he liked it or not (and the jolly young libertine didn't like it at all!), he would uphold the rule of their dour Calvinistic faith. Young Charles II had promptly tried to invade England, been completely routed by Cromwell and, after hiding in an oak tree, fled for his life. That was four years ago, but from his exile abroad the young king had been busily preparing to regain his kingdom ever since.

As for Cromwell, what sort of government had he offered? A Commonwealth, it was called. But take away the mask of a Parliament of squires and merchants hand-picked by himself and it was clear that the power was still entirely with the army. Not even the one that had won the Civil War, though, for the democratic Levellers had been crushed and their leaders shot. Cromwell was called Protector now and signed himself Oliver P., just like a king. Three months ago, when even his own chosen Parliament had refused to increase his army, he had dissolved it. "He's a worse tyrant than the old king ever was," they protested. With the royalists still plentiful on the one hand, Parliament men and even army democrats furious on the other, it was not unreasonable to hope that Cromwell might be toppled. As always in the affairs of men, however, the outcome would have nothing to do with the merits of the cause and everything with timing.

The news came on Thursday.

"They've been broken." It had happened during a night-time skirmish in a village down in the West Country. "Wagstaff got away, but Penruddock and Grove are taken. They're going to be tried. For treason."

It was only gradually that the full story emerged. The Sealed

Knot's great rising had not exactly failed: it had never really started. Despite the fury of the Parliament men at being dismissed, despite the fact that some of Cromwell's army was still in the north pacifying the Scottish Highlands, the senior men of the Sealed Knot had concluded, quite rightly, that their organisation wasn't ready for a full-scale rising. A flurry of confused messages to and fro between the Knot and the king in exile had not only left some agents, like Wagstaff, believing the rising was still on, but had also alerted Cromwell who had promptly brought extra troops into London and other key points. At one rendezvous after another the conspirators had either failed to turn up or quickly gone home. By the day before the events at Salisbury the whole thing had been completely called off.

But nobody had told Penruddock. It was just a question of timing.

Thomas had never seen his mother like this before. Although she had passed on the saturnine looks of the Martells to her son, she herself had a broad, open face with a mass of chestnut hair. She was a simple soul, she understood her household, but she had always left all matters of business and politics to her husband and followed behind him. She had seen him spend over a thousand pounds in the king's cause, and suffer a fine of thirteen hundred more. The last few years had been hard as they struggled to pay this off. But a trial for treason, as even Thomas knew, could mean stiffer penalties for the family. They could lose Compton Chamberlayne and everything they had. As his mother fussed about her household daily tasks, supervising her children, the kitchen, the larder, household servants and now estate workers too, he wondered if she knew and was trying to carry on as normal, or whether she just closed her eyes even to the thought.

But above all, he watched her for signs of what was happening with his father.

His first letter had been brought to them on Thursday night. It begged her to remain where she was and await further word. Within days another came with instructions.

Thomas could see his mother doing her best. His father asked her to use all her influence on his behalf, to approach all sorts of people. Such business did not come easily to her. She asked friends for help. The trouble was, almost all of them were among the gentry with royalist connections. After a fruitless week of seeing friends who couldn't help and writing to others who probably wouldn't, his mother announced to the family one day: "We're all going to the Forest tomorrow."

"Whom are we going to see?" Thomas asked.

"Alice Lisle."

"At least she can see us," his mother declared as the old carriage rolled across the Forest. She had learned that Alice Lisle was at Albion House, so they had spent a night at Hale before setting off again at dawn. "She may have married Lisle, but she's still an Albion. We used to know them," she had remarked plaintively.

By late morning they were at Lyndhurst and by noon they had passed Brockenhurst and were crossing the little ford from which the track led down towards the house in the woods.

As he looked at his two younger brothers and three sisters, Thomas thought of the conversation he had had with his mother the night before. "I think Mrs Lisle hates us, Mother," he had suggested.

"Perhaps, but she's a woman with children too," his mother had replied in her simple way. And then, with a sudden vexation he had seldom seen before: "Oh, these men! I don't know. I really don't."

So they rolled in through the gateway to Albion House and the surprised servants told their mistress who was there; and after a short pause Alice Lisle gave orders that they might come in. They were escorted into the parlour.

Alice Lisle was dressed in black, with a plain white apron, a big linen collar and cuffs. Her reddish hair was tucked into a linen cap. She looked every inch a Puritan. Mrs Penruddock had dressed as simply as she could, although her lace collar showed plainly enough that she was the wife of a cavalier. What's the use of pretending, she had thought?

Alice Lisle looked at Mrs Penruddock and her children. She was standing herself and she did not suggest they sit down. She had understood, of course, at once. The Penruddock woman had come to plead and was using her children. She didn't blame her. She supposed she'd have done the same. She saw the other woman look round for her own children but she had already had them swiftly taken to another part of the house. She didn't want the children to meet because it might suggest an intimacy that was impossible. She stood stiffly. She dared not show any weakness. "My husband is in London and will not return this month, I think," she said.

"It was you I came to see." Mrs Penruddock had not prepared a speech because she didn't really know how. "I remember your father very well. My grandfather and old Clement Albion were friends, you know," she blurted out.

"That may be."

"Do you know what they're doing to my husband? They've accused him of treason!" Her voice went up at this last as though it were something outrageous.

Dear God, Alice could have cried out, if you put yourself at the head of four hundred men, capture the sheriff and declare war on the government, what do you expect? But she understood. She looked at the children, saw the eldest boy watching her intently, wanted to look at him with pity, but knew she must not. Instead, she looked stern. "What do you want with me?" she asked.

"It can't be right," the other said, indicating the six children, "to leave these without a father, whatever he did. I mean, it was he who stopped Wagstaff harming those men in Salisbury. He never hurt anyone. And if the Protector lets him live, I know he'd give him his word never to take up arms again, or even have any dealings with the king at all."

"Are you saying you wish me to write all this to my husband? You think he can persuade the Protector?"

"Yes." A light of hope appeared in Mrs Penruddock's face. "Would you do that?"

Alice stared at her. She could see the hope dawning and she knew she must crush it. She could not add to this family's misery by awakening false optimism that would only be dashed. Her gaze fell upon Thomas again. The boy looked more sensible than his mother, she thought. "Mrs Penruddock." Putting on her sternest frown she addressed herself partly to the boy as well. "I must tell you that there is no hope at all. If the judges find him guilty he will surely die. That is all I have to say to you."

The woman's face fell, but she had not quite given up. "You will not even write?" she pleaded.

Alice hesitated. What could she reply? "I will write," she said unwillingly. "But it won't do any good."

"Well at least she said she'd write," said Mrs Penruddock to her children as they went back.

And write Alice did – a long and passionate letter. She described the interview to her husband and made all the points in Colonel Penruddock's favour, including some that his wife hadn't thought of. Whatever his intentions at the start of the ill-fated business, she hadn't the least doubt that if Penruddock gave his word to Cromwell he would keep it.

John Lisle's reply came a few days later. He agreed with Alice and had talked to Cromwell but, hardly surprisingly, he couldn't help much.

The leaders will be tried by jury and the judges they ill-used at Salisbury shall not sit in judgement lest it be thought they seek vengeance.

If Penruddock is found guilty – and surely he is so – the Protector will grant him a merciful death. But he cannot do more. If he pardons Penruddock, what encouragement he'd give to any other rebellion.

Thomas did not remember the details of the days that followed. There were letters, desperate appeals; for a time it seemed that a guarantee of safe conduct and pardon offered to some of their followers might be applied to Penruddock and Grove, too, but this was denied. Next the authorities appeared to hesitate about where the trials were to be, but by April it was decided that the rebels taken down in the West Country would be tried down there, in Exeter city, where they were being held. Every day he asked his mother, "When shall we go to see Father?" and always she replied: "As soon as he sends for us."

It was clear that his father still thought it might be necessary for his wife to go to London on his behalf, so they remained at home. But in the third week of April a message came. The trial was about to begin. Colonel Penruddock had sent for his wife.

"Can't I come too?" Thomas had begged. Not now, he was told. So once again, he had to stay at home and wait.

His mother was gone a week, but before she returned he had already heard the verdict. Guilty. They had sent to Cromwell for the death warrant. She was frantic now. Penruddock and Grove had issued an appeal to the judges.

She herself, the moment she reached her home, immediately despatched a letter to Alice Lisle. "I'm sure she can do something," she declared. Although why this should be the case, when they had never heard another word from her, Thomas did not know.

One blow, however, they had not foreseen. On the day after her return, when she was trying to comfort her children, a party of six soldiers under an officer came to the door of the house and informed the unhappy woman that she must leave.

"Leave? What do you mean? Why?"

"House is sequestered."

"On whose orders?"

"The Sheriff's."

"Am I to be turned out of doors, then? With my children?"

"Yes."

They spent that night at an inn at Salisbury; the next with their cousins at Hale. The following day, however, word came that they might return. There had been a mistake. No decision as to their property had been taken yet.

The fact that Alice Lisle, hearing about it the same day, had guessed that the sheriff, a greedy man, was probably trying to get the property for himself and sent an urgent message to her husband to have the order rescinded was something the Penruddock family never knew.

The day after that Mrs Penruddock and all her children set out for Exeter. It took them three days. By the time they reached it the warrant for the executions had arrived from Cromwell, written and signed in his own hand. Instead of the usual gruesome hanging, drawing and quartering of traitors, Penruddock was to be executed cleanly by having his head struck off with an axe. Never having seen a traitor's execution the family did not fully understand what a mercy this was.

They were allowed, in that last week, to see him twice. The first time came as a shock to Thomas. Although, thanks to his

wife, he had been provided with a clean shirt, Colonel
Penruddock was looking gaunt and haggard in his small cell.
His gaolers had not let him wash as often as he wished and
Thomas was aware of a certain grimy odour in his father's
presence. The effect of this, however, after the initial shock,
was to make him even more moved than he might have been
otherwise. The little children just stared at their unkempt father in confusion. He spoke to them all in his usual calm and
kindly way, blessed them and kissed them and told them they
must be brave.

"Perhaps," Thomas heard him murmur to their mother,
"Cromwell may relent. But I do not think so."

The second occasion was more difficult. With time passing,
although she tried to keep calm, his mother had become more
and more distracted. As the day of the execution approached
she seemed to think that her appeal to Alice Lisle was sure to
bring relief. "I can't understand why it's taking so long," she
would suddenly break out plaintively. "The reprieve must
come." She'd frown. "It must do." She also for some reason
would return in her mind, again and again, to the fact that the
sheriff's men had turned her out of her house for two days. "To
think they could do such a thing," she would exclaim.

They knew their second visit would be their last because the
execution was to be the following day. They went there in the
afternoon and entered the prison.

But for some reason there was a delay. They had to wait a
while in an outer chamber, where they found themselves in the
company of the senior gaoler who passed the time by thoughtfully eating a pie and picking his teeth. He had a dirty grizzled
beard, which he had not trimmed because, nowadays, there
was no one to make him. They tried not to look at him.

But he looked at them. They interested him. He did not
like royalists, especially cavalier gentry, which these
Penruddocks were. If the father of these children was about
to have his head cut off, so much the better. He observed
their aristocratic clothes – lace and satin for the girls; why,
the younger boy had little rosettes on his shoes – and wondered idly how they would look after he and his men had had
a chance to spoil them. He could see the clothes in tatters, the
boys with a black eye or two and the mother . . .

The mother was jabbering on about something now. She'd hoped for a reprieve. That was a joke. No one was going to reprieve Penruddock, even he knew that. But he listened curiously all the same. She'd hoped Judge Lisle would speak to Cromwell. He'd heard of Lisle. Never seen him, though. Close to Cromwell he'd heard. The woman had written to his wife. A useless hope, obviously, but the wives of condemned men sometimes got like that.

"Lisle, did you say," he suddenly interjected with a smile, to throw her off guard. "Judge Lisle?"

"Yes, good man." She turned to him eagerly. "Has anything been heard from him, do you know?"

He paused. He intended to savour this. "The warrant for your husband's death is made out by Lisle. In his own hand. He was with Cromwell when he signed it."

The effect was delicious. He watched her face fall into abject confusion. She seemed to collapse and wither before his eyes. He had never seen anything equal to it. The fact that he hadn't the least idea whether Judge Lisle was even within a hundred miles of Cromwell or the warrant made it even better. "'Tis well known," he added for artistic effect.

"But I wrote again to his wife," poor Mrs Penruddock wailed.

"They say it's she," he went on blandly, "who especially urged the poor Colonel's death." The suggestion that he pitied her cursed husband made the thing sound more plausible. The woman almost fainted. The eldest boy looked ready for murder. And he was just trying to think whether there was anything else he could invent to taunt these unhappy people when a signal from one of the guards told him that the prisoner was ready.

"Time to see the Colonel, now," he announced. And so the Penruddocks passed from his presence. Being unversed in the practices of malice, it had not occurred to them that every word the gaoler said had been a lie.

Colonel Penruddock had done all he could to prepare himself for his final meeting with his children. They found him washed, brushed and in good spirits. To each he spoke cheerfully and calmly, and told them to be brave for his sake.

"Remember," he said, "no matter what difficulties may face

you, they are still small beside the sufferings of Our Lord. And, if men revile you, that is nothing when He watches over you and loves you with a love far greater than they can ever know."

To his wife he spoke what words of comfort he could and then he made her promise that she would take the children out of Exeter at first light the following morning. "At first light, I beg you. You must be well clear of the city and on your way before morning is stirring. Do not stop until you get to Chard." This was nearly twenty-five miles, a good day's journey.

Mrs Penruddock nodded and murmured a few words, but she seemed to be in a daze. As for Thomas, he could only bow his head to hide the tears when his father embraced him and told him to be brave. Almost before he knew what was happening the door of the cell was being opened and they were being taken out. He tried to look back at his father. But they had shut the door again.

It was not until ten that night that Mrs Penruddock seemed to spring to life. The smaller children were asleep in the big chamber they all shared at the inn, but Thomas was awake when she suddenly sat bolt upright, with a look of horror on her pale face and cried: "I never bade him adieu."

She started to search for pen and paper on the table. "I know it's here," she murmured plaintively. "I must write a letter," she added with urgency.

Thomas found her what she needed and watched as she wrote. It was hard to know what to make of his mother. When she had the will to do so, when she concentrated her mind, she could express herself with dignity; but then, in almost the same breath, some other petty or homely thought would come into her mind and cause her suddenly to veer off her course entirely. So it was with her letter. It started so well:

My sad parting was so far from making me forget you, that I scarce thought upon myself since, but wholly upon you. Those dear embraces which I yet feel, and shall never lose . . . have charmed my soul to such a reverence of your remembrance . . .

Yet a few lines later the memory of the sheriff's men suddenly intruded.

> *'Tis too late to tell you what I have done for you; how turned out of doors because I came to beg mercy . . .*

And then returned once more, abruptly, to a lovely and passionate ending:

> *Adieu, therefore, ten thousand times, my dearest dear! Your children beg your blessing, and present their duties to you.*

It was eleven at night when she finished, but a groom, when handsomely paid, agreed to take the letter to the gaol and returned a little after midnight with a brief and loving reply in the Colonel's hand.

Not until the early hours, however, did Thomas fall asleep. It would never have happened if Mrs Penruddock had been on time. She had tried to be. By eight o'clock on that pale grey morning the carriage had already been waiting at the gateway of the inn for nearly an hour.

She wanted to be gone. She not only meant to obey her husband, but she wanted to remove herself from the scene, to close herself off – and her children, of course – from the terrible business, from the loss she could not bear to think about. This was no intentional delay. But first one thing was missing, then another; then the youngest girl chose that moment to be sick. By nine, Mrs Penruddock was in such a state of fretful agitation that she lost her purse and had a quarrel with the innkeeper who thought he might not be paid. Unthinkingly, she warned him that if he didn't mind his tongue she would surely see her husband should hear about it. Which made him give her such a strange look; and as she realised with an awful coldness that in a few moments, dear God, she'd have no husband and perhaps then not even money to pay any more innkeepers at all, she might well have burst into tears; except that now her native strength came back to her rescue again and she came to herself enough to realise where her purse might be, and to find it. So then, at last, with ten o'clock sounding

from a bell nearby, she mustered her children and bustled them
to the carriage, and called for Thomas.

But Thomas had gone.

He couldn't help it. He had walked along the street and followed the passing crowd which, he guessed, must be going towards the place of execution. For how, being in the city still,
could he lose the opportunity to see the father he loved so
much, and worshipped, one last time?

He could not get close when he came to the place because
there was such a crowd; and besides, even if he could have got
to the front, to the very foot of the scaffold, he did not dare, for
he knew that by his father's orders he should not be there.

But he found a cart to stand on, along with a dozen appren-
tices and other urchins, and from there he had a perfect view.

There was a platform in the middle of the place. They had
already set a block upon it. Half a dozen soldiers guarded it.

He had waited a quarter of an hour before the parties arrived. They came on horseback, followed by a cart with a
guard of foot soldiers carrying muskets and pikes. In the cart,
in a clean white shirt, his long brown hair tied back, stood his
father.

The sheriff mounted the platform first, then two other men,
then the executioner wearing a black mask, carrying an axe
that glinted silver. They escorted his father up next.

They did not waste undue time. The sheriff in a loud voice
read out the death warrant for the crime of treason. His father
moved forward with the executioner towards the block. He
said a word to the sheriff, who nodded; and the executioner
stood back while his father produced a piece of paper at which
he glanced. Then, looking calmly over the crowd, Colonel
Penruddock spoke.

"Gentlemen," his voice rang out. "It has ever been the custom of all persons whatsoever, when they come to die, to give
some satisfaction to the world, whether they be guilty of the
fact of which they stand charged. The crime for which I am
now to die is loyalty, in this age called high treason. I cannot
deny . . ."

The speech was clear, but long. The crowd was fairly quiet,
but Thomas could neither hear nor follow all of it. He

understood the sense, however. His father had some points to make about how he had been treated; also it was important that he clear others, especially those close to the Sealed Knot, of any complicity. All this he did simply and well. Only when it was done did he express the hope that England would one day be restored under its rightful king. Then he commended his soul to God.

One of the sheriff's men stepped forward and scooped up his father's hair under a cap he slipped over his head. He glanced at the executioner who nodded.

They were going to the block, now. His father knelt down and kissed the block, then, still kneeling, turned to the executioner. He said something. The executioner presented the head of the axe to him and he kissed it. The crowd was utterly silent. Colonel Penruddock said something else, Thomas could not hear what, then turned back to the block again. Silence. He was going to lay his head over the block.

It was the last moment. Thomas wanted to cry out. Why had he waited so long, until they were all so silent? He wished he had cried out, no matter that he had disobeyed, to let his father know that he was with him, even at the last. A cry of love. Was it too late? Could he not? He felt the terrible shock of parting, the surge of love. "Father!" He wanted to shout. "Father!" Couldn't he? He took a breath.

His father's head went down on to the block. Thomas opened his mouth. Nothing. The axe fell.

"Father!"

He saw a sudden spurt of redness, then his father's head, falling, with a small bump, to the ground.

1664

For Alice Lisle the years that followed Penruddock's Rising did not bring peace of mind. Superficially, it might have seemed that she had everything. Her husband's career went from strength to strength. In London they had acquired a fine house in the pleasant riverside suburb of Chelsea. They and their children were close to Cromwell and his family, joining the same Puritan group at worship. The Cromwell family even took an estate near Winchester, not far from one of the handsome places that John Lisle had acquired in that part of the county. The Lisles were rich. When Cromwell had made a new house of peers he had chosen John Lisle to be one of them, so that now the lawyer was called Lord Lisle and Alice was his lady.

The Protector was all powerful. His army had crushed Scotland and Ireland. England's trade increasingly dominated the high seas. The Commonwealth of England had never been mightier. Yet despite all this, Alice was uneasy; and there were days when she felt the same apprehension as she had that grey winter when her husband had gone to London to execute the king.

For the trouble was that the Commonwealth didn't really work. She could see it, often, more clearly than her husband. Each time the Parliament and the army, or some faction within either, failed to come to an agreement, and her husband would come home with some new form of constitution that he and his friends were going to try, saying, "This time we shall resolve matters," she could only nod quietly and hold her peace. And sure enough, months later, there would be a new crisis and a new form of government chosen. The months after Penruddock's Rising had been the worst. In order to crush any thought of further opposition, Cromwell had divided the country into a dozen regions, placed a major-general in charge of each and ruled by martial law. It had achieved nothing except to make all England hate the army and after a time even Cromwell had to give it up. But the underlying issue remained the same. Dictatorship or republic, army or civil rule, rule of the landed classes or rule of the ordinary people: none of these issues was decided; nobody was content. And as Cromwell tried one expedient after another she came to wonder: take Oliver Cromwell away and what have you? Nobody, not even her clever husband, knew.

There was something else that bothered her too. "All that we have done, John," she would say to Lisle, "if it were not done to establish a just and godly rule, then better it had not been done at all."

"That is what we are about, Alice," he would respond irritably. "We are establishing a godly rule."

But were they? Oh, the Parliament had made some fear-some laws. They had even made adultery punishable by death – except that juries quite rightly refused to convict in the face of such monstrous punishment. Swearing, dancing, all kinds of amusements that offended the Puritans were out-lawed. The major-generals had even managed to close half the inns where people went to drink. But what did this mean if, at the centre, she saw Oliver Cromwell, when his supporters put it to him, quite clearly tempted by the idea of taking the title of king, and who clearly meant his son, a nice but weak young man, to succeed him as Protector? Visiting Whitehall, she had been shocked, to find the other leading families of the new regime dressed up in silks and satins and brocades exactly like the old royalist aristocracy they had replaced. It seemed to her, though she was too wise to say it, that little had changed at all.

And so it was, as the years had passed, that while to all out-ward appearances Alice loyally supported her husband, whom she loved, in his busy public life, she withdrew, within herself, into a more private world. She found that she cared less and less what party people belonged to, and more and more about what kind of individuals they were. When poor Mrs Penruddock, a few months after her husband's execution, had finally been stripped of all his family's property and had peti-tioned Cromwell for mercy, Alice had vigorously argued on the family's behalf and been glad when a part of their estates had been granted back so that Mrs Penruddock could support her children.

"I don't know why you care about these people, who cer-tainly care nothing for you," Lisle had remarked.

Because Colonel Penruddock, deluded or not, was probably worth ten of our friends, she might have told him. But instead she kissed him and said nothing.

One thing she did like about the Commonwealth regime, however, was its tolerance in matters of religion. That toler-ance, of course, did not extend to the Roman Church. As a good Protestant she could not have sanctioned that. Popery meant the enslavement of honest people by cunning priests and brutal inquisition; it meant superstition, backwardness, idolatry and, like as not, domination by foreign powers. But within the broad range of Protestant congregations, stern Cromwell was surprisingly liberal. He had refused to allow the Presbyterians to impose their forms upon everyone; independent churches, choosing their own ministers and their own forms of worship, were allowed. Fine independent preachers, drawing their inspiration directly from their own religious experience, were encouraged. Alice liked the preachers. They were mostly honest men. When she thought of how they would have been treated by King Charles and his bishops – silenced, hounded out of house and home, even perhaps put in the stocks or sentenced to have their ears cut off – at least she could believe that the Commonwealth had brought some real improvement to the world.

Then Cromwell had suddenly died.

No one had been prepared. They'd thought he'd live for years. His son Richard had tried to step into his place, but he wasn't cut out for the job. It would be all right, Lisle told Alice. There were wise men like himself to guide the regime. But she had shaken her head. It wouldn't work. She knew it wouldn't.

It didn't. Even Alice was amazed, though, at how quickly everything had fallen apart. The very circumstances that the gentlemen of the Sealed Knot had hoped for at the time of Penruddock's Rising had now, only a few years later, come to pass. The people, after the brief rule of the major-generals, had come to hate the army. The army was divided within itself. The Parliament men wanted to have their own say again. The royalist gentry saw their chance. If the terms were right, people started to say, perhaps they'd be better off with a king again. Finally General Monk, who believed in order, and the city of London, which had had enough of the army, agreed together to restore the previous regime.

Young Charles II was ready and waiting. He had gone through the necessary period of adversity. If he had ever believed in his father's foolish doctrines they had long ago been knocked out of him. Tall, swarthy, affable, deeply cynical, longing to escape from exile, determined not to be thrown out again, ready to compromise, completely penniless – here at last was a Stuart who had been properly trained to be King of

England. Terms were negotiated. The king would return. The English prepared to rejoice just as though they had never cut off his father's head.

It was a bright day in early May when John Lisle arrived back from London. Alice had been sitting with one of her daughters by the window and they ran out to greet him. He was looking cheerful, yet Alice had thought she detected a trace of awkwardness in his manner. When she asked for news he had smiled and said: "I'll tell you as we dine."

As the family ate together he painted a pleasant picture. The Parliament men, the army, the Londoners, everyone was to be reconciled with each other and the king. It was all to be the friendliest business imaginable. There was to be no vengeance. Only after the children had left them alone did Alice ask: "You say there is to be no vengeance? None?"

John Lisle poured himself another glass of wine before replying. "Almost." He came to it slowly. "There is, of course, the matter of the regicides. As it happens" – he tried to speak easily, as if he were discussing some interesting case in the courts – "it is not the king who is pressing this, but the royalists. Those gentlemen want to see some blood shed for all the losses they have suffered."

"And?"

"Well . . ." He looked awkward now. "The regicides are to be tried. Executed probably. The king will decide, but I think it likely."

She stared at him blankly for a moment, before saying quietly: "You are a regicide, John."

"Ah." He put on his professional smile. "That can be disputed. You must remember, Alice, I did not in fact sign the king's death warrant. I think it could be said that I am not a regicide."

"Said by whom, John? They have always called you one. You were with Cromwell, you argued for the king's death. You helped draw up the accusations, the papers . . ."

"True. Yet even so . . ."

Was he trying to give her hope, break the news to her gently, or was it possible that her clever husband, faced by this crisis, was suddenly unable to face the obvious truth?

"They will hang you, John," she said. He did not reply. "What will you do?"

"I think I should go abroad. It would not be for long. A few months at most, I suppose." He smiled reassuringly. "I have friends. They will speak to the king. As soon as this matter of the regicides is over I can return. It seems wisest. What do you think?"

What could she say? No, stay here with your wife and children until they come to hang you? Obviously not. She nodded slowly. "I am sorry for it, John," she said miserably, then forced herself to smile. "We should rather have you alive, though. When shall you leave?"

"At dawn tomorrow." He looked at her earnestly. "It will not be for long."

She never saw him again.

He had been right about the king. Young King Charles II, whatever his faults, had no appetite for vengeance. After twenty-six surviving regicides had been hanged in October that year he quietly told his council not to look for any more. If they appeared they would have to hang, but if they stayed out of sight he was content to leave them alone. This vengeance being not quite enough for the king's royalist supporters, however, they hit upon what seemed to them a happy idea. The following January the corpses of Cromwell and his son-in-law Ireton were dug up from their graves, brought to the Tyburn gallows in London and hanged there for all to see. Much wisdom was shown, no doubt, in choosing January, rather than a warmer season of the year.

But Lisle had been wrong if he believed that he mightn't be viewed as a regicide. As he waited in Switzerland for news, it soon became clear: he had too many enemies.

"My dearest husband," Alice wrote sadly, "you cannot return."

There was talk, each year, of her going to join him in Lausanne, where he was now living. But it was not so easy. For a start, money was short. Most of John Lisle's property had been confiscated or removed. One estate had been given to some of his own relations on the Isle of Wight who had remained faithful to the royalist cause. Another went to the new king's younger brother James, Duke of York. The London house was gone. Alice alone had to support the family now on her New Forest inheritance and try to send money to her poor husband, too.

"We must live quietly," she told her children. With the estate to look after, and the children, it was hard to see how she could go to live in Switzerland.

The family was quite extensive. There were John's two sons from his previous marriage. They were young men now, but she had always brought them up like her own and with their father's fortune gone and his name in disgrace, how were they to make good marriages? As for her own children, her son, to her great grief, had died at sixteen, but there were three surviving daughters, Margaret, Bridget and Tryphena who would all be needing to find husbands.

And then there was little Betty – bright-eyed Betty, so small and full of life. She had been conceived that last night before her husband departed: that night when she had clung to him, praying that he would return, so afraid that he would not. Little Betty: the child John Lisle had never seen; the child she would remember him by.

Two years passed. Then another. And another. The baby had become a toddler; she ran about now, she talked. She asked about her father. Alice would tell her stories about him, what a fine man he was.

"I shall go and see the king one day and tell him I want my daddy back," she said. And who knew, thought Alice, given the genial character of Charles II, it might work. But not yet. It was too soon. So she wrote to her husband and told him every detail of what they all did and how Betty grew; and he wrote long and loving letters in return; and they both prayed that with the passing of time, he might come back – one day.

In the meantime, what was there to do? She was glad at least to be in the Forest. It was the country of her childhood and her family. In Betty she could relive her own happy early days. There was comfort in that. There was always plenty to keep her occupied, from day to day. Yet how could she fill the other void in her life?

To her surprise it was religion that did so.

She had never been especially religious before her marriage. Of course, she and John had been vigorous supporters of their congregation in London; but how much of that, she wondered, had been her husband's desire to keep close with Cromwell and his family? Her new interest had come from another source entirely and was quite unexpected.

Stephen Pride's wife. It was unusual for a Pride to marry someone from outside the Forest, but one fine Saturday morning, when the Pride family had gone down into Lymington to the little market there, Stephen Pride had met his future wife and that was it. Her family had come from Portsmouth, some years before. She was quiet, kindly, about Alice's age with light-brown hair and grey eyes very like Alice's own. "He says he married me because I reminded him of you," Joan Pride once confessed to her. Alice couldn't help being rather pleased about that.

Joan Pride was devout. All her family were. Like so many others in the small towns round England's coasts, these honest folk had read their Bible in the days of Queen Elizabeth and found nothing there about bishops and priests and ceremonies; so they had preferred to gather in small meeting houses, choose their own leaders and preachers, and lead a simple, godly life in peace, if only they were allowed. When Charles I had found such freedom intolerable, many of these folk had emigrated to the new settlements in America; some had fought the king in Cromwell's army. During the Civil War and under the Protector's rule they had been able to worship as they pleased.

Every Sunday, therefore, while her husband watched with a tolerant smile, Joan Pride had set out from Oakley, sometimes taking one or two of her children, and walked the two miles into Lymington where she joined her family at the meeting house. And now and then, when she was not in London with her husband, Alice had joined the congregation at their prayers. There was no reason why not. In matters of religion these had been democratic days. Although somewhat surprised to find such an important lady in their midst, they quietly welcomed her; and for her part, she liked them. "I've heard sermons there from travelling preachers quite as good," she had told John Lisle, "as ever I heard in London."

Often on these occasions she would lead her horse beside

Joan Pride and her children as far as Oakley, in pleasant conversation, before returning to Albion House. Their relationship
was entirely comfortable. As was the custom, she called her
tenant's wife Goody Pride and Joan called her Dame Alice.
When John Lisle had been made one of Cromwell's Lords,
properly she should have been called Lady Lisle, or My Lady,
but Alice noticed with amusement that Joan Pride continued
quietly to call her Dame Alice – which let Alice know what her
Puritan friend thought of lordship. In this way, over the years,
while they preserved the usual formality between landlord and
tenant, Alice Lisle and Joan Pride became friends.

It was the week after John Lisle had fled from England that
Joan Pride came to Albion House. She just happened to be
passing that way, she said. She had brought some cakes she
had baked. It would have been the height of bad manners not
to accept such a gift, even though she didn't particularly want
them, so Alice thanked her kindly, while Joan Pride's grey eyes
took in everything she saw in the big house she had never entered before.

"Perhaps we shall see you at the meeting house, Dame
Alice," she had said gently, as she left.

"Yes," Alice had replied absently. "Yes, of course."

She had gone to Boldre parish church, however, the next
Sunday and for several more afterwards. With her regicide
husband on the run she did not want to do anything that might
cause unfavourable comment in the new royalist regime.

She was riding by a small coppice she owned about a month
after this, when she noticed Stephen Pride at work on the
fence. Asked what he was doing, he showed her where a section had been broken down. "Don't want the deer getting in,"
he remarked. Had her steward asked him to see to this? she enquired. "Just noticed it as I was passing," he replied; and although she offered, he refused to take any payment. Gradually,
in the weeks that followed, she noticed a number of similar incidents. One of the cattle was sick: it was brought in to her
steward. When a tree fell across the lane that led to Albion
House, Pride and three of the Oakley villagers were cutting it
up and carting the wood to the house by early morning without even being asked. Her Forest friends were silently looking
after her, she realised.

She continued to go to Boldre parish church. She suspected that Joan Pride understood. But after some time, when it was clear that nothing she did was going to help her husband or save his fortune, she turned up at the Lymington meeting house again one Sunday and was quietly welcomed as if she had never avoided the place. She went often thereafter.

And she might have continued to do so indefinitely, had it not been for the English Parliament.

King Charles II was a tolerant man and, unlike his father, his tolerance seemed to extend to religion. He told his councillors that he was content to allow his subjects to worship as they pleased. But his council and his Parliament were not content with that at all. The gentlemen in Parliament wanted order. They had no wish to encourage the Puritan sects who had given so much trouble before. And besides, if people were free to worship as they pleased it might allow the Roman Catholic Church to flourish again and that was unthinkable. So the Acts of Parliament followed and the new king could not stop them. Only the Anglican prayer book with its formal services might be used in churches. Protestant sects – Dissenters as they were called – were banned from any church. Soon, it was said, a new Act would ban them from meeting within five miles of any town. Joan Pride's congregation at Lymington was practically illegal.

"It's monstrous," Alice declared. "What possible harm can these people do?" But the law was the law. She went to Boldre church, used the Anglican prayer book and held her peace. She told Joan Pride she was sorry for what had happened and the other woman made no comment. Indeed, for three months she did not even see her friend. And then one day she chanced to meet her in the lane that led south from Boldre church, and Joan Pride told her that there was a preacher, a certain Mr Whitaker, who was willing to come to Lymington. "But we daren't have him in the town, Dame Alice. So we've nowhere for him to preach," she explained.

Alice had heard of this preacher, a scholarly young man with a fine reputation. "I should like to have heard him myself," she confessed. After only a few moments' thought, and rather to her own surprise, she heard herself saying: "He could come to Albion House. He might stay as my guest and preach in the hall. Mightn't you and your friends come to hear him there?"

And so it was done. Mr Robert Whitaker proved to be a splendid preacher. Before the royal Restoration he had been a fellow of Magdalen College, Oxford. He was also very good-looking. Her daughter Margaret, especially, seemed to take an interest in him; and he, for his part, seemed to need little per-suading before he promised to come and visit them again. Alice was not sure what she thought of this new development. A young preacher, however eloquent, was not quite the match she had considered for one of her daughters.

She had hardly had time to worry about this, however, before a letter from her husband had driven all other thoughts from her mind. He had a friend who was to make a visit to Switzerland and who would be happy to convey her with his family, at no cost to herself, and bring her back again after a month. She could bring little Betty, the daughter he had never seen. They were to leave in three weeks. As John Lisle wrote:

> There being no time to carry messages back and forth be-
> tween us, I shall either rejoice to see you, my dearest
> love, and my daughter in Lausanne; or else learn with
> grief but understanding, that you cannot make this jour-
> ney.

What should she do? I must go, she concluded. "You are going to see your father," she told the little girl. She began to prepare and pack.

So it came as a particularly painful blow when, five days be-fore she was to leave, a messenger arrived with news that John Lisle had been murdered in Lausanne. It was not certain who was behind it. Certainly not the king himself. At no time did Charles II ever indulge in acts of vengeance of this kind. But there were other royalists who were certainly capable of such a deed. It was said that his French mother, the widow of the executed king, might have been responsible. Alice thought so.

Anyway, she had no husband now and Betty had no father. By chance young Whitaker came calling not long after.

1670

Zephyr was blowing his gentlest breeze through the green glades as King Charles II of England went forth in his New Forest, that warm August day, to hunt.

He had been there before. Five years back, when the terrible plague was raging in London, the king and his court had come down to the safety of Sarum; and while there he had made a small tour of the villages round about. "When I was running away from Cromwell, after I hid in the oak tree, I came through Sarum." This had included a ride into the Forest. "I slept rough in the New Forest two nights," he genially told his courtiers, "and not even the charcoal burners knew I was there."

And now he had decided to visit the Forest again, with a party of courtiers, for his royal pleasure.

Stephen Pride looked at his friend Purkiss and Purkiss looked at Puckle. Furzey should have been there too, but he had said he wasn't coming, not for any king. So it was the three of them and Pride's son Jim, who were waiting on their ponies by the gate of the King's House at Lyndhurst, where they had been told to report, as the king and his party emerged.

Then Stephen Pride looked at King Charles II of England and King Charles II looked at Stephen Pride.

The royal visitor was certainly a memorable figure. Tall, swarthy, with that mass of curling brown hair that fell to his chest so thickly that you might have thought it was a wig, Charles II exhibited both sides of his ancestry very clearly. His fine brown eyes and the long line of his mouth were those of the Celtic Stuart family, but to these features were added the heavy nose and the sensual, cynical power of his French mother's Bourbon ancestors. He glanced now at Pride with exactly the same cheerful cynicism he would have shown if he were addressing a pretty young serving wench or his royal cousin King Louis XIV of France.

Stephen Pride stared, but it wasn't so much the king whom Pride was looking at. It was the women.

There were several of them. They were dressed in hunting

clothes just like the men, with jaunty hunting caps. The queen was not among them that day, but there was a vivacious, dark-haired young woman who whispered something in the king's ear that made him laugh. This, Pride guessed, must be the comic actress, Nell Gwynn, whom all England knew to be the king's latest mistress. He noticed an elegant young Frenchwoman and several others. Were these all royal mistresses too? He didn't know. But as the independent New Forest smallholder looked at the French and Celtic prince he wondered, with a touch of secret envy, how the devil the handsome rogue got away with it all.

There were nine in the royal party including the king and four ladies. Pride did not know who the other men were, but one – a strikingly handsome youth, a delicate version of the king, really – he assumed must be Monmouth, the monarch's bastard son. In attendance was Sir Robert Howard, an aristocrat whose official title of Master Keeper meant he was nominally in charge of the deer in the bailiwick in which they were to hunt; there were also several local gentlemen keepers. The party was to hunt from Boldrewood lodge and, as Jim Pride was underkeeper there, he had recruited his father and Puckle to act as extra riders. There were usually some tips to be had on these occasions. Furzey had been asked, too, but as he'd refused they'd taken Stephen Pride's friend Purkiss from Brockenhurst. He had a reputation for being no fool, so they reckoned they were probably better off with him than with Furzey anyway.

They were all ready. Stephen Pride was sixty years old, but he had to admit he was quite excited. He'd been a happily faithful husband for over thirty years, but to his own amusement he found himself stealing glances at the king's pretty lady friends. Life in the old dog yet, he thought cheerfully, and was glad he was fit enough to participate with his son in what, he supposed, would be a tiring day.

"I should think we'll be taking a lot of deer today," he remarked to one of the gentlemen keepers, who gave him an old-fashioned look.

"Don't count on it, Stephen," he murmured. "I know the king."

And to Pride's astonishment they had not gone a quarter-mile before he saw the Master Keeper's hand shoot up and the king's voice rang out. "Nellie wants to see the Rufus tree."

"The Rufus tree!" his courtiers cried out.

So off they all went, instead, to the Rufus tree.

"It will be like this" – the gentleman smiled at Pride – "the whole day."

And indeed, they had only gone another quarter-mile when suddenly there was a further change of plan. Before seeing the Rufus tree the king wished to inspect his new plantation. This meant a couple of miles' extra riding and the party obediently swung round to go off there instead.

Pride looked at his companions. They were not very pleased.

"Doesn't look as if we're going to get much out of this," Puckle remarked with reproach to Jim Pride. Money and the odd haunch of venison tended to come when numbers of deer were killed. The gentlemen keepers were usually pretty good at making sure the riders like Puckle were looked after. But if they were just going to wander about like this all day, the prospects weren't so promising.

"It isn't Jim's fault," Pride defended his son.

"It's early yet," said Jim hopefully.

Pride glanced across at Purkiss. He felt bad about him because he had asked the Brockenhurst man himself.

Purkiss was a tall man with a long face and a quiet, intelligent manner. The Purkisses were an ancient Forest family, respected for their good sense. "They go quietly," Pride would say, "but they're always thinking. No one ever makes a fool of a Purkiss." If he felt guilty about wasting Purkiss's time, however, Purkiss himself looked content enough. He seemed to be meditating to himself.

The king's plantation, it had to be said, was a fine affair. So much timber had been lost during the lax administration and confusion of the last seven decades that everyone agreed something needed to be done. As so often with Charles II, behind his sensual indulgence, the king's keen intelligence was at work. Just as, after the city of London had suffered its great fire, he had studied every detail and firmly supported the huge rebuilding programme of Sir Christopher Wren, so now the royal patron of the arts and sciences had devised a practical and far-seeing project in his royal forest. On his personal orders three large areas – three hundred acres in all – were to be fenced off like coppices and sown with acorns and beech mast. Thousands of fine timber trees would result for eventual harvesting. "Future generations, at least, will bless me," he had reasonably remarked.

The party arrived at the big inclosure. The seedlings stretched away in lines like an army. The party dutifully looked and expressed their admiration. But the king, Pride noticed, although genial, was also surveying the scene with a sharp eye and, taking two companions, he cantered away round the perimeter to inspect the fence.

Having returned satisfied, he gave the order: "Now for that Rufus tree."

So back they went again. The four Forest men bringing up the rear of the cheerful cavalcade said little now. Jim was looking glum, Puckle bored. But Purkiss still seemed quite happy and, when Stephen Pride remarked that he was sorry to have brought him on a fool's errand, the Brockenhurst man just shook his head and smiled. "It's not every day I get the chance to ride with the king, Stephen," he said calmly. "Besides, a man may learn much and profit from such an occasion."

"I can't see much profit myself," Pride answered, "but I'm glad if you can."

If the Rufus tree had been old at the time of the Armada, eighty years later its long life was clearly nearing its end. The ancient oak was decrepit. Most of its branches had died back. A great rent in the side showed where a large limb had broken off. Ivy grew on the trunk. Only a little crown of leaves grew from its topmost branch. As a mark of respect it had been enclosed behind a stake fence.

The two acorns which had tumbled down and taken root after the Armada storms stood not far off, noble oak trees now. One was shorter and broader because it had been pollarded; the other, untouched, grew high.

They all surveyed the hoary old hulk with reverence. Several of the party dismounted.

"This is where Tyrrell shot my ancestor William Rufus, Nellie," the king announced. He glanced at Sir Robert

Howard. "That's almost six hundred years ago. Can this tree really be so old?"

"Undoubtedly, Sir," said the Master Keeper, who hadn't the faintest idea.

"What exactly is the story?" young Monmouth asked.

"Yes." King Charles looked sternly at Howard. "Let's have it exactly, Master Keeper."

And the aristocrat, a little red, had just started to bluster some vague and garbled version of the tale he'd obviously forgotten, when to everyone's surprise there was a movement from the back, and a tall figure stepped forward and made a low bow. It was Purkiss.

Stephen Pride watched in astonishment as his friend calmly made his way to the front. Now Purkiss, in a respectful voice and with a serious countenance enquired: "May I, Your Majesty, recount the true story of this tree?"

"You certainly may, fellow," King Charles said affably, while Nellie pulled a face at Howard.

And so Purkiss began. First he explained about the oak tree's magical Christmas greening and, when Charles looked doubtful, the gentlemen keepers assured him this was perfectly correct. The king leaned forward in his saddle after that, paying close attention to Purkiss's every word.

Purkiss was good. Pride listened with admiration. With the quiet reverence of a verger conducting the faithful round a cathedral, he gave the story of Rufus's death with every detail recorded or invented in the chronicles. He described the evil visions of the Norman king seen the night before; what he had said to Walter Tyrrell in the morning; the monk's warning. Everything. Then, solemnly, he pointed to the tree. "When Tyrrell loosed the fatal arrow, Sire, it grazed the tree and then struck the king. It left a mark, they say, which once could be seen up there." He pointed to a place some way up the trunk. "It was only a young tree then, Your Majesty, so the mark was carried higher with the years."

He explained how Tyrrell fled across the Forest to the River Avon at Tyrrell's Ford and how the king's body was carried on a forester's cart to Winchester. He concluded with a low bow.

"Well done, good fellow!" cried the monarch. "Wasn't that

well done?" he asked the courtiers, who agreed that it was excellent. "That's worth a golden guinea," he said, producing a gold coin and handing it down to the Brockenhurst man. "How do you come to know all this so well, good friend?" he then enquired.

"Because, Your Majesty" – Purkiss's face was as solemn as a judge's – "the forester who carried away the king's body on his cart was my own ancestor. His name was Purkiss."

There was a peal of laughter from Nellie.

King Charles bit his lip. "The devil he was," he said.

Pride stared at his friend with stupefaction. The cunning rascal, he thought. The cleverness with which the thing was done; the way Purkiss had carefully stopped and let the king draw this last, astounding piece of information from him. And the man was still standing there, without even the hint of a smirk on his face.

As for King Charles II of England who, whatever his vices or his virtues, was certainly one of the most accomplished liars who ever sat upon a throne, he gazed down at Purkiss with professional admiration. "Here's another guinea, Purkiss," he said. "I shouldn't be surprised if your ancestor's name appears one day in history books."

Which it did.

It was not often that Alice Lisle couldn't make up her mind. Some people would have been surprised to know that such a thing ever occurred. But this morning, as she looked coldly at her family and at Mr Hancock the lawyer, she hesitated; and her hesitation was not unreasonable. "I wish that somebody would tell me," she remarked in her usual business-like manner, "how I am to ask a favour of a man when my husband killed his father."

For they wanted her to ride across the Forest and see the king.

There were many who thought that Alice Lisle was hard. She didn't really care. If I'm not strong, she had long ago concluded, who will be? If she was attacked, who would defend her? She had looked about. She didn't see anybody.

It wasn't as if she had a husband any more. Sometimes she would have liked one: somebody to hold her, comfort her and love her; especially during that period, just after John Lisle's death, when she was passing sadly from her childbearing years towards the age of fifty. But there had been no one, so she had faced it all alone.

God knows there had been plenty to do. And she had managed fairly well. Her triumph had been the marriage of her stepson. With the help of family friends she had found him a handsome girl who was heiress to a rich estate near Southampton. Her late husband would have been proud of her, and grateful, for that. As far as her own daughters were concerned they had so far married godly men, but none of wealth; and this, Alice frankly admitted, was probably her own fault.

The religious meetings she had begun at Albion House had soon grown into something more. Word spread quickly among the Puritan community. Since the new restrictions upon them, men who had been living as well-beneficed ministers had to toe the line of the Anglican Church; those who refused lost their livings. So there was no shortage of respectable men who were only too glad of the hospitality of a country house from which to preach. Soon she found she was letting them stay at Moyles Court as well and people were coming to hear preachings from Ringwood, Fordingbridge and other villages up the Avon river almost as far as Sarum. Some of the preachers, inevitably, were handsome unmarried men.

Margaret, as she had foreseen, had married Whitaker. Tryphena had wed a worthy Puritan gentleman named Lloyd. But Bridget, Alice considered, had found the most distinguished man of them all, a scholarly minister named Leonard Hoar, who had been in America and studied at the new university of Harvard before returning to England as a notable preacher. There had been talk of his returning with Bridget to Puritan Massachusetts when a good position came up, perhaps at Harvard. Sometimes Alice thought there was too much nervousness in his disposition, but his brilliance was undoubted. She was sorry that she seldom saw them.

For the moment, then, Alice could consider her daughters settled, except for little Betty. And as Betty was still only nine, there was time enough before she needed to worry about her.

Other matters, however, were not so settled. Money was always a problem. None of her Puritan sons-in-law was rich and with the new regime there wasn't a chance of preferment. "And because I'm a woman," she told her family frankly, "men always think they can cheat me."

There was the Christchurch merchant who had owed money to John Lisle, although he denied it; there were the Lisle relations on the Isle of Wight, withholding part of her stepson's inheritance – they were still trying to wriggle out of that. When the Christchurch merchant told her she was a peevish, troublesome woman she had coldly demanded: "And if I weren't, would you pay me what you owe? Would you feed and clothe my children? I think not. First you try to rob them," she told him scornfully, "then you call me names if I complain." She had learned to be tough.

"No one is going to love me," she had remarked to Hancock the lawyer, "but perhaps they will respect me."

She looked at the three people before her now. Whitaker: handsome, honest, a fine man, but not a man of business. Tryphena: her husband was no fool, but he was away in London. Narrow-faced Tryphena herself was a good woman and a loyal daughter, but even now, in her thirties, she was as literal as a child; the idea of being subtle, or even tactful, had simply never crossed her mind. John Hancock the lawyer, however, had good judgement. With his neatly curled grey hair and his stately manners, he should really have gone to practise in London, but he preferred to live down near Sarum. Like all good advocates he understood that the law is a negotiation and that indirect means are as good as direct. It was to John Hancock that she would listen.

"You really think I should go and see the king?"

"Yes, I do. For the simple reason that you have nothing to lose."

Alice sighed. The problem involved no less a personage than the king's brother James, Duke of York. In this case it was Alice who was defending herself against the charge of withholding money. For after being given part of John Lisle's forfeited estate, the duke had somehow become convinced that Alice was secreting some of Lisle's money, to which he was entitled. He had even started a lawsuit against her, which had already dragged on for some years.

"I think that the Duke of York, who is an honest but obstinate man, really believes you are secreting this money and that if he were convinced you were suffering hardship, he would drop the case," Hancock explained. "He is of the opinion that you are cheating him because you are John Lisle's widow. The king is a much easier man than his brother. If you can convince him, he would persuade James. At least you should try. You owe it to little Betty."

"Ah. You hit me there, John Hancock."

"I know. I am ruthless." He smiled. Betty, playing outside: the threat of the duke's lawsuit was a cloud over her future fortune.

"I know why you are unwilling to go," Whitaker remarked amiably. "It's the king's reputation with women. You fear he'll make an attempt upon your virtue."

"Yes, Robert," Alice said drily. "Of course."

"I hardly think" – Tryphena had been listening carefully and now she frowned – "that the king would make any attempt upon Mother. His interest is only in women who are young and beautiful."

So it was agreed that Alice should go and that she should take little Betty with her. "Perhaps," Alice said wryly, "the sight of the child may soften the king's heart, even if the sight of me is unlikely to excite him."

While Tryphena prepared the girl for her outing, Alice did, all the same, take some trouble over her own appearance so that, as she surveyed herself in the glass, she could murmur a little wistfully: "John Lisle didn't marry such an ill-looking woman, at least."

It was noon when they left Albion House and started up the lane that led northwards towards the small ford. They missed their visitor, approaching from the south, by only a few minutes.

Gabriel Furzey rode slowly through the gate to Albion House. He'd been glad when Stephen Pride went off with his son Jim, so that none of the Prides was around to see him as he went on his errand.

The truth was Gabriel Furzey was in trouble.

The presence of Charles II in the New Forest that year was not entirely a matter of royal whim. The Forest was very much in the royal mind just then. The merry monarch was always on the lookout for extra income and, like his father before him, he had realised after a time that the royal forests might be a useful asset. The second King Charles was going about things in a much jollier manner; but he was just as thorough. He did more than institute a Forest Eyre; his Commission of Inquiry was going into everything. The regarders were checking every boundary in the Forest. The encroachments and land grants were all carefully recorded; timber selling, charcoal selling, the administration of the forest officers – all were inspected. The king was letting them know that his Forest was to be properly managed in future. There was even a deer census, which revealed that the New Forest still contained some seventy-five hundred fallow and nearly four hundred red deer. Clearly the king wanted to know exactly what the place was truly worth. And, the largest task of all, his justices were ordered to record exactly who held what rights in the Forest and what they should be paying for them.

"A complete register of claims, right down to the last hog to eat the acorns on the forest floor," Hancock the lawyer had described the inquiry to Alice. The justices in Eyre had already held two sessions about the claims. A final one, at which Alice's would be dealt with, was due shortly. "As well as establishing what everyone owes," Hancock had pointed out, "this will cut off any further claims. Either a claim is recorded, or it's invalid. It also seems to me," he added, "that the king is cleverly preparing the ground for the future. Once our claims are recorded, we can't complain about anything he may do at a later date. So long as he doesn't infringe what is already registered he can look for ways to profit from the Forest in any way he can."

Whatever the royal motives might be, one thing was very clear: these claims would be final and binding. If yours wasn't in here it would never be recognised in the future. Every landlord and peasant in the Forest had understood that perfectly by now and they had all turned up before the justices at Lyndhurst. The basis of most claims was the less formal register made thirty-five years before. Whatever was in that would be recognised. If there were further claims they could be added but would need to be proved.

And that, for Gabriel Furzey, was the trouble.

It was his own fault, that was the worst of it: a moment of obstinacy and bad temper a long time ago. Worse still, it was Stephen Pride who had urged him to go and make his claim with young Alice; Stephen Pride who knew he hadn't. So now the Prides of Oakley had all their rights and he didn't.

Not that it had made any difference. All through the years of political strife, when no one had bothered much about the Forest, the people of Oakley had gone about their lives as they always had before. He had pastured his few cows, cut turf, collected wood and no one had ever questioned it. Until recently he had clean forgotten about that business of claims back in 1635. And then this New Forest Eyre had come along.

It was his son George who had brought up the matter. Furzey had two sons: William, who had married a girl over in Ringwood and gone to live there, and George, who had stayed at Oakley. When Furzey died, George would take over the smallholding, so naturally he had an interest in the business. Furzey had heard about the coming registration of claims that spring and wondered if he ought to be doing something. Since he hated this sort of thing, though, and remembered the previous occasion with embarrassment, he had tried to put it out of his mind.

Then one evening George had come home with a worried look on his face. "You know this register of claims? Stephen Pride says we were never on it, Dad. Is that right?"

"Stephen Pride says that, does he?"

"Yes, Dad. This is serious."

"What does Stephen Pride know?"

"You mean he's got it wrong?"

"'Course he has. I fixed all that. Years ago."

"You sure, Dad?"

"'Course I'm sure. Don't you worry about that."

"Oh. That's all right then. Had me worried."

So George had stopped worrying and Gabriel Furzey had started.

It had to be all right, though, didn't it? A commoner's rights were his, weren't they? Always had been, long before all this writing of things down. All through the spring and summer Furzey had meant to do something about it; week after week he had put it off. He had half expected Alice or her steward to come and check the village; but Oakley was just the same now as it had been thirty-five years ago, so they probably assumed there was nothing to alter. Alice Lisle had many things to think about; she had probably forgotten about Furzey's failure to turn up all those years ago. The court had met, but he had heard that Alice was not presenting her claims until later. The court had met again. But now time had run out. He had to do something. He rode up to the house.

As it happened, his timing could not have been better.

John Hancock the lawyer would be presenting Alice's and numerous other landowners' claims before the court. As Furzey stood before him with his hat in his hand, he understood the situation at once. "The claims for Mast and Pasture will not be a difficulty," he reassured the villager. "Nor, I think, will the right of Turbary. These clearly belong to your cottage. However," he continued, "the right of Estovers is not so straightforward." And when Furzey looked mystified and mumbled that he'd always had that right the lawyer explained: "You may think you have, but I shall have to examine the records."

The ancient rights of the Forest folk, although they derived from common practices that went back into the mists of time, were by no means as simple as might be supposed. The common rights in the Forest belonged not to a family but to the individual cottage or holding. Some cottages had some rights, some had others. The right of Estovers – of collecting wood – was especially valuable and had been granted back in Norman times only to the most important village tenants, those who held their dwelling by the tenure known as copyhold. The Pride smallholding in Oakley, for instance, had always been a copyhold. Down the centuries, other villagers without copyholds had often claimed, or assumed they had, the right of Estovers and some had got away with it for so long that no one ever questioned it. From time to time, however, some new attempt was made to restrict this practice of helping oneself to the Forest's underwood; and the rule which applied to Furzey now stated that he might claim the right of Estovers only if the cottage – the "messuage" was the ancient legal term – he occupied had been built before a certain date in the reign of

Queen Elizabeth – an arcane dispensation of which Furzey himself had never even heard.

The estate records were kept at Albion House. Hancock knew where they were and, as he had nothing special to do until Alice returned from her mission, he thought he might as well see what he could find. It was the sort of burrowing the lawyer rather enjoyed. "When did your family first occupy your holding?" he enquired.

"My grandfather's day," Furzey told him. "We was in another cottage before then. Always in Oakley, though," he added firmly, in case it mattered.

"Quite. Sit and rest." The lawyer gave him a professional smile. "You don't mind waiting, do you? I'll see what I can find."

The hunt had lasted less than a quarter of an hour. Stephen Pride still couldn't quite believe it.

The thing had been beautifully managed, too. The king had been placed in a perfect spot in a glade. He was armed with the traditional bow. His ladies were grouped behind him. Pride and the Forest men, aided by the gentlemen keepers and two of the courtiers, drove some deer through and the king, in the most cheerful manner, loosed an arrow, which shot quite close over one of the deer before embedding itself in a tree.

"Well shot, Sire," cried one of the courtiers, while Charles, without the slightest show of disappointment, turned to his ladies for approval.

Stephen Pride, riding past an instant later, could have sworn he heard Nellie cry: "I hope you're not going to hurt any of those poor little deer, Charles." And after a moment or two later, just as they were about to begin another drive, there was a shout: "To Bolderwood!" And to the utter astonishment of the Forest men, the whole party prepared to ride back to the lodge, where refreshments were awaiting them. Did all kings, Stephen wondered, get bored so quickly?

But Charles II was not bored at all. He was doing what he liked best, which was to learn how things worked, with a shrewder eye than people supposed, and to flirt with pretty women. And an hour afterwards he was quite happily doing the latter when he observed, with no great pleasure, two

figures, cut, it seemed, from the same brown cloth, riding towards him. Who the devil, he murmured to the Master Keeper,
were they? Alice Lisle, he was informed. The child was her
daughter.

"Shall I send them away, Sire?" Howard enquired, as he
turned to meet them.

"No," came the answer, with a sigh, "although I wish you
could make them vanish."

She had done her best, Charles saw at once, to make herself
agreeable. Her reddish hair, streaked with grey, was parted in
the middle: she had curled and combed it to try to give it more
body. Her plain dress was long out of fashion, but the cloth
was good. She had made a little concession to him by wearing
a lacy cravat. She looked what she was: a Puritan gentle-
woman, a widow secretly sad that she had grown a little
hard – not the king's type at all. But he felt slightly sorry for
her. The small girl looked much more promising, though:
fairer than her mother; eyes more blue than grey; a twinkle
there, perhaps.

So when Howard returned and murmured that the widow
Lisle had come to beg a favour, Charles gave her a long, cool
look and then remarked: "You and your daughter shall join our
party, Madam."

Bolderwood was a charming spot. Situated nearly four
miles west of Lyndhurst, by the edge of open heath, it consisted of a paddock, a little inclosure of trees, including an ancient yew tree, and the usual outbuildings. The main house
was quite modest, a simple lodge, really, where a gentleman
keeper lived. Nearby, beside a pair of fine oak trees, was the
small but pleasant cottage that went with Jim Pride's job as
underkeeper. As the day was fine, the refreshments had been
set out in the open under the shade of the trees.

Dishes of sweetmeats, venison pie, light Bordeaux wine: all
were offered Alice and her daughter as they sat on the folding
stools provided. The king and some of the ladies lounged on
rolled blankets draped with heavy damasks. It was a scene typical of the Restoration, as Charles II's reign was often called:
courtly, amusing, easygoing, louche. Alice understood at once
that the king meant to punish her a little by making her take
part in it and she shrewdly guessed that he might deliberately

steer the conversation into areas designed to shock her. For the time being, nobody took any notice of the visitors at all, however, and so she was free to listen and observe.

They represented, of course, everything that she and John Lisle had fought against. Their cavalier clothes, their immoral ways said it all. She might, she suspected, have been at the court of the Catholic King of France. The stern, moral rule that the Cromwellians at least aimed at was wholly foreign to these pleasure seekers. Yet, if she didn't approve, she quite enjoyed their wit.

At one point the conversation turned to witchcraft. One of the ladies had heard there were witches in the Forest and asked Howard if it was true. He didn't know.

The king shook his head. "Every disagreeable woman is accused of magic in our age," he remarked. "And I'm sure a great many harmless creatures are burned. Most magic is nonsense anyway." He turned to one of the gentlemen keepers. "Do you know this spring my cousin Louis of France sent me his court astrologer? Said he was infallible. Pompous little man, I thought. So I took him to the races." Alice had heard of the king's latest passion for racing horses. At Newmarket Races he'd mingle with the crowds just like a common man. "I had him there all afternoon and, do you know, he couldn't predict a single winner! So I sent him straight back to France the next morning."

Despite herself, Alice burst out laughing. The king gave her a sidelong look and seemed about to say something, but then apparently changed his mind and ignored her again. The conversation turned to his oak plantation. Admiration was expressed.

Then Nellie Gwynn turned her large, cheeky eyes on the monarch. "When are you going to give me some oak trees, Charles?" It was well known that the king had given an entire felling of timber to one young lady of the court a few years back, presumably as a gift for favours received.

The king returned his mistress's gaze sagely. "You have the royal oak, Miss, always at your service," he replied. "Be content with that."

There was laughter, although not this time from Alice, who now felt a nudge from Betty at her side.

"What does he mean, Mother?" she whispered.

"Never mind."

"The trouble with the royal oak, Charles," Nellie rejoined, with a tart look towards the elegant young Frenchwoman who was sitting composedly on a small chair, "is that it seems to be spreading." From this Alice concluded that the king had also been turning his eye in the French lady's direction, but he seemed not in the least abashed about it.

Looking bleakly at the proud lady in question he replied with a slight crossness: "There has been no planting. Yet."

"I don't think much of her, anyway," said Nellie.

In the middle of this unseemly exchange King Charles suddenly turned to Alice. "You have a pretty daughter, Madam," he said.

Alice felt herself tense. She realised instantly that Charles had deliberately chosen this moment and this remark to vex her: the idea, insolently floating in the air, that her God-fearing little daughter might be viewed as a future royal conquest was as offensive as anything he could have said. Not, of course, that he had even implied it. If such a horror arose in her mind, he would say, it only proved her own antagonism towards him. He'd simply said the child was pretty. His game was plain: if she thanked him, she made a fool of herself; if she was insulted she gave him an excuse to send her packing. But always consider, she reminded herself, that my husband killed this man's father. "She is a good child, Your Majesty," she replied as easily as she could, "and I love her for her kindness."

"You rebuke me, Madam," the king said quietly and looked down for a moment, before turning back to her again. She noticed as he did so that his nose, at a certain angle, looked strikingly large and that, with his soft brown eyes, this made him appear surprisingly solemn.

"I will deal plainly with you, Madam," he said seriously. "I cannot like you. It is said," he continued with a trace of real anger, 'that you cried out with joy at my father's death."

"I am sorry if you heard that, Sire," she said, "for I promise you it is not true."

"Why not? It was surely what you desired."

"For the simple reason, Sire, that I foresaw that, one day, it would lead to my husband's destruction – which it did."

At this blunt failure to express sorrow for the death of the king's father, Howard began to rise as though he meant to throw her out; but King Charles gently raised his hand. "No, Howard," he said sadly, "she is only honest and we should be grateful for that. I know, Madam that you have suffered too. They say," he continued to Alice, "that you harbour dissenting preachers."

"I do not break the law, Your Majesty." Since the law now required that meetings of religious dissenters must be five miles outside any chartered borough, and Albion House was only four from Lymington, this wasn't quite true.

But to her surprise the king now addressed her earnestly. "I'd have you know," he said, "that you will have no cause to fear trouble from me on that account. It is Parliament that makes these rules, not I. Indeed, within a year or two I hope, Madam, to give you and your good friends liberty to worship as you please, so long as all Christians may have equal dispensation." He smiled. "You may have meeting houses at Lymington, Ringwood, Fordingbridge and I shall be glad of it."

"The Catholics, too, might worship?"

"Yes. But if all faiths are free, is that so bad?"

"Truly, Sire" – she hesitated – "I do not know."

"Think on it, Dame Alice," he said and gave her a look which, at another time and place, might almost have charmed even her. "You may trust me."

In his desire for religious freedom, so that the Catholics might have their churches again, Charles II was entirely sincere. For the time being. That he had also, that very summer, signed a secret treaty with his cousin Louis XIV promising to adopt the Roman Catholic faith and enforce it in England as soon as possible was a fact of which neither Alice, nor Parliament, nor even the king's close council had the slightest inkling. In return for this Charles was to receive from Louis a handsome yearly income. Whether the king was serious and really meant to betray his Protestant English subjects, or whether he was duping his French cousin to get some more money will never be known, except to God. Since, like so many of the Stuarts, the merry monarch was a habitual liar, he probably didn't know himself.

So while the idea of trusting the king would have caused

hilarity in any courtier, Alice had no reason to suppose that, for her dissenting friends, he might not be offering a genuine hope.

"And now, Dame Alice," he said, "do not forget that you came here to ask me for a favour."

Alice was very brief and straightforward. She explained the lawsuit with the Duke of York and assured the king: "I'm sure the duke believes I am hiding money and there is nothing I can say to persuade him otherwise. I come to you, Sire, with this little girl" – she indicated Betty – "whose interests I am bound to protect, to ask for help. The matter is as simple and as plain as that."

"You ask me to believe my brother is mistaken?"

"He is bound to hate me, Sire."

"As am I. And that you are honest?" To this Alice could only bow her head. The king nodded. "I believe you *are* honest, Madam," he concluded. "Although whether I can help you remains to be seen."

He was just turning back to the ladies when Alice caught sight of a solitary rider out on the heath. He was coming towards them at a trot. She supposed that it must be one of the forest keepers but as he drew closer she observed that it was a youngish man, in his middle twenties she guessed, whom she had never seen before. He was tall, with dark good looks. A very handsome young man indeed. Betty was staring at him open-mouthed. Alice observed the king turn to Howard enquiringly and saw Howard murmur something to him. She noticed that the king looked, just for a moment, a little awkward, but that he quickly recovered himself.

Who, she wondered, could the young man be?

Thomas Penruddock did not often come to the Forest. When his cousins at Hale, whom he was visiting the previous day, had told him that the king was to be at Bolderwood he had hesitated to go there. He was a proud young man and had no wish to risk further humiliation. It was only after his cousins had begged him to go that he had finally set out, with some misgivings, in the direction of the royal party.

Although the Penruddocks had managed to hold on to the

house and part of the estate at Compton Chamberlayne, the years since his father's death had been hard. There had been no fine clothes for young Thomas; the horses were mostly sold; nor were there any tutors. Side by side with his mother, the boy had worked to keep the family going. If there were lawyers to see in Sarum, which always particularly distressed her, he would accompany her. Often he would work in the fields; he became a tolerable carpenter. Sometimes his mother would cry fretfully: "You shouldn't be working like a farmhand. You're a gentleman! If only your father were here." To please her, as much as anything, he would sit down in the evenings, if he were not too tired, and make some attempt to study his books. And forever before his mind he kept one promise: one day, things will get better and then I'll be a gentleman, like my father; I shall be like him in every way. This was his talisman, the nearest he could do to get his father back, his hope of eternal life, his dream of love, his secret honour.

Always there had been the hope: one day the king will return. What joy there would be, then. The faithful would be rewarded; and who had been more faithful, who had suffered more for the king's cause, than the family of Penruddock? When the Restoration came, therefore, seventeen-year-old Thomas Penruddock was beside himself with excitement. Even his mother said: "I'm sure the king must do something for us now."

They heard of the festivities in London, of the loyal new Parliament and the bright new court. They waited for a message, a call to come and share the triumph of the king. And heard – nothing; not a word, not a whisper. The king had not remembered the widow and her son.

They sent word by friends. They even wrote a letter: which was answered with – silence. Friends explained: "The king hasn't any money to give, but there are other things he can do." An application was prepared, asking the new king to grant this Penruddock a monopoly for making glasses. "In other words," a worldly friend explained, "anyone who wants to make glasses has to pay you for the licence to do it." This was a popular way of rewarding a subject, since no money had to come out of the crown coffers.

"I'm sure I shan't know how to do all this," Mrs Penruddock fretted, but she needn't have worried. The monopoly wasn't granted. "I can't understand why he does nothing," she cried.

For young Thomas, despite all he had been through, this was his first and very important worldly lesson: he could trust no one, not even a king, to look after him if he did not look after himself. Those in power, even anointed kings, used people and then forgot them. It was the nature of their calling. It could not be otherwise. He had gone back to work with a vengeance.

And in the last ten years he had succeeded very well. Slowly, bit by bit, the estate was reverting to its former condition. Lost acres were being recovered. At twenty-seven, Thomas Penruddock was a toughened and successful man.

Today he wanted something specific. Already a captain in his country's local cavalry, he knew that his colonel, a pleasant old gentleman, meant to give the thing up shortly. He had let it be known that he wanted the colonelcy, but there were other older men who could quite reasonably expect to come before him. He was determined, though. It was not a question of profit: if anything, this colonelcy would cost him money. It was a question of family honour: the day he got the post, there would be a Colonel Penruddock at Compton Chamberlayne again.

"The lord-lieutenant of the county makes the appointment," he told his cousins. "But, of course, if the king says he wants me to have it then I'll get it." When he considered his family's sufferings and the fact that this would cost the king nothing, it seemed to Thomas Penruddock that it was the least the king could do. Nonetheless, he had felt uncertain of his reception, as he prepared to meet his monarch for the first time.

There was no mistaking him: the big swarthy fellow surrounded by women. Thomas doffed his hat politely as he drew up and received a nod in return. He saw Howard, whom he knew, and therefore guessed that the king had already been told who he was; he scanned his face for a sign of recognition – a welcoming smile for a loyal family, perhaps. But he saw something else. There was no mistaking it. King Charles was looking embarrassed.

As indeed he was. It had been one of the humiliations of his royal Restoration that his Parliament had made it almost impossible for him to reward his friends. A number of the rich and powerful men who had made his return possible, of course, had been sitting on estates confiscated from royalists, so he could hardly expect to ask for those back. But he had at least hoped that Parliament would give him enough funds to do something for his friends. Parliament didn't. He had been helpless.

But even so . . . The truth was that Charles winced inwardly whenever the name Penruddock was mentioned. Penruddock's Rising had been a bungled affair and that was partly his own fault. He'd been able to do nothing at first for the widow; but after that he'd felt so embarrassed that he'd tried to pretend they didn't exist. He'd behaved shabbily and he knew it. And now, here was this handsome, saturnine young man, like an angel of conscience, arriving to ruin his sunny afternoon. Inwardly, he squirmed.

But that was not what young Penruddock saw. For as he glanced round the group, wondering what was in the royal mind to cause it such embarrassment, his eyes fell upon a quiet figure sitting at one side. And his mouth fell open.

He recognised her at once. The years had passed, her red hair was greying now, but how could he ever forget that face? It was graven on his memory. The face of the woman who, with her husband, had deliberately set out to kill his father. In a single sudden rush, the agony of those days came upon him like a searing wind. For a moment he was a boy again. He stared at her, unable to comprehend; and then, as he thought, understanding. She was the friend of the king. He, a Penruddock, was scorned; while she, a rich regicide, a murderess, was sitting at the king's right hand.

He realised that he had started to shake. With a huge effort he controlled himself. In so doing, his saturnine face assumed a look of cold contempt.

Howard, seeing this, and ever the courtier, quickly called out: "His Majesty is hunting, Mr Penruddock. Have you come to request an audience?"

"I, Sir?" Penruddock collected himself. "Why, Sir, should a Penruddock wish to speak to the king?" He indicated Alice Lisle. "The king, I see, has other kinds of friends."

This was too much.

"Have a care, Penruddock," cried the king himself. "You must not be insolent."

But Penruddock's bitterness had overcome him. "I had come to ask a favour, it is true. But that was foolish, I plainly see. For after my father laid down his life for this king" – he was addressing them all now – "we had neither favour nor even thanks." Turning to Alice Lisle, he directed his years of suffering and loathing straight towards her. "No doubt we should have done better to be traitors, thieves of other men's lands and common murderers."

Then, in a fit of anguish, he turned his horse's head and a moment later was cantering away.

"By God, Sire," cried Howard, "I'll bring him back. I'll horsewhip him!"

But Charles II raised his hand. "No. Let him go. Did you not see his pain?" For a while he gazed silently after the retreating figure; not even Nellie attempted to interrupt his thoughts. Then he shook his head. "The fault is mine, Howard. He is right. I am ashamed." Then, turning to Alice, with a bitterness of his own, he exclaimed: "Ask no favours of me, Madam, who are still my enemy, when you see how I treat my friends." And the nod that followed told Alice plainly that it was time for her and her daughter to be gone.

So she was in some distress when she arrived back at Albion House to find Furzey sitting in a corner of the hall and John Hancock, with a large sheet of paper over which he was poring carefully, in the parlour. Anxious to get rid of the Oakley man so that she could discuss her meeting with the king, she demanded that Hancock deal with Furzey at once. Closing the parlour door, the lawyer explained Furzey's predicament in a few words and then showed her the paper. "I found it all in the rental records. You see? This cottage, which is the one Furzey occupies, shows its first rent here, in the reign of James I, just a few years before you were born. It was clearly built recently and Furzey's grandfather moved into it."

"So he had no right to Estovers?"

"Technically no. I can make application, of course, but unless we mean to conceal this from the court . . ."

"No. No. *No!*" The final word was a shout. Her patience had suddenly given out. "The last thing in the world I need now is to be caught out in a lie, concealing evidence from the court. If he hasn't the right of Estovers then he hasn't and that's that." She couldn't take any more today. "John, please make him go away."

Furzey listened carefully, as the lawyer explained, but he did not hear. The explanation about the building date of his dwelling meant nothing to him: he had never heard of it, didn't believe it, thought it was a trick, refused to take it in. When the lawyer said, "It's a pity you didn't make the claim when you should have back in the last king's reign – plenty of those claims are improper, but they're all being allowed," Furzey looked down at the floor; but since that made it his fault, he managed within moments to screen this information from his mind. There was only one thing Furzey knew. Whatever this lawyer had said, he'd heard it for himself. That shout – "No!" – from behind the door. It was that woman, the Lady of Albion House, who had denied him.

And so it was, in an excess of rage and bitterness, that he swore to his family that night: "She's the one. She's the one that's taken away our rights. She's the one that hates us."

Two months later, Alice was greatly surprised when the Duke of York dropped his lawsuit against her.

1685

People were often surprised that Betty Lisle was twenty-four and unmarried. With her fair hair and fine, grey-blue eyes she was pleasant to look at. Had she been rich, no doubt people would have said she was beautiful. She wasn't poor: Albion House and much of the Albion land was to come to her.

"The fault is mine," Alice would acknowledge. "I have kept her too much with me."

This was certainly true. Betty's older sisters were married and away. Margaret and Whitaker were frequent visitors, but Bridget and Leonard Hoar had gone to Massachusetts where, for a while, Hoar had been President of Harvard. Tryphena and Robert Lloyd were in London. Alice and Betty were often alone, therefore, in the country.

Mostly they were at Albion House. They both loved it. To Alice, no matter what hardships she had known, the house her father built her had remained a refuge where she felt secure and at peace. Once the Duke of York's threat of litigation had been withdrawn she had known that it would pass intact to Betty and what might have been lonely years for her were filled with the joy of watching her youngest daughter relive the happy years of her own childhood. For Betty herself the gabled house in the woods seemed the happiest place on earth: her family home, hidden away from the world. In winter, when the frost left gleaming icicles on the trees and they went down the snowy lane to old Boldre church on its little knoll, it seemed intimate and magical. In summer, when she rode up on to the wide heath to watch the visiting birds floating over the heather, or cantered down to Oakley, to see old Stephen Pride, the Forest seemed magnificent and wild, yet full of friends.

But the house was also a serious place, on account of the visitors: the men of religion. King Charles's promise to Alice at Bolderwood, that he would give his subjects religious freedom, had actually come to pass in 1672. But it hadn't lasted. Within a year, Parliament had struck it down. Dissenters were thrust firmly back to the margin of society and forbidden all public office. The only effect of the brief freedom was to cause all the dissenters to come out into the open so they'd be known in future. Alice quietly continued to provide a haven for Puritan preachers and was generally left alone; but it brought a certain air of seriousness and purpose into the house that was bound to affect the young girl living with her. There was something else, besides: although Alice hardly realised it, the preachers who came to seek her hospitality were older than they had been before.

For a few years Betty had been sent to a school for young ladies in Sarum; but while she had been happy enough there and made some friends, she had never really felt satisfied by the conversation of the other girls. Used to older people, she found them rather childish.

After this her mother had sent her, once or twice a year, to stay with relations or friends, on the assumption that she would meet young men. And she had; but often as not she had found them insipid until at last Alice had told her firmly: "Do not look for a perfect man, Betty. No man is perfect."

"I won't. But do not force me to marry a man I can't respect," she countered, ignoring her mother's sigh.

By the time she was twenty-four, Alice was near despair. Betty herself was happy enough. "I love the house. I love every inch of the Forest," she told her. "I can live and die here alone contentedly enough."

Until this June, while they were staying in London.

"And when you consider," her eldest daughter Tryphena remarked to Alice, "that this has occurred when all the world is thinking only of the great events now shaking the kingdom, I think she must be serious indeed."

But that, alas, for Alice, was just the problem.

Figures in a landscape. A July night. There had been thousands the night before. But most, by now, had melted away into town, farm and hamlet, hiding their arms, going about their business as if they had never been out at all, the days before, marching round the western towns, trying to seize a kingdom.

Not all would be lucky, however. Some would be named, others given away, and sent to join the several hundred captured.

Figures on horseback, keeping out of sight, moving through woods when they can or out on to the bare, deserted ridges with none to witness them but the sheep, or a lonely shepherd, or the ghosts, perhaps, in the grassy earthwork inclosures, those silent reminders all over the countryside of the prehistoric age. Figures moving eastward now, still out on the chalk ridges, twenty miles or more south-west of Sarum.

Monmouth's Rebellion was broken.

Nobody had expected King Charles to die. He was only fifty-four. He himself had expected to live many years and Sir Christopher Wren had been building him a fine new palace on the hill above Winchester where the king had looked forward to residing. But then suddenly, that February, Charles had been struck with an apoplexy. Within a week he was dead. And that left a huge problem.

Although Charles II had had numerous sons by his various mistresses, several of whom he had obligingly created dukes, he had left no legitimate heir. The crown, therefore, had been due to pass to his brother James, Duke of York. At first James had not seemed so bad a choice: he'd married a Protestant wife, had two Protestant daughters and one of those had married her cousin, the very Protestant ruler of the Dutch, William of Orange. But when James's wife died and he married a Catholic princess, the English were less pleased. And when he soon afterwards admitted he was a Catholic himself, there had been consternation. Wasn't this just what Protestant Englishmen had dreaded for a century? England was more Protestant now than it had been in the time of the Armada or even the Civil War. Charles, to appease them, assured everyone that, if his brother should succeed him, he'd uphold the Church of England whatever his private views. But could anyone really believe that?

Most of the Parliament did not. They demanded that Catholic James be debarred from the throne. King Charles and his friends refused; and so began the great divide in English politics between those who would keep a Catholic off the throne – the Whigs – and the royalist group – the Tories. The problem dragged on for years. There were endless discussions and demonstrations. Although violence was avoided, it was really the same debate that had led to the Civil War: who should have the last say, king or Parliament? King Charles II, however, wheeling and dealing, had pursued his merry way for more than a decade, racing horses, chasing pretty women, getting money from Louis of France; and because the English liked the jolly rogue and thought he'd probably outlive his Catholic brother anyway, they went along with it. Mercifully, also, James had produced no heir with his Catholic wife. Time seemed to be on Protestant England's side. Until this sudden death.

James became king. A Catholic on the throne – the first since Bloody Mary a century and a quarter ago. The country held its breath.

Then, in June that same year, Monmouth's Rebellion had begun.

In a way it was bound to happen. Charles II had always

adored his eldest natural son, Monmouth the handsome,
Monmouth the Protestant: when the Whigs in Parliament
wanted to exclude Catholic James, they told King Charles
they'd rather have Monmouth. Charles, a Catholic Stuart at
heart, protested that the boy was not legitimate, but the prag-
matic English Parliament told him they'd worry about that.
Charles had refused to allow such a thing but, as far as
Monmouth was concerned, the damage had been done. He was
a spoiled young man, forever getting into trouble, always protected by his doting father. It seemed the English wanted him
as king. Even before his father's death he had allowed himself
to be implicated in one aborted plot that might have killed
both Charles and James. Small wonder, then, if, with Catholic
James suddenly placed over a most unwilling English nation,
Monmouth, in his thirties now but vain and immature, might
have thought the English would rise for him if he gave them
the chance.

He had started in the West Country. People had flocked to
his banner – small farmers, Protestants from the ports and
trading towns – several thousand strong. The local gentry, the
men of influence, however, had held back, cautious. And
wisely so. For yesterday, at the Battle of Sedgemoor, the royal
troops had smashed the rising. Everyone had scattered, to hide
or flee as best they could.

Figures in a landscape, in the misty morning. Monmouth
was fleeing. He had only two companions with him now. He
needed to find a port from which to sail, somewhere he
would not be betrayed. "We had better go," he decided, "to
Lymington."

There were other fugitives, too, that July morning, heading
in the same direction.

"But isn't he everything you have taught me to love?" Betty
was looking at her mother in genuine confusion. "You can
hardly object to his family," she added, "since he is an Albion."

Alice sighed. There had been no news, yet, from the West
Country. Was Monmouth about to succeed? The whole business made her fearful. And now her daughter insisted on troubling her with a suitor. She wished the young man, just for a
month or two, could be made to disappear.

Peter Albion was a credit to his family. If his grandfather Francis had deserved her own grandfather's scorn, Francis's son had done better. He'd become a physician and married a rich draper's daughter. Young Peter had practised law and, with his parents' numerous friends to help him, had already, by the age of twenty-eight, established himself as a rising man. He was handsome, with the traditional Albion fair hair and blue eyes; he was industrious; he was clever, thoughtful, ambitious. It was Tryphena who had encountered him and invited him to call; and it was she who summed him up: "He looks an Albion, but he's just like father."

Perhaps, Alice thought, that was why Betty liked him so much. He fitted the description of the father she'd never known.

But that, unfortunately, was precisely why Alice wanted to discourage him. "I'm getting old," she told Tryphena. "I've seen too many troubles." Troubles in England; troubles in the family. She did not doubt that the causes her husband had fought for had been just; she was quite sure, when she helped the dissenters, that she did right. But was it all worth it – the fighting, the suffering? Probably not. Peace was worth more, it seemed to her, than any of the small freedoms won in her lifetime. And peace was what she wanted now, for her old age and, above all, for her daughter.

It wasn't so easy to come by. A couple of years ago, at the time of that stupid plot to assassinate the king and his brother, Tryphena's husband had been arrested and questioned for days. Why? Not because he had even the faintest connection to the plot, but because of his family associations and friends. Once you were an object of suspicion you would always remain so. It was inevitable.

But for young Betty things could be different. Her youngest child, having lost her father, had missed the joys of early childhood she had known; but the rest would be better: a life of peace and security – the sort of life that she, Alice, had always expected to live in her house in the friendly Forest.

The very day after news of Monmouth's arrival in the West Country Peter Albion had come to Tryphena's house to pay his respects to his cousin Alice and her daughter. He had been pleasant company, very polite, but quietly forthright.

"The English will not tolerate a Catholic king," he stated. "Nor do I think they should." He bowed to Alice as though he clearly expected she would endorse these views. "Let us hope Monmouth succeeds." He had smiled. "I have some friends in that camp, Cousin Alice. I expect word of success at any time. Then, I can assure you, we shall see King James sent packing."

As he spoke, she had felt herself go cold. It was her own husband again, John Lisle. "Do not say such things," she cried. "This is dangerous."

"I should not, I assure you, Cousin Alice," he said quietly. "Except in such company as this."

Such company as this; the phrase had terrified her. Was Betty already assumed to be a conspirator? Was Peter Albion going to drag her into that role? "Leave us, Sir," she begged, "and speak no more of this."

But he had, nonetheless, seen Betty again a few days later. And although she had not liked it, it had been difficult to refuse her kinsman entry to the house. Wisely, he had never made any reference to these dangerous subjects again, but as far as she was concerned the damage was done. She had begged her daughter to have no more to do with him, to no avail. It wasn't easy: Betty was twenty-four. And she might, that very day, have taken her back to the safety of the Forest if she had not received, this morning, a letter from John Hancock.

Do not, I urge you, return to Albion House. Rebellion has broken out at Lymington. They have sent to you for support already. For God's sake stay in London and say nothing.

She had hastily torn up the letter and thrown it in the fire.

Say nothing. Would young Peter Albion say nothing? And Betty? She looked at her daughter desperately. "Dear child," she began softly, "if you are not careful we shall soon be hunted." She shook her head at the thought of it. "Like deer in the Forest."

Stephen Pride walked slowly past Oakley pond. He was seventy-five, but he certainly didn't feel it. Tall and lean, he still strode about – more slowly, a bit stiffly perhaps – just as he had all his long life. Common sense told him he wouldn't live much longer, but whatever cause God had prepared to strike him down, he had no sense of it. "I've known men live to be eighty," he remarked contentedly. "Reckon I might."

It had been one of the small joys of his long life to watch the pond by the hamlet's green. Its fluctuations were always the same, year after year, with the seasons. By late autumn, after the rains had fallen, the pool was fairly full. In winter it often froze. Two years ago, in the coldest winter Pride could ever remember, the pond had been frozen solid from November to April. Then, when the spring showers came and the warmth of May, the pond's whole surface would be covered with white flowers, as though the water itself had broken into blossom.

The wonder of the pond was the way it filled. There was no stream, as such, not even a rivulet. But as the rains fell on the nearby heath, somehow, as by a miracle, they drained off invisibly, tiny trickles you hardly saw that gathered by the hamlet into a small snake of water that ran across the green and spread out into the shallow depression beside it.

By summer, however, the pond began to evaporate. The warm heath soaked up any showers that fell upon it. The snake of water disappeared. Day by day the animals cropping the lush grass by the pond's edge advanced a little further. By the fence month in midsummer the pond was only half its springtime size. By August it was often completely dry. As he looked at it now, two cows and a pony were grazing in the green depression beside the three or four large puddles remaining at its centre.

Stephen Pride was feeling relieved. He had been to Albion House that morning and had just walked back. The news there had been exactly as he'd hoped: Dame Alice was still in London and no word had come to say she was returning. That was good. He'd known and loved Dame Alice all her life, and he didn't want to see her back at present, not the way things were at Lymington.

Because of his wife and her family, Pride usually knew more than most of the Oakley people about what was going on in Lymington, but nobody could have failed to be aware of the way feeling was running there in the last few years. If the little harbour town had been seething, so had almost every borough in England.

There might be some in the county who still hankered for the old Catholic faith, but the century since the Armada had thinned their ranks greatly by now. As for the townsfolk, they wanted none of it. The merchants and small traders of Lymington had disliked Charles I and distrusted Charles II. A few years ago, when concerns about the Catholic succession had been especially high in Parliament, a rogue named Titus Oates had invented a Catholic plot to depose Charles and put James in his place. The Jesuits were to take over the country; honest Protestants would be murdered. The whole thing was a fiction from start to finish, by which Oates aimed to make himself a rich celebrity. But the English were so afraid of Catholicism by then that they believed it. Hardly a week went by without Oates creating some further tale. Up and down the country people started imagining Jesuits peeping from behind windows or lurking round corners. And the growing port of Lymington was no exception. Half the town was looking for Jesuits. The mayor and his council were ready to arm the citizens.

So when Monmouth had raised his banner for the Protestant cause, Lymington had not hesitated. Within a day the mayor had several dozen men under arms. The local merchants and gentlemen were mostly with him. Pride himself had seen half a dozen local worthies riding past Oakley on their way up to Albion House to seek Alice's support. A message had already been sent by a swift horseman to Monmouth to assure him: "Lymington is with you." The afternoon before, there had been a march through the streets with pipes and drums, followed by ale and punch for everyone at the house of one of the merchants. It was like a carnival.

And Stephen Pride the villager, like John Hancock the lawyer, looked on cautiously. "Let the townspeople get excited," he had told his son Jim. "But those of us in the Forest may be wiser. No matter what happens with Monmouth, I'll still have my cows and you'll still be underkeeper. I just thank God," he added, "that Dame Alice isn't here. They'd draw her in whether she wanted it or not."

He was in a reasonably cheerful mood, therefore, when he

caught sight, a hundred yards past the pond, of a group of people listening to an argument. He went towards them.

It wasn't often you saw the two Furzey boys together. They were actually middle-aged men now and, since Gabriel's death a few years ago, George Furzey had taken over his cottage; but to Stephen Pride they were still the Furzey boys. God knows they both looked just like old Gabriel. George was a little bigger, but they both bulged at the waist in the same way. And, Stephen thought privately, they were both just as obstinate as their father.

William Furzey had never made much of himself over at Ringwood: he worked for a farmer as a stockman, looking after the cattle. A long way to go for no good reason, it had always seemed to Pride, but then he could never quite approve of anyone who went to live outside the Forest boundary. He'd come over to see George Furzey about something, evidently, and now they were standing side by side like a pair of infuriated bantam cocks. The cause of their fury, he now saw, was his own son.

"You ain't got the right," George Furzey was protesting, "an' I ain't going to do it anyway." He looked at his brother who was too busy hating Jim Pride to take time off to speak. "So that's that."

The trouble, as Jim Pride had put it to his father only a week ago, was predictable. "George Furzey doesn't know how to keep his mouth shut."

If the Furzeys had never accepted the fact that they hadn't the right of Estovers – if, to this day, they refused even to acknowledge Alice Lisle with a nod when they saw her and called her a thief – then the one thing that had been intolerable to them was when, a year ago, Jim Pride had been transferred from the post of underkeeper at Bolderwood to that of underkeeper in the South bailiwick.

For Stephen Pride this transfer had been very welcome. Boldrewood was almost nine miles from Oakley, but now he could see his son and his grandchildren almost every day.

For George Furzey, however, Jim's presence meant something very different, for the underkeeper was responsible for supervising common rights, including that of Estovers. "I'm not answering to Jim Pride," he had told his family. He wasn't going to be made a fool of by the Prides. And he had made a point of collecting firewood from the Forest just to prove his point.

Yet even then, matters needn't have come to a head. Jim Pride hadn't been an underkeeper for fifteen years without learning some wisdom. If Furzey had quietly taken some underwood when he needed it, Jim would have ignored it. But, of course, George Furzey was incapable of doing that.

Two days ago at the little inn at Brockenhurst, he had announced for everyone to hear: "I don't take no notice of Jim Pride. If I want Estovers I take them." Then, looking round in triumph, he added, "I'll take wood for cooper's timber, too," and had given everyone a broad wink. The right of Estovers applied only to wood that was to be used by a cottager for his fire. Cooper's timber was wood that was to be sold for making barrels or fencing, and was illegal.

It was a stupid and unnecessary challenge, and it left Jim Pride with no option. "I've got to come down on him now," he told his father.

So that morning he had arrived at Furzey's cottage and informed him, as politely as he could: "I'm sorry, George, but you've been taking wood you aren't entitled to. You know the rules. You've got to pay."

George and William Furzey looked at old Stephen now – the sight of him, it seemed, only infuriated them more – and after William had taken time, with careful deliberation, to spit on the ground, George summarised his position with a shout: "I'll tell you who's going to pay, Jim Pride. You're going to pay. You and that old hag Lisle! You and that witch. You're the ones that are going to pay."

With that, the two Furzeys turned and stamped back to their cottage.

Colonel Thomas Penruddock sat on his horse and coolly observed the crowd which, whatever it really felt, showed signs of rejoicing. His cousin from Hale was beside him.

Behind the two Penruddocks was Ringwood church with its broad, cheerful square tower. In front of them was the vicarage with guards on the door. Inside the vicarage, being questioned by Lord Lumley, was the Duke of Monmouth. There was no small excitement in the air. Ringwood had never been at the centre of English history before.

The last two days had been hectic. As soon as it was known that Monmouth was on the run a huge reward – five thousand pounds – had been offered for his capture. Even a sighting would be worth something. Half the south-western counties were out looking for him. Lord Lumley and his soldiers had clattered into Ringwood and had been scouring the New Forest. They had raided several houses in Lymington, where the mayor had already taken ship and fled abroad.

But now Monmouth was captured and unless he could find some way to persuade his uncle, the new King James, to pardon him, he was undoubtedly going to die.

Colonel Thomas Penruddock felt no emotion, personally. If Monmouth had succeeded that wouldn't have worried him much either. He felt none of the emotion for the cause of James II that his father had felt for his brother Charles. Why should he? He wasn't a Catholic. The reigning Stuarts had never done anything for his family to repay their loyalty. The colonelcy he wanted had gone to another. He had finally obtained it only four years before. No, he felt nothing for the Stuarts any more.

But he did believe in order and Monmouth, by rebelling, threatened disorder. As he'd failed, he must die.

The fact that this was exactly what had happened to his own poor father did not make Thomas Penruddock sympathetic in the least. Rather the reverse. Monmouth should have learned from the other man's mistakes, he told himself grimly. The rebellion had been poorly organised and had come too soon. Very well, then. They killed my father, he thought. Let Monmouth suffer his turn now.

Monmouth's capture had been a wretched business. Penruddock and his cavalry squadrons had been out on the ridges below Sarum and been unlucky to miss the fugitive, who had somehow slipped past them. But he had finally been discovered about seven miles west of Ringwood, disguised as a shepherd, half starved and hiding in a ditch. The honour of spotting him had gone to a militia man named Henry Parkin. Penruddock had ridden down to Ringwood as soon as he received word of the capture, out of curiosity as much as anything, and had not been surprised to find his cousin, who was a local magistrate, already there.

But now the door of the vicarage was opening. They were bringing him out. The crowd was watching expectantly.

He had been given some clothes to wear, but he was still a bedraggled figure. He looked dead beat. In that haggard face, with a week's growth of beard, Penruddock found it hard to see the handsome, spoiled youth he had briefly caught sight of that day in the Forest, fifteen years ago, when he had gone to see the king.

They didn't waste any time. They hustled him down the street, past a row of thatched Tudor cottages, to a larger house by the market place where he could be conveniently held under guard.

"What will they do with him now?" Penruddock asked his cousin.

"Keep him here a day or two," the magistrate replied, "then to the Tower of London I should think."

"My men are still out looking for fugitives. I hear they've rounded up hundreds further west." He looked after the figure of Monmouth as he disappeared into the other house. "You think he has any chance?"

"Doubt it." The magistrate shook his head. "I'm sure he'll appeal to the king for mercy, but" – he gave his cousin a side-long glance – "with the feeling in the country the way it is, I doubt whether the king can afford to let him live."

Colonel Thomas Penruddock nodded. Even with Monmouth dead, Catholic King James II was unlikely, in his opinion, to be secure on his throne for very long.

His cousin the magistrate, echoing his thoughts, looked down at the ground. "Too little, too soon," he murmured.

The crowd was breaking up.

"I think I'm going," Colonel Penruddock remarked and was just turning his horse's head when he noticed a man who, it occurred to him, looked uncommonly like a turnip – a rather grumpy turnip, come to that. The fellow seemed to be watching them. "Who's that ugly fellow?" he asked his cousin. "Any idea?"

The magistrate glanced at William Furzey and shrugged. "No," he said. "Looks like a turnip."

• • •

Although William Furzey knew perfectly well who the magistrate was, and had been gazing with mild envy at the fine horses that he and the Colonel rode, his mind had not been on the Penruddocks at all.

If he was not looking his best that morning, it really wasn't his fault. He'd only just got back from Oakley when he heard about Monmouth's defeat and the reward. He hadn't wasted any time. He'd seized a cudgel and a short length of rope, put a loaf of bread and an apple in a napkin, sent word to the farmer that he was sick and prepared to set off.

Of course, he had known it was like looking for a needle in a haystack. On the other hand, it would have been foolish not to try. And, as he thought about it, William Furzey reckoned he had a chance.

After all, Monmouth had to be looking for a port. Lymington, therefore, was still his best bet. True, the king's troops were watching the place, but Lymington was full of sympathisers and you could hide an army of fugitives in the Forest. He'd only need to get word to some of the people down by the quay. The Seagulls, to William Furzey's knowledge, would take the devil himself as long as he paid.

How would the fugitive get to Lymington? He'd certainly avoid Fordingbridge and Ringwood, but he'd have to cross the river Avon.

Tyrrell's Ford, then. It was the obvious place.

So Furzey had sidled up to a group of troops gathered in Ringwood market place and asked casually if any of their number had gone south along the river. They had told him no. He'd already noticed that not one of the troops who had arrived was a local man. Typical, he thought, of the authorities to conduct a search with soldiers unfamiliar with the territory.

But it was good for him. Without another word, he'd set off for Tyrrell's Ford.

He'd waited down there a day and a night before he heard that his quest was in vain and Monmouth was already found: due west of Ringwood, though, and heading south. Monmouth had been heading for Tyrrell's Ford all right.

The thought that he'd been cheated of his reward so narrowly did nothing to improve his temper.

• • •

Colonel Penruddock and his men continued to search the area around Sarum for several more days. They found no one. Meanwhile, however, the numbers taken in the west went to over a thousand.

Then the search slowed and stopped. There was a watch kept at every town, of course, but all seemed quiet.

Figures in the landscape. There were still fugitives out there, however: men of the Protestant cause; men who had vanished into houses where they could find shelter; men who must keep moving on, cautiously, towards the Forest.

Two weeks after the arrest of Monmouth, Alice Lisle could bear it no longer. Peter Albion had been calling almost every day.

Although Monmouth had written to King James and even had an interview with him, it hadn't done him any good. A week after his capture, on the little green in the Tower of London, he was executed. Meanwhile, preparations were in hand to deal with the huge mass of his followers who had been captured down in the West Country. A huge assize, at which they would all be tried, was to be held in August, with James's hand-picked man, Lord Chief Justice Jeffreys, presiding.

Yet none of this seemed to alter Peter Albion's view. "The king is just going to make himself more hated. I predict nothing but trouble," he announced.

And I predict nothing but trouble for you, Alice thought, *if you don't keep your mouth shut*.

Her terror was that he was going to propose marriage. She had no doubt that Betty would want him. And then what was she to do? Refuse her consent? Cut Betty off?

When she confided her fears to Tryphena and even that she was afraid Betty might elope, Tryphena with her usual tact, nodded sagely. "We must consider, Mother, that although Betty loves you, if she had to choose between you and a young man she will certainly choose him."

The best course, surely, was to keep the two apart. Once Monmouth was executed and the search for his followers dying down, Alice felt she could safely return to the Forest. Indeed, it was looking a safer place than London every day, with the threat of Peter Albion so present. But she also feared that, if she announced their departure, it might bring matters to a head with Albion and provoke a proposal.

A week after Monmouth's execution, however, he announced that he must go down into Kent for a few days upon business. Telling him that she looked forward to seeing him on his return, Alice said a fond farewell. The very next morning she told Betty they were leaving for the country before noon.

By that night they were already at an inn twenty miles down the road.

"We should be in Winchester by tomorrow night," Alice said cheerfully.

Jim Pride was surprised, two days later, to see a carriage containing Alice and Betty Lisle passing through Lyndhurst. At the same moment he saw them, Alice Lisle caught sight of him and waved for him to come over.

Betty, he noticed, was looking a bit subdued, but Alice greeted him warmly, asked after his father and mother, and demanded to know all the news.

The Forest, as it happened, had been quiet for a week, until today. A rumour from somewhere had caused the authorities to think there might be fugitives about to embark from Lymington. There had been a house-to-house search there that morning, but nothing had been found.

"I reckon it'll all be quiet after this," Jim said.

Alice, however, had looked thoughtful. "I think, all the same, we won't go to Albion House just yet," she said. "It's too close to Lymington." She smiled at Pride. "Tell the coachman we'll go to Moyles Court instead," she requested. "We've still time to get there before dark." Moyles Court, right across in the Avon valley, seemed a safer bet altogether.

William Furzey had just finished work for the day and he was walking up the Avon to a spot where he intended to do a little unobserved fishing, when he came upon the man on the horse. The horse was not impressive. The man was a rather frail-looking fellow, with grey hair and mild, watery blue eyes. He seemed to be lost. "Could you tell me," he enquired, "the way to Moyles Court?"

William eyed him. A townsman by the look of him, a small trader or craftsman, perhaps. Didn't sound local. William Furzey wasn't stupid; he knew an opportunity when he saw it. The fish could wait. "'T'ain't easy to find," he said. The house was, in fact, less than a mile off by a straight lane. The stranger looked tired. "I could take you there," William offered, "but it'd be out of my way."

"Would sixpence repay your kindness?" A day labourer's wage was eight pence. Sixpence from an ordinary townsman like this, therefore, was handsome. He must want to find the place badly. Furzey nodded.

He took a circuitous route. Moyles Court lay in a clearing just below the ridge that led up from the Avon valley to the heathland of the Forest. This part of the valley was quite wooded, so it wasn't difficult for Furzey to stretch the journey to two miles, taking paths that sometimes doubled back on themselves. Since the stranger made no remark, Furzey concluded that his sense of direction wasn't strong. It also gave him the chance to find out more about him. Had he come from far? The man was evasive. What was his occupation?

"I am a baker," his companion admitted.

A baker, from a long way off, prepared to pay sixpence to find Moyles Court. This man was almost certainly a dissenter, then, looking for that damned Lisle woman. Furzey bided his time before speaking. "You seek a godly lady," he ventured in a pious voice, at the next wrong turn he made.

"You think so?"

"I do. If it is Dame Alice you seek."

"Ah." The baker looked pleased. His watery blue eyes brightened hopefully.

Furzey wasn't quite sure where this conversation would lead, but one thing was certain: the more he could learn from this man, the more chance he had of using it for profit. And the beginning of an idea was starting to form in his mind. "There are many good folk she has helped," Furzey continued. He thought of the hated Prides and mentioned the names of some of their Lymington relations. "But I must be careful what I say," he added, "not knowing who you may be."

And now the poor fool smiled gladly. "You may know me, friend," he cried. "My name is Dunne and I come all the way from Warminster. I have a message to deliver to Dame Alice."

Warminster: west of Sarum by twenty miles. A long way for a dissenting baker to be carrying a message. His first suspicions began to grow. This fellow might be useful indeed.

"By what name may I know you?" the baker asked eagerly.

Furzey hesitated. He hadn't the least intention of giving his name to this probably dangerous friend of the cursed Lisle woman. "Thomas, Sir. Just Thomas," he replied, adding cautiously: "These are difficult times for godly men."

"They are, Thomas. I know it." The baker's watery blue eyes gave him a look of tender understanding.

Furzey led him on another hundred yards before quietly remarking: "If a man needed shelter, in these dangerous times, this'd be a good place, I should say."

Yes. There was no doubt of it, the baker was looking at him gratefully. "You think so?"

"I do. Praise God," Furzey added devoutly. He had run out of detours now, but he knew all he needed to. "Moyles Court lies just up there." He pointed. It was less than a quarter-mile. "Your business and that of Dame Alice is your own, Sir, so I'll leave you here. But may I ask if you will be remaining there or returning?"

"Returning forthwith, good Thomas."

"Then, if you need a guide to conduct you on your way so that you will not be seen, I'll wait for you, if you please." With gratitude the baker thanked him and went upon his way.

William Furzey sat on a tree stump. There was no doubt in his mind now as to what this must mean. The baker was helping fugitives. Why else should he come and go again like this? He wanted to bring them to Dame Alice. He smiled to himself. He might have missed Monmouth himself – and several people who had helped find Monmouth had been handsomely rewarded – but if the baker's friends were of any importance then there'd surely be something in it for him. The question was, how and where to find them? He couldn't very well accompany this baker all the way home. But if the men were to be brought to Moyles Court . . . A grin spread over his face. That would bode ill, now, for that cursed Dame Alice, wouldn't it?

An hour passed before Dunne the baker returned. One look at his face was enough. He was smiling contentedly.

"You saw Dame Alice?" Furzey enquired.

"I did, my friend. And I told her of your kindness. She was curious as to who you were, but I said you were a quiet fellow who minded his own business and wished to know nothing of ours."

"You did right by me, Sir."

They said no more for a while, but after about a mile the baker asked: "If I come again, with my friends, would you take us by a discreet way to Moyles Court?"

"With all my heart," Furzey replied.

They parted near Fordingbridge.

"Meet me here, then, in three days' time, at dusk," the trusting baker said as they parted. "May I count upon you, Thomas?"

"Oh, yes," said William, "you may count on me."

Alice Lisle stared at the table, then at the letter again.

She and Betty had arrived back at Moyles Court themselves only an hour before Dunne called, so she had been rather pre-occupied when he gave it to her. Perhaps, she now considered, she hadn't paid the matter enough attention.

It was very brief. It came from a highly respectable Presbyterian minister named Hicks, whom she knew slightly. She thought she remembered him staying at Albion House once, years ago. Hicks asked if she would allow him and a friend to come for a night on his way eastwards.

It was a simple request and normally she would hardly have given it much thought. When she'd asked Dunne what this meant he had said only that he was a messenger but that Hicks seemed a most respectable man. So she had agreed that they might come there on Tuesday, which was in three days' time, and let Dunne go. She had wondered who this man Thomas might be, who had shown Dunne the way, but there were prob-ably many people in the area who had friends in the Lymington community. The man was obviously a well-wisher.

Yet as the evening wore on she began to have second thoughts. Had she been careless? Dunne had come a long way. What if these men were fugitives? Dunne had said nothing about that, but then he probably wanted to accomplish his mission, possibly even get them off his own hands. As for this man Thomas – could he really be trusted? The more she thought of it the less she liked it and the more she was cross with herself. A moment of weakness, a failure to keep watch, a slowing down, a weariness. Every creature in the Forest knew better than that.

She felt a sudden fear, a burst of urgency. She must put them off. She could send a messenger after Dunne in the morning. Assuming, of course, that he had returned to Warminster and not somewhere else. It was worth a try. She sighed. She'd sleep on it.

Yet every creature in the Forest, sooner or later, will be guilty of carelessness, for which the penalty can be high. In the morning, in the quiet shade of Moyles Court, she told herself that she was worrying unduly.

William Furzey didn't waste any time. As soon as he had parted from Dunne he had continued northwards. It was a four-mile walk up to Hale, but he wasn't taking any chances. If, by ill luck, the baker should be caught and questioned, Furzey couldn't run any risk of being accused as an accomplice. Penruddock of Hale, therefore, was his first objective.

It was twilight when he arrived. The magistrate, about to go to bed after a busy day, was not best pleased to see the man who looked like a turnip, but as soon as Furzey began his tale he was all attention. By the time William had finished he was looking approving. "Fugitives. I haven't a doubt of it," he said briskly. "You did well to come here."

"I'm hoping not to be the poorer for it, Sir," William Furzey said frankly. He'd considered bargaining at the start but wisely concluded this might irritate the magistrate.

"Certainly." The other nodded. "It'll depend on who they are, of course. But I'll see you're not the loser if we take them. You have my word." He gave Furzey a quick look. "They'll probably think you could be useful, you know, at any trial."

"Yes, Sir." Furzey understood. "Whatever is wanted."

"Hm." The magistrate didn't particularly care for this kind of business himself, but it was as well to know where one stood. "You say," he resumed, "you're to conduct them to Moyles Court on Tuesday night and that Dame Alice will shelter them?"

"That's what he told me, Sir."

Penruddock the magistrate considered silently for a few moments. Alice Lisle, he thought grimly to himself. How the wheel turned. "Tell no one. Not a soul. Meet them exactly as planned. Have you a horse?"

"I can get one."

"Ride straight to me as soon as they are at Moyles Court. Can you do that?"

Furzey nodded.

"Good. You can sleep in the barn here tonight, if you wish," Penruddock offered kindly.

That night, before he went to bed, the magistrate wrote a message to be taken to his cousin, Colonel Thomas Penruddock of Compton Chamberlayne, at dawn the next day.

George Furzey looked at William Furzey and shook his head in wonder. "You dog," he breathed. "You clever dog. Tell me again." So William repeated everything.

The magistrate had instructed him to tell no one, but William didn't count his brother, so as soon as he was able on Sunday, he had quit the farm and crossed the Forest to Oakley, to share the news. The joy it brought George Furzey was everything William could have wished for him.

George was not a man of deep imagination. He did not concern himself in detail with what might befall Alice Lisle. All he knew was that the woman who had cheated and humiliated his family was going to get her come-uppance. That thought was so large, and so beautiful, that all others were extinguished before it like stars before the rising sun.

"She'll be arrested, I reckon," said William.

The thought of Dame Alice being hauled off to the magistrate, humiliated in front of the whole Forest, seemed to William to be God's perfect justice: a fitting tribute to his father's memory. And then, as he considered the sweetness of it, another idea came into his mind like a flash of morning sunlight. "Know what?" he said. "We could send Jim Pride along there, too. If they found him at Moyles Court he'd have some explaining to do, wouldn't he?" He let out a chuckle. "We could do that, I reckon, William. We could do that, then!"

"How'd you do it, George?" his brother asked.

"Don't you worry about that." George was in a transport of delight. The Lisles and the Prides. All humiliated. All in one go. "That's easy, that is. Don't you worry."

Moyles Court was bigger than Albion House. It had a number of large brick chimneys rising from its various parts and a large open courtyard. It was set in a clearing, with trees all around, although there were two small paddocks on the slope up to the Forest opposite. The manor's main fields lay on the Avon valley floor, not far away.

Betty was standing in the courtyard when the letter from Peter Albion was brought on Monday morning. The messenger who delivered it had already gone to Albion House and been sent on there.

It was brief. Peter's business in Kent had been cut short and he had returned to London only the day after they had left. He had been shocked to find them gone, because he had an important matter to discuss with her. He was following in person and expected to arrive at Albion House on Tuesday afternoon.

As she read, Betty felt her heart quicken. She had no doubt what this must mean. In her mind there was only one question, therefore: should she tell her mother before she went to Albion House, or not? She realised that the servants at Albion House would surely send him on to Moyles Court anyway. He'd be there by Tuesday evening. And whatever her feelings, Dame Alice could hardly send him away. She was receiving other visitors that evening, wasn't she? But all the same, the thought of going to meet him was attractive.

George Furzey waited until Tuesday morning before going over to Jim Pride's. He found the underkeeper leaving his lodge.

Jim wasn't particularly pleased to see him, but he was civil enough, as George delivered his message: "Dame Alice wants to see you at Moyles Court."

"Moyles Court?" Pride frowned. "I can't get over there till evening. I've got things to do."

"She don't want you there till evening. She said she's out till dusk anyway but wants you to come by after that. She said sorry to ask you to come so late but it's urgent." He felt pretty pleased with this.

"What does she want me for?" the puzzled underkeeper asked.

"I don't know, do I?"

"How come it's you bringing me this message?" Pride demanded with a trace of irritation.

"How come it's me? 'Cause I was going by Albion House, that's why. And the groom said he had to go on with a message, but he was late, so I said I'd take it for him. That's why. I'm just being helpful, aren't I? There something wrong with that?"

No. No, Pride allowed, there was nothing wrong with that.

"You be sure to go, mind. I don't want to get blamed if you don't show up."

"I'll go," Pride promised.

"All right then," said Furzey. "I'm off."

The early evening was warm as William Furzey rode out of Ringwood, where he had borrowed a horse from a blacksmith he knew. There were two hours to go before dusk, so he took his time.

The River Avon between Ringwood and Fordingbridge is particularly lovely. Often, towards evening, when the fishermen come out, there is a magical mist that drifts across its watery meadows, as if the silence itself had coalesced into a damp but tangible form. The first hint of such a mist was just beginning to arise on the water as Furzey rode northwards through the dappled shadows cast, like fishermen's lines, across the lane.

Would they come? He certainly hoped so. He wondered how much the authorities would think they were worth. Five pounds, perhaps? Ten? What if they were captured on the way, though? Possible, but it seemed to him unlikely. He guessed the authorities would rather take them together with

Dame Alice, whom they could not possibly like, at Moyles Court.

He rode along cheerfully, therefore.

Stephen Pride had been feeling his age a bit that day, but he kept himself cheerful. A few aches and pains were to be expected. A walk usually eased the stiffness in his leg. It was because of the pain there, although he didn't care to admit it, that he had set off in the afternoon to call upon his son.

Jim Pride had been out when his father arrived, but his wife and children had been there and Stephen had spent a pleasant hour playing with his grandchildren. The youngest, a four-year-old boy, had insisted on making his grandfather try to catch him, which had left old Stephen a little more tired than he wanted the child to see. He was grateful when his kindly daughter-in-law took pity on him and called the children indoors for a while so that he could sit in the shade of a tree and take a nap.

Jim returned just after he awoke and told him about the message from Dame Alice. Stephen had no more idea than his son what this might be about, but agreed that if Dame Alice wanted him, he should certainly go.

At their insistence, he remained with Jim and his wife until early evening.

The lengthening shadows were providing a pleasant coolness under the blue August sky by the time Stephen Pride made his way slowly along the edge of Beaulieu Heath towards Oakley; and he had just passed the path that led across to Boldre church when he caught sight of a figure a little way ahead. It was a lone, mounted woman, quite motionless, gazing out across the heath, apparently unaware of his approach. Only as he drew close, and she turned to look at him, did he realise it was Betty Lisle.

She greeted him affectionately. "I'm waiting for my cousin Peter Albion," she explained.

She had been at Albion House since early afternoon. Rather than risk a confrontation, she had finally decided to tell her mother she was going for a ride in this direction; that way she could meet Peter without interference and return with him to Moyles Court in the evening.

Her mother had raised no objection to her ride and she had arrived at Albion House in good time; but there had been no sign of Peter. All afternoon she had waited at the house but at last, unable to bear it any longer, she had told the servants to keep her cousin there if he turned up from the Lyndhurst road and had gone out to the edge of the heath to watch, in case he decided to cut across that way. She was glad to see Stephen; at least she could talk to him and take her mind off her vigil.

Stephen was interested to hear about this cousin. He knew the Albions well enough to understand at once who Peter was. He told Betty that he could even remember seeing the young man's grandfather, Francis, once when he had been a boy.

"I meant to return with him to Moyles Court this evening," she told him. "If he doesn't come soon, I don't know what I should do. Go back without him, I suppose."

Pride told her next about the message Dame Alice had sent to Jim.

This puzzled her. "As my mother knew I was coming this way, I'd have thought she'd have asked me to carry the message," she remarked. "I didn't see any groom go off. Still," she added, "I suppose it's something to do with the men who are coming to the house this evening." And she told Pride briefly of the stranger who'd been brought to Moyles Court three days before.

Soon after this, Pride went upon his way.

William Furzey waited quietly. The shadows cast by the departing sun had merged into a general orange glow and then into brownness. The mist was spreading in ghostly patches all over the meadows. The Avon valley had entered a slow summer gloaming as the first stars appeared over the Forest in a pale turquoise sky.

He saw them now: three horsemen, coming quietly through the mists towards him.

George Furzey couldn't help it. It was more than he could bear. He put his two hands between his knees and rocked back and forth for joy, murmuring: "Oh my. Oh my."

In the east, the first faint stars were just appearing. Had the horsemen come to William by now? Possibly. Had Jim Pride left on his fool's errand? Any time now. Furzey had been so

excited he couldn't stay in his cottage. He'd come out into
the warm evening, found a fallen birch tree by the edge of the
heath and sat there, gazing with rapture at the beauty of the
sky. He rocked himself again. "Oh my."

And this was how Stephen Pride found him as he arrived,
rather weary after his long day, back at Oakley. "Well," he remarked, "you're looking cheerful for once, George Furzey."

George Furzey really couldn't help it. All his life, it seemed
to him, the Pride family had been looking down at him. But not
any more. Not after tonight. "Maybe I am cheerful. I reckon I
can be cheerful if I want," he replied.

"You be as happy as you like," said Pride. Was there a hint
of contempt in his voice?

Even if there wasn't, this was what Furzey heard. "Some
people may be laughing the other side of their faces, Stephen
Pride," he said with a note of malicious triumph that couldn't
be mistaken. "Some may, before long."

"Oh?" Pride looked at him carefully. "And what do you
mean by that?"

"Never you mind. I don't mean nothing. Or if I do, it ain't
none of your concern. Or if it is" – Furzey warmed to his
theme – "you'll find out when you find out, won't you?"

And rather pleased with this bit of high diplomacy, Furzey
gave him a look which, even in the fading light, plainly said
"You've got something coming to you."

Stephen Pride shrugged and walked on. This unexpected
aggression left him feeling suddenly very tired.

When he reached the door of his home, his wife took one
look at him and made him sit down at once. "I'll bring you
some broth. You rest a while," she commanded.

He leaned back and closed his eyes. Perhaps, he thought,
he'd just sleep a few minutes. But instead of sleeping he found
the events of the last few hours passing through his mind:
playing with his grandchildren, talking to Jim, meeting Betty;
the strange fact that she knew nothing about the message
Furzey had brought; the visitors coming to Moyles Court that
night; Furzey's unusual air of triumph.

Suddenly, he sat bold upright, with a shock – as though a
flash of lightning had passed, with a great thunderclap,
through his brain. A moment later a tide of cold panic surged

through him. He was horribly awake. "Lord Jesus," he cried and stood up, as his wife hurried anxiously to his side. "That devil!" he exclaimed. He did not know exactly what this business meant, but he saw the shape of it. The message Furzey had delivered must be a fake. That's why he was so pleased with himself. He had Jim going over to Moyles Court where visitors were expected. No doubt they were dissenters. Dissenters? Fugitives, more like. That was it. The Forest man's instincts told him at once that it was a trap.

"Got to get the ponies," he cried, pushing past his wife. "Don't worry," he explained, as he checked himself and gave her a kiss. "I haven't lost my wits. Come with me."

By the barn, saddling up both their ponies with feverish haste he explained to her what he knew. "You better take the small pony. Get up to Jim's, fast as you can. If he hasn't gone, tell him to stay home, but don't tell him why. I don't want him coming after me, see? Just tell him George Furzey made a mistake."

"What'll you do?"

"Go and warn them at Albion House. Tell them to stay put if they haven't gone."

"And then?"

"I'll ride across the Forest. Cut Jim off if you miss him. Then I'll go on to Moyles Court."

"Oh, Stephen . . ."

"I've got to. If it's a trap, that means Dame Alice . . ."

She nodded. There was no argument. Minutes later, husband and wife were cantering along the edge of the heath northwards. The dusk was gathering, but even the stars would be enough for these two, who knew every inch of the Forest. At the place where the track led towards Albion House, Stephen Pride and his wife of fifty years paused for a moment and kissed, before riding their separate ways.

"God protect you," she murmured, as she glanced back, with love and fear in her heart, at the dark path through the trees into which he had vanished.

Colonel Thomas Penruddock stared at William Furzey in the candlelight of the hall of the magistrate's house at Hale.

Although he had looked pleased with himself when he first

arrived, Furzey was a little nervous now. With their braided
uniforms and yellow sashes, their huge riding boots with folding tops, their broad leather belts and clanking swords the
colonel and his dozen men seemed larger than life.

"You are sure these men are at Moyles Court?" Colonel
Penruddock demanded severely.

But about this Furzey seemed confident. "They were when
I left them," he said. "That's for sure."

"We leave here at midnight," Penruddock ordered his men.
"We'll surround the house and move in before dawn. That's the
time to catch them off guard." He turned to Furzey. "You will
remain here until morning." Having completed his orders,
Colonel Thomas Penruddock bade his cousin goodnight and
went to an upstairs chamber and lay down.

But he did not sleep.

Alice Lisle. This was the third time she had come into his
life. Once when she murdered his father; once when he had
found her with the king; and now, caught with traitors. This
time, surely, would be the last: the completion.

Retribution. It was not only his father. She represented
everything he hated: those sour Puritan looks, that humourless
self-righteousness; the Puritans, it seemed to him, believed
that God's kingdom was only served by the cruel destruction
of all that was lovely, chivalrous, gallant. Alice Lisle the
Cromwellian, the regicide, the thief of other men's estates, the
murderer. This was how he saw her. How could it be otherwise?

Yet as he lay there, a colonel surrounded by his troops, with
all the authority of the kingdom behind him, Thomas
Penruddock found that he was conscious above all of his
power. The evil old woman down at Moyles Court seemed in
his mind's eye no less hateful, but small and frail. Like some
vicious old fox that has terrorised an area for many seasons,
she was in her decline now and all nature called for her to die.
He was not going to destroy the woman, he told himself; he
was just going, as one goes to a guttering candle, to snuff her
out.

Peter Albion had taken longer than he expected and Betty had
almost given up when at last, just as it was getting dark, he ar-

rived. He looked tired. At the suggestion that they might ride on across the Forest to Moyles Court that night he looked dismayed; and Betty was just wondering what to do when Stephen Pride arrived.

"I thought you'd still be here," he said. "I got a message for you."

He'd had to think hard on the way. If he told Betty the truth, that her mother was in danger, he was afraid she might go running back to Moyles Court whatever anyone said. So he'd prepared a lie – not a very good one, but he thought it would do.

"I just sent the groom back to your mother. Met him at Boldre bridge. I told him you were here. She says to stay. She doesn't want you riding across the Forest at night." The obvious relief on Peter Albion's face told him he need say no more.

"Thank you, Stephen." She smiled. "I don't think my cousin Peter has any desire to ride more today."

The young man smiled, too, and Pride nodded his head politely. A handsome young man, he thought. Just right for Betty. It seemed to him that Betty might think so, too. "I'll be getting home then," he said as casually as he could and rode back to the lane.

A minute later he was urging his pony forward as fast as he could, up the lane towards the quiet little ford. Soon after, he had crossed it and was making his way swiftly up the long track that led to the western heath.

There was no time to lose. Jim might be out there, ahead of him somewhere. And at Moyles Court Dame Alice had probably already received her visitors. Had the trap been sprung by now? Late at night was more likely, he thought. Such things were usually done late at night.

His heart was beating fast. He felt a little light-headed as he came out on to the edge of the western heath by Setley. It was many a year since he'd gone rushing about all day and all night like this. His physical exhaustion seemed to have evaporated, though. He was too nervous and too excited to be tired.

The stars were gleaming brightly now. He decided to cut straight up north, skirting Brockenhurst, then take the track that led out above Burley. That was the way Jim would be going. He pushed his pony along. Thank God it was a sturdy little creature. That pony could carry him all day . . . and all night.

He skirted Brockenhurst. Ahead of him lay a section of forest known as Rhinefield. A quarter-moon was rising. Its light caught the pale sand and gravel along the path. It was like a silver trail of stardust across the heather.

On any other errand his heart would have filled with joy at such a sight – the open heath of the Forest under starlight, the Forest he loved. His heart was pounding. He took deep gasps of the warm August air. The hoofs of his pony were beating, beating upon the path.

There was something out there, ahead of him. He felt a little strange. Something pale out on the heath: cattle probably. No, the moon. The moon was on the heath. He shook his head to clear it. And then a great white flash, like lightning, came with an awesome thunder into his head.

And just short of Rhinefield, Stephen Pride, having suffered a single stroke, fell on to the gentle warmth of the Forest floor.

Alice Lisle stood at the open window and looked out.

Above the trees on the small ridge opposite the starlit sky had clouded over, as though it had been muffled with a blanket. Moyles Court was quiet in the silence before the dawn.

No one had come since the visitors had arrived that evening. She had not been surprised when Betty did not arrive back, for the simple reason that she knew exactly where Betty was. A message from Tryphena on Sunday had warned her that young Mr Albion had arrived back in London early and that, having called at the house, he was almost certainly on his way to the Forest. Betty's suggestion that she should ride to Albion House hadn't deceived her mother for a moment.

She hadn't tried to stop her. If young Peter Albion was as determined as that, and if her twenty-four-year-old daughter had deceived her in order to meet him, it was clear that there was nothing more she could do. Albion House, quite likely, would return to the Albions. It was fate. Whatever her reservations, young Peter was actually a better match than any of her other daughters had found: better placed to succeed, more gently born. Perhaps it was the result of being back in the familiar surroundings of the Forest, but it seemed to her now that if this was what Betty chose it was useless to fight it any more.

But now, suddenly, there was shouting in the dark. Men were moving outside. There was a bang at the door. She heard a voice.

"Open! In the name of the king."

More bangs. Alice ran to the next chamber. Dunne and Hicks were in there. "Wake up!" she cried. "Quickly. You must hide." The other man, Nelthorpe, was in the next room. She found him roused already, pulling on his boots.

They ran down the oak staircase, all four of them, in the darkness, the men clumping so loudly in their boots that it was hard to believe they wouldn't be heard at Ringwood.

"The back," she hissed, leading the way to the kitchens. But even as they got there they could see shadows outside the window there. "Hide as best you can," she told them and hurried to the stairs. Running up, her heart beating wildly, she found two of the servants already standing on the landing, looking pale and frightened. "Close the beds," she whispered, indicating the two rooms where the men had been. "Leave no sign. Quickly." The hammering on the doors, both front and back, was growing louder. Another minute and they might start to break them down. Again she raced downstairs, seized a candle from a table where she had left it the night before, lit it from the glowing embers of the fire and went to the door. Taking a deep breath she began to turn the heavy key and slip the big iron bolt. The last thing she thought, before she opened the door, was that she must not show fear.

Thomas Penruddock looked down at the woman before him.

She was in her nightdress, a shawl covering her shoulders. Her hair, mostly grey, was hanging loose. Even in the candlelight she looked pale. She stared at him. "What is the meaning of this, Sir?"

"In the king's name, Madam, we are to search your house."

"Search my house, Sir? In the middle of the night?"

"Yes, Madam. And you will let us in."

There were two large troopers behind the colonel, Alice now realised. They looked as if they were about to push past her. She tried to appear calm.

But it was at this moment that she also realised her terrible mistake. If the troops entered the house, was there really any chance they wouldn't find the three men? If they had been sleeping innocently, it might not look so bad, but the fact that she was trying to hide them suggested guilt. What could she do? A panic seized her; she saw that her hand, holding the candle, had started to shake. She fought to master herself. Perhaps she could bluff. It was her only hope now. "By what warrant do you dare to invade my house, Sir?" She stared at him haughtily.

"My warrant is the king's name, Madam."

"Produce your warrant, Sir," she cried furiously, although she hadn't the least idea if a warrant were needed or not, "or be gone." Did he hesitate? She wasn't sure. "So," she cried again, "I see you have none. You are nothing but common trespassers, then." And she started to close the door.

Penruddock's boot was in the way A moment later the two troopers had pushed rudely past her. Then two more, out of the shadows, came blundering in.

"Lights," voices were calling. "Bring lights."

It did not take long to find them. Beyond the kitchen lay a large, barn-like room known as the malt-house. Hicks the minister, who was a large, corpulent man, and Dunne the baker had tried to bury themselves under a pile of refuse in there and were dragged out, looking foolish. Hicks's companion Nelthorpe, a tall, thin fellow, had tried to hide in the kitchen chimney.

Penruddock addressed them briefly. "Richard Nelthorpe, you have already been outlawed as a rebel; John Hicks, you also are known to have been with Monmouth; James Dunne, you are their willing accomplice. You are all arrested. Alice Lisle," he added crossly, "you are harbouring traitors."

"I am giving shelter to a respectable minister," she retorted scornfully.

"To traitors fleeing, Madam, from Monmouth's rebellion."

"I know nothing of that, Sir," she replied.

"A judge and jury will decide that. You are under arrest."

"I?" She glanced down at her nightdress. "And what sort of soldier are you, Sir," she said with contempt, "who comes to arrest women in the night?" She defied him; she despised him openly in front of his own troops.

How strange it was, he thought. He had expected to find an evil old witch; instead he found that same haughty, forceful woman who even now was ready to stare him down. Just as they had once before, the years seemed to fall away and he was looking at the terrible figure of vengeance who, if he were still alive, would strike his poor father down again. As she stared at him with those cold grey eyes, he could almost have trembled. And, taken by surprise, he suddenly felt, like a blow to the stomach, all the old pain of the loss of the father he had so loved. To his utter astonishment he found he had to turn away.

It was not so much with anger as with pain that, striding out into the darkness, he called back: "Arrest them all."

It took some minutes before they were brought out. He did not bother to interfere. When they came he saw that Alice was still dressed only in her nightclothes. He also observed that one of the troopers had obviously appropriated a silver candlestick and some linen. He did not care.

"Where are we going?" cried Dunne.

"To Salisbury gaol," he answered bleakly. And off they went, with Dame Alice incongruously made to ride pillion behind one of the troopers.

He shouldn't have allowed it, Thomas Penruddock thought, but he truly didn't care.

On 24 August in the Year of Our Lord 1685 there arrived near the city of Winchester a large cavalcade. Five judges, a flock of lawyers, Jack Ketch, the official and highly incompetent executioner, marshals, clerks, servants and outriders – the whole panoply of justice needed, in the reign of His Majesty King James II of England, to hang, decapitate, burn, whip or transport to the colonies the more than twelve hundred men unlucky enough to be caught after marching with Monmouth. At the head of this great legal deputation, as promised, was no less a personage than the Right Honourable George, Lord Chief Justice Jeffreys.

The assize which was to be held down in the West Country, after executing three hundred and thirty and sending eight hundred and fifty to the American plantations, would be known as the Bloody Assize; the presiding judge would go down in English history as Bloody Jeffreys. But before that great business began an introduction was to be held in the great hall of Winchester Castle: the trial of Alice Lisle.

As she looked around the great stone hall of the Norman and Plantagenet kings, Betty could not help being impressed by the ancient majesty of the setting. A soft afternoon light filtered into the church-like space through the pointed windows. On the dais sat the five judges in their scarlet robes and long white wigs; below them the lawyers and clerks like so many black old birds; before them a crowd of people. And alone, dressed in grey, sitting quietly in an oak chair on a raised platform, was her mother.

In a place of such solemnity, thought Betty, before such reverend and learned men, justice would surely be done and her mother – as Peter had explained the law to her – should undoubtedly go free. She glanced at Tryphena, who was sitting beside her and gave her an encouraging smile. On her other side Peter squeezed her hand.

The case to answer was straightforward. Her mother had taken in three men for the night. One, poor Dunne, was a comparative nonentity; Hicks the preacher was accused, but not yet convicted of treason; the third, Nelthorpe, had been outlawed.

"The case is dangerous," Peter had explained, "because it's treason. If you help a felon who's running away you are an accessory after the fact; but you are not held to be guilty of the felon's crime. With high treason, however, the case is different. If you give any aid to a known traitor you, too, are guilty of treason. That's your mother's danger. However," he had continued, "the prosecutor will have to show that she *knew* these men were part of Monmouth's rebellion. Nelthorpe she'd never seen before and she knew nothing about him. Furthermore, he was brought by a man known to be a reputable minister, namely Hicks. So," he expounded, "she takes in a respectable dissenter and a friend for the night – the sort of thing she's often done before. Does she know they're traitors? No. Unless someone can prove she had knowledge, most juries would give her the benefit of the doubt." He smiled. "I say she has committed no crime."

"As soon as she is acquitted, Peter," Betty had said, "I think we should celebrate."

He had asked her to marry him that very first night he had arrived in the Forest and, had it not been for the arrest, they would have spoken to Dame Alice about it the next morning. Since then, while the family was turned upside down, she had asked him not to speak of it; but as soon as this terrible business was over and things returned to normal she intended to tell her mother and get married as quickly as possible. "By Christmas," she had indicated.

For the next few hours she must put Peter out of her mind, though. She must see her mother safely acquitted.

It was late afternoon when the trial began.

The business started blandly enough. Witnesses said they had seen Hicks the minister with Monmouth's troops. Dunne the baker was called, to describe how he had gone upon the Saturday and Tuesday to Moyles Court. But then something strange occurred. Instead of interrogating Dunne, the prosecutor suddenly said he wished Judge Jeffreys to question Dunne himself. Betty looked at Peter, who only shrugged with surprise.

At first Judge Jeffreys seemed rather gentle. His broad, rather skull-like face bent forward, he called Dunne "friend" and reminded him that he must take great care to tell the truth. Dunne, his watery blue eyes looking hopeful, began his tale and got one sentence out.

But then, at once, Judge Jeffreys interrupted. "Take care, friend. Begin again. When do you say you first set out?" Another sentence or two and another interruption. "Sayest thou so? I know more than you think. How did you find Moyles Court?"

"With the help of a guide named Thomas."

"Where is he? Let him stand up."

To Betty's astonishment, William Furzey stood up. So this was the mysterious Thomas. But what did it mean?

Judge Jeffreys was in full flood, now, pausing for nothing. Dunne was asked a question, then immediately cross-questioned. Within minutes it was clear he was getting confused. Trying not to incriminate Furzey, whom he had not yet understood to be the one who gave him away, he foolishly said that Furzey had not brought them to Moyles Court the second time and was soon lost in a quagmire of contradictions.

"Alack-a-day!" cried Jeffreys with cruel sarcasm. "Come, re-fresh your memory a little." As the unhappy baker's watery eyes grew desperate, it seemed to Betty that the judge was like a cat, playing with a mouse. Increasingly confused, Dunne contra-dicted a tiny detail of something he had said before.

Jeffreys pounced. "Wretch!" His voice thundered so that the whole courtroom seemed to shudder. "Dost thou think the God of heaven not to be a God of truth? 'Tis only His mercy that He does not immediately strike thee into hell! Jesus God!" And for two entire minutes, glowering at the poor baker, the most powerful judge in the kingdom, with life and death in his hands, raved and bellowed at him until he was shaking so much it was obvious that nothing more could be got from him.

Betty herself was white. She glanced at Peter.

His mouth was open in astonishment. But he did lean down and whisper in her ear: "He still has no evidence that could convict."

Furzey was called, but only briefly, to relate what he saw. One thing he said seemed to interest Jeffreys.

"You say Dunne told you that Dame Alice asked him if you knew what business he had come upon?"

"That's right."

It was poor Dunne's turn to be questioned again – if that was what the process could be called. For the baker was now in a state of such fear and confusion that he was hardly coherent. What was the business, demanded Jeffreys. What business? The baker looked uncertain. Again and again the judge pounded, shouted, cursed. Dunne stuttered, finally fell silent. For long minutes he seemed to fall into a kind of trance.

The light from the windows was dimmer now, the great hall shadowy. A clerk lit a candle.

Then at last Dunne seemed to recover a little. "The busi-ness, my Lord?"

"Blessed God! You villain. Yes. The business."

"It was that Mr Hicks was a dissenter."

"That is all?"

"Yes, My Lord. There is nothing more."

Betty felt Peter touch her arm. "Our friend Dunne has beaten this judge," he whispered.

But not, it seemed, without a fight.

"Liar! You think you can banter me with such sham stuff as this?" He turned to the clerk. "Bring that candle. Hold the candle to his brazen face."

And poor Dunne, quaking again, cried out: "My Lord, tell me what you would have me say, for I am cluttered out of my senses."

Betty watched in horror. This was not a court of law. It was an interrogation. What would they do next? Torture the baker in public? She looked across at her mother.

And looked again, in astonishment.

For in the midst of all this, Dame Alice had fallen asleep.

Not asleep. Not really. But Alice had lived too long, seen too much. She remembered the Civil War, the trial of King Charles, so many other trials, her husband's fate. She knew already which way this business must end.

She would not show her fear. She was afraid. She wanted to tremble; she could have screamed at the terrible, cruel stupidity of it all. But there was no point. She already knew it and she would not give them the satisfaction of seeing her fear. So she closed her eyes.

They brought Colonel Penruddock on next. He was brief and factual. He said how he'd found the men hiding. He also said that Furzey had told him Dunne had hinted that the men were probably rebels. So they hauled the baker on to the stand again and asked him what he meant. But he stuttered now so hopelessly that he didn't even make sense. They had nothing.

They called one of the troopers who had been in the house making the arrests and who declared that the men were obviously rebels; but this testimony was so useless that even the judge soon waved him away.

But now, it seemed to Dame Alice, that she had a small opportunity. Pretending to wake, she stared at the trooper and then called out: "Why, My Lord, this is the man who stole my best linen."

But it did no good. Jeffreys passed rapidly on to other matters until at last he came to Alice: what, he demanded contemptuously, had she to say for herself?

It was simple enough. She told him she'd stayed in London

throughout Monmouth's rebellion. He interrupted this statement twice. She had no quarrel with the king. He treated this with contempt. She had no idea that her visitors were involved in the rebellion. She even produced a witness who swore that Nelthorpe the outlaw had never said his name.

But Judge Jeffreys knew how to deal with that. "We have heard enough," he cried. "Send this witness away." He turned savagely back to Alice. "Have you more witnesses to call?"

"No, My Lord."

"Very well." He turned to the jury. "Gentlemen of the jury," he began.

"There is, My Lord, one point of law," Alice now interrupted.

"Silence!" he cried. "Too late."

There was, quite clearly, no valid case against her. This did not slow Judge Jeffreys in his flow. He reminded the jury that the Lisles were regicides, that dissenters were natural criminals, that Monmouth's rebellion was horrible and that Monmouth's morals were unclean. That this was all both nonsense and irrelevant was not, to the judge, important.

Only at the end of his tirade did one of the jurymen ask a question. "Pray, My Lord," he desired to know, "is it a crime to receive Hicks the preacher if he has not yet been convicted, but only accused of treason?"

"A vital point of law," Peter whispered to Betty.

Indeed, it was the only point of law raised in the entire trial. For under English law you could not be accused as an accessory when the person you helped had merely been accused, but not convicted, of treason. Clearly this was only right, since otherwise an accessory might be sentenced for helping a man who was afterwards judged to be innocent. As Hicks was still awaiting trial, he wasn't yet a traitor. The case against Alice, feeble as it already was, would completely fall to the ground.

The Lord Chief Justice saw the trap. "It is all the same," he blandly declared. And the court was silent.

"That's a lie," Peter whispered. "That's not the law."

"Say something," Betty whispered back.

But the four judges beside Jeffreys, and the lawyers and the clerks, were all silent.

. . .

The jury returned in half an hour. They said she was not guilty.

Judge Jeffreys refused to accept their verdict and sent them away again. They came back a second time and said she was not guilty. He sent them off again. A third time they came and said the same.

And now Judge Jeffreys swore an oath. "Villains," he cried, "do you dare to mock this court? Do you not understand I can attaint every one of you for treason too?"

They came back once more after that and found her guilty.

Then Judge Jeffreys sentenced her to burn.

The room was not large, but it was clean and light. The bars on the window were not too noticeable. It was still morning. They could be grateful for these small mercies at least.

Dame Alice was not to be burned. The bishop and clergy of Winchester had appealed at once to the king. They did not want such a thing done in their cathedral city. Quite apart from anything, as news of the outrageous trial spread through the city and across the Forest, they were afraid of a riot. Today, then, in the afternoon, Dame Alice Lisle was to have her head struck off.

There were only Betty and Tryphena with her now. The others had all gone: children and grandchildren, she had said goodbye to them all. The room was quiet.

Peter was in London. Betty had not spoken of him to her mother and, strangely, she had not thought of him so much. Perhaps, if they had known each other longer, she might have wanted him there to support her. But instead, she had been so drawn into her own family and into the terrible business in hand that he had seemed to drift away in her mind, like a visitor after whose departure the door has been closed.

"Peter Albion." It was her mother who said the words and Betty looked at her in surprise. Dame Alice smiled. "I did not want to speak of him with the others present." She looked at Betty thoughtfully. "Do you still want to marry him?"

She had never actually confessed that she did, but there was no time for such prevarications now. "I don't know," she replied honestly.

Her mother nodded slowly. Tryphena, her narrow face

looking up suddenly, seemed about to say something but Alice cut in ahead. "I think better of him than I did," she said firmly. "This trial has been very good for him."

"But it was a mockery. An outrage. It wasn't justice at all," Tryphena interjected.

"That's why it was so good for him," said Alice evenly. "I thought him rather arrogant. Now he has seen that even the law may be bent to necessity. He is humbler."

"There is" – Betty hesitated, glanced at her mother and her sister and gave a small shrug – "something else."

"Tell me."

So Betty explained about the moment during the trial when Jeffreys had so flagrantly misled the jury, and how Peter had told her the judge had lied. "It wasn't the law. And I whispered that he should say something."

"You wanted him to stand up and contradict the judge?"

"Well . . ." It was hard to say quite, but she knew that she had thought about it afterwards and somehow his conduct had seemed . . . unsatisfactory.

"The other judges said nothing. The lawyers said nothing. You said nothing," her mother reminded her wryly.

"I know. I'm so sorry."

"Don't be silly, child. What you mean is that the man who wants to marry you proved to be less than perfect. He decided not to be heroic." She shook her head and sighed. "Do not fall into the trap of looking for a perfect husband. Women of your age often do. You'll never find him. Consider also, my child, if a husband were perfect, you'd have to be perfect too."

"But . . ."

"You saw a moment of cowardice?"

"Yes. I suppose so."

"Which I call discretion."

"I know. But . . ." Betty was not sure how to explain it, the silence that had fallen upon Peter at that moment in the court. It was not so much what he had done as the insight she had suddenly gained, just then, for the first time, of his inner nature. There was a wariness there, a calculation, a readiness, behind all his talk, to make deep compromises. "It was something," she said uncertainly, "in his nature . . ."

"Thank God." Alice sighed. "Perhaps he will survive."

"But my father did not compromise. He did what was right."

"Against my wishes. To further his own ambition. And your father was on the winning side. That makes men bold. Until, of course, he lost and had to run away."

"Yet what of right and wrong, Mother? Are they not important?"

"Oh, yes, child. Of course they are. It's not in doubt. But there is something else equally important. As I get older, I wonder if it is not more so."

"Which is?"

"God's gift to Solomon, Betty. Wisdom."

"Ah. I see."

"Don't marry Peter unless you both have a little wisdom." Her mother smiled at her very sweetly. "You'll be surprised how easy it is to be good if you are wise."

"You must be very wise, Mother."

Alice laughed quietly. "How fortunate, when I'm to lose my head this afternoon."

None of them said anything after that for a little while, each sitting silently with her thoughts.

Finally, it was neither Betty nor her mother, but Tryphena who spoke. "They say," she said thoughtfully, "that after a head is severed, life does not instantly depart; but the head remains conscious for a moment or two. It may blink or even try to speak."

This was greeted with silence.

"Thank you, dear," Alice said softly, after a pause. "You are a great comfort to me."

A further short silence ensued before Alice slowly got up. "I am ready to end my life now, my dear children, for I have nothing more to say. Let me embrace you, then you should go. I find I am a little tired."

They had set up the scaffold in Winchester's old market place. Half the population of the city had gathered there and many from the Forest, too. The Prides were there. So were the two Furzey brothers, although the Prides entirely ignored them.

She looked pale and smaller than the crowd had imagined when they brought her out. Her hair, just a few sad strands of red remaining in the grey, had been scooped up on top of her head and tied, leaving her bare neck looking thin and rather scrawny. There was to be no address on this occasion for she had not wished to make one.

The fact was that Alice was now in something of a daze. A few minutes before, with a large trooper on each side towering above her, she had known great fear. But now, like an animal which, at the end of a long chase, knows that it can do no more, and that the desperate game is up, she had yielded finally to resignation. She felt limp and numb, and she wanted only to get it over.

She scarcely saw the faces as they led her out. She didn't see Betty, nor the Prides, nor the Furzeys. She didn't see, some way off, Thomas Penruddock with a sad, grave face, sitting on his horse.

She saw the block as they helped her kneel down beside it, but scarcely took note of the axe. She saw the wooden boards, clumsily nailed, just below the block as they stretched out her neck upon it. And she realised that there would be a mighty bite, a blow that would crunch through her neck bones as the axe fell.

The axe fell and she was conscious of the huge thud.

It must have been a summer day, as they walked along the lane and turned down the track into the wood. The sun was slanting through the light-green lattice of the canopy; the saplings spread their leaves like trails of vapour through the underwood; birds were singing. She was so pleased that she had started to skip; and her father was holding her hand.

Albion Park

1794

There could be no doubt, no doubt of it at all: great things were afoot in Lymington nowadays – indeed, in the whole Forest.

"And when you think," said Mrs Grockleton to her husband, "when you think of Mr Morant at Brockenhurst Park with I don't know how many thousands a year and Mr Drummond now at Cadland, and Miss . . ." For a moment her memory failed her.

"Miss Albion?"

"Why, yes, to be sure, Miss Albion, who must have a large inheritance . . ."

It was no doubt part of the divine plan that, having been endowed with an insatiable desire to rise in society, Mrs Grockleton had also been created absent-minded. Only the week before, showing her children to a visiting clergyman, she had told him there were five, pointing them out by name, until her husband had gently reminded her that there were six, causing her to exclaim: "Why so there are, indeed! Here's dear little Johnnie. I had quite forgot him."

Her ambition, like her absent-mindedness, was quite without malice. It was, for her, a little ladder to a humble heaven. It brought with it, however, certain small peculiarities. Whether it was because she thought it a kind of wit, or whether she supposed it indicated her own roots in some gentle antiquity, she liked to use expressions or exclamations that hearkened from a former time. She would pick these up from

487

time to time and use them for several years before moving on to others. At present, if she wished to convey something of particular significance, she would say: "Methinks . . ." Or if she broke a cup, or told a funny story of a vicar getting drunk, she would conclude: "Alack-a-day." Expressions so dated that you might really suppose she had been present at the court of the merry monarch himself.

She was also the mistress, or at least the devotee, of the meaningful gaze. She would fix you with her dark-brown eyes and give you a look of such arch significance that, even if you had no notion what it meant, you felt privileged. When the look was accompanied by "Methinks . . ." you really knew you were in for something, quite possibly a state secret.

And when you considered that she was the daughter of a Bristol haberdasher and her husband a Customs officer, these social marvels could only be described as a triumph of the human spirit.

Mrs Grockleton was of medium height, but with a fine display of powdered hair. Her husband was tall and lean with hands curiously like claws. Mrs Grockleton's intention, which she planned to achieve as soon as she could, was to raise Lymington to the status of a social centre to rival Bath. And then to preside over it.

Samuel Grockleton inwardly groaned. It is not easy for a man to know that his wife is careering unstoppably towards her social doom, especially when he himself, through no fault of his own, must be the cause of the disaster. "You must not forget our own position in society, Mrs Grockleton," he observed. "And given my office, we can never raise our hopes *too* high."

"Your position is very respectable, Mr Grockleton. Quite gentlemanly."

"Respectable, yes."

"Why, Mr Grockleton, I declare you are held in great esteem and affection. Everyone has told me so."

"Neighbours are not always truthful."

"Oh, fie, Mr Grockleton," said his wife cheerfully. And a moment later she was off again, explaining her plans for the future.

You could say what you liked about Mrs Grockleton, but she

was never idle. She had not been a month in Lymington when she saw that it had need of an academy for young ladies; and since it happened that a lease was available on the big brick house next to their own, which lay a little way past the church at the top of the High Street, she had persuaded her husband to take it and here she had set up her establishment.

She had been skilful. First she had secured the mayor's daughter and her best friend whose father, an attorney, belonged to a landed family in the next county. Next she had gone to the Tottons. They lived nowadays in a handsome house just apart from the town. Although Mr Totton was certainly involved in the town's trade, his sister had married old Mr Albion of Albion House, so the young Tottons and Miss Albion were cousins. Edward Totton was up at Oxford. When Louisa Totton was snared, therefore, Mrs Grockleton could reasonably feel that this advanced the academy into the sphere of the local gentry. At the apex of the merchant families was another, more recently arrived in the area: Mr St Barbe gave his business as grocer, salt and coal merchant, but he was a most gentlemanly and philanthropic man, a pillar of the community. One of the St Barbe girls was duly obtained. Within a few months, by allowing some girls to come for only certain lessons and others, from further off, to board there, Mrs Grockleton had drifted almost twenty young ladies into her academic corral.

The academy had two features of which she was particularly proud. It taught French, which was done by herself. She had acquired this fashionable accomplishment quite humbly as a girl from a French dressmaker in Bristol, but her fluency certainly reinforced her claims to social authority in Lymington. And while a command of French would undoubtedly be an asset to any of the daughters of Lymington merchants who wanted to shine in the great London houses or the courts of Europe, it was surely an inducement that they could also practise upon the charming young French officers who had recently been stationed in the town.

The second was the art class. The Reverend William Gilpin had not only been the loved and respected vicar of Boldre for two decades; he was also a notable artist, selling his drawings and paintings from time to time for charitable causes. Mrs

Grockleton had purchased two and, soon afterwards, when Mr
Gilpin arrived to award prizes in the academy, he was astonished to discover it was his own work that the young ladies
were instructed to emulate or even copy. The vicar was no
fool, but it was hard, after that, to refuse the invitation to deliver a lecture and take a class at the academy once a month;
and in fact he rather enjoyed it.

So Mrs Grockleton's academy grew. Its growth, so far as
Mrs Grockleton could manage, was spiral in form – starting
with the better families in the town, then sweeping round those
whose gentility had taken them to the environs and finally, cir-
cling ever wider, like a great, revolving seashell, she hoped to
suck young ladies even from the distant manor houses of the
gentry into the pleasant vortex of her establishment. Thus
Miss Fanny Albion had already come to join her cousin Louisa
Totton for the French classes – a triumph that had brought the
academic huntress a deep joy – and no doubt there would be
others. The one family she had hoped for, and which had so far
eluded her, was that of Burrard.

The Burrards were very big in Lymington now. While the
Tottons had remained, as it were, at the top of the town, the
bolder and now much richer Burrards had long ago acquired a
country estate called Walhampton, which lay on the other side
of the river from Lymington. Their generations of marriages
into gentry families like the Buttons had entirely established
them in that class. But Lymington town was their base of operations and they ran the politics of the place. She had not yet
managed to get past the Burrards' park gates. But one day, she
felt sure, she would. Indeed, if all her hopes succeeded, it was
inevitable that she must.

For the school was only the beginning. Her plans for
Lymington were far larger. "I can see it, Mr Grockleton," she
declared. And indeed she could. On the ridge overlooking
Pennington Marshes and the sea, there would be rows of handsome Georgian houses and villas: with its ample supply of
clay, the New Forest nowadays boasted a number of thriving
brickfields; but in her mind's eye she saw stone, like that at
Bath. Perhaps, she considered, stucco painted white would do.
The old medieval houses along the High Street, although still
structurally intact, had mostly received squared-off Georgian

façades by now. Any lingering medieval gables, she considered, could be quickly covered. The modest bathhouse down by the beach would be converted into something more like the Roman baths at the great spa in the west. The present Assembly Rooms, adjoining the Angel Inn, would of course be quite inadequate for the new resort. Something new, classical and splendid would be needed, up at the top of the hill, she supposed, very near her own house. Well, perhaps she'd be in something grander by then.

Then there was the theatre. It wasn't bad. Similar playhouses had been set up at Sarum and other western towns. It had a modest pit with wooden benches for the poorer sort, a tier of boxes for the gentry and a gallery of cheaper seats above. During the season, from July to October, you could hear Shakespeare, or one of Mr Sheridan's comedies, and a varied repertoire of melodramas and tragedies. Lymington theatre usually contrived one or two offerings with a nautical flavour. No doubt, once the town was fashionable, the theatre could be redecorated. Mrs Grockleton's only regret was that it should have been near the Baptist chapel which, as far as she was concerned, should be moved well away from the fashionable public's sight.

No, the only complaint she had about the town lay down by the beach itself. Those salterns, with their grubby little furnaces and windpumps, and the dock where ships from northern Newcastle brought coal – coal of all things! – to fuel the furnaces: something would have to be done about them. The salt pans might still bring profit to the Tottons, but if the fashionable world was to take the waters there, the salterns would have to go.

Was her vision just a fantasy all of her own? Not entirely. The New Forest, after all, was a place with royal connections. For over twenty years the king's brother, the Duke of Gloucester, had been Warden of the Forest; and since his wife wasn't welcome at court, he had often chosen to stay at Lyndhurst. The Prince of Wales came to stay in the Forest, too. But Mrs Grockleton's hopes grew out of larger considerations.

In the great political calm that had graced Georgian England for several generations now, society itself was changing. A burgeoning commercial empire was bringing the island kingdom huge new wealth. Although land inclosures and new production methods had taken the traditional livelihood from some peasant farmers, the landowners had prospered. In London and the handful of big cities that dotted the vast stretches of rural England, speculators were building handsome Georgian squares. People were moving about. Even the open wastes of the Forest were now crossed by a turnpike road – the first return to such a civilised transport system since Roman times. Like the latter-day Romans they were, the fashionable English classes were going in search of health and leisure. In the West Country the ancient Roman spa of Bath had been revived and a gracious resort built around its mineral springs. More recently the royal court of King George III, in the belief that it might help cure the king's bouts of madness, had become interested in the benefits not only of mineral waters but of those of the sea. Several times in recent years King George III had come to the New Forest on his way to the little seaside resort of Weymouth, some forty miles further west along the coast. He had stayed with the Drummonds and the Burrards, and visited the Isle of Wight.

"Why go all the way to Weymouth, when Lymington is so much closer and surely just as healthy?" Mrs Grockleton declared. People came to bathe at Lymington, some of them very respectable. If the king and his court made regular stays there the fashionable world would surely follow. "And then," she explained to her silent husband, "our own position, what with the academy and my other plans, is assured. For we shall, you see, be *there* already. They will come to *us*." She gave him a delighted smile. "I have not told you, Mr Grockleton, of my latest idea."

"And what is that?" he enquired, as he knew he must.

"Why, we are going to give a ball!"

"A ball? Dancing?"

"Indeed. At the Assembly Rooms. You see, Mr Grockleton, with our girls at the academy, their families and friends – don't you understand? Everyone will come!" She did not say so, but she had already secretly included the Burrards in this number.

"Perhaps," Mr Grockleton said sagely, "nobody will come."

"Oh, fie, Mr Grockleton," said Mrs Grockleton again, but this time with some asperity.

Yet Mr Grockleton had a reason for these fears – something he knew, which she did not. Unfortunately, he could not tell her what it was.

It might have been supposed that in Georgian England the age of miracles was passed. Yet at the very moment when Mrs Grockleton was chiding her husband for his lack of faith in Lymington – that is to say, at eleven o'clock that spring morning – a few miles away on the Beaulieu estate a miracle of sorts was in progress. It was happening at the busy place on the Beaulieu River known as Buckler's Hard.

There, in the bright morning sunlight, a man had become invisible.

The Hard – the name meant a sloping shore road where boats could be drawn up – had a lovely setting. As the river made a westward loop, broad banks created gentle slopes, almost two hundred yards long, down to the water. Situated some two miles downstream from the old abbey and the same distance upstream from the Solent water, it was a peaceful place, sheltered from the prevailing sea breezes. Once, long ago in the days of the monks, a furious prior with hands like claws had nearly come to blows with some fishermen at the river bend above. But his shouts had been one of the few to disturb the habitual silence of the sheltered curve and the reedy marshes opposite. The abbey had been dissolved, the monks departed; Armada, Civil War, Cromwell, the merry monarch, all had come and gone; but nobody had troubled about the quiet place. Until about seventy years earlier.

The reason was sugar.

Of all the opportunities for amassing wealth in the eighteenth century, nothing could approach the fortunes to be made in sugar. The sugar merchants' lobby in Parliament was powerful. The richest man in England, who had purchased a noble estate west of Sarum, was heir to a sugar fortune. The Morants who had bought Brockenhurst and other New Forest estates were a sugar dynasty, too.

The old Beaulieu Abbey lands had passed by marriage from the Wriothesley into the Montagu family and the Duke of Montagu, like many of England's great eighteenth-century aristocrats, was an entrepreneur. Although the ruined abbey was not a place where he spent much time, he knew that the Solent's double high tide, extending up Beaulieu river, made it apt for navigation and that he still possessed all the old abbey's river rights. "If the crown will grant me a charter to found a settlement in the West Indies," he decided, "I could not only start a sugar plantation, but I could bring the sugar back to my own port at Beaulieu." While the river banks were mostly mud, at the sheltered curve they were gravel, perfect for building upon. Soon a plan for a small but elegant harbour town had been prepared. "We shall call it Montagu Town," the duke declared.

That, alas, was as far as it got. A private flotilla was sent to the West Indies with settlers, livestock, even prefabricated houses. It cost the duke ten thousand pounds. The settlement was planted. But the French kicked them out. Nothing more could be done. At Montagu Town the banks had been cleared and smoothed, and the outline of the main street down to the river had been laid down; but that was all. The site reverted, for twenty more years, to silence.

But it was ready for commercial use and, just before mid-century, with the duke's active encouragement, a use was found.

The British Empire was growing. Conflicts with the rival powers of France and Spain could not be avoided. Britain's army was negligible but its navy ruled the seas; whenever a conflict threatened, therefore, more ships had to be built and quite often nowadays the building of the hull was farmed out to private contractors. The cleared site on the Beaulieu River was a perfect location. For naval ships there was the timber of the king's New Forest close by; for merchant shipping there were oak trees in the private estates all around. An ironworks, established at the old monastic fishery of Sowley Pond, supplied any necessary iron. Buckler's Hard became a shipbuilding yard.

It was never large but often busy. Merchant ships were needed all the time. The naval building came in bursts, each time there was a conflict somewhere: a European dynastic dispute affecting the colonies; the American War of Independence; and now, after the dangerous business of the French Revolution, a threat to every established monarchy in Europe, Britain found itself at war again with France.

On each side of the broad, grassy street that led down to the water, a row of red-brick cottages stood. Behind them lay garden allotments, and further scattered cottages and barns. At the water's edge, set at an angle to the bank, were five slipways where the ships were built. Down the centre street and on sites all around were huge stacks of timber of various shapes and sizes. The men who worked on the ships were mostly quartered a mile or two away, either in lodgings up at Beaulieu village itself, or over at the western edge of the Montagu estate, at a new, straggling settlement of cottages known as Beaulieu Rails. At Buckler's Hard itself there was the master builder's house, a blacksmith's shop, a store, two little inns, a cobbler's and cottages for the most senior shipwrights.

Work had started early that bright spring morning. A cheerful column of smoke was rising from the blacksmith's forge. Mr Henry Adams, the owner of the business, eighty years old but still supervising, had just come out of his master builder's house; his two sons were at his side; shipwrights were busy at the waterside; men were carrying timber; a cart was standing in front of the Ship Inn.

Yet as Puckle arrived, hours late for work, from Beaulieu Rails, and walked down the street, nobody saw him. The men at the sawpit looked, but they didn't see him. The women by the village pump didn't see him. The cobbler, the innkeepers, the timber carriers, the shipwrights – why, even old Mr Adams with eyes like gimlets and his two sharp sons – not one of these good and worthy people saw Puckle as he walked past them. He was completely invisible.

The miracle was made greater yet by the fact that, by the time he stepped on to the vessel under construction at the water's edge, there wasn't a single person in the yard who couldn't have sworn, had you asked them, that Abraham Puckle had been there all morning.

"That's the best one, Fanny," said the Reverend William Gilpin with approval; and the heiress to the Albion estate smiled with pleasure, as she put the drawing back into her sketching book, because she thought so too.

They were sitting by the window of the library in the vicarage – a big Georgian house with a large beech tree just opposite its front door.

The vicar of Boldre was a handsome old man. A little corpulent, but powerfully built, he and the heiress of Albion House were very fond of each other. The reasons for loving the distinguished clergyman were too obvious to need explanation. His for loving Fanny, whom he had christened himself, were numerous: she was kind and thoughtful for others; she was also lively, intelligent and really drew quite well. He enjoyed her company. Her fair hair had a reddish tint; her eyes were strikingly blue; her complexion was excellent. Had he been, say, thirty years younger and not already happily married – he admitted it frankly, at least to himself – he'd have tried to marry Fanny Albion.

The drawing she had done was a New Forest view, looking across from Beaulieu Heath, past Oakley, to a distant prospect of the Isle of Wight and the hazy sea. It was altogether admirable: the near ground, which in truth had only a shallow undulation, had been judiciously raised at one point and a solitary stricken oak had been added. A small brick kiln nearby had, quite rightly, been expunged. The heath and woodland had a controlled but natural wildness, the sea a pleasant mystery. It was – and this was the highest term of praise he could use – it was picturesque.

If there was one thing – upon earth, that is – that the Reverend William Gilpin believed in, it was the importance of the picturesque. His published *Observations* on the subject had made him famous and was much admired. He had travelled all over Europe in search of the picturesque – to the mountains of Switzerland, the valleys of Italy, the rivers of France – and he had found it. In England, he assured his readers, there were landscapes entirely picturesque. The Lake District in the north was the best area, but there were many others. And his readers were ready to discover them.

The Georgian era was an age of order. The great classical country mansions of the aristocracy, the leaders of taste, had shown the triumph of rational man over nature; their broad parks, designed by Capability Brown, with sweeping lawns and carefully placed woods, had demonstrated how man – at least if he were in possession of a handsome fortune – could tutor nature into a state of graciousness. But as the Age of Reason swept on, people found its dictates a little too ordered, too severe; they looked for more variety. So now the successor to Brown, the genius Repton, had started adding flower gardens and pleasant walks to Brown's bare parks. People began to see in the natural countryside not a dangerous chaos, but the kindly hand of God. In short, they went for walks outside the park in search of the picturesque, as Gilpin said they should.

He was quite clear about how to recognise the picturesque. It was all a question of choice. The Avon valley, being flat and cultivated, did not appeal to him. For similar reasons the ordered slopes of the Isle of Wight, although admirable as a blue mass in the distance, were, if one actually took the ferry across for a closer inspection, quite intolerable. Open heath, however wild, he found dull; but where there was variety, a contrast of wood and heath, of high ground and low ground – where, in a word, the Almighty had shown good judgement in showing His hand – there the Reverend William Gilpin could smile at his pupil and say, in his deep, sonorous voice: "Now that, Fanny, is picturesque."

But pleased as he was by the drawing she had just shown him, this was nothing to the excitement he felt when, having put it away, she stared meditatively out of the window for a moment or two and then enquired: "Have you ever considered whether we should build a ruin at Albion House?"

For if there was one thing in the whole of God's creation that Mr Gilpin loved above even the countryside it was a ruin.

England had plenty of ruins. There were the castles, of course; but better still, thanks to the break with Rome of which Mr Gilpin's Church of England was the heir, there were all the ruined monasteries and priories. Near the New Forest were Christchurch and Romsey; across Southampton water a small Cistercian house called Netley, whose waterside ruins certainly qualified as picturesque. And then, of course, there was Beaulieu Abbey itself, whose ruins, despite two centuries of being plundered for stone, were still extensive.

Ruins were part of the natural landscape: they seemed to grow out of the soil. They were places of quiet reflection, mysterious yet safe. They were utterly picturesque. A man who owned a ruin owned its antiquity. For if the hand of time had reduced the buildings of these invisible ancestors, nature had joined in and he was the inheritor of the product. Lost ancestors were appeased; time, death, dissolution – even these former enemies became part of his estate. Often as not, he would build his own mansion close beside it. Thus, for the gentle English classes in the late Age of Enlightenment, even chaos and old night could be set, like a sundial, in a garden.

And if, by chance, no ruin stood nearby, then, in an age when good fortune could accomplish anything, you built one!

Some people favoured classical ruins, as if their classical houses were really built upon the site of some Roman imperial palace. Others favoured the Gothic, as the mock medieval was called, which charmingly echoed the taste for Gothic horror novels that were one of the fashionable amusements just then. There was only one problem.

"To build a ruin, Fanny," the vicar cautioned her seriously, "is a great expense." One needed stone in large quantities, expert masons to carve it, a good antiquarian to design it, a landscape artist. Then the stone needed treating to give it a mouldering appearance; then time, for mosses and ivy and lichens to grow in appropriate places. "Don't attempt the thing, Fanny," he warned, "if you haven't thirty thousand pounds to spend." It was cheaper to build a fine new house. "But there is something else I have often thought you could do, to the house itself when it becomes yours," he added cheerfully; for it could properly be admitted that, since old Mr Albion was now nearing his ninetieth year, the time of Fanny becoming mistress of the estate could not be far off.

"What's that?"

"Why, you could make it into a Gothic house. You should turn it into Albion Castle. The situation," he added persuasively, "is perfect."

It was certainly a very pretty idea. In a journey over to Bristol the previous year, Fanny had seen the thing admirably done. An essentially Georgian house could be remodelled, adding a few embellishments here and there, placing mock battlements round its roof, inserting Gothic tracery in the windows and plaster moulding like fan vaulting in the ceilings of some of the rooms. The result was highly agreeable – a picturesque blend of the Roman and Gothic, which especially appealed to families who wished their house to suggest both medieval ancestry and classical taste, or to echo the atmosphere of some of the grandest aristocratic families whose houses were built around the remains of the abbeys they had acquired in Tudor times. These mock fortresses, however small, were often called castles – which also sounded rather grand. Albion House, with its intimate setting in a clearing among the oaks in the middle of the ancient Forest, would make a charming little castle.

"It could be done," Fanny agreed. "Indeed, I really think it should." She looked thoughtful. "I do not think, though," she continued slowly, "that I should care to attempt such a thing alone. I should want the guiding hand" – she smiled a little mischievously – "or at least the willing co-operation of a husband. Do you not agree?"

William Gilpin bowed his broad, greying head, inwardly cursed fate for making him so old and ventured: "Have you anyone in mind, Fanny?"

She should, God knew, have no shortage of suitors. Because of her father's age and infirmity Fanny had not, by her own choice, made any attempts to show herself in society. But she was not in the least bashful. She was very cheerful. She knew perfectly well, at the age of nineteen, that although not a great heiress, her inheritance would recommend her wherever she went. It was an age when every young man and woman who claimed or aspired to gentility carried their incomes like a price tag round their necks. Every hostess knew the money value of each of her guests. It was probably a more mercenary period in English history than any before or since. And luckily for her, she was well placed in the system.

Whom ought she to marry? There was no single candidate whom neighbourly relations or family interest obliged her to consider. The greatest family in the Forest was that of the old Duke of Montagu, but the Beaulieu estate was split between the families of his two daughters now, who both lived far away; only the steward actually resided at the old abbey ruin. Next, in Fanny's own estimation, were the most ancient landed families like the Albions. There were still several in the Forest: the Compton family still had Minstead; just north of them a family named Eyre had reputedly been in the region since Norman times; on the eastern side of the Forest, the Mill family, who had done so well in Tudor times when Beaulieu Abbey was dissolved, had a large estate. Then there were the old Lymington families – which really meant the Burrards. And finally came the relative newcomers to the Forest area. There were many of these now, who had come in during the past two generations. They had built splendid classical mansions all the way along the coast from Southampton to Christchurch. Some had high titles; others came from gentry families, having made fortunes in the city or in trade, as had the Morants in sugar, or the Drummonds, from a noble Scottish family, who had become bankers to the king and financed his war in America. Nearly all these newcomers were very rich indeed.

Great mercantile families have often shown a predilection for the sea – no doubt because, for most of human history, trade has always been carried by water. And so it was, during the eighteenth century, that the New Forest had acquired this new layer to its ancient identity – as a pleasant coastline wilderness where the rich could build their mansions and enjoy the sea. It was a view of the world which the old Forest folk, for all their occasional shoreline activities, never entirely understood; and Fanny, coming as she did from the Forest interior, was, despite her genteel education, closer in spirit to the Prides than she was to some of the new landowners. But still, it could not be denied, marriage among them might be considered a desirable outcome. And even if, secretly, she yearned for something else, she didn't like to say so and didn't know what it was.

"No one at present," she told the clergyman.

"You are going to visit your cousin Totton at Oxford soon, I believe?"

"Next week." Edward Totton was just about to come down from the university, and she and his sister Louisa were going to pay him a visit there for a few days. It was an expedition she had been greatly looking forward to.

"Why, then, I'm sure some poor professor with a taste for the Gothic will impress you with his merits," her friend said playfully. "And now," he added, "I must go to my little school. We have a special duty to perform there today. As it lies on your way home, shall we walk together?"

• • •

Samuel Grockleton moved cautiously down Lymington High Street.

The size and shape of the town was almost the same as it had been in medieval times, even if nearly all the houses lining the broad slope had Georgian façades now, some arranged as shops with bow windows.

He passed the entrance of the Angel Inn. Mr Isaac Seagull, proprietor, standing in the door, gave him a bow and a smile. He glanced across the street. The landlady of the Nag's Head, dead opposite, also outside, was smiling too.

"Good morning, Mr Grockleton."

He didn't like it. He didn't like it a bit.

He noticed the wooden sign of the Nag's Head swing, just an inch or two, with a faint creak in the sea breeze. Was it a mere chance, or had people stopped all down the street? His feet alone were ringing on the cobblestones; the rest of the town had paused to watch him: a hundred masks, like painted figures in a carnival, or mummers at Hallowe'en. And behind those masks, so polite and smiling?

He knew. The long tail of his black coat, his starched cravat, his white knee-breeches, all suddenly felt as though they had turned to solid mortar, trapping him as securely as if he had been put in the stocks. His high, broad-rimmed hat seemed to be made of lead as he forced himself to raise it to a lady in front of the little bookshop. He knew what the friendly faces meant. They were all in on it.

There had been a run the night before and he was the Customs officer.

Customs and Excise. There had always been taxes to pay for the shipping and landing of goods. And traders had always tried to avoid them. The owlers of Lymington had shipped wool out of England illegally for centuries. But it was not the exports that were the main concern now. It was the goods coming in. And there lay the huge problem.

It was the scale of the business. As Britain's commercial empire grew the tide of imports swelled at an ever increasing rate. Silks and laces, pearls and calicoes, wines, fruits, tobacco and snuff, coffee and chocolate, sugar and spices – the list was huge. Fifteen hundred different items were liable to Customs duties now. And greatest of all were the two items without which, it would seem, Englishmen would lose all their vigour and their island would probably sink beneath the waves. Tea: if drinking coffee and chocolate was fashionable, everyone, from highest to lowest, drank tea. And brandy.

Brandy was the elixir of life. Its uses were manifold. It protected against the plague, cured fever, colic, dropsy. It stimulated the heart, cleaned wounds and kept you young. If you were frozen, brandy warmed you. Why, if the surgeon had to saw off your leg, he'd give you a pint of brandy first before he hit you over the head. Or, of course, you could always drink it for pleasure. And on every drop of brandy you bought, Customs were due. But nobody wanted to pay.

"It is unreasonable that people curse the Customs," Grockleton would observe plaintively to his wife, "when it is the Customs money that pays for the Navy vessels to protect the very trade which brings them the goods they desire."

"I am sure there is nothing rational about it," she would agree.

But however unreasonable – and Grockleton was perfectly right – everyone tried to avoid paying; smuggling was widespread. It was the job of the Customs officials to stop it. Customs officers were not popular.

The chief official for the whole region, the collector, was based at Southampton. The next most senior man was Grockleton at Lymington. Then there was another officer, rather less senior, in charge along the coast at Christchurch. In theory, the Customs officers had quite impressive forces at their disposal. There were sea vessels – swift cutters, usually – to intercept the smugglers' boats. There were riding officers, one every four miles, to patrol the coast. There were tidewaiters to check incoming ships, gaugers to inspect barrels, weighers, searchers – the titles changed as the Customs men thought of new ways to regulate the trade. The senior men like Grockleton were almost always posted in from outside, so as to be free of local ties; quite often they had just retired from some other branch of government service. Salaries were modest, but the officer was granted a handsome share of any contraband that was intercepted: a good inducement to be vigilant, one might have thought, yet to Grockleton's certain knowl-

edge, the supervisor at Christchurch had told his riding officers not to patrol and not to report anything they did happen
to see.

Not all the Customs men were so cowardly, though. Over on
the Isle of Wight, the Customs officer William Arnold had won
the grudging respect of the whole region by the way he had
gone about the job. With little support from the government,
he had paid out of his own pocket for a swift cutter to patrol
the local waters; and very effective it had been. If the other
towns had had such cutters, the smugglers along the coast
might have had a hard time of it. There were other ways to
catch them, though, and whatever Grockleton's faults may
have been, he had a strong sense of duty and he had courage.

That was why, if his plan worked, he was soon going to be
the most hated man in the county.

He continued down the street towards the quay. People were
moving about now, but they were still watching him. He could
imagine the looks behind his back, but he did not turn to see. At
the bottom of the street just off to one side was the Customs
house which was his official place of business.

He was just in sight of it when he happened to see the
Frenchman. The Frenchman, also, bowed and smiled politely.
But for a different reason. He and his compatriots were in
Lymington as guests of His Britannic Majesty. It was his duty
to be polite, therefore, even to a Customs official.

The count – for as well as commanding a regiment, he was
also an aristocrat – was certainly a most agreeable man and a
great favourite with Mrs Grockleton whom he treated as if she
were a duchess. Several of his relations having met their
deaths by the guillotine in the recent French Revolution, he
carried, at least in Mrs Grockleton's eyes, a certain aura of
tragic romance about him. With his fellow aristocrats and
troops quartered in Lymington, and some other émigré French
forces taking refuge in England, he was anxious to go and fight
against the new revolutionary regime in France at the first opportunity.

"Soon, Monsieur le Comte." Mrs Grockleton would sigh.
"Soon, we shall see better times, I trust." That England during
the last hundred years had been engaged in, or close to, hos-
tilities with royalist France for most of the time was a fact

which, faced with the charming French aristocrat, she had now entirely forgotten.

There was nothing very surprising, therefore, if, seeing the Frenchman, the Customs officer should have reached into his coat pocket, drawn out a letter and handed it to him with the words, overheard by a passer-by: "A letter from my wife, Count." Then he passed on towards the Customs house.

Only a little while later, in the privacy of his lodgings, did the count open the letter and read its contents with an expression of horror. "*Mon Dieu*," he murmured, "what shall I do now?"

From the Reverend William Gilpin's front door the lane ran straight between the hedgerows of small fields until it met another track at right angles. Down the lane, in pleasant sunlight, came Gilpin wearing a large clerical hat and carrying a stick, and Fanny in a long coat and cape. The two friends enjoyed the pleasant walk. Their object was the small building on the left just before the end of the lane.

Gilpin's school was a somewhat different establishment from Mrs Grockleton's academy, yet possibly just as useful. The Boldre parish never having had a school before, Gilpin had founded it not long after his arrival there and the little seat of learning had such charm that you might almost have called it picturesque.

The whole building was hardly forty feet long and built in the shape of a T. The long central section was a single high room, twenty-five feet long. The cross section was divided into two low storeys, with accommodation for a teacher and a classroom for the girls. The end of the central section facing the lane was charmingly shaped like a classical façade with a triangular pediment. This jolly little structure was perched on a tiny plot of ground. Below it the track led down towards the river and the bridge at Boldre. On the eastern side it led towards the old medieval vaccary, long since a hamlet, of Pilley.

"Who sold you the plot of land for the school?" Fanny had once asked him. She knew the ownership of almost every inch of land around there, but could not place that particular piece.

"I stole it," the vicar had replied amiably, "from the King's Forest. They made me pay a small fine later."

The purpose of the vicar's encroachment was simple enough: to take twenty boys and twenty girls from families in the Boldre parish hamlets, and teach them to read and write and cipher, as basic mathematics was then termed. For reading, naturally, they used the Bible, on which they were tested twice a week. Every Sunday, they put on the smart green coats with which the school provided them and paraded to Boldre church. This last feature also provided the vicar with a useful incentive. He knew his parishioners. If now and then a child was needed to help its parents in the field, no questions were asked about a day's absence; but the strong woollen and cotton clothes the school provided free along with the green coats were a powerful inducement for a country family. And if any of the parents expressed doubts about the value of so much learning for their daughter he could assure them: "As writing and arithmetic are less necessary to girls, we spend more time on practical things – knitting and spinning and needlework." Beyond this level of education the parish school did not venture. To go further might, everyone agreed, have been to make the village children discontented with their lot.

"Is it difficult," Fanny now asked as they reached the gate of the school, "for these children to learn to read and write?"

Gilpin gave her a sidelong glance. "Because they are simple country folk, Fanny?" He shook his head. "God did not create people with such disadvantages. I can assure you that a young Pride will learn just as quickly as you or I. The limits to his learning will be determined by what he sees – quite correctly, I may say – as being of use to him. Whoa, Sir," he suddenly exclaimed, as a small ten-year-old boy with a mass of curly black hair came rushing out of the schoolroom door and tried to get past them. "As for this young man." Gilpin smiled as he expertly caught the fleeing child and scooped him up. "This child, Fanny, would be a fine classical scholar had he been born in another condition – wouldn't you, you rascal?" he added affectionately as he held the boy securely.

Nathaniel Furzey had been a great find of Gilpin's. He didn't come from Boldre parish at all, but from up at Minstead; but the child was so precociously intelligent that Gilpin had wanted him for the Boldre school. Supposing that the Oakley Furzeys might have some family connection with the Minstead branch, he had enquired if they would take the child in during the school term, but the Oakley Furzeys weren't interested. The Prides of Oakley however who, even a century after the Alice Lisle affair, still scarcely spoke to their Furzey neighbours, had no objection to housing this child from the Minstead family; their own boy, Andrew, attended the school. And so each morning Gilpin could look out of his window with pleasure to see Andrew Pride and curly-haired Nathaniel Furzey going along the lane towards his school.

"I assume from your flight," the vicar said cheerfully to his prisoner, "that the doctor is already here." He turned to Fanny. "This boy does not trust doctors. I told you he was intelligent."

The doctor from whom Nathaniel Furzey was running was no less a person than Dr Smithson, the fashionable physician from Lymington, whom Gilpin had summoned at his own expense. He was standing in the main schoolroom with the children obediently waiting in line before him. The treatment he was administering was a vaccination.

Only eight years had passed since there had been a minor but troubling outbreak of smallpox in the Forest. Although it would be another two years before Dr Jenner would be able to test his cowpox vaccine, vaccination with minute quantities of the smallpox virus itself had been used recently with success. This, therefore, was what Gilpin had arranged for his pupils.

But even with Gilpin there, as the other children obediently went forward, young Nathaniel would have none of it. Standing beside the vicar, who held his hand, he shook his head slowly but with evident determination. "He's going to put up a fight, I think," murmured Gilpin. "I'm not sure what to do."

It was Fanny, in the end, who solved the problem. "If I do it, Nathaniel," she suddenly asked, "will you?" Nathaniel Furzey considered. His dark eyes rested first on her, then the doctor, then on her again. "I'll go first," she offered. Slowly he nodded.

Taking off her cape, she offered her bare arm while all the children watched; and moments later, his eyes fixed solemnly upon her, young Nathaniel underwent the ordeal too.

"Well done, Fanny," said Gilpin quietly and, indeed, she felt rather proud of herself.

She could tell that she was in high favour when, after the

vaccinations were all done and the doctor thanked, Gilpin announced that he would accompany her on her way home as far as Boldre church.

There were two ways to approach the church from the school: one was to descend to the river and then climb up to the church again; the other was to take a track through the hamlet of Pilley that led across the top edge of the little valley and round to the knoll. They took the latter and, since it was nearly a mile, they had time to talk of various things along the way.

The church was coming in sight when the vicar casually remarked: "I noticed today, Fanny, when you were being vaccinated, that you are wearing a silver chain round your neck. I have seen you do so before, yet upon each occasion I have also noticed that whatever hangs from it is hidden under your dress. What is this pendant, I wonder?"

By way of answer, with a smile she pulled it out. "It's nothing to look at," she said, "so I keep it hidden. But I like to wear it sometimes."

Gilpin stared at the pendant curiously.

It was a strange little object, a wooden crucifix, quite black with age. Looking carefully, he could just make out some antique carving on it; but of what kind or what date it was impossible to say. Whatever kind the carving was, the pendant was a simple wooden cross and the vicar approved of it. "You performed a Christian act this morning," he said warmly, "and I am equally glad to see that you choose to wear this simple cross – for you must know that to me it is worth far more than any gold or silver ornament." She could not help blushing for pleasure at such praise. "But tell me, Fanny," he continued, "where does it come from?"

She had only been seven years old at the time, but she remembered it well. Her mother had taken her to the house. She supposed it was in Lymington. She wasn't sure, but her mother had seemed to be cross about something.

The old lady had been sitting by the fire. She had appeared very old to Fanny – over eighty probably – all wrapped in shawls; but with a comfortable air: a nice, friendly old face and very bright blue eyes.

"Bring the child here, then, Mary," she had told Fanny's mother. There had been a trace of impatience in her voice. "Do you know who I am, child?" she had asked.

"No." Fanny had no idea. She saw the old woman glance at her mother and shake her head.

"I'm your grandmother, child."

"My grandmother!" She had felt a thrill of excitement. She had never met such a person before. Her father had been so old when he married that his own mother had died well before Fanny's birth. As for her mother, she had always supposed it was the same. She turned to her now. "You never told me I had a grandmother," she said reproachfully.

"Well, you have!" the old lady exclaimed sharply.

They had had a lovely talk after that. Fanny couldn't remember much of what they said. Her grandmother had spoken of the past and her own parents, and other family long departed. Their names had meant nothing to Fanny, but she had taken away a vague but unforgettable impression of sea breezes, ships, vague adventure: as though she had opened a hidden window and seen, smelled, tasted a world she had never known before – and never would again, for she was not taken to see the old lady any more. The woodland world of Albion House had enclosed her for many years after that. The house at Lymington and her long-lost grandmother had receded into her memory like a single childhood day, spent by the sea.

Only one tangible evidence of that meeting remained. Just before they left, her grandmother had taken the little wooden cross from around her neck and given it to her. "This is for you, child," she said, "to remember your grandmother. My mother gave it to me and it had been in her family for I don't know how long. Since before the Spanish Armada, they say." She had taken her hand. "Now if I give you this, will you promise to keep it?"

"Yes, Grandmother," she had said. "I promise."

"Good. Now give your old grandmother, whom you never saw before, a kiss."

"I shall come again, now I know you, and you must come to see us," Fanny had said happily.

"Just you keep that cross," the old lady replied.

She had been very surprised by how angry her mother had been when they got out into the street again. "Fancy giving a child that dirty old thing," she had exclaimed, looking at the little cross with disgust. "We'll throw it away as soon as we get home."

"No!" Fanny had cried, with unexpected passion. "It's mine. My grandmother gave it me. I promised to keep it. I promised."

She had hidden the cross, so that no one should steal it. A year later her mother had died. As for her grandmother, she supposed she must have died too. There was no more mention of her at Albion House. But she had always kept the cross.

"And who was your grandmother?" Gilpin now enquired.

"My mother was a Miss Totton, as you know," Fanny replied. "So she must have been old Mrs Totton. I know she was Mr Totton's second wife. His first, from whom my Totton cousins descend, was a cousin of the Burrards. So I should imagine she was one of those old Lymington families, connected with the sea."

"Undoubtedly," agreed Gilpin. "One of the Buttons, perhaps." He nodded. "It's probably in the Lymington parish register, you know, if they married there."

"Why yes. I hadn't thought about it. I suppose it is." She smiled. "Would you help me look, one day?"

Dusk: the two figures came independently, from opposite directions. No one would have guessed that they would meet at a prearranged place.

Charles Louis Marie, Comte d'Hector, general, aristocrat, as valiant a man as any of the legendary Three Musketeers, took good care to saunter up the High Street as casually as if he were enjoying an evening stroll. His trusted companion came down a back lane in a similar manner.

The Frenchman was an elegant sight. While most men were now wearing their hair naturally, he and his fellow émigrés wore the short powdered wigs of the French royal court. A silk coat and knee-breeches completed his attire, as though to say: "We not only deplore the Revolution in our country; we decline even to recognise its existence."

Whatever one thought of the old royal regime in France, the French Revolution of 1789 had turned into a desperately bloody affair. The initial experiments in republican democracy had given way to the guillotine, for the aristocracy and the royal family, and more recently, in the awful Terror, to the wholesale execution of thousands accused as enemies of the Revolution. Aristocrats and their followers, like the French community at Lymington, had fled if they could. All Europe had watched, horrified. The continental powers had prepared for war. Nobody knew where this turmoil across the sea might lead. Even in quiet Lymington, which seldom took much notice of anything that did not concern it, the French conflict was made real by the presence of the émigrés in their midst.

There were about a dozen gentlemen like the count in Lymington, several with their families, mostly lodging with the better local tradesmen. There were also three bodies of troops – four hundred soldiers at the town's small barracks, another four hundred artillerymen at the malt-house in New Street, and a further six hundred men of the French Royal Navy who had been quartered out in the farm buildings near Buckland. The men were, as was only to be expected, a considerable nuisance to the community, but were suffered on account of the gallant officers who led them. The count had caused eight of his men to be soundly whipped at the corner of Church Street the day before to make it clear to the people of Lymington that indiscipline would not be tolerated, and the entire cadre of officers had gone out of their way to make themselves agreeable both to the ladies of the town and to their husbands. For the time being, at least, they were still welcome guests. But the count was under no illusions. Put a foot wrong and life in Lymington could be made very unpleasant.

The packet Grockleton had given him that morning, therefore, had been very frightening indeed. Not the letter from Mrs Grockleton, inviting him and two fellow officers to dinner the following week, but the other message, slipped discreetly inside it by her husband after he had taken it from her. If the message meant what the Frenchman suspected, then it concerned a business that might take very careful handling; and this was why, as a precaution, the count had selected one companion to join him, as a witness, at this evening's secret rendezvous.

"I am not yet telling any of the other officers, *mon ami*," he had explained. "I am only telling you because I can rely not only upon your advice but upon your absolute discretion."

It was almost dark as he turned off the High Street near the church.

Of all the many inventions English builders had discovered in the last century or so, none was more charming than a particular kind of boundary construction often used in gardens.

The crinkle-crankle wall, they called it. Instead of running in a straight line like an ordinary brick wall, it was wavy, curving back and forth like a series of love seats. Most often these walls were to be found in the counties of East Anglia; but for some reason – perhaps an East Anglian builder had come to dwell in the town – there were a number in Lymington. They were mostly built quite high: some you could just look over, some not. The curves were big enough, usually, for a couple of men to stand in so that, if you were looking along the wall, you would not see them. And it was for precisely this reason that Samuel Grockleton had asked the French count to come at dusk, down the lane behind his garden, which was bounded by a crinkle-crankle wall.

Grockleton waited quietly until he heard the light tap, made with a coin, on the other side. He had scraped away some of the mortar on the outside of the wall between two of the bricks. When he pulled a brick out from his side, there was a neat little slit through which one could talk. He tapped the place, then spoke. "Is that you, Count?"

"Yes, *mon ami*. I came as you asked."

"Were you followed?"

"No."

"This precaution is necessary. Did you know that my house is watched?"

"It does not surprise me. It is natural, given your position."

"Even when you come to dinner, I cannot risk being seen in private conversation with you. Tongues would wag."

"I do not doubt it."

"Quite. I am instructed to say, Count, that His Britannic Majesty's government has need of your help." This was not quite true. No one had actually instructed him to say so because, knowing only too well the inefficiency, and quite likely the corruption, of official channels, Grockleton had decided to act on his own initiative without official approval. Of course, if he succeeded they *would* approve, so it all came to the same thing.

"My dear friend, I am at your government's service."

"Then let me tell you, Count," he began, "exactly what I need."

It was not only, as both men knew, a question of smuggling brandy and other goods. As well as the huge illicit trade there was traffic in gold and in information. The patriotism of a later age was not much developed yet and certainly not along the southern coast. British naval officers fought in the hope of prize money from captured ships; their men fought because they had been kidnapped by the press gangs and taken to sea. Even a commander as loved as Nelson dared not let his men ashore at an English port – for if he did, he'd never see most of them again. So would the smugglers of southern England buy brandy, trade gold, sell information to their country's enemies? They would. They did.

But above all, for the dwellers by the New Forest coast, it was a question of simple trade in contraband. And they were so well organised, in such large bands, that not all the riding officers together could have stopped one of their great night-time caravans. In order to do that you needed troops.

It had been tried. Detachments of dragoons and other regiments had been quartered at Lymington from time to time. There were plans for building a new barracks over at Christchurch. The cavalry were never locally recruited, of course; that would be useless. But even so, they were not always keen to take on the smuggling bands. In the last ten years there had been two pitched battles. On each occasion a number of troopers had been killed. And since the troopers were in sympathy with the smugglers anyway, it was not a popular assignment.

"My chances of intercepting contraband with English troops," Grockleton informed the Frenchman, "are not good."

But what about French troops? The idea had come to him a week ago and it might turn out to be a stroke of genius. The French troops had no local ties, no sympathies with the smugglers, nothing. They were bored, looking for something to do.

There were, altogether, more than a thousand of them. And they were only there on the sufferance of the British government. If he could make a major interception using them it would not only earn him the grateful thanks of the government; his share of the confiscated loot would make him a modest fortune. He might be unpopular but he could probably retire.

If, on the other hand, the Frenchman failed to support him he could let it be known in London at once. The king himself would hear and be seriously displeased.

All of this, without needing to be told, the Frenchman perfectly understood. "It will have to be done with total secrecy," he replied when he had heard Grockleton's plan.

"Certainly."

"I dare not tell my men even upon the day. A parade, some excuse to assemble under arms will be needed, and then . . ."

"My feelings exactly. I may have your co-operation, then?"

"Totally. It goes without saying. I am His Britannic Majesty's to command."

"Then, Sir, I thank you," said Grockleton and pushed his brick back into place.

For a moment or two the count and his colleague walked along the lane in silence.

"Well, *mon ami*," the count said at last, "you heard all that?" The other nodded. "It puts us," the count went on, "you know, in a difficult position. Do you think I did right?"

"I do. You have no choice."

"I'm glad you agree. Not a word of this must be known, I need hardly remind you."

"You may trust me."

"Of course. Now, as we came, let us return, by separate ways."

Night had come to Albion House and, as she had so often in her young life, Fanny was sitting in the parlour with two old people. In the fireplace the cindery logs produced only an occasional flicker of flame; the candles threw a gentle glow on to the dark oak panelling. Fanny might have ambitious plans for remodelling the house one day into a classical Gothic folly but, for the present, the old parlour had hardly changed since the days of good Queen Bess.

It was very quiet. Sometimes she would read to the old people, but tonight they had preferred to sit still in their chairs, enjoying the silence of the house, which was broken only by the soft tick of the long-case clock in the hall and, more occasionally, by the tiny rustle of a falling cinder in the fire. At last, her father spoke: "I can't see why she is going all the way to Oxford."

This was greeted with a silence during which the clock quietly sounded another forty ticks.

"Of course she should." Her aunt Adelaide.

Fanny knew better than to interrupt. Not yet, anyway. Only twenty ticks now intervened.

"How long shall you be gone, Fanny?" A hint of reproach, of sadness, bravely borne.

"Only six days, Father, including the journey."

"Quite right," said Adelaide firmly. "We shall miss you, but you are right to go away to see your cousin."

"She's going to see Oxford. It seems a long way." They had come full circle. A greying cinder fell.

Francis Albion was eighty-eight years old. People said he had stayed alive so long to see his daughter grown up and it was probably true. Then people said that he wanted to see her safely married. But since any mention of that subject seemed to fill him with dismay, this clearly could not be the case. And there were even those who wondered if, having grown so used to being alive for such a prodigiously long time, Mr Albion might not be doing it for himself.

The fact was that Francis Albion had never expected to have a child at all. The last of Peter and Betty Albion's children, who had expected his elder brother to continue the family line, he had been a wanderer much of his life. A lawyer in London, an agent in France, a merchant for a while in America, he had always made enough to live as a gentleman, but not enough to marry. By the age of forty, when the death of his brother left him heir to the Albion estate, he was a confirmed bachelor with no desire to settle. His sister Adelaide had kept Albion House going alone for another twenty years before he had finally returned, as he put it, to take up his family obligations in the Forest.

These were not onerous and he made sure they were profitable to him. They soon included the position of gentleman keeper of one of the walks, as the minor divisions of the Forest were now called. His discharge of this responsibility was typical. Even by the genial standards of the eighteenth century the administration of the New Forest had become notoriously lax. When the crown, in one of its occasional attempts to sort the old place out, had held a royal commission some years before, the commissioners, having pointed out that the woodward of the Forest had kept no accounts for eighteen years, also noted rather sourly that when they inspected the coppice in Mr Albion's walk, where the king's timber was supposed to be grown, they had found it used as a huge rabbit warren, with not a single tree to be found in the whole inclosure.

Having assured the commissioners that something would be done, Francis Albion's only comment to his sister was: "I had a thousand rabbits out of there last year and I'll have another thousand next."

What then, at the age of sixty-five, had induced Mr Albion to marry Miss Totton of Lymington, thirty years his junior?

Some said it was love. Others that, after his sister Adelaide had suffered a severe cold, it had occurred to Albion that she might not always be there to look after him. Whatever the reason, Mr Albion proposed and Miss Totton accepted, and came to live at Albion House.

It was strange, really, that Miss Totton had not married long before. She was pleasant-looking, respectable; she wasn't poor. Perhaps she had been crossed in love when young. Whatever the reason, at the age of thirty-five, she had obviously decided that marriage into the Albions, even as a nurse, was preferable to her present situation. Her half-brother, as head of the Totton family, was pleased with the Albion connection, and Adelaide seemed genuinely glad to see her brother married. She kept to her own wing of the house and the two women had got on well.

The marriage had been rather successful. Miss Totton had not expected much, but marriage seemed to have given Francis Albion a new lease of life. Even so, it came as quite a shock to him when, in his sixty-eighth year, his wife informed him that she was pregnant.

"Such things can happen, Francis," she told him with a

smile. They called the baby Frances, after her father; and, as was the fashion of the time, she was always known as Fanny.

There were no more children. Fanny was therefore the heiress. Old Mr Albion was happy because he had a daughter, which caused some pleasant admiration at his age. Fanny's mother was happy: not only had she a child to love, but to be the mother of the next owner of Albion House was a much finer thing than to be the married nurse to an elderly gentleman. Adelaide was happy because she, too, had a child to love. Mr Totton of Lymington was delighted, because now his children, who were the same age, had a close cousin who was heiress to one of the local estates. Why, even Fanny herself was happy, being rich and loved. And so she should have been. For all she had to do, in such happy circumstances, was to live up to everyone else's desires.

Fanny had been ten when her mother died. The family had been shocked, not only on account of their grief, but with concern for the future of the child.

"What shall we do now?" Francis Albion had cried to his sister.

"Live a long time," she had sternly replied.

They had both done so. Fanny had not been orphaned; if Francis and Adelaide had been more like grandparents, Fanny had nonetheless had a happy home. If her father, as he grew into old age, was somewhat timid and plaintive, her own youthful spirits and the frequent company of her Totton cousins easily overcame this influence. And if her aunt Adelaide tended to repeat herself, Fanny could, all the same, enjoy the intelligence that was still there, as sharp as ever.

And then there was Mrs Pride.

Mrs Pride. Were all housekeepers known as Mrs, regardless of whether they had been married? Fanny had never met a housekeeper who wasn't. It was a term of respect, a recognition that, within their own domain, they were mistress of the house. And there was absolutely no question about who ran Albion House. Mrs Pride did.

She was a very handsome woman: tall, her grey hair swept elegantly back, her walk stately; any man would guess at once that she must have a magnificent body. The only reason she had not married, in all likelihood, was that she preferred running a manor house to the much harder life she would have had as the wife of a farmer or forest smallholder, or even a Lymington shopkeeper.

She was always deferential. If the sheets needed renewing she would get permission from Adelaide to attend to it. When it was time for the spring clean she would enquire what date would be convenient. If a chimney looked about to fall down, even, she would politely ask Francis what he would like her to do about it. She knew every nook and cranny, every rafter, every store, every expenditure. Mrs Pride was, in truth, the mistress of Albion House; the Albions only lived there.

To Fanny she became a second, silent mother. For years Fanny did not know it. If she decided to go for a walk and Fanny went with her, Mrs Pride might want to sit a while so that Fanny could play in the water at the ford. When she happened to see sketching materials in Lymington she took the liberty of buying them, just in case Adelaide might wish to give them to Fanny. She remarked on Fanny's drawing prowess to the vicar after church and meekly supposed that there would be tutors visiting the house to give her lessons in other accomplishments, too – at which Mr Gilpin took the hint at once and saw that these things were attended to. And so quiet and effective was she that, at almost fifteen, Fanny still thought that she was just the loving, friendly figure who saw that she was clothed and fed, and who seemed always glad of a little company when she sat in her little parlour in the early evening for a pot of tea and some delicious brandy cakes.

Fanny glanced across at her father. He had closed his eyes, after these last remarks. It was strange, in a way, this timidity of his, when one considered his life. Sometimes, even now, he would tell her about his travels, describing the gorgeous French court of Louis XV, or the busy port of Boston, or the plantations of Carolina. He still recalled every great event.

"I remember the excitement in London, back in forty-five," he would say, "when the Scots tried to march south under Bonnie Prince Charlie." Every victory of the British on the high seas or out in India seemed to have a story to go with it, and when she was a child he used to relate these to her vividly, so that, without knowing it, she had learned much of the history of her times from him.

She was sad to see his decline, but glad that she was there to be at his side in these final years.

"Perhaps" – her aunt Adelaide's voice broke into the silence, now – "you will meet a handsome beau at Oxford."

"Perhaps." Fanny laughed. "Mr Gilpin told me today I should fall in love with a poor professor."

"I don't think that's what a Miss Albion would do, is it, Fanny?"

"No, Aunt Adelaide, I don't think it is."

She loved her aunt's aristocratic old face. She hoped she would look like that one day, too. It seemed to her that Adelaide could not have had a very happy life, but she never complained. If Mrs Pride ran the house in the practical sense, her aunt Adelaide was still its family guardian – the guardian angel, really.

It was evenings like this, when her father was dozing or had retired to bed, and she and Adelaide were sitting quietly together, that Fanny treasured most. The old house so silent; the shadows, like familiar ghosts, always in the same places on the panelling in the candlelight – at such times, her aunt would begin to talk. And she started to do so now.

Fanny smiled. Her aunt told the same stories over again, yet she was always happy to hear them. It was probably because, although her father's stories were interesting, they concerned only his own life; whereas Adelaide spoke about a more distant past – her mother Betty, her grandmother Alice, the story of the Albion inheritance going back centuries. Fanny's own inheritance. Yet the wonderful thing was that when her aunt Adelaide told it, all these things seemed to have happened only yesterday.

"My mother was born just after the Restoration of King Charles II," Adelaide could say. That was more than a hundred and thirty years ago. Yet Betty Lisle was a living memory. Adelaide had shared this house with her for forty years. "That's her favourite chair, where you sit now," her aunt would say. Or, one afternoon in the garden: "I remember the day my mother planted that rose tree. It was sunny, just like this . . ." The very house itself seemed to become like a living person too. "The brick skin of the house was put on when grandmother was a girl by her father. But he left the timbers and this old panelling," she would add, with a nod to the wall, "just as it was in Queen Elizabeth's day. Of course" – and here followed a vivid personal description of the terrifying figure in red and black – "it was from this room, on a night like this, that old Lady Albion went out to try to raise the county to join the Spanish Armada."

How could anyone fail to love such family history? But – here was the real difference between her aunt's and her father's stories – Adelaide's were told with such feeling for the people she spoke about. She would tell Fanny how this one had known hardship, or that one lost a child and grieved, so that the ghostly figures peopling the house became like friends whose joys and sadnesses one shared and whom, were such a thing possible, one wanted to sustain and comfort.

"I try to keep things as they were for my dear mother and father," Adelaide liked to say. And even if I do decide to add some Gothic features, thought Fanny, I, too, will continue as loyal guardian of the family shrine.

There was only one story, though, which used to move Aunt Adelaide to tears and that was the tale of her grandmother, Alice Lisle.

It was ironic, really, that Monmouth's rebellion and the execution of Alice Lisle should have come when they did. For within three years of Monmouth's attempt to seize the throne for the Protestant cause, King James II had so infuriated the English Parliament with his promotion of Roman Catholicism that they were ready to throw him out; and when, at this crucial point, his Catholic wife unexpectedly gave birth to a healthy son and heir, they did. The Glorious Revolution of 1688 effectively ended the civil and religious dispute that had been going on since the Stuarts came to the English throne. It was practically bloodless. The English didn't want Catholic rule and they got their way. James and his baby son were out. His Protestant daughter Mary and her Dutch husband William took over instead. Had Monmouth been alive then, Parliament might have chosen him but, like so many Stuarts, he had been vain and impetuous. So William and Mary it was. After them, the other Protestant daughter Anne. And after Anne, a grandson of one of Charles I's sisters, the Protestant King George, head of the German House of Hanover whose grandson George III was still reigning now.

Kings ruled through Parliament these days. Neither they nor their heirs were allowed to marry Catholics. Catholics and dissenters might practise their religion, but they could not attend university or hold any public office. Eighteenth-century England would not be quite what Alice Lisle might have wanted, but to a large extent the cause for which both she and her husband had been murdered had now been won.

Ironic politically, but the personal tragedy remained, like a tree that continues growing, almost the same, despite a change in yearly weather. A century had passed, but the Forest had not forgotten Alice. And in Albion House she was still a living memory.

Aunt Adelaide might have been born twenty years after those terrible events, but she knew them from her parents, and relations like her old aunt Tryphena, and local figures like Jim Pride, who had all been there at the time. Through their eyes and their descriptions, she had witnessed the arrest, the shameful trial and the execution. She still shuddered whenever she passed Moyles Court or the Great Hall at Winchester. Moyles Court had passed out of the family, now, but Albion House had been Alice's true home, the place she had loved, and her presence abided.

Yet perhaps Alice might have faded back, with time, to join those other shadows in the evening candlelight. If it had not been for Betty.

For the first year after her mother's execution, Betty had retreated back to Albion House and remained there in a state of shock. When Peter wrote to her she replied vaguely; when he came to see her she sent him away. She couldn't see him. She didn't quite know why, but everything seemed impossible. He persevered, though, for three long years and at last she came out of her depression enough to marry him.

Was their marriage happy? As she grew older, Adelaide sometimes wondered if it had been. There had been several children who died young; her elder brother who had later married and died without any heirs; then herself and lastly Francis. Peter had often been away in London while Betty remained alone at Albion House. By the time Adelaide was ten she had realised her mother must be rather lonely. A few years later, when he was not quite sixty, Peter had died in London; of overwork, it was said. He had been planning to spend more time in the country.

After that, with Francis sent to stay with an Oxfordshire vicar for his schooling and then away studying law, Betty had slowly contracted into the house, like a creature retreating into its shell. She would go out to visit neighbours, of course, or to shop in Lymington. But the house became her life, where Adelaide kept her company and, as that life stretched on down the years, the shadows of the house gradually gathered, enfolding them. The chief shadow was Alice.

"To think that I was here with Peter that terrible night," Betty would sometimes cry with self-reproach. And pointing out that she could hardly have done anything, and might have been arrested, did no good. "We should never have gone to Moyles Court anyway." True, perhaps, but useless. "She only left London because of Peter." Also true – Tryphena had told her – but equally useless to worry about now.

Adelaide was a sensible and quite a cheerful young woman. Her mind was strong. But hearing these litanies year after year raised around her a sense of life's tragedy and her mother's pain that was like a cloud.

With this tragic cloud came another – black, like thunder, rolling across the sky. The name of this dark shadow was Penruddock.

There were no Penruddocks in the Forest now. The Penruddocks of Hale had departed early in the century. The Penruddocks of Compton Chamberlayne were still there; but that was thirty-five miles away, over the horizon, in another county. Adelaide didn't know any Penruddocks in person, therefore. But she knew what to think of them.

"All royalists, of course," Betty would say. "But treacherous with it. When I think how my mother had actually tried to help them when they were in trouble. And this was their thanks."

The treachery of the Furzeys had never been fully understood by the Albions, as it had by the Prides. And even if it had, it would only have earned them a bleak contempt. But the cruelty of another gentry family was a very different matter.

"Sneaking around the house with his filthy troops all night. Trying to break down the door. Letting his men steal mother's linen. And then shoving her on the back of a trooper's horse in just her nightdress. An old woman like that. Shameful!" Betty would cry, her eyes flashing suddenly with rage and scorn. "Evil!"

Adelaide had a clear picture of Colonel Penruddock, with his saturnine face and cruel, vengeful nature. Such a crime between families could never be forgiven; nor, she believed, should it. "That family," she therefore told Fanny, in her turn, "are wicked, evil people. Never have anything to do with them."

She had said so once again that evening and Fanny had just assured her with a smile that she certainly wouldn't, when they both turned, Fanny in some alarm, at a terrible sound. It was a cough, a rasping, wheezing cough, followed by a gasp. It came from old Francis Albion. He seemed to be struggling for breath. Fanny went pale. She rose; hurried to his side. "Should we send for the doctor?" she whispered. "Father seems to be . . ."

"No, we should not." Adelaide did not move from her chair.

Francis had opened his eyes now, but they were staring up into his head in the most alarming way. He had gone pale. The cough began again.

"Aunt Adelaide," Fanny cried, "he's . . ."

"No, he is not!" said her aunt with some asperity. "Stop pretending to die, Francis," she cried. "Stop it at once." She turned crossly to Fanny. "Don't you see, child, he's trying to prevent you going to Oxford?"

"Aunt Adelaide! What a thing to say of poor papa." Her father was gasping for air now. "Of course I wouldn't go if he is unwell."

"Fiddlesticks," said Adelaide. But the awful sound went on.

Isaac Seagull, landlord of the Angel Inn, let the damp breeze play on his face as he gazed over Pennington Marshes.

He was a tall, wiry man, as tall as Grockleton if he stood straight. But usually Isaac Seagull stood with his round head stooped forward. His hair, still all black, was worn in a plait down his back. His face, as chinless as his Seagull ancestors, was usually cheerful; but at present it was serious. Isaac Seagull had something on his mind.

The organsation of smuggling in the New Forest area was a large and complex affair. First of all there were the ships that supplied the goods. These came from various ports across the sea, but the busiest were those of Dunkirk, which picked up Holland trade, Roscoff in Brittany, and the Channel Islands of Jersey and Guernsey. The main transports were called luggers, which varied in size but had broad, shallow draughts and huge capacity. They usually came across in armed convoys. When it was necessary to avoid the few Customs vessels sent against them the luggers could either turn into the wind and row away, or dash into the mudflats where the revenue vessels couldn't follow them. Sometimes the smugglers also used swift clippers, which could outrun almost anything.

The man in charge of the ship, or convoy, was the captain. But then, when the shipment came to shore it had to be met by a huge caravan that was to transport and distribute the goods. The organiser of this operation was the lander.

Isaac Seagull was the lander for the New Forest.

But behind the lander and the captain was another, more shadowy figure. The man who put up the money for the whole operation, who could buy the goods, pay for a clipper: the entrepreneur. This was the venturer.

Who was he? Nobody knew. Or if they did, they said nothing. The parish clerk at Lymington church kept all the books, so he must have known. A local bailiff took contributions from any of the farmers or merchants who wanted to invest in the enterprise; so he probably knew. The scale of operations was so large, sometimes, that it could only have been someone with very deep pockets, one of the local aristocrats, a member of the gentry.

Grockleton believed it was Mr Luttrell. Owner of a fine house called Eaglehurst, down past Mr Drummond's Cadland estate, at the junction of the Solent water and the Southampton inlet, Mr Luttrell had built a tower, which gave him a view of the whole Solent water and the Isle of Wight. That brandy shipments of some kind came to Luttrell's Tower was not in doubt, but this could be just some minor dealing for his own account. Was Luttrell really the secret figure, the venturer behind the whole huge New Forest coastal trade? Perhaps it wasn't even a single gentleman at all. Perhaps it was all of them.

Whether or not they were actual participants, two things could be said not only of the gentry, but of every inhabitant of the south coast of England at this period. The first was that, aristocrat or peasant, clergyman, magistrate or poacher, they were all at the very least the knowing recipients of illegal merchandise. The second was that nobody saw anything. Two kegs of brandy might be delivered to the Lymington magistrate's next-door neighbour, yet he was quite unaware of it. The pulpit might be full of brandy bottles but the vicar found plenty of room for his feet as he preached. Three hundred packhorses might wind along the edge of his lordship's park; his lordship never woke. Why, even Mr Drummond, His Majesty's personal banker, living in plain sight of Luttrell's Tower, never saw a thing. Nothing at all.

Why, for nearly a century, did the entire population of England's southern counties cheerfully connive at breaking the law? Because they did not like paying taxes? Nobody does. Were they all criminals?

Even the wisest legislators sometimes forget that, for the most part, government is just a business like any other. The entire population down to the humblest cottager now drank tea. The tax imposed on tea was so high that ordinary folk could not afford to pay it. Therefore they must either do without or find contraband. As much for this reason, probably, as any other, the smuggling business was not perceived as anything more than technically illegal. No one actually thought it was wrong. The law, in this instance, had no repute. Why, it was not even called smuggling. Free Trade was the name by which the enterprise was known; Free Traders were smugglers.

The case with brandy, and the many other goods shipped, was similar; but here a related factor came into play. The high level of duty actually created a potential profit margin: there was an inducement for a smuggling business to develop.

The obvious solution, one might have thought, would be to reduce the level of Customs duty. Ordinary folk might have had their tea and the smuggling trade become unprofitable. The Customs receipts would very likely have gone up. But this, it seems, never occurred to anyone – unless, of course, it had, and not every legislator wished to end the business.

The structure of the Free Trade was conventional. Profits on different commodities varied but on best brandy, the most favoured line, they ran roughly as follows.

A keg of brandy retailed in London, tax included, at about thirty-two shillings. Its cost price in France was half that. Selling at a discount of about thirty per cent off full retail price therefore left the Free Trader with a gross margin of around thirty per cent and the certainty that all his stock would be sold instantly for cash. After paying for the carriage of goods and other expenses, his profit would have been around ten per cent of his sales; so by making several runs a year he could earn a healthy return on capital employed.

Thanks to Isaac Seagull the lander, the distribution network was excellent. No cargo he had run had ever been intercepted.

Why then, as he gazed out over the marshes, should he betray by a twitch in his mouth that he was worried?

The venturer had some big plans for the coming year – very big. Nothing must go wrong. His job, as lander, was to make sure that nothing did.

So what could go wrong? Some time next year, if the reports were correct, there would be detachments of dragoons arriving at the new barracks at Christchurch. What would that mean? It was too early to know how many were coming, but it would be wise to get the biggest shipments through before they arrived.

Then there were events in France to consider. So far, the Revolution, the execution of the king, the reign of the Terror had all come to Paris. War had even been declared. But that had not stopped the big wine merchants of France concluding ambitious deals with the venturer. That was the venturer's problem, of course, not his. It exercised his agile mind, though, all the same.

Assuming the shipments could all be made before the new dragoons arrived, what else was there to consider?

Grockleton. Some Customs officers could be paid off, but they let you know soon enough if that was their game, and Grockleton hadn't. Isaac's feelings were mixed. Letting yourself be paid off was probably the most rational course, he supposed, but he quite respected a man who was prepared to fight. If he had a chance, that is. But could Grockleton really believe he had a chance?

Seagull could think of only one instance of the Lymington Customs men scoring a success and that had been five years ago, just before Grockleton came. A breakaway group of Free Traders had started operating out of a cave known as Ambrose Hole, in the river valley just north of Lymington. He'd known who they were, of course, and stopped using them for the smuggling run because they wouldn't obey orders. They'd taken to robbing people on the turnpike roads; then they'd killed several people. Everyone had had enough by then. The Free Traders were armed, but they scarcely ever used violence unless a convoy was attacked. Killing wasn't their style. The magistrate, the mayor, even he himself had all agreed it had to stop. So Seagull had told the Customs officer where they were, troops called in, the gang raided. They'd found a lot of stolen goods in the cave. And thirty bodies, too; buried in a shaft. He had been shocked by that.

The Customs officers and the troops had claimed that as a success. Seagull hadn't minded; it did no harm.

But Grockleton was still there. He had a determined look about him. He might be watched every hour, but he clearly could not be discounted. Isaac Seagull never discounted danger: that was why he was good at his job.

And now, as he considered the problem of Grockleton and what to do about him, another thought came into his mind.

What if Grockleton had a spy? A good one. Someone in the Free Traders. That was a further possibility. It might seem unlikely, but it had to be considered. An informer would be killed if caught of course. That was something the Free Traders would do. But still . . .

Isaac Seagull's mouth twitched. He was thinking.

Nathaniel Furzey liked living with the Prides in Oakley. They were a pleasant, lively family. He and Andrew Pride were fast friends. Andrew's father, besides keeping a small herd of cows, had a timber business, buying timber at a good price from the woodward and selling it on. Piles of his timber were stacked by the edge of Oakley green.

The first few weeks he had lived there he had been on his best behaviour. But before long, his natural high spirits had come out, and he had been getting into cheerful mischief ever since.

The fact was that curly-haired young Nathaniel Furzey was quickly bored. The schoolwork at Mr Gilpin's came so easily to him that he had usually finished when the rest of the children were only halfway through. Sometimes Mr Gilpin himself would come by and read with him. The vicar had even been tempted, once, to teach him a little Latin, but realised that Nathaniel was picking it up so fast that he had stopped the exercise quickly before it went too far.

"What do you think I should do?" Gilpin had asked a fellow cleric. "I'm not talking of natural intelligence. Young Andrew Pride has quite as much of that as any of the boys you'd find at the schools in Salisbury or Winchester. I'm speaking of a rare bird, a natural scholar, a fellow who could spend a life at Oxford or Cambridge." He sighed. "I dare say Sir Harry Burrard or the Albions would pay for it if I asked them to send him away to school – if the parents agreed of course. But . . ."

"You'd take him away from his family, his friends, the Forest," his friend had answered. "And if it didn't work . . ."

"Stranded like a boat on a sandbank."

"I think so."

"It's easier in towns. If he lived in Winchester, or London . . ." Gilpin mused. "I suppose the whole nation's like that, though. Trees growing deep in the forests. Wonderful trees dropping thousands of acorns. One in a million is carved into a piece of fine furniture. Nature's waste."

"True, Gilpin. But also England's stock. Always plenty of it."

So the vicar had left young Nathaniel in the little village school, after which he would doubtless grow up to enjoy a quiet Forest life. In the meantime he was mischievous.

One of the chief delights that occupied his active mind was that of playing practical jokes. Andrew liked these, too, but even he was awestruck sometimes by the ingenuity of some of the jokes that Nathaniel devised. His most recent had concerned the Furzeys.

Although he had the same name as the Oakley Furzeys,

Nathaniel soon came to share the Prides' view of their neighbours. Even setting aside the dark memory of their betrayal of
Alice Lisle, it seemed to the Prides that Caleb Furzey was a bit
slow in the head. What intrigued Nathaniel, however, was
Caleb's imagination. For it was full of fear and superstition.

"I always carries some salt with me," he assured the boy, "to
throw over my shoulder." Burley he was afraid to enter, "on account of the witches." He wouldn't go up to Minstead church
because he said it was haunted; and once, by mistake, he had
gone round Brockenhurst church widdershins – though few
Forest folk would have cared to do that – and had lived in fear
for weeks. But any evil sign would set him off. If he saw a solitary magpie, he spoke to it at once; he walked carefully round
ladders; and if he saw a jet-black cat with no white marking
he'd be off as fast as he could. "Black cat: witch's cat," he'd declare.

So Nathaniel had found a black cat. It was dead when he
found it and it wasn't really black, because it had some white
hair under its chin. But when he'd discovered a man who knew
how to stuff animals, and when he'd applied some black dye to
the white patch, he reckoned the cat looked pretty good. Then
he and Andrew Pride went to work.

There was nowhere that black cat didn't appear. Walking
along a forest path, Caleb would suddenly see it confronting
him, turn away in horror and never see the string that jerked it
quickly into the bushes. With luck he'd take another path and
the boys would be able to set up an ambush there too. Next
day, he'd see it at his window. Nathaniel was an artist, though.
Days would pass and Caleb would think himself safe before,
suddenly, the cat would appear in some new and improbable
place to terrify him. Soon the whole of Oakley was out looking for the mysterious feline. It was Andrew's father who
guessed the truth, cuffed the two boys and gave the stuffed cat
a discreet and decent burial. Nothing more was said about it
after that and the two boys certainly never knew that when the
timber merchant had told his wife about it privately the two
adults had laughed until they cried.

There were other things to interest Nathaniel at Oakley,
however. He had seen the Free Traders' packhorses up at
Minstead from time to time; but you couldn't help noticing a

lot more activity down at the coast near Oakley. Several times he had been aware that Andrew's father had disappeared for the night, returning at dawn looking cheerful, leading his pony and dumping a little sack of tea on the kitchen table without a word.

One morning three riding officers had arrived at Oakley and started inspecting Pride's pile of timber by the green. Pride had watched them with mild interest as they started dismantling it. They found this hard work; they took all morning. At noon Grockleton rode up and saw they had found nothing.

"I hope your officers are going to put my timber back the way it was, Mr Grockleton," Pride remarked.

"I don't believe they will, Mr Pride," the other replied with equal coolness.

Pride and the family had restacked the timber after they had gone. No word was spoken. That was the game.

Nathaniel encountered Grockleton himself one day, however. It was about two weeks after he had been given the small-pox vaccination. He and Andrew Pride had just come out of school and, instead of turning, as they usually would, to go past Mr Gilpin's house back to Oakley, they were walking the other way, towards Boldre church.

Their destination that day was Albion House, where Pride's aunt was the housekeeper. Andrew had been told to pay this formidable lady a visit after school and Nathaniel had been delighted to go with him. This was the house where the young lady lived, who had persuaded him to have the vaccination. It was a big house, too, Andrew had told him: a manor house. He had never been in such a house before.

They were just going along the lane to the church when they heard the horse behind them and turned to see the tall Customs officer riding up. As he came abreast he looked down and asked them politely where they were going.

Apart from his claw-like hands, Grockleton could make himself pleasant enough when he wasn't looking for contraband. Hearing their destination was Albion House, he pulled a sealed letter from his coat and asked with a smile: "Would you boys like to earn tuppence?"

"We each would, Sir," said Nathaniel, quick as a flash.

Grockleton hesitated a second, then chuckled. "Very well,

then. This is a letter from my wife to old Mr Albion. Will you
deliver it?"

"Oh, yes, Sir," they both cried eagerly.

"Then you will save me the journey." He reached for the
money, and as he did so casually remarked: "Now you must
see it's delivered at once. You know how to deliver letters, I
suppose?"

"I will deliver a letter anywhere in the Forest, Sir," said
Nathaniel firmly, "for tuppence."

"Good. Here you are then."

He gave them the money and watched them go off. But for
some reason, as if a thought had just struck him, Grockleton
did not move at once but remained where he was for fully a
minute, staring after them. And when Nathaniel glanced back,
he saw that Grockleton was staring at him, particularly, in deep
thought.

Now why, he wondered, should Mr Grockleton be doing
that?

Oxford! Oxford at last. There it was, ahead of them, its spires
and domes rising out of a faint morning mist that hung over
the broad green meadows and the gentle river that wound past
the colleges. Oxford on the River Isis, as the Thames is called
on this stretch of its long journey. It was useless to pretend
they were not excited.

"And to think, Fanny, my sweetest, dearest friend," cried her
cousin Louisa. "To think that we nearly did not set out at all!"

How very pretty Louisa looked today, Fanny thought with
pleasure. She had always admired Louisa's dark hair and lustrous brown eyes, and this morning her cousin was looking
particularly animated. How pleasant it was, she considered,
that her closest cousin should also be her best friend.

Their journey had almost been cancelled due to ill health.
Not that of old Francis Albion, who had been scolded by his
sister from death's door back to his usual state, but unexpectedly by Louisa's mother, Mrs Totton, who was to have accompanied them and who had fallen and sprained her leg so
painfully that she really didn't think she could travel. So they
certainly wouldn't have been able to go, if it hadn't been for
Mr Gilpin.

"My wife thinks I have been sitting in Boldre for too long," he assured the grateful Tottons just as firmly as if it had been true. "She positively insists I accompany you. Remember, I was up at Oxford myself, so to visit it again is nothing but a pleasure to me."

With the vicar as their companion there could be no doubt of the girls' safety. "Indeed," as Fanny reminded Louisa, "it is really a great honour for us to travel with such a distinguished man." And so, in high spirits they had set off in the Albions' best carriage to Winchester and thence up the old road that led, due north, the forty miles to Oxford.

By mid-morning they were installed in one of the city's best inns, the Blue Boar in Cornhill, the girls sharing one room, Mr Gilpin taking another. And promptly at noon Edward Totton called for them.

Having embraced his sister and his cousin, bowed and expressed his honour that Mr Gilpin should have accompanied them and seeing that they were all eager to explore the city, Edward suggested they should make a tour forthwith.

What a delight the city was. With its broad, cobbled main streets, and its curious medieval lanes, ancient Gothic churches side by side with splendid neoclassical façades, the university had been quietly growing there for more than five centuries. Its streets were busy with all kinds of people. Tradesmen and farmers from the countryside around mixed with clerics and poor scholars, rich young men with powdered hair, stern professors in academic gowns and visitors like themselves. Here they would pass a stately gateway and porter's lodge, like the entrance to a palace, and look into the huge cobbled quadrangle behind; there, down an alley, they would peep into some dark little yard that appeared to have been forgotten since medieval monks had used it four hundred years before.

Edward was very cheerful, the girls in high spirits; but Fanny did not fail to notice, with admiration, the role that Mr Gilpin assumed. He accompanied them in the most companionable way, but said little. Occasionally – when they came to the Bodleian Library, for instance, or the classical perfection of Sir Christopher Wren's Sheldonian Theatre – he would step forward and point out quietly, in his deep voice, a few of each building's finer points. Not to do so, after all, would have been failing in his duty. When they visited his own college, Queen's, he naturally took them round. But apart from these occasions he seemed to prefer to bring up the rear, letting Edward conduct the tour and not even allowing a hint of a frown to cross his distinguished brow when Edward got things wrong. Indeed, he seemed to be enjoying himself just as much as they were, as he poked his head into familiar old nooks and crannies with a delighted "Aha," to find them just as they had been fifty years before. They visited mighty Balliol College, stately Christchurch, pleasant Oriel and, towards three o'clock, came to Edward's own college, which was Merton.

"We say we are the oldest college," he informed them.

"Disputed." Gilpin chuckled.

"The first to be built, at least," Edward responded with a smile. "In 1264. We are very proud of ourselves. The Master of the college is known as the Warden."

Merton was certainly delightful. Its quadrangles were not large and grand, but more intimate and suggestive of its antiquity. Its chapel, however, was a very imposing affair, at the west end of which were a number of monuments and memorials. They had paused in front of a rather fine one to a Warden, Robert Wintle, who had died some decades before, and Gilpin had just begun to say, "A fine scholar, I remember Robert Wintle well," when Edward interrupted him with a happy cry: "Ah, here he is! I told him he'd find us at Merton."

And to their great surprise, Mr Gilpin and the two young ladies saw an elegantly dressed man, a few years older and somewhat taller than Edward, with a pale, aristocratic face and a good head of dark hair, which had been blown a little carelessly by the breeze. Seeing Edward, he nodded and smiled, then made Gilpin and the ladies a brief, formal bow.

"I said nothing, because I had no idea if he would come," said Edward. "He often doesn't," he added. "This is Mr Martell."

The introductions were quickly performed, Mr Martell bowing again, with grave politeness to Gilpin and each of the girls, though it was hard to tell whether he was really interested.

"Martell was in his final year when I came up to Oxford,"

Edward explained. "He was very kind to me. He used to talk to me." He laughed. "He doesn't talk to everyone, you know."

Fanny glanced at Martell to see if he was going to deny this. He didn't.

"You are of the Dorset family of Martell, perhaps?" Gilpin enquired.

"I am, Sir," Martell replied. "I know nothing about the Gilpin family, I confess."

"My family has Scaleby Castle, near Carlisle," Gilpin said firmly. Fanny had never heard him say this before and looked at her old friend with new interest.

"Indeed, Sir? You will know Lord Laversdale, perhaps."

"All my life. His land marches with ours." This having been duly noted, Gilpin glanced towards Fanny and continued more easily: "You know of the Albion estate in the New Forest, I dare say?"

"I know of it, although I have never had the pleasure of seeing it," said Mr Martell, again with a slight bow towards Fanny. There was, she thought, a faint tinge of warmth in his manner now, but it might just have been a trick of the light in the chapel.

"Let's go outside," said Edward Totton.

One of the delights of Merton College was its setting: for its buildings backed on to the open green space of Merton Field beyond which, across the Broad Walk, lay the lovely expanse of Christchurch Meadow and the river.

They made a pleasant group as they set out into this Arcadian scene, the two girls in their long, simple dresses, Mr Gilpin in his clerical hat, the two men in their tail coats and breeches and striped silk stockings. As they were leaving the college, Edward had kept up a lively discourse, explaining how his friend came to be staying in the vicinity, what a noted sportsman he had been at Oxford, and a scholar, too, it seemed. But as they started across Merton Field, his supply of conversation seemed temporarily to have dried up, and as neither Fanny nor Louisa wished to lead the conversation with the stranger, and Mr Martell himself showed no inclination to say anything, Mr Gilpin stepped in, walking beside Martell while the other three followed, listening, just behind.

"Have you taken up any career, Mr Martell?" he enquired.

"Not yet, Sir."

"You considered it?"

"I did. At Oxford I considered entering the Church, but the responsibilities of my position decided me against it."

"A man may be the owner of a large estate and be a clergyman, too," Gilpin pointed out. "My grandfather was."

"Certainly, Sir. But shortly after I completed my studies at Oxford a kinsman of my father's died, leaving me a large estate in Kent: this in addition to the estates in Dorset, which will be mine on the death of my father. The two lie a hundred miles apart; unless I relinquish one – which would betray a trust laid upon me – I conceive that it would be impossible to carry out my duties as a clergyman as well. I could, of course, engage a perpetual curate, but if I do that there seems little point in taking holy orders."

"I see," said Mr Gilpin.

"I think, perhaps," continued Mr Martell, "of entering politics."

"He's looking for a seat," Edward now interrupted from behind. "I've told him he should talk to Harry Burrard. He decides who the members for Lymington will be." He laughed. "I think Martell should represent us, Mr Gilpin. What do you think?"

But whether the vicar of Boldre meant to reply would never be known, for Fanny suddenly cried: "Oh, look, Mr Gilpin! A ruin."

The object at which she was pointing was a small bridge over the river, some way off to their right. If not exactly a ruin, it was certainly in a very dilapidated state, with its arches visibly crumbling. It looked most unsafe.

"Folly Bridge," said Mr Gilpin, who seemed glad to change the subject. "Now then, Edward, can you tell me the date of it? No? Mr Martell? No also. Well, it is believed to date from the late eleventh century, about the time of King William Rufus. If so, it is much older than the university."

This information having been received with respect, Fanny decided she could properly address the stranger. "Do you care for ruins, Mr Martell?"

He turned and looked at her. "I am aware" – he inclined his head momentarily towards Gilpin – "having read Mr Gilpin's

Observations with great profit, of the picturesque nature of ruins; certainly there is much to admire in, and much to learn from, the ruins of antiquity. But I admit, Miss Albion, that I prefer the vigour of a living building to the decadence of its remains."

"Yet there are some people who build ruins," she offered.

"I had a friend who did. But I consider it preposterous all the same."

"Oh." Thinking of her own plans she could not help blushing. "Why?"

"I should not care to spend so great a sum upon an object so useless. I see no sense in it."

"Come, Sir." Gilpin came to her defence. "Your argument surely has this weakness: you might say the same of any work of art. A painting of a ruin, then, should not be made either."

"I grant the justice of what you say, Sir," replied Martell, "and yet find I am not satisfied. It is, I think, a question of degree. The painter, no matter how great his labour, expends only his time, paint, canvas. Yet for the cost of even a small ruin a man might build a score of cottages that could be both useful and pleasing to the eye." He paused. Did he, perhaps, resent being obliged to speak for so long? "There is this further, Sir. A mansion is what it is, namely a house; a painting is a painting. But a constructed ruin pretends to be something it is not. It is false. The sentiments, the reveries it is intended to provoke, are also false."

"You do not care for the Gothic fashion in building, then?" asked Fanny.

"Taking a good house and adding Gothic ornaments to it to make it look like something else? Certainly not, Miss Albion. I abominate that fashion."

"Ha," said Mr Gilpin.

They went across, all the same, to inspect Folly Bridge, then walked along the river bank a little way. Edward had started to chatter again. It was very pleasant. By the time they had done this, Mr Gilpin and the two girls felt ready to return to the Blue Boar Inn to dine and rest. Edward and Mr Martell accompanied them to the inn and it was agreed that Edward should join them again the next morning to continue their investigation of Oxford. Mr Martell, it seemed, had other engagements. For their final day, however, Edward proposed that they should venture out to the village of Woodstock and visit the huge country mansion of Blenheim Palace, which lay in a magnificent park nearby.

"The duke is away at present," said Edward, "but one can visit the house upon application, which I have already made."

"Capital!" cried Gilpin. "The duke has some paintings by Rubens which must not be missed."

"Martell," asked Edward, "you will accompany us, perhaps?" His friend seeming to hesitate, he asked: "Have you visited Blenheim?"

"I have stayed there once or twice," Martell replied quietly.

"Oh God, Martell," Edward cried, not at all abashed, "I should have guessed you would know the duke. So come now, will you keep these ladies company – or do you only go to Blenheim when the owner is there to receive you?"

To Fanny's astonishment Martell merely shook his head, half smiling, at this sally. It seemed he did not mind Edward's puppyish teasing. "I should be delighted to accompany you," he said with a slight bow; although whether he really wanted to Fanny could not guess.

Mr Martell left them after this and so the two girls dined with Edward and Mr Gilpin. Fanny decided that this was preferable, really, since it relieved them of the necessity of conversing with a man who had no great desire for their company. She did ask Mr Gilpin for his opinion of Edward's friend, though.

"His intellect," Gilpin said cautiously, "is strong, although perhaps too rigid. But I should need to know him better." Which, while interesting, wasn't quite what she'd meant.

"He's damnably rich," said Edward. "I can tell you that."

Later, in their room, she had asked Louisa what she thought. She always enjoyed discussing things with Louisa. Her cousin and she were very close, perhaps because they were so different. They both had a good eye and enjoyed painting; but while Fanny would take time to seek some particular effect of the light or weather on the landscape, Louisa after a while would content herself with a few quick dashes of colour and say she was done. Or sometimes, when Mr Gilpin was instructing, she would make some flippant addition to the scene and, as the distinguished artist passed, point to it and ask: "Do you like my rabbit, Mr Gilpin? It has floppy ears."

But as it was done in a cheerful way and was so in tune with her character, he would just smile and say, "Yes, Louisa" and not take offence.

Louisa had a talent for mimicry – her imitation of Mr Grockleton was beyond praise – but she was not malicious. She read books, as much as she wanted to; she spoke enough French to amuse the French officers in Lymington. With her lovely eyes and dark-haired good looks, Louisa had long ago concluded that her role as a pretty daughter of Lymington's richest merchant suited her ambitions very well. And if she could have been cleverer or more hard-working if she wished, then she must have concluded that it was not in her self-interest. "What do I think of Mr Martell, Fanny? Why that he is a great catch and he knows it."

This was clearly true.

"But what of his character and his opinions?"

"Why, Fanny, I hardly know. It was you who spoke to him." Fanny had not thought of it, but she realised now that, unusually, Louisa had kept almost silent through their walk with Mr Martell. "I did observe one thing, Fanny," her pretty cousin continued with a smile.

"Tell me what, Louisa?"

"That you liked him." And now Louisa burst into a laugh.

"I? Oh, no, Louisa. I do not think so. Why do you think such a thing?"

But Louisa refused to discuss the matter further and instead went and sat in a chair by the window and, taking up a book, started to make a little drawing for herself upon the flyleaf. She busied herself in this way, refusing all conversation for some time, while Fanny began to prepare herself for bed, until finally she called Fanny over and, quietly handing her the book, let her look at the drawing by the fading light.

It was of a rutting stag: a great red deer, on the twilit forest heath, his head with its magnificent antlers thrown back about to emit his roar. It really was a very good likeness of the creature and well observed. With this one alteration: the face was that of Mr Martell.

"It is as well we are not to see him tomorrow," said Fanny, "as I should be afraid of laughing."

They did not see Mr Martell, or even think of him, the next day, which passed delightfully. But the following morning he was at the door of the inn, wearing a brown coat and riding breeches, and a tall brown hat to match. While they rode in the carriage, he mounted a magnificent bay, explaining that, as the day was fine and his horse had now been stabled for two days, he thought it best to give it some exercise. While this made perfect sense, Fanny could not help but reflect that it also meant that he was spared the need of talking to them on the journey.

With Mr Martell riding easily beside the carriage, the journey nonetheless passed very pleasantly. Of the Oxfordshire countryside Mr Gilpin had a poor opinion. "It is too flat. I can describe it," he told them, "only as a cultivated dreariness." But if the landscape was sadly wanting in the picturesque, its history was more encouraging. At Woodstock, the vicar reminded them, a medieval English king had kept his lady love, the fair Rosamund. So jealous of this lady was the queen that she wanted to poison her. And so, it was said, the king built a maze around her house, and only he knew the way in. "A pleasant story, even if untrue," as the vicar remarked. With these and other tales he regaled them until they reached the park gates of the great palace of Blenheim.

John Churchill had been a genial fellow, with only a poor squire's fortune at the court of the merry monarch, with whom he had shared a mistress. But he was also a formidable soldier. Having won a string of brilliant victories for Queen Anne, he was made Duke of Marlborough and rewarded, as successful generals were, with a great estate. As their carriage rolled along the drive this sunny morning, Fanny looked out eagerly to see the mansion. And soon enough, looking across a great sweep, she did.

It came as a shock. She felt a little intake of breath, a sense of cold fear. She was familiar with the mansions of the New Forest; she had visited the great house of Wilton up at Sarum; but she had never seen anything like this before.

The vast classical palace of Blenheim, named after the

duke's most famous victory over King Louis XIV of France, did not sit in the landscape: it spread across it like a cavalry charge in stone. Its baroque magnificence utterly dwarfed even the largest of England's manor-mansions. It was not an English country house. It was a European palace, of a kind with the Louvre, or Versailles, or one of the great Austrian palaces that stretch across the horizon at Vienna – behind whose classical façades one may sense a spirit of almost oriental power, like that of the Russian tsars, or the Turkic khans of the endless steppe.

For even in England, in that age – when portraits of aristocrats depicted them in the poses of classical gods – the founder of the Churchill family was not to be housed like a mortal. It was a quarter of a mile from the kitchens to the dining room.

They toured the house first. The Duke of Marlborough's marbled halls and galleries had a haughty grandeur she had never encountered before. This, she realised, was an aristocratic world quite outside and beyond her own. She felt a little overawed. She noticed that Mr Martell looked quite at home, though.

"There is a connection between Blenheim and the New Forest," Mr Gilpin reminded them. "The last Duke of Montagu, whose family owns Beaulieu, married Marlborough's daughter. So the lords of Beaulieu now are partly Churchills too."

They admired the Rubens paintings. "The first family picture in England," announced Gilpin of one. Although of the picture of the Holy Family he roundly declared: "It is flat. It possesses little of the master's fire. Except, Fanny, you may agree, in the old woman's head." But despite all the wonders of the palace, Fanny was not sorry when Mr Gilpin finally led them out to survey the park.

The park at Blenheim was very large, one of the greatest that Capability Brown had ever undertaken. There were no small comforts like those favoured by Repton: no modest walks or flower beds, but great sweeps across which all Marlborough's armies might have marched. God, it seemed to say, in framing nature, had only presumed to make a rough preparation, to be ordered and given meaning by the authority of an English duke. So it was that the park at Blenheim, with its broad arrangement of stream and lake, belts of woodland

and endless open vistas, rolled away towards a conquered horizon.

"Every advantage has been taken, which could add variety to grandeur," declared Gilpin as they began their promenade.

They all chatted together quite easily by now. As she walked with Mr Gilpin behind the other three, she saw that even Louisa was saying a few words to Mr Martell, about the scenery or the weather no doubt; and if Mr Martell did not say much, he seemed to be replying, at least. One could not deny, whatever one's opinion of him, that Mr Martell looked very handsome in this setting.

At one point, when a particularly fine vista, cunningly contrived by the genius of Brown, opened out before them, Gilpin cried out: "There. As grand a *burst*, I should term it, as art ever displayed. Picturesque. A scene, Fanny, for you to sketch. You would do it admirably."

Mr Martell turned. "You draw, Miss Albion?"

"A little," Fanny replied.

"Do you draw, Mr Martell?" Louisa asked; but he did not turn back to her.

"Badly, I fear. But I have the highest admiration for those who do." And looking, now, straight at Fanny, he smiled.

"My cousin Louisa draws quite as well as I do, Mr Martell," said Fanny with a slight blush.

"I do not doubt it," he said politely and faced round again to resume his conversation.

Having walked some distance, they turned to look back at the palace of the Churchills and, by way of making conversation, she asked what was the origin of the family.

"Royalists in the Civil War, certainly," said Gilpin. "A West Country family. Not one of the oldest or noblest, though, I think."

"Not like you, Martell," Edward laughed. "He's a Norman. The Martells came with William the Conqueror, didn't they?"

"So," replied Martell with a slight smile, "I have always been told."

"There you are," said Edward cheerfully. "No drop of lowly blood pollutes his veins; no contact with trade has ever blotted his escutcheon. Confess it, Martell. It's very good of you to talk to us."

Martell greeted this with an amused shake of the head.

Fanny was a little surprised to hear Edward raise the subject in this way when, as a Totton and undoubtedly still in trade, it might have seemed to place him at a disadvantage. But watching Martell's amused reaction, she realised there was an element of calculation in her cousin's boyish candour. With his own mother, she realised, belonging to a minor gentry family, his links to the Burrards – his close relationship, come to that, with herself, an Albion – young Edward Totton was already within the circle of relationship of the gentry. His oblique reference to his own family being in trade was therefore a subtle invitation to the aristocrat to tell him it didn't matter.

"I amaze myself sometimes," Martell finally remarked, rising very creditably to the occasion, "that I talk to anyone at all."

At which Edward grinned and Louisa laughed; and Fanny, if the truth were told, could not help being secretly pleased that she was an Albion.

They walked back to their carriage after that, the two girls together with Mr Gilpin, Edward and his friend talking to each other. Everyone seemed in high spirits, except for Mr Gilpin, who had fallen rather silent.

Before they got into their carriage, however, it was time to bid farewell to Mr Martell, who had to ride on to another house in the neighbourhood.

"But we are not parting for very long," Edward announced, "for Martell has agreed to come and stay with us, in Lymington. Quite soon, he says. It's all agreed."

This was a surprise indeed: yet not, Fanny had to confess, entirely unwelcome. After all, if he were at the Tottons' house, she should not be obliged to see him more than she wished.

So they all said goodbye and watched him ride off, and then returned to Oxford for their final dinner before their departure with Mr Gilpin, whom they did not forget, at dinner, all to thank.

Fanny found as, with the help of the inn's maid, she packed her clothes, that she was in a very cheerful mood.

She was somewhat taken aback, therefore, when Louisa suddenly declared: "Are you sure, Fanny, that you do not like Mr Martell?"

"I? I do not think so Louisa. Not really."

"Oh," returned Louisa, giving her a strange little look. "Well, I do."

Puckle set out soon after dawn. Nobody took any special notice. You didn't ask where Puckle was going. He was a man of secrets.

Only a handful of the men who worked at Buckler's Hard actually lived there; and although there was a village just outside the gateway to Beaulieu Abbey, not many of the labourers and carpenters lodged there either, since neither the owners of Beaulieu nor the villagers wanted them.

The reason was simple. If a labourer lived in Beaulieu parish and fell sick or grew old, he might become a charge on the Poor Rate, which meant that the parish, by law, would have to support him, his widow, possibly even his children. Naturally, therefore, all over England, parishes did their best to unload their poor upon their neighbours, sometimes going to great trouble to discover the distant birthplace of some poor person, for instance, in order that the charges could be levied there.

The solution for the Buckler's Hard workers had consisted of a new settlement. Down the western boundary of the Beaulieu estate, along the edge of the open heath, a straggle of cottages had sprung up. Technically they had no right to be there, for each plot was actually an encroachment upon the king's forest, but although there had been some talk of their removal, nothing had been done. As the settlement lay along the estate's boundary, it was known as Beaulieu Rails, although sometimes called East Boldre. It was only two miles or so from the shipyard, so the workers had no further to walk than if they'd lived at Beaulieu village.

But they were off the parish.

Puckle had lived at Beaulieu Rails for many years, but would still go over to the western side of the Forest once in a while, where most of his relations lived, so when he set out across the heath that Sunday morning his neighbours assumed he was going there. They might have been surprised, therefore, when, across the heath, he instead made his way northwards through the woods, past Lyndhurst and even Minstead. It was mid-morning when he came along the edge of the trees to the meeting place, which he had selected both for its distance from his home and because, from there, it would be easy to retire into the deeper seclusion of the woods nearby. As he drew close, he noted with satisfaction that the place was deserted.

The Rufus tree was gone. Its hollowed old hulk had finally rotted down into a stump which had disintegrated half a century earlier. In its place, however, a stone had been erected to commemorate the historic site. For although its miraculous winter greening was still remembered by some, it was the tree's false reputation as the site of King William Rufus's death that was now enshrined in stone. Nor was this all: even Purkiss and his cart had now become a matter of historical record.

At the stone, Puckle stopped and looked around. A short distance away stood the old tree's two sons. One had been pollarded, the other had not. Puckle's expert eye took in both at once. The pollard oak would not make good ship's timber, for the pollarding process made for weaker joints; but the other, he noticed, had been marked for felling any time. And it was from behind this tree that a figure now emerged, to whom he nodded.

Grockleton was on time.

He walked over and joined the Customs man under the oak, where they stood together. Puckle glanced around again.

"We are alone," said Grockleton. "I've been watching."

"That's all right, then."

Grockleton waited a moment, to see if the Forest man was going to open the conversation; but as it seemed not, he began: "You think you can help me?"

"Maybe."

"How?"

"I might tell you things."

"Why would you do that?"

"I has my reasons."

The scene Grockleton had witnessed was still vivid in his mind. What this fellow had done to annoy the landlord of the Angel Inn he had not discovered, but it had clearly been more than a question of brawling or drunkenness. Indeed, Puckle had appeared to be quite cool and sober at the time. But

whatever it was that had caused Isaac Seagull to drag him to
the entrance of the Angel and, quite literally, kick him into the
High Street in front of him, Grockleton would never forget the
look this fellow had given Seagull as he picked himself up. It
wasn't drunken anger: it was pure, undying hatred. Customs
officer although he was, Grockleton had never received a look
like that. He hoped he never did.

Shortly afterwards he had ridden after the Forest man as he
went home and, passing him on a deserted stretch of the lane,
remarked quietly that he would pay well if there was anything
Puckle ever wished to tell him. It was just a hunch, of course,
but it was the job of a Customs officer to make such ap-
proaches.

He hadn't really expected anything to come of it; but two
days later Puckle had made contact. And now they were talking.

"What sort of things could you tell me? Things about Isaac
Seagull?"

He couldn't be sure that the landlord of the Angel was actively involved in the smuggling. Normally speaking, you
could assume that the landlord of any inn received contraband,
but he had long suspected that Seagull might be doing far
more.

"He's a devil," Puckle said bitterly.

"I had the impression you quarrelled."

"We have." Puckle paused. "'Tain't only that, though." He
looked down. "You heard about when they raided Ambrose
Hole a few years back?"

"Of course." Although the raid on the gang of highwaymen
had taken place just before his arrival in Lymington,
Grockleton could not fail to be aware of it.

The other man now spat with disgust. "Two of them taken
was my family. An' you know who gave them away? Isaac
damned Seagull. He knows I know, too." This was cause for
hatred indeed. Grockleton listened carefully. "He treats me
like a dog all the same," Puckle continued with heartfelt bitterness, "because he reckons I'm afraid of him."

"Are you afraid of him?"

Puckle said nothing, as though unwilling to admit it. His
gnarled face reminded Grockleton of a stunted oak, just as

Seagull's made him think of a jaunty lugger, with a sail run up before the breeze.

"Yes," the forest man said quietly at last, "I fear him." And then, looking straight at Grockleton: "So should any man."

Grockleton understood. Violence between the smugglers and the Customs men was rare, but it could happen. Once or twice, if he had given them too much trouble, a riding officer might get a knock on the door and a bullet in the head. His claw-like hand clenched, but he gave no other sign. He was quite a brave man.

"So what do you want?" Puckle asked.

"To intercept a big run. On shore. What else?"

"You haven't the men to do it."

"That's my business."

Puckle looked thoughtful. "You'd have to pay me a lot of money," he said.

"A share of what we take." They both knew this could be a small fortune.

"You'd take Isaac Seagull?"

"So long as he's there, yes."

"Kill him," Puckle said quietly.

"They'd have to shoot at us."

"They will. I'll need money before. Plenty. And a fast horse." Seeing Grockleton look doubtful he continued: "What d'you think they'll do to me if they find out?"

"They might not."

"They would. I'll have to leave the Forest. Go away. A long way."

Grockleton tried to imagine Puckle outside the Forest. It wasn't easy. People did leave, of course. Not often, but it happened. And with plenty of money . . . He tried to imagine Puckle with money and couldn't do that either, but then he sighed to himself. People changed when they acquired wealth, even a man like this. Who knew what he would become with money in some other place? Puckle was mysterious. "Fifty pounds," he said. "The rest later. We can arrange for you to collect your share in Winchester, London, wherever you like."

He saw Puckle react, then try to hide it. The sum had impressed him. Good.

"Won't be for a while, yet," Puckle said. "You know that."

Grockleton nodded. The big smuggling runs were usually done in winter when the nights were long.

"One thing," the Forest man went on, looking thoughtful. "I'd need a way of getting word to you. Can't be seen near you myself."

"I know. I've thought about that already. I may have a solution."

"Oh. What's that, then?"

"A boy," said Grockleton.

It was some weeks before Mr Martell came to Lymington, but when he did, he chose his time carefully.

On a fine summer morning he rode down the turnpike into the town. He was feeling optimistic. He had preferred to ride ahead, leaving his manservant to follow in the chaise with his dressing case and portmanteau. As he rode past the turnpike's tollgate at the entrance to the borough, he realised that he had never been here before.

He had no doubt that he would have a pleasant visit and an interesting one, too. He liked young Edward Totton. They might not have a lot in common, but he had always liked the younger man's cheerful spirit and the fact that Totton wasn't frightened of him, which many people were. He actually quite enjoyed his stern reputation: it protected him from those who would have liked to take advantage of him; but it amused him when a young fellow like Totton refused to be abashed. Besides, in this case it was actually he who was intending to make use of Edward Totton.

Mr Wyndham Martell was in an enviable position: he didn't have to please anyone. Master of a large estate, heir to another, a graduate of Oxford, of good character: in the society in which he lived there was no man, unless such a person were impertinent, to find fault with him. If he was courteous – and in his somewhat reserved way he was – this was because he would have despised himself for being anything else. The only danger to his enviable estate might have been if he were a gambler or a debauchee and Martell, whose natural inclinations were towards the pleasures of the intellect, was far too proud to be either. He had enough personal vanity to present himself well; he had concluded, quite reasonably, that for a man in his position to be without vanity would be an affectation. He intended, for himself and for his family name, to make a figure in the world and he could afford to do it on his own terms. That is to say, he had decided to enter public life as that phenomenon, so rare in the politics of any age, an independent man who cannot be bought. And if this should be adduced as evidence that his pride was really quite above the usual, why then, so it must have been.

His real reason for coming to see young Edward Totton, besides his kindly feelings towards the young man, was that Lymington, which lay conveniently between his two estates, returned two Members of Parliament.

"And I think that at the next election," he had informed his father, "I might like to be one of them."

Why had the modest borough of Lymington two Members of Parliament? The short answer was that good Queen Bess had granted them a few years before the Armada when she wanted some extra political support. Did two Members for such a small place seem excessive nowadays? Not very, when you considered that Old Sarum, the so-called pocket borough on the deserted castle hill above Salisbury, returned two Members – and had practically no inhabitants at all.

The system of elections evolved in the borough of Lymington was actually typical of many of England's towns in that Age of Reason and, it must be said, it had the merits of safety, convenience and economy. Indeed, its electors considered it a model for all times and places.

Elections in some boroughs, alas, were not so well managed. Scurrilous pamphlets about the candidates provoked bad feeling. There was expense, for electors had to be bribed; there was trouble, when electors for another candidate had to be made drunk and then locked up; there could be still more trouble if they got out. Even a limited democracy, it was agreed by all parties, was a dangerous thing and nothing showed it more clearly than the drunken brawling of an election. They ordered this matter better, however, in Lymington.

The two Members of Parliament were chosen by the town's burgesses, of whom there were about forty; and the burgesses, in theory anyway, had been elected by the modest tradesmen and other obliging freeholders of the borough. Who were elected to the position of burgess? Sound men, worthy men, trustworthy men: friends of the mayor or whoever had the responsibility of running the town. Quite often the burgesses of Lymington actually lived there; but the quest for good men might lead much further afield. Twenty years ago when Burrard, as mayor, had decided to create thirty-nine new burgesses, he had chosen only three from the town itself; his search for other loyal men had taken him all over England. Why, he had even gone to the trouble of finding one gentleman who lived in Jamaica!

There were hardly ever disputes between the burgesses as to which Members they should elect. Until twenty years before, the Burrards had shared the control of the borough with the Duke of Bolton, who had large interests in the county, and there had been a slight disagreement once over whether the duke's friend Mr Morant should or should not be given a seat at one election. But since then the duke had ceded the borough entirely to Burrard, so that even that possibility for disagreement had happily vanished.

But how were things managed, it might be asked, when an election came? How were the burgesses who might live two hundred miles away – let alone the good gentleman in Jamaica – to get to Lymington to record their votes? Even this had been taken care of, by a simple expedient. Elections were not contested. There were no rival candidates. If there were but two gentlemen standing for the two seats available, then the trouble and expense of an election poll were clearly superfluous. All that was necessary was for a proposer and seconder to appear before the mayor upon the appointed day and the thing was done. So easy were these arrangements that it was agreed that there was no need even for the candidates themselves to appear, thereby saving them what might have been a tiresome journey.

Thus, in the eighteenth century, were the Members for Lymington chosen. Whether a different method would have produced better representatives cannot be known; but this at least is certain: the burgesses, and the Burrards, were entirely satisfied.

Martell's father would have preferred his son to stand for a county seat as these tended to be Tory, whereas Lymington, like most trading towns, was solidly for the Whig party. Traditionally the Tory party was for the king, the Whig for the post-1688 Parliament which, although loyal, believed in keeping the royal power in check. Country squires were often Tory, merchants usually Whig. But these differences were not always real. Many of the greatest landowners were Whigs; often as not, one's party depended upon family alliances. Even the king would sometimes prefer a Whig leader to a Tory. The interests and beliefs of Sir Harry Burrard, baronet, and the gentlemen burgesses of Lymington were unlikely to differ from aristocratic Mr Martell's in any significant way.

Indeed, there were only two things about Mr Martell's behaviour this morning that would have struck his contemporaries as odd. If Martell wanted a Lymington seat, why the devil go there when he could easily write to Burrard or meet him in London? And stranger still, why was Martell deliberately going to Lymington when he knew – for he had made careful enquiries – that the baronet would be away?

To ask such questions, however, was not to know Wyndham Martell.

He was always thorough. At Oxford, unlike many young bloods, he had chosen to work quite hard. He had already made the most careful study of the estate he had been left and started a series of improvements. Had he been a clergyman, no matter how high his social position, he would certainly have paid attention to the welfare of every parishioner. So if he thought of applying for a Lymington seat, he meant first, like a good general, to reconnoitre the place thoroughly.

Of course, he knew it was possible that Sir Harry Burrard might not care for such intrusive behaviour. There was a well-known case where a borough patron, afraid that a candidate might charm his own burgesses away from him, had only agreed to give him the seat on the condition, set out in writing, that once elected the said Member swore never to set foot in the constituency he represented. Even in the eighteenth century this was thought a trifle eccentric. But without going so far as this, Burrard might not approve of his sniffing around his borough, so he had decided to do it discreetly by visiting young Totton. One thing was sure though; by the end of a week he'd know a good deal about it and make up his own mind whether, and upon what terms, he wished to take the business further.

In the meantime, apart from Edward, there were two pleasant young women to pass the time with. Louisa Totton was a good-looking, lively girl. As for Miss Albion, while not quite so pretty, he thought her agreeable.

"You must admit," Edward Totton remarked quietly to his sister, as they waited for their guest to emerge from the house, "I bring you only the best."

Mr Wyndham Martell was the third eligible bachelor he had brought to the house in the space of a year. One had been a young fellow – too young, really, but heir to a large estate – who was still at Oxford with him. Another young blood he had brought with the promise of attending the local races had shown a strong interest in Louisa – so strong that when he got a little drunk she had to fight him off and he was asked to leave. Still, even these encounters had added to her small store of knowledge of human nature and the outside world; and her attitude to these encounters – although she would not have used such words – might best be expressed as: keep them coming.

Martell, however, was quite another story. Martell, as her brother put it, was "serious business." He supposed she might be rather afraid of the stern landowner.

"I've watched him," she replied. "He's proud – after all, he has so much to be proud about. But he likes to be amused."

"So do you mean to amuse him?"

"No," she said thoughtfully. "But I shall let him suppose that I might." She glanced at the door of the house. "Here he comes."

Martell was in an excellent humour. He had not been quite sure what the Tottons' household would be like, for he had never stayed with a member of the provincial merchant class before. So far he had been agreeably surprised. The house was a handsome Georgian place with a sweep of drive and a view to the sea. It was about the size of a good rectory, the sort of home that might belong to the younger brother of the landowner, an admiral, or someone of that sort. Mrs Totton turned out to be a handsome woman of his own class, related to several families he knew. As for Mr Totton the merchant, they had only had time to speak a few words, but he seemed both sensible and easy, entirely a gentleman. If young Edward Totton had any idea that his position in society was lacking in some way, Martell considered, he should be told not to be silly, and not to insult his parents.

"We'll make a tour of the town first," said Edward as Wyndham Martell joined them. And it being a fine day, they decided to walk.

They made a leisurely progress into Lymington and down the High Street. Martell admired the shops – Swateridge the watchmakers, Sheppard the gunsmith, Wheeler's china store – and the numerous signs of the place's prosperous gentility. He insisted on spending some time in the bookseller's. He noted the brass plate on the fashionable doctor's house and that Mr St Barbe the merchant had even started a High Street bank. He learned that the postal service came down the swift turnpike road from London four days a week, arriving at the Angel Inn; as did the diligence, as the stage coach was called, from Southampton – that fifteen-mile journey being covered in as little as two and a half hours. He was impressed.

They went down to the quay, where there were several small vessels tied up, then round by the salterns before returning to the house with a good appetite for dinner.

Mr Totton and his wife kept an excellent table. The meal began with a light pea soup and bread, followed by a fish course; this was then removed to make way for the first main course, which consisted of dishes of sirloin of beef, turkey in prune sauce, stewed venison and fried celery. The men drank claret; Louisa, who usually drank currant wine at home, joined her mother today with champagne.

The conversation was light and sociable. Mrs Totton spoke of the ancient forest deer, the king's recent visit, of places he should see and told stories about them. Louisa, her large eyes, it seemed to Martell, hinting at reserves of humour behind her demure countenance, gave a good account of some of the plays to be seen at the playhouse and how they were acted.

Edward told him about the racecourse that was now laid out above Lyndhurst. "And we don't only race horses, Martell," he remarked. One amusing local gentleman, it seemed, had a racing ox which he rode himself and challenged all comers to compete in a similar manner.

By the time the second course was served – potato pudding, anchovy toast, syllabubs, jugged pigeon and tarts – Martell could reasonably conclude that the seaside town below the ancient forest was probably one of the most pleasant to represent in all England.

The tablecloth had been removed, however, the jellies, nuts, pyramids of sweetmeats and plates of cheese set out, port appeared for the men and cherry brandy for the ladies, before Martell remembered to ask after Fanny Albion.

"Poor, dear Fanny," cried Louisa. "She has, I declare, the disposition of a saint."

There was, it seemed, small likelihood of her appearing. "Although you may be sure," said Edward, "that we shall try to coax her out." Her aunt Adelaide's lifelong friend having fallen sick in Winchester, the intrepid old lady had insisted upon getting in her carriage and going over to stay there, despite her own advanced age, leaving Fanny and Mrs Pride in charge of old Mr Albion. Before leaving, she had given her brother strict instructions not to be ill until she came back – instructions he had already disregarded. And if the nature of his present malady remained unclear, this was only because it was too advanced, he told them, to be identified. So Fanny was stuck at home with him and didn't feel she could get out.

"Perhaps we should call upon your cousin," Martell suggested.

"I'll suggest it," said Edward, "but I think she'll say no."

Shortly after this the ladies retired and Martell was able, over the port, to question Mr Totton about the business of the town. As he had expected, Totton was thoroughly well-informed.

"Salt, of course, has been one of our main trades here for centuries. As in other towns, you'll find that most of the larger merchants have several businesses and salt is usually one of them. St Barbe, for instance, deals in groceries, salt and coal. The coal, by the way, fuels the furnaces in the salterns. Salt, remember, is not only used to preserve fish and meat; it's a medicine against scurvy – vital for the Navy, therefore – it's used in curing leather, as a flux in glass-making and metal smelting, a glaze in pottery."

"There are cheaper ways of making salt than from the sea, I believe."

"Yes. In the long run Lymington's salterns will be threatened. But that's a long way off yet."

"You export timber?"

"Some. Less than before. The Navy and other shipbuilding seems to take most of our local supplies. The port is busy, though. Coal comes in from Newcastle. There are various merchantmen sailing to London, Hamburg, Waterford and Cork in Ireland, even Jamaica."

"And the local industries?"

"Apart from those mentioned, most of the parishes have clay, so there are a number of brickworks. That's why you'll find some handsome brick barns in the area nowadays. Brockenhurst's got the biggest works. Then there's a rope factory at Beaulieu Abbey. Rope for the Navy, of course. Some of the Forest people drift into Southampton, too. Apart from the port, there are some very big coachbuilding works there now."

"But our greatest hope for the future," Edward interposed with a smile, "lies in quite another direction. We are going to become a fashionable resort, a second Bath."

"Ah, yes." Totton laughed. "If Mrs Grockleton has her way. You have not met Mrs Grockleton yet, Mr Martell?"

Martell confessed that he hadn't.

"We are going to take tea with her," Edward chuckled. "Tomorrow."

The next morning was occupied by a visit to Hurst Castle. Although the day was bright, a fresh breeze was coming across Pennington Marshes, causing the little windpumps by the salterns to click loudly. Mrs Beeston's bathing house, which was situated near one of the windpumps by the beach, was deserted. In the channel between the fortress and the Isle of Wight the running waves were flecked with foam, while out in the sea beyond the waters were churning green. There was a rich, salty smell in the air. Louisa, her face a little flushed and wet with spray, looked uncommonly well as the wind blew her dark hair; and Martell, too, was conscious of his own strong heartbeat as they walked rapidly, laughing together, over the wild coastal marshes.

They were halfway back when they met the count. He was walking alone, looking sad.

Martell had already remarked upon the presence of French troops in the town and Edward had explained about them. He introduced the count to Martell, who addressed him in excellent French, and it was not long before the Frenchman, discovering a fellow aristocrat, was anxious to make a friend.

"You are one of us," he cried, taking Martell's hand in both of his. "How charming that we should have found each other in this wild place." Although whether this referred to the marsh or to Lymington was not quite clear. He asked about Martell's estate, his Norman ancestry, insisted that they were related, therefore, through the line of Martell-St Cyr – of which Martell blandly assured him he was entirely unaware – and enquired whether he liked to hunt, receiving an affirmative.

"At home we hunt boar," he said wistfully. "I wish, my friend, that I could invite you to join us, but unfortunately if I go home at present" – he gave a shrug – "they will cut off my head. Have you fishing also, perhaps?" Martell assured him that he had some excellent fishing. "I like to fish," said the count.

As this elicited only a polite bow and a brief silence, Edward cut in to inform the Frenchman that they were going to take tea with Mrs Grockleton and that they must return home.

"A remarkable woman," the count replied. "I must bid you *au revoir*, then, my dear friend," he said to Martell. "I love to fish," he added hopefully; but his English friends were moving on and so he continued, sadly, towards the windpumps by the sea.

"As you see, Mr Martell," said Mrs Grockleton at three o'clock that afternoon as, brushed and sedately dressed, they took tea in her drawing room, "there are great possibilities for Lymington."

Mr Martell assured her that he found the town admirable.

"Oh, Mr Martell, you are too obliging, I'm sure. There is so much to be done."

"No doubt, Madam, you will transform the landscape just as Capability Brown would make a park."

"I, Sir?" She almost blushed at what she took to be flattery. "I can do nothing, although I hope I may encourage. It is the situation of the place, and its residents, and its royal patrons who will effect the transformation. And it will come. I think I see it clearly."

"The sea is bracing, Madam," said Martell, non-committally.

"The sea? To be sure the sea is bracing," cried Mrs Grockleton. "But have you seen those ugly windpumps, those furnaces, those salterns? They will have to go, Mr Martell. Would any person of fashion wish to bathe under the gaze of a windpump?"

The question seemed unanswerable; but considering that the leading merchants of the town, including his hosts, were in the salt trade, Martell felt bound to disagree. "Perhaps a suitable bathing place may still be found," he suggested.

Whether Mrs Grockleton would have allowed this he did not learn since at this moment the master of the house appeared.

Martell had been told what to expect in Samuel Grockleton and he saw that Edward's description had been accurate; although to insist upon referring to the Customs officer as "The Claw" was, perhaps, a little cruel. He had no sooner sat down and accepted his wife's offer of tea when the maid who was assisting Mrs Grockleton tripped and upset the cup of hot tea on his leg.

"Alack-a-day!" cried Mrs Grockleton. "You have scalded my poor husband. Oh, Mr Grockleton." But that gentleman, though he winced, got up and, with admirable presence of mind, took a vase of flowers from a table and poured the cold water over his leg. "What are you about, my dear husband?" she demanded a little crossly now.

"Cooling the scald," he replied grimly and sat down again. "I may as well have that walnut cake, Mrs Grockleton," he now observed.

Martell, who rather admired this blunt good sense, decided to engage his host in conversation at once, so asked him frankly if he considered the trade in smuggling to be large in the Forest.

"The same as Dorset, Sir," the Customs officer replied.

Since Martell knew perfectly well that from Sarum westwards, across the whole of Dorset and the West Country, there was probably not a single bottle of brandy on which duty had been paid, he contented himself with a nod of the head. "Can the trade ever be stopped?" he enquired.

"On land, I should say not," Grockleton answered. "For the simple reason that it would take too many officers. But one day it can and will be severely limited by sea patrols. As in all our nation's affairs, Sir, the sea is the key. Our land forces are generally of small use."

"Ships to intercept the goods at sea? They'd have to be swift, and well armed."

"And well manned, Sir, too."

"You'd use naval captains?"

"No, Sir. Retired smugglers."

"Brigands in royal service?"

"By all means. It always worked before. Sir Francis Drake and his like in the days of good Queen Bess, Sir, were all pirates."

"Mr Grockleton, fie," cried his wife. "What are you saying?"

"No more than the truth," he replied drily. "You will all forgive me, now," he observed, getting up, "if I go to change," and with a bow he was gone.

"Well," said Mrs Grockleton, obviously disappointed by her husband. "What will you think of us, Mr Martell?"

Rather than answer, Martell calmly observed that he understood her academy had enjoyed a growing success.

"Why indeed, Mr Martell, I truly think it has. Tell Mr Martell, Louisa, about our little academy."

So turning her large eyes in his direction, Louisa gave some account of the art classes and the other scholastic attainments of the academy in a way that neither made light of them nor took them too seriously.

"In particular," Mrs Grockleton added, "I myself instruct the girls in French. I make them read the finest authors, too, I assure you. Last year we read . . ." Her mind failed to supply the name.

"Racine?" offered Louisa.

"Racine, to be sure, Racine it was," and she beamed at her

erstwhile pupil for her cleverness. "You speak French perfectly, no doubt, Mr Martell?"

It was at this moment that Martell decided he'd really had enough of Mrs Grockleton. He looked at her blankly for a moment.

"*Vous parlez français,* Mr Martell? You speak French?"

"I, Madam? Not a word."

"Well, you greatly astonish me. In polite society . . . Did Edward not say you spoke with the count?"

"Indeed, Madam. But not in French. We spoke in Latin."

"Latin?"

"Certainly. You teach the young ladies to speak Latin I am sure."

"Why no, Mr Martell, I do not."

"I am sorry to hear it. In the politest circles . . . The horrors of the Revolution, Mrs Grockleton, have given many an aversion to the language. In my opinion it will soon be Latin, and Latin alone, that is spoken in the courts of Europe. As it was formerly," he added with a scholarly air.

"Well." Mrs Grockleton, for once, looked flummoxed. "I had not supposed . . ." she began. And then, gradually, a light dawned in her broad face. She raised a finger. "Methinks, Mr Martell," she said with a knowing smile, "methinks you are teasing me."

"I, Madam?"

"Methinks." There was just a hint of warning in her eyes now, enough to make even the aristocrat realise that her academy was not built without some ruthless cunning on her part. "Methinks that I am mocked."

Unless he wanted enemies in Lymington it was time to bail out fast. "I confess," he said with a smile, "that I speak some French, but not enough, I suspect, Madam, to impress you; so I hardly like to admit it. As for my jest about Latin." He looked at her seriously now. "After the horrors we have just seen in Paris, I do indeed wonder if French will continue as the chosen language of society."

This seemed to pass. Mrs Grockleton made noises about the fate of the French aristocracy that almost made it sound as though she were one of them. It was agreed that the sooner the gallant count and his loyal troops in Lymington could return to France and restore order the better.

From here on, Mrs Grockleton was back in her element. The necessity for a new theatre, new Assembly Rooms and very likely new citizens were all warmly agreed to, so that she felt no hesitation in announcing, as they were about to leave: "I am intending to give a ball in the Assembly Rooms before long. I do hope, Mr Martell, that you will not disappoint us by refusing your company."

And given all that had passed, Martell found it difficult not to respond that, if he were anywhere in the vicinity he would be delighted to attend – a form of words that normally would have committed him to nothing, were it not for the fact that he had a curious, uncomfortable feeling that, somehow, she would contrive things so that he was there.

"Well," whispered Edward, as soon as they were out in the street, "what did you think of her?"

"Give me 'The Claw' any day," murmured Martell.

No further mention had been made of Fanny Albion, nor was it at dinner that evening.

The next day in the morning they took the carriage to call upon Mr Gilpin, who received them in the Boldre vicarage very cordially. They found him in his library, amusing himself by giving mathematical problems to a curly-haired boy from his parish school who, he informed them, was named Nathaniel Furzey.

The vicar was happy to show Martell his library, which had some fine volumes in it, and to let them see some of the recent sketches he had done of New Forest scenes.

"From time to time I have a small auction of them," he explained to Martell, "and men like Sir Harry Burrard pay foolish prices for them because they know the money goes to endow the school and some other charities with which I concern myself. The life of a clergyman" – he gave Martell a sidelong look – "is quite rewarding."

There was no question that Mr Gilpin's vicarage, which was three storeys tall and capacious, was a very handsome residence for any gentleman, and from the gardens behind he could display an admirable view across to the Isle of Wight.

The breeze of the day before had remained about the same, but banks of grey clouds were starting to pass over the Solent water now which, with their silver linings, gave the scene an atmospheric heaviness, a contrast of shafts of light and areas of darkness that was certainly picturesque. It was as they were surveying this natural picture that Martell happened to ask after Fanny.

"She is at Albion House now," Gilpin remarked. "Which reminds me," he added thoughtfully, "that I have something to tell her. But that can wait." He looked at Edward. "Were you intending to call on her?"

Edward, after only a second's hesitation, said that they were uncertain whether she would wish it at present.

Gilpin sighed. "I should think she must be lonely now," he remarked. Then, calling the curly-haired boy to him: "Nathaniel, you know the way to Albion House. Run up there and enquire, from me, whether Miss Albion will receive Mr Martell and her cousins."

Some refreshments were brought and, answering numerous questions put to him about the area, he entertained them very well for something more than half an hour, when young Nathaniel returned.

"I am to say yes, Sir," he reported.

It was not quite what he had expected. He could not say exactly why: perhaps it was the closeness of the trees as they turned in at the gate from the lane; or possibly it was the advancing grey clouds which, just as they had come down from old Boldre church, passed with their shining edges overhead, drawing behind them a shadow. All Martell knew was that, as the carriage approached the corner of the narrow drive, the sky above was sunless, and he felt strangely dull and ill at ease.

Then they turned the corner and came in sight of Albion House.

It was only the light, he told himself; it was only the grey glow pressing through the clouds that made the house so sombre. How old it seemed with its bare gables; how closely the green circle around it was hemmed in by the trees. Its brick skin was dark as a bloodstain. Its wrinkled roof told of the old Tudor skeleton of timbers within. The windows stared out so blankly that you might have supposed the place was empty and dwelt in now only by the spirits who would remain there year by year as the house fell slowly into ruin, until it crumbled away so that even their habitation was gone.

They came to the entrance. A tall woman was standing at the door. "Mrs Pride, the housekeeper," said Edward quietly. There was, Martell thought, a guarded, anxious look in her eyes.

The last few days had not been easy for Fanny. Her father had been very poorly. Several times he had been petulant; once, which was unusual, he had even had a fit of temper. She had sat with him most of the time in his room the day before and today, although he had taken some tea and some broth, and a glass of claret, it seemed unlikely that he would leave the big wing chair beside his bed where he was sitting, wrapped in a shawl.

So it had come as a shock to her when Mrs Pride had come to tell her, half an hour ago, that the young Tottons and Mr Martell were about to call.

"But we are not in a state to receive them," she cried. "As for Father . . . Oh, Mrs Pride, you should have asked me first. You should not have told them to come." But once Mrs Pride had apologised and said she supposed Miss Albion would have wished it, there was nothing to be done. "We shall have to make the best of it," she said.

Yet to her great surprise, when she went to tell her father about the unwanted visit and promised to send them all away as soon as she decently could, old Mr Albion seemed to make a miraculous recovery. Although somewhat querulous, he insisted that she bring him a looking glass and a clean cravat, scissors, hairbrush, pomade. In no time he had everybody running in every direction so that it was all Fanny could do to slip away and make a few small preparations in her own appearance.

She was standing on the staircase looking down into the hall as they came through the door with the grey daylight behind them. Edward entered first, then Louisa and Mr Martell just behind her. They paused for a moment before they noticed her. Edward looked around and, just before the big door was closed behind them, Louisa half turned to Mr Martell to say something and she saw her lightly touch his arm.

How pale she looked in the shadows of the staircase, Martell thought, as Fanny advanced towards them. In her long dress she seemed like some ghostly figure in a drama from antiquity. He saw at once the signs of strain in her face.

She led them quietly into the old panelled parlour, apologised for the fact that she was not better prepared to greet them, and asked politely after his health and his family. There seemed to be a slight constraint in her manner as she did so, however, and Martell wondered if perhaps she would have preferred it if he had not come.

However, they made polite conversation; Louisa gave a lively account of their tea with Mrs Grockleton, which brought a smile, if a rather weak one, to her face. And when Louisa produced a perfect imitation of Mr Grockleton pouring the vase of water over himself and then replacing the flowers, Fanny, too, joined in their laughter.

"You could go on the stage, Miss Totton," Martell declared with an amused shake of the head and a warm glance in her direction. "Your cousin, Miss Albion," he observed, "is a most amusing companion."

"I am delighted you have discovered it," said Fanny, but she looked tired.

The light-hearted conversation came to a sudden end, however, with the entrance into the room of old Mr Albion. With one hand he leaned on a silver-topped stick; the other arm was supported by Mrs Pride. His silk breeches and waistcoat and cravat were in perfect order; his snow-white hair was neatly brushed; his several days' growth of beard was not shaved but trimmed close. His eyes, old though they might be, were the most startling blue that Martell had ever seen. His coat hung loosely; he was thin and frail; but as he moved slowly across the room to an upright chair, he seemed to have discovered an almost fierce old dignity with which to meet his guests.

As is often done when a very aged person is in a room, people took turns to come and speak to him. Martell, as the visitor, went first. After the usual compliments, which were well enough received, he remarked that they had all enjoyed his daughter's company in Oxford that spring. It was hard to be sure, but this seemed to please the old man less. Martell then remarked that he was come recently from Dorset and was planning to proceed to Kent, since this sort of geographical information usually opened up a conversational response of some kind.

"Dorset?" Mr Albion enquired, then looked thoughtful. "I'm afraid," he confessed regretfully, "I never liked it much."

"Too many long hills, Sir?" Martell offered.

"I never leave here now."

"I understand you travelled to America," Martell attempted, still in hope.

The old blue eyes looked up at him sharply. "Yes. That's right." Mr Albion now appeared to be considering something and Martell supposed he might be about to make some reflection upon the subject. But after a few moments it seemed that if he had been going to, he had thought better of it, for his eyes wandered to Louisa instead and, raising his silver-topped stick he pointed to her. "Very pretty, isn't she?"

"Indeed, Sir."

Mr Albion seemed rather to have lost interest in Martell now for he pointed at Louisa again. "You're looking very pretty today," he addressed her.

She bobbed a curtsy and, smiling, took this as a cue to come to his side, where she knelt down very charmingly by his arm.

"Are you comfortable down there?" the old man asked.

"I'm always comfortable," she said, "when I come to talk to you."

It being plain that the old man had no further use for his company, Martell withdrew while Fanny went to make sure there was nothing her father needed.

"I feel sorry for Miss Albion," he murmured to Edward. "Where did you intend we should go tomorrow?"

"To Beaulieu, if the weather's fine," said Edward.

"Could we not ask your cousin to accompany us?" Martell suggested. "It must be grim for her being in this house with her father all the time."

Edward agreed and thought the plan a good one. "I shall do my best," he promised.

After this, Fanny returned and Martell had the opportunity

to talk to her for several minutes. She seemed to recover her former cheerfulness somewhat and they enjoyed a little of the pleasant conversational intimacy they had experienced at Oxford, but as well as appearing rather older, there was, he thought, a hint of sadness, even tragedy in her person, now that he saw her in the setting of her home. She must get away from here, he decided. Someone must save her from this. But he could quite see that such an escape would not be easy. Perhaps the visit to Beaulieu might raise her spirits. Out of the corner of his eye he saw Edward approaching the old man. Young Totton's affable manner, he supposed, would do the trick nicely.

"I think, Sir," Edward addressed Mr Albion with a charming smile, "that Louisa and I shall beg you, if the weather is fine, to let us steal our cousin Fanny from you for an hour or two tomorrow."

"Oh?" Mr Albion looked up quite sharply. "What for?"

"We mean to visit Beaulieu."

For a second, not even that, a tiny shadow might have appeared on Louisa's face, but in an instant it was gone. "Oh, yes!" she cried. "Do let Fanny join us. We shall not, I'm sure," she declared, "be gone for more than half the day." And she gave Mr Albion a smile that really should have melted him, had he not looked away.

"Beaulieu?" They might have announced an intention to travel up to Scotland. "Beaulieu? That's a long way."

No one quite liked to point out that it was scarcely more than four miles from where they were, but Edward, to his credit and with a pleasant laugh, remarked: "Scarcely further than we have come to see you today. We'll be there and back in no time."

Mr Albion looked doubtful. "With my sister away and in my state of health . . ." He shook his head, frowning. "There's no one else to take care of matters . . ."

"You have Mrs Pride, Sir," said Edward.

But this interference in his domestic arrangements did not suit Mr Albion at all. "Mrs Pride has nothing to do with it," he snapped.

"I think," Fanny interposed gently, not wanting to see her father upset, "that it would be better, Edward, if I remained here."

"There," Mr Albion said crossly, yet with a triumphant gleam in his eye. "She doesn't even want to go."

This was so outrageous that Martell, who was not used to being crossed himself, could scarcely remain in passive silence. "You will permit me to observe, Sir," he said quietly but firmly, "that a brief excursion might benefit Miss Albion."

Had this intervention done any good? For a second or two, as Mr Albion sat, his head momentarily sunk down in his cravat, in total silence, it was impossible to tell. But then, suddenly, it became all too clear. The old man's head shot up on its stalk so that he suddenly looked like an enraged old turkey. The neck might be withered but the startling blue eyes were blazing. "And you will permit *me* to observe, Sir," he shouted, "that my daughter's health is none of your concern. I am not aware, Sir, that the arrangement of this house has passed into your hands. To the best of my knowledge, Sir" – and now he raised his silver-topped stick and drove it down into the floor with all his force, to accentuate each word – "I – am – still – master – of – this – house!"

"I had no doubt of it, Sir," answered Martell, flushing, "and I had no wish to offend you, Sir, but merely . . ."

Mr Albion, however, was no longer of a mind to listen. He was white with rage. "You *do* offend me. And you will oblige me, Sir" – he spat out the words with venom – "if you make your observations in some other place. You will oblige *me*, Sir" – he seemed to be struggling to rise from his chair now, grasping the arm with one hand and the stick with the other – "if you will leave this *house*!" This last word was almost a shriek as, unable to get up, he fell back into the chair and began a gasping cough.

Fanny, now white herself and obviously fearing her father was about to have an apoplexy, gave Martell an imploring look and, with some hesitation – in case Mr Albion really was having a fit and Fanny in need of assistance – he backed into the hall, followed by Edward and Louisa. Mrs Pride, by now, had already miraculously appeared and, having inspected her employer, signalled to the visitors that it was safe to retire.

Once outside, Edward shook his head with some amusement. "Not a great success, I fear, as a visit."

"No." Martell was still too surprised to say much. "That is the first time," he remarked wryly, "that I have ever been thrown out of someone's house. But I fear for poor Miss Albion."

"Poor, dear Fanny," said Louisa. "I shall go back there this afternoon, Edward, with mother."

"Well done, Louisa," her brother said approvingly.

"They say there's bad blood in the Albion family," continued Louisa sadly. "I suppose that's what it is. Poor Fanny."

An hour later, after she had helped Mr Albion to his room and sat with Fanny while she wept, Mrs Pride slipped out of the house and made her way across to Mr Gilpin's.

The weather was perfect the following morning when Edward and Louisa set out with Mr Martell. Unfortunately, because Mrs Totton was already engaged, Louisa had been unable to go back to see her cousin; but she had sent Fanny a most loving letter, which the groom had taken across that very same afternoon, so her conscience was clear.

She really felt quite cheerful, therefore, as the carriage bowled up the turnpike towards Lyndhurst where they meant to pause briefly before crossing the heath. Mr Martell was in a conversational mood. It was very agreeable, of course, to be asked questions so attentively. Although always polite, she noticed that if Martell became interested in a subject he would pursue it, at least in his own mind, with a relentless thoroughness that she had not encountered before but which, she acknowledged to herself, was proper in a man.

"I see, Mr Martell," she remarked upon one occasion, "that you insist upon knowing things." And this he acknowledged with a laugh.

"I apologise, my dear Miss Totton, it's my nature. Do you find it disagreeable?"

He had never addressed her as "dear Miss Totton" before, nor asked her opinion of his character.

"Not at all, Mr Martell," she said with a smile that had just a hint of seriousness in it. "To be truthful, no one in conversation ever asked me to think very much before. Yet when you issue such a challenge, I find it to my liking."

"Ah," he said, and seemed both pleased and thoughtful.

The village of Lyndhurst had changed very little since the

Middle Ages. The forest court still met there. The King's
House, somewhat enlarged, with a big stable block opposite
and extensive fenced gardens on the slope behind, was still
essentially the royal manor and hunting lodge it had always
been. There were two gentlemen's houses in the near vicinity,
one called Cuffnell's, the other Mount-royal; but Lyndhurst's
scattering of cottages only really amounted to a hamlet. The
status of the place was signalled rather by the fine church
which, replacing the ancient royal chapel, had been erected
on Lyndhurst's highest piece of ground beside the King's
House and could be seen like a beacon for several miles
around.

They paused only briefly at the King's House before going
to look at the racetrack. This was an informal affair, laid out
on a large expanse of New Forest lawn, north of Lyndhurst.
There were no permanent stands: in the usual manner of the
age, people watched the races from carriages and carts if they
wanted a better view.

"One of the attractions here," Edward explained, "is the
New Forest pony races. You'd be amazed how fast they can run
and they're wonderfully sure-footed. You must come back for
a race meeting, Martell." And something about the look on
Martell's face told Louisa that he probably would.

They set out for Beaulieu now. The lane to the old abbey,
which ran south-east across open heath, left Lyndhurst from
just below the racetrack. In so doing, it passed by two most curious sights, which immediately engaged Martell's attention.
The first was a great, grassy mound.

"It's known," Edward explained, "as Bolton's Bench."

It was the great Hampshire magnate the Duke of Bolton
who, early in the century, had decided to take the little mound
where once old Cola the Huntsman had directed operations
and raise it into a great mound that overlooked the whole of
Lyndhurst. The duke was well known for these sweeping alterations to the landscape. Elsewhere in the Forest he had ar-
bitrarily blazed a huge straight drive through miles of ancient
woodland because he thought it would make a pleasing ride
for himself and his friends. But what struck Martell even more
than Bolton's man-made hill was the great grassy earth wall
that stretched across the landscape just beyond it.

"That's the Park Pale," said Edward. "They used it once for catching deer."

The huge deer trap where Cola the Huntsman had once directed operations was still an awesome sight. Enlarged even further some five centuries before, its earthwork wall strode across the landscape for almost two miles, before making a mighty sweep round into the woods below Lyndhurst. In the clear morning sunshine the great empty ruin might have been some prehistoric inclosure in a genteel world; yet the deer of the Forest were still there, men still hunted; only the turnpike road nearby and the church on Lyndhurst rise had altered the place since medieval days. And who knew, as they gazed at the earthwork in silence, if suddenly a pale deer might not appear from beside the green hill of Bolton's Bench and run out across the open ground?

It was at this moment that they heard a merry cry from behind them and turned to see a small open chaise coming round the track behind Bolton's Bench; inside it sat the sturdy figure of Mr Gilpin, who was waving his hat cheerfully. Beside him was a curly-haired boy. And on the other side of the boy sat Fanny Albion.

"Oh," said Louisa.

They all walked into the abbey together. Mr Gilpin was in high good humour.

He had been surprised by Mrs Pride the housekeeper's call the day before, yet rather intrigued and delighted to do something to help Fanny. He quite agreed with her that Miss Albion needed to go out with her cousins, especially after the behaviour of old Francis Albion. But he pointed out to her that, if the old man continued in his present mood, it would scarcely be possible to extract Fanny.

But while Mrs Pride acknowledged that this was true, she also assured him: "Some days, Sir, Mr Albion sleeps right through the day and would not even know if Miss Albion were out."

"You think tomorrow might be such a day, do you?" the vicar asked.

"He was so excited this afternoon, Sir, I shouldn't be surprised."

"I do believe," the amused Mr Gilpin remarked to his wife, after Mrs Pride had gone, "that she's going to drug him."

"Is that proper, my dear?" his wife asked.

"Yes," said Mr Gilpin.

So he had set off very cheerfully that morning in his light two-wheeled chaise. Calling at the school on the way, he had also collected the Furzey boy. He knew he shouldn't, but the child had such a sparkling intelligence that it was almost impossible to resist the temptation to educate him.

Arriving at Albion House, he found Mr Albion sunk in a profound sleep and, tempted yet again, sent up a secret plea to God that the old man's sleep might be eternal. Fanny, however, proved more of a problem. It was not so much the fear of leaving her father that worried her, but the prospect of encountering Mr Martell after what she felt had been her humiliation the day before.

"My dear child," the vicar assured her, "there was no humiliation whatsoever. Although quite unjustified, I gather that for a man of his age, your father put up rather a fine display."

"But that Mr Martell should meet such a reception in our house . . ."

"My dear Fanny," remarked Gilpin shrewdly, "Mr Martell has people fawning upon him wherever he goes. He will have relished the change. Besides," he added, "I don't even know for certain that your cousins will have carried out their intention of going to Beaulieu at all. So you may have only me and young Furzey for company. Pray come along, for I have a letter to deliver up at Lyndhurst on the way."

He insisted, now, upon walking beside the two Tottons, leaving Fanny and Mr Martell to follow.

If Fanny felt a sense of embarrassment after yesterday's events, Mr Martell was able to dispel it. Indeed, he made a great joke of the business, said that he'd never been thrown out of a house before but no doubt would be many times in future. "Indeed, Miss Albion, your father reminded me very much of my own although, if we could set the two of them to fight each other, like two old knights in a tournament, I think your father might prevail."

"You are kind, Sir, for I do confess," she owned, "that I felt mortified."

Martell considered. It was not her mortification that he remembered from the day before. It was her pale form advancing across the hall, her air of inner sadness, even tragedy, his own desire, perhaps scarcely realised at the time, to protect her. Yet here she was, flushed with the ride in the morning air, warm flesh and blood, very much so. Two images in a single person, two aspects of a soul: interesting. He would see if he could not keep the tragic shade at bay.

"Ah," he continued cheerfully, "if only we could all control our parents. But when they flash, you know, your father's eyes are very fine." He glanced down at her, somewhat searchingly. "As indeed are yours, Miss Albion. You have your family's wonderful blue eyes."

What could she say, or do, but blush? He smiled. She had never seen him so warm.

"I believe your family is very ancient in the Forest," he went on.

"We say we are Saxon, Mr Martell, and that we had estates in the Forest before the Normans came."

"Dear heaven, Miss Albion, and we Normans came and stole from you? No wonder you throw us out of your houses!"

"I think, Mr Martell" – she laughed – "that you came and conquered us." And without especially meaning to, as she said the words "conquered us," she looked up into his eyes.

"Ah." He gazed straight back, as though the thought of conquest had suddenly struck him, too, and their eyes remained looking into each other's for several moments before he looked thoughtfully away. "We old families," he said with a hint of intimacy that seemed like a comforting cloak around her shoulders, "perhaps dwell upon the past too much. And yet . . ." He glanced in the direction of the Tottons in a way that suggested that, although fine enough people, there were things that a Martell or an Albion could never quite share with them. 'I think we belong to the land in ways that others do not."

"Yes," she said quietly. It was how she felt too.

"So." He turned to her with such easy playfulness that it was as if he had already put his arm round her. "Are we ruins, or are we merely picturesque, you and I?"

"I am picturesque, Sir," she replied firmly. "But pray don't tell me you're a ruin."

"I promise you," he said gently, "that I am not."

The Beaulieu River being tidal, the tide was out as they crossed the bridge to the old gatehouse and the big pond on their left was almost empty of water, the reeds around the edge of this muddy expanse greeting them with a soothing rustle as they approached.

Although the abbey was long since ruined, it still preserved remarkably its ancient character. Nor was it all destroyed. The gatehouse and much of the inclosure wall was still there. The abbot's residence had been restored and somewhat enlarged into a modest manor house. The cloister inclosure also remained, with the huge lay brothers' *domus* still taking up one of its four sides. And while the great monastic church had been almost all dismantled, the monks' refectory opposite had been converted into a handsome parish church. The present Montagu heiress was seldom there, having made another of the family's brilliant marriages, this time to the descendant of Monmouth – for although Charles II's unlucky natural son had lost his head when he rebelled in 1685, he had still, thanks to his wife, passed down huge estates to his descendants. And these were now united with those of Montagu. The family kept a kindly eye upon the place, however, and its grey stones retained their air of ancient peace.

"So, Mr Martell." Louisa turned back to them as soon as they had passed the gatehouse. "Have we lost you to Fanny?" She gave Martell a curious little look when she said this, as if there were something slightly odd about Fanny, but Martell smiled and took no notice.

"I have been enjoying her conversation as much as I enjoy yours," he replied amiably. "Will you not join us?" And so, with one young lady upon each arm, he proceeded into the precincts. They had not gone far before he suddenly remarked: "This abbey hath a pleasant seat; the air . . ." He paused. Louisa looked blank.

Fanny laughed. "Nimbly and sweetly recommends itself," she continued. And, seeing Louisa still looking confused, she cried: "Why, Louisa, 'tis from Shakespeare's *Macbeth*. We read it together with Mrs Grockleton. Only it is a castle, not an abbey, in the original."

"I had forgotten." Louisa flushed and frowned irritably.

"But Mr Martell, you surely remember that after the king makes that remark he meets his death," Fanny reminded him. "Perhaps you had better be careful."

"Well, Miss Albion." Martell looked from Fanny to Louisa. "I believe I am safe, for neither of you looks to me like the fearsome Lady Macbeth."

"You haven't seen me with a dagger," said Louisa with mock fierceness, trying to recover her position. It seemed to Fanny that it was perhaps herself, rather than Mr Martell, into whom Louisa might plunge a dagger just then and she decided to make sure there were no more embarrassments for her cousin.

She was on her guard, therefore, when, as they reached the abbot's house, Martell casually enquired of Louisa what order of monks had inhabited the place in former times.

"Order?" Louisa shrugged. "They were just monks, I suppose." Hardly wishing to do so, she glanced towards Fanny.

"I'm really not sure," said Fanny carefully, although in fact she knew perfectly well. "Didn't they keep many sheep, Louisa? I should think they might have been Cistercian."

"So in that case," said Martell, who had not been deceived by this protection of her cousin for a moment, "there would have been lay brothers and granges?"

"Yes," Fanny confirmed. "Some of the big barns out at the granges still remain." And she indicated in the direction of St Leonards Grange. Martell nodded, interested.

Ahead of them Mr Gilpin had just paused to take note of some trees the Montagus had planted in straight lines, of which he was expressing his strong disapproval to Edward and the Furzey boy; and they were waiting for him to finish, when over the gatehouse, from the south quite unexpectedly, a redshank swept across the sky. It was such a lovely sight that they all paused to watch. And what, Fanny wondered, could have possessed Louisa to point to the slim, elegant wader and cry out: "Oh, look, a seagull."

For a second Martell and Fanny assumed she must be joking, but at the same moment they both realised that she wasn't. Fanny opened her mouth to say something, then thought better of it. She and Martell looked at each other. And then – they didn't mean to, they couldn't help it – they both burst out laughing. Worse, scarcely thinking what he was doing, as he leaned away from Louisa towards her and she towards him, he took Fanny's arm and squeezed it affectionately. So there they were, while Louisa looked on – there was no disguising it – sharing a joke like a pair of lovers and at her expense. Louisa's face darkened.

"Mr Gilpin!" It was, no doubt, a providence that they should have been interrupted by a cry, at this moment, from the direction of the cloisters as a figure came hurrying forward. "We are honoured indeed." Mr Adams, the curate of Beaulieu – the resident clergyman, actually, since the man who nominally held that benefice never came there – was the eldest son of old Mr Adams who ran the shipyard at Buckler's Hard. While his brothers had gone into the business, he had been educated at Oxford and then taken holy orders. After Gilpin had greeted him warmly and introduced everyone the friendly curate offered to conduct them round and took them at once into the abbot's quarters – "For reasons which remain unclear, we nowadays call it the Palace House," he explained – and they admired its handsome vaulted rooms. Martell, ever polite, was giving his full attention to the clergyman, while Fanny was entirely content to fall a little behind with young Nathaniel Furzey, who so evidently considered her his personal friend.

From there they passed into the cloister and the curate led them towards the old monks' refectory, which now served as his parish church. As Fanny knew it well, however, and young Nathaniel was getting a little restless, she told them she would wait outside with him while they went in. And so, as they disappeared, she found herself alone with him in the cloister.

If, in the abbey's heyday, the cloisters had always been a pleasant place, in their ruin they had acquired a new and special charm. The north wall with its arched recesses was more or less intact. The other walls, clad with ivy, were in various states of crumbled ruin, with, here and there, a little arcade of empty arches remaining like a screen beyond which the foundations of former buildings, all grassed over, provided an intimate vista. Wisely, therefore, having no need to build themselves a ruin, the Montagus, laying out a lawn and placing small beds of plants by crumbling walls and broken pillars, had created a delightful garden where one could walk and enjoy the friendly company of the old Cistercian shades.

She let Nathaniel run about and, having taken a turn around the garden, looked for a place to sit. The sheltered arches of the monks' carrels in the north wall looked inviting, screened from the breeze and catching the sun's warm rays. She selected one near the centre, sitting on the stone seat and resting her back on the wall behind. It really was quite delightful. In front of her across the cloister the big end wall of the former refectory made a stone triangle in the blue sky. The others were all inside it. No sound issued. Nathaniel, too, had vanished somewhere. She took a deep breath and closed her eyes for a moment, feeling the sun on her face.

Why did she feel so happy? She thought she understood. She was not so foolish, she told herself, as to believe that Mr Martell's liking her – for she was sure he did – would necessarily lead to anything more than that. Mr Martell had, there was no question, the pick of almost any young lady in England. But it was very pleasant, all the same, to feel that he admired the things she had to offer: her family, her intelligence, her gentle humour. She had had no dealings with men before. Yet the first she had met, and one of the most eligible, clearly valued her and was attracted to her. It gave her a sense of confidence that was most agreeable. That, she thought, was why she was so happy and relaxed.

But even this was not quite all. No, the contentment she felt derived from something even simpler. Something she had just felt when she was walking and laughing with Mr Martell and it took her a few minutes to realise what it was.

She had felt so easy in his presence. That was the answer. She had never been so comfortable in her life. It gave her a strange feeling of lightness. It really seemed to her, just then, as if she had entered a world in which there was no more pain.

She smiled to herself and, for no particular reason, pulled out the wooden cross she often wore and felt the faint lines of its ancient carving. She sat there for some minutes, enjoying the peace of her surroundings.

After a little time Nathaniel came back and sat down contentedly beside her. "What is that?" he asked, noticing the little cedarwood crucifix.

"A cross. My grandmother gave it to me. It's very old, I believe."

He inspected it and nodded solemnly. "It looks old," he agreed and leaned back, testing the seat for comfort. Having satisfied himself, he let his eyes wander round the cloisters. "Do you like it here?" he asked and, when she said she did: "I like it here too."

They had sat together for another minute or two before Nathaniel pointed to a place on the wall just behind Fanny, causing her to turn and look. For a second she did not know what he had seen, but then she noticed it: a letter "A" that someone had scratched in the stone. It was quite small, very neat and the script looked Gothic, as if it might have been carved long ago by some monk's hand. She smiled. A letter "A" left in the stone, a tiny record of a life, vanished, deep beneath the ground.

"How surprised the monk who carved that would be – if monk it was – to see the two of us sitting in his cloister now," she remarked. "And not at all pleased, we may be sure," she added with a smile.

It was a pity, therefore, that Brother Adam could not have appeared to tell his descendants that, on the contrary, he was very pleased indeed.

A minute later Mr Gilpin emerged to tell them they were going to inspect the rope works and then go down to the ship-building yard at Buckler's Hard.

Slowly, slowly, the great tree moved forward. Slowly the six mighty carthorses, harnessed one behind another, hauled on the chains, and the huge cart behind them creaked and lurched under its load. They were bringing a forest oak tree to the sea.

Puckle sighed. What had he done?

He had been right, the day he had met Grockleton, to spot the value of the spreading oak near the Rufus stone. Normally trees were felled in winter and transported in summer when the ground was hard. But for some reason Mr Adams had allowed this tree to be felled late. And so, while its pollarded brother had been left to live another century or two, this splendid son of the ancient, miraculous oak had felt the sharpened axes swing and thud into its side, biting their way into its two-hundred-year-old core until at last, in sight of the place where its magical old father had grown, it had toppled, and fallen and crashed down upon the moss and leaves of the forest floor. Then, with their saws and axes, the woodsmen had gone to work.

There were three parts to a fallen oak. First, the outer reaches, the lop and top, of no use to the shipyard and quickly cut away, along with the twigs that were carted for firewood. Then there was the main part of the tree, the mighty trunk, cut into huge sections to be used in the body of the ship; and then there were the all-important joints, known as knees, where the branches grew out from the trunk, which would form the supporting angles within the ship. There was also a fourth part, the bark, which some timber merchants would strip off and sell to the tanners. But Mr Adams would never allow this to be done, so the great oaks that came to Buckler's Hard arrived with their bark still on.

Now, chained and spiked in place, the main section of the huge trunk, its widest or butt-end foremost, was being hauled across the Forest to the shipyard, where it would be seasoned for a year or two before use. To make the great stem and stern posts of a ship, a tree with a girth of at least ten feet was needed. A large tree like this one would provide about four loads, or tons of timber. A naval battleship would use over two thousand loads – about forty acres of oak trees. All the time, therefore, the woodsmen's axes were at work, constantly felling, as the ancient oaks dropped from the canopy and the endless supply of timber made its way towards the sea like so many streamlets running off the Forest.

Now the tree had reached the end of its journey on land and Puckle, walking beside the lead horse, looked down into Buckler's Hard.

What had he done? For some reason that particular morning, the terrible realisation had come over him like a wave. As he gazed at the two little terraces of red-brick cottages he could have wept. He was going to have to leave all this: everything that he loved.

Buckler's Hard had become his home. How many years had he worked here upon the wooden ships? How many years had he gone down the river to the quiet spot where the lugger brought casks of the finest brandy and brought the precious load up to the cobbler's shop in Buckler's Hard from whose secret cellar bottle upon bottle would be discreetly conveyed to the manors on the eastern side of the Forest? How many times had he walked by Mr Adams the master, or any of his other friends at the yard – or even young Mr Adams the curate of Beaulieu come to that – at some strange hour, and never been noticed?

For Mr Adams's rule was simple. He was to see nothing. No contraband landed at the Hard. If the cobbler's shop had a cellar, goods came and left after dark. If a bottle of finest brandy arrived at his door, he never asked how. And as long as these requirements were met, it was remarkable what he could fail to see. Whenever Puckle turned up late after one of the big runs on the other side of the Forest – and sometimes he missed an entire day – Mr Adams could always have sworn he was working in the yard all the time and paid him accordingly.

Puckle the trusted man; Puckle among friends; Puckle in the Forest. How could he leave?

He'd thought about it, of course, even told himself he could talk his way out of it. But it was no good. Some things you might get away with, but not this. There would be no forgiveness shown. Weeks, even months might pass, but you would pay the price.

If only, now, he could refuse. Could he? A vision of Grockleton's claw-like hand and Isaac Seagull's watchful face came up before him. No, it was too late. He could not refuse. Detaching himself from the haulage team, now, as other men came to take over, he made his way down towards the slipway. He always felt better when he was working on the ships.

Just before he reached it he noticed that Mr Adams was standing in front of his house, talking to a party of visitors.

Although two of his sons were there, it was old Mr Adams who fascinated Fanny. With his flint-like face, his old-fashioned white wig, his stiff, upright walk, at over eighty years of age he would still ride to London to get the contracts for the yard's naval vessels. While clearly not best pleased to be interrupted by visitors, he was courteous enough as he showed them round.

But equally interesting, Fanny soon discovered, was the subtle change in Mr Martell. She had seen him as a proud aristocrat, a man of education and – she might as well admit it – a charming companion and no doubt lover. But as he went round with old Mr Adams she saw something else. His tall frame stooped forward just a little to catch everything the shipbuilder said; he asked sharp questions, to which the older man was soon answering with obvious respect. His handsome, saturnine face had grown concentrated and hard. This was the face of the powerful landowner, the Norman knight who knew his business and expected to be obeyed. To her surprise, she felt a little shudder pass through her body as she watched him. She had not realised he possessed such power.

The building of a great sea-going vessel, as the eighteenth century drew towards its close, was a remarkable business. Like so much industry at that time it was still a rural affair, small in scale and done by hand. Yet the little shipyard at the Forest's edge was highly productive: as well as numerous merchant vessels, more than a tenth of all the new naval warships built had come from the Beaulieu River yard.

Taking them first to a large barn-like wooden building just above the slipways and beside the blacksmith's, Mr Adams showed them a large, long space where a series of line patterns had been marked out on the floor. "This we call the mould loft," he explained. "We lay out the designs to scale on this floor; then we make wooden moulds so that we can check the shape of every inch of the ship as we build it."

Then he walked them up to the huge sawpit. Two men were busily at work on a section of tree trunk, which they were sawing with a huge saw, the man holding the upper end standing up on the trunk, the man with the other end down in the pit.

"The fellow on top is the master. He guides the saw," Mr Adams told them. "The man below is his junior. He has the harder work for he pulls the saw."

"Why is the man in the pit wearing such a big hat?" asked Louisa.

"Watch and you will see," answered Mr Adams with a wry look. And as the great saw swept downwards, the reason was all too clear as a cascade of sawdust fell down on the poor man's head.

Inspired, it seemed, by the stern, practical mind of the aristocrat at his side, Mr Adams was becoming quite affable. He took them by several spots where individual men were at work on particular projects. One was shaping a huge rudder with a gouge and mallet; another was making holes in a timber post with an instrument like a huge two-handed corkscrew.

"He makes a hole with the augur," the shipbuilder explained, "and then it will be fastened with one of these." He picked up a great wooden spike as long as his arm. "This is a wooden nail. We make them here. We always use the same wood for the nail as the timber it is to fasten, otherwise it will work loose and the ship will rot. Some of them are even bigger."

"Don't you use any iron nails in the ship?" asked Edward.

"Yes, we do." A thought seemed to strike the old man. "You passed by the rope works up at Beaulieu, I believe? Well, the monks over at Sowley built a great fish pond in times past. And now it is used by an iron works. That's where our nails come from." He smiled. "So even a monastery" – he clearly meant, "even something so useless and popish as a monastery – may be changed, with time, to serve a useful purpose." And, clearly delighted with this reflection, he led them down towards the river.

There were three vessels of different sizes and stages of completion in the slipways.

Martell looked at them appraisingly. "I assume you try to build a smaller vessel alongside a larger, for reasons of economy," he remarked.

"Precisely, Sir. You have it," Mr Adams responded. "The larger ship," he explained to the others, "uses the larger timbers and the lesser ship the smaller, all from the same tree. Even so," he remarked to Martell, "there is huge wastage of wood, for only the inner part of the tree is hard enough to be used. We sell off all that we can, but . . ." It was evident that any kind of waste was offensive to the shipbuilder.

"Are they all New Forest oaks?" asked Fanny.

"No, Miss Albion. This" – he indicated the surrounding Forest – "is our first timber yard. But we go further afield. Nor are ships made only of oak. The keel is made of elm, the ships' wall planks are beech. For the masts and spars we use fir. Come, let me show you."

On the largest slipway, a big man-of-war stood almost ready for launching.

"That's *Cerberus*," announced Mr Adams. "Thirty-two guns, almost eight hundred tons. The biggest battleships are only forty feet longer, although they have double the tonnage. She'll launch in September and be towed along the coast to Portsmouth for fitting in the naval dockyards there. The smaller ship we have started work on beside her is a merchant ship, bound for the West Indies trade. She'll complete next year. The little fellow in the third dock is a fifty-ton lighter for the Navy. As you see, we've just got the keel down, whereas for the merchant vessel we have the whole frame completed."

"Do you build the great battleships, too?" Fanny asked.

"Yes, Miss Albion, but only once in a while. The biggest we built was *Illustrious*, five years ago. A seventy-four-gun monster. The finest ship I think we ever made was a sixty-four-gun called *Agamemnon*." He smiled. "The 'Am an' Eggs, the sailors call her."

"And do you follow their progress after they leave the yard?"

"We try to. *Agamemnon*, for instance, has just been placed under a new commander. A captain called Horatio Nelson." He shrugged. "Can't say I'd ever heard of him." He glanced around. Nor had anyone else. "Well," he continued, "would you like to enter *Cerberus*?"

Puckle was alone between decks. A moment ago there had been the sound of hammering from above as the last planks of the deck were being fastened; but now, for some reason, the noise had ceased and the ship had fallen silent.

How cavernous it seemed in the sudden quiet, with the light coming in through the empty squares of the gunports. There was nothing between the decks except the occasional supporting posts: no partitions, no guns, no galley equipment, no hammocks or ropes or casks. Everything beyond the empty shell of the ship would be fitted at Portsmouth. All he could see was wood: wooden deck, wooden walls, stretching away for a hundred feet, the grain of the timber visible in the soft light, the scent of the planking, and of the pitch used to seal it, sharp in his nostrils; and in the corners, where the deck heads met the hull, the angle brackets made of the knees of oak as though the decks above his head were not made of planks but a spreading canopy of branches forming natural layers within the silent echo of the ship.

Then he heard footsteps and down the ladder from the deck above came Mr Adams with the party of guests.

How curious the fellow looked, Martell thought, with his stooped shoulders, his shaggy brown hair and oaken face. One by one the party descended the ladder and looked at him.

Mr Adams came last and gave him a curt nod. "This man's name is Puckle," he told them. "He's been with us, it must be fifteen years."

"Seventeen, Sir," Puckle corrected.

"Puckle." Edward laughed. "Funny name."

"It's a good old Forest name," said Fanny at once, thinking her cousin sounded rude. "There have been Puckles in the Forest as long as Albions, I'm sure. Over at Burley mostly, isn't it?" she asked Puckle with a friendly smile.

"That's right." Puckle knew who the Albion girl was and she met with his approval. She belonged.

The Tottons were still gazing at Puckle with amusement, as though he were a curiosity. Martell was looking around, noting the way the deck and hull were joined. Mr Gilpin was apparently meditating.

"Down here." Fanny hesitated because she wasn't quite sure what she meant. "It has such a strange feeling." She looked at the others, who didn't seem very interested, then turned to the Forest man. "Do you feel it?" she asked, hearing as she did so, to her great irritation, Louisa giggle behind her.

Because he had just been feeling the same thing and because he liked her, for the first time in his life Puckle tried to put a complex idea into words. "It's the trees," he said, with a nod towards the hull. He paused for a moment, wondering how to put it. "When we go, Miss, there isn't much left, really. Not after a year or two in the ground, anyway."

"There is your immortal soul, man," Gilpin interrupted his reverie to remark firmly. "Pray do not forget that."

"I won't, Vicar," Puckle concurred politely, if not, perhaps, with great conviction. "Only trees," he said to Fanny, "not having souls they say, when they're cut down, they get another life," and he waved all around him now. "Sometimes, down here," he added, with simple feeling for the mystery of the thing, "I feel as if I was inside a tree." He smiled at her, eager, yet a little embarrassed. "Funny, really. Stupid, I expect; but a man like me doesn't know much."

"I don't think it's foolish at all," said Fanny warmly. But she got no further, for Mr Gilpin indicated with a cough that he and Mr Adams had had enough and a few moments later she found herself out in the bright sunlight again.

Louisa had started to laugh. "I do declare," she cried, "that strange fellow looked exactly like a tree himself. Did you not think so, Mr Martell?"

"Perhaps," he agreed with a smile.

"Yet I liked what he said." Fanny turned to the landowner hopefully.

"I agree, Miss Albion," he replied. "His theology may be deficient, but these peasants have a kind of wisdom, in their way."

"It is hard to believe," Louisa maintained, "that such a creature is a man at all. I believe he is a troll or goblin of some kind. I'm sure he lives under the ground."

"As a Christian, I may not agree," Martell laughed. "Although I know what you mean, my dear Miss Totton."

It was time to depart now. The Tottons with Mr Martell would take the lane that led across by Sowley to Lymington; Mr Gilpin wished to take another track that would bring them across the heath towards the ford above Albion House.

Before they parted, however, Mr Martell came to Fanny's side. "My stay here will shortly end, Miss Albion," he said quietly, "but I fully expect to return. I hope when I do I shall find you here and that I may call upon you."

"By all means, Mr Martell. Although I fear I cannot answer for my father, it seems."

"I can assure you, Miss Albion" – he looked her straight in the eye – "I am quite prepared to brave his wrath."

She inclined her head to hide her pleasure. "Then come by all means, Sir," she softly said.

Minutes later, with young Nathaniel tucked beside her, she was bowling across the wild heath with Mr Gilpin, her heart singing in the breeze.

• • •

Puckle stayed down in the ship for a while after the visitors had gone. Though he despised the Tottons, he had been glad to speak to Miss Fanny Albion. He had liked something in her blue eyes. But after her departure, as he gazed sadly round the great wooden space, the thoughts that had troubled him returned with even more insistence than before.

In a few months' time Miss Albion would still be here, in the Forest. But where would he be, cut adrift?

What had he done? What could he do about it?

The chaise had drawn up by Albion House, and Mr Gilpin had just handed Fanny down and was conducting her to the door, when he turned to her casually and remarked: "There is something, by the by, which I had been meaning to tell you, Fanny. Do you recall that we spoke of your grandmother and of her marriage?"

"Why, yes, indeed," she answered brightly. "We were going to look it up, were we not?"

"Indeed. And as I chanced, a little while ago, to be examining the parish register in Lymington I took the liberty of casting back to see what I could find."

"And did you find it?" She felt quite eager.

"Yes. I think so, anyway." He paused. "It may come as a surprise, perhaps a shock."

"Oh?"

"Of course, such connections in any family, especially in the maternal line are quite commonplace, you know. Entirely normal. You would be surprised."

"Please tell me, Mr Gilpin."

"It would appear, Fanny, that Mr Totton, your mother's father, as his second wife, married a certain Miss Seagull, of Lymington. The family is well known, as you may be aware, in the town."

"My grandmother, the old lady who gave me this" – she fingered the wooden crucifix round her neck – "was born Miss Seagull?"

"Yes."

"Oh. Not of any gentle family, then. Hardly even respectable."

"I'm sure she was respectable herself, Fanny, or Mr Totton your grandfather would not have married her."

"Do you suppose" – she frowned – "that Edward and Louisa know this?"

He smiled wryly. "I have always supposed that the Tottons were pleased by their connection to the Albions. That is all they think of."

"Perhaps the Seagulls . . ."

"It is a long time ago, Fanny. I think you may assume that no one except ourselves has any knowledge of this at all. It is nothing my child, I assure you, of which you should be ashamed." This was the only time she had ever heard Mr Gilpin tell an obvious lie.

"So what should I do?"

"Do? Nothing. I only thought to tell you myself . . ."

"To save me an embarrassing discovery, perhaps in front of some curious parish clerk." She nodded. "Thank you, Mr Gilpin."

"Put it out of your mind, Fanny. It has no significance."

"I shall. Goodbye. And thank you for taking me to Beaulieu."

She did not go inside at once, but watched the chaise roll away round the corner of the drive. Then she went over to a bench under one of the trees and sat there, considering this new revelation for a while. She wondered what Mr Martell, without a blot upon his aristocratic escutcheon, would think of the fact that she was connected, and closely, to the lowly Seagulls of Lymington.

"I have great hopes," said Mrs Grockleton, well before the summer ended, "that our situation is about to improve. Indeed," she asserted, "I think I may say, Mr Grockleton, that I have never been more happy." This proposition filled her husband with some anxiety: for Mrs Grockleton's happiness was a fearsome thing to behold. "And to think," she went on, for she was very honest about such things, "that we have that clever girl Louisa to thank for all this."

As Mr Grockleton couldn't for the life of him think why he should be thanking Louisa Totton for anything in particular, but was too wise to say so, he gave her a look of enquiry that seemed also to signal agreement and she soon rattled on.

"I shall always be quite persuaded that it was Louisa who decided Mr Martell to take such an interest in Lymington. Now it seems that he has spoken to Sir Harry Burrard about standing for Parliament."

"That may not be Louisa's doing," Mr Grockleton observed.

"Yes, yes, my dear. It is, I do assure you. And if proof were needed, Louisa and Edward are invited to visit him at his place in Dorset. They leave next week. There now! I tell you, Mr Grockleton, he means to marry her."

"It would not be unnatural, since the Tottons had him staying in their house, to return the hospitality," her husband pointed out.

"Oh, Mr Grockleton, you do not see these things," she cried. "But I do. And surely you understand what this means for us?"

"For us, Mrs Grockleton? I do not think I do."

"Why Mr Grockleton, it means everything. Our dear, dear Louisa, my favourite protégée, my most talented pupil, married to the Member of Parliament – and a notable landowner – and all tied up in every conceivable way with the Burrards."

"And the Albions?"

"The Albions?" She stared at him blankly. "I fail to see the significance of the Albions. There's only the two old people and . . ."

"Fanny."

"Fanny, to be sure. Fanny. Poor girl. But please do not stray from the point. Fanny is of no importance. With Louisa and dear Mr Martell our friends, why you may be sure we shall be in the Burrards" house in the twinkling of an eye. It will all be" – she beamed at him – "so natural." She considered the prospect in the spirit of an explorer who has at last come in sight of a fabled land. "Next time Mr Martell comes here," she said thoughtfully, "I shall give that ball and I truly think the Burrards might come."

"He had better come by autumn, then," the Customs officer muttered, although his wife did not hear him.

Even if she had heard him, Mrs Grockleton could have no idea what her husband meant by this cryptic statement; nor did he wish her to know. But it was this secret consideration that caused him, now, to raise a subject that had been increasingly on his mind. "I wonder if it has ever occurred to you, Mrs

Grockleton, that the time might come when we decide to leave Lymington."

"Leave Lymington?" She turned to look at him and it seemed that her eyes took a moment or two to focus upon him. "Leave?"

"It is a possibility."

"But Customs officers are never moved, Mr Grockleton. You are here to stay."

It was quite true, of course. A position like his led to no possibility of advancement or transfer. You kept it until you retired. "True, my dear. But we might choose to move."

"But we shan't, Mr Grockleton."

"What if," he proceeded very cautiously, "I cannot say it is likely but what if, Mrs Grockleton, we were to come into money?"

"Money? From what source, Mr Grockleton?"

"Have I ever spoken to you, my dear, of my cousin Balthazar?" The question was somewhat devious, since he had only invented this relative the day before.

"I do not think so. I am sure you have not. What an extraordinary name."

"Not," he said calmly, "if your mother was Dutch. My cousin Balthazar made a great fortune in the East Indies and retired to the north, where he lives in utter seclusion. He has no children. Indeed, I gather that I am his only kinsman. As I hear that he has a malady from which he is unlikely to recover, I think it possible that his fortune may come to me."

"But Mr Grockleton, why have you never spoken of him? You should go to see him at once."

"I think not. He greatly disliked my father although to me, as a boy, he was always kind. A year ago I wrote to him. He wrote back, fairly warmly, but said quite plainly that he did not desire any visitors. His malady, I suspect, makes him unsightly. Should he die and remember me, as I say, our circumstances will alter and I mean to retire."

He watched her carefully, rather pleased with himself. It was clear that she believed him; and it was important that she should. For the last part of his statement was entirely true.

It had been his interview with Puckle that had finally decided him. As he watched the fellow's obvious fear – and he had no doubt it was well founded – he could scarcely help thinking of what the forest smugglers would do to him, too, after his great attack upon them. Perhaps they would be cowed; maybe respectful; possibly even broken. But he was not so foolish as to rely upon it. No, he had considered, as the days and weeks passed, it was far more likely, one dark night, that he would be ambushed somewhere and receive a pistol shot in his head for causing them so much inconvenience. Was he prepared to wait for that? On balance, he had concluded, he wasn't. He was brave enough to take on the smugglers, but if he won and made a small fortune from the business, then he would do as Puckle meant to do. He'd take his winnings and leave, get out, retire. No one would blame him and, frankly, he no longer cared much if they did.

As he certainly couldn't tell his wife the truth, since she was quite incapable of keeping such a secret, it had occurred to him to invent his cousin Balthazar and the legacy as a way of preparing her for the possible change of circumstances. He watched her face, therefore, with interest; and after she had reflected a few moments, he saw her smile.

"But, my dear husband, should this happy event transpire and you acquire a fortune, there would be no cause to leave Lymington at all. We shall be able to live here, with only a little more money, I promise you, in the greatest style. Oh, indeed . . ." It was clear that prospects of future balls, graced by Burrards, Martells, perhaps even royal visitors, were entering her mind one after another, like swans landing upon a river.

"Ah." This was not at all what he wanted. "But think of the places we could choose to live. "Why," he suggested cleverly, "we could even go to live in Bath."

"Bath? I have no wish to live in Bath."

"But Mrs Grockleton." He looked at her in astonishment. "You speak constantly of Bath. Surely . . ."

"No, no, Mr Grockleton,' she cut in. "I speak of Bath as a model for Lymington, but I have no wish to live there. Bath is already taken. Whatever our fortune, we should be nobody in Bath. Whereas here, with our many dear friends . . ."

"Our friends here," he gently suggested, "may not be quite as close as you think."

"They are as good," she retorted sharply, with one of those flashes of brutal realism that could be so disconcerting, "as any that you and I are likely to get."

"Well, my dear," he said in a conciliatory tone, "there is no need for us to consider the matter now, I dare say, for perhaps my cousin Balthazar will leave me nothing at all."

But if he thought this would do, he was sorely mistaken, for by now his wife's hackles were up. "I am quite persuaded to stay here, Mr Grockleton," she said, with a deliberateness that struck a chill into his heart. "Quite." She looked at him solemnly. "I will not be moved."

For a fleeting moment Mr Grockleton imagined himself alone with his fortune in London, without Mrs Grockleton, and a wistful look passed across his face. Then he corrected himself. "Whatever you wish, my dear," he replied, and prepared to leave for the Customs house. "Do you really think," he asked, to change the conversation, "that Mr Martell is so taken with Louisa Totton?"

"I saw them together in the High Street just the day before he left," she replied, "and I observed his manner towards her. He likes her very much. And she means to marry him, you may depend upon it. She is a clever and determined young woman."

"Do determined women always get their way?" he asked with genuine curiosity.

"Yes, Mr Grockleton," she answered quietly. "They do."

Isaac Seagull was very seldom taken by surprise.

The August sun was shining pleasantly on the High Street. As usual, he was standing by the entrance of the Angel Inn, surveying the scene. There was a particular reason why Mr Seagull liked to be where he was and it had nothing to do with the street scene before him. It pleased him to stand there not because of what was in front of him, but because of what lay under his feet.

A tunnel. It ran from under the Angel, across the street to the smaller inn opposite. Then it proceeded down the hill all the way to the water. There were other tunnels and chambers leading off it. By this means, Seagull knew, he could move goods from his boats to inns and hiding places all over Lymington without anything being seen. When he stood where he did, therefore, and thoughtfully tapped his foot on the ground, he could feel like the master of some ancient labyrinth filled with secret treasure.

There was nothing unusual about the Lymington tunnels. Most of the coastal towns in southern England had them. Christchurch had an elaborate labyrinth centred on the old priory church. Even villages thirty miles from the coast, up on the chalk downs near Sarum, often had tunnels for hiding contraband. Indeed, at a time when the revenue men were having little effect upon the smugglers' trade, some of these systems may have reflected the human love of underground passages and hiding places as much as any real necessity.

Isaac Seagull was thinking quietly about his plans for the coming months and the use to which his tunnels might be put when he noticed, out of the corner of his eye, that Miss Albion was strolling, under a parasol, in his direction. This was hardly of interest and he paid no attention until she came directly up to him and asked if they might speak. She had, she said, a private question.

As there was nowhere very private inside the inn, he led her through the courtyard into a small garden just behind. No one was there but themselves.

Then she lowered her parasol, looked up at him with a curious smile and a pair of wonderful blue eyes, and asked: "Mr Seagull, are you my cousin?"

That surprised him, all right.

It had taken her a long time to decide to come to him. Ever since Mr Gilpin had told her about his discovery in the parish register she had thought about the matter. She had asked her father and, after she had returned from tending her sick friend in Winchester, her aunt, if they knew anything about her mother's family; but it was clear from their lack of interest in the subject that they didn't. As far as they were concerned she had been a Totton, which was well enough, and she had married an Albion, which was the only thing about her that really mattered; that was the end of it. Fanny had not relished the thought of going to inspect the parish registers herself. At the very least, if she wanted to find out anything more about her mother's connections, this could be a tedious and unsatisfactory process. The sensible course, undoubtedly, was to follow Mr Gilpin's advice and forget the whole business.

And that was what she had tried to do. With Aunt Adelaide back, the normal pattern of their life had been peacefully resumed. She had gone visiting with her Totton cousins, shown her sketches to Mr Gilpin for his approval and secretly hoped that, if Mr Martell did return to the area and called upon her at Albion House, her aunt would ensure that this time he was given a better reception.

Yet she couldn't forget it. Not quite. She herself was not sure why. Perhaps it was just that her curiosity had been aroused, or that she wanted to know more about the mother she had lost. But if she was honest with herself, there was more to it than that and the truth was not very comfortable.

For if I really am connected to such people, she thought, then I am ashamed of it. I am afraid to acknowledge members of my own family. How can I defend such cowardice?

It was in this frame of mind that she realised there was one person who almost certainly knew: Edward's and Louisa's father, her mother's half-brother – Mr Totton. Perhaps she could ask him. Yet here a certain discretion held her back. If he knew and had never spoken of it, he might have his own reasons. Living, as he did, practically in the town, Mr Totton might not thank her for making him talk about even a half-sister's connection to its less respectable elements. Whatever her curiosity about the matter, she decided not to approach him.

That left only one other source of information, potentially the most dangerous of all: the Seagulls themselves. Even if there was a connection, did the present Seagulls know it? Perhaps not, or maybe they had chosen to keep silent. Or, yet another possibility, possibly they and others in Lymington knew, but it had never come to her ears. What would happen if she approached them? Would they suddenly claim her as one of their own, embarrass her, annoy the Tottons and – it came back to this after all – undermine her own position in society? It would surely be folly to go near the Seagulls.

She had proceeded no further with this delicate matter when news of a different kind drove it, briefly, out of her mind.

"Fanny, have you heard?" Her cousin Louisa had taken a chaise by herself and come all the way to Albion House to share the news. "My dear, dear Fanny, what do you think? Mr Martell has asked Edward to stay with him in Dorset. And he has particularly asked that I may come, too. We are to leave next week. Oh, kiss me, Fanny," she cried in delight. "I am so excited."

"I am sure" – Fanny managed to smile – "that it will be a delightful visit."

She had wondered, after Louisa had gone, if perhaps she might also be invited, but days passed and no invitation came. She told herself it was natural that Mr Martell should repay the Tottons' hospitality, yet still continued, despite her better judgement, to hope. Perhaps, she thought, Mr Martell will write or send some message. Although I really don't know, she scolded herself, why he should. He didn't, anyway, and ten days after Louisa's visit, the two young Tottons left for Dorset, after which she felt very much alone.

She had been sitting outside, three mornings after Louisa's and Edward's departure, trying to read a book; and, hardly aware that she was doing so, she had started to finger the little wooden cross she wore, when suddenly the thought struck her. The old woman who had given it to her: how lonely she must have been. Did my mother ever go to see her, Fanny wondered? Probably not. I'm quite sure I was taken to see her only once. And why? Almost certainly because my mother was ashamed of her. She didn't even want me to keep this wooden cross, the only thing the old woman was ever able to give her granddaughter. Here am I, she considered, feeling sorry for myself because I have not been invited to the house of a man I hardly know and who has probably forgotten me; but how many years was my grandmother left to sit in that house in Lymington all alone, denied the love and affection of a granddaughter, all for a worthless vanity. For the first time in her life Fanny realised that nature is as wasteful of the affections as it is of the acorns that fall upon the forest floor.

"I don't care what they think," she murmured. "I shall go into Lymington tomorrow."

• • •

Isaac Seagull gazed at her with interest. He understood exactly the daring of her question, as she calmly set out across the great social chasm that divided them, like an explorer upon a flimsy bridge. This one's got courage, the master smuggler thought. He answered her carefully, all the same. "I've never thought of it as such, Miss Albion," he said. "It would be very distant, you see, and a long time ago."

"Did you know my grandmother, old Mrs Totton?"

"I did." He smiled. "A fine old lady."

"Was she not born a Miss Seagull?"

"So I believe, Miss Albion. In fact," he admitted straightforwardly, "she was my father's cousin. She had no brothers or sisters. That line of the family's all gone."

"Except for me."

"If you wish to think of it that way."

"You don't advise it?"

Isaac Seagull looked towards the end of the small garden. His curious, chinless face, in reflective repose, had an unexpected fineness, she thought.

"I shouldn't think, Miss Albion, that anyone in the town would remember about old Mrs Totton being a Seagull. I expect I'd be the only one who knows." He paused, apparently doing a quick reckoning. "You had sixteen great-great-grandparents and one of those was my great-grandfather. Only through your mother's mother, too. No." He shook his head wryly. "You're Miss Albion of Albion House as sure as I'm plain Isaac Seagull of the Angel Inn. If I said I was related to you, Miss Albion, people would just laugh at me and say I was getting above myself." And he smiled at her kindly.

"So if my grandmother was the daughter of a Mr Seagull," she persisted quietly, "who was her mother?"

"I can't say I remember. Don't think I ever knew."

"Liar."

It was not often that anyone dared to say that to Isaac Seagull. He looked down into the girl's startling blue eyes. "You don't need to know."

"I do."

"If my memory serves me," he said reluctantly, "she might have been a Miss Puckle."

"Puckle?" Fanny felt herself go pale. She couldn't help it. Puckle, the gnome-like figure with the oaken face she had seen at Buckler's Hard? Puckle, the family of woodsmen and charcoal burners, the lowliest peasants in the Forest? Why some of them, she had heard, used to live in hovels. "One of the Puckles of Burley?"

"He was very taken with her, Miss Albion. She possessed a rare intelligence. She taught herself to read and write which, forgive me, none of the other Puckles has ever done, I'm sure. My father always told me she was a remarkable woman in every way."

"I see." She was dazed. Entire landscapes were suddenly opening up before her. In her mind's eye she saw vistas of underground places, deep burrows, gnarled roots. They were peopled, too, with strange creatures – loathsome, subhuman, hag-like – who turned to look at her or came to her side, claiming her for their own. She felt a cold panic, as though she had been trapped in a cave and heard the flocking sound of bats. She, Fanny Albion, a Puckle. Not a Totton, not even a Seagull, but with the blood of the lowest charcoal-burners running in her veins. It was too horrible to contemplate.

"Miss Albion." He was calling her back to daylight. "I may be mistaken. These are only things I believe I heard when I was a child." He wasn't quite sure if she had heard. "It makes no difference to anything," he told her kindly. But all she did was bow her head, and murmur some thanks; and then she departed.

A few minutes later Isaac Seagull was back in his usual place, enjoying the sun. The Albion girl's secret was safe with him. He'd been keeping secrets all his life. But he contemplated her embarrassment with a philosophical wonder all the same. That, he supposed, was the price you paid for belonging to the gentry, where you had to display your ancestors like plumage and your acres were laid out for all to see. Too high a price, he reckoned; and not for the first time, the clever Free Trader shook his head at the all-embracing vanity of the landed class.

Personally, he was comfortable with all things dark and subterranean. Besides, his fortunes were always riding on the wild and open sea.

Fanny had gone halfway down the High Street when she encountered Mrs Grockleton, who greeted her most warmly. "You have not heard from your clever cousin Louisa, yet?" She was positively beaming.

"No, Mrs Grockleton. But I don't think I expected to. Why do you call her clever, by the way?"

"Oh, come now, my dear." Mrs Grockleton wagged her stout finger at her. "You and your cousin must not suppose you can hide your secrets from all us old people." She gave her a knowing look. "Methinks we may expect news from that quarter before long."

"I really have no idea what you mean."

"My dear child, I caught sight of Mr Martell with Louisa the day before his departure. Do not tell her so, mind. But these eyes can see. And sure enough, he has asked her to Dorset with her brother. Just the two of them. Had he not been serious I should think very likely he'd have asked you as well."

"I see no reason why."

"Oh, Fanny, you are a good and loyal friend, and I shall ask no more. But my dear child, we both know Louisa means to marry him and I can assure you, knowing the world as I do, that I think she will succeed." She patted Fanny's cheek. "What celebrations you and I may enjoy with her then."

She did not wait for any further comment, but billowed away, under full sail, up the street.

September came: the days were warm, but the oaks' first golden leaves appeared, hinting at the sharp excitement of the rutting season ahead. At Boldre, Mr Gilpin's school resumed, and the troop of girls and boys in their green coats were to be seen walking up the hill to Boldre church on its knoll each Sunday morning.

Among them was Nathaniel Furzey. The weeks of summer he had just spent with his own family up at Minstead had certainly done nothing to lessen his appetite for cheerful mischief. In school, he was more or less in order. Mr Gilpin had given him a book of simple algebra and geometry to study, since he had long ago mastered all the sums the other children were doing. Also, somewhat against his judgement, the vicar had agreed that one day a week he might read a history book. But the rest of the time, he was to confine his reading to the Bible. "For there is quite enough there, young man," the vicar told him sternly, "to occupy you for a lifetime."

Even so, the schoolmaster found him a trial. He would start playing curious games with numbers instead of the problems set; if he was set to learn a text he would do so, but then rearrange the words to make foolish rhymes. More than once it had been necessary to punish him for practical jokes – and this was all since the term began. As for his questions, his infuriating habit of demanding the reasons for things instead of simply learning what he was told, the schoolmaster had to report to the vicar: "His mind is too active. It must be curbed."

The Prides, however, were more indulgent. If Nathaniel tempted young Andrew into mischief there was always a wit to the business, which appealed to Pride the timber merchant. "Let them get into trouble," he told his wife. "I always did. Can't do any harm." And if they got into trouble and were punished, which they were, Andrew and Nathaniel somehow knew, although nothing was ever said, that the grown-ups at home did not entirely disapprove of these activities.

But when, one afternoon after school, Nathaniel told Andrew about his new plan, even young Pride was awestruck. "You can't do that," he whispered. "Not really."

"Why not?"

"Because . . . well, it's too difficult. And anyway, I daren't."

"Nonsense," said Nathaniel.

September also seemed to have a strange effect upon Aunt Adelaide. It came out unexpectedly one evening when she and Fanny were sitting together in the usual way.

The shadows were falling, but Aunt Adelaide had decided not to light any candles yet and, sitting in her wing chair, was only dimly visible in the penumbra as the orange glow outside the windows slowly ceased. Apart from the soft ticking of the hall clock, the house was silent and it seemed that Adelaide might have fallen asleep when instead she suddenly said: "It's time you married, Fanny."

"Why?"

"Because I shan't be here for ever. I want to see you settled before I die. Have you ever thought of anyone?"

"No." Fanny paused only for a moment. "I don't think so." And having no wish to pursue this conversation just now she asked in turn: "Did you never think of marrying, Aunt Adelaide?"

"Perhaps." The old lady sighed. "It was too difficult. There was my mother: I did not feel I could leave her and she lived such a long time. I was over forty when she died. Then there was this house. I had to look after this, you see. I was doing it for her and for the family."

"For old Alice, too?"

"Of course." She nodded and then, with such feeling that Fanny could not fail to be moved, said: "How could I not keep Albion House as they would have wished? And whomever you marry, you will do the same, won't you, Fanny?"

"Yes." How many times had she made that promise? A hundred at least. But she knew she would keep it.

"You must never dishonour your family, you see. When I think," she burst out, as she had a thousand times before, "of that cursed Penruddock and his filthy troops, and my poor, innocent grandmother, made to ride through the night half naked like that. At her age. Thieves! Villains! And Penruddock calling himself a colonel, the common blackguard."

Fanny nodded. This was her cue to keep her aunt diverted. "Was Penruddock at the trial, Aunt Adelaide?"

"Of course he was." Fanny expected her aunt to plunge straight into a relation of the trial in the usual way, but instead the other fell silent for long moments and Fanny was wondering if she was going to have to listen to the tick of the clock, when Adelaide spoke: "My grandmother was wrong. I have always thought so."

"Wrong?"

"At the trial." She shook her head. "Weak, or too proud. Foolish Alice." She suddenly burst out, "You must never give up, child. Never! You must fight to the end." Fanny hardly knew how to reply to this when her aunt continued: "At the trial, you know, she scarcely said a word. She even went to sleep. She let that liar Penruddock and the others take away her name. She let that evil judge bully them all and sentence her . . ."

"Perhaps there was nothing she could do."

"No!" her aunt contradicted with surprising vehemence. "She should have protested. She should have stood up and told the judge his court was a mockery. She should have shamed them."

"They would have carried her from the court, and sentenced her anyway."

"Probably. But better to go down fighting. If ever you find yourself accused in court, Fanny, promise me you will fight."

"Yes, Aunt Adelaide. I don't think," Fanny added, "it's very likely I shall be in court, though."

But her aunt didn't seem to be listening to this last remark. Her eyes were gazing thoughtfully at the dimming light of the window. "Have you ever heard your father speak of Sir George West, Fanny?" she now enquired.

"Once or twice." Fanny tried to remember. "A friend in London, I think."

"A fine old family. His nephew Mr Arthur West has just taken the tenancy of Hale. As I mean to visit my old friend the vicar at Fordingbridge, which lies nearby, I thought to call upon him."

"I see." Fanny smiled to herself. Evidently her ruse to divert her aunt had not been successful. "You think Mr Arthur West is eligible?"

"He is presumably a gentleman. His uncle is to leave him part of his fortune, which is ample. That is all I know, so far."

"You mean to inspect him, then?"

"We shall, Fanny. You are to accompany me."

September also brought Mr Martell back to the Forest. He came, this time, to stay with Sir Harry Burrard.

Fanny had heard a good deal about Mr Martell and his big estate in Dorset since Louisa's return. "Oh, Fanny, I do declare I am in love with the house, and so would you be," she cried. "I was sorry you could not have seen it. The situation is so fine, with the great chalk ridges all around; and he is quite lord of the village, you know."

"The house is old?"

"The part behind is very old, and that I own is dark and

solemn. I should pull it down, I dare say. But the new wing has large rooms and is very fine, and has quite a noble prospect over the park."

"It sounds delightful."

"And the library, Fanny. How you would have loved that if you had been there. It has more books, all finely bound, than you ever saw, and on a table they place all the London journals, which are especially sent down, so that you can follow the world of fashion. I spent quite half an hour up there I swear."

"I am glad Mr Martell found you so studious."

"Oh, he is very easy at home, Fanny, I do assure you. Not at all the scholar. We amused ourselves in all kinds of ways. He draws – very well, I must say – and he even seemed to take pleasure in my poor efforts. This one in particular he liked." She had pulled out a small sketch. "Do you remember the day we all went to Buckler's Hard?"

The sketch, Fanny had to admit it, was good. Very good. It was a caricature, of course, yet it caught the subject, as he seemed to her eyes, quite perfectly. It was Puckle. She had drawn him like a gnome, half tree, half monster. He was grotesque, absurd, rather disgusting.

Fanny shuddered. "You do not think it a little cruel?" she asked.

"Fanny, you cannot suppose I should let the fellow see it? 'Tis only for ourselves."

"I suppose that makes it different." But what would you say, she thought to herself, if you had any idea that I, an Albion, might be related to this peasant. And how, then, she wondered, would you draw me?

She also learned from Louisa that Martell had already written to Sir Harry Burrard about the parliamentary seat.

The very day that Mr Martell arrived at the Burrards', Louisa came to tell Fanny that she and Edward were invited to dine there – "Sir Harry being our kinsman, you see." This did not seem surprising. And as Mr Martell was reported to be staying a week or more, she supposed that in due course he would call upon her. So it was with some dismay that she heard Aunt Adelaide announce: "We go to Fordingbridge on

Tuesday, Fanny. My friend the vicar will give us shelter that night. In the evening, we are all invited to dine with Mr Arthur West."

"Might we not delay a little?" Fanny asked. It was Saturday today. What if Mr Martell did not appear until Monday? Or Tuesday, in which case he would miss her entirely?

"Delay? Why no, Fanny. We are already expected. Besides, I think we should be back by Wednesday afternoon as you have an engagement that evening in Lymington."

"Oh?" Fanny felt her heart leap. "With the Burrards?"

"The Burrards? No. But I have just received this message, a rather tiresome invitation no doubt, but I supposed, as a matter of courtesy, that you would wish to go." And she handed Fanny the invitation.

Mrs Grockleton was going to give a ball.

"It's perfect, don't you see, Mr Grockleton." His wife was chirping like a bird. "Mr Martell is here. Louisa assures me she will bring him. Besides, he knows he promised me himself and he is far too much a gentleman to break his word."

"That may be," Mr Grockleton said gloomily.

"Between Louisa and Mr Martell, who is after all their guest, I do not see how they can fail to bring the Burrards. Think of that, Mr Grockleton." Mr Grockleton did his best to think about the Burrards. "Dear Mr Gilpin will be there, of course," she continued. "And he is certainly a gentleman."

"And Miss Albion?"

"Yes, yes, she too." If Fanny was a less exciting catch, she was, of course, of impeccable family. Indeed, Mrs Grockleton started to think, if she could have an Albion, a Martell and the Burrards, perhaps she might be able to snare yet another member of the local gentry. A Morant, perhaps. "We shall have refreshments, dinner, the orchestra from the playhouse – they will be delighted, you may depend upon it – and there must be wine, champagne, brandy. You must see to that, Mr Grockleton."

"I shall have to buy it, you know."

"To be sure, you will buy it. How else would we come by it?"

"You forget," he said drily, "that I'm the only man between

Southampton and Christchurch who has to pay full price." But Mrs Grockleton, if she heard this, ignored it. "Apart from the presence, or otherwise, of Mr Martell," he enquired irritably, "why must everything be done at such short notice? Why Wednesday?"

And now Mrs Grockleton looked at him with genuine astonishment. "But Mr Grockleton, of course it must be Wednesday," she cried, pausing an instant to give him time to realise for himself. "Wednesday is a full moon."

Tuesday morning was clear and bright, and Aunt Adelaide was in such good humour that you might have thought she was twenty years younger than her age. "Francis," she told her brother, "you shall be quite happy with Mrs Pride." As this was virtually an order, Mr Albion did not disagree. Taking just the coachman to drive and one maid to look after them, she and Fanny set off early in the morning on the track across the Forest to Ringwood, from where it was an easy road up to Fordingbridge. "We should," Aunt Adelaide announced brightly, "be there by noon." And it was with just a trace of reproach, as they came up towards the wide open space of Wilverley Plain, that she remarked: "You don't seem very happy, Fanny."

He had not come. He had been, with the Burrards, to dine at the Tottons' – who might, she thought, have invited her – but he had not come to Albion House. Perhaps, considering his previous reception, that was not surprising; but after what he had said when they parted, she had expected at least a message of some kind. There had been nothing, though: no letter, no word.

"No, Aunt Adelaide," she replied, "I am quite happy."

As they came up on to Wilverley Plain they noticed some small boys in the distance, but thought nothing of it.

The problem was the pig. A full-grown pig is a formidable creature. Not only is it heavy, but it can move with remarkable speed. A harness was needed in order to lead it. Then there was a further difficulty.

"We'll have to keep it somewhere for the night," Nathaniel had pointed out. That had seemed an almost insuperable obstacle until one of the gang remembered a cousin who had a shed at Burley.

They did not take the main track but kept a few hundred yards to the north of it. At one point the track passed by a lonely, bare old tree.

"That's the Naked Man," Nathaniel said, and the boys gazed at it solemnly. "That'll be where we do it."

The vicar was a tall, thin, grey-haired man who welcomed them to his pleasant vicarage very warmly. He appeared delighted at the chance to accompany them to Hale for dinner. The new tenant, he assured Adelaide, seemed in every way a gentleman and had taken the place for five years. "Hale has had several owners and tenants in recent decades," he explained, "and nobody has taken much care of the place. But I understand that Mr West intends to take the house in hand."

Aunt Adelaide wished to rest after her journey and Fanny was glad to let the vicar conduct her round the small town of Fordingbridge. The five rivers of Sarum, which lay about eight miles to the north, had all joined the Avon's stream by now and the river, with its long river weeds, made a delightful scene as it passed under the handsome old stone bridge. By the time she returned to prepare for their evening excursion, she was able, at least, to put on a reasonably cheerful face.

Certainly, she thought, as the vicar's carriage slowly climbed the slope of Godshill that led up to the manor of Hale, the place had the most charming views over the Avon valley. As they came up the long drive to the house, she could see that its handsome Georgian façade showed signs of neglect; but as soon as they reached the entrance it was clear from the two smart footmen who issued from the door that Mr West intended to maintain himself in style. And the appearance of the gentleman himself made everything clearer still.

Mr Arthur West was a fair-haired, rather stocky, thirty-five-year-old gentleman whose brisk, masculine manner told you at once that if anyone had an estate that lacked a master, he was equipped by birth and in every way to satisfy the attendant obligations. His inheritance, if it would not quite allow him to set himself up as a landowner on the scale he desired, was enough for him to look any heiress in the eye. No one would think him an adventurer. He deserved the heiress of a fine estate and he meant to have one; and this very self-assurance made him attractive to many women of that sort. At least, such a woman would know, if Arthur West fixed his blue eyes upon her, he knew what he wanted. And that, as every woman sooner or later discovers, is something to be grateful for.

Towards Aunt Adelaide he was solicitous and gallant, which was very pleasing to her. As for Fanny, he immediately made himself agreeable in a quiet and practised way so that she felt both that they had an understanding and that, if she wished it, he would pursue her. Not having encountered such treatment from men before, she was a little cautious, but as his behaviour was, at the same time, impeccable, she could explore the situation safely and found it not unpleasant.

"My uncle has told me many tales of your father and his travels, Miss Albion," he said with a quiet smile. "He sounds a most adventurous man."

"Not nowadays, I'm afraid, Mr West."

"Well." He looked at her in a companionable way. "Each age has its season. It is probably our turn to be adventurous now."

"I'm not very adventurous, perhaps, living down here."

"I don't believe it, Miss Albion." He gave her an almost boyish grin. "There are always enough adventures in the countryside to satisfy good people like us, don't you think?"

"I love the Forest," she replied simply.

"And I quite agree with you," he answered.

He entertained them all very pleasantly in the big salon. While he was talking briefly to the vicar, Aunt Adelaide found the occasion to tap Fanny lightly on the arm and whisper audibly that she found their host a very proper man – by which Fanny understood very well that she meant that, having no estate of his own to distract him, Mr West might do very well for Albion House. She was spared the embarrassment of having to reply to this, however, since dinner was then announced and Mr West came to escort the old lady, upon his arm, into the dining room.

The dinner was excellent. Mr West made delightful conversation. He told amusing stories about London, asked, and was kind enough to seem very interested in, the views of both Aunt Adelaide and Fanny upon the great events of the day, was fascinated to learn about the French garrison in Lymington and glad to hear anything they cared to tell him about life in the Forest.

He was also engagingly frank. For when Fanny remarked that their lives were really very quiet, his blue eyes flashed with genial amusement and he replied: "Of course they are, Miss Albion. But I assure you I think none the worse of the countryside for that. Our armies fight and our ships patrol the seas precisely to safeguard such quietness."

It also turned out that Mr West liked to race horses, to hunt and to fish.

When the dessert course had been served, Mr West proposed that instead of the men sitting over port, they should all retire to the library; which clearly suited Aunt Adelaide, who said she hoped he would forgive her if, at her age, she did not linger long.

"But I should like to see something of the house, Mr West," she said, "for strangely enough, the place always being empty, or tenanted by people who seldom stayed, I have never been round it before."

"Why then," their kindly host said, rising, "if you will forgive the fact that I have not yet had time to do much to the place, let us explore it together." And taking a candlestick in one hand himself, and calling to the footmen to bring more, he led them all out into the hall.

There were two smaller formal rooms besides the library on the ground floor. The decorations were what one would expect in a manor house of the Georgian period, but somewhat faded. The better furniture had been brought by Mr West, but some of the pictures and a few old tapestries had come with the house and evidently dated from the century before; so there was a hint of the Jacobean era in the place, which reminded Fanny of the darker intimacy of Albion House.

When they had done looking at these rooms, it seemed to her that it was time to leave; but her aunt was not quite finished. "What lies upstairs?" she enquired.

"A landing and small gallery, and a parlour," Mr West replied, "and the bedchambers, of course. But they are hardly touched as yet, I fear, and are scarcely fit to be seen."

"May we not look, Mr West?" the old lady asked. "As I am here, I confess I am most curious."

"As you like." He smiled. "If the stairs . . ."

"I go upstairs every day," she replied, "do I not, Fanny?" So up they all went, at a slow pace, Adelaide upon Mr West's arm, two footmen carrying candlesticks, and the vicar discreetly following Adelaide like a shadow, a step below, in case she should fall. Up on the landing they paused for a moment, then Mr West went forward and opened one of the chamber doors, which swung with a soft creak.

It was pitch-dark inside, but as the footmen went in with the candles, faint shapes could be seen: a tall four-poster bed with heavy old curtains in tatters; the faint glow from a polished oak chair, the ghostly flicker of reflected candlelight in a blackened looking-glass.

"I really think no one has touched these rooms in almost a century," Mr West declared. The next bedchamber was the same and, having seen it, Aunt Adelaide signalled that she was ready to descend again.

They were just coming to the head of the stairs when, down a short passage, the old lady caught sight of a large portrait in a heavy gilt frame facing them, but whose lineaments were hidden in the shadows. Seeing her peer towards it, Mr West obligingly bade one of the footmen to hold the candles closer and by their light there now emerged a striking image.

He was a tall, saturnine and darkly handsome man. He had been painted three-quarter length and his clothes suggested that the picture must be about a century old. His long dark hair, falling to below his shoulders, was his own. His hand rested upon the hilt of a heavy sword and he stared out at them with the cold, proud and somewhat tragic air that is often found in those who were friends to the Stuarts.

"Who is that?" Adelaide asked.

"I do not know," Mr West admitted. "It was here when I came." He went over to the picture with a candle and searched the base of the frame. "There is a label," he said, "but it is hard to read." He studied it a moment. "Ah," he called out, "I think I have it. This gentleman is . . ." He struggled a moment more. "Colonel Thomas Penruddock."

"Penruddock?"

"Of Compton . . . Compton Chamberlayne. Does that mean anything to you?"

Of course. The former Penruddocks of Hale, Fanny realised, must have been responsible. But who could have known that they had a portrait of their kinsman, or that they would have left it behind like this? What ill fate had arranged this ghastly shock for them?

The effect upon Aunt Adelaide was terrible to see. The old lady went white and grasped the oak banister of the staircase as though she might stagger. She let out a tiny moan and seemed to sag as Fanny moved swiftly to her side. But never had Fanny been so moved, or so proud of her aunt as, not wishing to embarrass their host, she righted herself and bravely replied: "The name is familiar to me, Mr West. The Penruddocks owned this house a long time ago. And now," she continued, taking Fanny's arm, "I should like to go down. I must thank you, Mr West, for a most agreeable evening."

So Fanny took her safely down into the hall and only she was aware that her aunt was still shaking.

But as the carriage was being brought round, it was the turn of sharp-eyed old Adelaide to look at Fanny and softly enquire: "Are you quite well, child? You look pale."

"Yes, Aunt Adelaide, I am well," she answered with a smile.

Yet in truth she was not, although she had no desire to tell her aunt the reason why. For the picture of Colonel Penruddock had been only too familiar to her: so much so that it had been all she could do not to gasp out loud when it emerged in the candlelight.

The figure and face were those of Mr Martell. To the life.

Caleb Furzey had set out at dawn on Wednesday morning from Oakley. The journey to Ringwood was one that he made every month or so to visit the market there. Sometimes he had piglets to sell, or some illicit venison. He would arrive by midmorning, take his horse and cart to the inn, wander about in the market and, sooner or later, encounter one of the Ringwood Furzeys. By the end of the afternoon, he would be sitting in the inn, drinking and talking with anyone who cared to do so. Towards sunset, or even after dark, his cousins or the innkeeper would load him on to his cart and, while he slept in the back, the horse, who knew the way quite as well as he did, would walk slowly along the track past Burley and over Wilverley Plain and so take him home.

Given his superstitious nature and the vaguely mysterious reputation that Burley had always possessed, Caleb Furzey might have hesitated to drive past Burley on a night when the moon was full, but today, as he had proudly told his neighbours some time before, was a special occasion. It was the fiftieth birthday of one of his Ringwood cousins. "And if I ain't there," he had told a surprised neighbour, "they say it won't be a proper party at all."

So it was with great expectations of family warmth and cheerful drinking that he was crossing the Forest now. He was up on Wilverley Plain when he saw the Albions' carriage returning and, as they passed, he saluted the occupants respectfully enough.

The red sun was already sinking over Beaulieu Heath that evening when Wyndham Martell began to ride across it. He had just spent an interesting two hours with Mr Drummond of Cadland, but now it was time to return. Indeed, he was going to be somewhat late for Mrs Grockleton's ball.

Hardly anyone was going to be there, as far as he could gather. As Martell gazed across the open Forest before him he saw it, very naturally, through the eyes of the gentry. And to the gentry, although the ordinary Forest folk did not realise it, the whole Forest was just a kind of lake. There were the Mill and Drummond families in the east, various others along the coast; in the centre the Morants and the Albions; there were landed families around the north of the Forest and the estates down the Avon valley, like Bisterne, on its eastern border. But as far as their social world was concerned, the forest villages and hamlets, and even the busy town of Lymington, scarcely existed. "There's no one there," they would say, without the least sense of incongruity. Thus Mrs Grockleton's desire to tempt the members of this class into her social orbit was not mere snobbery, but a more primeval instinct: she wanted, quite simply, to exist.

Her hopes that the Burrards would come were going to be

disappointed. When she had heard he was calling upon Mr Drummond of Cadland, she had sent an urgent message through Louisa begging him to bring that gentleman and his entire family with him if he could – a suggestion Martell had quietly ignored. But the Tottons were going, and he had promised to accompany them. And besides, Fanny Albion was going to be there.

Why hadn't Wyndham Martell been to see Fanny?

On the face of it his excuses might be reasonable enough. He had come there to get to know Sir Harry Burrard and he wished to place himself at that gentleman's disposal. Indeed, Sir Harry had kept him quite busy, both in conversations with himself and in meetings with other people of local importance like Mr Drummond. It was surely right to attend to these matters first and it would certainly have been wrong to raise Fanny's hopes with the prospect of a meeting that might have to be deferred. There was, besides, another problem. It was by no means clear that he would be welcome if he did call at Albion House and he wasn't sure he really wanted to be thrown out a second time. Seeing Fanny, therefore, was not without complications.

But couldn't he at least have sent her a message of some kind during all the days he had been there? He could have and he hadn't.

The truth was – and he knew it perfectly well – he had deliberately kept her waiting.

He liked her, certainly. No, he conceded, he liked her very much. She was kindly and intelligent. She was well-bred. She came from an ancient family and she was a modest heiress. If he were to marry her, it might not be called a brilliant match, but then, as he had overheard a young blood remark jealously in London a week before: "With two fine estates, that damned Martell can marry anyone he pleases and still look a hero."

If he secured one of the Lymington parliamentary seats and married the heiress of the Albion estate he had no doubt that his father and his friends would say he had done well, and he wouldn't deny that such things were important to him. And if, perhaps, secretly he yearned for something more than such conventional pleasures, he supposed his own political career might provide it.

There was something else he liked about her, too. She was modest and she had not attempted to captivate him. Many women in London had tried to do so; it had been flattering at first but soon became a burden. He didn't mind when some cheeky girl like Louisa Totton set her cap at him, because, whatever her drawbacks, he didn't think she was sophisticated enough to deceive him much, and she was amusing. But Fanny was an entirely different case. Fanny had a simpler, purer nature, as well as being more intelligent.

And she was waiting for him. If he chose – and he wasn't sure he did, yet – she was waiting to be his. He did not fear competition. He liked to play and win. But in the matter of marriage, if there were competitors, there was always the chance that the woman's heart had been divided. And Mr Wyndham Martell wanted a heart that belonged to him and him alone – first to last.

He did not care for games, therefore, in matters of the heart. Unless, of course, it was he who was playing them. Every man knew that if a woman is waiting for you it is no bad thing to make her wait a little longer.

She would be there tonight at Mrs Grockleton's ball, waiting.

Some people might have said there were too many plants. But the infallible maxim had been applied: if there is any doubt about the appointments of a room or the quality of the guests, then fill the place with flowers. And, so far as the September season allowed, this was what Mrs Grockleton had done. Every imperfection was masked by a late rose or a shrub. The entrance to the Lymington Assembly Rooms this evening might have been mistaken for a plant house.

"Mr Grockleton," she declared as, accompanied by her husband and her children, she surveyed the verdant scene, "I am quite in a flutter." And if a stout lady in a ball gown can be said to be fluttering, she was. "We have refreshments, dancing, cards. I'm sure I've done my best. And the guests are . . ." She trailed off.

The guests were what in social terms might be described as mixed. Their core, naturally, was provided by the young ladies of her academy. The dance, officially, was for them. They gave Mrs Grockleton her cover. They, their parents and their brothers were the participants, she the presiding headmistress. Were the Burrards to come and not to care for the company of some of the parents there, it would be churlish of them indeed to be ungracious to the local school's young ladies or to insult the headmistress. If she could not quite resist trying to make small social sorties beyond this defensible position, she could at least fall back upon it.

A huge asset were the French officers. Glamorous, undeniably aristocratic and God knows – although there was no need to say it – only too glad to go anywhere that offered dancing and free food, the Frenchmen would dance with the tradesmen's daughters and speak to Mr Martell as equals. She would happily have entertained a hundred regiments upon such terms. "It will really seem," she said to her husband, "as if Versailles has come to Lymington tonight."

But even so, unless a romance should develop between a French aristocrat and one of the girls, the Frenchmen ultimately were pawns in the grand game of connections she meant to play.

Could the town's fashionable doctor be introduced to Mr Martell? Surely, yes. Some of the other girls' merchant parents? Probably not. The encounter she dreamed of was that of the blessed discovery. If, say, the Burrards were to come and meet some other major family, and note that she was already their friend – why, then, they would accept her too. Thus, if Mr Martell brought Mr Drummond, Mr Drummond would find that she knew the Albions. And, of course, if she could then have got herself into Cadland and met the Burrards there . . . "These are connections, Mr Grockleton," she would explain. "It is all a question of making connections." Perhaps a quarter of Mrs Grockleton's huge mental energy was - expended in dreaming about discoveries and connections. "Whoever comes," she said – by which of course she meant only people like the Drummonds or the Burrards – "they will find the Tottons and ourselves and the Albions and Mr Martell all friends together. Just so long as it all goes well."

"It will, my dear," said her husband. The main room really looked very well. The card tables were all set up in a side room. The food, which Mr Seagull of the Angel had provided, the wine and brandy, which Mr Seagull had also sold the Customs officer at full price, without a twitch of his face – all were in place. In half an hour, when the guests began to arrive, he was sure they could not fail to be delighted. "And as soon as the music starts," he said cheerfully, "and the dancing begins . . ."

Mrs Grockleton nodded. Then Mrs Grockleton stopped. And then Mrs Grockleton let out a cry that was almost a shriek: "Oh, Mr Grockleton, Mr Grockleton, whatever shall we do?"

"What is the matter, my dear?" he cried in alarm.

"Everything is the matter. Oh, Mr Grockleton, I have forgot the band!"

"The band?"

"The orchestra. The musicians. I forgot to engage them. We have none. Oh, Mr Grockleton, how are we to dance without any music?"

Mr Grockleton had to confess he did not know. His wife stared wildly round at her children, as if she could transform them, like a magician, into so many fiddlers. But as no such miracle occurred, she turned back to her husband. "A dance without music! What is to become of us?" Then a worse thought: "What if the Burrards should come? Quick, Mr Grockleton," she cried, "run to the theatre and see if the musicians are there."

"But if there is a play . . ."

"A play is only words. They must come here."

"There is no play tonight, Mama," cried one of the children.

"Find the musicians, then. Hurry. A piano. Mr Grockleton. Bring me a piano. Mr Gilpin shall play. I know he can."

"Mr Gilpin may not wish . . ."

"Of course he must play. He must." And crying out frantic orders, Mrs Grockleton soon had her husband, children, servants, even Isaac Seagull rushing about in every possible direction. Twenty minutes later there was a piano in the room, albeit somewhat out of tune. Moments after that a fiddler with his violin appeared. He had not shaved that day and he might, perhaps, have had a drop or two to drink, but he said he was ready and gave directions as to where a colleague might be found; and as the first of her pupils appeared with her father the coal merchant, Mrs Grockleton was relieved, if disconcerted, to hear her solitary violinist start to play a hornpipe from behind a potted plant.

The full moon was already rising when the carriage left Albion House.

Mrs Grockleton's desire to hold her ball on the night of the full moon was entirely natural. In country areas, if people were to return several miles home late at night, they always preferred to do so when the moon was as bright as possible and balls were arranged accordingly, at seasons when there was the best chance of the sky being clear. Although the forest roads had been free of criminals since the Ambrose Hole affair, people still preferred to be able to see their way home.

Tonight, however, Fanny did not expect that they would be returning late. In the first place she had her own reasons for anticipating a less than enjoyable evening. But secondly there had been another development, which had entirely taken them by surprise.

Mr Albion had decided he was coming too.

They had found him already fully dressed when they arrived home that afternoon. He had positively insisted he would go. Whether old Francis had suddenly acquired a new lease of life or whether he was just cross at being left alone for two days it was hard to be sure; but since he refused all attempts to dissuade him and seemed likely to become angry, there was nothing to do but take him. Mrs Pride was accompanying them in case of any difficulty.

Aunt Adelaide was tired, but in a good humour. Although she did not say much to her brother – except to pass on Mr West's kind remembrances and to state that the new tenant of Hale was entirely a gentleman – the old lady had already made her views clear to Fanny. "He is very suitable," she had stated. "Do you not think so?" And when Fanny had agreed that he seemed a sensible man: "Do you like him, child?"

"Truly, Aunt, I do not know," she had replied. "I have only just met him." Her aunt was satisfied to leave it at that and question her no further. Fanny could tell by her manner, however, as the old lady sat in the carriage with a shawl wrapped around her, that Aunt Adelaide felt the effort required to go across the Forest had not been wasted and that she had done something important for Fanny's future.

As for her real feelings, Fanny hardly knew what she felt any more. The silence of Mr Martell, the knowledge – for she had asked Mrs Pride – that even after her departure no word had come from him and the eerie likeness of the picture of Penruddock had been a series of blows. She was not sure she wanted her poor aunt to catch sight of Martell, as Adelaide's eyes, old although they were, could not fail to notice this awful likeness; and she would prefer to spare her another shock.

She had quite decided that she hoped he would not be there as they clattered up the High Street towards the Assembly Rooms. Minutes later, as they made their way slowly through the plants into the main hall, it seemed to Fanny that she felt nothing at all.

The Burrards had not come. But all the Tottons were there, and the count and his wife, and all the French officers. The bevy of young ladies from Mrs Grockleton's academy looked very charming; and if, perhaps, one or two of their parents wore coats of a somewhat rustic cut or more powder than was desirable, or laughed a little too loudly, or tittered too bashfully, you would have been a black-hearted villain to take any notice. Mr Gilpin was also there, looking rather cross. Of Mr Martell she saw no sign.

Her father and Aunt Adelaide both desired to sit down, and Fanny had to acknowledge that here Mr Grockleton behaved admirably, putting chairs for them in a corner, bringing suitable people like the doctor and his wife to talk to them and looking after them in every way, so that she was free to go and talk to her friends. Having greeted her cousins, she thought it her duty, given her social position, to make the rounds of the room; so for some time she was too busy making herself pleasant to the various Lymington families and the French contingent to notice anything much, but she did glance round once or twice and see that Mr Martell had not yet arrived. She was rather astonished, however, when Mrs Grockleton had clapped her hands and her husband gravely announced the dancing, to observe Mr Gilpin, looking none too pleased, sit down at the piano and, accompanied by two men with violins, begin to play.

"A minuet," cried Mrs Grockleton. "Come, Fanny. Come Edward, lead us in the minuet."

Fanny and Edward both danced well. The count and his wife fell in behind, the other French officers were not slow to take partners and the business got under way very nicely; although when Edward whispered to her that Mr Gilpin was at the piano because Mrs Grockleton had forgotten the band it was all Fanny could do not to collapse with laughter. The minuet was followed by several more dances. Mr Gilpin then indicated that he felt he should be relieved and rose from the piano. But the two fiddlers, having got quite into their stride, struck up a country dance on their own, and this brought most of the Lymington folk on to the floor; so that it was a very jolly, if not very elegant scene that greeted Mr Martell's eyes as he quietly entered from the far end of the room just as refreshments were announced.

Fanny did not see him at first. With Edward's help she had brought her aunt a little fruit pie and a glass of champagne, which was all she wanted; but old Francis Albion, who seemed to be enjoying himself enormously, demanded a plate of ham and some claret. Not only that, he gave his daughter quite a naughty look – which she had never seen before in her life – and suggested that she bring some of the young ladies to talk to him. She was quite astonished at this transformation in the old man and dutifully did as he asked.

A few minutes later, talking to one of the French officers, she suddenly became aware of a presence beside her and knew at once, with a little tremor, who it was.

"I had been searching for you, Miss Albion," said Mr Martell and, almost unwillingly, she looked up at his face.

The tiny gasp she gave was quite involuntary, as was the expression of horror she must have shown, since the sight of it made him frown. Yet she really couldn't help it. For at her side stood the man whose portrait she had seen the night before.

The thing was uncanny. This was no mere likeness – a similarity of hair, saturnine features or proud, handsome look. This was the man himself. Indeed, it seemed to her, she could only assume that up at Hale House at this moment the frame in the shadowy passage was empty, and that Colonel Penruddock himself had stepped out from it, changed his clothes, and was now standing beside her, tall, dark, very much alive and threatening. She took a step back.

"Is something wrong?" No wonder he was puzzled.

"No, Mr Martell, nothing."

"You are not unwell?" He looked concerned, but she shook her head. "I should have called upon you before this but Sir Harry has kept me rather busy."

"You would not have found me anyway, Mr Martell, these last two days. I have been away."

"Ah." He paused a moment.

"In a house I recently visited, Mr Martell, I saw a picture that bears a striking resemblance to you."

"Indeed? Was it such a disagreeable face, Miss Albion?"

If this was intended to draw a smile from her, she remained serious. "A Colonel Thomas Penruddock, of Compton Chamberlayne. About the time of Charles II or a little after."

"Colonel Thomas?" His face grew most interested. "Pray where did you see this?"

"At Hale."

"I had no idea of its existence. What extraordinary good fortune, Miss Albion, that you should have discovered it. I must go and see it." He smiled. "Colonel Thomas Penruddock was my mother's grandfather. My ancestor. We have no picture of him, though."

"You are a Penruddock?"

"Certainly. The Martells and Penruddocks have married each other for centuries. I'm a Penruddock many times over." He grinned. "If you get one of us, Miss Albion, you get both."

"I see." She kept very calm. "There was some trouble between the Penruddocks and a family called Lisle in the New Forest."

"So I have heard. The Lisles of Moyles Court, I believe – although I confess I have never known the details. The other branch of that family were more respectable, weren't they?"

"I couldn't say."

"No. It was a long time ago, of course."

Fanny glanced across to where her father and Aunt Adelaide were sitting. Mr Albion was chatting happily with two young ladies, but her aunt appeared to be falling asleep. So much the better. There was little point in her being made aware that there was a Penruddock in the company.

"Perhaps, if your father is in better humour," he was saying, "I may call upon you . . ."

"Better not, I think, Mr Martell."

"Well. There is to be a dinner tomorrow at the Burrards. I have a note here from Lady Burrard asking you to come. May I tell her . . ."

"I am afraid that I am already promised elsewhere, Mr Martell. Would you please thank her for me. I will send a letter to her tomorrow." She suddenly felt very tired. "I must look after my father now," she said.

"Of course. When the dancing begins again I shall claim you."

She smiled politely but non-committally and retired to the far corner, leaving Martell a little puzzled. It was evident that a distance had opened up between them, but he was not certain of the cause. Was it because he had neglected her during his stay? Were there other reasons? No doubt the matter could be put right, but he felt anxious to do so, and had it not been for the dangerous presence of her old father he might have followed her there and then. A moment later, however, Louisa appeared and as she remarked that she was hungry, he could hardly fail to escort her towards the refreshments. Nearly half an hour passed before the sound of the violins signalled the resumption of dancing and even then she did not move.

It was at this point that some of the more discerning guests in the main room began to notice that all was not quite well with Mrs Grockleton's ball. The two fiddlers were working away hard enough, but one of them was getting rather red and the second, between dances – or even during a dance – was pausing to drink out of a tankard that contained something other than water.

Was their playing a little out of tune? Was a note missing here and there? It would have been inappropriate to ask. Mr Grockleton did murmur to his wife that he might remove the tankard. "But if you do that," she cautioned, "he might stop playing." So he left it where it was.

A country dance was in full, if slightly lurching, swing when Mr Martell finally emerged and saw Fanny standing alone. He did not waste any time in moving towards her, but she did not see him approach. Her eyes were upon other things.

Aunt Adelaide was asleep, quite comfortably propped in her chair. But old Francis Albion was in a remarkable state. She had never seen anything like it. He was well into his second glass of claret and looking very cheerful on it. The ladies in general, from her friends at the academy to the count's wife, had all decided to adopt him. There were at least six of them sitting around him and at his feet, and if his gleaming blue eyes and their peals of laughter were anything to go by, he was entertaining them thoroughly. Fanny could only shake her head in wonderment and suppose that, in the long years of his travels before she was born, her father might have had a more active social life than she had realised.

"Perhaps you would do me the honour of granting me the next dance."

She turned. She had already made up her mind what to do if this happened. Now she must see if she could carry it out. "Thank you, Mr Martell, but I do not care to dance at present. I am a little tired."

"I am sorry. But glad if it means that I have the chance to speak with you. My stay here will shortly end. Then I return to Dorset."

She inclined her head and smiled politely. At the same time she glanced around the room in the hope that, without being rude to him, she could interrupt his attempt to converse with her. She caught sight of the count and nodded to him; she could see Mr Gilpin, but he was not looking in her direction.

The interruption came blowing in, however, from a different quarter, in the form of Mrs Grockleton.

"Why Mr Martell, so there you are! But where is dear Louisa?"

"I believe, Mrs Grockleton, she . . ."

"You believe, Sir? Pray do not tell me you have lost her." Had Mrs Grockleton, perhaps, had a glass of champagne or two? "You must find her, Sir, at once. As for this young lady." She turned to Fanny and wagged her finger. "Methinks we hear interesting news of a young lady visiting a certain gentleman up at Hale." She beamed at Fanny. "I have been speaking to your aunt, Miss. She has formed a very good opinion of your Mr West."

"I scarcely know Mr West, Mrs Grockleton."

"You should have brought him with you," cried Mrs Grockleton, oblivious to Fanny's embarrassment. "Methinks you are hiding him."

How she might have silenced her hostess Fanny did not know, but at this moment the gallant count appeared at her side, asked for the minuet just beginning and, murmuring quite untruthfully to Mr Martell that she had already promised the count this dance, Fanny gratefully took this means of escape.

"When this dance is over, Miss Albion," the Frenchman asked with a twinkle in his eye, "shall I return you to Mrs Grockleton?"

"As far away as possible," she begged.

For another quarter of an hour she managed to avoid Mr Martell. She saw him dancing with Louisa, then she sought refuge in the company of Mr Gilpin, with whom, for a little while, she could safely watch the proceedings.

Unfortunately, it could no longer be denied by now that Mrs Grockleton's ball was not going quite so well. They should have taken the fiddler's tankard away, since it contained a potent mixture of claret laced with brandy and his fingers were slipping. Strange sounds were beginning to emerge. A few people had started to giggle. Glancing towards the entrance, Fanny noticed Isaac Seagull standing there quietly, looking in with amusement; and wondered what thoughts were passing through his cynical mind. It suddenly occurred to her that his presence, reminding her of the grim secrets of her own ancestry, was not unlike the discordant notes in the music.

"Something must be done," muttered Gilpin. "If Grockleton doesn't act, I shall have to." And, as if to prompt him, the violin now made an excruciating screech that stopped the dancers in their tracks.

At that moment the vicar caught Grockleton's eye. A sign and a brisk nod from Gilpin were enough, and with good grace the Customs officer stepped forward, clapped his hands, raised one of those claw-like appendages and announced: "Ladies and Gentlemen, the evening is growing late, I know, for some. So Mr Gilpin has kindly consented to give us a final – no, you are very generous, Sir – two final minuets."

The first started off well enough. Fanny partnered one of the French officers. Louisa again danced with Mr Martell, but she tried not to look at them. Mr Gilpin on the piano acquitted himself admirably. Only towards the end did trouble break out.

The two violinists decided they had not done. They were both of them now at that stage of drunkenness where they believed they were enjoying themselves and took quite unkindly to any interference. They felt sure that Mr Gilpin needed accompaniment. Suddenly, therefore, the dancers became aware of the sound of strings. Even this might have passed, since Mr Gilpin was holding his own with firmness, had the other two not come to the conclusion that accompaniment was not enough. The vicar needed leading. And so it was that now the dancers became aware of a more strident sound from the strings, one of greater and greater urgency, but which, most unfortunately, was not the same tune that the vicar of Boldre was playing. In fact, it seemed to be a country dance. The dancers came to a halt. Mr Gilpin stopped and looked furious.

Mr Grockleton stepped forward, tried to speak to the fiddlers, who were still playing, put out his arm to restrain one of them and was promptly tapped on the head with a fiddle. Pale with annoyance, now, he grasped one of the fiddlers and began to drag him away, whereupon the other, who still had his tankard with him, emptied its contents over the Customs officer and started to belabour him with his bow. He might even have hurt him had he not suddenly, with a yelp, felt the finger and thumbnails of Mrs Grockleton close like piercing pincers upon his ear as that lady marched him away, past a grinning Isaac Seagull, past the plants and straight out into the night air.

The good people of Lymington laughed and applauded, and laughed again until they almost cried, which, all semblance of dignity having been lost anyway, was probably the sensible thing to do. Mr Gilpin, considerably irritated now, but unwilling to see the evening end in shambles, waited patiently for a moment or two by the piano, then bravely continued the minuet, which the dancers very loyally took up again and brought to a conclusion. But as the Grockletons had now returned and the room was still awash with ripples of laughter, the good vicar had in common charity to do his best to save the day.

He rose to the occasion admirably. "Ladies and gentlemen." He advanced to the centre of the room. "In the days of ancient Rome it was the custom to grant victorious generals a triumph upon their return. Such a triumph, I think you will agree, has been earned by our kind host and hostess. *For they have expelled the barbarians from our gates.*"

There was stamping, "hear hears!" and a round of applause. Fanny, standing to one side, heard a voice she knew to be Martell's quietly murmur: "Well played, Sir."

"And now, for a final dance, I am at your service. Mrs Grockleton, what shall it be?"

It would not be true to say that the room fell silent. All around, murmurs arose from behind hands, or other people's backs, or into handkerchiefs and fans. And Mrs Grockleton heard them. She smiled as gamely as she could. "Let it be a country dance," she said.

It really seemed they all would dance: the French aristocrats, the local coal merchants, the doctor, the lawyers. Fanny was not at all sure that Mr Isaac Seagull was not dancing as well. Mr Gilpin struck up, with the obvious intention of giving them a good five minutes' worth.

But Fanny did not dance. She stood at the side, content to watch, unnoticed. She looked for Martell but did not see him. Louisa was dancing with a young Frenchman. Fanny frowned. And then she slowly realised. She had heard his voice just behind her before the dance began. He must, therefore, be standing there now. She dared not look round in case he should ask her to dance. For she had no wish to do so. She was sure she hadn't. But if he was behind her, what was he doing? Did he mean to speak? How could she speak and what was the point, when he cared so little for her and when, besides, he was a Penruddock? She wished, if he was there, that he would disappear.

Something was happening on the dance floor now. A little gaggle of young ladies had gathered, like an eddy, about Louisa. She was saying something to her partner, who shrugged amiably and smiled. The eddy was moving out towards the edge in the direction of her father. Louisa had detached herself. She was going up to the old man, saying something to him. Mr Albion was looking rather flushed; Aunt Adelaide, awake now, was also speaking but he was evidently ignoring it. Her father was getting up, a girl on each side of him; the others were squealing and starting to applaud. Dear heaven, Louisa Totton was leading the old man out to dance!

And he was dancing: stiffly, of course, with Louisa effectively holding him up. But Francis Albion was dancing a country dance. The other dancers were parting, they were forming a ring, everyone was applauding as a very old man who hadn't been out in years came dancing through their midst with a pretty young girl and, if she was holding him up, why then so much the more gallant they both appeared. Fanny rose on her toes to see, her heart beating half in fear and half delight. Her father, of almost ninety, was dancing before all the world. Louisa was laughing with pleasure and real admiration. With a gesture that said "I'll show you a thing or two now," old Francis stepped free, treated them all to a little jig by himself and, as the room erupted into applause, turned back to Louisa, suddenly went deathly pale, choked, felt wildly for his collar and crashed face downwards on the boards, while Mr Gilpin, unaware of what was passing, continued to play for several more bars until the awful silence alerted him to stop.

"Oh, my dear Miss Albion." She heard Martell's voice behind her, but did not look back as she rushed forward through the dancers to the place where, miraculously, Mrs Pride's strong arms were already raising the little old gentleman up. Without a word she carried him towards the entrance and the fresh air, where she was quickly joined by Mr Gilpin and the Lymington doctor.

Minutes later, still uncertain of the outcome of this scene, the guests were collecting their cloaks and coats to leave.

And poor Mrs Grockleton, having been through so much that night, could only turn helplessly to her husband and wail: "Alack-a-day!"

They had the pig ready and the moon was high as along the track on the gorse-strewn bareness of Wilverley Plain the cart containing Caleb Furzey trundled towards them.

The sky was clear and clustered with stars; the moon shone

down with that intimate, frightening urgency it often has when
it is full.

The six boys waited by the tree called the Naked Man. The
pig was surprisingly quiet, probably because it had been well
fed. It grunted a bit, that was all.

The cart was drawing closer. The horse was going at a
slow walk. Caleb Furzey's feet could just be seen resting on
the side. From within the empty box of the cart his snores
were magnified, as if by some magic of the moon.

Nathaniel and Andrew Pride moved out first. The old horse
recognised them, and when Nathaniel took his head, he
stopped quite willingly.

Taking him out of the harness was not too difficult. Andrew's
task was to lead him away across the plain and tether him
to a stunted tree trunk behind a large gorse brake a few hundred yards off. The next step was to put the pig in the horse's
place.

The makeshift harness they had made worked well enough,
but the shafts of the cart were far too high. Two of the boys
now tried to pull them down, but couldn't.

Two more boys added their weight to the shafts. The shafts
came down, but not far enough. The pig didn't like the look of
it. Nathaniel was holding firm but the pig was large; if he
made a run for it, there would be no stopping him. But now, as
he clung on to the pig's harness, he heard a sound from the
cart. Caleb's feet were moving; the snoring was interrupted.

Suddenly the cart tipped forward. They heard a bump.
Caleb had rolled to the front.

"Quick."

It was the work of a moment to attach the traces to the harness. Nathaniel was still holding the pig, soothing him as the
others stepped back. They all looked apprehensively towards
the cart but, miraculously, Furzey was still asleep.

"Now."

They fled, but not far. A hundred yards away, behind a gorse
brake, Andrew was already waiting.

"You know what to do," said Nathaniel, as he started un-
dressing. So they did as he had told them and went to their sta-
tions. It was time for the fun to begin.

The pig, surprisingly, did not react for more than a minute. Then it decided to move.

The pig was much smaller than the horse, but it was heavy and very strong. The cart inched forward, but the sensation of something not only holding but following it was displeasing to the pig. It grunted loudly and tried to make a run. Again, the cart seemed to be holding on, as though it were determined not to let the pig escape its clutches. The pig didn't like this a bit. It let out a bellow of rage, bumped the shafts from side to side and squealed loudly again.

Behind, Caleb Furzey frowned in his sleep. He opened his eyes, blinked, and awoke.

The full moon was high over Wilverley Plain. All around him, a magical silver light gleamed eerily; close by, the Naked Man stood with its bare arms raised as if it meant to reach down and strike him. He blinked again. What was that strange sound that had awoken him? He got up and started forward. His horse had disappeared. Something else was in the traces. That something made a strange sound which so startled him that he stepped back. The cart tilted.

The pig was lifted off the ground. It squealed, screamed, paddled furiously with its legs. And Caleb Furzey let out a howl of fear.

His horse gone at full moon, a pig in its place. Every rustic knew who did such things – the witches and the fairies. He'd been bewitched! And he was about to clamber out of the cart when he saw another even more terrifying sight. From gorse bush to gorse bush, small, naked figures were flitting, emitting cries. They were all around. They had to be fairies. He must have been mad to come out, past Burley of all places, on the night of a full moon. As the figures flitted about, the squeals of the pig rose to a terrifying pitch. The cart tilted back wildly. For a terrible, mad moment Caleb saw the pig, outlined against the moon. He yelled again with fright, covered his face and threw himself down into the cart, which tilted forward once more.

And there poor Caleb Furzey lay, curled up in a ball, cowering with terror, for upwards of half an hour, until, after there had been silence for some time, he finally peeped out.

The moon was high. The Naked Man was still standing in its threatening attitude; but the pig was gone and the fairies, it seemed, had disappeared into the ground. Out in the silver light of Wilverley Plain, about two hundred yards off, his horse was peaceably grazing.

A mile away, Nathaniel was giving his final instructions. "Not a word – not even to your brothers and sisters. Remember, if anybody tells, then we're all dead." He looked at them solemnly. "Swear." They swore. "All right, then," he said.

Wyndham Martell couldn't sleep. The Burrards' big house was quiet; everyone else had long gone to bed, but he still sat in his room, wide awake.

The moonlight flooded in through the window. He told himself it was the full moon that was keeping him from sleeping. Perhaps. But it was also the girl.

Old Francis Albion had been taken home. At first the doctor had thought he had suffered an apoplexy, but then concluded he hadn't. They had waited an hour, given him a little brandy to revive him and packed him off home, with the good Mr Gilpin accompanying him.

Although his presence was clearly not desired, Martell had waited about all the same, requesting the landlord of the Angel to give him news, before returning himself. He had caught sight of Fanny as she left, but she had not seen him. She had looked composed, but very pale. He had no doubt she must feel embarrassed by the whole business even though, in his opinion, she had no need.

But that brought him to the other question. Why had Fanny changed so abruptly towards him? Of course, it might be that he had been mistaken all along and that she had never been interested in him in the first place. Perhaps he was guilty of mere vanity in supposing otherwise. But a man has to trust his instincts, and he believed she had liked him. Why the sudden coldness? Had he neglected her? In her eyes, yes. And, he had better confess it, she was right. But he felt there was more. Mrs Grockleton's word in such matters was probably unreliable, but Mr Arthur West undoubtedly existed, might be considered eligible and was therefore a factor. I should have returned sooner, he thought. I shouldn't have tarried. But was that enough to explain her coldness? And what should he do?

What, come to that, did he want to do?

It was no good. The moon was making sleep impossible. He seized a pair of boots, went softly down the stairs and outside. The night was really very fine. The stars over the Forest were sharp as crystal. He started to make for Beaulieu Heath, by the moon's light.

The September night was not cold. He walked very comfortably along the edge of the heath, past Oakley, with the woods on his left. He was not going anywhere in particular. He had continued like this for about a mile when he realised that Boldre church must be not far off and, sure enough, after following a track for a little time he came upon it, standing in a friendly way upon its knoll in the moonlight. He walked round it, then realised that he could not be far from Albion House. So he went down the lane into the valley and took the track that led northwards, under the trees, although it was rather dark, and just as he heard the river splashing over some stones he turned away into the still darker drive until, emerging into the clearing, he saw the ghostly old gables of the house, apparently wide awake in the harsh moonlight. He moved cautiously, now, keeping to the edge of the grounds, not wishing to wake any dogs or alert whatever guardian spirits might be up there, like sentinels upon their watchtowers, in the ancient timbers or the chimneys on the roof.

Which room was hers, he wondered, and where did old Francis Albion sleep? What history and what secrets was the old manor keeping? Could it be that Fanny's rejection of him was caused by something more than mere indifference or the presence of another lover, some part of her soul, perhaps, secreted in this house?

He supposed he was being fanciful, yet he did not leave. Taking up a station where he had a good view of the most likely windows, he remained there, he really could not say why, for an hour or so.

And some time before dawn, when the moon was still casting long shadows on the bright lawn, he saw a pair of wooden shutters open and a window go up.

Fanny was in a white nightdress. She was staring out at the moonlit scene. Her hair fell loosely upon her shoulders and her face, so beautiful yet so tragic, seemed as pale, as unearthly, as any spirit. She did not see him. After a time, she closed the shutters again.

There was a cold snap in the October evening air as Puckle came to Beaulieu Rails; and out in the misty brown gloaming of the heath beyond, the ancient roar of a red stag announced that the rutting season had at last begun.

Puckle was tired. He had been working down at Buckler's Hard all day. Then he had stopped briefly to see a friend at the farmhouse which had once been St Leonards Grange. Now, walking along the straggle of cottages by the heath's edge as dusk was falling, he was ready to go to bed. He had just reached the door of his tiny cottage when a noise made him turn: the sound of a horse walking up the track towards him – a single horse and rider. As he swung round, instinct told him who it would be.

Even in that dim brown light there was no mistaking the chinless face and the faint, cynical smile of Isaac Seagull as he came towards him.

The lander did not speak until he was right beside him. "I'll be needing you soon," he said quietly. Puckle took a deep breath.

It was time.

There had been no small amusement in the village of Oakley when Caleb Furzey told them he'd been bewitched.

"You was drunk at the time, remember," they jovially told him. "Have another drink," they'd cry, "and tell us how many fairies you see." Or, "Careful of that horse, mind. He might turn into a pig!"

But Furzey stuck doggedly to his story, and his description of the pig and the sprites up on Wilverley Plain was so vivid that there were some folk in Oakley who were almost ready to believe him. Only Pride gave young Nathaniel a slow and thoughtful look; but if he had his suspicions he evidently concluded that it was better to say nothing. So the days had passed and then the weeks. And aside from a few titters and jokes about the gullible cottager, nothing of any note occurred in the quiet New Forest hamlet on the edge of Beaulieu Heath.

It had not been long before Mr Arthur West had called at Albion House. He had turned up, driving himself in a smart chaise, explaining that he was staying a day or two with the Morants at Brockenhurst. He was dressed in a heavy coachman's coat and hat, smiling very amiably at the joke, and looked every inch the brisk sporting gentleman that he was.

He was received with enthusiasm by Aunt Adelaide and, since he was the nephew of a friend, even old Francis felt obliged to be polite to him. To Fanny he was friendly, relaxed and cheerful. He did not make the mistake of issuing any invitation that might seem to remove her from her father's company, but contented himself with remarking that he felt sure they would meet again at one of their neighbours' soon and that he would greatly look forward to it.

All in all, Fanny thought to herself with a smile, he had played his hand very well. She realised that she was grateful, too. You knew where you were with Mr West. He was there; he was marriageable; he would make himself known to the young ladies of the county and if he received an indication that his attention might be welcome, he would advance, sensibly, one step at a time. They would meet at a dinner here, a dance there; and if something developed, well and good.

Mr West also brought another small piece of news. "I received a call recently from a gentleman you know, a friend of the Tottons: Mr Martell."

To her embarrassment, Fanny felt herself go rather pale and then colour. Seeing Mr West glance at her in surprise she quickly explained: "I'm afraid Father and Mr Martell had an altercation when he came here."

If Francis Albion had given everyone a fright at Mrs Grockleton's ball, he certainly seemed quite his old self again now – which was to say you could never be sure that he mightn't have a fit and drop dead on the spot, or, as the doctor confided to Mr Gilpin, "He may just as well live to be a hundred." One thing was certain at least: as long as he did live he meant to have his way. "Martell? A most insolent young man," he piped, without a shade of embarrassment.

"Well, anyway," said Mr West, "he was most anxious to see one of the pictures in the house: one of his ancestors. And I must say, when we inspected it, the thing was quite extraordinary. It was his double. You saw the picture." He turned to Aunt Adelaide. "The dark-haired gentleman we looked at upstairs, Colonel Penruddock."

"That young puppy was a Penruddock?" cried Francis, while Aunt Adelaide's face was like a mask.

"I'm sorry," Mr West said, looking from one to the other, "there is evidently some family dispute of which I was not aware."

"There is, Mr West," Aunt Adelaide replied graciously, "but you could not possibly have known of it. However," she said with a polite smile, "we do not mix with the Penruddocks."

"I shall remember in future," Mr West promised with a bow.

Certainly this faux pas did not do Mr West any harm in Adelaide's eyes and she made clear to him when he left that he would be welcome to call again at any time.

"I think him a very agreeable man," Fanny said in answer to her aunt's questioning glance; and when Francis remarked that he hoped the man wasn't going to come buzzing around the place like a fly she was able to assure him, with a laugh, that Mr West had a great many other places to go.

Mr West was not the only visitor to Albion House, however. Whether it was by chance, or whether some friend like Mr Gilpin had lent encouragement, a number of people called to see that Fanny was not deprived of company and even Francis Albion could hardly complain if she went out to dine from time to time. One of the most charming of these visitors was the count, who came once with his wife and once without.

Nathaniel had just emerged from Mr Gilpin's school one afternoon when he was hailed by the fellow trudging down the lane. He didn't know him, although he reckoned he might be one of the Puckles, judging by the look of him. But when the man asked if he'd like to earn sixpence Nathaniel was all attention.

"I was up at Albion House and Miss Albion gave me this letter to take into Lymington. Didn't like to say no to her, but I ain't going that way. Here's the sixpence she gave me if you want to take it down there. It's to a Frenchman, she said."

"I can see." Nathaniel could read and Fanny's hand was clear. The letter was addressed to the count. Sixpence was a handsome sum indeed. "I'll take it," he said. "Straight away."

A deep November night. Moonless. Better, a thick blanket of cloud had snuffed out even the starlight, so that there was only the pitch-black texture of nothingness over the sea. The faint sound of small waves upon the formless shore gave the sole hint that there was anything yet created in the void beyond. Smugglers' weather.

Puckle waited. He was standing on a small rise on the coast below Beaulieu Heath. In front of him the mudflats extended hundreds of yards at low tide, cut by long inlets known locally as lakes. To his left, a quarter-mile away, lay the little smugglers' landing place known as Pitts Deep. The same distance away on his right was Tanners Lane, and past that the park of a handsome coastal estate called Pylewell. The Burrards' land lay beyond that and then, about two miles away, the town of Lymington.

It was a quiet spot. The farmer at Pylewell's home farm had long been suspected as a large operator in the Free Trade. It was said that hundreds of casks of brandy were buried at Pitts Deep.

In Puckle's hand was a lantern. It was a curious object because, instead of a window, it had a long spout. When he pointed the spout out to sea, by covering it with his hand and then moving his hand on and off, Puckle could send pinpoint light flashes out there, which were invisible to all but the smugglers in the vessels on the water. The tide was coming in.

The plan, as Puckle had explained it to Grockleton, was very simple. First, as the tide came in, the luggers would bring the contraband to shore. They would leave it and depart. The main body of Free Traders would then come down Tanners Lane along the beach and remove the contraband. That would be the moment when Grockleton and his troops could pounce. This was a typical procedure, but the cargo on this occasion was particularly valuable: best brandy, a huge quantity of silk, lace – one of the most profitable runs ever made.

"Another hour," he remarked quietly to the tall figure at his side, trying to sound calm. Grockleton nodded, but said nothing.

He had taken enormous trouble. So far everything had gone according to plan. The note from Fanny Albion had been a good idea. Using one she had written to his wife some time ago, it had been an easy matter to forge a short letter. Nor were the contents anything to arouse comment if they had fallen into the wrong hands: thanks for a book he had lent her, good wishes from her father and Adelaide. The note had been left with Puckle. When he gave it to Nathaniel to deliver to the count, who was under instructions to inform Grockleton at once, the smuggler sent a signal that the big shipment was due and that he and Grockleton must meet at the Rufus stone again the next day.

The preparations for the military contingent had been even more careful. In the first place Grockleton had told nobody, neither his wife nor his own riders, that anything was afoot. The colonel had arranged for sixty of his best troops to be transferred up to Buckland. At dusk, he had called a muster and then, taking another twenty mounted men from Buckland, he had slipped out with them, split them into small parties and brought them under cover of darkness to the rendezvous, in a little wood immediately above Pitts Deep. A dozen men were already lying, well concealed, overlooking the beach. Their orders were strict. No one must interfere with the landing of the goods or give any sign.

"We have to catch the landsmen red-handed," Grockleton had impressed upon the count. His own role was to be heroic and quite certainly dangerous. While the twenty horsemen raced out of the woods along the shore to cut off their retreat, and twenty of his men ran with lanterns along the line of the smugglers' caravan, he intended to call out to offer them terms of instant surrender, or a devastating salvo if they resisted.

There was nothing to do but wait. He intended to remain with Puckle until the luggers came to shore. Just to make certain he didn't change his mind.

Even Isaac Seagull's keen eyes could not pierce this darkness. He was supervising personally. This shipment was the big one.

Behind him, two hundred men and eighty ponies waited quietly in a long, well-ordered line.

Each pony could carry a pair of barrels with flattened sides, roped together over its back. These barrels were called ankers and each held eight and a third imperial gallons. The men would mostly carry a pair of half-ankers, one on their chest, the other on their back, each weighing about forty-five pounds – a heavy load when they had a ten- or fifteen-mile march ahead of them.

The tea was packed in waterproof oilskins, known as dollops. A pony could carry several of these. The bales of silk were also in oilskin packages, but for these Seagull had devised a special form of transport. Half a dozen tall, strong women were standing just behind him. They wore long dresses that hung very loose on them. As soon as the silks were brought to shore, however, their dresses would come off. The silks would be wound round them, yard after yard, as though they were being embalmed, and at last, when they had all they could carry and were twice the girth they had been before, they would put their dresses back on, and ride and walk their way to their various markets. Within a couple of days, two of these women would be up at Sarum and another over at Winchester.

As he waited in the dark, Isaac Seagull smiled to himself.

There were so many routes you could choose when you were landing goods on the shores of the Forest. For the smaller drops Luttrell's Tower in the east was useful. So was the Beaulieu River. It amused him, on occasion, to use the old fortress of Hurst Castle: the Customs had actually put an agent there a few years back, so Isaac Seagull, in his genial way, had gone to see him and asked: "Would you like me to break your head or pay you?"

"Pay," the fellow had said promptly and, although he reported to Grockleton, he had followed Seagull's orders ever since.

On the west side of the Forest, along the coast between the spit of Hurst Castle and Christchurch, there were two wonderful landings. These were the narrow gullies coming down to the shore where a string of packhorses could wait unseen. Bunnies, these little defiles were called: Becton Bunny lay just below Hordle; Chewton Bunny a mile or so further west. Chewton was good because the beach on each side contained treacherous quicksands, to impede the Customs men. From Chewton you went up a mile or so to the Cat and Fiddle Inn, then across the Forest, up the track called the Smugglers' Road between Burley and Ringwood. There was the first of several Free Traders' markets held quite regularly up that way. And from the Smugglers' Road you passed up into the northern forest and far beyond.

But back in the eastern forest there was also Pitts Deep. There were advantages to that, too. You could go eastwards, skirting Southampton; or you could go by Boldre church and across into the western forest by the ford above Albion House, picking up the Smugglers' Road a few miles further on. Pitts Deep was good, and less obvious. That was why a shipment was coming in there now.

Grockleton tensed. Without his realising it his claw-like hands gripped Puckle's arm, causing Puckle to curse quietly as the lantern shook.

For a moment more the Customs officer failed to see anything, but then he did: a faint blue light, winking out at sea. Puckle flashed the lantern again. Two more blue winks. Two from Puckle. Then a long blue flash.

"They're coming in," the smuggler said quietly. A partial break in the cloud gave them a little starlight now. Just enough to make out the water's edge and the white lines of the lapping waves. Grockleton felt his pulse racing. The moment of triumph. Soon it would be his.

Beside him Puckle did not feel any excitement at all. For him, he knew, this was the final action that must seal his fate. "Don't worry," Grockleton, meaning to be kind, murmured beside him, "there'll be plenty in this for you." But it wasn't true. None of it was true.

Long moments passed. Then the sound of oars and, two hundred yards out, the vague shapes of three large luggers rowing towards Pitts Deep.

Grockleton was gone. Running, stooped over, below the line of the little cliff, now that he was satisfied that the goods really were coming in, he was anxious to ensure that the French

troops didn't move too soon. It was all going exactly to plan.
The three luggers were beaching; men were leaping into the
water. A moment later they were starting to unload.

Even from where he stood, Puckle could see that they were
unloading a prodigious amount. Casks, boxes, oilskins – one
could not see exactly, but there appeared to be a long dark line
of goods stretching for about fifty yards along the shoreline.
Pitts Deep had never received such a cargo. The luggers were
finishing their work. The speed of these mariners was remarkable. In the faint starlight, he could see one of the luggers
pulling away. A few yards out it started coming towards him.
The second lugger was beginning to move out.

Puckle sighed. It was time for him, too, to move.

Grockleton waited patiently. An hour passed. Puckle had told
him that the Free Traders often waited a good while before
coming down, to make sure the coast was clear. The goods on
the shoreline looked so tempting that he longed to go down
and inspect them; but he knew he must not. There must be no
risk of giving away the ambush.

His eyes scanned the shoreline. Puckle had been ordered to
stay at his post because this was what he would normally have
done. There was a risk here. He might signal the smugglers to
warn them not to approach. But if he did, Grockleton would
have him arrested and bring the entire weight of the law down
upon him. He smiled to himself grimly: even this would not be
the worst outcome. He'd be able to appropriate the entire cargo
without the risks of a fight.

Another hour passed. He strained, listening for some sound.
At last he could bear it no longer. Moving carefully, bent low,
almost holding his breath in case that sound should alert anyone, he crept back to Puckle's station. It took him ten minutes.
He worked his way up on to the tiny knoll.

It was vacant. He peered around. Perhaps the fellow had left
his post to attend to a call of nature. Or possibly the Free
Traders were close by and they had called him down. He
peered around into the gloom. No sound. No movement. He
waited five minutes. Surely if the smugglers were here they
would have come by now.

Grockleton was a patient man. He waited another half-hour.

The silence was complete. Puckle must have warned them. He got up and started to move stiffly. As he did so, his foot struck something, making a sharp tinny crash which, it seemed to him, would have awoken the dead. It was the spout lantern. He looked around, then shrugged. There was nobody to hear.

He walked back to where the troops were waiting and called for a lantern. Holding it aloft, he went down towards the contraband. There was a huge quantity: a fortune at his feet.

Curiously, he reached down to one of the ankers of brandy to see how heavy it was. He tried to tilt it. The anker fell over. He frowned, took hold of the one next to it. The barrel rose easily when he tugged. It was empty. He kicked the one next to that. Empty too. He ran to one of the oilskin dollops of tea, started to unwrap it. Loose straw. He started to lope about. Kicking ankers, dollops, boxes. Empty, all empty.

Then, in the middle of the night upon the Forest shore, Grockleton turned to where the darkness covered the deep and let out a great howl.

Isaac Seagull watched the long cavalcade make its way up the Smugglers' Road. There was a profusion of tracks, defiles and gullies to mystify any Customs riders or dragoons trying to find the Free Traders caravans as they wound their way northwards; but there were no riders out looking for smugglers tonight. The Customs contingent was safely away in the eastern forest where he had so skilfully diverted them.

The run into Chewton Bunny that night had been the finest moment of his long career: a prodigious cargo. He was sorry about having to force Puckle to act as decoy. The poor fellow's agony had been pitiable.

"You mean I have to leave the Forest?"

"Yes."

"When can I come back?"

"When I tell you."

The tale they made up about their quarrel and a little play-acting in the street had taken in the Customs officer completely. Puckle was already safely at sea by now. He'd gone out in one of the luggers. He'd be well paid. Handsomely. Not that the money meant much to him when he was being exiled like his. But once Seagull had known that Grockleton meant to use the French garrison, he'd needed to do something drastic.

When Mr Samuel Grockleton walked down Lymington High Street that afternoon everyone greeted him very politely. They were all there in their usual places, except Isaac Seagull who seemed to be away.

In a strange way the people of Lymington were getting to like Mr Grockleton. He took his humiliations like a man. As he walked down the street towards the Customs house by the quay, he acknowledged each greeting and, if he didn't exactly smile, you could hardly blame him for that.

Near the bottom of the street he saw the count, who came up and, giving him a melancholy smile, touched his arm with an affection that was real. "Next time, *mon ami*, perhaps we shall have better luck."

"Perhaps."

"I'm always at your service."

Grockleton nodded and passed on. He had already requested a warrant to be made out for Puckle's arrest. That, together with a full description, would be sent to every magistrate in the country. It might take time, but sooner or later Puckle was going to pay for this. Meanwhile, if he ever got the chance, he'd use those French troops to shoot every damned smuggler in the Forest.

Only one aspect of the business had not occurred to him: that as long as he proposed to use French troops, the lander's information would always be better than his.

For the companion the count had brought to his rendezvous at the crinkle-crankle wall that night in spring was Mr Isaac Seagull.

The count felt a genuine affection for Mr Grockleton and his preposterous wife. But he wasn't stupid.

Francis Albion knew, sometimes, that he was behaving badly and he also, occasionally, felt a twinge of guilt. But when a person comes close to the end of his life it is not unusual for him to feel it only fair that his selfishness should be indulged a little longer. So, if he felt any guilt, he was able to suppress it.

By mid-December, although she did not go out much, Fanny had met the ubiquitous Mr West upon three more occasions. She also seemed distracted and sad. Francis wondered if she were in love with him. If Fanny must marry, he supposed the West fellow was not a bad choice. He could give up the lease of Hale and come to live at Albion House. After all, that way he could learn to run the estate and Fanny would not be taken away. So he brought up the subject with her one winter morning when she had come to sit with him as he rested in his room. "Do you have feelings for Mr West, Fanny?" he mildly enquired.

"I like him, Father."

"Nothing more?"

"No." She shook her head and Francis could see that she meant it. "Why, Father – did you wish me to marry him?"

"Oh, no. There is no need."

"I know Aunt Adelaide does. And if I were forced to do so, I have no doubt he would be an agreeable husband. But . . ." She spread her hands.

"No, no, my child," he said tenderly. "You should consult your heart." He paused. "There is no one else? You seem a little sad."

"There is no one. It is only the weather."

"I am glad to hear it." He gazed at her watchfully. "You have your whole life ahead of you, my child, an inheritance. Looks that are very pleasing. I have not the least fear of you remaining unmarried. But" – he smiled with satisfaction – "there is not the least hurry."

"You do not wish to see me married, Father?"

Old Francis paused a moment before answering carefully. "I do not fear for you, Fanny. I trust your judgement. And I should not like you to marry with the thought only of pleasing me. As for the rest." He gave her such a sweet little smile, "I like to have you here with me for what, you know, cannot be much longer. I dare say your aunt will outlive me, but if anything should happen to her, you see, I should be quite alone." He made a sad face now.

"You shall never be alone, Father."

"You promise me, Fanny, that you won't go away and leave me all alone?"

"Never, Father," she promised, suddenly moved. "I will never leave you."

Fanny had not been in love before and so she did not know about the pain. There was, besides, this further problem: she had no idea she was in love at all.

If Mr Martell came into her mind, as he often did, it was only as a figure of fear and repulsion. If she suddenly fancied she saw his dark image through a window or, hearing a horse's hoofs, turned, half expecting it would be him, or listened carefully whenever her cousin Louisa spoke of her visits to the Burrards', in case she spoke of him, these were only examples, she told herself, of a sort of morbid interest, just as one might think of some threatening, ghostly figure from a Gothic novel. To think that she could have been on terms of near intimacy not merely with a Penruddock, but with the very image of her great-grandmother's murderer – for that was effectively what he was. What could she make of her own feelings, of his smile, of his hints, even of tenderness? She did not know; she told herself she did not care. It was all useless and meaningless anyway. But with these reflections came one other new and insidious thought.

Could it be that her judgement was at fault? Bad blood. She had bad blood, low connections: she was tainted. Her gentility, her claims to consideration were, in a sense, a fraud. At least the peasants like Puckle are honestly what they are, whereas I lack even that excuse for my existence, she thought. Even if Mr Martell were not an impossible Penruddock, he could scarcely wish to touch me if he knew the truth.

Although hardly aware of the process, she found that by Christmas she had less and less energy. Sometimes she would sit all morning in the parlour, apparently reading a book yet in reality not even doing that. If a visitor like Mr Gilpin called, she could rouse herself into a liveliness, so that she seemed her normal self. But the instant he was gone she would relapse into lethargy, staring out of the window. If Gilpin invited her to tea she would agree to go; she would mean to go; but for some reason she did not understand herself she would sit, hardly able to move until Mrs Pride, standing there with her coat, would induce one of those little bursts of energy that would carry her through the visit.

She got through her days. She did all that was required. One might have accepted, if one did not know her, that the weather was making her listless. No one could know, since she could not tell them, that, hour after hour, she felt not sadness as much as a great, grey sense that everything was pointless.

By mid-January Mrs Pride and Mr Gilpin were seriously worried about her.

Fanny Albion was not the only worry upon the vicar's mind that month. Of no less concern was the fate of another even younger life.

Nathaniel Furzey had been found out.

It was inevitable that sooner or later someone was going to talk. Over the Christmas season one of the boys told his sister; she told her mother. Within a week it was all over the Forest. Some people laughed, others were scandalised. With the exception of the Prides, who were embarrassed, the parents of the other boys involved were up in arms. To induce the boys to slip out of their cottages at night; to run around naked; to play at witchcraft. They came to see the vicar.

So did the master of the school. "This cannot go on," he told Gilpin frankly. "The boy is a bad influence. I do not think I can continue if he is there. Perhaps," he added with a viciousness he had been storing for months, "you have been teaching him too much."

It was useless to argue with so much opposition and Gilpin was far too wise to do so. Nathaniel was sent home to his parents in Minstead. His career at Gilpin's school was over.

But what to do next? It was normal enough for the boys at the school, by the time they were eleven or twelve, either to return home to work for their parents or to be apprenticed to some shopkeeper or craftsman. Yet as Gilpin reflected about the boy, he found it hard to see him settling down into a humdrum life with any craftsman. He could foresee some unfortunate shopkeeper being plagued with practical jokes and, no doubt, throwing Nathaniel out long before his apprenticeship was completed. He could imagine the boy wandering about Southampton looking for work, getting picked up by some

Navy press gang and thrown on board a ship. The press gangs were out in force these days. And then? The Navy was England's greatest glory, her oak-walled defence. But what was life like for the press-ganged men who worked the noble ships? "Rum, sodomy and the lash," an old mariner had once told him. He hoped it wasn't quite as bad as that. But whatever the truth, it wasn't what he wanted for Nathaniel Furzey.

Given the boy's lively intellect and enterprise, Gilpin found he could see two possible destinies. One, that he receive a proper education, perhaps go as a poor scholar to Oxford and, quite possibly, end up in the Church. The other that he would remain in the Forest, Gilpin thought, and develop into a first-rate smuggler, in which case he might as well go and apprentice to Isaac Seagull right away. After all, since somebody was going to run the smuggling it might as well be someone intelligent. The irony of these two choices was not lost upon the vicar; when he discussed the case with Mr Drummond and Sir Harry Burrard, each of those worthy gentlemen seemed to consider both alternatives with interest.

The solution finally came, however, from a slightly unexpected quarter: Mr Totton the merchant. He had been at dinner with the Burrards and heard about the case. "With no more children to educate," he told Gilpin in his easy way, "I'd be glad to help this boy if you recommend it. He sounds a little wild, though."

"He's bored, I think. But you'll be taking a chance."

"That," said Totton cheerfully, "is what merchants do. So tell me, where shall we send him to school?"

"There's a first-rate school in Winchester," said Gilpin.

And since one good deed almost always begets another, it was only days after young Nathaniel was packed off to Winchester that Mr Gilpin set about doing something definite for Fanny Albion.

"Bath!" cried Mrs Grockleton. "Bath! And with Fanny Albion as our charge. We should be as good as her parents, Mr Grockleton – *in loco parentis.*" She pronounced the Latin phrase as though it were a state secret. "Think of that. It's not as if," she added with a certain want of tact, "you had anything to do here."

"And are the Albions in agreement with this?"

"Well, old Mr Albion, you may be sure, is against it as he is against most things. And Fanny is reluctant to leave him. But Mr Gilpin has persuaded her to consider it and Mrs Pride, the housekeeper, who's really like an old nanny to her, you know, has been helpful, too, I understand. And then Mr Gilpin has quite persuaded old Miss Adelaide. So I think the matter is decided."

"Although Mr Albion is against it?"

"Well, my dear, it's the women who take the decisions in that house, you know."

"Ah," said Mr Grockleton. "Then I suppose," he continued after a pause while he reflected that this was the best chance he was likely to get of quitting Lymington for a while, "that we had better go to Bath."

"Thank you, Mr Grockleton." His wife beamed. "I told them you always see things my way."

They left two weeks later.

"Oh, Fanny, we are well up the hill," cried Mrs Grockleton as they arrived, "which is quite the fashionable place to be," she added, in case Fanny had not understood. They were to stay six weeks. After such a period it was fashionable to be bored of Bath although there were those who, for reasons of health or inclination, lived there all year round.

The house Mr Grockleton had found was certainly a fine one. Like most of Bath's houses, it formed part of a handsome Georgian terrace and was built of a creamy stone.

The houses rose up the steep hills in rows and tiers, in elegant terraces and crescents, staring out at the sky and down into the city's valleys through which the local river snaked between cliffs of stone. If God had asked Mrs Grockleton how she thought He should create heaven, she would probably have told Him: "Make it like Bath." She might, however, have added, considering her own plans: "You can put it by the sea."

Fanny, although she did not say so, liked the look of it less. The house, while certainly well-proportioned and elegant, had no garden. Few houses in Bath did. Nor, except in one or two parks, which were anyway given over mainly to lawns and flower beds, did there seem to be any trees. But when she gen-

tly remarked upon this to Mrs Grockleton, that lady was able
to put her right at once. "Trees, Fanny? But have you not considered, in a place like Bath, all those leaves would make such
a mess. And besides," she added with perfect truth, "there are
woods in profusion on the hills all around where, I dare say,
they look very elegant."

The house was quite big. The Grockletons had brought their
children, but there was a nursery for them on the upper floor.
The main reception rooms were on the level above the street
and had splendid views down over the city. Fanny quite enjoyed sitting and looking over this prospect. She even tried to
sketch it. But there was seldom time for sitting long when Mrs
Grockleton was in charge.

She certainly gave Fanny a change of air. They went down
to the Pump Room where, by the old Roman baths, one took
the medicinal waters. In the big yard, with an old Gothic abbey
church making a charming contrast, men in blue coats and
gold buttons waited to convey people in sedan chairs. Mrs
Grockleton insisted that she and Fanny use these upon the first
occasion.

The next day they attended a concert at the Assembly
Rooms. These were large and very handsome. They learned
that there was to be a subscription ball two evenings later,
which Mrs Grockleton insisted they must attend.

The next day was taken up chiefly with shopping – which
was not to say that they bought anything, but they inspected
the fashionable shops and observed all the people in them.

"For Bath sets the tone, Fanny," Mrs Grockleton obligingly
explained. "Bath is where polite society is born. Bath is" – she
was delighted by the sudden thought – "like our academy.
Even the most charming young ladies, those of the highest
birth who have lived all their lives in the country, can benefit
from being exposed in Bath."

The ball turned out to be a slight disappointment. If the
fashionable world was at Bath, it had not descended on
the Assembly rooms that night. Instead, a large collection of
the spa's widows, invalids, half-pay officers and eager tradesmen danced the night away very cheerfully and with a certain
decorous noise. They encountered the family of a Bristol
merchant whose two sons asked Fanny to dance. So did a very

pleasant army major, whose coat collar had taken on that slightly greasy look, which cloth has just before it starts to fray. "You need have no fear of me," he genially remarked to her. "I'm here to find a rich widow."

The major, in fact, turned out to be an amusing man, who told her much that was useful about the town. "For people like yourself in the higher part, there are the upper rooms to go to in the evening. Better company up there. But the best sort, the gentry, don't come to the Assembly Rooms often. Not unless there's something worth seeing. They have private parties. That's where you belong."

In her different way, Mrs Grockleton had come to a similar conclusion. "I'm afraid," she remarked to her husband when they were alone that night, "the Rooms were full of people like us."

"You don't care to meet people like ourselves?" her husband mildly enquired.

"If we wanted to meet people like us," Mrs Grockleton very reasonably pointed out, "we could save our money and stay at home."

The succeeding days went off well enough, though. When it was sufficiently warm, in the mornings, they took the children to see the sights, or to walk round by the river to view the splendid wooded slopes of Beechen Cliff. Another day they went out of the city to wonder at the splendour of Prior Park, past which much of the stone for the building of the city had been brought on a specially constructed railway track which, being on a long incline, operated by the force of gravity. Mr Grockleton was much taken with this.

Mrs Grockleton was thorough. Soon Fanny felt she knew the city as well as most visitors: handsome Queen Square, the Circus, the elegant Pulteney Bridge designed by Adams, the Assembly Rooms, upper and lower, and the Royal Crescent, where one walked on a Sunday, to be seen. There was no defined social season at Bath, for with people going there all year round it was always a season of a kind. The place was very agreeable, on the whole, even if they didn't know many people. At the end of the first week it rained, almost continually, for three days and Fanny might have felt a little depressed if she had not received a most loving letter from Louisa saying

that she and her brother were planning to make a short visit to
Bath themselves, to enjoy her company.

It was halfway through the second week when the strange
little incident occurred. Having spent an hour or two playing
rather listlessly with the Grockleton children in the house,
Fanny had gone down to the centre of the town alone. There
were shops in the arcaded streets selling every kind of luxury,
but her attention had been especially taken by one window in
which there was a fine display of Worcester china. The set,
which was decorated with depictions of English landscapes in
the classical style, had seemed so appropriate in this English
Roman spa that she had decided to come back and peruse it at
her leisure. And, for quite half an hour, the listlessness she had
felt almost disappeared as she inspected one charming scene
after another. At last, however, she emerged and started to
walk up the hill.

She had gone only a little way and come to an intersection,
when, a couple of hundred yards away down the street on her
right, she saw Mr Martell. He was stepping out of a carriage.
He turned, with his back to her, and handed down a very handsomely dressed young lady. A moment later they entered a
large house together.

Mr Martell. Her heart missed a beat. With a lady. Why not
with a lady? Was it Mr Martell, though? She hadn't actually
seen his face. A tallish, saturnine man, dark-haired. The carriage, drawn by four beautifully turned-out horses, certainly
belonged to someone rich and aristocratic. The way he moved,
the general look of him were so exceedingly like Mr Martell
that she had assumed it must be he. But then, she reflected, Mr
Martell had a double in an old picture; there could be other
visitors to Bath who resembled him.

Was it Mr Martell? She felt her pulse quicken sharply. She
wanted so much to know. She hesitated. What would she do if
she encountered him? Would they speak? Would she speak?
What could she say to Mr Martell and a handsome young
lady? If he was staying in Bath, would they meet, or would he
move across the upper horizon of the city, from one private
house to another, hidden from her view?

Since he is living in a world quite beyond mine, where he
has certainly no further desire for my company; since his heart

is probably engaged by now; and since, besides, he is a Penruddock, with whom I cannot and do not wish to have anything to do, she thought, these speculations are quite useless. The only thing is to move on.

She didn't. Looking around for an excuse, she found a view to admire and lingered there several minutes, in case he came out. After all, he might have been returning the lady to her house. But no one emerged. The carriage remained where it was. After a further pause she began to walk along the pavement towards it. She was only curious, she told herself, that was all.

Her heart was beating faster, though. What if he appeared now and bumped into her? She would be polite but cool to him. She would certainly rebuff him. If there were any lingering doubts in his mind about her attitude towards him she would be able to settle them. Fortified with this intention, she walked casually in the direction of the big wheels of the carriage.

The door of the house was closed. The coachman was sitting calmly but very smartly in position. He was wearing an elegant chocolate-brown coat and cape. She looked up at him and smiled. "You have a very handsome carriage," she said pleasantly. He touched his hat and thanked her kindly. "And who does it belong to?"

"To Mr Markham, My Lady," he replied politely.

"Markham, did you say, or Martell?"

"Markham, My Lady. I don't know any Mr Martell. Mr Markham just stepped into the house."

"Oh. I see." She forced another smile, then walked on. Had she made herself look foolish? She didn't think so. Was she relieved? She thought she must be. So why was it, then, as she turned the next corner, that the energy she had experienced in the last few minutes seemed to drain from her? Her feet suddenly felt heavy. Scarcely knowing it was doing so, her head hung forward and her shoulders seemed to wilt. Ahead of her, up the steep stone hill, the sky inadvertently grew a duller grey.

When she got back she went up to sit with a book by the window of the drawing room and when Mrs Grockleton suggested a drive she excused herself, saying she had a headache.

And there she sat for some hours, doing nothing, wishing for nothing. That night she slept badly.

Fanny's curiosity as to the whereabouts of Mr Martell was to be satisfied early the following week by a letter from Louisa.

It informed her that as Mr Martell was expected at the Burrards' in a few days, she and Edward had decided not to come to see her in Bath.

> *Indeed, Fanny, I'm sure you will be glad to hear that Mr Martell is to go to London afterwards and has proposed that Edward and I should travel with him. Great as the delights of Bath must be, I'm sure they cannot compare with London, so I fear we shall not be seeing you and Mrs Grockleton there.*

That was it. Louisa had forgotten to enquire after her health or even to seem sorry at their not meeting. There was something else, too, about the letter. At first Fanny could not quite put her finger on what it was, but gradually, as she pondered it, she saw the intention clearly enough. A note of triumph: her cousin was telling her plainly that she had done better. A coldness: behind the brief, throwaway regret at not seeing her, Louisa was really saying that she had more exciting things to do and she didn't care if Fanny knew it.

So, Fanny thought grimly, my cousin and close friend doesn't love me. Apart from her father and Aunt Adelaide, did anyone? Mr Gilpin, perhaps, but it was his duty to love. Maybe there was little to love about her anyway. And the sense of her worthlessness and the pointlessness of all things overwhelmed her, so that life itself seemed like a great, grey winter wave breaking and then receding upon an empty shore.

The incident that took place at the end of February in the fashionable spa city of Bath was, you might think, an almost trivial event. Yet it was not seen in that way at the time. Within days there was hardly a person in the whole of Bath, despite the fact that practically no one knew the unfortunate young lady in question, who had not taken sides. The matter was of such curiosity because it was so hard to explain. Theories

abounded. It cannot be said that all this talk, none of it even
known to the unfortunate young lady, did anyone much harm
or good. Except, that is, for the impoverished major who had
danced and talked with her at the Assembly Rooms. For on the
strength of this intimate knowledge of the subject, he was soon
much in demand, invited to dine in houses where he'd never
been asked before, with his chances of finding a rich widow
enhanced considerably.

Fanny Albion, meanwhile, was in gaol.

"Mrs Pride must come with me." Aunt Adelaide was firm and,
in such circumstances, even old Francis could hardly argue;
but he did somewhat plaintively enquire who was going to
look after him. "You are going to stay with the Gilpins," his
sister told him.

Mr Gilpin had wanted to go to Fanny himself but Adelaide
had persuaded him that he could be more help in looking after
her brother. "I could have no peace of mind leaving him without Mrs Pride," she told him and so the old man was conveyed
down to the vicarage, with which he pronounced himself well
enough pleased. Mr Gilpin, meanwhile, contented himself
with a letter.

> *My dear child,*
>   *How or why this strange business has arisen I can*
> *scarcely guess. Nor can I imagine that you could ever*
> *perform any act of malice or dishonesty. I am praying for*
> *you and ask you to remember – more than that, to know*
> *that you are in God's hands. Trust Him, and know that the*
> *Truth shall make you free.*

To Adelaide he said only: "Get a good lawyer."

So the intrepid old lady and Mrs Pride set off together to
make the seventy-mile journey to Bath. On the turnpike roads,
with changes of horses, they could arrive there upon the second day.

It was a source of fury to Mrs Grockleton that Fanny should be
held in prison at all, but all that good lady's efforts had been in
vain. For some reason – perhaps it was something he had

eaten, or merely the fact that the trial judge was to arrive shortly – the magistrate had ordered that Fanny was to be held in the city gaol. Not even Mrs Grockleton's threat to have the Customs men inspect his house had moved him.

Insofar as was possible, the small prison where she was held had been made comfortable for her. She had her own cell, food, everything she could need. She was treated with politeness as those set to guard her had no wish to displease the generous and slightly frightening Mrs Grockleton, who was constantly visiting. Mr Grockleton, meanwhile, had already secured the services of Bath's leading law firm to defend her and the head of the firm himself had been to see Fanny three times.

Surely, therefore, it should not be long before this regrettable matter was cleared up and Fanny set at liberty. It should be so. Yet, on each of the three occasions, the distinguished legal gentleman had come away shaking his head. "I cannot obtain a statement from her," he confessed.

So that finally Mr Grockleton was moved to suggest to his wife what had been in his mind for some time. "Supposing she did it," he said.

The outrage with which this was received did that stout lady credit. "If you ever say such a thing again, Mr Grockleton, I shall box your ears."

So Mr Grockleton said no more. But he wondered, all the same.

The shop was not a large emporium, but a busy one: buttons and bows, ribbons, every kind of fine lace. You might find ladies, dressmakers, all sorts of people in there, buying the small oddments without which, in Bath, life would be almost meaningless.

It had been a slow, dull day and the afternoon was already losing light, as though someone were drawing down the blinds, when Fanny Albion had started to move towards the door. She had been in the shop for some time, drifting listlessly round the tables, inspecting pieces of silk and other fashionable fripperies. She had no real desire to buy anything and had only come in there because she lacked the energy, or the will, to walk up the hill towards her lodgings. Her mind had been full of melancholy reflections. During her wanderings the bag on her arm had come open. After spending about twenty minutes in this way, she had lingered, in an abstracted way, for several minutes by a round table on which were displayed a large number of pieces of fine lace, some of which she had picked up. Then, calmly closing her handbag, she had moved towards the door.

The shop assistant who had been watching her had run out to apprehend her the moment she was through the door. This girl had been joined by the manager of the shop only seconds later. They had made her open the bag, in which – this was not in doubt – lay a neatly folded piece of lace, value ten shillings. Passers-by were called to witness. Fanny was taken back inside the shop. The beadle was summoned.

In all this it was noticed that Fanny seemed dazed and said nothing.

"But my dear child, what can you possibly mean?"

Despite her long journey, Aunt Adelaide had insisted upon being taken to see Fanny as soon as they came to the Grockletons' house. Now, looking very frail in these strange surroundings, but with a steely determination, the gallant old lady gazed at her niece with a piercing look.

But even that did no good as Fanny sat there and slowly shook her head, while her aunt and Mrs Pride looked on.

"What can you possibly mean, child?" Adelaide's long, arduous effort at self-control had stretched her nerves, now, almost to breaking point, so that her question rose in exasperation until it was almost a scream. "*What can you mean, you don't know whether you did it or not?*"

The dinner at the Burrards' was a fine affair. The Tottons were all there and Mr Martell, who had just arrived that afternoon; also Mr Arthur West, who by now was known to the Burrards and always a useful addition at any dinner.

The first remove had just been served and the company was investigating the venison, duck, rabbit stew, fish pie and other dishes supplied when Mr Martell, having taken his first taste of the first-rate claret, politely enquired of Louisa: "What news of your cousin Miss Albion?"

As the table fell silent and Louisa blushed red, it was Sir Harry himself at the end of the table who very sensibly interposed: "If you wish to help yourself and Fanny Albion, you must be prepared with a better answer than a blush, Louisa. For I must tell you plainly, the whole Forest is talking about her and the news is already in London." He turned to Martell. "That poor young lady, Sir, has been accused of stealing a piece of lace from a shop in Bath. It's the most absurd and unconscionable thing imaginable. She is being held in the common gaol and will be tried, I believe, very soon. As the business cannot be anything but a misunderstanding she will, of course, be acquitted. Her aunt, despite her age, has gone to her. She is a most courageous old lady. Her father is with Mr Gilpin." He fixed his eyes upon Louisa. "Everyone at this table, Louisa, and all our acquaintance unite in defending Fanny Albion and we shall welcome her back soon." He said it sternly.

"Hear, hear," said Mr Totton firmly.

"I wish," remarked Mr Martell, with a deep frown, "that I could offer my services in some way. I know an excellent lawyer in Bath." He paused. "Unfortunately I fear I may have offended her in some way."

The Tottons and the Burrards glanced at each other questioningly and Mr Totton remarked that he had never heard this was so. Mr Arthur West leaned forward helpfully. "I believe, if you will permit me, Sir, that I can tell you why that is. You will recall the picture of your great-grandfather you came to see at Hale?"

"Indeed."

"To whom, Sir, you bear so striking a resemblance. Perhaps you were not aware that old Mr Albion and his sister Adelaide are the grandchildren of Alice Lisle and, in their eyes, you are a Penruddock."

The effect of this information upon the table was dramatic. Burrard and the Tottons stared at him in amazement.

"You are a Penruddock?" There were so many other significant items of information about Martell – his two estates, his education, his good looks, his interest in the Church and in politics – that the question of his late mother's family had somehow never come up.

"The Martells and Penruddocks have married each other for centuries. My mother was a Penruddock," he said with pride. "I had not realised the connection of the Albions with Alice Lisle, but surely Colonel Penruddock was only arresting a known troublemaker, and the business is long forgotten now."

"Not in the Forest." Sir Harry shook his head. "The Albions, at least, would regard you with horror."

"I see." Martell fell silent. He remembered, now, Fanny's questioning him at Mrs Grockleton's ball and her sudden coldness.

"Old Miss Albion, in particular," Mr Totton explained, "feels passionately about the subject. Her mother brought her up, so to speak, in Alice Lisle's shadow. Alice was born Alice Albion, you see, and Albion House was her true home."

Martell nodded slowly. The vision he had had of Fanny the first time he had come to that dark old house came back to him with vividness. His impression had not been wrong, then. She was, indeed, a tragic figure, trapped with those two old people in a house full of memories and ghostly shadows. But this information also meant something else: he had been correct, almost certainly, in thinking she cared for him. It was the discovery that he was a Penruddock that had caused her to avoid him and push him away.

It is the shadow of Alice Lisle that stands between us, he thought. Curse her. The thing was ungodly. And now, thinking of her terrible situation, a wave of pity swept over him. How must she feel, facing such an ordeal, almost alone? "I am deeply sorry to hear of her predicament," he said quietly and the dinner continued with no further mention of such a painful subject.

When the ladies retired, leaving the men to their port, he did venture to bring up the subject with Burrard and Totton.

"It's a strange business," Burrard informed him. "Gilpin and I, without interfering, have tried to get information. The shop in question, having accused her, is unwilling to back down. The magistrate insisted she be held. But worst of all is the state of mind of Fanny herself." And he explained, briefly, how Gilpin had persuaded the Grockletons to take Fanny to Bath. "She had fallen, during the winter, into a very melancholic state. Alas, it seems the visit to Bath, as yet, has effected no cure. She is utterly lethargic and says nothing to help her cause. And, even for people of our sort, Martell, theft is theft. I will not conceal from you that, privately, I fear for her. The case is grave."

Theft: the penalties for theft in eighteenth-century England were harsh indeed. Sentences of death or transportation were frequent. The value of the goods stolen seldom interested the courts much: it was the moral character of the criminal and the attack upon property that concerned them. Theft, of the kind of which Fanny was accused, was theft pure and simple, and even gentlefolk could be severely punished for such an offence. After all, it provided an example to society at large that the law was absolute.

"Do we know why she should have fallen into melancholy when she did?" Martell ventured to ask.

"No." It was Edward Totton who answered now. "I think it was after Mrs Grockleton's ball that she seemed to become withdrawn. I suppose her father's making a spectacle of himself may have caused her, however unjustifiably, embarrassment. Louisa and I are at fault, I believe. We didn't realise; we should have done much more for her at that time. But we didn't and I feel rather ashamed."

Just after the ball. Her melancholy, thought Martell, might also have another cause. Yet what the devil, he wondered, as they went to join the ladies, could he do about it? It was hardly to be imagined that the family would have failed to obtain good legal counsel. His involvement could not possibly be welcome.

Only one phrase from all this conversation kept recurring, nagging at his mind: "She is utterly lethargic and says nothing to help her cause." She must be persuaded to help her cause. The case was far too serious to be left to chance. She must help herself in every way she could.

The gentlemen and ladies were making up two tables of cards, but Martell was not in the mood for play just then and nor, it seemed, was Louisa; so they moved away to a sofa and began to talk.

There was no doubt, Martell considered, that Louisa was a very pretty and amusing young woman. He liked her; enjoyed her company. He had even, once or twice, thought of more. A

Totton might not have been quite his style, but within a broad range he could marry whom he pleased. Perhaps the shock of the news about Fanny had added a tenderness to his mood, but he looked at Louisa now with affection. "I must confess," he told her, "that I am very distressed about Miss Albion."

"We all are," she said quietly.

"I only wonder if there is not something I can do. Perhaps," he continued, thinking aloud, "if Edward were to go to see her, I could accompany him."

A little cloud crossed Louisa's face. "I had not known you wished to involve yourself with Fanny," she remarked softly. "I am not sure she wants even Edward's company at present."

"Perhaps. And yet" – he shook his head – "I suspect it is precisely company – I truly mean affection – that she needs."

"I see." It scarcely required the female instinct, with which Louisa was well endowed, to see in which direction Martell's feelings might be tending. "It is not easy to be sure," Louisa said carefully, "exactly how matters lie. For that reason, perhaps, we are cautious."

"Your meaning? It cannot surely be that Miss Albion is guilty of this crime."

"No, Mr Martell." She paused. "Yet even so, we cannot at this distance know anything for certain. There may be something . . ."

He gazed at her, half astonished, half curious. Louisa was no fool. She was trying to hint something. But what?

"I will tell you something, Mr Martell, if you will promise never to repeat it."

"Very well." He considered. "I will not."

"There is a circumstance of which my cousin may not herself be aware. You know, I think, that my father and her mother were brother and sister."

"I do."

"But they were not. She was his half-sister. And her mother . . . well, my grandfather's second wife came from a different station of society. She was a Miss Seagull. The family are of the lowest kind: sailors, innkeepers, smugglers. And further back . . ." She made a little grimace. "It's better not to ask."

"I see."

"So that is why, perhaps, we wonder . . . we cannot be sure . . ." She gave him a sad little smile and he stared at her.

For he saw – he saw it quite clearly – that she was not herself even aware of the incalculable malice behind what she had just told him. "It is good of you to confide in me, Miss Totton," he said quietly and made up his mind, that very instant, that he would go straight to Bath, at dawn the very next morning.

Adelaide shook her head. She had been in Bath for over a week, without success. At moments she had been so near the end of her tether that she had almost decided she could bear it no more and that she would return home. But she had been guarding the temple of her family for so long now, tenaciously holding on for her mother, her brother and her niece, that she could scarcely have let go had she wanted to. She was so locked, clamped, riveted to the house of Albion that she couldn't have given up on Fanny if she'd tried.

This did not mean, however, that she was hopeful of success. "You'll be like Alice," she cried bitterly. "She wouldn't defend herself: falling asleep in front of that judge; never protesting. Are you going to let them murder you too? Are there to be no more Albions?"

But Fanny said nothing.

"Can you" – the old lady turned wearily to Mrs Pride – "say anything to persuade her?"

For a week, now, Mrs Pride had conveyed Aunt Adelaide to and fro, had listened quietly to all that passed in the Grockleton household and brought, as far as possible, a sense of comfort by her presence. She had also observed Fanny and drawn her own conclusions. So now, although she spoke gently, the Forest woman was firm.

"I've known you all your life, Miss Fanny," she said. "I've watched over you. You were always bold and sensible. But they're hunting you now." She looked straight into Fanny's eyes. "You've got to save yourself. That's all there is to it, really. Just save yourself or there won't be anything left."

"I'm not sure I can," said Fanny.

"You just have to. That's all," Mrs Pride repeated.

"You must fight, Fanny," cried her aunt. "Can't you see? You must fight. You must never give up." She stared at Fanny, then turned to Mrs Pride. "I think we should go now." She rose stiffly to her feet.

As they left, Mrs Pride glanced back at Fanny and their eyes met. There was no mistaking the older woman's message: "Save yourself."

After they had gone, Fanny took out Mr Gilpin's letter and read it again in the hope it would give her strength, but it didn't really help and she put it away again. Then she closed her eyes, though she did not sleep.

Save herself. If only she could. Sometimes, when no one was looking, she would curl up into a ball, like an unborn child and lie like that for an hour. At other times, she would sit staring vacantly ahead of her, unable to do anything at all. It seemed to Fanny that there was no way out of her predicament. Her life was enclosed by walls as blank, as unyielding and as close as those of her prison. There was no way out, no alternative, no end.

Yet how she yearned for an escape, for someone to come and save her. Aunt Adelaide could not do it. Even Mrs Pride could not. They told her to save herself when all she needed now was to be saved and comforted by another. But who? Mr Gilpin, had he been there, might have helped. Yet in the end she knew he could not.

She longed to be forgiven. For what she scarcely knew. For her very existence, perhaps. She longed for the one she loved to come and comfort her and tell her he forgave her. She could face anything, then. But it was, from first to last, impossible. So she stayed, in utter misery, where she was and kept her eyes closed to shut out the pain of the light of the world.

She did not, therefore, see him as he came to her door.

How long does it take for a man to know, absolutely, that he loves a woman?

Wyndham Martell looked down upon the pale figure sitting in silence in her cell, as a pale ray of sunlight through the small window caught her face, making it look ethereal. He thought of her vulnerability and all he now understood about her, and he knew in that moment that this was the woman whom destiny had given him to love. After which, as all who have loved have known, there is nothing further to say. His life was decided. It took, approximately, one second.

Then he stepped through the door and she looked up in the most entire astonishment. He did not pause but moved straight to her and, as she started to rise, he took her in his arms and with a tender smile said: "I have come, Fanny, and I shall never leave you."

"But . . ." She frowned, then looked desperate, "you do not know . . ."

"I know everything."

"You cannot . . ."

"I even know the dark secret of your Seagull grandmother and her forebears, my dearest." He shook his head affectionately. "Nothing matters, so long as I am with you and you are with me." And, before she could speak further, he kissed her and held her in his arms.

Fanny began to shake, then she broke down and, clinging to him, she wept and wept, hot tears that came in a shaking flood that would not stop. He did not try to soothe them but let them come and held her tightly, murmuring only words of love. And there they remained, they did not know how long.

Neither saw Aunt Adelaide return.

For a moment or two the old lady could not understand what was happening. Fanny was in the arms of a strange man, whose face was turned away. Who he was or why Fanny was clinging to him she had no idea. She put out her hand to steady herself on the arm of Mrs Pride, who was standing just behind her. Several seconds passed before she spoke.

"Fanny?"

The two young people sprang apart. The man turned and looked towards her. Aunt Adelaide stared and then went very pale.

Whether she realised that this must be Mr Martell or whether, for a moment, she supposed that the figure in the picture she had seen at Hale had miraculously come to life and she was looking at Colonel Penruddock himself it was hard to guess; but whichever it was, as she gazed at him in horror, she hissed only a single word. "You!"

He collected himself quickly. "Miss Albion, I am Wyndham Martell."

If Aunt Adelaide heard him, she chose to ignore it. Her face was white and wore a look of anger and hatred unlike any that Fanny had ever seen before. When she spoke, it was in a tone of contempt that she might have used to a thief. "How dare you come here, you villain! Get out."

"I am aware, Madam, that in the past there has been bad feeling between your family and that of my mother."

"Get out, Sir."

"I think it is unnecessary . . ."

"Get out." She turned to Fanny now, as if Martell no longer existed. "What is the meaning of this? What are you doing with this Penruddock?"

It was not only the cold, angry question; it was the look of hurt, of shattered disappointment, of betrayal in the poor old woman's eyes that was so terrible to Fanny.

She has looked after me all my life, Fanny thought, trusted me, and now I have done this to her: the most terrible thing that I could do – the worst, betrayal. "Oh, Aunt Adelaide," she cried.

"Perhaps," her aunt said, with a quietness that went like an arrow through her heart, "you have no need of your family any more."

"I do, Aunt Adelaide." She turned to Martell. "Please go."

He looked from one to the other. "I shall come again," he said.

There was silence as he left.

"Do you wish," her aunt asked, still coldly, "to give me any explanation?"

Fanny did her best. She confessed that she had developed feelings for Martell without knowing about his ancestry. "I do not suppose," she added, "that he knew of my ancestry either." She explained how she had discovered and, effectively, sent him away; and how she had not seen him since, until he had so unexpectedly walked into her cell.

"You kissed him."

"I know. He was tender. I was overcome."

"Overcome," her aunt said with bitterness, "by a Penruddock."

"It shall never happen again."

"He may return."

"I will not see him."

Her aunt looked at her with suspicion, but Fanny shook her head.

"Fanny." Aunt Adelaide did not speak with anger now; her voice was very quiet. "I am afraid that if you see that man again I can no longer see you myself. We shall have to part."

"No, Aunt Adelaide, please do not leave me. I promise that I shall not see him."

Adelaide sighed. She turned towards Mrs Pride. "I am tired. I think we should go back after all. My child." She embraced Fanny gently. "We shall meet again tomorrow." Having, thus, done all she could to preserve the family, the old lady retired.

Fanny did receive one unexpected visitor that night, however. It was Mrs Pride. That worthy lady stayed with her nearly an hour, during which time she learned exactly what had passed between Mr Martell and Fanny, and saw only too well what the true state of Fanny's affection was.

"He came to save me," the girl wailed, "but it is impossible. I know it to be impossible. Everything is impossible." And though she held her, and let her cry, and comforted her as best she could, even Mrs Pride could not deny that what Fanny said was true. As long, she thought grimly, as the memory of Alice Lisle dwelt at Albion House, no Penruddock could ever come there. It could not be otherwise. Memories were long in the Forest.

The next morning Mr Martell came to call, but on Fanny's instructions he was turned away. The same thing happened that afternoon. The day after, he tried to leave a letter, but it was refused.

There had been so many false alarms in the past that only when the doctor was absolutely certain that Francis Albion was dying and could not last more than a day or two did Mr Gilpin finally send a message to Adelaide.

The arrival of the letter placed the old lady in a quandary. She felt she must return to her brother yet did not wish to leave Fanny, the more especially since she dreaded the thought of her receiving another visit from Mr Martell. But when Fanny pointed out that there had been no sign of Martell for three days and once again renewed her promise not to have any contact with him, she felt somewhat reassured.

"Besides, how could I bear to think that I had kept you, his only comfort, from him at such a time?" Fanny cried. "Go, I beg you, and take my love to him so that he may know I am there in spirit if not in body."

There was much truth in this and Adelaide agreed to go. There remained, however, the paramount question of the coming trial. It was only ten days away now. The best available lawyer was ready and waiting to defend her in court. But Fanny's own state of mind remained unclear. One day she would seem to have the energy to defend herself, another she would sink into a lethargy so that, as the lawyer very fairly pointed out: "I cannot be sure what impression she will make in court, nor even how she will answer any questions put to her."

"No matter what my brother's state of health," Adelaide assured him, "I shall return well before the trial. We shall have to do the best we can then. Perhaps," she added, "I shall bring Mr Gilpin with me."

Upon these terms, therefore, Aunt Adelaide departed on the arm of Mrs Pride, leaving Fanny, for the time being, alone.

As the carriage rolled along the swift turnpike between Bath and Sarum, Mrs Pride had time to reflect carefully on all that had passed in the last few days. She only wished that she could see a solution to the terrible dilemma ahead.

About Fanny she had no confidence at all. The trial, it seemed to her, could very well go against her even if she made a strong defence. As to her state of mind and the presence of Mr Martell, both raised large questions to which she could see no solution.

As far as Aunt Adelaide was concerned, Mrs Pride didn't blame the old lady for her view of Mr Martell. If the Prides still remembered the treachery of the Furzeys, how could old Adelaide forgive a Penruddock? In her place, thought Mrs Pride, she would have felt the same. As for finding him with Fanny like that . . . It must have nearly killed her.

Again and again, though, her mind returned to that tearful interview with Fanny. She had no doubt about the state of Fanny's heart. She wished it were otherwise. But it was surely this impossible love that lay, at least partly, behind Fanny's helpless condition. They reached Sarum in the evening without Mrs Pride seeing any way out of the dilemma.

They took the Southampton road out of Salisbury, over the high chalk ridge with its view over the Forest, and picked up the Lymington turnpike later in the day. By late afternoon, as the day was closing, they came along the lane to Mr Gilpin's vicarage.

The vicar himself came to the door to greet them, which he did gravely, leading Adelaide straight to the drawing room, where he asked her to sit down. To her enquiry after her brother's health, he paused a moment and then quietly told her: "Your brother died, just before dawn, this morning. It was entirely peaceful. I had been praying with him, then he slept a little, and then he slipped away. I could wish for such an end myself."

Adelaide nodded slowly. "The funeral?"

"With your permission, tomorrow. We can wait if you wish."

"No." Adelaide sighed. "It is better that way. I must return to Bath as soon as possible."

"You wish to see him? He is in the dining room, all ready."

"Yes." She got up. "I will see him now."

Mr Gilpin had made all the arrangements and done so thoughtfully. When Adelaide had spent a little time alone with her brother he explained briefly the form of service he proposed at Boldre church, where the Albion family vault had been made ready. The Tottons, Burrards and other local families had all been informed and would be coming unless she wished otherwise. She herself was most welcome to stay at the vicarage, he added, but this, with many thanks, she declined as she preferred to stay in Albion House. Though some of the servants had been allowed to return to their homes in her absence, enough were still there to take care of her.

"Promise me to rest at least a day or two before your return to Bath," he begged her. "You have time to do so."

"Yes. A day. But after that I think I must go. I cannot leave Fanny alone."

"Quite so. Perhaps, then, the day after the funeral, I may call upon you; for there are certain matters in that connection I wish to discuss."

"Of course." Indeed, she let him know, she was most anxious for his advice.

He saw her safely off, watching her carriage from his door until it was out of sight. Only then did he come back, cross the hall and enter his library, the door of which had been kept closed during Adelaide's visit. He turned to the figure with whom he had been closeted for most of the afternoon. "The day after tomorrow, then. I shall talk to her. But I want you to come with me. You may have to speak to her too."

"You think it wise?"

"Wise or not, it may be necessary."

"I shall be guided by you, then," said Mr Martell.

The funeral at the old church on its little knoll had been an intimate occasion. The Tottons, the various Forest neighbours, the tenants and servants of Albion House had all been there. Mr Gilpin had kept the service short but very dignified. He had alluded to Fanny in his brief address and in the prayers and, as they parted from Aunt Adelaide, the congregation did not fail to send her kindly messages.

Adelaide had wished to return quietly to the house alone when the service was over and this was respected, so that it was only she and Mrs Pride who were conveyed up the drive to the old gabled house. When she was installed in the oak-panelled parlour, Mrs Pride brought her some herbal tea and left her, so that the old lady could doze a while before eating a small dinner of ham and retiring early.

Mr Gilpin appeared at eleven o'clock the next morning and Adelaide was ready to receive him.

You had to admire her, Mrs Pride thought. As she sat, very erect, propped up with cushions in a big wing chair in the parlour, she might be frail but, despite all she had been through, she was sharply alert.

When Mr Gilpin entered, Mrs Pride started to withdraw, but Adelaide summoned her back. "I should like Mrs Pride to remain," she said to Gilpin. "We could not manage without her."

"I quite agree." The clergyman smiled at the housekeeper warmly.

"Let me tell you first," the old lady began, "how the case rests with Fanny."

She described exactly the state in which Fanny remained, her inability to come up with any defence, the lawyer's concern, the whole dismal business. She spoke briefly of the Grockletons' kindness, but she did not mention Mr Martell. When she had finished Mr Gilpin turned to Mrs Pride and asked her if she had anything to add.

Mrs Pride hesitated. What should she say? "Miss Albion's recollection is very precise," she said carefully. "Miss Fanny's case seems grave. I fear for her."

"Her lack of defence is strange," Gilpin remarked. "I wonder, is it possible, do you suppose, that the lawyers have any thought that she might have – for whatever reason – actually taken this piece of lace?"

"The idea is absurd," replied her aunt.

Gilpin looked at Mrs Pride. "I cannot say, Sir, what they may think. I do not believe, even now, that she has ever addressed the question."

"She is in a strange state of mind, most evidently. Almost, forgive me, a derangement. She is clearly, my dear Miss Albion, not herself."

"Quite."

"Yet why" – he looked at her searchingly – "could this be? Is anything disturbing her mind, or her affections?"

"Nothing of consequence," snapped Adelaide.

"I believe, Sir," said Mrs Pride quietly, "that her emotions are greatly disturbed." She got a sharp look from Adelaide, but she had to say it.

And now started the most difficult part of Mr Gilpin's mission. He began by making very clear to Adelaide the extreme danger he believed Fanny was in. "She is accused. There are respectable witnesses. Her position in society will not, in these circumstances, protect her. Indeed, as a point of honour, the judges might even sentence her to transportation, to show they make no distinctions. Such things have happened." He paused to allow this awful consequence to sink in.

But even he had not fully reckoned with the fixed nature of

Adelaide's mind. "Justice," she replied scornfully. "Do not speak of justice when I remember what the courts did to Alice Lisle."

"Justice or not," the vicar pursued, "that is the risk. You will surely agree that we must take every possible step to save her." This received a curt nod. "I believe I should accompany you to Bath. Would that be agreeable to you?" Again a nod. "I must, however, caution you," he went on, "that I do not believe my presence will necessarily induce Fanny to save herself – and save herself she must. I am now convinced that the answer lies elsewhere."

If Adelaide guessed what he meant, she gave no indication beyond a slight frown. Gilpin pressed on.

He really showed great wisdom. He dwelt – how as a Christian could he not? – upon the need for reconciliation. He dwelt upon the evil of ancient feuds. "The sins of the father, Miss Albion, cannot be visited upon the son." He dwelt, above all, upon the paramount need to save Fanny. "I think," he said penetratingly, "that you know to what I am referring."

"I have not," old Adelaide said invincibly, "the least idea."

"And yet, Madam," another voice came quietly but firmly from the doorway, "I believe that you have."

And Mr Martell entered the room and made her a polite bow. Although told by Gilpin to wait in the covered carriage outside, he had entered the house and been quietly listening for some time.

Adelaide went pale, looked from Martell to Gilpin and then enquired acidly: "You brought this villain here?"

"I did," the vicar confessed, "but I am convinced he is no villain. Quite the reverse, in fact."

"Kindly leave, Mr Gilpin, and take this villain" – she deliberately used the word again – "with you." Her eyes seemed to fix themselves upon a distant point beyond the panelling. "I see, Sir, that even clergymen betray the trust of their friends nowadays. But my family are accustomed to dealing with villains, murderers and seducers, even if this is the first time that a clergyman has introduced them to our house."

"My dear Miss Albion."

"I suggest, in future, Mr Gilpin, that you keep your own

company. You are not to approach my niece in Bath. Good day."

If even Gilpin was reduced to speechlessness by this, Wyndham Martell was not. "Madam," he explained, calmly and politely, "you may abuse my mother's family as much as you wish. If what you say of them is true, then I am very sorry for it. If it lay within my power" – he raised his hand – "to take away my Penruddock ancestry by cutting off this hand, then I assure you I should gladly do it to save your niece."

She stared at him in silence. Perhaps he was making progress.

"I discovered that I resemble an ancestor about whom I knew little, and then that this man was held in contempt and abhorrence by the family of the young lady to whom my affections had already become deeply attached and who, without explanation, then rejected me because of it. But each generation, although we honour our parents and our ancestors, is still born anew. Even the Forest grows new oaks. I am not, I assure you, Colonel Penruddock and have no wish to be. I am Wyndham Martell. And Fanny is not Alice Lisle."

"Get out."

"Madam, I think it is possible that I can induce Miss Albion to defend herself. Whatever your feelings, would you not even allow me to attempt to save her?"

Gilpin chanced to glance, just then, at Mrs Pride and saw, clear as day upon her face that, whatever she knew from Fanny, she thought that Martell could save her too. "I beg you, consider above all the possibility of saving Fanny," he interposed.

"A Penruddock save an Albion? Never."

"Dear heaven, Madam!" Martell burst out in exasperation. "You will make your niece the inhabitant of a living tomb."

"Get out."

He took no notice. "Do you love her, Madam? Or is she loved only as the servant of this family temple?"

"Get out."

"I tell you, Madam, that I love Miss Albion for herself. In truth I scarcely care at this moment whether she is an Albion, a Gilpin, or" – he suddenly found himself looking straight into the eyes of the tall, handsome woman, not unlike himself, really, who, he realised, was closely following his every word – "or a Pride. I love her, Madam, for herself and I intend to save her, with or without your leave. But your assistance might have greatly helped her."

"Get out."

At a sign from Gilpin Mr Martell, considerably heated now, withdrew with him and a few moments later the sound of Mr Gilpin's carriage could be heard leaving.

Adelaide sat in complete silence for some time, while Mrs Pride hovered behind her. Then, at last, whether to the house-keeper or only to herself it was hard to say, the old lady finally spoke. "If he saves her she'll marry him." She shook her head sadly. "Oh, my poor mother. Poor Alice. Better she died than that."

It was at that moment that Mrs Pride saw what she had to do.

Martell and Gilpin sat late together in the vicar's library that night, discussing what to do.

"I want to go," Gilpin said. "And I have no doubt Fanny would see me. But two questions remain. With the old lady so implacable, would my presence create still more confusion? And besides, it is you she needs now, Martell, not me."

"I have no qualms about the old lady," Martell responded. "I shall go first thing in the morning. But I still have to gain admittance to her. I can't break in the door of the prison."

"You shall take a letter from me. I shall beg her to see you. I can tell her you speak with my blessing. That may help."

Gilpin had just sat down to write the letter and Martell begun to read a book when there was the sound of someone arriving at the door. Moments later the manservant entered and came to murmur something in Gilpin's ear. Gilpin got up and went into the hall, disappearing for a minute or so before he returned, in a hurry. "Get your coat, Martell!" he cried. "We shall need you. The horses are being saddled."

"Where are we going?" Martell called, as he ran up to his room to get his coat and boots.

"Albion House. And there's not a moment to lose."

• • • •

No one could say where or how it had started, for the whole house had apparently been sound asleep. So much so, indeed, that it was only when the one manservant happened to wake on the top floor and hear a strange crackle that he realised anything was amiss. As soon as he came out of his little room, however, he found the passage already filling with thick smoke. A second later he encountered Mrs Pride, who had obviously just awoken too, in her nightclothes.

"The whole house is on fire," she cried. "Quickly, find all the servants. The back stairs are clear. Take them all to the stables, then make sure none is missing."

"Where are you going?"

"To get the old lady. What else?"

The smoke was already choking as Mrs Pride made her way to the main landing. She went swiftly along to the chamber where Adelaide slept, walked in and went to the bed.

It was empty.

She cast around the room swiftly. Nothing. She tried the next chamber, found that empty too, went to the stairs.

Fire was licking up a tapestry. At the bottom of the stairs she saw flames coming out of the parlour. She ran down and tried to go in but the heat was too intense. She opened the main door and went swiftly out.

"Has anyone seen Miss Albion?"

The entire household was assembled in the stables now. No one was missing. The men were already gathering buckets in the hope of making a chain down to the river. She could see it would be useless but did not try to dissuade them.

No one had seen the old lady.

"She must have got up. She may be outside," offered one.

"Perhaps she started it. Fell over with a lamp," said a housemaid.

"No one is to go inside," ordered Mrs Pride and went back to the house.

The roof had started to smoke, now, and flames were leaping from some of the upper windows. The cottages in Boldre had obviously seen the flames because men were running along the drive. She directed them to help with the buckets. Someone had already gone to tell the vicar.

"Search for the old lady outside," she told the cook and the other women. "She may have wandered out."

By the time Mr Gilpin and Martell arrived the flames were leaping high from the roof and cinders poured upwards into the dark night sky. The doorway, surprisingly, was still passable, but inside there was only a strange flickering darkness.

All searches for Adelaide had proved fruitless. No one could guess where she had gone. If to the parlour, then she must be burned to a cinder already.

"She could have fallen," Gilpin said. "It is possible she is still alive." He glanced at Martell. "Well. Shall we?"

But, as the two men dismounted, Mrs Pride was ahead of them. "Wait," she cried, "you don't know where to look." And before anyone could prevent her she plunged again into the house.

The flames licking round the edge of the roof gave the blank stone triangles of the gables a strange look, as though they were trying to break away from the raging heat behind them. Flames were bursting out of half the windows. It seemed almost impossible that anyone could stay alive in that furnace. Yet, a moment later, the tall form of Mrs Pride appeared at one window, then vanished and reappeared at another. Then vanished once more and did not reappear, so that Gilpin and Martell were both starting to run towards the door when, out of it, appeared Mrs Pride, striding into the flickering night, carrying in her arms a frail white burden.

It was Adelaide. She was not burned, although her white nightdress was blackened and singed. But she was limp. And quite dead. She had apparently fallen, perhaps knocked herself out, and asphyxiated in the thick, choking smoke.

They hadn't a prayer, without a fire engine, of saving Albion House. The fire was a long one, for the great Tudor framework of the house burned slowly and some of the huge oak timbers, although they charred outside, did not burn through at all. But by the early hours the place was a great red shell and, by dawn, a glowing ruin. Albion House had fallen. It was over. And with it the two inhabitants, Francis and the house's guardian Adelaide, had departed from the scene.

Nor did it fail, that night, to occur to good Mr Gilpin that

his accident had left Fanny Albion free, if she wished, to allow
herself to be saved by Mr Martell and, remembering that other
day when Francis Albion's deep sleep had allowed him to take
Fanny out to Beaulieu the vicar, shortly before midnight, gave
Mrs Pride one searching look.

But Mrs Pride's face registered nothing as her noble profile
was caught by the light of the glowing fire and the vicar wisely
remembered that things were not always what they seemed in
the Forest.

The courtroom was hushed. There were three cases of theft before the judge that morning. The accused, each sitting with a
beadle guarding them on a bench, had to watch as, one after
another they were made to stand forward for trial.

First came a young man who had held up an elderly gentleman and relieved him of his money and a gold watch. He had
a mass of curly black hair and as a boy he must have resembled Nathaniel Furzey. But if he had once been a mischievous
boy, there was little sign of it now. He stared ahead, dully and
hopelessly. It did not take the jury long to find him guilty. He
was sentenced to hang.

The poor girl of sixteen who had stolen a cooked ham to
feed her family was let off more lightly. Fair-haired, blue-eyed,
those observing her could see that she might have been as
pretty as one of Mrs Grockleton's young ladies, if she had not
spent three months in a filthy cell with only thin gruel and a
little bread to eat. It seemed a pity to hang her. So she was
merely transported to Australia for fourteen years.

These were routine cases. Although tragic for the families
of the condemned, they were not especially interesting.

But the case of the young lady accused of stealing a piece
of lace was quite another matter. The back of the court was
crowded. The jury sat up with interest. The lawyers in their
black coats and wigs watched her curiously. Why, even the
judge had stopped looking bored.

If the case evoked their interest and the young lady their curiosity, this was nothing to the impression made when, the
judge asking who represented the accused, the young lady
calmly replied: "If it please Your Lordship, I have no lawyer. I
intend to represent myself."

This was met with a murmur all round the courtroom. She really had their attention now.

For anyone who had seen Fanny Albion a week before, the change in her now was remarkable. She was dressed simply in a white dress whose fashionable high waist gave the wearer a look of particular chastity. Yet a glance at the lace fringe, the satin sash and her silken shoes told you that Miss Albion, although modest, was obviously rich. And if, under the dress, there hung a curious little wooden crucifix that had once belonged to a peasant woman, no one but Fanny and Mr Gilpin knew it was there.

She was quiet and confident as she was led to her place, and when the charge was read out and she was asked how she pleaded, her answer came in a clear, firm voice. "Not guilty."

A glance around the courtroom told her she was well supported. The Grockletons were there. Mr Gilpin, who had urged her to tell the truth in the simplest way, was sitting next to them. Then Mrs Pride. How earnestly the housekeeper had urged her, the day before: "You must save yourself, Miss Fanny, after everything that has happened. You have your own life to lead now." But it was the other figure, smiling at her, who had asked her to marry him – it was Wyndham Martell who had made her promise to fight, at last, when he begged her: "Do it, dear Fanny, for me."

The prosecution's case was straightforward. First, the shop assistant was called. She stated that she had watched the defendant for some time, seen her bag open, seen her inspecting the lace and drop a piece into the bag, which she then closed before making her way swiftly out of the shop. The shop assistant described how she had run after the thief, stopped her outside and how, with the manager present, the lace had been found in Fanny's bag.

"What did the accused say when confronted with this theft?"

"Nothing."

The court buzzed for a moment, but the judge called for silence and told Fanny that she could cross-question the witness.

"I have no questions, My Lord."

What did this mean? People looked at each other.

The manager was called. He confirmed the events. Again Fanny was offered the chance to question him. She declined.

A woman who had witnessed the confrontation gave her testimony. Still Fanny did not challenge anything. Mr Grockleton was looking concerned, his wife ready to spring out of her seat. Mrs Pride's lips were pursed.

"I call the accused, Miss Albion," the prosecuting lawyer announced.

He was a small, plump man. The tabs of his starched lawyer's collar moved back and forth against his thick, fleshy neck when he spoke. "Would you please tell the court, Miss Albion, what took place on the afternoon in question."

"Certainly." She spoke gravely and clearly. "I proceeded round the shop exactly as the court has heard."

"Your bag was open?"

"I was not aware of it, but I have no reason to doubt that it was."

"You came to the table on which the lace was displayed? And do you deny that you took a piece of lace, dropped it in your bag, and went towards the door?"

"I don't deny it."

"You do not deny it?"

"No."

"You stole the lace?"

"Evidently."

"The same piece of lace that was found in your bag outside the shop, as described by the manager and a witness?"

"Precisely."

The lawyer looked a little puzzled. He glanced at the judge, shrugged. "My Lord, members of the jury, there you have it from the mouth of the accused. She stole the lace. The prosecution rests its case." He returned to his place, murmured something to his clerk about the foolishness of women trying to defend themselves without lawyers and awaited the defence, as the judge indicated to Fanny that she might proceed.

The court was absolutely silent as Fanny stood before them. "I have only one witness to call, My Lord," she declared. "That is Mr Gilpin."

Mr Gilpin took the witness stand with great dignity; he confirmed he was the vicar of Boldre, the holder of various degrees, the author of certain well-respected works and that he had known Fanny and her family all her life. Asked to describe her position in life, he explained that she was the heiress to the Albion estate and a considerable fortune. Had she ever been short of money to spend, she asked him, and he replied that she had not.

Requested to describe her character, he did so very fairly, explaining the nature of her somewhat quiet life and her devotion to her father and her aunt. How was it, she asked him, that she had chanced to go to Bath? He himself, he told the court, had arranged with the Grockletons that they should take her there for a change of air. In his judgement she had spent too long living in seclusion with the two old people in Albion House.

"How would you describe my state of mind at that time?"

"Melancholy, listless, abstracted."

"When you heard that I had been accused of theft, were you surprised?"

"Astonished. I did not believe it."

"Why?"

"Because, knowing you as I do, the idea that you should steal anything is inconceivable."

"I have no further questions."

The prosecution bounced up now and rolled towards the vicar. "Tell me, Sir, when the defendant says that she stole a piece of lace, do you believe her?"

"Most certainly. I have never known her tell an untruth in her life."

"So she did it. I have no further questions."

The judge looked at Fanny. It was up to her now.

"I may address the court on my own behalf, My Lord?"

"You may."

She bowed her head and turned towards the jury.

The twelve members of the jury watched her carefully. They were tradesmen, mostly, with a couple of local farmers, a clerk and two craftsmen. Their natural sympathies were with the shopkeeper. They felt sorry for the young lady, but couldn't see how she could be innocent.

"Gentlemen of the jury," Fanny began, "it may have surprised you that I did not seek to contradict a word of the evidence given against me." They did not say anything but it was plain that it had. "I did not even try to suggest that the assistant in the shop had made a mistake." She paused for only a moment. "Why should I do so? These are good and honest people. They have told you what they saw. Why should anyone disbelieve them? *I* believe them."

She gazed at the jury, now, and they at her. They were not sure where this was leading, but they were listening carefully.

"Gentlemen of the jury, I would ask you now to consider my situation. You have heard from Mr Gilpin, a clergyman of the highest repute, as to my character. I have never stolen anything in my life. You have also heard as to my fortune. Even if I were inclined to a life of crime, which God knows I am not, is there any reason *why* I should not have paid for a piece of lace? My fortune is large. It makes no sense." Again she paused to let this sink in.

"I now ask you to remember the testimony as to what occurred when I was confronted outside the shop. It seems that I said nothing. Not a word. Why should that be?" She looked from face to face. "Gentlemen, it was because I was so astonished. Honest people told me I had taken a piece of lace. The evidence was before my eyes. I could not deny it. I did not suppose them to be lying. They were not. I had taken the lace. I say I took it now. Yet I was so astonished that I did not know what to answer. And I tell you very truly, I scarcely have known how to answer for my actions ever since. For I must ask you to believe: *I did not know that I had done so.* Gentlemen, I make no denial, I simply tell you, I was unaware that I had dropped that piece of lace into my bag. I was never more astonished in my life." She looked at the judge, then back to the jury.

"How can this be? I do not know. It is true, as Mr Gilpin said, that I was at that time in some distress. I remember, that afternoon, that my mind had been much upon my dear father, who had been unwell. I had been considering whether to return from Bath to be with him, because I had a strong intimation that he might be close to his end – an intimation, alas, which proved to be correct. It was with a mind full of such thoughts that I wandered, somewhat abstracted, around that shop. I do not even remember looking at the lace, but I suppose that, with my mind entirely elsewhere, as I passed by the table, I must have placed it in my bag. Perhaps, in my abstraction I imagined I was somewhere else, at home perhaps. For gentlemen." Her voice now rose. "How, under what influence, for what possible motive should I steal a piece of lace for which I had no need? Why should I, heiress to a great estate, devoted to my family and to preserving their good name, suddenly risk all for a crime I had no possible reason to commit?"

She took a deep breath before continuing. "Gentlemen, I have been offered the best lawyers to represent me, and I considered using them. They would, I have no doubt, have tried to throw doubt upon the motives, the veracity, the reliability of the good people who are my accusers. During the time before this trial I have been kept in the common gaol. I have lost my good name, my father, my aunt, even my family house. God has seen fit to take everything from me." She spoke with such feeling, now, that just for a moment she was unable to go on. "But this terrible passage of time has convinced me of one thing. I must come before you and speak nothing but the most simple truth. I throw myself entirely upon your wisdom and your mercy." She turned. "My Lord, I have nothing more to say."

It did not take the jury long. Even the shopkeeper was ready to believe her. How did the jury find her?

"Not guilty, My Lord."

She was free. As she left the courtroom with her dear friends, however, Fanny felt no elation. Just outside the door, standing with a beadle, she saw the poor girl who was to be transported and paused a moment. "I'm sorry about what they did to you."

"I'm alive," the girl replied with a shrug. "Can't be worse for me there than here."

"But your family . . ."

"Glad to see the back of them. They never did nothing for me."

"I might have been joining you," Fanny said quietly.

"You? A lady? Don't make me laugh. They'd have let you off anyway."

"Don't be impertinent," said Mr Gilpin, not unkindly.

But even so, Fanny still looked back to give the girl a pitying glance.

• • •

The marriage of Miss Fanny Albion and Mr Wyndham Martell took place later that spring. There had been some uncertainty about where the celebrations should be held, but the matter was resolved to everyone's satisfaction when Mr Gilpin offered his vicarage, where Fanny had in any case been staying. Mr Totton, as her nearest relative, gave her away, Edward was best man and Louisa the senior bridesmaid. If the Tottons had sensed a faint coolness towards them on behalf of the bride and bridegroom, there was no sign of it upon the day, when everyone congratulated Louisa on how pretty she looked and gave it as their opinion that it could not be long before she, too, found a husband.

Three days before the wedding Fanny received one unexpected guest. He came to the door of the vicarage, bearing a gift and, although a little nervous, Fanny felt she could hardly refuse to receive him, which she did in the drawing room.

Mr Isaac Seagull was looking very spruce that day, in a smart blue coat, silk stockings and a perfectly starched cravat. With a slight bow and a curious smile, he handed her the present, which was a very fine silver salver. Fanny took it and thanked him, but could not help blushing a little, for she had not seen fit to invite him to the wedding.

Guessing her thoughts, the landlord of the Angel with his cynical, chinless face gave her a smile. "I shouldn't have come to the wedding if you'd asked me," he said very easily.

"Oh."

She looked out of the window at the lawn, which was still somewhat untidy after the spring rains. "Mr Martell knows about our relationship."

"Maybe. But no need to speak of it, all the same. Nothing wrong with secrets," remarked the man who lived by them.

"Mr Martell is not here at present. I'm sure he would be glad to shake your hand."

"Well," said the lander with a humour that Fanny missed, "I dare say I shall have the pleasure of shaking his hand one of these days."

Then he left. And it was half an hour later that Mr Gilpin, with a wry smile, found a bottle of the very best brandy outside his back door.

• • •

"They were all there, Mr Grockleton, did you see? The Morants and the Burrards and I don't know who else out of Dorset." After her own wedding day – she had enough sense to say that – Mrs Grockleton declared it had been quite the happiest day she could remember. And nothing, nothing could compare with the moment when Fanny and Wyndham Martell, standing with her, had called to Sir Harry Burrard, who had come over smiling, and Fanny had said with such simple warmth: "Mrs Grockleton, I'm sure you know Sir Harry Burrard. Mrs Grockleton," she smiled, "is is our true friend." Which, although she scarcely knew it herself, was all that Mrs Grockleton had been waiting for someone to say all her life.

For everyone else, however, the most notable event of the day came when Mr Martell made his speech.

"I know that many of you may be wondering," he declared, "if it is my intention to take the last Albion out of the Forest. I can assure you it is not. For while our interests must, of course, take us to Dorset and Kent, and London, too, it is our intention to build a new house here, to replace Albion House." It was not to be on the old house's wooded site, however, but upon a large open area just south of Oakley where he intended to lay out a park with views towards the sea. Plans for a fine classical mansion were already being drawn up. "And to make it clear that in our new order we have not forgotten the old," he cheerfully declared, "we have decided to call it Albion Park."

1804

Everything was ready at Buckler's Hard, that warm evening in July.

The last three days had been especially exciting. Over two hundred extra men had arrived from the naval dockyards at Portsmouth to help with the launching. Riggers, they were called. They were camped all around the shipyard.

The launching tomorrow would be one of the most impressive that the shipyard had ever undertaken. Two or three thousand people were coming to watch. The gentry would be there, and all sorts of great folk from London. For tomorrow they were going to launch *Swiftsure*.

It was only the third time in the yard's history that they had built a great seventy-four-gun ship. Even *Agamemnon* had been only a sixty-four. At seventeen hundred and twenty-four tons, the ship towered over the dock. The Adamses were to be paid over thirty-five thousand pounds for building her.

Business had been brisk at Buckler's Hard. At the age of ninety-one, old Henry Adams was still seen about the yard, but his two sons ran everything nowadays. In the last three years they had built three merchant coasters and a ketch; three sixteen-gun brigs, two thirty-six-gun frigates of which the second, *Euryalus*, had been built alongside *Swiftsure*, and the mighty seventy-four-gun herself. Another three brigs, twelve guns each, were already in production. Indeed, the yard was so loaded with work that the Adamses were often behind schedule and their profits were not all they should have been. But the completion of mighty *Swiftsure* was still a cause for celebration.

Puckle certainly meant to celebrate. He had been working on *Swiftsure* ever since the keel was laid.

They had been long years, the years of exile before that. He'd been busy enough. Isaac Seagull had dropped a discreet hint to old Mr Adams; Mr Adams had spoken to a friend at the shipbuilding yards at Deptford, on the Thames outside London. And a month or so after he had slipped away out to sea, Puckle the smuggler had been patriotically employed building ships for His Majesty's Navy again.

The Navy had needed ships, as never before. Ever since his arrival in London, England had been at war, or close to it, with France. Out of the Revolution there had now emerged a formidable military man, Napoleon Bonaparte, a second Julius Caesar, who had made himself master of France and who, quite likely, meant to be master of the world as well. His revolutionary armies were sweeping all before them. In England, only the unbending minister, William Pitt, and the great oak ships of the British Navy stood, implacably, in his path.

They had been hard years. The war, bad harvests, French blockades had all hit Britain's economy. The price of bread had risen sharply. There had been sporadic riots. Puckle, working hard in Deptford, had been well enough provided for; but although he could go upstream to the busy port of London, or wander up on to the high ridges and bosky woods of Kent, he missed the soft, peaty soil, the gravelly tracks, the oaks and heather of the Forest. He had longed to return. He had waited six years.

Not Mr Grockleton's fictitious cousin, but an aunt of his wife's, from a rich Bristol tradesman's family, left the modest legacy that allowed the Grockletons to retire. It was with some surprise, however, that her many friends, who even included – more or less – the Burrards, learned that Mrs Grockleton did not intend, after all, to stay in Lymington. Her academy was thriving. No less than four girls from prominent landed gentry attended some of its classes. The yearly ball she now gave for the girls had become a very pleasant fixture at which only the very best of the merchant families like the Tottons and the St Barbes were to be seen with the gentry. Mr Grockleton, who had never intercepted a single cask of brandy, had even been known, rather wryly, to drink the occasional bottle left at his door by order of Isaac Seagull, who had grown quite fond of him. Why, then, should they want to move?

The fact was, although she was too polite and kind to say it, Lymington had failed Mrs Grockleton. Indeed, so had the Forest. "It's those salt pans," she would say sadly. For the salt pans, the little windpumps and the boiling houses were still there. True, there were one or two very agreeable houses built recently at Lymington with views of the sea. A captain and two admirals graced the place, with the promise of more to come: and admirals, though they might be fierce, were very respectable.

Yet something was missing from the town even so. Perhaps it was the French. In 1795 most of them had departed on a campaign against the revolutionaries in France. They had landed there in force, fought bravely, but in vain. The expedition had not been very well supported by the British government. Few of the brave Frenchmen returned. All that was left to remind Lymington of their sojourn there were one or two aristocratic widows, a larger number of local girls who had either fallen in love with, or married, French troops and, inevitably, a number of illegitimate children, all of whom were likely to be a charge to the parish.

No, it was not enough. With its salt pans and its smugglers, Lymington, while well enough, was never going to become a place of fashion.

But what of her own position? Wasn't she a friend of Fanny and Wyndham Martell? And of Louisa, dear Louisa, who had married Mr Arthur West? Wasn't she, if not a regular guest at dinner, at least on terms of friendly acquaintance with the Burrards, the Morants, even Mr Drummond of Cadland? She was and that was just the trouble. She had achieved her objective. The enemy had been vanquished. She had met them and they were mortal. It might have surprised these good people to know it, but in her own capacious mind, at least, Mrs Grockleton had moved past them. The Forest was no longer large enough to contain her.

So the Grockletons went to Bath.

And with Mr Grockleton's retirement and departure, the coast had been clear for Puckle to return.

It was all done very quietly. Isaac Seagull saw to that. His old cottage was ready for him. So was his job. And, by some Forest magic, when he walked back into the shipyard you really might have thought that no one even knew he had been gone.

And indeed, he discovered one other pleasant continuity upon his arrival. For the great tree he had escorted across the Forest from the Rufus stone was also there, as it were, waiting to greet him. So large and fine were its timbers that Mr Adams had been holding it at the yard until he had a ship that was worthy of it. That ship had been the mighty *Swiftsure*. In this way, the acorn from the magical, midwinter-leafing tree had entered and become a part of one of Nelson's finest ships.

That had been four years ago, as work had just started on *Swiftsure*, and he had been working on her ever since. Her launching tomorrow, therefore, in some strange way seemed a kind of affirmation to him. He had returned home, and brought a great ship into the world. At least, he would have, after tomorrow when she was launched.

The launching of a great ship was a complex and tricky business. Essentially it was necessary to transfer the vast weight of the vessel from the keel blocks on which it had been built to a slipway down which it must safely enter the water.

For days, now, Puckle had been helping the men building the wooden slideways. These were railtracks made of elm and, since they had to run down well into the water, most of the work on them had to be done at low tide. It was a muddy affair.

The business of transferring the huge weight of the ship had to be done with the utmost care. While it was being built, the ship had rested upon keel blocks made of elm wood, about five feet high and placed five feet apart. Around the outside of the hull, tall wooden poles, thirty or forty feet high, like ship's masts, acted as scaffolding. Starting from the end nearest the water, the riggers had swiftly moved, driving in huge wooden wedges to lift the ship off the blocks and then putting in the timber props that would guide her on her path down the rails. It was a long operation requiring great skill. For everything had to go right. If the ship lurched, it could crash on its side. If the angle of the slideways were too shallow she might not launch. Too steep and she might rush down into the water and go careering off, to get stuck on the mud banks across the river. Such things had happened. If all went well, however, the rising tide coming up under the stern would just ease the ship off the blocks, the wedges holding her would be knocked away and, slowed by drag ropes, she would slide gently down into the Beaulieu River, stern first, to be towed away downstream and out into the Solent.

Puckle walked round the ship. He loved the line of the huge keel and the workmanship that had gone into it. The inner keel was made of sections of elm. Outside this was another outer keel of oak. When the ships ran down the sliderails, or if ever, later, they ran aground, it was this outer keel that would endure the scraping, protecting the inner keel from harm.

He would be staying at the yard that night, for before the ship could be launched there was still one vital job to do.

The normal time to launch a ship at Buckler's Hard was an hour before high tide. At lowest tide, therefore, which, that night, would come shortly before dawn, gangs of men would go down to grease the slideways with melted tallow and soap. Puckle had asked to be one of them. He wouldn't have missed this last pre-dawn preparation for anything.

• • •

There was a quarter-moon that night and the sky was full of stars. At Albion Park the pale, classical façade of the house stared across the faintly glimmering sweep of its lawns to the gently shelving belt of small fields and woods that sank down, as though in a contented dream, to the Solent water. Beyond that, clearly visible in the moonlight, the long line of the Isle of Wight lay like a gentle guardian.

In that handsome, ordered house, everyone was asleep. The five children of Fanny and Wyndham Martell slept happily in their nursery wing. Mrs Pride, a little elderly, now, but still very much in control – not a fly stirred in that house without her permission – slept peacefully. The entire household would be driving across to join the more than a hundred carriages, which would arrive to watch the launching of *Swiftsure* in the morning.

Everyone slept. Or almost everyone.

Mr Wyndham Martell was not asleep. He had been awakened an hour before by a sound from his wife and now he sat watching her thoughtfully.

It was just in the last few weeks that she had taken to talking in her sleep. He did not know why. She had done so before, usually in little bursts that lasted for a week or two and then subsided, as though there were complex hidden tides in her mind about which he scarcely knew. Sometimes he could make something out. She had murmured about her aunt, about Mrs Pride, about Alice Lisle. There had also been conversations with what appeared to be Isaac Seagull. Mr Gilpin was the recipient of some of her confidences, too. But there was one dream she had which seemed to cause her particular distress; she would toss and turn, and even cry out. She had just had it again tonight.

Wyndham Martell loved his wife very much. He wanted to help her, yet was not sure what to do. Most of the conversations she had made no particular sense. Even when she was in distress, it was not always possible to understand the moans and cries she emitted. And by morning, when she awoke, she would smile at him lovingly and be well enough.

Tonight, however, he thought he had understood something more.

Wyndham Martell got up and walked to the window. The night was warm. Across the park he could see to the coast, out past the distant spit of Hurst Castle and the open sea beyond. He smiled to himself: that was the province of Isaac Seagull the smuggler. His wife's cousin. He remembered well the night Louisa had told him that and how her malice had made him feel so sorry for Fanny. Perhaps, he thought wryly, it was the very unfolding of that dark secret that had led him to the wife he loved.

Maybe everyone, he reflected, had dark secrets within them of which they might or might not even be aware.

And then, because he loved his wife and all her secrets, he quietly left the room, went down to his private library and, sitting down at his desk, took out a piece of paper. He was going to write his wife a letter.

He paused a little while, thinking carefully, then began.

My dearest wife
Each of us has secrets and now there is something which
I, too, have to confess.

It was a long letter. Dawn was almost breaking before he finished and sealed it.

At Buckler's Hard, Puckle was busily at work. The tide was out. Slipping about contentedly in the riverside mud, he moved the heavy soaked leather rag over the wooden rail. Above him the dark bulk of *Swiftsure* loomed beneath the fading stars like a friend. Across the Beaulieu River a bird suddenly started singing and, glancing eastwards, Puckle saw the first faint hint of the light of dawn.

Swiftsure would be launched that day. As he glanced up again at the vessel, although he had not the words quite to express it, Puckle reflected once again how, in this huge wooden ship, the trees had become transmogrified into a second and perhaps equally glorious life. And his heart was filled with joy to know that the Forest itself, with all its secrets and many wonders, would, in this manner, pass down the slideway to be joined with the endless sea.

Pride of the Forest

1868

Brockenhurst railway station: a sunny day in July. The tall-funnelled steam engine had a burnished coppery gleam, like a snake that has just shed its skin, as it hissed and smoked by the platform. Behind it a line of thickset brown carriages, their windows wiped and their brasses buffed by the smartly uniformed guards, stood waiting to receive their passengers, who would be taken with a proud rattle and at speeds of over thirty miles an hour the seventy miles to London.

The London and South-Western Railway line was a fine affair, a symbol of all that was best in the new industrial era. A decade or so before, it had been extended westward across the Forest to Ringwood and down into Dorset. But as well as paying compensation to the Forest for this intrusion, the director of the line, Mr Castleman, had agreed to follow a winding route that would inflict minimum damage on the woodlands so that his line was known as Castleman's Corkscrew. At Brockenhurst, where the cattleyard and pony-yards abutted the station, the engines would also pause to take on more water.

The two figures who walked along the platform made a curious contrast. The older man, almost sixty, was every inch a Victorian gentleman. As the day was warm he wore no outer garment over his grey frock coat. His wing collar was encircled by a cravat tied in a floppy bow. He carried a silver-handled cane. His tall black top hat had been brushed until it shone; there was not a speck of dust upon his trousers. As for his shoes, the boot-boy had spat and polished to such good effect before dawn that they gave off little flashes as they caught the sun. Florid faced, blue-eyed, white-haired with a long drooping moustache, Colonel Godwin Albion would have been pleased to know that he resembled his Saxon ancestor Cola the Huntsman and, in all probability, would have agreed with him on most matters of importance.

If Colonel Albion was even a fraction nervous at the prospect ahead of him he no more showed it now than he had, a dozen years before, when he led his men into battle in the Crimean War. If he could face the Russians, he reminded himself, then he could certainly face a Select Committee of his fellow countrymen, even if they were all peers of the realm. He squared his shoulders, therefore, and went forward bravely.

The figure beside him, about ten years younger, was also looking his smartest, in a different manner. He was dressed in his Sunday best – a rather more shapeless frock coat made of sturdy material. On his head, a wide-brimmed countryman's hat. His boots, under the Colonel's strict instructions, were shining. Like most working men, he couldn't see the point of the high polish that the gentry and the military favoured on their boots, which were bound to get dusty again. His beard was neatly combed and his wife had continued brushing his coat until the Colonel had come for him. But as Mr Pride, tenant smallholder of Oakley, strode cheerfully along with a slightly loping gait, beside his landlord, he was probably less concerned than the Colonel about the prospect before him.

Besides, if the Colonel wanted him to do this, then as far as Pride was concerned, that was reason enough. He'd known the Colonel all his life and his parents, too. As well as being his landlord, the Colonel was a man you could trust. When, a few years back, the Colonel had started a local cricket team on Oakley green, and Pride had shown a distinct aptitude as a spin bowler, there had sprung up an extra bond between them which, as far as social position allowed, could almost be called a friendship.

Only one cloud darkened his horizon. His son George. They'd scarcely spoken these last few years. Until three days ago when the boy had turned up begging him not to go, afraid he'd lose his job. His brow darkened when he thought of that; he didn't want to ruin his son.

"You shouldn't have gone to work for Cumberbatch then," he'd said coldly. And he'd gone with the Colonel.

He had never been to London before. He had read about it. Like his father Andrew before him, he had attended the little school founded by Gilpin and he took quite an interest in the newspapers. But this would be his first time in the capital; so the day was rather an adventure. The fact he was about to face a panel of peers meant nothing in particular to him. He supposed they would be like the gentlemen verderers. And anyway, whether they were devils incarnate or a choir of archangels, he knew who he was. He was a Pride of the Forest. That was good enough for him.

The Colonel, however, with subtler distinctions on his mind, was not sorry as they came along the platform to see another top-hatted figure, with a rich brown beard, waiting by the entrance of the first-class carriage. For though his fellow landowner, the lord of the great Beaulieu estate, was only a little over half his age, he was the son of a duke, which was no small thing to be in Victorian England.

"My dear Colonel." The aristocrat raised his hat and even gave Pride half a nod.

"My dear Lord Henry."

"We are here, I believe," Lord Henry smiled at them both, "to save the New Forest."

In the year 1851, the fifteenth of the reign of Queen Victoria, the British Parliament had passed an Act that was to mark the greatest change in the New Forest since the days of William the Conqueror.

They decided to kill all the deer.

Nobody knew exactly how many deer there were: surely seven thousand; perhaps more than ten. Red and fallow, stags and hinds, bucks and does, calves and fawns – they were all to die. The Deer Removal Act was the title by which this measure was to be known.

Of course, it was centuries since, as a deer farm, the New Forest had had any economic justification. The deer culled each year went to the ancient officers, or to landowners whose property lay in the area. Indeed, it was calculated that each deer killed actually cost the Crown the astonishing sum of a hundred pounds! The Forest was an anachronism, its offices were sinecures, its lovely deer served no purpose. But that was not why they were all to die.

They were to die to make way for more trees.

Ever since the first, late medieval coppices, the Crown had taken an interest in its Forest trees. When the merry monarch Charles II had begun his plantations, he had started a more organised approach to the question of timber; but the first time that Parliament had really addressed the subject was an Act of 1698, when it was decided to set up inclosures for growing timber. Stock – deer, cattle and ponies – would be fenced out until the saplings were too well grown to be eaten by them. Then the inclosure would be opened up again for the stock to graze the undergrowth, and a new inclosure made elsewhere. But although some inclosures of oak and beech had been made, the business had never been followed through. Indeed, most of the oaks felled for the naval ships at Buckler's Hard came from the open Forest, not from plantations. The old medieval woods and heaths stayed very much as they had always been.

Wasn't it all a shocking waste? The British Empire was expanding, the Industrial Revolution had ushered in a modern world of steam and steel. In the year 1851 the Great Exhibition in London, with its huge Crystal Palace of iron and glass, was drawing trainloads of eager visitors from all over Britain to see the results of industrial progress on a world-wide scale. In the countryside farm machinery was coming to the land; a huge new programme of inclosure had partitioned the wasteful old communal fields and common wastes into efficient private units. People had been thrown off the land, admittedly, but there were jobs for them in the growing manufacturing towns. Surely it was time to create tidy plantations in the Forest's unreformed wilderness.

In 1848 a House of Commons Select Committee investigated the Forest. They were shocked by what they found: Forest officials paid for doing nothing; those in charge of the woods selling off timber for themselves; venality, criminality. In short, the place was much as it had been for the last nine hundred years. They saw that reform was needed at once.

They proceeded with a logic which could only evoke admiration. The deer, since they served no purpose, must go. But if the Crown was no longer farming the deer, then it must be compensated. Any voices protesting that by getting rid of the deer the Crown was actually saving itself from a loss, were stifled. The compensation was fixed at fourteen thousand acres to be enclosed for woods – this in addition to the six thousand or so designated, though not all taken up, under the old 1698 Act. Finally, to make the new interest of the Crown very clear, the commoners who shared the Forest were to fall under the control of the Office of Woods. There was no consultation with the commoners. In the brief period before the proposal and the legislation the five greatest landowners in the Forest managed to have the proposed new inclosures reduced to ten thousand acres. Then the measure was whisked through.

Soon after this, the day to day administration of the Forest was placed in the hands of a new Deputy Surveyor. His name was Cumberbatch.

Had he been wrong to bring Pride? Not many people in the Forest had any use for the Office of Woods, but Pride's loathing of Cumberbatch was legendary. On the other hand, he could be a wonderful witness. The best sort of smallholder the Forest had to offer. It was a risk, of course, but he'd coached his tenant carefully.

Just so long as he kept his temper.

The presence of Lord Henry, by contrast, was deeply reassuring. Not only was Lord Henry's elevated social position a help, but as the owner of Beaulieu also sat as a Member of Parliament in the House of Commons, he had real influence at Westminster.

In a way, Albion considered, their situations were similar. When Wyndham Martell had died, he had divided his estates between his three sons: the old Dorset estates going to the oldest son, the land in Kent to the second, and the smaller New Forest estate deriving from Fanny going to Godwin who had taken his mother's name instead of his father's as more fitting for the owner of the old Albion inheritance. Large though Wyndham Martell's possessions had been, those of the duke were vast. Though a descendant of the Stuart kings through the unfortunate Monmouth, as well as being a Montagu, a large part of his ancestry came from the Scottish aristocracy. His lands, north and south of the border, ran to hundreds of thousands of acres. It was a small matter for him to grant his second son the eight thousand acres of the Beaulieu estate as a wedding present; but it was a great matter for the New Forest. For although the duke and his family had always been good landlords of Beaulieu through their stewards, it was hardly the same thing as having an owner in residence; whereas now Lord Henry – as the son of a duke the title of lord was placed as a courtesy before his name – had set about plans for rebuilding the ruined abbey as a family home and was taking a keen interest in the place.

It was time to board the train. The Colonel had given Pride a ticket for the second-class carriage. He and Lord Henry prepared to step into the first-class and he had just got one foot in through the door when a voice hailing him from further down the platform caused him to turn, start violently and almost lose his balance.

"Watch out," said the voice, cheerfully. "You nearly fell down."

The owner of the voice, who now came with an easy, swinging gait towards them, was in his twenties. He was dressed in a loose velvet coat and a wide felt hat. Under his arm he carried a satchel. These attributes, in addition to his small pointed goatee beard and the long curls of fair hair that reached his shoulders, all suggested that the young gentleman was an artist of some kind.

"Going to London?" he enquired amiably.

The Colonel did not reply, but his jaw set and his hand clenched as though he were about to slash a Russian with his sabre.

"I'm going up to look at some pictures," the young man continued, then, glancing at Lord Henry: "Have we met?"

And now, if only to stop this infuriating flow, Colonel Albion turned to face the young man. "I have nothing to say to you, Sir," he roared. "Good day!" And he hurled himself forward into the carriage as furiously as if it were a Russian battery.

"Suit yourself," said the young man cheerfully, and went to

another door. The engine at the front, no doubt in sympathy with the Colonel, let out a huge huff of steam.

Only some time later when the engine was puffing them with a busy rattle towards the environs of Southampton, did Lord Henry venture to enquire: "Who was that young man?"

And now poor Albion buried his face in his hands and through gritted teeth informed him: "That, Sir, was my son-in-law."

"Ah," Lord Henry enquired no more. He had heard of Minimus Furzey.

It wasn't long before Albion saw their game. The Committee Room was crowded. Cumberbatch and his friends, the Forest landowners, everyone was there; and sitting behind the long table facing the room were ten men, law lords or peers of the realm, every one. He saw their game by the way they looked at him.

Colonel Albion had always felt rather proud of the fact that he was descended from two of the most ancient families in southern England. He wasn't arrogant about it but there was a satisfaction in knowing that no one, not the mightiest in the land, could ever tell him he wasn't a gentleman or that he didn't belong. He was also proud of the fact that, though he had purchased his captaincy, he had advanced to the rank of colonel entirely on his merits. His social place amongst the Forest gentry was as solid as a castle on a rock.

But the aristocrats who faced him now were of a different sort. Their families mightn't be as ancient, but they didn't care. Their estates were far larger; they belonged to that more rarefied club that governed the country. And to them – they were too polite to say so but he saw it in their eyes – he was just a florid-faced squire.

"Colonel Albion, you are a Commissioner, arc you not, of the Deer Removal Act?"

"I am." There were thirteen Commissioners whose job it was to oversee the working of the Deer Removal Act and, in particular, to approve any new inclosures. Three came from the Office of Woods, including Cumberbatch then there were the four verderers, chosen by the county, though their power was only a shadow of what it had been in medieval times. The rest were the gentlemen or freeholders who held rights of commoning on the Forest. Albion, with extensive rights and numerous tenants, was a natural person to sit on the Commission.

"And why, Colonel, in your view, has there grown up such opposition to the Crown?"

Opposition? Of course there had been opposition: fences broken, young plantations set on fire. These were the ways the poorer Forest folk let you know their feelings and frankly he didn't blame them. Cumberbatch might like to characterise this as a rebellion against the monarch, but he wasn't going to let him get away with it.

"There has been opposition to the Office of Woods," he said calmly, "but the New Forest Commoners like myself are loyal Englishmen and have always enjoyed the special protection of the Crown. Until recently," he added.

"Colonel, would you care to summarise what, in your view, have been the causes of the bad feeling in the Forest since the Deer Removal Act?"

"Certainly." He might have been only a bluff soldier and country squire, he might have missed the Oxford education that his father Wyndham had enjoyed, but the statement of Colonel Godwin Albion to the Committee of the House of Lords would have made his father proud. It was concise, accurate and elegant. "My statement falls into two parts," he explained. "The first is political, the second material."

It was a melancholy tale.

Why, the Colonel used to wonder, had they chosen Cumberbatch? He was far too young, only in his early twenties when he first arrived. He looked and behaved like a pugilist in the ring. He knew nothing about the Forest and cared even less. And straight away he had attacked the Forest folk with a vengeance.

His first assault had been absurd. In the days when the Forest was an actively managed deer preserve, the commoners were supposed to keep their stock off the Forest during the fence month, when the deer gave birth, and throughout the winter heyning, as the cold months were called, when food was scarce. Not that these rules had been enforced for decades. It was generally assumed that the fees the commoners paid entitled them to year-round grazing. And with the deer gone there was no possible reason to apply these medieval rules anyway. Yet no sooner had he arrived than Cumberbatch had tried to order all the stock off the Forest during these times. It was a senseless harassment which, if followed up, would have ruined most of the commoners.

Yet that had only been the beginning. Next, a new register of commoner's rights had been compiled – essentially an update of the old register of 1670 – but with one great difference. Almost every right of common claimed, from the big claims like those of the Albion estate down to those of the smallest freeholder, was now disputed by the Crown.

"Your Lordships, this could only lead any reasonable person to conclude that the intention was to destroy the commoners. The legal costs alone have been crippling. Yet even this is overshadowed by one other business."

Despite the fact that the Deer Removal Act had made sweeping changes, many people still expected more drastic change to come. The reasoning was simple: if the Office of Woods and the commoners couldn't agree about how to share the Forest, then why not partition the whole place once and for all? The commoners could have their land, the Office of Woods their inclosures, and they need never trouble each other again – the big problem being to ensure that one side did not get all the best land at the expense of the other.

"I refer, of course," Albion went on, "to Mr Cumberbatch's famous letter."

Famous. Infamous. It was perhaps unfair that this document – a private letter to his superiors pointing out the most advantageous position for them to take – should have been made public. But in 1854 it had been published in a report on the Forest and everyone had read it. The point that the young Deputy Surveyor made was clever and brutal. Since there was a good chance the Forest would end by being partitioned, he argued, the Office of Woods should make all its inclosures as fast as possible, on the best land. With that land, for all practical purposes, withdrawn from the equation, the commoners' future share was bound to be worth far less.

"Nothing in the last twenty years has caused such bad

feeling," Albion pointed out. "The commoners have been told, without a doubt, that it is the intention of the Crown to destroy them. That, Your Lordships, is the politics of the Forest now."

Did they care? It was hard to know.

"I come now to the material threat." He looked at them severely. "Your Lordships must understand the underlying problem. Trees grow best on the richest land and that's where the best grazing is, too. So the tree-growers and the commoning farmers both want the same pieces of the Forest. Secondly, it is often supposed that once you inclose land for trees and let them grow to a certain height you can open the inclosure for grazing again. That's not true. With today's planting methods the trees are grown so close together that little ground cover grows underneath them. The new inclosures are lost to grazing for generations. Inevitably, therefore, the tree-grower seeks to deprive the farmer of his best land, for an indefinite period."

"You say 'seek to deprive,' Colonel. Doesn't that presume the Office of Woods to be aggressive in its claims?"

"It is not presumption. I have absolute material proof that it is highly aggressive. That is my point. First, they have frequently said they will inclose their allotted acres, reopen the inclosures later – which I have just explained won't work – and then inclose the same amount all over again. I don't think the Act allows this, but if so, they will plainly end by taking most of the Forest.

"More immediately, however, they have done something rather clever. They have said that there were still authorities to make inclosures, deriving from the ancient legislation of 1698, which had never been exercised. So they added those to the ten thousand acres allowed under the Act and came up with several thousand more." He gave their lordships a wry look.

"Your lordships, it may be legal. But let me show you the deviousness of the thing. You will recall that under the Deer Removal Act it was agreed that no inclosure should be less than three hundred acres. That was precisely to stop the Office of Woods picking off little pieces of the best land all over the Forest. But by saying they were taking up their unused quota from the earlier legislation, they neatly evaded Parliament's intention. Here is a list of the inclosures. I invite you to look at them."

He had done his work thoroughly. The list showed exactly what he said: a few score acres here, a hundred there, two hundred somewhere else – all on the best land.

"Nor is that all," the Colonel went on. "We now come to the inclosures made under the Act. About four of the ten thousand acres have been taken up so far. Each individual inclosure must be a minimum of three hundred acres, you will remember. Did they obey the Act? Of course they did. And let me show you how. I have made some maps. It's something we old soldiers learn to do," he added drily. "Perhaps you would kindly consider them?"

As they looked at his maps even some of their lordships could not repress a smile. The new inclosures might be three hundred acres, but the shapes were fantastic. Here a long arm along a line of rich pasture; there a great curve to avoid a patch of poor soil. One of the inclosures was shaped like a huge "C."

"Your Lordships," the good Colonel said pleasantly, "we have all been taken for fools."

Year after year it had gone on. Cumberbatch and his men, under legal sanction, stealing the best of the common land, quietly but steadily. There had been nothing anyone could do. Until two years before.

The meeting which had precipitated the crisis took place when the Commissioners, who had not met for some years, were suddenly called and told, without any consultation or warning, to approve inclosures taking up all the rest of the land allowed under the Act. Six thousand acres: the biggest land grab ever attempted. When they expressed their shock, Cumberbatch said he would have them thrown off the Commission.

The time had come to fight. Within weeks the larger Forest landowners had met and formed a league – the New Forest Association. The Colonel had joined it, of course. So had one of the verderers, a Mr Eyre, whose family had extensive land in the northern Forest. Other families like the Drummonds, the Comptons of Minstead, and the lords of the old Bisterne estate were all ready to defend their heritage. Lord Henry, with the biggest estate of all, was a key member. There was also one most welcome addition to their number: a certain Mr Esdaile who had bought an estate at the dark old village of Burley some eighteen years before – a newcomer in Forest terms, therefore – but whose legal training made him invaluable. They had prepared a petition. The Office of Woods had been forced to pause. And now here they were, in the august setting of the House of Lords itself, fighting for the Forest.

"Colonel Albion." Another peer, younger than the rest, addressed him now. "May I ask you whether your fellow Commissioners, other than the three from the Office of Woods, are equally opposed to these inclosures?"

Albion stared at him gravely. He knew what this meant. Grockleton. Damn the man. Why the magistrate from Southampton should have decided to involve himself in Forest affairs he had never been sure, but some years ago he had purchased a hundred acres with commoning rights, and then got himself put on the Commission. He and the Deputy Surveyor seemed to agree about everything. As far as anyone could discover, Grockleton wanted to see the entire Forest as a huge commercial plantation without any humans in it at all.

"I could not say," the Colonel answered calmly. "Most, I believe, do; but it is not my place to speak for them."

"I see. You make these complaints on behalf of the commoners in general, do you not? Of whom there are, in round terms, about a thousand?"

"Commoning rights vary. I believe that there are well over a thousand households with rights of one kind or another."

"Yet," the young peer had a little glint of triumph in his eye now, "isn't it the members of the New Forest Association, the main landowners like yourself, who have most to lose or gain in this?"

That was it: the Colonel saw it clear as day. Cumberbatch and Grockleton had got at this young peer. For this was always the line taken by the Office of Woods: if you opposed them, you must be doing it out of self-interest. He smiled sweetly.

"Quite the reverse, in fact." He saw the young peer frown. "You see," he went on blandly, "while it is true that I can rent out an acre with commoning rights for far more than one without those rights, this business isn't going to ruin me. And if one day the Forest is broken up and partitioned – *disafforested* is the technical term, as you may know – we big landowners will probably receive fair compensation. But the little people, without the huge open Forest, will be ruined. And, speaking for my-self, I don't want to see such a thing happen." He paused. "Of course," he added, as though the thought had just struck him, "there may be landowners who feel otherwise. My fellow com-missioner Mr Grockleton, for instance, has land and some ten-ants. Whether he cares about their fate I couldn't say." That thrust went home. But the young peer wasn't quite done yet.

"The smallholders and tenants in the Forest, Colonel, are not a very settled population are they? I mean to say, you could hardly call them solid farmers or yeomen, could you?"

He might have guessed that was coming. Sooner or later, whenever you talked to outsiders, it always did. The landed classes have always had clear views about peasants. Good peasants lived on open lands and touched their forelock to you. Once you got into hilly country, watch out. And as for the dark forest, outlaws lived there; poachers; charcoal burners and tinkers. Who knew what sort of people these New Forest commoners descended from? Should the legitimate interests of the Crown really be held up for a population of shiftless vagabonds?

And now Albion smiled. "I suggest that Your Lordship judge for yourself," he replied amiably. "For the next person you are to interview is one of them. My tenant, Mr Pride."

Outwardly the Colonel smiled; inwardly he said a prayer. Now he'd find out if he'd been right to take the risk. Just so long as he didn't become abusive and weaken their case. God knows he'd spoken to him about it frankly enough, and Pride had promised to be circumspect.

The other problem was young George, Pride's son.

Personally, Albion didn't blame George Pride for taking a job with the Office of Woods. Others had done the same. A job was a job. George had a young family to think of. But Pride senior had felt otherwise. There had been a furious row. He'd vowed never to forgive him; and since George had started working for Cumberbatch, his father had not spoken to him. Family loyalty was close in the Forest and this rupture was a sad and serious matter.

Whether Cumberbatch understood all this was another issue. As far as the Deputy Surveyor was concerned, the father of one of his employees was coming to testify against him, and he wouldn't be best pleased. He couldn't actually dismiss George because of it, but the young man would be under suspicion. Albion was sorry about that but if necessary, he had decided, he must sacrifice George Pride to the greater good. If Pride senior kept his head he was a powerful witness.

Would he?

They looked at Pride with interest as he stood, and was then gently induced to sit down before them. He sat bolt upright. Even the young peer couldn't help noticing that Mr Pride looked very respectable. The Chairman addressed him kindly.

"Whereabouts do you live?"

"At Oakley."

"How long have you lived there?"

"Always."

"Always?" The Chairman smiled. "You cannot always have been there, Mr Pride, but I take it you mean all your life?"

"I meant my family was always there, Your Lordship. I mean," he frowned, "not always, but before King William."

"You mean King William IV, before our present queen, or King William III, perhaps?"

"No, Sir. I meant King William the Conqueror, that made the Forest."

The Chairman looked somewhat astonished, glanced at Colonel Albion, who smiled and nodded.

"You have a smallholding of how many acres?"

"It was eight. Now I have twelve. The eight rented are off the Colonel, the four I bought freehold."

"You have a family?"

"Twelve children, Sir. Praise God."

"You can support a family of twelve on these few acres?"

"In the Forest, Sir, we usually reckon twelve acres a good size. It can be worked without the expense of hiring extra hands. I make a profit, depending on the year, of forty or fifty pounds." This was no fortune, but a decent living for a small farmer.

"How do you go about it?"

"The greatest part of my holding is pasture, on which I make hay. Then I have a strip where I grow cabbages, vegetables, roots . . ."

"Turnips?"

"Yes. Also oats."

"What livestock have you?"

"I have five milking cows, two heifers, two yearlings. The milk and butter we sell at Lymington. As to pigs, I keep three brood sows. They produce two or three times a year. Then we have several ponies. The brood mares are run all year upon the Forest."

"The New Forest cow, I have heard, has special virtues. Would you describe them?"

"Mostly brindled, in looks, your Lordship. Quite small but they are hardy. They can live on the heather and heath grass if they have to. They are good milkers. The farmers from the chalk downs of places like Sarum come down to Ringwood to buy our cattle. They cross them with their own and up on the richer pastures the crosses produce huge quantities of milk."

"You depasture your livestock on the Forest?"

"I could not keep them otherwise. I should need many more acres."

"You could not support your family without your commoning rights?"

"I could not. There is another thing besides. It is a question you see, Sir, of the children. I have two sons grown now. One of these lives with me and works as a labourer. But he also has two acres from which he turns out stock on to the Forest. That way he doubles his wages. In a few years this will allow him to start his own smallholding, and raise a family."

"You also have rights of turbary?"

"Yes. That, and the wood from the Forest, is how I heat my cottage."

"Without those rights . . . ?"

"We should be cold."

"How have the commoners been affected by the Deer Removal Act?"

"In several ways. Firstly, the absence of the deer itself has reduced the grazing for my livestock."

"How so? If the deer aren't feeding, there must be more for the other animals."

"So I would have thought, Sir, but it turns out otherwise. The lawns, where the best grass is, are getting overgrown with scrub, which the deer used to eat up. I was surprised, but it is so."

"Otherwise?"

"Though Mr Cumberbatch has said we may not turn out our stock in winter, which we used to do when the deer were there. This has only been partly enforced. If it is, I don't know how I shall manage."

"And the inclosures?"

"Some commoners now have to drive their cattle for miles to find grazing. The best pasture is being taken. The inclosures, when reopened, provide little for the cattle to eat and the drains made for the plantations are a hazard to the livestock."

"So you fear for your future?"

"I do."

The Committee was silent. The smallholder had impressed them. This was no furtive forest scavenger, but a free farmer of a kind, they dimly realised, which went back in their island history to ancient days, before even the feudal lords ruled the land. Only the young peer seemed ready to test Pride any further. Cumberbatch had just passed him a note.

"Mr Pride," he gazed at the forest man thoughtfully, "I understand that there has been bad feeling towards the inclosures. Indeed, the fences of some have been torn down. Others have been set on fire. Is it not so?"

"I've heard about that, yes."

"I suppose, until now, that is the only way the commoners could make their feelings felt. Wouldn't you agree?"

It was a trap. Colonel Albion looked at Pride sharply, trying to catch his eye. Pride stared fixedly at the wall behind the Committee.

"I couldn't say, Your Lordship."

"You feel some sympathy for them, I dare say?"

"I'd be sorry for any man that had his livelihood taken away, I suppose," said Pride calmly. "But of course they shouldn't break the law. I don't hold with that."

"You wouldn't do such a thing yourself, then?"

Pride looked at the young peer dispassionately. If he felt anger, or contempt, there was not a sign of it on his face.

"I have never broken the law in my life," he said, gravely.

Well done, man, thought Albion. He watched the young peer, to see if he had finished. Not yet, it seemed.

"Mr Pride, you seem much opposed to the Office of Woods. Yet you have an eldest son do you not? One George Pride. Would you please tell us by whom he is employed?"

"Yes, Sir. He is employed by Mr Cumberbatch."

"By the Office of Woods, then?" The young peer looked triumphant. He'd caught this peasant out. "If the Office of Woods is such a monster, why does your son work there? Or is he consorting with the enemy?"

Albion held his breath. He had foreseen most things but not this. He hadn't imagined that, in such a setting, anyone would stoop to baiting the smallholder about his son. Quite possibly the young peer didn't understand the question he had been told to ask. Albion glanced across at Cumberbatch. The swine.

He saw the hair bristle on the back of Pride's neck. Dear God, this was the lighted match that was going to set off the powder keg. He tensed, bit his lip.

Pride gave a quiet laugh, and shook his head. "Well, well. I reckon a young man gets a job where he can, Your Lordship. Don't you? As for Mr Cumberbatch, he isn't any enemy of mine." He turned his head round to look at the Deputy Surveyor and gave him a forester's smile. "Not at present he isn't, anyway. Of course," he turned back to the young peer, "if Mr Cumberbatch makes so many inclosures that he ruins me, and my children go to the poor house, you might say he makes himself my enemy whether I like it or not. I only came here, Your Lordship, hoping you could help, so that Mr Cumberbatch and me could stay friends."

Even the Chairman smiled broadly now, and the young peer gracefully indicated defeat.

"I think," said the Chairman, "we have met the Pride of the Forest. Perhaps this would be a good moment to adjourn."

The white-haired woman waited nervously in the big empty church on the hilltop. She had not told her husband about her rendezvous.

When Mr Arthur West had married Louisa Totton they had produced two sons and four daughters; the sons had been brought up to make their way in the world, the daughters to obey – first their parents and then their husbands. When Mary West had married Godwin Albion it had been on the clear understanding that she would obey him, and so she always had. It was no small thing for her, therefore, to be having a secret assignation in Lyndhurst church; and especially when the man she was meeting had such a dangerous reputation as Mr Minimus Furzey.

Women were always forgiving Minimus. They had been all his life. Minimus, the smallest, the last child of a large family, the pet, the one who could get away with the things his brothers and sisters never could. He was so charming that women could forgive him anything. Men, especially husbands, did not always forgive Minimus. Nor did fathers.

His family had not been shocked when Minumus became an artist. They were all talented. His grandfather Nathaniel had taken up the law and become a solicitor in Southampton. His father had also followed the legal profession but graduated to London and prospered. His eldest brother was a surgeon, the next a professor. Two of his sisters had married rich men in the city, and it was these two who had provided Minimus with the modest income that allowed him to follow his inclinations without any financial worries.

Three years ago Minimus had come to the Forest and decided he liked it. He was not the first artist of his time to do so. If Gilpin in the last century had written of the picturesque beauty of the Forest, numerous artists and writers had come to visit in recent years. The author, Captain Marryat, whose brother had bought a house on the old smuggling route known as Chewton Glen, had even immortalised the area in his *The Children of the New Forest* twenty years before. "Is it the play of the light on the heath or the beauty of the oaks that brings you artists here?" one enthusiastic lady had once asked Minimus.

"Both, but principally it's the railway," he had replied.

The fact that the Forest was full of humble Furzeys who were undoubtedly his relations neither embarrassed nor even interested Minimus. About all social matters he had a reckless innocence. It was not that he ignored social conventions: he only had the vaguest idea of their existence. If something felt agreeable, Minimus usually did it and he was genuinely surprised when people became angry. This included his relationships with women.

Minimus did not set out to seduce women. He found them delightful. If they were charmed by his boyish innocence; if they thought him poetic and wanted to mother him; or if perhaps he found himself suddenly drawn to some pretty young woman: to Minimus these were all wonders of nature. He scarcely stopped to think whether they were ladies or farm girls, married or unmarried, experienced or innocent. All things, to Minimus, were wonderful. He could not really see why the whole world did not operate in this carefree way.

He favoured the western side of the Forest, finding himself a pleasant little cottage near Fordingbridge which he had set about furnishing with gusto. The walls were hung with his own paintings and watercolours; an annexe he built on contained a studio and a study already filled with specimens of plants and insects, in which he took a scholarly interest. But the possession that gave him most delight was in the bedroom upstairs.

He had found it when he was walking near Burley one day. He had noticed an old cottage, badly damaged by a fire, which a group of men were preparing to demolish. Always curious, he had gone inside. Upstairs, exposed to the open sky, covered with ash and charred rafters, he had discovered the shape of a broken bed. Broken but not destroyed. The dark old oak had survived the fire. Cleaning off the ash, he had seen that the rustic piece was magnificently carved. And by the time the men had brought the thing downstairs for him, Minimus realised that he had stumbled on a treasure. Squirrels and snakes, deer and pony, the thing was alive with every creature of the Forest.

"This must be preserved," he declared, and for a few shillings he both purchased it and had it carted to his own cottage where he restored it for his own use. So Puckle's bed found a new home.

Mrs Albion had been waiting for him in the church, now, for some time. But she knew better than to be cross. Minimus was always late. In the cavernous space, with the warm light filtering in through the richly coloured windows, she had time to reflect on why her daughter Beatrice had chosen to marry Minimus Furzey. He was almost ten years younger than Beatrice was. And she had had to face her father's bitter rage.

"She only wants him because she thinks she'll never get a husband," Colonel Albion had fumed.

"She is nearly thirty-five," Mrs Albion had gently pointed out.

"The man's a common adventurer."

The fact that Minimus was of the same family as some of his humblest tenants could not be expected to please Albion, kindly landlord though he was. It upset the order of things. With neither a proper occupation, nor any income except his sisters' charity, you couldn't possibly deny that he was an adventurer.

Yet Mrs Albion knew perfectly well that Minimus hadn't married for that reason at all. The amount of money her husband had been going to settle upon Beatrice was quite modest, and the fact that he had refused to do so had meant very little to Minimus. Her own suspicion was that Furzey had been a good deal less interested in marrying Beatrice than she had been in marrying him.

"The damn fellow just sees her as a free housekeeper," the Colonel had once muttered, and Mrs Albion suspected this might not be far from the truth. Certainly they lived in the most extraordinary manner, with only a woman coming from outside to cook and clean. Even the meanest shopkeeper in Fordingbridge had a servant or two living in.

But what, she wondered, had Beatrice seen in him? As if in answer to her question, the door of the church opened and there, with the golden sunlight behind him, stood Minimus Furzey.

"You are alone, aren't you?" he enquired as he shut the door.

"Yes. Quite." She smiled and, just for a moment, had to fight down an idiotic little fluttering of her own heart as he came towards her.

He looked about the church. "Strange place to meet." His musical voice made a brief echo that quickly died away in the surrounding silence. "Do you like it?"

The new church which had replaced the eighteenth-century structure on Lyndhurst's hill was a tall, ornate, redbrick

Victorian affair with a tower. The tower had only just been completed and it now rose, a monument to the age's commercial pride and respectability, over the oak trees of the old royal manor at the heart of the Forest.

"I'm not sure." She didn't like to say either way, in case he didn't approve.

"Hmm. The windows are fine, don't you think?" The two that he indicated, one at the east end, the other in the trancept, were certainly impressive. They had been designed by Burne-Jones, the Pre-Raphaelite painter who had been a visitor to the Forest in recent years. With their huge, bold forms, they were very striking. "Those two figures," he pointed to the trancept window, "were actually done by Rossetti, you know, not Burne-Jones."

"Oh." She looked at them. "I suppose you know all these artists personally."

"I do as it happens. Why?"

"It must be . . ." she was going to say "so interesting," but that sounded so banal she stopped herself.

The light from the trancept window just caught his fair hair. "I love the fresco," he said with a smile.

The huge painting of *The Wise and Foolish Virgins* by Rossetti's friend Leighton dominated part of the interior. The bishop had been concerned that the Pre-Raphaelite images were too "popish and ornamental," but they had been allowed all the same. So they stood below the wise and foolish virgins, admiring both.

"I asked you here," Mrs Albion said, "to talk about Beatrice." She took a deep breath. "There's something I want you to do."

Bognor Grockleton was in a cheerful mood. As he passed his claw-like hand over his pale, clean-shaven face to wipe off the beads of perspiration, he was smiling contentedly.

To appreciate Bognor Grockleton – he was named after the seaside resort where his parents liked to go on holiday – it was necessary to understand that he meant well. Perhaps there was something of the missionary in him, or perhaps it was the genetic legacy of his grandmother who, after leaving Lymington, had lived to a formidable old age in Bath; but whatever it was that drove Bognor Grockleton relentlessly forward, he always acted in the belief that the world was there to be improved. Few people, in the Victorian age, would have disagreed with him.

He had been trying to improve the Forest ever since he came there. It was natural that he should soon have found an ally in the Deputy Surveyor. The two men in fact were very different. To Cumberbatch the Forest was a material resource like a coal mine or a gravel pit. The Forest folk were a nuisance. If he could have chained them like galley slaves or culled them like the deer, he probably would have. To Grockleton, the Forest folk needed to be helped. Many of them lived in miserable little cottages with only an acre or two. It was primitive. Even the best sort, like the Prides of Oakley, only made their modest living because they had the run of the Forest, and that was a terrible waste of resources. Once the Forest was economically run though, there would be work for many of them in timber production. A few of the larger farms round the Forest edge would doubtless survive. The factories and enterprises growing up in Southampton and the local market towns like Fordingbridge and Ringwood should absorb the rest. The new productive world was going to be so much better. Once the Forest people saw this, they would understand.

The visit to the House of Lords in London had been interesting, but though the Select Committee had not reported yet, he had little doubt of the outcome. The plantations would continue. They had to. This was progress.

He'd been glad when Cumberbatch had offered him young George Pride as a guide this afternoon. If old Pride represented the past, his son George was the future. The job he'd taken was a good one. The keepers and underkeepers were no longer needed now the deer had gone, but there were several positions, known as woodsmen, looking after the plantations, which brought a cottage with them. Young George might be working for Cumberbatch, but he lived on the Forest and he was well paid.

"He'll be very anxious to please you," Cumberbatch had remarked with a grim smile. On his return from London the Deputy Surveyor had summoned George to his office and informed him bluntly: "You may not be able to control your father, but I wasn't pleased to see him at the Committee. I'll be

watching you," he told him. "One false move, any hint of dis-
loyalty, and you're out."

So when Grockleton approached the meeting place, he
found the young man practically standing to attention. This
alone would have made him well disposed towards George;
but even without this reception he would probably have been
in a sunny mood.

Because they were meeting at Grockleton's Inclosure.

It was a fine thing to have a building or a street bear your
name. But when this inclosure had been made a few years ago
and Cumberbatch had announced it would be named after him,
Grockleton had realised with a sense of wonder that this was
something more: a whole wood, a feature on maps for generations to come. Grockleton's Inclosure: it was his greatest pride
and joy.

It lay in the central area of the Forest, west of Lyndhurst. It
covered over three hundred acres. But best of all, as far as
Grockleton was concerned, was the timber with which it was
planted. For Grockleton's Inclosure was nearly all Scots pine.

They had been planting fir trees in the Forest for half a century. Usually they were used as a nurse crop to protect young
oak or beech from the wind. Though great firs would sometimes be grown as masts for ships, it was oak and beech that
the Navy really needed. Or used to need. For wooden ships
were giving place to ships of iron. Buckler's Hard made ships
no more; its pleasant building yards were all grassed over, its
cottages let to artisans and labourers.

Since 1851 the new plantations had contained a different
mix of trees. Slow-growing, broadleaved oak and beech,
whose wood was hard, had given way to softwood trees, quick-
growing cash crops of Scots pine and other conifers. Though
recent, this process had already begun a subtle change in the
character of the Forest. The ancient, gentle pattern of oak
grove and heath was becoming interrupted by the straight-
edged military lines of the fir plantations, dark green all winter. Further, the pines would spread, growing here and there on
the open heath, or even sending up stunted seedlings on the
acidic bogs.

What pleased Grockleton most of all about his plantation,
however, was its wondrous efficiency. "See how close-planted

they are, Pride," he remarked with satisfaction. The trees were so closely set that you would be constantly brushed by their needles if you tried to walk between them. "All the goodness of the ground goes into them. There is no waste." The greensward and undergrowth between the spreading oaks had always seemed wasteful to Grockleton. Beech plantations were better: the ground under the beech woods was mostly moss. But under the fir trees there was neither light nor space. Nothing grew, not even grass and moss. It was lifeless. "That is the utility of the pine plantation, Pride," he explained to the woodward. "A great improvement."

"Yes, Sir," said George.

They went along the path through the plantation and admired its wonderful uniformity. When the Commissioner was finally satisfied, he announced that he wished to make a tour of the northern part of the Forest. So, walking their horses across the open heath, they made their way northwards.

George Pride was a pleasant-looking young man. His fresh, clean-shaven face was framed by a soft fringe of beard that ran down the line of his jawbone and under his chin. He seemed willing and eager. This was a good opportunity to educate him and Grockleton did not fail to make use of it.

"You'll find me very straightforward, Pride," he explained. "And I like people who are straightforward with me."

"Yes, Sir," said George.

"The Office of Woods," said Grockleton, as they descended from a tract of high ground towards the stream known as Dockens Water, "is making great improvements in the Forest."

"Yes, Sir," said George.

"I'm glad you agree," remarked Grockleton. So many did not. The state of the Forest roads was a typical example. When the old turnpike roads had started falling into disrepair around the middle of the century, it was usually the local parish councils, in most parts of England, who had taken over responsibility for repairing them. But would the New Forest villages cooperate? Not at all. And when people like himself and the gentlemen from the Office of Woods had protested, what had the Forest people replied? "If the Office of Woods wants roads, let the Office of Woods pay for them. We don't need them." What could you do with such people?

"We must all move with the times, Pride."

They forded the stream. Ahead of them rose a long heathery slope at the crest of which lay the stretch of open heath known as Fritham Plain. Here and there Grockleton could see cattle grazing, and as they came out on to the plain, he counted a dozen ponies. He sighed. The commoners and their stock: men like George's father were so wedded to these useless animals. The cows he could understand, but the sturdy little ponies hardly seemed worth keeping. About the time of the Deer Removal Act the queen's husband, Prince Albert, had lent an Arabian stallion for a few seasons to breed with the local mares. One could sometimes see a trace of Arabian in some of the ponies now, but the experiment hadn't yielded much. His friend Cumberbatch, for some reason, had interested himself in the ponies and introduced some fresh mares from other places. But the stocky creatures still looked ugly to Grockleton.

"We mustn't blame men like your father for wanting to keep their stock on the Forest you know, Pride," he said kindly. "It's a way of life that has to go, but we must be patient."

"Yes, Sir," said George.

"There were some new plantations planned up here, I believe," Grockleton continued. "I want you to show me where."

"Yes, Sir," said George. "This way."

There was no question, Minimus Furzey considered: the northern Forest was another world. There were individual vantage points, of course, in the wide tracts below Lyndhurst, from which you might enjoy some fine views. But as you made your way northwards up the rising ground above Lyndhurst and went past Minstead and climbed the high slope up to Castle Malwood, you realised that you had come out on to a broad ridge that swept westward right across to Ringwood. Below the ridge, in descending shelves, the southern Forest spread out; but above, in a huge north-western triangle, a high, heather-clad plateau extended for a dozen miles all the way past Fordingbridge and up to Hale.

This was the table-land that Minimus Furzey loved. Up here in its airy silences, under the open sky, a huge panorama opened out beyond the plateau's edge: eastward to the downs of Wessex, westward to the blue hills of Dorset, northward to the chalk ridges of Sarum rolling away into the distance like a sea. It was a high, bare, brown and purple place, a land in the sky, a world apart.

This afternoon, as he often did, Minimus had chosen a pleasant spot up on the high ground to sit and sketch. He and Beatrice had walked up from their cottage together, and she had continued across the high heath while he sat down to work.

It was delightfully warm. At his feet, Minimus noticed the bright emerald backs of the tiny Forest insects known as tiger beetles. Across the heather and gorse, he could hear a Dartford warbler, the click of a stonechat and the faint sounds of one or two other heathland birds. He had not remained alone for long, however.

The lone gypsy caravan that had come slowly westward along the track was not an unusual sight. No one was sure when the gypsies had first appeared in the Forest. Some said it was back at the time of the Spanish Armada, some said later. But whenever it was, these strange eastern people who wandered all over Europe made a colourful addition to the Forest scene. With their brightly painted caravans and strings of horses they would pass across near Fordingbridge, then follow the ancient prehistoric tracks along the ridges below Sarum towards the horse fairs in the West Country.

Minimus would often talk to passing gypsies. Once he had gone off with them for several days, leaving Beatrice only a note to say where he was going. He had returned with an armful of sketches and a rich vocabulary of gypsy words so that, nowadays when he talked to them, only they and he knew what was being said.

He was deep in conversation with the gypsy man and woman when he noticed Grockleton and George Pride approaching.

Grockleton did not like Minimus Furzey. It was one of the few things he and Colonel Albion could agree about. In Grockleton's case, there was no specific reason for this dislike: it was more instinctive. Furzey, it seemed to him, represented disorder. It was a pity the disruptive artist should have chosen to sketch at just the lace he wished to inspect, but he certainly wasn't going to let it nterfere with him. He gave Furzey and the gypsies a bleak stare, lismounted and began to pace the ground.

The spot Minimus had selected lay on the edge of a ridge rom which a slope swept down into a marshy dip below. Across it, a quarter of a mile off, a Scots pine plantation had een laid out upon the heather recently, its seedling trees only nee-high as yet. Having walked over to inspect the plantation, Grockleton strode back and stood gazing down the slope houghtfully.

"Buy a posy, Sir. Flowers for your wife."

He whirled round. The gypsy woman had come up behind im. He noticed now that she had a small basket of flowers on er arm and she had tied them into little nosegays with tufts of urple heather. He glared at her. The flowers, he thought, had robably been stolen out of somebody's garden. The Forest olk seemed to tolerate this, but as far as he was concerned it vas theft. As for the heather, there must surely be some law gainst these wretched people taking that.

"Damn your flowers," he said irritably.

"Better buy them," Furzey called out. "Bad luck if you lon't, you know."

"When I need your advice I'll ask for it," he retorted harply. He turned to George Pride who was standing awkvardly a little way off. "Move these people away, Pride."

"Yes, Sir," said George.

"Buy a flower, Sir," the woman insisted. She did it just to nnoy him – Grockleton was sure of it.

Pride's attempts to move the woman didn't amount to much, ut she retreated back to Furzey who said something that nade both gypsies laugh. Then they got into their caravan and lrove away. Grockleton knew he should have ignored Furzey ntirely after that, but the tiresome thought of what the fellow night have said to the gypsies niggled at him. After surveying he landscape for a minute or two, therefore, he walked over to vhere the artist was working, glanced at the sketch, pronounced, "Not bad," and continued a little further to where a lump of ferns that had been trodden down made a small platorm from which he could survey the scene with dignity.

Minimus glanced at him, smiled to himself and continued to sketch. After a while he looked up.

"Do you know what you're standing on?" he asked. Grockleton stared at him blankly.

"It's the nest of a hen harrier. The Forest people call them blue hawks."

"I fail to see why that is of interest."

"They're visitors. Very rare. Sometimes they don't come for years. This is one of the few places in Britain where they've been seen. They're one of the treasures of the Forest, you might say."

"Treasures to you, Furzey," replied Grockleton. "Not to anyone else." And, quite pleased to see Minimus shrug with irritation, he kicked the remains of the nest and began to pace along the edge of the slope again. "I'll tell you what, though," he remarked as he passed the artist, "there is something useful we can do with this place." He paused a moment to smile, grimly. "We can make a plantation."

"Here? You'll ruin the place."

"Don't be foolish, Furzey. There's nothing here except your damned bird's nest." He nodded to himself with satisfaction. "We can run it right along this ridge and down the slope. Three hundred acres I estimate."

"No good planting on the slope," said Minimus crossly. "It's a bog."

Grockleton stared at him. There was no doubt Furzey could be very irritating indeed.

"The bog is at the bottom of the slope, Furzey," he pointed out. "The water runs down the slope and enters the bog at the bottom. Any fool can see that, you know." He shook his head. "I know you don't want the plantation, Furzey, but if you want to invent objections, couldn't you think of something more intelligent?"

"It's a bog," said Furzey.

"No it isn't!" Grockleton suddenly shouted. He began to stride down the slope. "It is a slope, Furzey." He called back the words deliberately, as though to a slow-witted child. "A slope and not . . . ." He never reached the end of his sentence, however. Instead, he let out a loud cry as he suddenly disappeared up to his waist.

There are several kinds of bog in the New Forest. In the
lower-lying southern region, where the valleys are wide and
shallow, the great peat bogs drawing moisture off the Forest's
gentle gradient extend for hundreds of yards. Some have alder
trees along the line of the water flow. Purple moor grass, bog
myrtle, ferns, tussocks of sedge and reeds grow there. The
edges are flanked with moss. Even after centuries of cutting,
the peat in these bogs is often five feet deep, sometimes more.

In the steeper, narrower gullies of the northern Forest there
are smaller bogs. But it is up in the high sweeps of the northern ridges that a different and unexpected kind of bog occurs.
These are the step mires.

In fact their formation is quite logical. As the water seeped
down through the gravel of the high terraces, it often encountered a layer of clay. Seeping sideways now it would undermine the gravel above and create a ledge, even hollow out a
bench in the ledge, from which it would seep down into the
valley below where, if the drainage was poor, a bog would
form. Down the main part of the slope a covering of mosses
and clumps of purple moor grass would indicate that this was
wet heath. But towards the top, where the moisture drained
swiftly, the covering of bare grass might lead the unwary to
suppose the slope was dry. And the ledge? The centuries had
filled it with watery peat and covered it over with vegetation.
It seemed a level part of the slope but it was in fact a deep bog.
This was the step mire. And Grockleton had just walked into
one.

"Told you so," said Minimus pleasantly.

It was unfortunate that as he climbed, wet and filthy, back
up the slope, Grockleton should have seen Beatrice returning
from her ramble. She was wearing a straw hat. She looked
down at him, her blue eyes concerned.

"You poor man. I did that once."

He was grateful for that. Even Furzey, he noted, had the
grace not to laugh.

But George Pride was laughing. He hadn't meant to but he
just couldn't help it. He was biting his lip now, but his body
was shaking.

Grockleton looked at him. If the young woodman hadn't
been so respectful all afternoon he mightn't have minded so

much. But seeing him laughing now, Grockleton couldn't help wondering if George hadn't been secretly mocking him ever since they met. These damned Forest people were all the same. He'd speak to Cumberbatch about that.

It had been quite soon after her marriage that Beatrice had started to dye her hair. Sometimes she would dye it black, and Minimus would call her his raven. With her slim, pale body and her full breasts – Minimus said they were voluptuous – she had soon learned that if she lay across the carved bed with her dark hair draped across her breasts, it excited him very much.

Sometimes she would dye it red, and put waves in it so that she looked like a gorgeous figure from a Pre-Raphaelite painting. Her face had a strong, rather classical bone structure, so she could carry off these transformations with effect. The changes were not merely decorative; there was magic in them. There was also some calculation. When Furzey was out, she would sometimes take her clothes off and practise attitudes in front of the glass. And then of course she would also return to being the golden-haired landowner's daughter she was originally, and Minimus liked that, too.

The attitude of her parents to her way of life, in so far as they knew about it, contrasted sharply. Once, when her father saw her walking towards him down Lyndhurst High Street with her hair in rich, crimson curls, he remarked that she looked like a harlot and refused to talk to her. Mrs Albion though she could not approve, was more curious and asked Beatrice why she behaved in this strange way.

"Minimus likes variety." Beatrice could have added that she rather enjoyed these transformations herself, but she didn't.

"I have sometimes been afraid," her mother ventured, "that his love of variety might . . ." She left the thought unfinished.

"Extend to other women?" Beatrice looked at her mother thoughtfully. "He is younger than I am, of course." She smiled and gave a little shrug. "It is a risk, Mother. I have always known that." She paused, fingering the little blackened crucifix her grandmother Fanny had given her. "I amuse him, you know. I have some education." Though she had little formal education, Beatrice had always been a voracious reader in the library at Albion Park. Many young men had found her too clever by half. "He says I have talent."

One of the things that had originally drawn her to Furzey was the interest he took in her mind. Instead of praising her harmless watercolours extravagantly, as her dear mother did, he had quietly showed her how to improve them. If she wrote a verse, he talked of other poets, read from their works, gave her new standards by which to judge her own. Sometimes poets or painters came to visit them, and they would all go out together to ramble or sketch out of doors. Occasionally they would take the train to London, visit studios, galleries, or attend lectures. To Beatrice these things were all new, and wonderful.

And most surprising of all, he had opened her eyes to the Forest. She loved it, she had lived there all her life, yet now she realised that she had never really known it at all. Poring on the ground, inspecting a fallen branch, or wandering by a lowland bog, he would utter a cry, and suddenly she would see a damsel fly, a stag beetle, or some other tiny creature she would never have thought of noticing before.

"The Forest is a naturalist's paradise, you know," he would tell her. "There are probably more species of insect here than anywhere else in Europe."

Sometimes they would go out with butterfly nets. She had seen people doing this in the past and thought them rather comical. But now, when they brought their specimens back, mounted and catalogued them, and when she saw the papers in naturalist journals, including some notes from her husband, she began to realise that this was a scientific enquiry to be taken seriously.

If she had waited many years, and quietly rejected several conventional suitors before she had encountered Furzey, it was probably also true that Beatrice was the first woman he had met who was able and also willing to be his life companion. His friends were impressed with her; he rather liked that. They were really very happy together.

"And children?" Mrs Albion had recently asked. It had surprised her that there had been no children yet.

"Minimus and I don't mind waiting a little. One can try to avoid them you know."

"Oh."

"But I was thinking recently . . . I think we may soon. We'll see."

"You should," said her mother. "You should." And it was really the prospect of having grandchildren that had impelled Mrs Albion to seek the meeting with Minimus in Lyndhurst church. Her two sons were abroad, one in India; neither was yet married. Since Beatrice had married, she had scarcely come to Albion Park, and Furzey was not allowed to set foot there. She couldn't bear to think of such a situation greeting the arrival of a grandchild. Besides, she felt sure, Beatrice would be needing money.

Her own attempts to make peace, so far, had been to no avail. Colonel Albion was adamant. He wouldn't see Furzey. Beatrice had made no great efforts since she knew her husband hardly cared whether he saw Albion or not. The only hope was for Furzey himself to make an approach. A letter: serious, respectful, humble even. If he didn't apologise for marrying Beatrice, he should at least show a proper gratitude and sense of humility at the sacrifice Beatrice had made in marrying him. He should ask for a reconciliation for her sake and that of any children. All this and more besides. It was not the sort of letter that Minimus was very good at. But this was what, in Lyndhurst church, Mrs Albion had begged him to do.

She had dictated much of it herself. She had taken out his ironical asides, his humour, his references to Beatrice's improving education. She had watched him write it and then taken it away before he could add anything more.

And, amazingly, it had worked. With no very good humour, and after she herself had pointed to some of the respectful passages in the letter of which she was particularly proud, the Colonel had grudgingly agreed that Beatrice and the artist might come to dinner.

The dinner went surprisingly well. There is nothing like misfortune for bringing people together, and it happened that the day of the dinner also brought the bad news of the House of Lord's decision. Their Lordships had concluded, not unreasonably, that since there were two parties, the Office of Woods and the commoners, whose interests were diametrically opposed, the only long-term solution was to partition the Forest between them. They did agree that the commoners should be fairly treated and that Cumberbatch and his men should not be allowed to steal all the best land.

"But that's what will happen in practice," Albion remarked gloomily. "I'm not sure even Pride will survive."

"If I understand it correctly," Minimus was respectful, on his best behaviour, "this Select Committee report isn't binding."

"That is true. It is only an opinion. But it carries weight," explained Albion. "The government may not find time to prepare legislation on the Forest for a year or two, but when they do they'll almost certainly follow the Committee's advice."

"We must fight on, then," said Minimus.

This earned a smile from Mrs Albion and a grunt of approval from the Colonel. But Minimus did even better with his next suggestion.

"I refuse to believe," he remarked, "that we can all be browbeaten by people who walk into step mires." And he gave them an account of Grockleton's recent accident.

The Colonel was delighted with this. "You mean he just marched in?" he asked, incredulous.

"I swear to you," said Minimus with a smile, "I behaved perfectly. I warned him. I told him it was a bog. And he wouldn't listen. Straight in, up to his armpits!"

The meal became quite cheerful after that and it was almost with good humour that, after they had drunk their port, Colonel Albion led Minimus into his office for a private talk.

Colonel Albion's office perfectly expressed the man; it also told you much about the state of the New Forest. On the shelves were the usual works of geneaology and county history, the foundation stones and buttresses of the gentry's world. There were the bound eighteenth century Parliamentary Reports on the New Forest, a shelf of parchment inventories of the Albion estate, and several volumes of minutes of the Verderers' Court which he had borrowed from Lyndhurst ten years ago and forgotten to return. There were literary works too. A set of Jane Austen's novels were lodged beside Mr Gilpin's works, not so much for their literary merit, but because the author had lived in the same county. There was also, given to him by a kinsman who owned the Arnewood estate where the story was set, a copy of Marryat's *Children of the New Forest,* whose numerous technical errors on Forest matters were neatly underlined and noted in the Colonel's own hand.

Hanging near the door, resplendently scarlet, was the Colonel's hunting coat. There were two leading hunts in the New Forest now. One hunted the fox, the other the deer which, despite the Deer Removal Act, were still to be found in the area. As a reminder of the days of the medieval deer Forest, they had been granted royal permission to wear the ancient insignia of the Lord Warden on their buttons. Colonel Albion, descendant of Cola the Huntsman, hunted with both.

Upon a table was a case containing a pair of guns. For the two hunts were not the only sports flourishing in the Forest. The area was becoming increasingly stocked with game. Since with the removal of the deer, the old keepers' lodges had become redundant, Cumberbatch had soon realised that they could be refurbished and let as shooting lodges. A steady stream of sporting gentlemen were taking the train down to the Forest for this purpose nowadays. Better yet, in Albion's opinion, were the opportunities for wildfowling over the marshes down by the Solent shore.

It might have seemed odd that Albion should keep these items, which really belonged in his dressing room and the gun room, in the place where he did his paperwork. But his wife was probably correct in thinking that they were there to comfort him with the thought of future pleasure while he attended to all the letters he so hated writing.

It was while Albion fiddled with some papers on his desk that Minimus caught sight, on a leather chair, of the game book in which the Colonel recorded the results of his shooting, and began to turn its pages.

Minimus had only drunk a little port: just enough to let him think that he was on more friendly terms with Colonel Albion than was truly the case. It did not occur to him therefore that he must still be careful.

"Good Lord!" he exclaimed.

"What's that?" the Colonel looked up.

"I'm just looking at what you've been killing. It's astounding." The Colonel's record was certainly one that any sportsman of his day would have been proud of. His bag for the previous year, as well as the usual snipe, geese, duck, wigeon and plovers included: 1 wild swan; 6 pintail; 4 curlew and 1 oystercatcher. "It's wholesale massacre," said Minimus. "A few more years of this and there won't be any game left. Do you know how many oystercatchers there still are in the British Isles?"

"No," said the Colonel, "I do not."

"Nor do I. But it isn't many." Minimus sighed. "You'll have to be stopped, you know, if you go on like this," he said in a friendly way.

"You are not a sporting man, I gather," said the Colonel through gritted teeth.

"More a naturalist," said Minimus. "By the way," he turned to face Albion, "now that we're getting on so much better, do you mind if I say something about saving the Forest?"

The Colonel indicated that he was listening.

"You're doing it all wrong, you know," said Minimus blithely. "You see," he continued, "if you want to influence the government then you've got to get public opinion on your side. That's the key."

"Public opinion?" Like many of his kind, Colonel Albion's views on political matters were not as consistent as he supposed. If he was faced by the commoners like Pride, with a concrete grievance, he was on their side. Had he read a newspaper account of the same business which referred to Pride's complaint by any general term, even one so mild as public opinion, then to Albion it sounded like revolution and he became suspicious.

"Exactly. What does the public know of the Forest? What they can see from the train. Its beauty, its wildness, its untouched nature. They don't understand Pride grazing his cows, though I dare say they like the look of it. But they do understand if you say that Pride and the heritage he represents are being taken away from them. Because the Forest belongs to them, you see. The Forest belongs to the public."

If, during the beginning of this speech, Albion had seen a glimmer of interest, this final statement snuffed it out at once. "No it does *not* belong to the public!" He glowered at Minimus, then with an effort at self-control: "To be precise, it belongs to the Crown and the commoners."

"But the public comes here, don't you see? It's not only the gentlemen who take the train down here to go shooting. Ordinary people are starting to move about. Shopkeepers from Southampton or London; even working men, skilled labourers and their families. They're starting to visit the Forest for the day."

Colonel Albion had noticed this trickle of folk coming from Brockenhurst station, wandering out across the big open spaces of Balmer Lawn, and paddling in the gravelly streams. He wasn't sure what he felt about them. He knew that he and Pride loved the Forest and walked about it with pleasure every day. If some child from the grey streets of London came to play in the stream as any Forest child had always done, he could hardly blame them. He supposed it did no harm, so long as there weren't too many of them.

"These people are public opinion?" he growled, dubiously.

"They have votes, many of them. They receive ideas from the leaders of public opinion."

As far as Albion was concerned, down in the Forest, he was a leader of public opinion, but he didn't think that was what Furzey meant. "And who are these leaders?" he enquired grimly.

"Writers, artists, lecturers, scientists," said Minimus. "People who write in newspapers."

"People like you?" asked Albion, in even deeper gloom.

"Exactly," said Minimus happily. "What you need is a petition, letters to the press from artists. The new plantations are ruining the landscape. Then there are the naturalists. They will tell you that the Forest is unique. There are all kinds of species here found almost nowhere else. We could make an outcry in the press, the universities. The political men are frightened of such things. Anyway," he concluded, "if you want to save the Forest, you take my advice. I could help. I'm on your side," he added encouragingly.

The thought of having Minimus on his side did not seem to bring Colonel Albion much happiness. "Thank you for your advice," he said drily. Then, remembering the pleadings of his wife, he took a very deep breath and addressed his son-in-law as kindly as he could. "There is another matter, Minimus," he forced himself to say the name, "that I think we should discuss. It is the question of money."

"Really? I haven't any, you know," said Minimus.

"I know," said Colonel Albion.

"We get by. I sold some paintings last year. I'm writing a book. That might bring in something."

"A book. On what subject?"

"Beetles."

The Colonel breathed deeply. "Were you to die," he asked hopefully, "have you made any provision for Beatrice? Do you know what would become of her?"

"She can have my pictures and my collections. She'd have to go back to you I should think. You'd take her back wouldn't you?"

"Have you considered how you would live if you had children?"

"Children? Beatrice wants them, you know." He smiled vaguely. "I suppose they just run around, don't they?"

"They also have to be paid for. There are expenses."

"Perhaps," Minimus said dubiously, "I could ask my father. I don't know if he'd help, though. He thinks I should be employed."

Colonel Albion had never met Mr Furzey the solicitor, but he felt for him. How was it possible, he wondered, that this irresponsible young man had dared to tell him how to organise the affairs of the Forest?

"How would you educate them?"

"Oh, that I do know. Beatrice and I want to educate them at home."

"Sons?" Daughters of course could be educated at home but sons were another matter. Some aristocratic families still engaged tutors, but that was hardly possible here.

"Well, we certainly wouldn't send them to any of these new boarding schools," said Minimus.

There had been boarding schools in England since the Middle Ages. A few, like Eton and Winchester, had even been patronised since the eighteenth century by the aristocracy. But the passion of the richer classes for sending their sons away to such institutions was a recent phenomenon, and these establishments were springing up everywhere.

"They're the most terrible places," Minimus continued. 'They blunt the intellect, destroy the sensibility. Do you know they flog the boys and make them play games? Did you go to a place like that?"

Colonel Albion looked at him in stupefaction. "I went to Eton," he said coldly.

"There you are, then," said Minimus.

"This is not the manner," said Albion, with rising anger, "in which I wish to see my daughter living, Sir."

Minimus stared at him in genuine surprise. "Of course it isn't," he said. "But if she married me," he glanced around the room at the volumes of geneaology and the Colonel's hunting coat, 'I suppose she must have wanted to get away from all this. Don't you think?"

That this observation was probably true did not improve Albion's temper in the least. He ignored it. "When you enticed," he gave the word an insulting emphasis, "my daughter into marriage, did it ever occur to you to consider her welfare?"

Even Minimus noticed that he was being insulted now. "It was she who wanted to marry, actually," he said. "She's quite old enough to know what she wants, you know. After all," he added, "she could have just come to live with me. I suggested that."

"You are telling me, Sir," the Colonel was starting to go very red, "that you intended to seduce my daughter and persuade her to live with you in sin?"

"But I married her," said Minimus plaintively. "There's no need to get so shirty." He shook his head. "Several people I know live with their mistresses."

"People?" Albion's voice was rising to a new plateau. "People like you, Sir. *Artists.*" He might have said lepers. "And do such people have children, too?"

"Of course they do," Minimus cried. "I always told Beatrice, she didn't have to marry me to have children."

It was too much. Colonel Albion was now the same colour as his riding coat. He gasped. "You villain!" he shouted, "you . . ." he began to search for a word, "you absolute . . ." he searched, and it came at last: "you *bounder!*"

1874

George Pride was devoted to his inclosures. There were three of them under his charge.

The job of woodman was a pleasant one. He had to keep up

the inclosure fences and maintain the drains. That was easy enough. More interesting was the management of the woods themselves, supervising the felling, replanting and thinning of the timber. He was also in charge of assigning the lops and tops of trees to the commoners with rights of Estovers, and to the cutting of turves from the peat bogs and bracken from the area.

Each woodman also received fifteen shillings a week, and a cottage with a paddock where he could keep a pony. He had the right to graze a cow on the Forest all year round, an allowance of fern for bedding as well as turves for his fire.

There were twelve woodmen in the Forest now. George Pride's inclosures all lay on the high ground, about three miles east of Fordingbridge. It was a beautiful, deserted area. Two miles to the east, perched on a wooded rise, in the middle of nowhere, was the hamlet of Fritham. The old Free Traders used to come up there from the Smugglers' Road, according to the old folk. But the coastguard service had pretty much killed off that fine old trade before George was born, and Fritham was quite a law-abiding place now. Apart from this, wherever you looked was lovely open wilderness.

George Pride's inclosures were delightful. The conifer plantations, of course, were fairly lifeless, but the mixed inclosures of oak, beech and chestnut were pretty places. With the grazing animals fenced out, they were carpeted with bluebells in May. Columbine, violets and primroses grew there. In one spot George even had wild lily-of-the-valley.

George was particularly proud of his fences – both those of the inclosures and around his cottage. He had wanted the best and so he had gone to Burley and employed Berty Puckle.

Berty Puckle's fences weren't like anyone else's. For a start, he made the planks the proper way.

"There are people," Puckle would say, "who get their planks from timber yards, where they've been sawed." This last word, his personal version of "sawn," was said in tones of the deepest disgust. The way to make a plank, he would explain, was to take a length of wood and split it carefully with a wedge and a hammer. Working his way gently down, following the grain of the wood, the skilful carpenter could produce wafer-thin planks, getting far more from the wood than any clumsy fellow with a saw ever could. Yet they would last for ever. "Natural is best," he'd say. "Takes longer, lasts longer."

His particular speciality was his gates. "I think I got the idea when I was a child," he once told George. "Down at Buckler's Hard. My grandfather was still working down there, although my dad had moved back to Burley. He was an old man then. We used to go and see him, and I remember seeing the oak knees they used in the ships, like wall brackets, to support the decks. They're so strong, you see, you can't ever break them. That's what gave me the idea, I reckon."

For his gates Berty Puckle would take a tree fork to form the upright and the diagonal. Then he'd fit other pieces of wood, dovetailing, and nailing with wooden or iron pegs until the resulting gate seemed more like a natural growth than any man-made object. Sometimes he would even take some complex knotted growth and work round that. You could spot one of Berty Puckle's Forest gates at a hundred yards. George Pride had fifteen of them.

Yet it was also the inclosures, their fences and gates that provided George with his only serious worry. For that was the other part of the woodman's job: he had to guard them.

And they were likely to be attacked.

After the setback in the House of Lords, the Forest had had one piece of luck. A Member of Parliament named Professor Fawcett who had taken an interest in the area had passed a Resolution that halted all further inclosures or felling of ancient trees until new legislation for the Forest could be framed. The government was led by the liberal Mr Gladstone now, who hesitated to attack the commoners. So the Forest was granted a breathing space. But no one knew for how long. And if men like Colonel Albion and Lord Henry were preparing for the next battle in Parliament, the Forest people indicated their feelings.

They set fire to the inclosures and stole the fences.

In these years of uncertainty, with the hated Office of Woods temporarily checked, it was hardly surprising if the Forest folk had been having quite a few very satisfactory little fires. Cumberbatch had even employed some extra men as constables – not, of course, that it had the slightest effect.

"We haven't been up your way have we, George?" a Forest

man remarked to Pride cheerfully in Lyndhurst one day. He was a large, burly fellow, not the sort of man you'd want to get into a fight with.

"No. And please don't," said George.

"I wouldn't worry about that, George, not if I was you," the other replied. "You just sleep sound at nights."

"I really don't know what I'll do if they come," George confessed to his wife. "But I'm not letting them destroy my inclosures."

Apart from these worries, however, they had been happy years. His family was growing. Gilbert, his eldest son, was ten years old now. When he watched the boy come back happily after catching rabbits, or go running down by one of the Forest brooks, he relived his own childhood, and it gave him a deep satisfaction.

He had four children now, but it was the two eldest, Gilbert and Dorothy, that he usually took with him on his rambles. Sometimes they would go down by the amber streams, and walk along the greens where the ponies came to avoid the flies – to shade as the Forest people called it. They would watch a kingfisher flash by or observe the tiny Forest trout and he would teach them all that he knew about the Forest lore.

If he saw himself in Gilbert, he could not quite pinpoint who Dorothy was like. She had the same features as his wife, but her wiry body seemed more like the tall Prides. Her eyes were such a dark blue they were almost purple. As he watched her helping her mother about the house, baking dough cakes and bread, or making apple jelly in the autumn, he would smile to himself at what a good wife she would make some lucky man one day. Yet she could also run like a deer. Gilbert couldn't catch her yet. George was prouder of her than he knew.

It was one day in summer, when she was nine, that he made a small discovery about his feelings that made him feel ashamed.

A deer had somehow got into one of the inclosures and, as he was allowed to do, he had shot it. After he and his wife had skinned it and cut it up, he had taken the haunches across to Fritham where the landlord of the Royal Oak – the only inn for miles around in that part of the Forest – had agreed to smoke it for him. Once smoked, the venison would be wrapped in muslin by his wife and hung in the broad chimney of the cottage where the flies wouldn't get at it.

He had gone across, leading the pony, to collect it from Fritham on a sunny August day, taking his daughter with him. At Fritham, he had drunk a little cider, exchanged a few words with the landlord of the Royal Oak, and then, having loaded the pony, started back again very contentedly towards his home. Dorothy was dancing about in the sun. The smoked haunches of venison bumped against the pony's flanks. They passed by a stony outcrop where some gorse was growing and he saw her go running in there like a wild thing. It had made him laugh.

When he heard her cry, he thought she must have fallen in some gorse, and calling to her to come in, he continued walking with the pony. He heard her cry again, and stopped.

"It's a snake," she cried.

An adder. There were harmless grass snakes in the Forest, but there were adders too. He ran back.

"Was it a big one?"

She nodded and pointed at a hole in the ground a few yards away. The snake had already disappeared.

She pointed to the place on her leg. It was already starting to swell. He could see the marks left by the creature's fangs. A bite from a large adder could be a serious matter for a young child. He felt for the knife he always carried.

"Sit." He ordered. "See the pony?"

She nodded.

"Look at it," he said. "Don't take your eyes off it."

She did as she was told. He cut. She tensed sharply, but didn't cry out. He cut again. Then sucked, and spat, and sucked again. He could taste the venom, a sharp and spiteful taste.

He continued for a quarter of an hour. She was shaking like a leaf but never said a word. Then he put her on the pony and took her home.

It was on the way back that he realised he loved her more than his other children.

A wet February day: Mrs Albion, in a tight little closed carriage, bowled down the lane past Brook, carrying her secret package to her house. She was anxious to get home before her husband's train steamed into Brockenhurst.

The windows of her carriage had fogged up, so she drew one down and stared out.

There are times in winter when it seems as if the whole Forest is turning into water. A misty haze enveloped the trees, clinging to the ivy-wrapped trunks of ancient oaks, seeping into the interstices of stricken branches, soaking into softening logs. The Forest floor was waterlogged. Huge puddles covered paths and greensward and leafy carpet, turning everything to a brownish, peaty slush. Above, below, in every direction, an all-pervading dampness seemed to be offering to sink into the soul. The Forest was often like this in the months of the old winter heyning.

She had just been to see her grandchildren. Colonel Albion and Minimus had never met again after their interview. The break was not exactly formal. If anyone mentioned the Colonel to Minimus he just shrugged and said: "He shouts at me." If anyone was unwise enough to speak of Minimus to the Colonel, he said nothing, but his face began to go dangerously red. Perhaps Minimus sometimes felt a little weary of their stand-off; perhaps Albion a little sad. But still they did not meet. And there was no money.

Actually there was a little money. Mrs Albion was quite clever at gleaning small amounts from her allowance – enough to buy clothes and hire a maid – which she would pass to her daughter on her clandestine visits to the cottage near Fordingbridge. Not that her husband actually forbade her to go there, but she wisely hid her visits from him. If Colonel Albion saw his daughter in the street, which he scarcely ever did, he would give her a bleak nod, but would not stop to speak. He had never seen either of the two grandchildren who had since been born. "They are being brought up as godless heathens, keeping the lowest company," he had stated glumly. It was true, and it greatly shocked Mrs Albion, that neither Beatrice's boy nor girl had been baptised. "No doubt," the Colonel concluded, "they will lead their lives accordingly. There is nothing to be done." He had been to see the family lawyer. The Furzeys were, in the best manner of the age, cut off. The Colonel's eldest son had married since. He already had a child. The future of the family lay there. Most men in his position would have done the same. It was how families survived.

Beatrice's children were fair-haired and pretty. Intelligent. Indeed, because their parents took such interest in these things, they were learning to read and write sooner than most. If they ran about the Forest, as her husband put it, like godless heathens, they seemed to thrive on the regime.

But the Furzey household was a mess. There was no denying it. The day before, the maid they employed could take it no more and had left. There was no nanny, no maid, only a charity girl from an orphanage in Sarum who worked in the tiny kitchen. Beatrice had been wondering what to do. So Mrs Albion had felt rather pleased with her suggestion that George Pride's daughter Dorothy should help out.

Beatrice knew the woodman well. The daughter was twelve or thirteen now. "I'll go over there tomorrow," she had told her mother. Coming from the Pride household, Mrs Albion had no doubt she'd be a steady girl and a good influence upon the children.

Mrs Albion's true mission that day, however, was more devious. She had never despaired of bringing the Furzeys back into the family fold, but she knew that it would have to be a long and carefully organised campaign. Her strategy today involved two acts of deliberate deception. The first had involved a request to her cousin Totton, her uncle Edward's son, who lived in London. He had obliged and she had his letter with her. The second was the collection of the brown paper parcel that lay on the seat of the carriage beside her.

Colonel Albion was in a thoughtful mood when he arrived back home that evening. The day in London had proved to be more eventful than he expected and as soon as he arrived at Albion Park he hastened to give his wife the news.

"Gladstone's resigned! The government's fallen." The news was grave indeed.

It wasn't that he cared for Gladstone so much; but the implications for the Forest were important.

"There's no doubt, it seems, that he will lose the elections," the Colonel reported. "That means, you know, that we lose our protection."

It was a technical, constitutional point, but an important one. The Resolution in the House of Commons that had forbidden the making of any new inclosures was only binding on the present Parliament. When the Commons met again after the election, it would be a new Parliament.

"You can be quite sure that the Office of Woods knows that, too," he said grimly. "We can expect the worst."

Not that the Forest had been idle. The landowners of the New Forest Association had been preparing their case assiduously. Another group, a Commoners' League, representing the smaller folk, had begun to agitate too.

"We shall give battle," the Colonel said.

It was after he had had his dinner that his wife produced the letter and the package.

"Do look," she said, "at what my cousin Totton has sent us. I do think it's very kind of him." The letter announced that her cousin had come across a picture in a gallery. It wasn't signed, so he couldn't tell them who the artist was, but he was almost certain the scene depicted came from the New Forest. He'd thought they might like it.

Colonel Albion grunted. He didn't take much interest in pictures usually but out of courtesy to Totton he inspected it.

"That's looking down from Castle Malwood," he announced. "That's Minstead church." The fact that he could identify the terrain triggered his interest. He inspected it more carefully. The painting showed a summer sunset. After a moment or two he smiled. "That's exactly how it looks," he said. "The light. Shines exactly like that."

"I'm glad you like it."

"I do. It's really damned good. How very kind of Totton. I'll write to him myself."

"I was wondering where to put it." She paused. "It could go in one of the bedrooms I suppose." She paused again.

"I'll have it in my office," said the Colonel. "Unless there's somewhere you'd rather."

"Your office. Why not, Godwin? I'm so glad you'd like it in here."

Although he didn't know it, the Colonel had just looked at his first Minimus Furzey.

• • •

Colonel Albion was right about the elections. Gladstone lost. March saw a new Parliament. Within weeks, Cumberbatch and his men were felling timber. George Pride himself had been forced to witness one ancient oak come down, over by the Rufus stone.

"He just did it to make a point really," he told his wife sadly.

His own inclosures were in good order. One in particular was due for thinning that year; so when Cumberbatch called him in and demanded a list of timber to be felled, he was able to satisfy him quite easily.

"Good man, Pride," the Deputy Surveyor said with a brisk nod. "We may be giving you a new plantation to look after soon. Mr Grockleton suggested we could drain some of those bogs and plant them."

"Yes, Sir," said George.

Apart from this, the spring passed without incident. Young Dorothy was happy going over to the Furzeys. "It's a funny sort of place," she told her father. But the Furzeys were very kind to her and she liked the children. "They're brought up just like Forest children in some ways," she reported.

Beatrice she liked. "You can see she's a lady, Dad. But she doesn't live like one I must say." Minimus she found funny, but strange. "It's amazing what he knows, though." George himself had often wondered how the artist had managed to marry the landowner's daughter. The whole Forest knew the two men didn't speak.

"Even worse than me and Dad," he'd say, for although the two Prides still avoided each other, they didn't actually refuse to speak if they chanced to meet.

Spring turned into summer and the Forest remained quiet.

They had met at midnight up by Nomansland, the remotest hamlet on the Forest's northern edge. By the light of the stars and a quarter moon they had ridden their ponies across, past Fritham, like a pack train of smugglers from the good old days. There were about a dozen of them, good Forest men all, led by the big fellow who had spoken to George at Lyndhurst.

When they reached George's inclosures they stopped and cut some gorse and dry bracken and started a small fire. They had some torches coated with pitch. At various points along the fence they stacked dry material that would burn.

"I should think we'll have ourselves a nice little fire here," said the burly man.

"What about the gates?" asked one of the men.

"Makes a very nice gate, does Berty Puckle," said the big fellow. "You don't want to burn those. That'd be a crime." He was pleased with this joke. "Now that *would* be a crime." He laughed. "Be a crime that would, don't you reckon, John?" There were several laughs in the darkness. "We might take some of those gates. Come in useful those will."

A few minutes later, several of the smaller gates had been removed from their places.

"All right then, let's start," the big man cried, and the men with the torches started to light the fires.

They had a quarter mile of fencing burning nicely when George Pride came along. He was carrying a gun.

There were cries and whoops.

"Here he comes. Here comes trouble. Whoah there, George!"

But George wasn't smiling.

Nor was the big man.

"Thought I told you to stay in bed," he cried.

George said nothing.

"Go home, George," called several voices. "We don't mean you no harm."

But George only shook his head.

"You stop that," he cried.

"What are you going to do, George?" asked the big man in his big voice. "You going to shoot me?"

"No. I'll shoot your pony."

There was a pause.

"Don't be stupid, boy," said a voice.

"If I shoot a few ponies," George called out, "you'll not only walk home. You'll have to explain to the Deputy Surveyor how your pony came to be there."

"You might miss and shoot me, George," said another voice from the dark.

"That's right," said George.

"I'm not very pleased, George," said the big man.

"I didn't think you would be," said George.

So they left, and George tore down the burning fences and, by a miracle, only lost a few trees.

"So who were they?" demanded Cumberbatch, the next morning.

"They rode off," said George.

"We know who the ringleader is, Pride. You must have seen him. All you have to do is say who it was."

"I can't, Mr Cumberbatch," he answered, looking him straight in the eye. "That'd be a lie because I didn't see him. They ran off when they saw my gun."

"You're lying."

"No, Sir."

Cumberbatch looked at him curiously. Was George Pride such a loyal forest man? If he had been on the side of the burners, he could have pretended to sleep through the whole episode until they'd gone. But he obviously hadn't.

"You've got one hour to change your mind," he said, and waved him away.

An hour later, George Pride said the same thing, and Cumberbatch sent him home.

"Couldn't you have given just one of the names?" asked his wife. But even to her he said nothing. The risk was too great.

He couldn't tell even her that one of the voices he had heard in the dark belonged to his father.

The next day George Pride was dismissed.

1875

The Select Committee of the House of Commons that sat in the summer of 1875 was the most thorough investigation of Forest administration since William the Conqueror founded it. For eleven days they took testimony: from Esdaile and Eyre, from Professor Fawcett, from Cumberbatch and a host of others. The chairman of the Committee, Mr W. H. Smith, had been a stationer and bookseller who, having already made a fortune, had entered politics and proved a considerable statesman as well. He was fair and thorough. If the government intended to legislate for the New Forest, they wanted to be certain they got very good advice. For the public was greatly concerned.

It was remarkable – Colonel Albion was bound to admit – what had happened in the last year. When Esdaile and Lord Henry had both impressed upon him the need to gather public support, he had dutifully gone to his London club and talked to all sorts of people like himself who had written some well-considered letters to *The Times*. And they had certainly done some good. But what he had not been prepared for was the public outcry from other sources. While Mr Esdaile had mastered the commoners' legal case, it was the landowner from the northern Forest, Mr Eyre, who had proved brilliant at marshalling this new public support. Scientists, artists, naturalists: the newspapers were bombarded with letters. "Where the devil do you find these people?" he had genially enquired. "Wherever I can," Mr Eyre had replied. "These are the people, you see, who form public opinion. We need them most of all."

"Oh," said the Colonel.

And now the Committee hearings had begun. Though Albion was not giving evidence himself, Lord Henry had arranged for him to attend. It was a strange sensation to find himself going through a process so like the one he had witnessed seven years before when he had come up to London with Pride.

There had been a great change in the Pride family recently, and he had been pleased to see it. After young George had been dismissed by Cumberbatch, it seemed that he and his father had been reconciled. Albion had given George a cottage to tide him over and employed him on the estate. But though he'd been happy that the Pride family was reunited, the whole incident of the dismissal had made the Colonel more determined than ever to see the efforts to save the Forest succeed.

He had a different companion this time. For some reason his wife had insisted on coming with him.

Generally he was glad of her company, but on the fifth day of the hearings he was not a little irritated when, because of some quite unnecessary shopping, she had caused him to

arrive late. By the time they reached the Committee Room, it
was already full and they had been obliged to sit at the back.
He didn't even know who was being called that day.

So he was entirely taken by surprise when he heard Mr
W. H. Smith addressing the next witness.

"Mr Furzey, you are an artist living in the New Forest, I believe."

Colonel Albion wanted to leave. Even his wife's restraining
hand on his arm might not have kept him there, but for the fact
that, to get up now would have caused an embarrassing com-
motion. He therefore sat there, bemused and furious, while
Minimus gave his evidence.

"You believe, Mr Furzey, that the New Forest is an area of
particular value to artists?"

"Without a doubt. I would draw your attention to the petition that has recently been signed not only by me, but by some
of the most distinguished members of the Royal Academy."

The petition had certainly achieved massive publicity. Many
of the greatest names in British art had given their opinion that
the New Forest was superior even to the Lake District for its
natural beauty.

"There is a romantic wildness in the Forest, a sense of primitive nature untouched, that is without equal in southern
Britain," he heard Furzey say. "The play of the light is quite
extraordinary upon the ancient oaklands."

The Colonel stared. Was it really possible Furzey could get
away with this sort of florid stuff in a Select Committee of the
British Parliament? Yet several of its members were nodding.

"I should also like to mention the extraordinary resource
that the Forest represents for the naturalist," Minimus continued. "You may not be aware, but the following species . . ."

Colonel Albion listened in a daze. Flies, insects, stag beetles, English and Latin names he did not know; Furzey gave
them a list of bugs that must surely have bored these gentlemen to death. Yet again, several of them were looking impressed. And so it went on. Opinions that mystified him,
terminology he only vaguely understood. Minimus was in his
element. Then he came to his peroration.

"This extraordinary area is a national treasure without

equal. I say national for, although historically it was a hunting forest for the Crown, it is now a source of inspiration, of study and of recreation for the people of this island. The New Forest belongs to the people. It must be saved for them."

Minimus had ended. The Committee took a brief pause. People started to file out. As Colonel Albion sat there, hardly knowing what to think, Mr Eyre came smilingly towards him.

"That was strong stuff," he remarked. "Just what was needed, don't you agree?"

Albion was still in a daze when his wife took him up to Regent Street at the end of the day. Mr Eyre and Lord Henry had arranged a reception there and, though the place they had chosen was hardly one where he would feel comfortable, the Colonel had felt it would seem like discourtesy not to attend.

There was no doubt that the exhibition of New Forest art that Mr Eyre had organised in the Regent Street gallery had been a very clever idea, and it had attracted favourable attention in the newspapers. Paintings of animals and landscapes were always liked in Britain, and since Queen Victoria had made the wild scenery of Scotland so fashionable, almost any landscape containing heather or a stag was sure of a ready market.

With as good a grace as he could muster, therefore, the Colonel let himself be led inside.

There was already a throng of people in the gallery when they entered. Mercifully, as far as Albion could see, most of them did not seem to be artists, but looked like respectable people. It was not long before he found himself having a perfectly reasonable conversation with a retired admiral from Lymington with whom, the previous year, he had shot a large number of duck. And he was feeling considerably cheered when his eye happened to be caught by a small painting of a sunset, seen from Castle Malwood, looking down over Minstead church.

"That's a lovely thing," he remarked. "I've got one just like it. Don't know the artist."

The admiral didn't either. But just then they were joined by Lord Henry who, glancing at the picture, gave Albion a puzzled look.

"My dear friend," he said genially, "you are right to like it because it is a very good painting indeed, by a very fine artist. It is by Minimus Furzey."

The *New Forest Act* of 1877 was to settle the shape of the New Forest for generations to come. The provisions of the Act, following the report of the W. H. Smith Committee, could hardly have been more decisive for the commoners. The Office of Woods were to have no new allowance of land. They were to protect and not pull down the Forest's ancient trees. The commoners, on payment of the usual fee, were explicitly to have their year-round grazing on the Forest.

But the real sting in the tail came in a provision the W. H. Smith Committee thought of themselves.

The ancient order of verderers, which had ruled the medieval Forest through its Swainmote courts, was to be given a new life in a new form. Under an Official Verderer, nominated by the Crown, six local landowners were to be elected as verderers by the commoners and parishioners of the Forest. They were to rule the Forest. It was they who would now make the bye-laws, administer the grazing, collect fees, hold judicial courts and, above all, protect the interests of the Commoners. If the Office of Woods misbehaved in the Forest, they would have to answer to the verderers. It was a complete reversal. The Office of Woods had, so to speak, been railed off in their own inclosures.

Mr Cumberbatch, on hearing the news, left the forest, never to return.

At a celebratory party given by Lord Henry at Beaulieu, Colonel Albion gravely, albeit hesitantly, took the proferred hand of his son-in-law Minimus and declared:

"We've won."

1925

It was Jack's wife Sally, George Pride's daughter-in-law, who persuaded the old man to talk. He was still the same spare, upright figure she had always known, but he was eighty-three years old.

"Once you've gone," she reminded him, "who's going to remember all this?" Sally's family came from Minstead. She had trained as a nurse, and was a great one for writing things down. So in the spring of 1925, George Pride sat in the wooden chair he loved in his little cottage at Oakley and talked for an hour or two, until he got tired, each afternoon.

Sally had been quite surprised, once he had started, how soon she had filled the notebooks she had bought. Indeed, she had already used up two before, at the start of the fifth afternoon, he reached the point that really interested her.

"Your Jack was the last of our children born," he began. "I think we knew he would be.

"That was the summer of 1880. And three days later," he smiled, "I was summoned to Lyndhurst.

"The Queen's House, next to the Verderers' Court is quite an impressive sort of building, so you can imagine I was a bit nervous the few times I ever went in there, and this was the first time I'd had occasion to meet the new Deputy Surveyor that took over after Cumberbatch. But say what you like about him, Mr Lascelles was a gentleman. A tall, sporting sort of man, very polite. He looked at me, as if he was measuring me, and then he said:

"'I've heard all about you, Pride. Both the good and the bad." He smiled when he said that. "My predecessor dismissed you. How would you like your job back?"

"As you can imagine, I was nearly bowled over. But I thought I'd better be careful, so I said: 'May I give you my answer on Monday, Sir?' It was a Friday that day. And he said: 'Yes, you may.' So off I went.

"The first thing I did was go to Albion Park to see the Colonel. After all, he was employing me then and he'd done everything for me. He was also one of the verderers on the new Verderers' Court. And I told him: "Mr Lascelles just offered me my old job back with the Office of Woods."

"'Did he?' said the Colonel. "You come back here on Sunday evening and we'll see about that."

"That was when he offered me the job as Agister.

"The Agister's job was much the same then as now. You're in charge of all the stock in your part of the Forest. It's a riding job, chiefly, checking the cattle and ponies. Sometimes you help collect the marking fees and licences. The pay was better than the other job: sixty pounds a year. You had to find your own cottage. "But I'll help you buy one," the Colonel said.

"Above all though, it meant a choice. I could work for the verderers or the Office of Woods. Those were the two sides in the New Forest then. They are now and I should think they always will be. I had to choose whose side I was on.

"So I said yes to Colonel Albion and no to Mr Lascelles.

"My patch was the northern part of the Forest. I was glad to go back up there. The cottage we found was up at Fritham. So that's where Jack was brought up almost from birth.

"We were very happy up there. I had a good horse and I'd ride out each day. I'd got rid of my whiskers and grown a long moustache then. They say I looked somewhat dashing. I'd take my son Gilbert out with me on his pony because I imagined that was the sort of job he might like to have one day, too. He could spot if a cow was getting sick even better than I could and I'd send him off to tell the owner. He was sixteen or so then and a great help to me.

"But it was Dorothy who was the best of all. The Furzeys had been very good to her during the years after I lost my job with Cumberbatch. They'd kept her in their house and paid her, which was a considerable help to us. And besides being a good training for her, they had taught her a great deal. She had read books quite beyond what the other girls had. Every year she would do my wife and me a painting – they were really lovely – as a present for Christmas. We had them up on the wall. We were so proud of her. And although I say it myself she was a lovely-looking girl, tall and slender, with her long, dark hair. She was wonderful at keeping house, a second mother to the children so that when we moved up to Fritham my wife was very glad to have her there. We imagined she could have the pick of the Forest when it came to a husband.

"She decided to work from home then as many girls do, taking in laundry. She'd go round the local villages. But every week or two she'd go to collect from the Furzeys. By the time Jack was two years old she had as much as she could handle. Sometimes she'd be out delivering for hours. She must have been twenty then.

"Do you ever go up to Eyeworth pond? I can just remember when Eyeworth was a pretty little keeper's lodge. It's only half a mile walk, as you know, from Fritham. But then the Office of Woods sold it – to a man who wanted to make gunpowder there. Can you imagine such a thing? A gunpowder factory right in the middle of the Forest? But that's the Office of Woods for you. Then a German company bought it. So the Schultze Gunpowder Factory it became and they made the pond as a little reservoir for their factory. They had quite a collection of sheds up there, though fortunately they were mostly hidden by the trees. But they made their presence known in other ways.

"The waste that trickled out of that place! Dark and sulphurous. Stinking. And it seeped down into the Latchmore Brook, which runs past that place and so it got carried westward for miles across the heath. Part of my job as Agister was to make sure the cattle stayed away from that stream because if they drank the water it made them sick. One or two died.

"I was riding past Eyeworth one summer afternoon about two years after we got to Fritham when I saw Dorothy, looking very pale. I could tell she'd been waiting for me.

"'I've got to talk to you, Dad,' she says. I asked if we couldn't talk at home but she shook her head and said: 'I can't go home.'

"So I got down and we stood by that stinking little brook. And then she told me she was going to have a child.

"As you can imagine, I was so surprised because I knew nothing of any young man. And I thought to myself, I hope it's a good man at least. And then I thought, I hope he doesn't work for the Office of Woods.

"'Oh,' I said, 'I reckon you'll be getting married, then.' But she just shook her head again. 'If you want me to go and have a word with this young man,' I said, because sometimes they needed a little persuading, you know.

"'It isn't a young man,' she said. 'And he's married.'

"'Oh,' I said.

"'I don't know what to do, Dad. So I came out looking for you. I can't face Mum,' she said.

"It's funny really it should have been me and not her mother she went to. Just then I remember thinking of that day when she got bitten by the snake. Because it wasn't very far away from where we were then. I suppose that's why it came into my mind.

"'You'd better tell me who it was,' I said. 'At least he can help you.'

"'I don't think he can, Dad,' she said. She didn't want to tell me who it was, but I talked to her quietly for a while and in the end she shrugged and said, 'It doesn't make much difference, anyway.' And then she told me it was Mr Minimus Furzey.'

George stopped. For a moment Sally wondered if he was going to continue. Then she realised that he was weeping. There was no sound, just a gentle shaking of his broad shoulders.

Sally waited.

"I suppose it was foolish of me to have let her go there," he said at last. "I shouldn't have trusted him, should I?"

"I don't know about that, George," said Sally.

He remained silent for a few moments more.

"The next day I went to see Mr Furzey. I was very angry, as you can imagine. Betrayed, really. But when I got over to their cottage I was very polite. I asked if I could have a private word with him. So he came out, looking a bit awkward. And when we were standing in his little garden where no one could hear us I told him what I knew and asked him what he was going to do about it. And do you know what he said?

"'Oh dear,' he said, 'I'm always doing this.' And he just shakes his head. 'I haven't any money, you know.'

"I'm not sure what I might have done just then. But at that moment Mrs Furzey came out, smiling at me kindly, and I realised she didn't have an idea of what was going on.

"'What's this?' she said to me. 'Is there anything we can do for you?'

"'Nothing much,' I said. 'I just wanted to ask Mr Furzey about a bird's nest I found.' I was so angry about Dorothy, but when I saw Mrs Furzey like that, I felt sorry for her too.

"'That's good,' she said. 'He knows more about the wildlife in the Forest than anyone.'

"'Well,' said Furzey quickly, 'we'll talk about this further, Pride. Give me a day or two.' And because I didn't want to say anything in front of Mrs Furzey, I left. But of course I never did hear from him. That's the way he was. He was a devil, really, you might say, but there wasn't that much you could really do about it.

"It was my wife who made me go and see the Colonel. I'd waited a week before I told her. She was very angry. And she let Dorothy have it. Didn't mince her words at all, which perhaps was a pity.

"I wasn't so sure about going to see the Colonel. God knows none of this was his fault. And you've got to be careful, haven't you? The Colonel was a verderer and the verderers employed me. It isn't such a good idea to embarrass your employer. But my wife went on at me so hard that in the end I rode across to Albion Park.

"I felt so awkward, but I just explained as simply as I could what happened that how I was still waiting for Mr Minimus Furzey to say something to me.

"The Colonel went so red I was afraid he was going to have a heart attack.

"'You did quite right,' he said, 'to come and see me.' I was glad he said that. 'That man,' he was shaking with anger, 'ought to be horse-whipped.' Then he was silent a few moments. 'Does my daughter know?'

"'No Sir,' I said. 'And I don't mean to tell her.'

"'Good. I appreciate that, Pride.' He shook his head. 'I'm very sorry about your daughter. This isn't the first time.' He looked thoughtful, then he started: 'I assume you're certain . . .' but then he stops himself and banged his fist on the desk. 'No, no, of course it was him, damn him. Pride,' he said, 'leave it with me. Something will be done.' He gave me a look. 'I don't wish it spoken of. Can you manage that?'

"'Yes, Sir,' I said.

"And sure enough, a week later, Furzey turned up to see me, looking pretty sheepish and gave me ten pounds with a promise of more when the baby arrived. I dare say it came from the Colonel, really. 'We shall take an interest in the child,' he said to me. 'I'm to tell you that. It'll have all it needs.'

"So Dorothy stayed at home and had the child. I rather wished we'd been at the woodman's cottage in those days instead of up at Fritham, since then no one would've seen. But here was nothing you could do about that. Things like that happen in the Forest the same as anywhere else I dare say, but it was shaming for all of us, of course. We never said anything about the father. What others may have thought I wouldn't know.

"The baby was a girl. A pretty little thing I must say." He paused. "It only lived six weeks though. Caught a fever. Dorothy cried for days.

"A couple of months after it was born, I was summoned down to Albion Park, to see Mrs Albion this time.

"'Do you know the Hargreaves at Cuffnells?' she asked me. I knew Cuffnells as being a fine house just outside Lyndhurst, but I'd never had occasion to go in there. The Hargreaves family had bought it years before and recently young Mr Hargreaves had got married to a Miss Alice Liddell. You still see her about nowadays, of course, but she was the Alice, as you may know, that figured in *Alice in Wonderland*.

"'They are very good friends of ours,' Mrs Albion went on. 'And they have a position for a girl to work as a maid to young Mrs Hargreaves. Actually,' she smiled, 'I think it might be as a nanny before too long. I had a long talk with them two days ago and I wondered if your Dorothy might be interested. It's really a very good position and naturally I should be glad to recommend her. Would you like to ask her?'

"Well, you can imagine my feelings as I rode home. This was a very respectable position. A new start in life for Dorothy.

"When I got home, I saw they were all looking a bit glum, but I told them: "I've got news that'll cheer you all up."

"'I don't think it will,' said my wife. And then she told me: 'Dorothy's gone.'

"She'd gone away. We didn't know why. We didn't even know where. Nor did we for a month, when we had a letter from London. No address. Just to say she was sorry and she wasn't coming back.

"We couldn't do anything. The Colonel hired a man to try to find her for us, but nothing came of it. So that was the end of Dorothy, as far as we knew."

He looked down at his hands and then out of the window. "I don't think I can talk any more today," said George Pride.

• • •

"Your Jack was only five, hardly old enough to be a nipper, as we say, when he got into the newspapers," George began the next day. He went over to the dresser and pulled out an old brown envelope stuffed with papers and slowly unfolded a yellowed newspaper cutting. "He made headlines, too."

"It was a year I'd remember anyway. We had a very cold winter. It was the year that Lord Henry was given the title of Lord Montagu of Beaulieu, on account of all he'd done for the Forest. The commoners were pleased about that.

"It was a sign of the times, I suppose, that ordinary people were coming to retire down by the coast. We saw it all the way from Hordle along to Christchurch: little brick villas, semi-detached mostly, springing up like mushrooms. But the biggest area of building was further west, beyond Christchurch.

"When I was young, Bournemouth was just a fishing village a few miles west of Christchurch. Open heath all round it. But then it turned into a little town and by the time of these events there were already houses, hotels and boarding houses spreading right along the coast.

"The old railway line, Castleman's Corkscrew, went from Brockenhurst over to Ringwood, miles inland from the sea. So now they wanted a coastal line across to Christchurch and on to Bournemouth. A good enough idea you might think. Mr Grockleton had a new enthusiasm now: he was one of the directors of this railway line.

"Quite a few young men from the Forest had gone to work on it. The pay was quite good. But I hadn't been at all pleased when Gilbert told me he was going to. I'd been training him to be an agister.

"The trouble was, there weren't any jobs working on the Forest just then and he wanted to earn some money.

"'It'll only be for a year or two,' he'd said to me. 'The line will be finished then anyway.'

"'About a week after Gilbert signed on I had a visit from Mr Minimus Furzey. It wasn't often he came over to my house, as you can imagine.

"'Don't you let your son work on Grockleton's line,' he said. 'It's not safe. They're mad trying to go down there. They've only got to look at the geology.'"

"Well, I wasn't in much of a mood to hear anything from

Furzey, after what he did to us. So I said, 'I don't suppose you know more than the engineers of the London and South-Western Railway line." After all, like him or not, Mr Grockleton was a magistrate and an important man. You couldn't imagine him starting a big thing like that if he didn't understand what he was doing.

"'That's Headon clay and gravel,' says Furzey. 'The whole Forest is running off through it,' or words to that effect. I didn't know what he was talking about, so I didn't listen. And Gilbert went off to work there.

"We found out soon enough what Furzey meant though. At first the digging of that line seemed easy. Going across from Brockenhurst through Sway, it's all sand and gravel which is hardly difficult to shift. The first year or so they were very pleased with themselves. But things aren't always what they seem, in the Forest.

"You know on a beach, you can be sitting on the sand and it seems quite dry? But any child with a bucket and spade that digs down soon discovers that it's all watery underneath and the wet sand's runny and won't stay still. It turned out the southern Forest was like that. There were tiny streams coming down by Sway – you could see them – but underneath there was a huge seepage, water just oozing down through the clay and the gravel. Every time they made a cutting and tried to build up the banks, everything just collapsed again. Several people were injured. The treacle mines, they called those workings, because the clay was a golden colour and as runny as treacle. The work was soon months behind schedule.

"Only Grockleton didn't seem to mind. 'It'll come right,' he'd tell them. 'It's the path to the future.'

I suppose the land of the Forest didn't feel the same way." He shook his head ruefully. "But eventually it looked as if things were getting sorted out. The line by Arnewood and Sway, where the worst of the trouble had been, was duly laid. The banks of the cuttings looked solid.

"And to celebrate, Mr Grockleton announced there was to be a picnic on the heath beside the line. I think he felt it would be good for morale, as they say.

"He did that picnic in style. There was a brass band, tables of pies and cakes, more than you could eat. Beer and cider. It

was like a fair, and a lovely, hot August afternoon he had for
it, too. All sorts of people were invited: the families of the men
working on the line; people from Lymington and Sway, and
even Christchurch. Colonel and Mrs Albion came along, the
Furzeys, too.

"It must have looked a bit strange, in a way – two or three hundred people, with a brass band, sitting around by a half-finished
railway line, under the hot sun, in the middle of a heath. There
was an even stranger sight, though, to keep us company.

"Have you ever noticed that when people make a lot of
money they often get a bit strange? There was a man like that
who'd retired to Sway. His passion was for concrete. He
might've been a bit like Mr Grockleton I should think.
Everything he could lay his hands on he wanted covered in
concrete. And he was building this concrete tower. A huge
thing – you can see it for miles around today. They say he
wanted to be put up at the top of it when he died. It was about
half-built then and I shall always remember it, pointing up into
the blue sky not half a mile away from where we were that day,
like a great broken pillar.

"People were in a cheerful mood. Even Grockleton, who
could be severe, was doing his best to be friendly. He organised games for the children; and when we had a race and
Furzey organised a tug-of-war, he joined in too.

"It was late afternoon and the Albions and some of the
Christchurch people had already started leaving when I noticed little Jack had gone.

"He was already a very daring little boy, with dark hair and
bright eyes. Always climbing things. He was always getting
into trouble, but you couldn't help loving him because he was
so cheerful and so courageous.

"I knew he couldn't be far away. He'd found another boy a
bit older than he was – a big draw to him of course – called
Alfie Seagull, from Lymington, and the two of them had been
playing; so I felt sure if we found one we'd find the other. And
it wasn't long before someone pointed out the little Seagull
boy playing over near the railway cutting.

"'Is Jack with you?' my wife called out, and he nodded and
pointed down into the cutting, so we reckoned that was all right.

"Mrs Furzey came over to talk to us then, who we were always glad to see, and we had a good chat. I did notice out of the corner of my eye that Furzey was walking along the edge of the cutting, some way off. Inspecting it, I dare say. But I didn't pay him any particular regard.

"And then I saw him running. I don't believe – and I've seen many things – that I ever saw a man run as fast as he did then. I truly think he was faster than a deer. And I do not know how it was that he knew what was going to happen. At any event, he flew towards the place where Alfie Seagull was standing and just as he got there we heard the sound.

"You'd think when so much earth and stone is in motion that you'd hear some sort of a rattle or a roar. And maybe in some landslides you do. But from where we were, as that cutting gave way, all we heard was a kind of hiss.

"Furzey ran straight over the edge. He never paused, he went straight over. He must have actually run down that landslide as it was moving. And somewhere before the bottom he scooped up our Jack and kept on running with him. I reckon the weight of all that gravel and clay and stones must have reached him and overwhelmed him within a few yards of the base. He must have held Jack high then, and thrown him forward as he was toppled over.

"By the time we got to the spot a few moments later, Jack was bruised and bleeding, but he was quite clear of the slide, which would certainly otherwise have buried him.

"We could see Furzey's hands. But we had to be careful digging him out because we soon realised both his legs had been badly crushed. I think he may have twisted as he threw Jack forward.

"So your Jack had his life saved, which caused him to be in the newspaper. And Furzey got a lot of mention, too, which I must say he deserved.

"He never really walked properly after that. You couldn't help being sorry for him. He was in a bath chair mostly, though it was remarkable how he managed to get himself about. Anyway, my wife would go over to his house to bring him one of her cakes now and then. I suppose, in her eyes, he'd redeemed himself, as you might say."

• • •

"I've often thought it strange," said George Pride the next day, "considering it almost killed him, that the one thing Jack loved more than anything else, was to go down to the railway line." Sally noticed that the lines of his face seemed to harden and his old hands tightened on the arms of his chair.

"There were a lot of small cattle-bridges over the Forest railway lines, so that the stock could move about, and he'd trained his pony not to be afraid when the engines went underneath. He was always down by one of those bridges.

"Perhaps one incident, though, should really have warned us of what was to come.

"The Office of Woods never got over the victory of the commoners, and though he was polite about it, Mr Lascelles never lost an opportunity to undermine the verderers if he could; and you may be sure the verderers gave as good as they got. We had to be constantly on the look-out for those people planting trees where they shouldn't – which they did – or messing up the Forest generally. They call the Office of Woods the Forestry Commission nowadays, don't they? But it's exactly the same and I dare say it always will be.

"I was just saddling up with Jack to go out one morning when Gilbert came riding up. He'd just become an agister by then. 'You'd better come with me,' he said. So off we all went, down to a place near the new railway line where there was a lovely lawn where the ponies liked to shade.

"Normally, when timber is cut, it is taken to a sawmill in some appropriate place. The sawdust and chips make a terrible mess and ruin any grazing. But here, right beside that lawn, was a hideous sawing machine, a steam engine, puffing away, belching smoke, with sawdust blowing all over the lawn. 'Who said you could do this?' we demanded. 'Mr Lascelles,' the foreman replied.

"We were furious. But next thing we knew, young Jack was round the other side of the machine, learning how it worked. And the next day he was down there again, we found out. And for weeks after that.

"The verderers with Mr Lascelles went to law over that machine. The law case dragged on for years, not because the

sawing engine was so important but to show who was in
charge of the Forest. It was a stalemate in the end. But young
Jack didn't care about that."

Jack had never talked to her about this. She watched with
interest. She had never realised the bitterness that had come
between her husband and his father. But she could see it now,
in George's face. His jaw was clenched.

"Even if I forbade him," he continued, "he'd sneak off to
play with that infernal thing so that whenever Lascelles saw
me he'd just nod and say: 'At least your son appreciates us,
Pride.'

"Anything mechanical: it was during these years that they
started having military manoeuvres in the Forest. It was just a
wasteland for the military of course. We were always clearing
up after them. Stock were killed. But did Jack care? Not a bit.
He'd be off learning how the guns worked and firing them, too,
when the soldiers would let him.

"Much as I loved him, I must confess that by the time he
was eighteen I had no control over him. So I suppose it was inevitable that in due course we should have parted from one another.

"We had gone riding one day, he and I, out past Lyndhurst.
We'd just come by the old park pale where the deer used to be
caught, when all of a sudden, along the lane from Beaulieu,
the most extraordinary vehicle came towards us. It was a sort
of little metal cart; it made the most horrible rattling noise, and
smoke came out behind. I had read about the motor car, of
course, and seen a picture, but this was the first time we'd actually seen one in the Forest. And a very unpleasant experience
it was, too.

"It was the Honourable John Montagu, Lord Montagu's son,
who was driving this contraption, and I was very sorry to see
that his father allowed him to do it. But Jack, needless to say,
thought it was wonderful.

"'That's the future, Dad. That's the future,' he cried.

"And it was this talk of the future, on our way home that
day, which led me to raise the subject of his own."

George levered himself out of his chair and went over to the
window. Outside, the poles that carried his favourite runner

beans seemed to occupy his attention for a while. Then he shook his head almost angrily and turned round.

"You must understand that around the turn of the century the New Forest was going through a period of what you might call success. Many farmers and landowners in England had been badly hit, even ruined, by all the cheap grain coming in from America. But there was a big demand for dairy products. So the smallholders in the New Forest were doing quite well. The ponies were fetching good prices. Some went to the coal mines as pit ponies – they were very sturdy, you see; and others, sad to say perhaps, went over to Flanders to the horsemeat market. There was also work to be had doing jobs for the new people coming to live at places like Lymington. The price of land was going up, so some people made a bit by selling building plots. All in all, life in the Forest wasn't bad.

"I'd been working as an agister many years now. I'd saved up a bit. It seemed to me a good idea to start Jack off with a little smallholding, which I was in a position to do. So I made my offer.

"'Thank you, but no thank you,' he said. Just like that.

"'Oh?' I said. 'Then what plans have you, might I ask?'

"'I'm going to be an engine driver on the railways,' he said.

"I wasn't best pleased, as you can imagine. 'Well, I suppose,' I said, 'you could get a place by Brockenhurst,' thinking this was near the railway station. But he shook his head.

"'I'm leaving the Forest,' he said.

"'Leaving the Forest? Where would you go?'

"'Southampton, I should think. Or London.' He gave me this rather pitying smile, which I didn't appreciate. 'I don't just want to stare up the back of a cow all my life. It's boring.'

"And then I argued with him. And then he said some things that I don't care to think about as they don't matter any more. One thing he did say, I shall always remember. 'Before long, Dad, we won't even be needing horses any more.'

"I thought he must be daft."

George sat down heavily and closed his eyes. Then he sighed. "So he left us and went to Southampton. He had to work on the railways a few years before he had his wish. But drive the engines he did.

"He also, strange to say, became considerably better acquainted with the Honourable John Montagu.

"When the railway had been built across the northern bit of the Beaulieu estate, a bargain had been struck. The line could go through, but a little station was put in, right in the middle of the open heath. If his Lordship wanted a train for himself and his guests, a signal would let the driver know, and the train was to stop for him. It wasn't long before Jack was driving the train and saw the signal. So he stopped all right; but to his surprise the Honourable John Montagu steps up and says: 'I'll ride with you if you don't mind.' He was already a very mechanical man, you see, and a qualified train driver. You can be sure Jack lost no opportunity to ask if he could inspect the Montagu motor car in return. So the next time we saw Jack he'd learned all about the motor car. As for the train, you could never be quite sure when it went past whether it was a Pride or a Montagu driving it.

"After ten years, Jack moved away from Southampton further up the line. He still wrote us a letter now and again, but we didn't see much of him.

"It was no surprise to us, really, that when the Great War came, Jack was mad keen to join a motorised unit. He volunteered at once. And in due course he did manage to drive a vehicle near the front. His letters were full of it. Of course none of us quite realised what was happening, let alone what was going to happen, up at the front; and I suppose somehow we felt that if he was in an armoured vehicle of some kind he must be safer. I dare say he was safer than many of those poor boys in the trenches. But not safe enough."

He cleared his throat. "Well, we got the telegram telling us he'd been wounded. They said it was bad and that we'd have to wait. So wait we did. And of course, when he finally did come back – you remember it, Sally – we were shocked. The idea that he could ever be near normal again, let alone marry and have a family – well, he didn't have much of his face left, so you can't say we held out much hope. But he was alive."

Oh, yes. Sally remembered. The poor shattered invalid they brought into the Southampton hospital where she had been nursing. Even the doctors hadn't thought they could do much for him. Nor had the other nurses.

But she had. And she'd proved it, too. She'd brought him back to health herself. And then she'd married him. She smiled. She'd earned her happiness.

But George was talking now.

"'I heard them say it, you know, Dad,' he said to me once. 'I heard the officer young Captain Totton come by. A good officer he was. Lost a leg. He came hobbling by asking after me. And the nurse – I never knew what she looked like, of course, but she sounded pretty, if you know what I mean – she said to him: "I'm afraid he's going." And he said: "Why's that?" And she said: "I don't think he wants to live." And then she whispered something and he said: "Oh."

"'And then there was a bit of a pause, and I heard him come up, tick-tock with his crutch and say quite loud to me: "Come on, now, we can't have that. I know it's hard, but you've got to fight. Don't give up." I didn't make any sign, Dad. I mean, I knew he was doing his best. "Think of England," he says. But though I tried, it didn't seem to do much good. If I thought of England I just thought of driving my train, and of course I knew I wasn't going to be doing that any more. So I just lay there and I thought, well, that's it then. I may as well go really, and no harm done.

"'And then, about an hour later, I hear this sort of rustling sound by the bed. And even with all my dressings and all the disinfectant I could smell something, mud and sweat, I suppose, that wasn't altogether unpleasant. And then I hear this voice. "Your name Jack Pride?" it says. "Well if it isn't you can die and it's all right. I just got here and my name's Alfie Seagull. But if you happen to be the Jack Pride I'm thinking of, I watched you nearly get buried under a gravel slide in a railway cutting. Is that you, then?"

"'So I tried to make some sort of sign that it was. "So it is you then," he says. "You can't die here," he says. "Blimey! Have you forgotten who you are? You're a Pride of the Forest." And it's funny, but then I remembered our cottage, and the woods, and how we used to ride out together in the early morning; and when I thought of that, somehow it did give me strength, Dad, and so here I am.'

"And I suppose it's foolish," said George, "but I was always so pleased he told me that."

The Forest

April 2000

Sunday morning. Dottie Pride had only arrived at the Albion Park Hotel the evening before, but already she felt the familiar flutter of nerves. There was a whole week to go – a week in which to work out what the story was and find the angle. Plenty of time. But this was the stage at which she always began to panic.

She decided to visit Beaulieu first. She would be going there on Saturday to set up the shoot, but she wanted to have a private look around the place in advance. Perhaps it would give her some ideas. It was only a ten-minute drive, even at the forty-mile-an-hour speed limit which was in force to protect the ponies and the deer.

She was impressed. If the stately homes of Britain needed tourists to pay for their upkeep, the present Lord Montagu had shown considerable flair. Taking his father's interest in the first motor cars as his starting point, he had built up the Motor Museum at Beaulieu into a huge national institution. Dottie wasn't particularly interested in mechanical things, but she spent a fascinating half-hour gazing at Victorian Daimlers, Edwardian Rolls-Royces, and even the later cars of the fifties. As she left the museum and walked the short distance into the abbey itself, however, the mechanical age seemed discreetly to vanish, and she entered the quiet peace of the medieval world.

It was all very well done. After the house, she walked through an exhibition of monastic life in the huge *domus* where the lay brothers had lived when they were not out at the granges. And when she went out into the ruined cloisters, she could almost see the Cistercian monks, moving quietly about their business amongst the old grey stones. In one of the carrels where they used to sit, she noticed with disapproval that some vandal had carved a little letter A.

Beaulieu would open the documentary and the timing was perfect. Lord Montagu had chosen the twenty-fourth of April, Easter Sunday, to mark the nine-hundredth anniversary of the killing of King William Rufus in the New Forest. He had organised a large archery competition at Beaulieu with the actor Robert Hardy, who happened also to be a world authority on the longbow, opening the proceedings. Lord Montagu was to act – this was the medieval term for the patron of such an event – as Lord Paramount of the day. A colourful day, full of pageantry. Excellent television material.

With an historical surprise. A prominent local historian, Mr Arthur Lloyd, had shown beyond much doubt that the killing of Rufus had been recorded at the time as taking place at Througham, on the coastal stretch below Beaulieu. The famous Rufus stone, one of England's best-known tourist sites, was actually in the wrong place.

And then? She spent the rest of the day driving round the Forest. First she went down to Buckler's Hard. There was a maritime museum by its grassy banks now. There was a model of the shipyard as it would have been during the building of one of Nelson's ships, the *Swiftsure*, which caught her eye. She noted that sections of the great Mulberry Harbours used for the D-Day landings in World War II had also been built on the Beaulieu River. Interesting stuff, certainly.

East of Beaulieu lay Exbury Gardens and Lepe County Park. Along the edge of the Forest on the Southampton side were a nature centre and a model farm. A little further north she found a leisure park with children's rides. The message was clear. The modern New Forest had equipped itself in a very professional way to attract large numbers of visitors. Nor was this only a matter for the larger operators. When Dottie drove across to the dark little enclave of Burley in the afternoon, she found that the village was busily trading on its reputation for witchcraft with at least three shops selling witch's trinkets of every kind. Tourism and recreation: was that the future of the king's old hunting ground?

• • •

Monday morning was bright. Dottie was quite excited as she
made her way up the steep curve of Lyndhurst's main street.
On her left, the high Victorian tower of the church soared into
a pale blue spring sky.

When she had telephoned the New Forest Museum, she had
not only been told she should go to this morning's meeting, but
they had offered to have someone there to meet her. "Don't
worry," the voice on the telephone had laughed. "We'll find
you."

As she came to the top of the street, she saw why. The
Queen's House, the ancient royal lodge and manor, was a handsome old red-brick building. Outside a door to the side of it, a
group of about twenty people had already gathered to wait. It
was obvious from the way they were talking that they all knew
each other. She was the only stranger. She looked around.

"Would you be Dottie Pride?" a voice asked behind her.

"Yes." She turned. A hand was held out. A nod. A smile. Did
he say his name? If so, she did not catch it.

All she knew was that she was looking at the most beautiful
man she had ever seen in her life. He was tall and slim, Celtic-
looking. He might have been Irish. His hair fell in dark ringlets
to his shoulders. With his pale, sensitive face, he looked like
the pictures of the metaphysical poets of the seventeenth century. His brown eyes were soft, wonderfully intelligent. He
was wearing a brown leather jacket.

"We can go in now," he said pleasantly. "The door's opening."

The Verderers' Hall was a large rectangular chamber. At the
far end a raised dais ran the width of the room like a magistrate's bench, with the royal coat of arms on the bare wall behind it. Round the walls were deers' heads and antlers and
glass-fronted showcases. In a place of honour, the ancient stirrup was displayed through which dogs had to pass unless they
were to be lawed. The floor was taken up with wooden benches
except for the space at the front where there was a table and a
witness stand. Old oak beams crossed the ceiling. Dottie, somewhat dazed, sat at the back, trying not to stare at her companion.

"The Verderers' Court meets on the third Monday of the
month, ten months a year," he murmured. "The Official

Verderer's appointed; a few represent official bodies; the rest are elected. They have to have commoning rights to stand."

"This is the court set up in 1877 to replace the old medieval court?" She'd done her homework. She wondered if it impressed him.

"Modified once or twice, but basically, yes. Here they come." The verderers were filing in. He gave her quick sketches of them as they appeared. Two had published books on the New Forest. The Official Verderer was a prominent landowner. Most of them had roots in the Forest that went back centuries. There were eight present on the dais that morning. In front, in green uniforms, stood the two agisters. The Head Agister, by the witness stand, called out:

"Oyez, oyez, oyez. All manner of persons who have any presentments to make, or matter or things to do at this Court of Verderer. Let them come forward and they shall be heard." She was back, Dottie thought, in the Middle Ages.

A brief report was read out. Then came the list of ponies knocked down by cars: a melancholy record at every meeting. When the meeting was opened to the floor, a succession of people came up to the witness stand to make their depositions, known as presentments. Each time, her companion would murmur a word of explanation in her ear. One man, with a broad face and fair hair, came to complain of litter from a nearby campsite. "That's Reg Furzey. Smallholder." Another man, with a curious gnarled face that seemed to her to have been carved out of oak came to complain of a new property whose fence was encroaching upon the Forest. "Ron Puckle. Sells wooden garden furniture in Burley." The young man smiled. "It's funny, when you come to think of it," he whispered. "For centuries the old Forest families spent their time making encroachments on the Forest; now they spend their lives making sure nobody else does!" At the end of each presentment, the Official Verderer would politely rise, thank the person concerned and promise to consider their point. Some of the issues raised concerning Forestry Commission activities on local bye-laws were too technical for Dottie to follow. But the sense of the meeting was very clear: this was the ancient heart of the Forest. And the commoners with their verderers were determined to protect its ancient character.

It was still before noon when they emerged from the court. Her next appointment was in the museum early that afternoon, and it seemed that her companion was now preparing to leave. She wondered how she could keep him with her.

"I've got to go to see Grockleton's Inclosure," she said. "Could you show me where it is?"

"Oh. All right." He looked surprised. "I suppose so. You'll have to walk a bit."

"That'll be fine. By the way, what did you say your name was?"

"Peter. Peter Pride."

"Pride?"

She had never walked that fast before. She wondered, if she stopped, whether he would just continue on his way, and didn't dare find out. Fortunately, however, he did pause frequently to show her some lichen, or a strange beetle under a log, or some small plant which, to the trained naturalist, made this ancient area such an ecological paradise. At one point, as they came out onto some open heath, she had noticed that the holly trees on a nearby ridge had a curious profile against the sky.

"They're flat underneath, like mushrooms," she remarked.

"That's the browse line," he explained. "The ponies and deer eat the leaves up as far as they can reach." And she realised that most of the trees she could see exhibited this feature. In the distance, it gave them a magical, floating effect.

And so the lessons went on. If she couldn't always follow the scientific information with which he constantly plied her, she could at least get a sense of the subject. And then she could watch his tall, athletic form striding ahead of her again.

He was an ecologist by training, but a Forest historian too. And knowledgeable. Impressively so. She wondered how old he was. Early twenties, twenty-five perhaps. Maybe a year or two younger than she was, but not more. She wondered if he was attached.

He was amused by her name. "I'm just one of them," he explained. "But there are Prides all over the Forest. Are you sure you don't come from here?"

Her father had told her when she was a girl that she reminded him of his grandmother Dorothy, and indeed she'd been named after her. She had also discovered from him, more recently, that his grandmother had never been married. "She led a bit of a life, actually," her father had said. "Lived with an art professor for years. Then another one. She seemed to have a talent for attracting artists. The first one left her a lot of pictures, which turned out to be quite valuable. Who his father was, my own father was never quite sure. But he took her name anyway, which was Pride."

"My great-grandmother was born Dorothy Pride," she said. "But she came from London."

He nodded quickly, but said no more on the subject.

He was curious about why she wanted to see Grockleton's enclosure. When she explained that her boss, John Grockleton, was connected with the Forest, he seemed to think it very funny. "Grockleton was a Commissioner of the hated Office of Woods," he explained. "Built a railway line where several people were injured. Not a popular name here."

"Oh." She would have to think of something else to tell him.

"Here we are," he said cheerfully, a few minutes later. "Grockleton's Inclosure."

The plantation, though it had been harvested several times, was much as it had been a century before. The lines of conifer seemed endless. Beneath the trees, in what little space there was, all was dark, silent, dead.

"Let's go," she said.

They were a few minutes early at the New Forest Museum back in Lyndhurst, so they took a quick turn round the exhibits. Every facet of Forest life, from a recent famous snakecatcher to a detailed diagram of how to build a charcoal fire, was covered. By the time they went upstairs to the library she was longing to ask some questions.

The figure who rose from the big central table proved to be a short, white-bearded man with a kindly face and twinkling, observant blue eyes. Peter Pride had already explained that, although the older man's manner was quiet, he was the discreet force behind much of what went on in the Forest museum.

He was immediately welcoming to Dottie, introduced her to

several friendly people working there, explaining that the place was also manned on a daily basis by a team of volunteers.

"This is Mrs Totton," he indicated a rather distinguished-looking lady, who must have been a stunning blonde in her youth. "She's on duty today." He gave Dottie an encouraging smile.

"What would you like to know?"

Dottie had prepared carefully for this meeting, and it proved informative. Was the Forest facing a crisis, she asked?

"The challenges of the twentieth and twenty-first centuries are new; but they grow out of the past as you'd expect," the careful historian answered. "The reason for the protests and fires is simple enough. The commoners aren't only having a hard time as farmers, with terrible prices for cattle, pigs and ponies. The newcomers, from outside, are paying such high prices for their pony paddocks that the price of land is being driven beyond the farmers' reach. Above all, they feel that the modern world – Forestry Commission, local government, central government – just despises them. And yet they really are the Forest, you know.

"Then you have the degrading of the ancient Forest environment: careless campers and tourists generally."

"Thousands of cars?" she suggested.

"Yes. But ninety per cent of people in cars never go further than fifty feet from the road. The new influx of bicycles may prove more damaging. We'll see." Dottie had noticed a lone bicyclist on her way to Grockleton's Inclosure, riding through the trees, churning up the ground as he went. She nodded.

He smiled ruefully. "As always, we want tourists for their income but not for the damage they do. That's another big subject, of course.

"But there is a third, long-term danger – the great threat of the new century, you might say."

"Building?"

"Exactly. The massive increase in housing needs, the existence of a huge area scarcely touched by housing development. Some people think we should protect the Forest by making it a National Park, which would make development extremely difficult; others, especially the commoners, fear that might take away from the power of the verderers who, for the last hundred and fifty years, have been their one protection." He smiled again. "We could discuss any or all of those."

They did, for some time. They helped her put together a list of people to whom she should talk.

"May I add myself to that list?" Mrs Totton enquired. A gentle nod from the kindly historian indicated to Dottie that she should accept. "Good," said the elderly lady. "Come to tea on Friday. Come a little early, say at four."

"If you really want to get the feel of the commoners," Peter Pride now cut in, "you ought to go to a pony sale. There's one this Thursday."

"That sounds colourful. Perhaps we should film it." She glanced at Peter Pride. "Will you be there?"

"Could be. Would that be helpful?"

"Definitely," she said.

It was just after the meeting had broken up and she was about to leave that she paused to ask one last question.

"By the way," she said, "people often associate the New Forest with witchcraft. Do you think there's any witchcraft here?"

The friendly historian shrugged. Mrs Totton smiled and said she didn't think so. Peter Pride shook his head and said it was a lot of nonsense.

"I just wondered," said Dottie.

The camera crew were busy. A scene like this was a challenge to be enjoyed. The past two days had been busy; but she'd been looking forward to Thursday.

The pony sales at Lord Montagu's old private station of Beaulieu Road were always lively affairs. Leaving Lyndhurst by the park pale, they had driven south-east across the open ground towards Beaulieu for about three miles before the hump of the bridge over the railway line announced that they had reached the place. And as they came over the bridge, immediately on their left, there it was: a wooden railed sale ring with pens beside it.

The lorries and horse boxes started arriving early. Apart from the usual refreshment stalls, there were stands selling riding tack and another selling boots. But these were strictly on the sidelines. The sale ring was the sole point of the exercise and the pens were soon full of ponies.

And people. Forest people. Peter Pride was already there when they arrived and he strolled over, smiling. "You'll see the real Forest today," he remarked. "These pony sales, the pony drifts – that's when they drive the ponies off each area of the Forest and check them – and the point-to-point on Boxing Day: these are the real Forest events."

"And how do they feel about us being here?" Dottie asked.

"Suspicious." He shrugged. "Wouldn't you be?"

They were all arriving now: countrymen in cloth caps, shaggy hair and whiskers; women in all kinds of garb to keep out spring showers; children in brightly coloured gumboots. The stands round the ring were crowded. Children were standing on the rails inspecting the ponies. Suddenly the auctioneer was at his place beside the ring, tapping his microphone, and the sale had begun.

The ponies were let into the ring in ones or twos usually. The auctioneer's descriptions were brief, the bidding fast. The ponies wheeled as the men tapped them, waved their hands and shouted to control them. Dottie noted with interest that within the sturdy wild ponies a strain of Arabian fineness could sometimes be seen. But not all the ponies were pure Forest either. Some quite handsome small mares came into the ring, too.

The camera crew were happy. They didn't need her. There would probably be plenty of footage to use. Peter Pride at her side was now giving her a quiet running commentary.

"That's Toby Pride over there. That's Philip Furzey next to him. That's James Furzey and that's John Pride and his cousin Eddie Pride over there. That's Ron Puckle. You saw him at the Verderers' Court. And Reg Furzey, remember? That's Wilfrid Seagull, who's a bit devious. Then that's my cousin Mark Pride. And . . ."

"Stop," she begged. "I got the message." What was interesting, she noticed, was that as you looked round the ring, you could see perhaps half a dozen strong physical traits coming out in all these cousins. One Pride might not necessarily resemble another, but the Furzey standing next to him was obviously related.

"We're like the deer," said Peter. "We move around the Forest o breed. That's probably why we haven't all got three eyes."

"Do you ever let outsiders in? I mean, really into the orest?"

He pointed across the ring to where a very pretty girl with a Slavic face and blond hair was standing. Her ponies were just coming into the ring.

"They came from outside." He indicated a fair-haired man n one of the pens with one of the Prides. "They're serious about commoning. They're part of the Forest now."

Dottie looked at the girl. She really was stunningly beautiful. She suddenly felt a stupid rush of jealousy.

Peter meanwhile was shaking his head in sympathy while he beautiful girl opposite was looking furious. The prices for ner ponies were really shockingly low.

"Hardly enough to pay the transport and fees," he sighed. "Something'll have to be done."

They watched for another half an hour. Then Dottie decided she needed something to drink. As they went over towards the van selling refreshments, he turned to her thoughtfully. "By he way," he said, "I did some checking. Around 1880 there was a young woman in my family called Dorothy Pride. She went away to London."

Like many Georgian mansions, Albion Park had converted very naturally into a hotel. The dining room was elegant, and although he had taken a little persuading, Peter Pride had finally agreed to come and join her for dinner that evening. Apart from the pleasure of seeing more of him, she was also glad of the chance to discuss some ideas. She had interviewed nearly a dozen people since Monday: local historians, Forestry Commission people, the owners of the Nova Foresta Bookshop, who knew every book ever written on the place; commoners, verderers, ordinary residents – everyone had a view of their own about the Forest. But now she had to start sifting them to see what approach she wanted to take.

They talked generally first though. She discovered they both iked similar music. He was a good chess player. That didn't surprise her. She preferred cards, but no matter. Sport? Hikes. He smiled. "You have to like walking. You're a Pride."

They had to agree that the fact a Dorothy Pride left the Forest and another appeared in London didn't really prove much.

"If she'd married," Dottie explained, "we'd at least have her parents on the marriage certificate. But she didn't."

"Never mind." He gave her a charming smile. "Perhaps we'll adopt you." She thought that sounded rather nice.

In answer to her questions, he was helpful. Why did everyone hate the Forestry Commission?

"Habit really. Remember, they took over from the old Office of Woods, the commoners' natural enemy."

Was the Forest going to be turned into a series of hideous conifer patches like Grockleton's Inclosure?

"No. In fact, after years of conifers, the Forestry Commission today is planting a mix of broad-leaf and conifers and taking quite a creative approach to ecology." He grinned. "Not that anybody's perfect of course."

But it was when she got him on to the subject of ecology in its broadest sense that his eyes shone and his mind really seemed to take wing.

"Why is the New Forest so important ecologically?" he asked her eagerly. "Why does it contain more invertebrates," he grinned, "than any other ecological site in Europe? Why do we have all these wonderful mires? Such a diversity of undamaged habitats? Such highly unusual ecotones? That's the rich area where two habitats merge. You always get the largest number of species there." He gazed at her. "Well, why?"

"Tell me," she smiled.

"Because nine centuries ago a Norman king made it a game preserve, and by the luck of history woodlands have remained in their natural state, bogs have not been drained. Ecology is history."

He looked at her triumphantly.

"Except of course that if man had never come along, the Forest would be in its truly perfect state."

"No such thing. Man is part of the natural equation along with the rest of God's creatures. Think about it. Why is the Forest biomass poor at ground level? Because the ponies and deer eat it up. Yet strangely enough, that leads to a diversity of species. Are you going to take them away? They were probably there before man came to the area. There's no such thing as a perfect system. Only a system in balance. And even that balance is in flux. Left to themselves, animal populations, woodlands, all natural systems die and regenerate at a varying pace. Whenever you try to impose a static order on nature, it doesn't work. The entire system changes anyway. There used to be four Needles at the end of the Isle of Wight. Now there are three. The sea washed one away in the eighteenth century. Anyway, the entire landscape has entirely changed since the Ice Age ended, and that was only ten thousand years ago. Less, in fact.

"An oak tree lives in a four-hundred-year time-frame. Human time-frames are always too short. So we get it wrong, and we don't really understand the natural processes half the time."

"So what's your rule for the Forest?"

"Look for a balance. But know that nature will find a better one." He looked straight into her eyes. "I think that's how to live, really. Don't you?"

Dottie Pride was silent for a while.

"Will you be at Beaulieu on Sunday?" she asked.

She really didn't want to go to tea with Mrs Totton. It was Friday. The last five days had given her so much to think about that the only thing she wanted to do now was to go over her notes and make her plans. She had devoted the morning to this and made good progress. She had a strong opening, but something was missing. She couldn't quite pin it down – that magic ingredient that, in her own mind, she called the story. With Dottie it always came at the end of the process and so far it had always happened in time. Just. It had to happen by Saturday.

She really didn't want to go to tea with Mrs Totton at all.

Mrs Totton lived in a charming whitewashed cottage with a walled garden and a small orchard behind. The cottage was set in the lush little valley near the point where the river was crossed by Boldre Bridge.

"And I thought, as it's a nice day, we might walk over the bridge and up to Boldre church," she announced, as she met Dottie at the door.

The church on its wooded knoll was a friendly building. Its

dark, wooded setting did not seem eerie, but it did, Dottie thought, feel very old. There were several plaques recording members of old Forest families on the walls, and one in particular caught her attention.

It was to Frances Martell, born Albion, of Albion Park; and most unusually, it also recorded her devoted housekeeper and faithful friend – those were the words – Jane Pride.

"Albion Park. It's the name of the hotel where I'm staying," Dottie remarked.

"It's also the house where I was born," her hostess told her. "I was an Albion before I married Richard Totton." She smiled. "A lot of the larger Forest houses are hotels now." On the way back she suggested, "If you like, I'll tell you the story of Fanny Albion. She was tried in Bath for stealing a piece of lace."

There was another guest for tea. A pleasant woman in her fifties called Imogen Furzey who Mrs Totton introduced as "a cousin of mine." Dottie correctly guessed that in Mrs Totton's world a cousin might be someone removed by many generations, but she did not enquire into the details. "She's an artist, so I thought you'd like to meet her," Mrs Totton said confidently, in the manner of those who assume that anyone involved with the media must belong in the company of artists of some kind.

Imogen Furzey was a painter. "It runs in the family," she explained. "My father was a sculptor. And his grandfather was quite a well-known New Forest artist named Minimus Furzey."

Dottie decided she liked Imogen Furzey. She dressed eccentrically, but with a simple elegance. The smock she was wearing had evidently been designed by herself. So, probably, had the silver bracelet she wore. Around her neck, on a silver chain that matched the bracelet, there hung a curious, dark little crucifix. "An heirloom," she said, when Dottie remarked on it. "I think it must be extremely old, but I don't know where it comes from."

The tea was delightful. It even turned out to be useful. Both Mrs Totton and Imogen Furzey were able to tell her an enormous amount about the Forest, and seemed happy to do so.

"The only thing we both wonder," Mrs Totton remarked, as

they ended tea, "is whether with a name like Pride you aren't connected to the Forest yourself."

Dottie told them of her conversation with Peter Pride on the same subject and its inconclusive outcome. "There was a Dorothy Pride who left for London, and a Dorothy Pride in London. But whether they are one and the same, there's no means of knowing."

Mrs Totton was looking thoughtful at this.

"Years ago, when we were selling Albion Park, my brother and I went through old Colonel Albion's papers. It's a long time ago, but I think there was something about a Pride girl who had run away to London amongst them." She glanced at Dottie. "Would it interest you to have a look?"

Dottie hesitated. She ought to go back to her work. On the other hand . . .

"If it's not too much trouble . . ."

"No it's quite easy." She smiled. "That is, if all these papers are where I think they are. Imogen dear, it's too heavy for me, but in the store room you will see one of the boxes is labelled 'Colonel Albion.' Perhaps the two of you could bring it here."

The store room of Mrs Totton's cottage turned out to be a carefully contrived solution to the problem so many people of her kind faced when they moved from a large country house into a small one: what to do with the mass of family papers, pictures and other records of the past which will not fit into a cottage? Her solution had been to build on a large store room. On the walls, frowning down, were the large family pictures that would have overwhelmed the rooms in the cottage. Arranged neatly by her late brother, on racks, were some twenty trunks, each labelled, containing the papers and mementoes of this or that ancestor. There were racks of swords, old cane fishing rods, whips and riding crops, and several cupboards of uniforms, riding coats, lace dresses and other finery all duly mothballed. It was a family treasure house. They found the leather trunk easily enough and managed to drag it along the passage into the sitting room. They opened it.

The Colonel had hated writing letters, but he had made a copy of almost every one so that his record not only of incoming, but also of outgoing correspondence, was almost complete. For a man who hated paperwork it was a commendable achievement. The letters were arranged not chronologically but by subject, each batch placed either in an envelope or wrapped in a piece of covering paper and neatly labelled in the Colonel's firm hand.

They went through them all, looking for anything labelled "Pride." There was nothing.

"Oh dear," said Mrs Totton, "I'm sorry. I must have remembered it wrong."

"It doesn't matter," said Dottie. "It was kind of you to think of it."

They started to put the letters away.

"Look," said Imogen, and held up a packet. It was labelled: "Furzey, Minimus," under which the Colonel had drawn a short, angry line. "May I?"

"Of course."

There were a number of letters, mostly brief. But one was much longer. It began, curtly: "Sir, It may interest you to know that the agent I employed some two years ago has recently furnished me with a reply."

"Whatever can this be about?" Imogen wondered aloud. She scanned the letter further, and then said: "Oh." She read a little more. "Dottie," she said, taking her arm. "I think I've found her."

The Pride girl is found. She is alive and well. For that we may thank God, I suppose. She is living, in sin, with a person said to be an artist, of no moral repute. A person, I dare say, therefore, very like yourself.

She has been offered an inducement to return to her parents, or at least to let them know that she is alive. This she utterly refuses to do, whether because she has sunk and accustomed herself to a life of sin, or whether out of shame I do not know. In the circumstances I think it best to say nothing to her parents.

You may come to reflect upon the fact, Sir, that it is you and you alone who is responsible for the ruin of Dorothy Pride.

I say you may care to reflect: I should rather say that you might care to reflect, if I did not know that it is not in your character to draw any moral conclusions under any circumstances.

I can only conclude by assuring you that I, for my part, have learned with each passing year to feel for your character an ever-increasing revulsion and disgust.

"I think that must be your great-grandmother, Dottie."

"It has to be. Living with an artist."

"And my great-grandfather . . . I'm sorry."

"Well, we've found her," said Mrs Totton. "It was a long time ago. But welcome home, Dottie, anyway. At least we can say that." She looked at the clock on the mantelpiece. "My dears, it's quite time for a drink."

But Dottie excused herself. She needed the evening to work. She thanked them both and prepared to go.

"Would you like a hand to put the papers back in the store room?" she asked.

"No. I think I may look at some of them myself this evening," said Mrs Totton. "Perhaps," she smiled, "we shall see you here in the Forest more in the future?"

"Perhaps."

Her evening's work went well. The mass of material she had gathered was beginning to separate out, then fit itself together in new shapes. That was usually the prelude to getting her story.

It was strange about her great-grandmother and Minimus Furzey. She had little doubt that she had found Dorothy and, therefore, her own roots. Once or twice she nearly picked up the telephone to tell Peter Pride, but she forced herself not to. She could tell him on Sunday, if he turned up.

He was her cousin – a very distant one, of course.

Mrs Totton sat alone that evening in a state of contentment. It had been a good day. She liked the Pride girl. As for discovering her family, that had been a gift from above. To be connected with the Forest, in Mrs Totton's eyes, was the greatest gift you could hope for.

She read a book for a little while, dozed for perhaps half an hour, and then, putting a chair beside the trunk on the floor, idly went through some more of old Colonel Albion's letters. Many were routine matters connected with the estate; some concerned the disputes of the verderers with the Office of Woods. After the Furzey letters, none of them seemed very exciting. Perhaps she was not in the mood.

She was just about to put the bundles back and close the lid when a slim envelope detached itself from the rest. It seemed to be a single item with no accompanying correspondence. On it, in the Colonel's hand, was written a single word: "Mother?"

Curious now, she picked up the envelope and opened it. There was only one sheet of paper inside, closely written on both sides, in a fine, rather academic hand, certainly not Colonel Albion's.

"My dearest wife," it began, "each of us has secrets and now there is something which I, too, have to confess."

Yet if it was a confession, it was a strange one. It seemed that the writer's wife, whom he clearly loved, had been having nightmares, calling out things in the night. And from this he had learned that she was guilty, or believed herself to be, of a great crime. Others, it seemed, had suffered transportation, even death. But she had got off free.

Because she had lied. Guilt, remorse, deep in the night, was visiting her in dreams. She was obviously in an agony which she could share with no one, not even her husband. Awake, no word was spoken. The nightmares, it would appear, came then departed for months at a time, then came again.

So what had her husband to confess? Firstly that he had, as it were, eavesdropped upon these confidences. He was still apparently undecided about whether to speak to her or not. Then came an urgent section. He knew her too well, he said, to have any doubt about her goodness. As a wife, a mother, mistress of their estates, there was not an evil thought or intention in her soul.

Had she really stolen that piece of lace, he asked, or was it possible that she herself had come to imagine it? He did not know. The crime itself, even if it were so, should never merit the punishments given; and she herself, by her goodness, had long ago earned forgiveness.

Perhaps, my dearest Fanny, I shall be able to persuade you of these things. Perhaps these terrible dreams will end. But I wish, in any case to leave you this letter to read, after I am gone.

For I, too, have an equal confession to make to you. When I came to you in Bath and implored you to save yourself and told you I knew you were not guilty of this crime, my beloved wife, I lied. I did not know. But I desired above all that you should be my wife, guilty or innocent. And even now, though I do not for one instant believe you are bound for anywhere but Our Father's Heavenly Kingdom, I tell you truly that were you to be consigned to the fires of Hell, I should follow you there, even to the bottomless pit, and do so gladly a thousand times.

Your loving husband, Wyndham.

"Well," murmured Mrs Totton. "Well."

Dottie Pride awoke before dawn. It had come. She could feel it. She was going to get her story today.

She could not sleep any more. She got up and pulled on some clothes and, proceeding down the dimly lit stairs of Albion Park, made her way out through the big front door. The gravel drive scrunched under her feet. Faintly embarrassed at the thought of waking the other guests, she walked along the grass verge until she reached the gate.

It was quite chilly, but she didn't care. For no particular reason of which she was aware, she wandered up the lane and into Oakley. The village was asleep. Not a soul was stirring yet. She came to the green where the cricket pitch was already fenced off. She could just make that out in the gloom.

Oakley. If she was a Pride, she suddenly realised, she must have come home. She walked across the wet, dewy grass to the edge of the heath. Her shoes would be sopping. She didn't care. She took a deep breath, scenting peat and heather. She shivered for a moment.

The grey-black spring night still lay like a blanket over the sky. It was quiet, as if the whole New Forest was waiting for something to happen in the silence before the dawn. She stared out across Beaulieu Heath.

And then, suddenly, a skylark started singing in the dark.